A NOTE OF PARTING

Even Dunrathway itself was coming to feel like a prison . . .

All it expected of her now was that she should conform to its tastes, customs and standards: early marriage to a fisherman, children who would be raised the same way everyone's were, eating the same food, wearing the same clothes, watching the same drivel on television. Physical survival was all that mattered, spiritual malnutrition would never even be noticed, much less considered important.

If she didn't get out, now while she had the chance, she would wizen and wither, dry out like a clump of seaweed beached far back in the sand dunes. Ten or fifteen years hence Aran Campion would be just another piece of jetsam, rough on the eye, stiff to the touch.

She didn't know yet what she really wanted, but she knew what she needed, and it wasn't that. She must get out. Was going to get out . . .

She went to the telephone, picked it up and dialled the number.

Also by Liz Ryan

Blood Lines

About the author

Liz Ryan has been a journalist with the Dublin *Independent* and *Herald* for fourteen years, and a regular contributor to many magazines and radio programmes. This is her second novel.

A Note of Parting

Liz Ryan

CORONET BOOKS
Hodder and Stoughton

First published in Great Britain in 1996 by Hodder and Stoughton
A division of Hodder Headline PLC
First published in paperback in 1996 by Hodder and Stoughton
A Coronet Paperback

10 9 8 7 6 5 4 3 2 1

A CIP catalogue record for this title is available from
the British Library.

ISBN 0 340 62458 2

Printed and bound in Great Britain by
Cox & Wyman Ltd, Reading, Berkshire

Hodder and Stoughton
A division of Hodder Headline PLC
338 Euston Road
London NW1 3BH

ACKNOWLEDGEMENTS

For my late father John Greenhalgh, whose memory remains so inspiring. Also for Lil, Rob, Lorraine and the children, for everyone in the family who takes such an interest.

Once again the support of my friends has been invaluable, and I thank them all: Gerry, Helen, Nell, Sarah, Susan and Frank, Tom and Eithne, Brendan and Aine, Sheila and Dominique, Helen and Lahcen.

For their help with research, much gratitude to Mr Pandhi at the Indian embassy, David Agnew of the RTE Symphony Orchestra and Dominic Rihan at Bord Iascaigh Mhara. Also to my colleagues at Independent Newspapers and the other media, who helped in ways too numerous to mention.

Finally, very special thanks to my lovely editor Carolyn, who says it with flowers, and to my endlessly wonderful agent Richard Gollner.

Chapter One

'Mr Campion, don't do this. Please don't.'

Eimear Rafter's tone was beseeching, and it tore the guts out of Conor Campion. He hated what he was saying, deplored what he was doing. But he had gone through it all with Molly, over and over again, and they could find no alternative. Twisting his cap in his hands, he looked down at the floor, his shoulders hunched in defeat.

'We wouldn't do it, Mrs Rafter, if we had any choice in the matter. But things have gone from bad to worse this past two years, and we have the boys coming up . . . we just can't afford it, ma'am, not all three of them.'

Eimear shifted on her chair, uncomfortable that he should call her ma'am, a man twenty years older than herself. But no matter what he called her, he knew he could command no respect in this damning situation. Education was the key to the future, everyone knew that. To deprive your child of it was a desperate resort, an admission that you could not even get through today for the sake of all your tomorrows. Mr Campion might as well have commandeered the pulpit down in the church and announced to the entire community that he was now officially a pauper.

Behind him, his daughter stood silently, hanging her head, her mass of fair hair hiding the eyes that were, Eimear guessed, filling with tears. Feeling the shame of the moment stamp itself on the girl like a seal on hot wax, she groped for some word of comfort.

'But Mr Campion, education is free, you know you don't have to pay to keep Aran at school. So if it's just a question of the extras, of books, lunches, equipment, please don't worry about those. We have . . . there are ways . . .'

Mrs Kelly should be here to handle this, she thought, properly and diplomatically. She would get the man to accept help without making him feel belittled. But the principal had left the building unusually

1

early today, and so Mr Campion had insisted on seeing Mrs Rafter, his daughter's favourite teacher, instead. Having made up his mind, Eimear supposed, he could not be delayed or deflected, forced to come back tomorrow and deliver his painfully rehearsed speech at Mrs Kelly's convenience.

'No, Mrs Rafter. It's not just those things. Aran already has her sisters' books, clothes, everything. The fact is that we can't afford to support her any longer. We need her to go out and find work, start bringing some money into the house.'

There. He had said it, flat out. He had failed as a father. Burning with humiliation, he bowed his head before all three women: his wife, his daughter and the teacher who had always been adamant that Aran was the brightest pupil in Dunrathway school.

In three weeks' time, according to Mrs Rafter, Aran would acquit herself with great credit in her Intermediate exam, and when the results arrived she would have at least eight, maybe all nine honours. Aran was indeed very bright, and he was proud of her. But after that he couldn't keep her. Times had changed since Val and Sher were at school, and there were Achill and Dursey still to be got through to the age of sixteen. Aran was sixteen now, and must leave school so that her brothers could stay on until the law permitted them, too, to start work.

The girl understood that herself. She had seen those big foreign trawlers being towed into the harbour, time and time again, their crews laughing as the Irish coastguard impounded their nets and gear, tied them up to await the next sitting of the local court which would fine them some derisory sum already built into their budgets, and reluctantly release them to do it all over again. Far from repelling them, the new twelve-mile fishing limit imposed by the EEC merely attracted them, a joke and a challenge which proclaimed that Irish waters must hold something worth defending. The Spaniards and Russians were the worst offenders, blatantly encroaching well inside the limit, their floating factories scooping up more fish in an hour than the little native trawlers could catch in a week. The situation was a free-for-all, survival of the fittest, and Conor Campion recognised, as his daughter must, that he was far from the fittest.

Looking at the man, Eimear remembered everything her mother had told her about him while teaching his two older daughters, and thought much the same thing. Conor Campion had never been a fighter. After thirty-five years he didn't even skipper a boat, let alone own one, because his hard work had never been fired by ambition. He was modest and honest, but those were qualities his peers had lately come to regard as superfluous; feeling that the government had betrayed and failed to protect them, they had turned their minds to all manner of ingenious scams and schemes, outwitting Dublin and Brussels in any way they could. Conor was by no means the only one of them in financial difficulty, but he was the only one who stood here now, hopeless.

Or was he merely the first?

Beside him, his small tense wife stood clutching her handbag before her, in both hands as if it might defend her from Eimear's ire. Eimear had met Molly often before, and thought her a joyless woman whose horizons coincided with her laundry line. Tight and thin, her face and voice proclaimed a mind pre-shrunk by the media and the Church, the twin forces which dictated her every thought. Not that Molly read much, to Eimear's knowledge, but she listened to the neighbours and the wireless religiously, righteously, taking all her cues from the society which depended on precisely such impressionable women. As soon as 'they' said something was right or wrong, Molly said so too. Bird-like, she reminded Eimear of a fledgling swallowing premasticated food from its mother's mouth.

Even before poverty had begun to pinch and age her, Molly Campion had not been known to smile much, or laugh at all. Yet she worked hard, to augment her husband's dwindling income, raising chickens and vegetables, knitting woollens for the co-op which sold them on to crafts shops which, in turn, sold them to tourists during the summer. Like Conor she was industrious, but she was certainly not garrulous. Eimear turned to her, feeling like a dentist pulling a painful tooth,

'But Mrs Campion, what about your knitting? We're just coming into the summer, won't you make a little money then?'

'I will. A little. Not enough to keep three growing children for the rest of the year.'

'But if only Aran could stay on for another two years, and do her Leaving Certificate, she'd get a much better job than anything she might get with only her Intermediate Certificate. It's an investment.'

Immediately, Molly fell back on what 'they' said.

'They say the school certificates soon won't be much use at all, Mrs Rafter. Aran can stay the few weeks till she does her Inter, but she won't be coming back in September. Even if we could keep her on the extra two years, the Leaving will be worthless by then, it'll be university degrees the employers will want. So where's the point?'

'But you kept the older two girls on until they were eighteen. They got both certificates.'

'Aye. And where did that sorry struggle get us? Away to be married, the two of them, before they ever brought a penny into the house.'

3

It was true. Val and Sher had never worked at anything other than finding husbands. But perhaps they might contribute something yet?

'Well, Mrs Campion, they did get married, as you say. Val married a newsagent in Cork city and Sher, I believe, married quite a prosperous American. Couldn't they help a bit now? It really wouldn't take much, would it?'

Eimear put as much wheedling encouragement into her voice as she could, attempting to inject some optimism into the woman's dejected tone and Conor's defeated stance. But he raised his blue eyes to her.

'No, ma'am. It wouldn't take much. But we wouldn't ask them. It wouldn't be fair, or right.'

'But it's not fair to take Aran out of school!'

'We're very sorry, ma'am. But Aran has got to get a job, as soon as possible. Will you tell Mrs Kelly for us, or do we need to put it in writing?'

His tone was weary, his wife's expression resigned. They had done all they could for their middle child, and Eimear might as well save her breath. As she looked at her, Eimear felt the girl pleading with her, imploring her not to prolong this ordeal. Clearly battle had already been done at home, and lost.

'Very well, Mr Campion. If there's nothing I can say to change your mind, then I'll tell the principal for you. There's no need to put it in writing. We'll give Aran references when she starts looking for work, and all the help we can.'

Thanking her, he nodded and shuffled away, taking his wife with him. As they left the room, Eimear could almost hear their daughter's dreams crunching under their feet.

At home that evening, Eimear informed Daniel that the school was about to lose its star pupil, and was not much consoled by his pragmatic response. But then Dan was usually pragmatic; it was one of the things that made their relationship balanced and even.

'She's their child, Eimear, not yours. If the law says she can leave in June, and they say she must, then you'll have to accept it.'

'I can't let her go, Dan, just like that! She deserves at least as much education as her sisters got – and more.'

Teachers were not supposed to have favourites, so Eimear was careful to hide the affinity she had felt for Aran Campion since she had begun teaching her three years before. But there was little she hid from Dan, except when the cows were calving or the mares were foaling and he was exceptionally busy.

'What does Mrs Kelly say?'

4

'I haven't had a chance to tell her yet. But she'll go a few rounds with the parents before she'll let them do it.'

'I dare say she will. Aran reflects a lot of credit on her school. But if Conor and Molly need the money their daughter can earn, what can she say to them? The fishing really is bad, Eimear. You know it is.'

'But there's the dole, and the children's allowance. Conor isn't even the type to drink it.'

'The children's allowance might well be what's behind this, though. Now that Aran is sixteen, Molly won't be getting it any more.'

'No – but as long as Conor has a child at school, he can claim tax relief for her.'

'Tax relief on what? He isn't earning anything! Or not enough, at any rate.'

'Oh, Dan . . . how is it that some of the other fishermen are coping? Look at Joey Devlin, building that big house up on Fenner's Hill, and Rowan Farmer driving an Audi. A brand new one.'

'Rowan and Joey are very different to Conor. They're clever enough to take evasive action when times are bad, and speculate when times are good. Clever enough to go after every loan, grant and subsidy they can get, and then find ways to repay slowly if at all. Whereas Conor Campion wouldn't know an opportunity if it leaped up and bit him. He has no imagination and no drive.'

No. Yet his daughter had both, and a cheerful spirit besides. Her two younger brothers wanted only to be fishermen like their father, yet her future was to be sacrificed so that their education could continue. Well, they were too young to be taken out of school, of course, at twelve and fourteen years of age. But neither Achill nor Dursey had a shred of their sister's intelligence.

'Conor had drive once, Dan. He stood up to the priest and insisted on having all his children baptised with those ludicrous names.'

Dan smiled as he thought of it: Valentia, Sherkin, Aran, Achill and Dursey, each one called after an island. When the priest had pointed out that children were supposed to be named after saints, not islands, Conor had retorted that in that case he wouldn't let them be christened at all. They could become Moonies or Holy Rollers or whatever they liked. Shocked, Father Carroll had acquiesced; but it was a good thing that Conor's pursuit of propagation had flagged after Dursey was born, because he was running out of islands. Had there been any more children, they might well have been called Whiddy, Blasket or Spike.

As Eimear said, the names had been Conor's one rebellious gesture in an otherwise meek, watery lifetime, and Dan began to share his wife's irritation. To put so much energy into such a pointless crusade, and so little into what was important! But the sea had eroded the man over the years, engulfing and quenching whatever spark might once have existed.

'Maybe Aran has a perverse streak too, Eimear. Perhaps she'll go to night school and get ahead in spite of everything.'

'The nearest night classes are nearly thirty miles away, Dan, and the Campions don't have a car, much less a driving licence between them. I'd give her private tuition myself, but history and English alone aren't enough. Some of us here in Dunrathway – the other teachers, I mean – have discussed starting night classes locally. But not everyone is willing to do it for free. In fact I'm the only one.'

That was predictable, Dan supposed, and reasonable; the other teachers had children of their own to support, busy homes to run in the evenings. There was no call for Eimear to bang those plates away in their cupboards so loudly.

'Look, Eimear, you're going to have to face facts. You've got thirty-six years of teaching ahead of you before you collect the gold watch. During that time you'll see many bright students going off to pump petrol or wait tables. You must learn not to take it so personally.'

'I'll take it any way I like. They're my responsibility. It made me so angry today, to see Conor standing there so – so *humble*, at his age. I'd have screamed at him, if it hadn't all been so pitiful. And the mother, with her mind as narrow as her mouth, and poor Aran looking ready to cry.'

'It's not their fault. They've done their best and they can't help it if that's not enough.'

'Oh . . . I suppose you're right. At least they're not fraudsters or debtors, like some of those people who call you out to deliver a litter of piglets in the middle of the night and then take six or ten months to pay you.'

'Farming can be just as hard as fishing, Eimear. You grew up here and it was you who chose to settle here after we graduated. You should know that.'

And you would know it, he thought, if we had children to feed and clothe ourselves. Perhaps a time will come when we'll be up to our ears in bills and nappies like everybody else, too busy to worry about other parents' problems.

Perhaps.

Putting down his newspaper, Dan got up and went to his wife, noticing how the setting sun brought out the dark sheen of her hair, the lustre of her warm, troubled brown eyes.

'Term is nearly over, love. When the summer comes I want you to promise me you'll stop worrying about Aran Campion, and relax. Will

6

we take the car and tent to France, go camping again? Would you like that?'

Briefly, she smiled at him, but then turned away again, looking out the window across the garden to where Sammy their spaniel was chasing butterflies. Sammy had been a gift from a farmer, in lieu of payment as it turned out, and the man had said the little dog was a good luck token to the newlyweds, whose children would be wanting a pup to play with. Sammy was five years old now, but he still had no playmates.

'I will relax, Dan. But I won't go anywhere until I've thought what's to be done about Aran.'

Silently he put his arm around her waist, and looked with her out over the sloping fields to the sea. On the horizon, the home-coming trawlers were black silhouettes, gliding into harbour on water calm and golden as buttermilk, the holds of the luckier ones half filled with fish.

With a mixture of relief and nervousness, Aran Campion made her way down the corridor to the staff room where, she had been told, Mrs Rafter wished to see her. As soon as she knocked on the door it opened, but rather than asking her in Mrs Rafter came out, wearing a duffle coat and a scarf around her neck.

'Go get your jacket, Aran, and let's have our sandwiches down on the beach.'

Surprised, Aran fetched her jacket and the waxed paper packet of sandwiches which looked so clumsy compared to Mrs Rafter's neat plastic box. Not that the jacket was much better, but at least it fitted, Val having been of the same slight build and medium height as herself. Feeling it would be impolite to open the conversation, and incapable of raising the emotional subject of her terminated schooling anyway, Aran said nothing as they walked across the yard, out through the gates and down the sandy lane that led onto the long white beach.

Were her eyes red? Could Mrs Rafter tell that she had been awake all night, sobbing into her pillow, listening to the muffled voices of her parents assuring themselves that they had done the right thing, taken the only course? But at least Val or Sher had not been there to make fun of her, tease her for a boring little bookworm; nowadays she had the bed and the whole bedroom to herself. But then, even if Mrs Rafter could tell, she wouldn't make fun of something so terrible. Even though Mrs Rafter was so much older than her, she sometimes seemed more like a sister than Val or Sher ever had.

Reaching a large rock after quite a walk that took them well out of

7

sight of the school, Eimear sat down on it and motioned to Aran to do the same.

'Do you like cheese, Aran? Have a cheese sandwich?'

Eimear held out the box and Aran gazed into it: four large sandwiches, for one person! Made with some kind of bread she had not seen before, lavishly filled with a kind of cheese that did not look at all like the kind that came in cellophane, from the shop. Unable to resist, she lifted one out, and shyly offered her own package in return.

'Mine are lettuce and tomato. We have lots, at home.'

In fact this produce was meagre enough, but it made a vital difference to the Campion diet. At this time of year lunch rarely consisted of anything else, but Mrs Rafter was not to know that. In winter, it would have been worse: she would have had to offer her a fish sandwich, when the entire village was sick to death of the stuff. Yet somebody must like fish, because the iced crates of it went away in lorries to Dublin, some even went on as far as London, by ferry. And a Frenchman had moved into Dunrathway recently, to farm the oysters and mussels for which he claimed there was growing demand on the continent. That was the good side of the EEC, it had done away with export restrictions, even if it had also brought big ships which ransacked and polluted the clear waters in which the harvest grew. A simple question, her father said, of harmony and balance. Only it was not turning out to be simple at all.

Putting down her lunchbox, Eimear accepted the swop with a smile, wondering why so many people, evidently including Molly Campion, preferred the factory-made, ready-sliced bread to the nutty nutritious kind they could bake themselves. Her neighbour Annie McGowan did bake it, and made wonderful cheeses as well, but her attempts to market the two commodities locally had met with indifference. People only wanted what they saw advertised on television, shiny snazzy wrappers that often disguised bland industrial contents.

'Mm. Delicious.'

At least this lettuce was fresh and homegrown, but if Molly had heard that chemical pesticides were good for her vegetables then that, Eimear realised, was what she was eating. Forcing herself to take another bite, she studied Aran, wondering where such a mother could have got such a daughter. In the May sunshine the girl's fair curls gleamed like silver, her skin pale and smooth as ivory, tinted only by natural colour. The wind and sea roughened most complexions in these parts, but they had as yet given her only a rosy glow. Where her parents were husked and bent she was supple and lush, her grey eyes clear and innocent. Small white teeth nibbled busily at the food she ate, and Eimear saw that she was hungry. Well, that was normal; all the children always were, even Joey Devlin's and Rowan Farmer's.

Childhood ended quickly in this village, as in most rural villages, there were few teenage boys who did not already help their fathers on the boats, few girls who got beyond twelve or thirteen without having raised a clatter of siblings. And of course they had all seen lambs and calves being born, knew about the mating ritual which, therefore, their parents felt little need to explain in human terms. For most, life simply happened to them as dictated by nature; but for Aran Eimear was determined to find a less brutal fate.

'So, Aran. We're going to lose you.'

'Yes, Mrs Rafter. Thanks for not making a scene with Mam and Dad yesterday. It was hard enough for them.'

'You're not angry with them, then? Even though they won't ask Val or Sher for help?'

'No. I'm not. Sher's in America, she'd worry herself sick if she knew how bad things were, and Mam says she mustn't be worried when she's pregnant. Val would . . . Val wouldn't . . . well, she doesn't come here very often.'

No. She didn't. Eimear had heard all about Val Campion's attitude to Dunrathway, now that she had escaped to Cork and left the smell of fish well behind. The fish that had put her through school until she was eighteen, old enough to marry her newsagent and, rumour had it, serve him with steak four times a week. Cork and Dunrathway were little more than an hour apart, but Val preferred the members of her family to visit her in the city rather than go out to them. That way she only had to see them one at a time, because the whole family never had bus fare all together, and so it was Molly who usually made the pilgrimage to the hallowed shrine of prosperity, where Val would meet her at the terminus in her little white Mini. And how Molly loved that! Even if her own neighbours never got to see the Mini, Val's did.

'Is there anything I can do, Aran?'

'Oh, no, Mrs Rafter!' Aran looked alarmed. 'Mam and Dad wouldn't hear of it! I'll be all right, really!'

'What will you do?'

'I'll – I'll try the hotel. It'll be busy for the summer, they'll be looking for staff.'

Dismally Eimear thought of the hotel, an ugly concrete affair built in the sixties by a developer who had misunderstood what tourists were looking for in Ireland. It had turned out that this was the very type of architecture they were seeking to escape in their own

9

countries, and the hotel had been sold twice since, its paint scruffy now, its manager surly and discouraged.

Even if he took Aran on, the girl could not be allowed to begin her young life anywhere so hideous, so hatefully dispiriting.

'Tell me, Aran, what would you really like to do? If you could choose?'

Aran finished her cheese sandwich and took a first bite out of the one that remained in the paper wrapper. It did not taste nearly so good, but her face radiated enthusiasm as if she had stumbled on something delicious.

'I'd like to get an honours Leaving Cert. and then go to college. Business college.'

Business? Eimear was taken aback. Certainly, the girl's grades were equal to it, but what about the poetry she wrote, the oboe she played so sweetly in Mr Lavery's music class?

'Well – that's a surprise! I thought I had a young Keats on my hands, and Mr Lavery thought he had a young Mozart on his.'

'Oh, I love poetry, Mrs Rafter, you know I do. But people only laugh at it, it's not much use for anything. And even if I weren't leaving school I couldn't keep on asking Mr Lavery to lend me the oboe to practise at home, when it's meant to be shared between everyone. Lucy Reilly plays it much better than I do, and her Mam doesn't – doesn't say what mine does.'

'What does yours say?'

'That music gives her a headache, especially when it's me who's playing, and that it's not a proper subject like maths or geography, it doesn't get you anywhere.'

'Look where it got Beethoven, and the Beatles.'

'Oh, yes! If I thought I had talent like theirs . . . but I haven't, Mrs Rafter. I can play pretty well, and I can make words sound musical on paper, but I can't hear music in my head. Not real music. The best I could ever do is sing or play somebody else's, and I don't want that. I want something of my own.'

'Such as?'

'Something that – that doesn't depend on the weather, like fishing! Something I could control.'

'Some kind of business, then? At a desk, in an office?'

'Yes.'

Surprised by such pragmatism, which sounded almost as worldly-wise as Dan's, Eimear leaned back on the rock to consider the student who, she always thought, had such a much more romantic streak. Her essays were wildly imaginative . . . but then, was it just her own lack of imagination, that found the concept of business so

10

dull? After all, many people found commerce very challenging, and money altogether fascinating. Some of them might even say that teaching was far less interesting, repeating the same things year in and year out, that it would drive them round the bend. Personally she loved all the children with their lively, funny ways, even the slow ones who always seemed to compensate with such charm or earnest effort. But much of the curriculum they studied was dry and dated, yes, even redundant in 1975.

'What about marriage, like your sisters? Does a husband come into the picture, or are you going to get to be a corporate magnate all by yourself?'

Aran smiled mischievously.

'If I could find a nice husband like yours, I'd marry him. But not till after I'd got my career going.'

'Well, Aran, that's not always so easy to control. You can decide who you don't want to marry, but only fate can send someone you do.'

'It sent you Mr Rafter. He's lovely. All the girls think so.'

'Do they now? Aren't they the grand bunch of little gossips.'

'Oh, I'm sorry – I only meant—'

Eimear laughed.

'Never mind, Aran, I'll take it as a compliment. Daniel is a good, kind man and it was a very lucky day I met him.'

'Definitely. Was it love at first sight?'

Aran gasped at her own audacity. Mrs Rafter was still her teacher! *How* could she have said such a nosy, cheeky thing? But Eimear only laughed again.

'Well, not the very moment I saw him. But the moment he opened his mouth and we got talking, I knew he was the right man for me.'

Just in time Aran grabbed back the next question that sprang to mind: everyone knows you don't have any children, Mrs Rafter, and why is that? We all like you easily the best of our teachers, and we reckon you'd make a great mother. Your classes are strict and hard work, but they're fun too, and you're always so kind when anyone is in trouble, like I am now.

And I'll be in a lot more, if I ask another word about your private life that's none of my business.

'Well, I hope I'll know the right man for me, when he opens *his* mouth.'

'And then what? Children, I suppose?'

'Oh, no.'

'No?'

'No thanks. I mean – not all women want them, Mrs Rafter, or have to have them. My own Mam often says little Dursey was a big

11

mistake, that she should have got a cat instead. Cheaper to run, she says.'

'But Aran, you can't put money first when it comes to children.'

'But look where the lack of it has got me.'

'Oh, Aran! If your parents had thought about it, you probably wouldn't have existed at all.'

'Maybe not. But since I do, I'm going to make my own money somehow, and keep them in comfort when they're old. I'll be too busy for children. I'll have a nice husband and a career instead, like you, with no hungry mouths to feed.'

And what can I say, Eimear wondered, to that? Where she's coming from, it's no wonder she wants to go where she does. She's only sixteen, and has no idea of the turns life can take – or not take, sometimes. She has no idea what children can mean to a woman, or to a marriage. She doesn't know how Dan and I – nor is it my place to tell her, or dampen her ambition, her wonderful energy. Ten years ago, I might have said exactly what she's saying now.

'Well then, Aran, we'd better get you started, hadn't we?'

'We?'

'Yes, of course, the two of us. I'm not going to let my best student wander out into the world all by herself. If I can't get you through to college, then at least I can help you find a job that might teach you something about business.'

'God, would you really, Mrs Rafter?'

'I would and I will. For the moment, I don't want you to think about what it might be, because for one thing I don't know yet myself, and for another you have your exams coming up. Concentrate on those, and I promise you I'll have something by the time they're over.'

'Oh, Mrs Rafter . . . if you really could, I'd never be able to thank you enough. You couldn't be nicer to me if – if you were my own mother!'

Now, Eimear thought, there's a compliment.

Conor Campion paused, a hunk of bread halfway to his mouth, and put it down again. At the other side of the kitchen table, his daughter sat fresh and neat in her blue pullover and grey skirt, eating her porridge with one hand while the other turned the pages of a book. It was the morning of her first exam and she was, he supposed, cramming some last-minute information into her head.

'Child.'

Reciting something in a low murmur, she did not hear him, her expression so absorbed she might have been on the other side of the world. He didn't want to distract her, but he must say it.

12

'Child.'

She looked up.

'Yes, Dad?'

'Good luck. Do the best you can, and you'll do well.'

'I will, Dad. Thanks.'

Her gaze fell back on the page, leaving Conor irresolute. He was a man of few words. But he wanted to find some now. The right ones.

'You know – you know we'd let you stay, don't you? If there was any way?'

'Yes, I do. But you're not to feel bad, Dad. It can't be helped.'

She smiled at him, with no trace of anger or bitterness, not even the sorrow that had shadowed her these many past days.

'You're a good girl, Aran. You'll find work you like, and new friends.'

'Yes I will. Mrs Rafter is going to ask around for me. She knows all sorts of people.'

'Aye. Work can be hard, Aran, but it's an honourable thing.'

'I know, Dad. You work hard for us and that's already got us further than you ever got, or Mam.'

He had left school at thirteen, as had his wife, in the days when the law did not meddle in such things. 'Honourable' was one of the longest words he knew.

'Do you remember the day we went to Dungarvan?'

It lay sunk deep in her memory like rusty gold. She had been only nine at the time, but she would never forget that day, the day Conor had got hold of a boat to call his own from dawn to sunset, and taken the whole family out in it. Turning east out of the harbour, they had set course on the long voyage filled with sunshine and sights she had never seen before or since, places she could remember to this day: Roscarberry, Courtmacsherry, Kinsale, Ballycotton and Youghal, each one different but somehow linked to the next, where distant figures had gone about their business on foot or on bicycles, sometimes waving at the boat when it came in close to shore, receding again as the boat pulled away. Now, Conor seemed to be narrowing the horizons he had opened up to her, but she would push them back again. Some day, she would see more of her country. Maybe even some of the others, too, that made up this European Community she lived in. Mr and Mrs Rafter had been as far as France.

Only as she thought of that trip to Dungarvan did she realise what it must have cost her father to take a whole day off work and pay for the fuel that had powered the chugging boat.

'I remember it, Dad. I'll always remember it, and someday I'll take

13

you somewhere you'll never forget. When I have money I'll take you somewhere – somewhere special!'

Special? Neither he nor Molly had ever been anywhere, unless you counted Cork, to see Val. Aran might get further than that, he hoped – but hardly much further, the way things were going. Yet he was touched by her impetuosity, the way she said, 'when I have money', as if the mere saying of it would make it happen. Everyone else in this house said 'if', not 'when'.

'Money's a grand thing, Aran. But you have to be careful of it, too.'

'What do you mean, Dad?'

'It can buy an awful lot of nice things. But the problem is that people get attached to those things. They get one, and then they want another. And another.'

'What's wrong with that? There are lots of things we need.'

'Aye. But there comes a time when some people can't tell the difference between what they need and what they only want.'

'Well, there are lots of things I want.'

She said it innocently, and he knew she didn't mean to wound him. Of course there were, and some of the other young girls already had some of them – a pretty dress, a new coat, a pair of shoes for the dances on Saturday nights. He wished he could get them for her, but if he couldn't, then maybe he could give her something else instead. Inarticulate, he sought to express it.

'Do you know what the very best thing is, child? The best thing money can buy?'

'No. What?'

'Freedom.'

'Freedom from what?'

'From cold and hunger, from the wind and the rain, but above all from doing anything you don't want to do, for people you don't want to do it for.'

What did he mean? That he didn't like the fishing, or Paddy Clafferty who owned the boat?

'But you like what you do, Dad, don't you?'

'Aye. But I don't like it as much as I used to, getting up at all hours to go out in all weathers, with no say in anything and no notion what'll happen when I get old. If I had my own boat, I'd be able to decide things, and plan them. And that's the difference, child. When you have something of your own, you're in charge. Even if you save all your money in the bank, people know you have it, they respect you and treat you different. They know you can tell them to go to hell any time you like.'

Control? Was that what he meant? Control and choice, the two

14

things she wanted herself? But he couldn't have gone after them, or he'd have got them. He was a quiet gentle soul, and she loved him dearly. But she was going to go after them, and get them.

'I'll buy you a boat, Dad, before you get old. And do you know what?'

He smiled. 'What?'

'It won't be a trawler. It'll be the kind you can take people out in – tourists, during the summer. You can take them out round the coast the way you took us when we were little, and show them where to fish for shark. Then you'll earn enough to keep you right through the winter.'

Tourists? Well, there were a few, and they did occasionally ask about shark. But after a day or two in Dunrathway they usually drifted away, and you couldn't blame them, when it was only a plain working village, with that bleak hotel they didn't like. It would never get enough of them that you could make the kind of living Aran said. She was talking nonsense. But maybe for once he shouldn't discourage her. She'd been discouraged enough already, and he was tired of feeling that way himself. Besides, she'd soon be fully grown, learning reality the hard way, forgetting these childish daydreams.

He looked at her eager eyes, and she looked at the net of lines around his, the darns in his sweater, the patches on the elbows. On the chair where Sher used to sit, his oilskins lay in a heap.

'We'd better get moving, Dad. You've got work and I've got school.'

'I wish you'd got a lot more of it, lass.'

'Well, stop wishing. If I need more I'll get more, one way or another, and then I'll get us both what we want.'

'What do we want?'

'What you just said. Freedom.'

Such resolve was beyond him. Getting up, he pulled on his oilskin jacket, folded the trousers over one arm and put the other around her shoulder.

'You'll forgive us, then? Your Mam and me, for putting you out to work?'

'There's nothing to forgive. Don't think about it any more.'

He thought about it all the way down to the harbour. His daughter's attitude should make him feel much better. But somehow it made him feel worse.

Dunrathway's community school was new, a great improvement on the draughty old building in which Eimear's mother Hannah had taught a whole generation of students. That one had been run by nuns, exclusively for girls, but this one took boys also, albeit in a separate building on the same land. Often the sexes mixed, for sports or drama, and while the girls were taught carpentry and basic electrical work, the boys learned to cook and sew. That was unusual, but as adults each would have to cope without the skills of the other while the men were away at sea.

The two nuns on the board of management had been quite agreeable to the idea of their girls learning traditionally male skills, outvoting Father Carroll who wasn't nearly so keen on letting his boys make omelettes and repair their own clothes. But he had been mollified when he realised he was going to get his way on another matter – namely, discipline. Appalled by what he heard of some of the big secular schools in Cork and Dublin, where pupils ran amok and made their teachers' lives a nightmare, he had resolved to set a certain tough tone come hell or high water – which would come, if he didn't set it. Surprisingly the staff had sided with him, and the result was an orderly establishment which functioned crisply and efficiently.

Eimear enjoyed her work there, and knew that today's ill humour had nothing to do with the children, who were sitting in total silence before her, completing the last of their exam papers with an air of great concentration. When they finished, they would jump up whooping with glee and rush out into the ten weeks of summer that awaited them. With equal if less noisy pleasure, the teachers would lock their rooms and enjoy a final chat about holidays to be taken, gardens to be dug, projects to be completed.

But her own two projects were getting nowhere.

After casting about for three weeks, she still had not found anything for Aran Campion, anybody who needed a young girl's labour. And she had a cramp in her stomach – the low dull ache that told her she had failed, yet again, to conceive.

The bell rang, and a minor riot broke out. Returning her attention to her duties, she gathered up the papers, assured everyone that they would pass in a blaze of glory and made her way quickly out of the room before Aran's hopeful gaze could fall upon her. Tomorrow, when she was in a better mood, she would go round to the Campion home, apologise and say something that would keep their morale up. Since Aran had told her parents that Mrs Rafter was going to help her find a job they had come not only to believe it but expect it, and twice already Molly had accosted her in the street, almost accusingly, to know whether there was any news.

Oh, blast Molly. Eimear decided to slip home, feed Sammy and then go have a cup of tea with her own mother. Hannah's house was high up on Fenner's Hill, with its nose in the air some people said, but she always found it welcoming and soothing. Recovering from an attack of shingles, Hannah would be at home, and probably even more glad to see her than usual.

When she arrived, Hannah was glad, but also preoccupied.

'Come in, dear, and meet Mr Allen.'

Mr Allen, whoever he was, sat ensconced in an armchair, looking rather as if he owned it. But he stood up as Eimear entered the room, offering the kind of hearty handshake that bespoke a salesman. On a table, empty teacups testified that he had been here for some time, and Eimear noticed that the top of Hannah's bureau was down, littered with papers.

He must be selling something. Life insurance? Double glazing? But Hannah didn't need the former, and already had the latter.

'Mr Allen is a solicitor, dear. I've been tidying up my affairs, and found I needed some help.'

'Oh, Mother! You've only had shingles! You're almost perfectly well again.'

'Yes, of course I am. But I am sixty-eight, you know.'

Eimear sighed. Hannah's mother, her grandmother, had died at an age vanity had never permitted her to disclose, but which was reckoned to be ninety-six or -seven. Longevity ran in the family – but then, so did this fussy need to organise things, keep everything straight at the corners. No wonder teaching ran in it too. Tactfully, Eimear didn't enquire about the affairs, which would leave everything to her automatically, as Hannah's only child.

Anyway, it appeared that the business was concluded. With something of an effort, she resigned herself to making small talk with Mr Allen. His practice was in Leemanway, he said, and she wondered that Hannah hadn't found somebody nearer. Leemanway was twenty miles inland. What was wrong with Harry Sigerson, the tall chimney of whose house could be seen here from this very window? Too close to home, she supposed. Hannah wouldn't want everyone to know her business, not even Harry who was discreet as the grave.

For some time they chatted, and with irritation she found that Mr Allen showed no inclination to leave. Settled and cosy in his armchair, he talked about anything and everything until, belatedly and reluctantly, he turned the conversation away from himself.

'Mrs Lowry tells me you're a teacher, Mrs Rafter, eh? Like mother like daughter, eh?'

'Yes. I started just before she retired. I work at the community school.'

'Oh yes? I've heard of it. A fine school, by all accounts.'

'It is. We have some fine students.'

17

Hannah turned to her.

'What about the Campion girl, Eimear? Have you got anything for her, yet?'

'No, Mother. I'm afraid nobody seems to have any use for her, smart as she is. It looks as if Aran is going to end up washing dishes at the hotel after all.'

'Who's Aran?' Mr Allen looked as if he couldn't bear to let the conversation go off anywhere without him.

'She's one of my students. Sixteen, looking for a job.'

Eimear's tone indicated that that was all she was going to tell him, but he leaned forward, unctuously.

'Is she any use?'

'She's very clever, if that's what you mean.'

'But not too clever? That she'd be bored with a bit of filing work, typing, that kind of thing?'

It dawned on Eimear that Aran couldn't even type. Also that this man seemed to be suggesting something. She should be pleased to hear it, but somehow she wasn't; he didn't appeal to her at all. However, beggars couldn't be choosers. She'd better find out what it was.

'She can't type, but she would learn quickly. Why do you ask? Do you have a vacancy?'

'No. I don't. But I heard Philip Miller over in Ferleague saying that he has one. I'm sure he'd be delighted to get someone from Dunrathway school, with the reputation it has. No nonsense at that school, eh?'

Eimear hesitated.

'No. None. Tell me, Mr Allen, who is Philip Miller?'

'He's the solicitor in Ferleague. I don't know him very well, but we meet now and then on the court circuit.'

'What kind of person is he?'

Mr Allen blinked. Surely an interview was for Philip to conduct, not this woman to whom he was only offering a little favour in return for her mother's business – and maybe her own, if she ever had any legal documents needed drawing up?

'Why he's a grand chap, Mrs Rafter, you couldn't meet nicer. He does a lot of conveyancing, and his son has just joined him in the practice. It's expanding a bit, and they need an office junior.'

Ferleague. It was a small town, fifteen miles north east of Dunrathway. But there was a bus that went through it every morning, en route to Dublin. And a solicitor's office – well, it was not a commercial venture, in the strict sense of the word, but it would teach Aran something about the way other people handled their

18

businesses, and maybe a bit about law as well. It was a start.

She bestowed a smile on Mr Allen.

'Would you have a word with him, then, perhaps? Or if you'd give me the number, I could telephone and say that you'd referred me?'

'Certainly.'

There and then, Mr Allen extracted his diary from his leather briefcase, flipped it open and handed Eimear a pen and pad.

'Here we are. Philip Miller, 24 Main Street, the number is . . .'

'Thank you very much, Mr Allen. That's very kind of you.'

'You're welcome. If you'd care to call him, say, this day next week, I'll have a word with him in the meantime.'

'He won't regret it, you can tell him. Aran's very obedient and industrious, she comes from an honest family and she's most anxious to learn. If he's agreeable to meet her, I'll take her over there myself.'

'Good, good. And now, ladies, I'd better be on my way.'

Court experience had taught Thomas Allen the advantage of quitting while he was ahead. Mrs Lowry's daughter hadn't seemed very well disposed to him when she arrived, but she was now. And might be again, in the future.

Philip Miller couldn't believe his luck. Without even the expense of putting an advertisement in the local newspaper, or the bother of putting one in shop windows, this dazzling blonde creature had fallen into his lap. In fact his lap was the very place for her. But the girl's chaperone sat watchful and attentive in the room with them and, feeling that he was being sized up, Philip adopted a tone at once businesslike and paternal.

'Nine honours?'

'Yes, Mr Miller.'

'But no typing?'

'No, but I'd learn in a week, you could put me on trial.'

'Yes, solicitors often put people on trial, hah hah!'

The girl's dutiful laugh was delightful, and her lack of experience was a bonus. He wouldn't have to pay her quite so much until she proved her worth.

'Fifteen pounds a week? That suit?'

Aran glanced uncertainly at Mrs Rafter. She had no idea what the going rate was, or what she was worth. But Eimear did.

'For a month – then up to seventeen, when she can type?'

'Sixteen.'

He'd go the seventeen, if he had to. The girl was bright as a button, and would be a splendid advertisement for him. But he mustn't look too eager.

'Very well. Sixteen. With a bonus at Christmas.'

'Done.'

Eimear smiled, glad she hadn't forced his hand, or let him see she'd have settled for fifteen if need be. The Campions' need was urgent, and Aran's anxiety obvious. Not that she would have let her take this job if there had been anything she could find fault with; but she had made enquiries, and been informed that Mr Miller was a perfectly respectable man, long established and long married. His office was clean and pleasant, the bus stopped right outside it, everything was really quite ideal. Standing up, she shook his hand, and Aran followed her example.

'Nine o'clock on Monday, then, young lady. Don't be late.'

Mr Miller escorted them to the door and, once it was safely shut between them, both parties laughed aloud.

'Oh, Mrs Rafter, you were great! I'd never have dared ask for the extra money!'

'Not this time, perhaps. But in future you must. You'll soon learn what value to put on yourself, and fight for it. This time next year, tell him you want twenty pounds, and he'll give you eighteen.'

'Right. I will, if you say so.'

'Good. Now, let's go shopping.'

'Shopping? Oh – but I haven't any money.'

Aran flushed as she said it, realising that Mrs Rafter must want to buy something for her husband or for herself. If she'd only kept her mouth shut, she'd have got through the day without having to make the confession.

'Never mind. Come on. You can't start work in the clothes you wore to school.'

Oh, Lord. Aran supposed that she couldn't.

'What'll I do? Would he mind if I wore them just for a week, until I get my first pay packet?'

Pay packet! Didn't it sound grown-up, and wonderful!

'Probably not, but you did so well at that interview, I'm going to give you a little reward.'

Stammering and protesting, Aran found herself taken firmly by the arm, marched into Ferleague's large drapery shop and propelled in front of a rack of dresses.

'Let's see . . . the lilac one, with the white collar. Do you like it?'

'Oh yes, but—'

'Try it on.'

Ninety minutes later, Aran found herself sitting at a table with a real linen tablecloth and flowers on it, a menu in her hands, her head spinning. *Lunch*! In a *restaurant*!

On one side of her, Mrs Rafter sat calmly reading another menu, and on the other a pile of packages sat as if under a Christmas tree in a fairytale. A dress, a pair of shoes with heels an inch high, six pairs of tights, and a tube of pink *lipstick*. It was unimaginable. And what would Mam say, when she saw the blouse for her, what would Achill and Dursey say, when they saw the huge box of sweets for them?

If she lived to be a hundred, she could never thank Mrs Rafter enough. Also, if she lived to be a hundred, she could not order a starter, a main course and a dessert from this menu. What was consommé? What was curry? What in God's name was baked Alaska?

Sole. She knew what that was, and she knew from French class that bonne femme meant good woman, even if she didn't know what good women had to do with sole. When the waitress came, she would order that. It was petrifyingly expensive, but so was everything else that this good woman seemed determined to give her.

Eimear looked up.

'Why don't you try the beef Wellington, Aran? I sometimes make it at home myself, it's delicious.'

And so Aran had beef for the first time in two months, discovered what baked Alaska was, and cleared both plates. But over and again her mind returned to the sole: one pound and fifty pence, for one piece! She was sure Paddy Clafferty didn't get that for a whole crate of it.

What did Paddy get, exactly, and how much of it found its way into Dad's pocket? What caused the price to rise so much by the time the fish arrived on a restaurant table in Ferleague, only fifteen miles away? Even as she applied herself to holding an adult conversation with Mrs Rafter, something in the back of her mind went on trying to work it out: transport – the lorry, the driver and the ice – cooking, the electricity and the chef – and then all these extras, the linen, flowers, waitress in her frilly white apron. Decor, laundry, dishes, cutlery, glasses . . . everything, she realised, was built into the astronomical prices.

Plus profit, of course. What percentage was that? And what if the hotel bought enough fish for thirty people, but only twenty ordered it? What if the—

'You will, Aran, won't you?'

Eimear was amused. She never lost Aran's attention in class, but clearly she had lost it now. Guiltily, the girl stared at her.

'I'm sorry, Mrs Rafter. What did you say?'

'I said I want you to keep on writing your poetry.'

Suddenly, poetry seemed very irrelevant. But she did enjoy writing it, useless as it was, and if Mrs Rafter wanted her to continue, then she would. It would be an excuse to stay in touch with her.

'Yes. I will, I promise.'

'Good. But while you're at work, I want you to concentrate on that. Learn everything you can.'

'That's exactly what I intend to do.'

Pleased, Eimear noted her firm tone. People might underestimate Aran, at first, because she only had a minimal education or because she was a pretty blonde. But they would be mistaken. That mop of angelic curls camouflaged a brain that was going to take her places.

Only not, Eimear hoped, too far away.

If Philip Miller couldn't believe his luck, Molly Campion was even more stunned. Sixteen pounds a week, Aran said? And Mrs Rafter had bought all these things, including the cream blouse which, she suspected, was pure silk? Battling an urge to check the label, Molly gazed at her daughter and her teacher.

'Well, Mrs Rafter, I can't think what possessed you to do such a thing.'

'Oh, we enjoyed it, didn't we, Aran?'

That Aran had enjoyed it was abundantly obvious. Tumbling breathlessly out of Mrs Rafter's car, she had not stopped talking since, her face glowing with excitement, her eyes gleaming like newly-polished pewter.

Well, a few weeks of hard work would soon bring her down to earth. For this evening, she might as well have her fun and get it over with. And Mrs Rafter had better have a cup of tea. Praying that the boys wouldn't come in and brawl over the box of sweets before the woman's eyes, Molly opened her top cupboard and took down the good china that Val had given her for Christmas. Until now, Val had always been the daughter who meant most to her.

Aran continued to regale her mother with an account of the shop and restaurant in Ferleague as Eimear sat down, taking in the small room which, when the entire family was in it, must be very constricting. As she might have expected it was almost aggressively clean, with a narrow window from which she could see the yard in which the few chickens and vegetables were raised, and from the opposite wall Pope Paul looked down on her from a gilt frame. Painted several years before in a muted shade she would call fawn, the walls carried evidence of perpetual damp, the steam that rose from pots and laundry and, at this moment, the large tinny kettle. It was a standard fisherman's kitchen, and it took Eimear a few moments to put her finger on what was missing: colour. In other such houses, the drabness was almost always relieved by some floral pattern, on curtains or a couple of cushions, often there was a vase of fresh flowers which, in such surroundings, stood out as if arranged by Vincent Van Gogh. Here, the only visual relief lay in a basket of wool which Molly, presumably, was about to knit into a sweater or cardigan. The violent red and screeching yellow were as arresting as a set of traffic lights, demanding attention.

'I see you're busy with the knitting, Mrs Campion.'

'Aye.' Molly put the tea things down on the table.

'Have you done much this year? Is there a good demand for it?'

'Not bad. The crafts shops say they're fairly busy so far.'

Those were in other villages, Eimear knew, Dunrathway didn't have one of its own. Abruptly, Molly dived on a cardboard box in a corner of the floor, bent down and took out a pile of knitted garments. If Mrs Rafter was trying to suggest she was slacking, not doing her best for her family, she was wrong. Dumping the evidence on the table, she left her to see for herself. There were perhaps ten or twelve assorted items in the pile, all in howling colours, and as Eimear conscientiously admired each one, she felt the harshness of the wool, the rigidity of the stitches in her hand. Little love, she thought, had gone into the making of these. Yet they were technically impeccable, neatly finished, of sound serviceable quality. To their owners' eventual horror, they would probably last for years.

Aran beamed.

'Mam's great at the knitting.'

It was Molly's cue to say they were all great, Eimear for having found her daughter a job and driven her to the interview, Aran for having got it. But she didn't.

'Indeed she is. It must be very difficult. I couldn't even make a scarf myself if my life depended on it.'

'Neither could I. I'm no help to Mam at all in that department.'

They both smiled, and for the first time Molly noted the air of complicity between them, as if they were friends rather than teacher and pupil. Ex-pupil. Why was Eimear doing so much for the girl, taking such an interest in this family? Of course she, Molly, didn't have a car, and could never have afforded to buy Aran those new things . . . but still, Mrs Rafter hadn't even apologised for having taken over what was really a mother's role.

Oh well. The job was got now, the matter finished. Mrs Rafter wouldn't be coming round here every day of the week to sip tea and make idle chat. Let her go home now and get on with providing her husband with the daughter they should have of their own, after five or six years of marriage. There was no room in this house for a career woman with her fine clothes and long summer holidays, for every day

23

of which she would be paid as if she were working.

Wiping her hands on her apron, Molly gathered up the woollens and replaced them in their carton. Admittedly the woman had been some help, and the silk blouse was very nice, but where was she supposed to wear it? Out feeding the chickens, or while blacking the boys' shoes, peeling the spuds?

It's more than a silk blouse I need, she thought. But when is anybody ever going to help *me*?

Chapter Two

Dad was right, Aran thought. Work was indeed an honourable thing. It gave her great satisfaction to see the pride in his face, the pleasure in her mother's as she handed them her pay packet every Friday evening. It did not contain as much as she had expected, the government first levying a quantity of tax on it that made her feel as if she had been robbed by masked bandits, but what remained was enough to ease the stress on the household budget and earn her a position of some status. From having been a burden, she had become an asset.

Since she wasn't sure how to open a bank account, much less run one, Philip Miller agreed to her request to be paid in cash, and Molly counted the notes vigilantly, tucking all but four into a tea caddy before returning those to Aran for bus fares and whatever sundries she might need. Aran found she needed remarkably little, once she'd got an extra skirt and shirt for work, and by the end of August fourteen pounds had mounted up between the pages of the book in which she kept her savings. Taking Achill and Dursey into Ferleague with her one Saturday morning, she bought them each a pair of trousers for school, an ice-cream apiece and two of the action-man comics on which their gaze hovered lustfully.

Mrs Rafter had introduced her to the joy of receiving, but the joy of giving proved even greater, and in her brothers' faces she saw one of the first things she wanted. On the bus home they sat almost quietly, spoke respectfully as they calculated the extent of this new force in their lives. It was an exercise that rendered them briefly but wondrously mute.

But its effect did not extend beyond the family. In the office Mr Miller called her a 'grand little girl' while Moira his secretary offered no help with the typing or anything that might undermine her own position. Lorcan, Mr Miller's son and junior partner, was friendly, but had a sharp enough tongue in his head if his coffee was not hot enough or paperwork not arranged to his liking. Aran found the arranging of it dull enough, but the contents quite fascinating. So this was how people went about buying a house or a farm, this was how you set things up! Of course it cost more, if you undertook to do it slowly over a long period of time, but you could do it. It was not the way her father paid his debts, but she could see the advantage of it – to the lender as well as the buyer. Then there were the wills that people drew up, and those were a revelation too; who'd ever have thought that these little old ladies, who crept like mice into the office and smiled coyly at Mr Miller, would have so much? Where they got it she couldn't imagine, but clearly there was more to the frail creatures than met the eye. Once, one of them burst into tears and sobbed all over Mr Miller's desk, mystifying her as he called for tea and tissues, but Moira seemed to know what it was about, sniffing curtly that there was 'a man in it'.

Men, Aran noticed, seemed to deal in larger sums than women, but less often and less competently, seeking the solicitor's advice only after things had gone wrong and bluffing it out even then. Where bailiffs were involved, or the situation was askew beyond redemption, they were usually and speedily referred to Thomas Allen over in Leemanway. Moira called Mr Miller 'Mr Teflon' and Aran laughed when she worked out what it meant, impressed by her boss's ability to control the conditions under which he worked. Conscious that she was learning things no business school could teach her, and that her mind was rising to them, she began to drive her colleagues crazy with her questions; those that went unanswered were the ones that intrigued her most of all.

But she was finding out a lot about other things too. Every day Mr Miller brought two newspapers with him into the office, the *Cork Examiner* and the *Irish Independent*, and in the evening he let her take them away to read on the bus. It was soon evident to Aran that a great many things were going on in the rest of the country, things that put Dunrathway into a very small, unimportant context. Dublin sounded so strange it might as well be on another planet, while Cork was busy and angry, coping with a wave of crime that seemed to be afflicting Limerick as well. In Dunrathway, the worst thing she could remember ever happening was Gerry Dineen's accidental shooting of his own brother, a disaster in which drink and darkness had played a mitigating part. Personally Aran didn't see how drink could mitigate anything, but at least the brother had lived to see another day.

Mitigate. She liked the new words she was learning, and it was a comfort to think Dunrathway was safe if nothing else. Every evening she asked the bus driver to let her off a mile short of it so she could walk the rest of the way, enjoying the exercise and the long bright light, the salty smell of seaweed as she got closer, the gulls circling over the hills and harbour until the first trawler appeared and they flew out to escort it noisily home. Her former classmates reported that they were having a wonderful summer, but Aran was just as happy with hers. Only when the school reopened did she feel a twinge – quite a twinge, as if someone had tweaked a broken bone. But that day she decided to do something none of her friends could do.

'Mr Miller, how does a person open a bank account?'

'Hah! Easiest thing in the world, my girl. Easiest thing in the world.'

And so it was, when she finally braved the big granite building and went up to the counter marked Enquiries.

'Current or deposit?'

Deposit. That had a lovely solid, weighty sound. Of course there wasn't anything very weighty about six pounds, and she could see that the clerk was trying not to smile – but had he had six pounds of his own at her age? How much might she have by the time she was his? With interest on it too, just as they had been taught at school. Some of the things she had learned there were becoming real now, falling into place. But for some reason she did not want to tell her parents about this major accomplishment. She wanted to tell Eimear. This evening she would take up the standing invitation to visit her, call in on the way home.

Eimear. It still sounded strange to call her by her first name, but Eimear had insisted, just as Dan had insisted too, as if he were a friend instead of a vet. But then he was so friendly, quite the nicest man in Dunrathway, Aran thought, and their house must be the nicest too; not the biggest, but certainly the warmest and sunniest. From its kitchen window you could see right across the harbour, up to Fenner's Hill where Eimear's mother lived and Joey Devlin was building a massive house for which, rumour had it, he had ordered a carpet with his initials woven into it. Aran thought that was the silliest, vainest thing she'd ever heard. As if he might forget his own name, or let anyone else forget it! And where was he getting such money, with the fishing the way it was? Not that it was any of her business . . . was it? Anyway, the Rafters' house had no carpets at all, it had pale polished floors with rugs to brighten the wood, and white tiles in the bathroom chequered with tiny green diamonds. Aran suspected there might even be another bathroom somewhere, but didn't dare ask.

Nicest of all, it had lots of bookshelves to which she was invited to help herself. There were pottery vases filled with yellow roses that Dan and Eimear grew themselves, and there was a record player. Often Aran could hear music as she knocked on the door, not always the serious kind you'd expect of a teacher, but songs sung by the people Mam always snapped off when they came on the radio: Carly Simon, Bob Dylan and, amazingly, the Rolling Stones. Aran just couldn't reconcile the Rolling Stones with the woman who taught Shakespeare and actually understood what T. S. Eliot was talking about.

Nor could she reconcile the sight that greeted her, this warm evening in early September, with the disciplined purveyor of Dickens and the Home Rule Bill. Eimear opened the door in a pair of denim shorts – not just denim, not just shorts, but ragged ones frayed at the ends. In her hand she held a messy wooden spoon, her cropped pink top revealed three inches of midriff, and she wasn't wearing any shoes.

Aran stared: Eimear smiled.

'Come in, Aran! You're just in time for supper, if you'd like to stay?'

Mesmerised, Aran followed the tanned bare legs down the hall into the big kitchen where, to her even greater astonishment, an open bottle of white wine stood on the pine table. She had never tasted alcohol in her life, and Eimear seemed to know it.

'Would you like to try a little drop?'

Aran swallowed. She wouldn't even be seventeen till April, and Mam would kill her if she found out. But then Eimear couldn't intend to tell her, since she was the one offering it – or else she must assume that Mam would give permission.

And it was something new. Something that had caused trouble this summer down in the pub, where her former classmates had begun to congregate in the evenings, swigging beer until they got noisily aggressive, driving Father Carroll up into his pulpit to read the riot act. But how could it cause any trouble here, with a teacher on the premises?

'Yes please. Just a tiny drop.'

A small amount was duly poured into a stemmed glass shaped like a tulip, and Eimear picked up her own glass.

'Sláinte, Aran. Wish me a happy birthday!'

'Oh Eimear, is it your birthday?'

If she'd only known, she'd have brought something, a card and chocolates maybe, some little thing she could afford now. How old could Eimear be, anyway? In those shorts, with her hair twisted into a slide and no make-up, she looked about eighteen.

'Yep. Twenty-nine today.'

Goodness, Aran thought, I hope I look like her when I'm as old as that. She's years older than Sher and Val. But she wears shorts, she listens to the Rolling Stones, she even has legs, a figure! Sher hasn't got one any more, judging by those photos she sent when the baby was born, and the things Val wears make her look forty. You wouldn't get Val into shorts at gunpoint.

Speculatively Aran took a first taste of her wine, thinking at first it tasted awful, thinking after a second go that it was something you might get used to, but you would have to really set your mind to it. Mrs Lowry must have been incredibly old when Eimear was born . . . but then everyone knew Mrs Lowry hadn't got married until she was thirty-six, the astonishing event had been the talk of the whole village Mam said, just as Mr Lowry's death had been four years later. How old would Eimear have been then? Just a baby. A tiny baby, with no Dad.

No wonder Eimear had got married so much younger herself, to Dan who must now be over thirty. And that would be why she was always going to see her mother, taking her out for drives or into Cork for shopping. Yet she didn't seem in any great hurry to have a baby of her own. Maybe she was afraid Dan would have a heart attack like her father? But he looked very fit. Probably the kids at school were enough for her – or had even put her off the whole idea. One look at Billy Devlin would be enough to put you off kids for life.

Something smelled funny.

'What are you cooking, Eimear?'

'Spaghetti bolognese, with melon to start. Your mother won't mind if you stay, will she?'

'No. She'll guess where I am. But I'd better be home before dark.'

'Oh, that gives us plenty of time. Dan will run you home. He'll be here any minute, with a birthday cake if he knows what's good for him.'

Wistfully, Aran surveyed Eimear as she went to stir her spaghetti thingy. How her eyes sparkled when she mentioned Dan! How happy and comfortable she looked, in her bare feet, in her lovely airy home! Aran always felt the same way in it, welcome and relaxed, sinking into the sofa while Sammy nuzzled up to her, accepting her as if she were one of the family.

'Can I do anything?'

'No thanks. I've had hours to prepare supper. Dan wanted to take me out to a restaurant in Cork, but it's such a long drive, and then he wouldn't have been able to drink anything. I thought a cosy supper at home would be nicer.'

Oh. Was this meant to be a romantic birthday meal? Was Dan going to arrive with a present, even flowers? He had a car, he wouldn't have to be seen carrying them down the street . . . perhaps she'd better not stay.

'Uh, Eimear, maybe it would be better if I . . . some other evening . . .'

'Oh Aran, don't be silly. You couldn't have picked a better evening. We'd have been lonely all by ourselves, just the two of us. Look, if you want to feel useful, get the cutlery out of that drawer and set the table. I'm going to pop upstairs and change.'

Eimear was gone as soon as she said it, leaving Aran to do as she was asked, and glance curiously under the lid of the saucepan that simmered on the stove. What could be in it, that smelled so strong?

'Garlic.'

She jumped out of her skin.

'Oh, Mr Rafter! D-Dan! I didn't hear you come in!'

He looked as amused as she was sure she must look guilty. In one hand he carried a huge bunch of flowers, tied with a red ribbon, while the other juggled the bakery box Eimear was expecting.

'How are you, Aran? Where's my lovely wife?'

He had a way of talking like that, humorous and yet romantic. Aran couldn't imagine either of her brothers ever doing it, if any girl was ever fool enough to go out with them.

'She's upstairs changing her clothes. She'll be right down.'

Changing for supper was another thing no one would ever do in the Campion house: when Dad was there to eat with them, the smell of mackerel made everything taste of it. But even if it meant extra laundry it was well worth the effort on Eimear's part. She looked even more beautiful when she reappeared, wearing her hair loose about her shoulders, a long white skirt patterned with apricot blossoms, a white smocked blouse and simple leather sandals. Aran caught some light scent as she floated into the room, saw that she had done something to her eyes. Going straight to Dan, she held up her face to be kissed.

'Happy birthday, my darling.'

God. Did married men really talk this way, kiss their wives like that? Aran felt something smoulder and crackle as if a fire were burning, and thought of her own parents as if from a great distance. She had only ever seen Dad kiss Mam once, and Mam had hardly even looked up from the ironing she had been doing, only muttering 'Dia leat' because Conor was going to be away at sea overnight, and the weather was rough. When he returned safely, there had been no kisses at all. But then he had not come bearing a fragrant bouquet, and Mam had not looked like some dreamy nymph in a painting.

Well, she supposed that the gap between the two couples was wide. Dan and Eimear didn't have to strive and worry as her parents did, they didn't have five children and they were a lot younger. Was it possible that once Conor and Molly had been visibly in love, the way they were now? It must be, or why would they have married? And she knew that they did love each other, in a stolid kind of way; like everything else affection was simply unspoken between them. If they didn't kiss, neither did they argue, and as a child she had always felt some secure, invisible thing that bound the family together. It just wasn't in Conor's nature to be demonstrative, any more than it was in Molly's to wear a drifting skirt like Eimear's, or the stuff which now made her eyes look so dark and dewy. It was a question not only of money but of attitude.

That attitude, whatever it was, seemed to have hardened in Molly with the years, shrunk her somehow. But, even as a child, Aran could not remember her mother playing with her like other mothers, laughing at childish misdeeds, holding hands with Conor as they walked to Mass together on Sundays. Something was either missing in her altogether, or had curdled in her, turned sour and resentful from lack of use and light. Like her hair, she had become grey and stringy, repelling people when they came close to her.

In recent weeks, Aran had tried to come closer. Sensing the shift in their relationship as she made the transition from child to woman, and the chance it offered for new beginnings, she had broached subjects she could hardly put a name on, vague things that had no particular rhyme or reason. But Molly's mind was nailed to the here and now, impossible to budge; she did not deal in nameless things, speculate in emotional rates of exchange. It was not that she did not follow what Aran was trying to say or do, it was that she chose not to query her lot, quest for things that might prove unattainable or disruptive, or both. Her world began at her front door and ended in her back yard, encompassing nothing that could not be seen or touched.

The result was conversation that became more strained as it became more civil, polite but meaningless, leaving Aran frustrated and baffled. Whenever she had something important to ask or say, Molly somehow reduced or diluted it, while inflating things that were trivial, turning difficulties into problems. Only last night, Aran had paused for a word while writing to Sher, and asked Molly how best she thought the point might be expressed.

'How should I know? Look it up in your books, and stop cluttering up my table on me!'

Every obstacle seemed to fall 'on' Molly from a malevolent sky: her chickens died on her, her potatoes burned on her, her stitches dropped on her. Some unknown demon waged a personal vendetta against everything she did; yet she never sought or accepted whatever advice anyone might offer, thought the problem through or went at it from a different angle. The gods had singled her out, she was their hapless victim, as blameless as she was impotent. When Aran was younger this attitude had been mystifying, confusing: now it was alienating. Yet for all the impediments to her own efforts, Molly could be quick to criticise others, judgemental and patronising.

'They say Annie McGowan is making cheese, when the shops are full of it, did you ever hear such nonsense.' Or, 'tie your hair back the way Val does, Aran, you look a fright.'

And so Aran had learned to turn to her father. If Conor didn't say much, or help much either, at least he listened. As Eimear listened, thoughtfully, never turning questions into barriers, discussions into hostilities. Even at this moment, as Aran looked at her, she appeared to be shedding some protective mantle, the cloak of authority that had kept an appropriate distance between them at school. Without reserve or discretion she was letting Aran glimpse into her personal life, see the nature of their love as she poured Dan a glass of wine, which he accepted as a relay runner might accept a baton from a team-mate, without glancing or confirming it was what he wanted. In his free hand he lifted a long packet aloft.

'Time for this to go on?'

Fascinated, Aran watched him open the packet and slide its contents into a pan of boiling water. Was he actually able to cook, and willing? What were those long narrow things?

'Spaghetti, Aran. That's what it looks like raw. It doesn't only come in a tin.'

It always did at home, with red sauce that soaked into the toast on which you ate the chopped soggy pieces. And they must guess that, if they were explaining without being asked. Searching for something to redeem her dignity, she came up with a winner.

'Guess what? I opened a bank account today!'

Dan grinned, but Eimear beamed.

'Good for you! Every woman should have five hundred pounds a year and a room of her own.'

'What?'

'That's what Virginia Woolf said she needed to become a writer.'

'Really? Did she get it?'

'Yes.'

'And then, did she still need it, or only want it?'

32

'Well! Who's been talking to you?'

'My Dad.'

It was a fair distinction, Eimear supposed, one of the many that Aran should learn to make. But if only Conor quibbled and demurred a bit less himself, he might achieve more. Corking the white wine, she put it back in the fridge and took a red one from a rack on the floor.

'This goes with the bolognese. Would you like to try it as well?'

What the hell. She might as well be hanged for a sheep as a lamb.

'Please.'

Dan pottered amid the pans as Eimear put the finishing touches to the table, and in due course they sat down to the melon that was served in small glass dishes, moulded into tiny balls which must, Aran thought, take hours of patience to do. Without incident she got through them, but was completely undone by the spaghetti.

'Wind it round your fork, Aran – look, like this.'

She wound, and the strands shot off her plate, onto the floor and down Sammy's throat, Oh, horror! Mam would have deplored the mess, decried her lack of dexterity and interrupted the whole meal to mop and mutter. But Eimear laughed.

'Lucky Sammy! Go on, Aran, try again.'

Gradually she got the hang of it, not caring that her chin was smeared because, by golly, it tasted wonderful. Especially with the powdery cheese dusted on top, that Eimear said was Parmesan.

'Where do you get this cheese? In Cork?'

'Yes, for the moment. But Annie McGowan next door is going to try making a variety of it herself. There's no demand here, but the deli in Cork says it might take some.'

'What's a delly?'

Eimear explained, and Dan smiled.

'We'll take you into Cork some day to see it. You might be better off putting your money into it than into the bank – this could be a good time to speculate in the Parmesan market.'

She smiled back, knowing but not minding that he was teasing her. She hated the way her brothers teased, pointlessly and viciously, even if they had cut back on it lately . . . what did that mean exactly, 'speculate in the Parmesan market'?

Obligingly Dan told her as he cleared the table, noting the way her eyes widened and latched onto him. What a funny little thing she was, so serious! But he knew there was something she probably wanted to hear even more, and went through to the other room where the record player was kept. Moments later, a slow sweet sound welled up like water in a rock pool, swirling through the whole house as two

33

male voices joined it, strong and clear but somehow sad, as if each had something the other wanted.

Aran sat transfixed.

'Oh, that's beautiful! What is it?'

'It's the duet from *The Pearl Fishers* by Bizet.'

As she listened she could see Dunrathway's fishers through the wide window, steering their boats home in the dusk, looking somehow lonely in a way she had never noticed before, small figures on the decks, vulnerable. How hard life could be, here! And must have been in Bizet's village, too.

'Who is Bizet? Or is he dead?'

Odd if he was, because his music was distinctly alive. But Mr Lavery had explained that that was the point about great composers; their music always was. That was how you could tell a classic from a piece of crap. Mr Lavery didn't mince his words about music he didn't like.

'Yes. He died a hundred years ago, when he was thirty-six. But he was only twenty-four when he wrote this.'

Twenty-*four*?! Sweet Jesus. She'd thought all composers must be at least sixty or seventy, if not a hundred. Except Mozart, who everybody knew had been a child prod – prodigy. But Bizet was only a year older than Val when he wrote this? In silence, she listened to it, forgetting Dan and Eimear until the music stopped, and Dan ushered them into the other room.

'Now, Aran, no more music for a minute. You and I are going to sing together, a cappella!'

Mentally Aran saluted Mr Lavery, who had told her that a cappella meant without accompaniment. And what were they going to sing, without it?

'Happy birthday, dear Eimear, happy birthday to you . . .'

Triumphantly Dan carried his cake out from the kitchen, over his head, with a circle of candles blazing on top.

'Blow, Eimear!'

'Oh, no, Mr Rafter – I mean Dan – she must make a wish first!'

A wish was important, if they were going to do this properly. But what could Eimear wish for? She had everything.

Slowly, Eimear looked up at Dan, and then turned round to her.

'Yes, Aran. You're right. I will make a wish.'

Closing her eyes she was still for a moment, concentrating as if she meant it, bowing her head over the candles almost the way Mam bowed hers, at devotions in church. Aran had learned not to trust wishes much, herself, but she was curious.

'What did you wish for?'

Slightly, but audibly, Eimear's voice wavered.

'I – I can't tell you, or it won't happen.'

Suddenly there was distress in her face as well as her voice, such pain that Aran leaned across to her before she knew what she was doing, and threw both arms around her shoulders.

'Oh, Eimear! Of course it will! I promise!'

Gently Dan put down the cake and sat beside his wife.

'Go on, darling. Blow out the candles. Aran has promised you you'll get your wish.'

Dan, too? Looking so sober, so sadly into the small flames? What had caused the mood to change, to echo the yearning music Bizet had written? And what had she promised? How could she get it for them, if she did not know what it was?

Abruptly, Eimear blew out all the candles, her face shadowed with some sorrow that Aran could feel as sharply as if it were her own.

'It's getting dark, Dan. Let's all have a slice of cake, and then you must take Aran home.'

Home? Until this moment, Aran had been so happy, so completely content that she felt she already was at home.

In the misty autumn evenings Aran thought of Eimear's birthday over and over. She had not known until then that there were men who really did bring flowers to their wives, like actors on television. Men who knew what raw spaghetti was, did not growl when presented with it, even helped to cook it. Men who preferred wine to beer, and did not fight or shoot their brothers after a surfeit of it. Here in this village, there was a man who adored his wife, a wife who ran a lovely happy home yet was, in some secret way, unhappy.

If there was any way in which she could help Eimear, she would offer to do so. But if there was any way, Dan would already have found it. He was the kind of man everybody liked, even those who envied him, because he was slow to send bills, quick to help. At night he drove miles to emergency cases, never complaining or remonstrating, he often dropped in on Mrs Lowry when Eimear was working late at a meeting or school debate, he even gave blood to the travelling blood bank. He would do anything, Aran was sure, for his own wife. This thing, whatever it was, must be something completely outside his power.

Meanwhile, her own power seemed to have peaked. Her parents and brothers accepted now that she was a worker, a wage earner whose contribution could be taken for granted. At work, she began to fear that she might soon have learned as much as she ever would be allowed to learn, as long as Moira was running the show in her senior and inviolate capacity. Clients never got past Moira until she chose to let them, and Aran didn't even have their status. She was just a necessary evil. Only Lorcan seemed to regard her as a grown woman, and she was grateful that somebody did.

'What are you doing tonight, Aran?'

It was a black night in late November, and she wasn't doing anything.

'Oh, nothing. Why? Do you want me to work late?'

It was not unusual to be asked, because everyone knew her bus didn't come until six, so she was always available to do any little last-minute chores. But Lorcan often stayed even later, catching up on things he didn't care to do early in the morning. He rarely came in before ten, but rarely left before seven.

'Yes. There are all these documents on the Regan case to be sorted out, I have a meeting with Jim Regan tomorrow.'

The office was quiet and peaceful after Philip and Moira left, and Aran worked methodically, labelling things in folders, stacking them in the order in which they would be needed. Now that dark fell so much earlier she didn't visit Dan and Eimear quite so often, saving up all her news for weekends. Anyway, Mam had said she was making a stew tonight, which would keep until she got home; on the odd occasion Lorcan kept her past the time at which the bus left, he drove her back to Dunrathway himself. Mam liked to see the Renault pulling up outside, but never asked him in.

It was ten to six when she heard the door of Lorcan's office open, and he came into the outer one in which she sat at her desk.

'Hungry?'

'Yes, a bit.'

'Well then, why don't we go out for something? I'll take you to the hotel for dinner when we're finished.'

She thought of the hotel with pleasure, the one where Eimear had taken her the day she got this job. But somehow the idea of having dinner in it, with Mr Miller's son, was less appealing. Conversation would be stiff, and then he would have to take her back to Dunrathway at God only knew what hour of the night.

'Thanks, Lorcan, but my mother has a meal ready at home.'

'Call her and tell her, then.'

'I can't. We don't have a telephone.'

It was embarrassing to have to admit it, and provoking that he should smile. He was quite handsome, but she didn't like that smile.

'Oh, come on, Aran, you can't be mother's little girl forever. Why don't you just do what you want to do, and come on with me?'

36

To her surprise he came around to her side of the desk, took her hand and pulled her to her feet.

'But I don't want to! I said I'd be home in time to mind my brother Dursey tonight, everyone else is going out—'

'Except our Cinderella?'

Suddenly his tone was cold, his eyes hard. And his grip was very strong.

'Lorcan, please let me go.'

She was frightened. But frightened to let it show, too; tomorrow she would have to work with him again.

His right hand held her wrist, his left one chucked her under the chin.

'You're too pretty to be let go, Aran.'

In a single lunge he was on top of her, pulling her blouse so that she heard it rip as she leaped away from him, wrenching her wrist free with all her strength.

'Lorcan, don't, stop—'

She ran to the other side of the desk, trying to put it between them, but he came after her with such deadly intent that she raised her arm and hit him, hard, across the face.

He stopped dead.

'That hurt, Aran. That really hurt. You shouldn't have done that.'

'You made me do it!'

'No. I never made you do anything. Nobody will believe that. I'm a solicitor. You're just a fisherman's kid who tried to seduce a solicitor. That's what everyone will say.'

Seduce? Everyone would say that, *when*? That was the question that sent her hurtling to Moira's desk as he advanced yet again, and that was what inspired her to pick up Moira's typewriter and hurl it at his chest with every ounce of force she possessed.

He fell with a loud yell as it thudded into his ribcage, but she did not stop to ascertain the extent of his injuries. Yanking open the door she flew down the stairs and out into the street where the bus, to her sobbing relief, was just pulling in.

'I – I'm sorry, I've lost my bag, I'll give you the fare tomorrow—'

The bus driver was the regular chap she knew, friendly as a rule, concerned at this minute.

'You all right, love?'

'Yes, yes, I just—' She was panting so hard she could not get the words out. 'I just thought I was going to miss the bus.'

'Oh, don't you ever worry about that, I'd always wait a minute or two. Sit down now and get your breath.'

She sat rigid with fright all the way to Dunrathway, where she did not get off as soon as the lights came in sight, but stayed on all the way to the terminus. The moment she stepped down off the bus she thought of Eimear, and automatically turned in the direction of the Rafters' house. Eimear would be horrified, and would know what to do about Lorcan. But then she remembered that Eimear had got her this job. How upset she would be – and what might Mam say, about teachers who fixed young girls up with would-be rapists? Perhaps it would be wiser to say nothing, not until she calmed down and got her thoughts together at least.

Her teeth chattered like castanets as she made her way home, coatless and dishevelled, trying to figure out what to do. Of course Mam would be angry if she were told, but she would not make her return to work in the morning – in fact she would not let her go, no matter what the loss might be to the family budget. And that loss would be considerable.

What would Mam do, exactly? First of all, Aran was sure, she would blame her for having got into such a situation. She would say she must have been careless, created some misunderstanding, because a man like Lorcan Miller couldn't have behaved so badly of his own free will. If she could be convinced that he had, she would despatch Conor over to Ferleague to challenge him ineffectually, and then she would storm up to Eimear to rant and rave, blame her for whatever part of it she, Aran, was not to blame herself. There would be endless scenes, and the result would be enmity and bad feeling that might fester for years.

Eimear would feel dreadful, as if she were responsible for Lorcan's behaviour, while in turn Lorcan would deny the whole thing – before suggesting, probably, that disgruntled employees suffering delusions of grandeur should not bother returning to work. His father would back him up, and she would lose her job for sure.

Well, she was going to lose it, one way or another. She couldn't stay in such a place. At best, she could only try to hang on for as long as it took to find another one, and she could only do that by remaining silent. The unfairness of it made her want to kick something, break something with her bare hands.

At least Lorcan might not be there in the morning. With any luck he would be at home licking his wounds, unable to explain them. That typewriter had struck him like a ton of bricks. But sooner or later he would return, to make her life a misery, even dangerous. Should she report him to the police? But they would say what he said they would – that he was a rising, respectable solicitor whose little filing clerk had designs on him.

Oh, if only she could confide in Mam, get some help!

Molly was in the kitchen when she came in, serving up stew to Achill and Dursey.

'Look at the state of you! Where's your coat, Aran, and your bag? What happened to your blouse?'

The tone was accusatory, and Aran was glad of the few minutes she'd had to pull her wits together.

'They're in the office. I didn't realise the time until I saw the bus coming, and had to run for it. I caught my blouse in the door on the way out.'

'Well, get on upstairs and tidy yourself. I hope nobody saw the cut of you.'

'No, Mam, they didn't.'

Up in the bedroom Aran found that she was shaking, on the brink of tears. Oh, why couldn't Mam guess, like a proper mother? Why couldn't she gather her up into a big warm hug, and take charge of the whole thing? Why couldn't she *sense* something was wrong? Eimear always could, when one of her pupils was out of sorts, she would take them to the canteen for tea and biscuits, a little chat full of sympathy and helpful advice.

Maybe Mam would guess, after all. It might just be taking her a few moments to work it out. Slowly Aran changed her clothes and combed her hair, washed her hands and face until she had scrubbed away every trace of Lorcan Miller, and returned to the kitchen.

'Here, Aran. It's nearly cold.'

Molly passed her a plate of stew. As she reached out to take it, it slipped from her trembling fingers and crashed to the floor.

'Oh, now look at the mess! You're worse than the boys! And you've broken my good plate on me!'

'I – I'm sorry, Mam. I'll buy you a new one.'

'Oh, that's it, money buys everything now, we can break what we like! New plates grow on trees, new blouses are ten a penny!'

Suddenly Aran did not recognise her own voice, the voice that was screaming at her mother at the top of its lungs.

'Shut up, Mother! Shut *up*! I've said I'm sorry, what more do you want?'

It was the first time she had ever called Molly 'Mother', and the timing of it made her want to weep. But she did not weep, as some door slammed shut in her head. It would take a lot, she thought, to ever prise that door open again.

Molly was reeling up against the sink, white and almost faint with shock. Uncertainly, they looked at each other. But Aran felt something coagulate inside her, and when she spoke again her voice was steady, almost indifferent.

'If you're going to your knitting circle tonight, Mother, you'd better be on your way. It's nearly eight.'

Wordlessly Molly took a mop and dustpan, swept up the broken debris and removed the apron from over her head.

'Yes. There's a bit of stew left in the pot. Heat it up if you like. I'll be home by eleven.'

Surprised by her meek tone, Aran nodded, feeling the fire of her anger wane. But the chill that replaced it did not wane, nor did a small invasive sense of guilt. Molly had all the sensitivity of a block of wood, but who knew what forces had combined to so dull and harden her? If she could not forgive her, she could not wholly blame her either. She was not sixteen like her daughter, not fighting fit in the way Aran suddenly felt. In those few fierce seconds, the balance of things had shifted between them.

Achill and Dursey were gazing at her, awestruck. Coldly, she turned to them.

'What's the matter with you two? Finish your food, and be quick about it. Achill, you're not going out until you've washed those dishes. Mother, there'll be frost tonight, you'll need your boots.'

They looked at her as if it was the picture of the Pope above her head that was speaking.

'Good morning, Mr Miller. Good morning, Moira.'

'Good morning, Aran.'

'Where's Lorcan? Not in yet?'

She glanced at the clock so pointedly, spoke so tartly that Philip raised his eyebrows, irked and rather aggrieved.

'Lorcan's not well. He took a nasty fall down the stairs last night. Working too late and too hard. I've given him the rest of the week off.'

'Oh dear. Poor Lorcan. Please give him my sympathy.'

She knew her expression conveyed none whatsoever, knew also that Moira was dying to know why her coat was dangling from the coat stand, her bag still on the floor where she had left it the night before. Hang Moira. Seating herself at her desk, she immersed herself in the mountain of waiting post, so studiously that neither Philip nor Moira addressed another word to her. But covertly she watched Philip turning the pages of his newspapers, her imagination ferreting into the small ads, wondering what jobs might be advertised. If anything remotely suitable came up, she would go after it right away, today, before she lost her nerve. But endless hours seemed to elapse before the clock crept round to lunchtime, and she got her chance. The moment she was alone she snatched up the *Cork Examiner*.

Office Staff. There were a few jobs in that section, but nothing for which she was qualified. Nursing, teaching, factory work, farm labour ... nothing, until her eye fell upon a category entitled Domestics.

'Au pair wanted to live in and help with Oliver, aged two, and new baby due February. Own room £20 a week all found. Must be energetic, reliable and cheerful. Telephone Holly Mitchell, London ...'

It gave a number, with a code in brackets. Letting the page lie open before her, Aran leaned back to think.

Twenty pounds a week, with bed and board included? It would take years to work up to a sum like that here; as her mother frequently reminded her, food and electricity cost ten pounds a week for each member of the family. In London, they probably cost even more.

London. It was as distant to her as any of the cities she had studied on maps in Mrs McKenzie's geography class, Rio, Nairobi or Barcelona. You had no option but to fly to those places, but London took just as long to reach, because most people who went there took a train to Dublin, a boat to Wales and then another train. It was a very long journey, that made London seem absolutely miles away.

But that, today, was exactly what she wanted to be. Miles away from Lorcan Miller, from Molly, from everything she felt snapping at her like a mousetrap. Even Dunrathway itself was coming to feel like a prison, since leaving school so prematurely she knew it was dismissing her, relegating her to a position of complete unimportance. All it expected of her now was that she should conform to its tastes, customs and standards: early marriage to a fisherman, children who would be raised the same way everyone's were, eating the same food, wearing the same clothes, watching the same drivel on television. Physical survival was all that mattered, spiritual malnutrition would never even be noticed, much less considered important. If she didn't get out, now while she had the chance, she would wizen and wither, dry out like a clump of seaweed beached far back in the sand dunes. Ten or fifteen years hence Aran Campion would be just another piece of jetsam, rough on the eye, stiff to the touch.

She didn't know yet what she really wanted, but she knew what she needed, and it wasn't that. She must get out. Was going to get out.

There was nothing to keep her from calling Mrs Mitchell, right this minute. If she got the job, she could send money home, her parents would be better off, not worse. Only the thought of Conor made her hesitate, and the thought of what Dan and Eimear would say. She had become almost as fond of them as she was of her father

41

... but she couldn't stay here on their account. Not with Lorcan coming back next week.

Would Eimear be angry? Or hurt, even, after all the trouble she had gone to? Would Conor mope and miss her? Yes. Of course he would miss her, of course Eimear would too. But she couldn't live her life for them, or through them. She could write, keep in touch, maybe even come home some day when she'd saved up some money and there were more jobs to be had in Ireland. And London was so big, there was bound to be a night school of some kind in it somewhere, lots of buses that would make everything accessible.

The phone sat on Moira's desk. She had never used it, only taken incoming calls, but all she had to do was dial the digits as they appeared in the paper. Mr Miller would certainly query a call to London when the bill arrived, but if she got the job she would be gone by then, and it was his son who had brought this about. As Aran thought of Lorcan, she could feel the exact spot under her chin where his finger had touched her.

She went to the telephone, picked it up and dialled the number.
'Hello?'

She was amazed by the speed at which Mrs Mitchell answered, all those miles away, and the clarity of her voice, so near she might as well be just round the corner.

'Hello, Mrs Mitchell, my name is Aran Campion, I'm calling from Ferleague in Cork, about your ad in the *Cork Examiner*, for a—'

A what was it? Oh God, what was that word again? She knew it meant child minder but she couldn't remember what it was.

'Oh, yes! I've had a few calls, it's lovely to hear all these accents from home. I'm from Clonakilty myself, I know Ferleague.'

She sounded so friendly that Aran's fist unclenched from around the phone, her nerves relaxed – but other people had called too, she said?

'Have you got someone already, Mrs Mitchell? Is the job gone?'

'No. I wish it was, because I'm about to pop in eight weeks, I'd like it all settled. But nobody has been quite right so far. Tell me about yourself – Aran, is it? How old are you? What experience do you have?'

'I'm eighteen, I have two little brothers, I've looked after them since they were babies—' *Pop*? What did she mean, *pop*? Pop away somewhere? She hoped she'd figure it out before Mrs Mitchell figured out that she was only sixteen, and had been only four when her youngest brother was born.

'Two little brothers? Oh, good. You know all about small boys, then! Ollie's at the why stage, very lively. Would you be prepared to

42

work odd hours, five days a week? Can you cook?'

'Oh yes. I make wonderful spaghetti bol – bolognese.'

'Oh, Ollie loves that! You'd have to take complete responsibility for him, you understand, because I'm out at work all day. And for the other little one when it arrives. What I need is a good bright girl who won't get homesick like the last one, or complain about anything when I come home in the evenings, someone who'll look after the children properly, amuse them as well, and pitch in with a bit of cooking or cleaning when need be. Would you be prepared to do all that?'

'Oh, yes. I'm very good with children, and I don't mind what hours I work.'

'Well, that sounds great. I tell you what, why don't you send me a letter with more details about yourself, a photograph and some references? Let me give you the address.'

References. Desperately, Aran thought of Eimear.

'Yes, I will, Mrs Mitchell. I'll write it this evening, and post it first thing in the morning.'

'Good. I'll look forward to it. Thank you so much for calling, Aran.'

The line went dead. Frantically, with mixed excitement and terror, Aran urged the day on until she could rush round to see Eimear.

'London? Oh, Aran, but why? You've only been six months with Mr Miller! Aren't you happy there?'

'Yes, of course I am, it's just that – oh, Eimear, I can't explain! But please say you'll write a reference for me, and take my photograph, I'll have to take the film into Ferleague with me tomorrow and get it developed right away – please?'

'Have you even talked to your parents about this?'

'No, but I will, I know they'll let me go, the house is too small for all of us . . .'

'But you don't know anything about this Mrs Mitchell's house, or what kind of person she is. You'll have to find out more about her.'

'She's from Clonakilty, and she sounds really nice.'

Something, Eimear saw, had taken hold of Aran. Something that seemed to be driving her away at top speed.

'Aran, is everything all right?'

'Yes. Really it is. Eimear, when you take the photograph, will you lend me some make-up, help me to look a bit more – well, you know, mature?'

'But you're not mature. That's the point. You're far too young to go to London, all by yourself.'

'But I'd be staying with a family – look, here's the newspaper, you

43

could ring Mrs Mitchell up and talk to her yourself.'

'Well, I will, if you're serious about this. But your mother will have to talk to her too.'

Oh, why was Eimear putting so many obstacles in her path? Only because she was concerned, of course, and cared about her. She really did seem to care.

'All right. I'll ask Mother to come up here and you can both speak to Mrs Mitchell.'

So it was Mother now, was it? Eimear thought a bit about that.

And she thought how much she would miss Aran, how quiet life would be without her chatty visits, her quaint questions, her lovely smile. But the smile was different this evening. It wasn't a child's smile, but a young woman's. A young woman who had made up her mind, for some very private reason, to go away.

What had happened? What could be behind this rupture, this haste? Eimear felt the most terrible wrench, and knew that Dan would feel it too. Somehow Aran had got under their skin, come bounding into their home and their hearts like a little gazelle, shy but trusting, lapping up all the affection they could offer her. Why were those big eyes of hers so fearful tonight – fearful, and yet fixed on the future, in a foreign place? If she did not invite questions, she would not force them upon her . . . but why so far, and why so soon?

'Could we take the photograph now, Eimear? Does your camera have a flash?'

A flash. Aran would be gone in a flash. Gone to this woman in London – tonight, if she were let.

'Aran, calm down. This is going to take a little while.'

'But the job will be gone! She'll give it to someone else.'

'No, she won't. If she thinks you're right for her, she'll wait. People always wait for what they know is right for them.'

It took two weeks, finally, but it was done. Eimear was as wretched as Aran was elated, but she forced herself to draw comfort from the shining grey eyes, the bouncy step with which Aran came to see her almost every evening now, chattering and asking incessant questions about the city that was about to become her home. Eimear had been to London often as a student, and was glad of all the information and advice she could supply. Forewarned was forearmed.

'It's beautiful, Aran, but it's very big. People don't know each other as closely as they do in a small village. You mustn't be disappointed if nobody has much time to talk to you.'

'Oh, I'll talk to them! I'm going to find a night school and try to get into a business course, I'll make friends there.'

'Good. When they ask what nine honours in the Intermediate Certificate means, tell them it's the same as nine O-Levels. They'll let you in on the spot. And I'll write you another reference, as your teacher.'

'Great. I'll write too, Eimear. All the time. I'm thrilled to be going, but I'm really sorry to be leaving you and Dan.'

'Are you?'

'Yes. You've been so good to me . . . I love it here, in your house, you make me feel – oh, I don't know – almost like your own daughter.'

Eimear's head was bent over the Christmas pudding she was stirring, and for several seconds she did not look up.

'I'm glad you're not going before Christmas, Aran. That would have been awful for – for your parents.'

Did Eimear's voice sound a little bit wobbly? Was she really going to miss her, that much? Climbing down from the ladder on which she was decorating the Christmas tree, Aran crossed the room and went to her.

'I wouldn't do that to them, Eimear. I wouldn't do it to you and Dan. I'll come up here after Mass on Christmas morning, with a present for you, and we'll have a lovely time.'

'Yes, we will. Dan and I have a present for you too, something we hope you'll really like.'

'Oh, Eimear. You've given me so much already . . . I feel terrible about not staying in the job you got me.'

'Did anything go wrong with it, Aran? Did someone upset you?'

'No . . . it was just that I could see I'd never get promoted as long as Moira was there, or learn anything more than I'd learned already.'

'You won't learn much from minding a toddler – and I thought you said you didn't like babies?'

'No. I said that I didn't want them myself. Not that I didn't like them. D'you know, it was funny, I was passing by the church this morning and I went in to see the crib, there was this big chubby infant Jesus in it and I wondered if he looked like baby Ollie!'

Eimear paused.

'Aran, you will be careful in London, won't you?'

'Yes. Mother says it's full of vice and wickedness and I'm to carry a hatpin with me everywhere I go. Watch out for pickpockets, carry my bag under my arm and lock all doors at all times.'

'She's spoken to you, then? There's nothing you – you'd maybe like to ask me?'

Aran thought for a moment, plunged her hands into the pockets of her skirt and took a deep breath.

'Could I – would you – Eimear, would you ever explain about men?'

45

Her face was so nakedly curious, so naive but resolute that Eimear had to laugh.

'Certainly. Where would you like to start?'

'At the very beginning. All I know is that Achill is a horrible lout, and Dursey's getting as bad, and some of their friends are disgusting little brats. Other than that, I haven't a clue.'

'Well then, let's sit down and get comfortable. Men aren't all horrible, but they're not all like Dan or Conor either. Some of them are overgrown children, a menace to themselves and everyone else.'

Exactly, Aran thought, like Lorcan Miller. I know what he wanted to do is called rape, but I don't know precisely what that is. Something dreadful unless you're married and want to do it yourself. Some of the girls say they want to do it, Deirdre Devlin even says she has done it. I suppose I should read the same magazines they read, but they're so expensive, and anyway I'd rather ask Eimear. If she and Dan do it, it can't be so bad.

An hour later, Dan came home to find his wife howling with laughter on the sofa with Aran Campion, wiping away tears of incoherent hilarity. It was good to see someone making her laugh, but he was bemused by the extent of it.

'What's the joke, girls?'

Speechless, Aran burst into renewed shrieks and giggles, shaking her mass of hair helplessly at the mere sight of him, leaving Eimear to make some stab at explaining.

'I – I'm afraid you are, Dan!'

'Me? What did I do?'

The two collapsed again, clutching each other as they fought for composure. Eventually Aran staggered breathlessly to her feet, gasping and grinning from ear to ear.

'I think I'd better go. Thanks for a great afternoon, Eimear. Thanks a million.'

Dan thought she looked unusually fetching as she pulled a pink sweater on over her skirt, its colour matching her blushes. She rarely laughed aloud like this, but he thought she should do it more often, it made those serious grey eyes look altogether stunning. But he couldn't imagine what he had done that she should survey him so acerbically, suddenly, on her way out.

Early on Christmas morning Aran slid quietly out of the house and cut through the grey dawn down to a cove on the far side of the harbour. Christmas Day was always busy and crowded, but she felt in need of a few minutes to herself first. With her hands muffled up into her sleeves she crunched across the shingle, squinting into the

mist until she thought she heard a watery plop, then a splash – and
there they were. Swimming close into shore, the two dolphins poked
their snouts up into the air, checking that it was a familiar face before
they began to dive and play, cavorting as if they knew Christmas was
a time for celebration. Aran wished she could swim out to them, as
she did in the summer; they were so tame they would let her catch
hold of their fins and tow her along, filling her with the most
exhilarating sense of friendship and freedom. Everyone in the village
knew them, and had christened them Fred and Barney, but she
thought such cute names unworthy of the wild, magnificent
creatures. As she watched they leaped and splashed, jumping
gradually higher above the water until they were reaching a height
of ten or twelve feet, twirling and tumbling through a diaspora of
glittering crystals like lovers racing through a rainstorm. Every time
they vanished they streaked back into sight, and she knew they
would play with her for as long as she stayed. But often people took
advantage of their good nature, wearing the lovable things out with
shrill cries of encouragement, and she would not do that. It was
privilege enough that they had come in at all today; in winter they
tended to stay much further out, resting and recuperating.

With a smile and a wave she left them, thinking how they were one
of the things she loved about Dunrathway, a symbol of hope and joy
whose grace and shining speed left her invigorated yet soothed,
secure in some larger scheme of things. Some day she would see
them again; some distant day when things were different.

When she got home it was time for church, the bells ringing from
both the big Catholic spire and the smaller Protestant one. Of the two
buildings Aran preferred the latter, a dignified place of grey stone
which made the other look brash by comparison, its concrete harsh
and domineering. But as she arrived with her family it was filling up
with neighbours exchanging greetings, bedecked in their colourful
best, twittering like sparrows until Father Carroll came out on the
altar and the ceremony began. Aran loved the Christmas mass, with
big white candles burning as the organ played the first notes of *Adeste
Fidelis*, filling the whole congregation with a palpable sense of
community and continuity. Sweetly and clearly she began to sing,
joining in all the carols for nearly an hour until they reached the last
and most favourite of all, *Silent Night*. As a schoolgirl she had been
in the choir, high up at the back of the church, but she was glad today
to be in a pew with her family, this last Christmas they might ever
spend together.

Already Val and Sher were gone, and she knew Conor had shed a
few quiet tears over them last night. Slipping her hand into his, she

squeezed it, and he squeezed hers in turn, very hard. But he was awkward and uncomfortable in his suit, the one that got him through the few formal or celebratory events of the year, and so they did not linger long after Mass was over. But Aran had found the ceremony a balm to her soul, directional to her uncertain spirit, and the reason why came to her: music was her religion. Her God resided not in the church, but in the voices gathered there.

At home, she picked up the small gift she had found for Eimear and Dan, and told her mother she would soon be back.

'You're not going out on me, with all the cooking to be done?'

'I prepared everything last night, Mother, you only have to put it in the oven. Achill will help you, and I'll be back in half an hour.'

Not waiting for the answer, she ran out and round the harbour, up to the Rafter house where the lighted tree was twinkling in the window. Effusively Dan flung open the door, but she slowed down as she went in, intimidated by the sound of several voices. In the lounge, quite a little party seemed to be in progress: clustered round the fire she recognised several of her former teachers including her music tutor Luke Lavery, three or four other people she didn't know, and Eimear's tall elegant mother, Hannah Lowry. They smiled at her, but she felt like a gatecrasher.

'Happy Christmas, Aran.'

Eimear came to hug her, leading her into the centre of things, making introductions, her face glowing with the warmth of the fire.

Nervously Aran shook everyone's hand, noting the smartness of the women's dresses, the large ruby brooch at Hannah's throat, the way the men did not run their fingers round the inside of their collars as Conor did. On the record player, some resonant choral music was playing, and Dan was looking very dashing in a check jacket with matching waistcoat.

'Will you join us in a little sherry, Aran? Cream or dry?'

'Oh, Dan!' Eimear's voice was reproving. 'Just give her a dry one – not too much, mind.'

The sherry was cold and biting, making her eyes water as she tried not to splutter, feeling Hannah's eye upon her. It was just as well, she thought, that she couldn't stay long.

'I just wanted to give you this, Eimear, and Dan.'

She held out the small, oddly-shaped package and to her horror Eimear opened it on the spot, with great ceremony.

'Oh, look! Isn't this lovely!'

It was a small stone urn, with a cherub leaning his elbow languidly over its lip, smirking naughtily into the bowl which was intended to contain flowers.

48

'It – it's for your garden. I didn't know what kind of flowers you might like to plant in it, so I got those packets of seeds as well, so you could choose. The man in the shop said alyssum would take well, or pansies or lobelias.'

She was encouraged by the way Eimear and Dan seemed to genuinely like it, turning it round in their hands, passing it to everyone for approval as they debated which seeds to plant.

'It's gorgeous, Aran, and we have just the place for it – an old pedestal Dan bought at an auction last summer – see it out there, in the corner of the garden? It's nice and high, Sammy won't be able to knock it over. Thank you so much!'

Aran's smile was shy, but Eimear's was huge as she turned to Dan.

'Go on, Dan, take Aran to the Christmas tree.'

He led her to it, and she was touched to find a present underneath with her name on it. You handed gifts to friends, but those for relatives or family members always went under the tree. Gingerly she picked it up, but it felt solid, not fragile or breakable.

'Oh, what is it?'

'Open it up.'

Suddenly excited, she undid the curly gold ribbon and starry green paper, lifted out a long, heavy black box. Everyone was curious, but she was no longer aware of their attention as she raised the lid.

'Oh!'

On a bed of white satin lay a gleaming silver oboe.

'Oh, m-my God, it – it—'

Everyone laughed as they finished her sentence for her, in chorus.

'It's an oboe!'

But she felt like crying as she took it up, feeling the smooth weight of it, the fluid length. It was an instrument such as she never imagined could exist, light years beyond the battered one Mr Lavery loaned everyone at school, completely unrelated to the recorder she had played before that. Almost dazed she took it out and caressed it, hardly hearing what her former music teacher was saying now as he stepped forward to exclaim over it. But Dan put his hand on his forearm, and restrained him.

'No, Luke, let her enjoy it a moment. What do you think, Aran? Will you be able to knock a tune or two out of it?'

A tune? But this wasn't for playing tunes on! This was a serious piece of craftsmanship, exact and precise, intended for someone who could rise to the standard it demanded. It was far too good for her – but now she would be able to play every day until maybe, some day, she could draw forth all the beautiful melody it promised.

Luke Lavery was incoherent with excitement.

49

'Dan, Eimear, where on earth did you get it, it's superb, I've never seen the like – Aran, if you don't play something on it, right this instant, I'm going to snatch it out of your hands and play it myself. Come on, let's hear you!'

She was to play here, now? But they all stood waiting, and unexpectedly she found that she was equal to the situation, willing and able although she had not played for six months.

'I must warm up first.'

Swiftly she ran through the scales, then a little snatch of *Jingle Bells* and *Rudolf*, just to loosen her lungs and her fingers as she wondered what to play for real.

The Pearl Fishers. She had never seen the sheet music, but she had heard the song many times in this house since that first time. She could play it by ear. She knew she could.

Taking a deep breath, she poised her fingers and lowered her lips to the cool smooth instrument, thinking of the dolphins who were as happy as the pearl fishermen were sad, and of her own father, a simple fisherman whose sadness she had felt this morning. Filling with confidence, she was unaware of her own eyes beginning to shine like the pearls of the song.

The first notes rose, and then the next, carrying true and strong out into the room, taking her audience with them as they gathered power, reaching the window through which everyone could see the sea. Softly, Dan began to hum, not knowing the words, but Luke Lavery knew them, and came in at just the right moment in the tenor part, overlaying the French lyrics with his rich Cork accent.

Rolling and rising the music mounted like a wave on the ocean, sweeping them all up on it as it reached its crescendo and came crashing down, surging in on a soft shore, fanning out and fading away until nothing was left but the promise of another tide, another time. Aran did not raise her eyes until the very end, but when she did they locked instantly with Luke's, one musician recognising another, both knowing it would have been perfect if only he had his oboe here too, to provide the counterpoint and the harmony.

But it seemed the performance was pleasing to its audience, and Hannah's voice rang into the silence.

'Well! I shall be keeping a close eye on you, young lady!'

As soon as she put down the instrument Aran's shyness returned, and she had to make herself smile, thinking that Hannah's eye was rather close for comfort already. It was the first time she had met Eimear's mother, but she felt as if the woman expected something of her, was setting some standard to be met.

Luke said nothing, knowing his look said it for him, but turned jovially to Dan.

'And where was our baritone, when we needed one? You're feck all use, Dan Rafter.'

Aran thought Dan was the most wonderful man in creation, and wished she could play another piece as he, and everyone, was asking her to. But Molly was waiting.

'I'm sorry, I have to go. Really. Please forgive me.'

Amidst protests she edged to the door, clutching the oboe as she said her goodbyes, remembering something for Eimear.

Fishing in her pocket she found the envelope, took it out and handed it to her.

'It's only a little poem, Eimear. Just so you'll know I haven't forgotten, or given up.'

With a quick diffident hug she opened the door before Eimear could open the envelope, and ran out into the mist.

'Of course,' Molly said grimly, 'there's no competing with *that*. But I hope you'll like it just the same.'

'That' was the oboe, and Aran knew what 'it' was: the sweater her mother knitted for her every Christmas. It was always a sturdy affair, designed to last. But this year it was different. Reaching into the carton from which she had already doled out Conor's, Dursey's and Achill's sweaters, Molly extracted a haze of lilac angora, so fine Aran was astonished. Not only did angora cost a lot more than ordinary wool, but the design into which it was knitted was loose and relaxed – almost, she thought, as if Molly knew she was losing her daughter, trying to let go in a graceful way she could not articulate. It was by far the best piece of work she had ever done.

Conor blinked.

'Isn't that nice, child? Try it on.'

It felt light as air as Aran threw it over her head, brushing her cheek as Molly's hand never had, falling gently over her shoulders.

'Mother – I never knew you could knit like this! I love it!'

The rare glimmer of a smile threatened to illuminate Molly's tight lips.

'I won't pretend it was easy. But I must say it looks well on you.'

There was no mirror in the room, but Aran knew that it did.

'It's so different to anything you've done before.'

'Aye, and I hope I'll never have to do such a difficult thing again.'

'Oh, but you must! Now that you've done one, the next will be much easier – Mother, people would buy dozens of these. And they'd pay more – not just for the angora, but for the work. You could wear

51

something like this anywhere, to a party even, or out somewhere fashionable.'

It wasn't that the sweater was fashionable, as such, but there was a timelessness about it. Rather than outlasting its welcome, the fine wool would fray from constant wear – and, she realised, create need of another one. Need, or want – whatever, the demand would increase.

For the first time, Molly seemed to be paying attention to her. 'D'you think so?'

'Yes, I do. Definitely.'

'Well then, maybe I will try a few more.'

'Please do. You must.'

She had given her mother perfume for Christmas, the light floral one of which Eimear had told her the name, but she saw that these few words meant much more, and might linger much longer. If only Molly would believe them, and act on them. *Use* them, as she would probably never use the perfume. But even as she spoke Molly whirled around and ran to the oven.

'My turkey! My turkey is burning on me!'

'Eimear, I can't. I truly can't. Please take it back.'

'No. Put it in your bag safe, and do as I say.'

Eimear spoke in the same tone she used in the schoolroom, the one that didn't permit disobedience. Tearfully, Aran opened her bag and shoved the wad of British pound notes down into it.

'I'll repay you then, as soon as I can. It's a loan, and you'll get interest on it.'

'I'll be very interested, to know whether it's enough for your fees. If it isn't, let me know.'

Aran felt overwhelmed to the point of being ashamed. First the plane ticket, the offer of the drive to Cork airport, next the arrangement that Mrs Mitchell would meet her at the airport in London, reducing a fifteen-hour journey to a mere two hours. And now this. It was too much.

Aran had been looking forward to London, but now she found she didn't want to leave at all.

But Dan was packing her suitcase into the back of the car, with the oboe which she would not let out of her sight no matter where the suitcase might go, and Eimear had turned to her parents, was opening the car door for them, ushering them inside. They had not seen the money, and Aran could not bring herself to tell them; it was bad enough that they could not offer her any parting gift themselves, the humiliation of such penury visibly eating into Conor.

The January morning was fine and bright, but something of a silence descended on all five occupants of the car as they drove away, leaving Achill and Dursey waving from the door. Sensing that Conor and Molly felt not only uncomfortable but miserable, Dan switched on the radio, leaving Eimear to utter assurances that London really was safe once you knew what to watch out for, and that she had warned Aran what to watch out for. And had not the Mitchells promised to take good care of their daughter, did they not sound like a very nice couple, was not Holly Mitchell originally Holly Clifford of Clonakilty? Of course Aran would be all right, and get on well with them. Not once did Eimear's face or voice betray the terrible anguish she felt, the anxiety or the inexplicable, awful pain. If anyone had a right to feel those things, it was Molly. But Molly sat silent and impassive in the back seat, with Aran wedged between herself and Dan.

'It'll be nice to see Val, Dad, won't it?'

'Aye, lass.'

Val was coming to see her sister off at the airport, and Conor's wan expression lifted marginally at the prospect. But it fell again as the car continued inexorably on its way, winding along the rackety country roads until finally Cork city came into view in the distance. But Dan turned away from it, following the signs with a plane on them, concentrating on the driving to the exclusion of all else. In recent times he had become unreasonably fond of Aran, and now he found he could not trust himself to speak.

Once again he busied himself with the luggage, leaving the others to go on ahead into the terminal. Val was waiting in it, and everyone was inordinately glad to see her, grateful for the distraction of greetings and conversation. Sizing up the situation, Val took Conor and Molly under her wing, steering them as if she knew the airport well. In fact she had never been in it, but now that Aran was going to London there might be the chance of a trip to that fabulous mecca, even mightier on the social scale than Montenotte.

Not that Aran looked as if she appreciated her destination at all, the way she hung back with her eyes the size of plates, as if she were a country bumpkin. Well, no matter, London would soon put a gloss on her.

Conor had insisted on allowing an absurd amount of time, but although they were early it seemed to fly by. The suitcase was checked in and swallowed up, drinks were offered by Dan and accepted by everyone except Eimear, who knew that one mouthful of anything would destroy her composure. Desperately, almost feverishly, Val chatted away, recalling her schooldays with Mrs

53

Lowry, the Rafters' house, the Rafters' spaniel, anything that would keep the whole group from disintegrating into tears. But finally the flight was called, and they stood up.

'What's in the box, Aran?'

'My oboe, Val. Dan and Eimear gave it to me.'

'Did they? I thought you'd have given that old thing up by now.'

'Oh, no! Well, I had to for a few months, while I hadn't got one, but you should see this, it's a work of art.'

'Aren't you the lucky one! I'm made up if Finbarr gives me a packet of cigarettes out of the shop.'

Val could afford to make little jokes like this; everyone knew she had Finbarr well under her thumb, and woe betide the man if he didn't keep her sweet. But why would the Rafters give Aran an oboe? It was out of all proportion.

'Well, here we are and off you go, my spoilt little sister. Have a great time, and be sure to let me know whether these Mitchell people have a spare room.'

Aran thought she would do no such thing – it was a job she was going to, not a hotel! But she was grateful to Val for keeping things light, and tears at bay. Determined to keep them that way, she ran to Dan and Eimear in a rush, then to Molly and Conor, hugging them all, even Molly who looked as if someone had come at her with a blowtorch.

'I'll write tonight, the minute I get there – Dad, you're to remember what I promised you, d'you hear?'

Conor swallowed and looked down at his shoes. He didn't want a boat from his daughter, he didn't want any dreams or flights of fancy at all, only that she should be well and safe, and come back to him. He wished he could express his gratitude to the Rafters, for giving her the plane ticket that had averted a long lonely journey, but he could not. He could not say anything.

'Have a good trip, sweetheart, and don't forget us, will you?' Dan's voice was so husky that Aran could only shake her head vehemently, clutch Eimear's hand one last time and make a headlong dash for the departure gates. By the time she got through the various security checks on the other side of them, her tears were flowing like a baby's.

Back on the concourse behind her, Conor managed to put together enough words to ask what he had to ask.

'Mr Rafter, would there be anywhere we could watch the plane taking off?'

Dan led them away to where it was possible, and with Molly he followed meekly, gratefully. Only Eimear held back, feeling that she could not bear to watch Aran's irrevocable departure. Yet she could

54

not bear not to watch it either, and when she reached the viewing area she found herself far from the only distressed person in it. On either side of her, many parents jostled for a last glimpse of their departing children, including a couple she recognised as the parents of a boy she had taught until the year before. He was their only son, and she knew what sacrifices had been made for – for this? But for Conor and Molly it must be even worse; they had already lost Sher, their eldest. This was the second time for them, the second airport, the second child.

Oh, she thought, why must Aran go? She had a job, she was not desperate like these others. But Ireland just keeps on losing them, these bright beautiful children for whom there seems to be no work, no hope, no alternative. If only they could stay, would stay, then there might be work, and hope, because there would be a bigger population, greater demand for all they can offer. Some day, this vicious circle must break.

Some day I want to return to this airport and not see a single emigrant in it. I want to see a time when there will be smiling parents, happy children, productive and fulfilled, setting off only on the holidays they have earned, and can afford.

Today, they are able, they are educated, but they are wasted. We equip them to go, we know they must, and then we break our hearts when they do. It can't be right, to prepare them for a future that takes them away the moment they reach it, forces them to flee.

Aran wouldn't tell me why she had to go, but she did have to, like all these other youngsters. I want something so much better for them, here at home, for her and for all our country's children, even if my own are never to be amongst them. This is a beautiful island, fertile and bountiful, but it is bereft.

Every parent I know has lost a child, to Britain or America, and now I know how they feel. I too am bereft.

Chapter Three

Look at them, Holly Mitchell thought, just look at them. It's sixteen years since I was amongst them, and they still haven't changed. The youths and the men with the red faces and the loud laughs, that they think will disguise their rawness, their uncertainty. The girls with their eyes down, their clumsy clothes, their awful lack of confidence. And these are the lucky ones, who came by plane, who will find work in pubs and shops, hotels and maybe even offices. At least they won't dig ditches or doss down in doorways, they won't turn to drink or drugs. But they look as lost and guilty as if they already had. Dammit, why don't they lift their heads up, let this country know that they have something to contribute? Since they must come, someone should organise courses for them, teach them to put a bit of style and sparkle in their step.

There she is. At least she hasn't tied her suitcase up with string. But she's been crying, and she'll cry again tonight, every night this week. That's OK, so long as it doesn't go on forever. The last one could have cried for Ireland – and she did. This one had better give us a smile by Sunday, or else.

'Aran! Aran Campion? Hello, over here!'

'Mrs Mitchell? Hello!'

The girl came bounding over, with a smile that left Holly to eat her words. Now this, she thought, bodes better. Much better. But eighteen? My eye! She's just a baby. She dolled herself up for that photo – but at least that shows a bit of initiative. Shows she must have really wanted the job, too, and might stick at it.

'There you are, Aran. I'm Holly Mitchell. Welcome to London.'

'Thank you. But where's the baby? Where's Ollie?'

'Oh, at home! I don't take him with me everywhere I go.'

But Mother did, Aran thought: Mother took us with her everywhere she went, until we were old enough to be left by

56

ourselves. Who's minding Ollie? Surely – surely the *father* can't be? Fathers don't mind babies.

But whatever about the father, this is the most glamorous mother I've ever seen. Imagine looking like that, when you have one child and are going to have another! She's not beautiful, but she's so striking, she doesn't look a bit Irish, you'd nearly think she was French, or Italian like that woman who asked me for directions in Ferleague last summer. She's the kind of woman you'd see in that magazine Eimear gets. She must think I look like a right Mary Hick.

That was exactly what Holly thought, at first. But, looking more closely as she led the way to her car, she became aware of the girl's natural grace, which negated the clothes she was wearing, drew the eye to her fresh, fine face, innocent eyes and delicate lips, her cloud of milky curls. Her step was so light, her look so fragile, there was something almost faun-like about her, some sweet note that made Holly feel rather protective.

The Mitchell home was in Islington, and Aran talked all the way to it, shyly but openly, her naïveté obvious as she admired the Rover when they reached it, the city as they drove through it, her grey eyes absorbing everything with endearing solemnity. Such was her interest that Holly knew she too was under scrutiny, felt Aran taking note of her well-cut coat and hair, polished nails, glossy shoes and scarf. It was the wardrobe of a working woman, yet of a much richer tone and texture than anything Aran had ever seen Eimear wear.

'Have you always lived in London, Mrs Mitchell?'

'Call me Holly, Aran.'

'H – Holly. When did you leave Cork? Do you like it here?'

'Yes. I love it. I came as a nurse when I was nineteen, and started the nursing agency when I was twenty-eight. I've put thousands of young Irish women through my hands since then. They make great nurses.'

'Do they? Why?'

'Because they care about their patients – not just for them, but about them. They take an interest, they put their hearts into their work and they have a sense of humour, never let anyone feel alone or depressed. Some can be a bit giddy at first, because they're traumatised by the tragedy they see around them. They realise you should live life to the full while you can, go in for a bit of wild partying . . . but then they settle down, get brisk and bossy just as a good nurse should be. They never lose the old blarney, though.'

'I've never kissed the Blarney Stone, Holly, have you?'

'With all those germs? You must be joking. I don't know anyone from Cork who has – although I thought you might have, when I

57

saw you. You're not eighteen, are you?'

'Oh – oh – I am nearly—'

'Never mind. Either you can do the job or you can't. I'll give you a week to be homesick, but after that you'll have to get cracking. Anyway, as I was saying, I set up the agency, married Walter when I was thirty, had Oliver when I was thirty-three. He's a little demon, but I love him to bits, and hope you will too. I'd stay at home with him myself if I could bear to give up the agency, but in a way that's my baby too, and will provide a good education for him. When the next one comes along my hands will really be full, but I'll expect you to take charge and cope properly.'

'I will, Holly. Eimear said there was no point in coming unless I was prepared to take London as I found it and set my mind to doing well.'

'Eimear? That's the teacher I spoke to over the phone?'

'Yes. We're great friends. She knows London well.'

Aran smiled, hoping that might make her sound a bit older, by association. Holly seemed very nice, but she also seemed the sort of woman who knew what she wanted, wouldn't stand for any nonsense.

'I'm glad to hear she advised you, and now let me give you another little bit of advice.'

'Yes?'

'Stay away from the Irish hangouts, the places where emigrants congregate. It's tempting to go to them in the beginning, when you're lonely, but if you do you'll end up in a ghetto. You'll never get anywhere. You must meet British people, mix with them, make the effort. That doesn't mean losing your identity or your culture, but it does mean no moping. No running home to Mummy, literally or figuratively.'

'I don't want to run home to M – Mummy.'

'Good.'

'But Holly, you advertised for an Irish girl. Why didn't you look for an English one?'

'Ah, aren't we quick! Well, yes, I do like to see faces and hear accents from home, especially around my own house. But I also wanted an Irish girl because they're good with children, and because it's a way of giving someone else the same chances I got myself. People helped me when I came here, so now I try to do the same for them. This is a big country, Aran, and you can do very well in it if you try. There are a lot of opportunities.'

'Would there be a night school I could go to?'

'Good Lord – you don't waste any time, do you? Yes, there are several. What do you want to study?'

'Business. How to run things, manage them.'

'I see. Well, I can help you with that, and so can Walter. He owns five antique shops.'

Then there must be money in antiques, Aran thought as they pulled into the driveway of a tall terraced house with a long narrow garden. Her parents' house was terraced too, but there the resemblance ended: this was a mansion by comparison, painted cream, with two stone lions on either side of the front door, a polished brass knocker and a second car outside. It was very impressive, but something about the smoking chimney and the child's trike flung on the grass gave it a friendly air.

The scarlet door shot open, expelling a small boy with fair hair cut square around his pudgy face, tiny round glasses and big blue eyes, who flew out to greet them as if fired by cannon.

"'Nuther one! New one, 'nuther one!'

Holly smiled, satisifed with the way Aran bent to embrace and scoop him up, wincing but not protesting as he plunged his fist into her fluffy hair and tugged on it experimentally.

Yes, Ollie, another one. Only I think this one might be different. She isn't blathering on about her mother, not gazing round her like a goon, not telling me how she's brought plenty of bacon and black pudding in her suitcase. I don't know yet why she's come, but let's hope she's going to stay. It would make such a nice change.

It took Aran a month to get properly settled, and another month to become thoroughly unsettled.

That first night, she wept for her home and family. The next night, she wept again, but in the comforting realisation that she need not muffle her sobs in the large secluded bedroom up on the top floor, which got a lot of sunlight and even had its own bathroom. If you had to howl like a child, she thought, this was a very nice place in which to do it. The third night, she found herself thinking about her oboe. One moment she could hear Conor's soft voice in her head, the next she could hear the first notes of the *Pearl Fishers*.

After a week her routine became established, and although there was a lot of work Holly let her do it in whatever hours and order she chose, chiefly concerned that she should form a good rapport with Oliver. Aran found the little boy as winsome as he was demanding, but usually his batteries wore out by early afternoon, leaving her with two hours to call her own while he took his nap. Bedding him down one day, she went to her own room and took the oboe from its case, closed the door and put it to her lips. Minutes later, she was horrified to hear the child crying and, thinking that she had woken him, rushed to soothe and lull him back to sleep.

59

But it was four o'clock. She had been playing for two hours. And two hours flew by every afternoon thereafter, an oasis of peace from which she drew strength and joy, feeling increasingly at home in the solid, happy household.

Every morning she took Ollie out in his buggy for a walk, patiently permitting him to get out and stagger into people's gardens, examine everything she wanted to examine herself. Islington was a lively village with long leafy streets, and she found a new corner of it every day, looking forward increasingly to the time when Holly would allow her to explore further. But she had agreed to wait a few weeks before striking out on her own at weekends, because Holly felt she should get her local bearings first, become acclimatised.

Walter Mitchell was so quiet she thought at first he must dislike her, but gradually she realised that he simply didn't see her; au pairs came and went with the anonymous regularity of milkmen. But on the third weekend it rained, so heavily that she was forced to spend her free time indoors with the family, and to her surprise he thawed as he talked about his business A serious man, he spoke to her as if she were an adult, fascinating her as he explained just how much there was to running it. So much more to be learned than she had thought! The following day she applied her attention to finding a night school that might take her, and finally located a small college two miles away which, to her delight, accepted her for the spring term which had begun only the week before.

Holly was a little perplexed.

'I thought you must want to play that oboe professionally, Aran, you're so keen on it and so good at it.'

Aran had to laugh; the first time Holly heard the sound she had called upstairs to enquire whether Aran had a hen in her room, and was forcing it to smoke a packet of cigarettes. But that was the day on which she had first attempted to play from sheet music she had found in a nearby bookshop, and in the interval she had mastered it.

'I'd love to play professionally, Holly, if I thought I was good enough. But at that level you need something – something extra. Sometimes I think I'm just on the verge of finding it, whatever it is, but then it slips away again.'

That was not the case with her business studies, which did not tantalise in the same elusive way. Although the pace of the course was challenging she found herself rising to it, finding solace and confidence in her ability to hold her own from one session to the next. Amused by her youth, her tutors and classmates were helpful, friendly once she got to know them, and she began to enjoy the four nights a week she spent in class with them, the coffee and chat afterwards. Music made her breathless with its joys and difficulties, but at business college she felt her feet coming to rest on solid ground.

Books and sheet music were both expensive, but she budgeted carefully, allowing for the fact that, every week, half of her wages had to be converted into a postal order and sent home to her parents. The letters that were received in return were not effusive, but she felt her duty done, her conscience clear.

Still . . . how long would she have to do it? A year, two years, ten years? All her life? Guiltily she admonished herself for wondering whether the fishing might ever improve at home, any way ever be found to supplement the family's income that would take the focus off her. It was not that she begrudged her contribution, but it was hard for a young girl to have to pass up all the exciting things she saw in the shops: Islington's temptations were far more numerous and enticing than Dunrathway's or Ferleague's. On the rare occasion she succumbed, she found she could never fully enjoy the item she had bought. Then there were bus fares, because Holly would not let her walk by herself to or from college at night, and although she did not mind that her classmates mimicked her accent, she did mind the way they smiled at her clothes. But her studies were the most important thing, leaving her increasingly torn between all the reading to be done and the oboe which glistened in the lamplight as she did it.

At home, her domestic ineptitude was quickly discovered, and Holly shrieked in horror one day to find her boiling the bejasus out of an artichoke.

'Aran, it's not a cabbage! Oh, dear God . . . look, take my cookery books – here, this one and this one – and read them. If you can master the principle of supply, demand and curve you can master the principles of grilling, roasting and frying.'

Frantically Aran read them, relieved to find herself not put on the next plane home. Holly and Walter were really remarkably patient, she felt more at ease with them every day, even if Walter did blink at her mystified whenever she ventured to tell a joke or recount a funny episode. He did not have his wife's sense of humour, but he was kind and tolerant – except for the awful day she left Ollie's buggy out in the rain, and it was soaked. Nobody, she supposed ruefully, could be expected to put up with such a featherheaded ninny . . . but later that evening she played *Greensleeves* for him, at his own request, and was amazed by the soothing effect it had.

Her resolve to write regularly to Eimear was distracted by the many things to be done, seen and learned, and by the end of January her long chatty letters had turned into brief cheerful postcards, twice a week and then once a week until Holly proposed a better solution.

'Since you've tried so hard, Aran, and come on so well, I'm going to let you use the phone once a month if you'd like, you can call Ireland for ten minutes. Do it on Saturdays or at night, when the rate is cheaper.'

In fact Holly was thankful that Aran had not already tried to abuse the phone, as the previous au pair had done, for long weepy calls every other day. Delighted, Aran wrote to Eimear naming a time when she should be at home and ask her parents round to the house as well, so she could talk to everyone. This proved ideal, and in turn Eimear began to call her once a fortnight, establishing regular communication that banished whatever lingering homesickness remained. It was impossible to be lonely or unhappy with the Mitchells, even less so to find any time for brooding after she had got through her day's work, practised her oboe, gone to class and completed her quota of study. Life fell into a busy, even rhythm, so absorbing that she slept like a stone, and dreamt of nothing at all.

The early weeks of February sped by, until the week arrived in which Holly's baby was due, and she summoned Aran for a little conference.

'You know I'll be taking six weeks off, Aran, and not going back to work until the middle of April. The baby is due on Thursday, and when I come home from hospital I want to spend as much time as possible with it myself – and with Ollie too, so he doesn't feel left out. So you'll have a little more time to yourself. You haven't seen much of London yet, but I think now you should be capable of getting round on your own.'

'Oh, yes, Holly, I'll manage.'

'Good. Then let me give you some maps and guidebooks, you can start taking the Underground and doing a bit of exploring. I'll still need you in the mornings and evenings, but most days you can have four or five hours free.'

Aran's excitement was lost in the even greater excitement when, on Thursday, Holly duly gave birth to a baby daughter. The two came home on Saturday and, after much debate with paternal grandparents in Wales, it was decided to name the little girl Morag. For a week Aran was almost as busy as Holly and Walter, as thrilled and as besotted by the beautiful infant who snuggled into her cot, into the family and into everyone's hearts. What a grip a child can get on you, she thought in surprise as she listened to Morag's sing-song cry, stroked the child's incredibly soft pink cheeks, felt the tiny fingers twining round one of her own.

But then a kind of dormant lull came over the house, and she realised that a process of regrouping was taking place, a knitting together of the new unit from which she was wordlessly, very gently excluded. Isolated, she was tempted to volunteer for work whether Holly wanted her or not, because Morag was such a pleasure and Ollie had become such a little pal, but Holly gave her the maps and tactfully, pleasantly sent her on her way.

Having fibbed about her age, she could not tell Holly that it was her seventeenth birthday. No card or gift came for her; Eimear did not know the date, her brothers and sisters had forgotten it, and Molly did not believe in such extravagances. Conor would have written, she knew, if anyone had reminded him, but evidently they had not. She could not even tell her classmates without sounding childish, and so she pocketed the maps as a kind of token, a sign that she was becoming an adult and must make her own way into the future. But in that future she could not help hoping that she would find someone who believed in birthdays, someone who would remember, celebrate and share in them. For now, she could only look on her solitude as a kind of freedom, and make the most of it.

But it was that very freedom which unsettled her. From the sanctuary of Islington she was flung out into a much wider world and a curtain went up on the theatre of London. The scale of it amazed her, the drama and pace and colour, the history, character, tone and diversity, the fabulous wealth and the spectacular poverty. On the same streets where huge houses towered, huddled forms slept in cardboard boxes; on one corner was an outstretched hand, on the next was a Rolls Royce. Here a street vendor cried his wares, there a shop window glowed with jewellery, everywhere punk rockers flaunted their black leather, pink spiky hair and enormous, aggressive chains and medallions. And the mixture of people, the cacophony of languages! Aran had never before seen a black or brown skin, and she had to stop herself from staring, avert her eyes from the strange costumes, not knowing whether or not they were for effect. Were these people dressing for shock impact, like the gritty rockers, or did they really wear such clothes in the countries they came from? Whatever the reason, she thought it wonderfully invigorating, that if she lived in London for a hundred years she would never tire of all the buzz, the technicoloured contrasts.

In all weathers she dashed about, conscious that the Mitchells would soon reclaim her time, cramming in every possible adventure while she could. Gripping her travel card as if it were a ticket into the Arabian nights, she raced down into the Underground, lost her way and bobbed back up again in Soho, Bond Street, Trafalgar Square, Chelsea, Chiswick, Cheapside. Some days she selected destinations in advance, spending them entirely in Kew Gardens, Madame Tussaud's, Regent's Park or the City; on others she window-shopped in Oxford Street, then took a notion to see Greenwich, Kensington or Piccadilly. Her senses quivered with the vibrant delight of it, the vivacity of the fruit and vegetable markets, the flying balls flung aloft by a street juggler, the sound of a piccolo or a purring Aston Martin, the tang of a lemon tart extravagantly purchased in a French bakery whose window display was like a work of art. Whenever she spoke to Eimear her words tumbled out garbled and exclamatory, a mile a minute as she strove to describe it all.

Only her studies kept her feet on the ground, but now she brought her books with her to Hyde Park where the first tulips were opening, to the cafés and squares, even on the water bus and walking tours she took. Walter had helped her get a ticket for Islington library, but everything else was as expensive as it was exciting, and again she found herself wishing she could keep just a little more of what she earned.

There was little chance of that. Mournfully Molly wrote that the fishing was still bad, winter gales often prevented the boats from going out at all, Achill was growing at a rate of knots and needed new shoes, the wind had torn a dozen tiles off the roof and the new ones had cost a fortune. Dursey broke a tooth and had to be taken to the dentist, there was a new tax on fuel, the price of wool had gone up . . . Aran gritted her teeth and wondered whether providence would ever spare her, deliver her from it all.

Yet Molly's voice keened and moaned in her ears, making her feel selfish and guilty, impelling her to even send a little extra whenever she could economise by passing up on coffee with her classmates, ignoring a book on Bizet, walking away from the cosmetics on which she longed to splurge in Boots. But in April Holly returned to work, reluctantly relinquishing Morag and Oliver into her care, and Aran had to slow down then anyway, rein herself in with a new sense of restlessness. Really she *must* concentrate on the children, and on her studies; there was an exam to be taken at the end of May.

She stood at the cooker one evening, stirring the spaghetti bolognese which no longer caused anyone to dive for the bathroom, with one eye on it and the other on the textbook propped open on the worktop.

'Annual rental of square footage should be calculated according to the . . . oh, hi, Holly. Had a good day?'

'Yes, thanks, Aran, how are my little darlings . . . ?'

She flew straight to them, so fervently that Aran saw the conflict in her, the look that told her how Holly loved her children even more than her work, and missed them much more than she would admit. Or did absence make the heart grow even fonder? Well, she did not intend to find out. She did not want to feel the way Holly clearly felt now, her mind half on the office when she came home, half on the children when she was at her desk. Both, she thought, must suffer a little, neither getting the full attention or devotion they deserved. If she ever had children, it wouldn't be until she was at least thirty-six like Hannah Lowry . . . but Holly was nearly thirty-six now, and yet she was caught in this fix even with her business so well established. Why did Walter not seem to fret as she did, why did men not experience this irresistible pull to their children? He could go out in the morning without a backward glance, he didn't phone home five times a day, he wasn't the one who read Ollie a bedtime story or prepared Morag's late-night feed. She liked Holly very much, and admired her greatly, but in that respect she wanted to be like him.

'I'm making spaghetti, Holly, is that OK?'

'Oh yes, that's lovely, I'm so tired this evening I was going to send you out for a takeaway. You really don't have to cook for us as well as the children, you know.'

'Oh, it's no bother, I don't have a class tonight anyway. Here, I'm putting some Chianti in the sauce, why don't you have a glass?'

'Oh, Aran, you're a treasure. Let me get my coat off and put my feet up for two minutes.'

Gratefully Holly sank into a chair, settling Morag in one arm as she accepted the wine with the other, smiling at Ollie's chatter and the music that Aran always had playing in the background. Aran looked very well tonight, and something popped into her mind that she had been meaning to ask for ages.

'I love that sweater you're wearing, Aran. Where did you get it?'

'My mother made it for me, last Christmas.'

'Did she really? My goodness, she's gifted. Would she make one for me, do you think? I'd pay her whatever she considers appropriate.'

Would she? Amazed and flattered, Aran spun round.

'Why yes, Holly, I'm sure she would! Would you want this colour, or another? What size . . . just a little larger, maybe?'

'Well, a little. And a different colour I suppose, so we don't look like twins – or mother and daughter! I know – I could choose the wool myself, and post it to her.'

'Yes – well, don't buy it until I write and ask. But I'm sure she'll do it for you.'

Serving and eating supper in a welter of impatience, Aran went to her room as soon as the meal was over, and wrote to Molly. Filling the letter with praise and enthusiasm, she couched it in the most coaxing terms, but its tone was firm. An opportunity had been found here, and it was to be taken.

Two months later, on a June morning so sunny nothing could dampen her spirits, Eimear ran into Molly Campion in the butcher's shop.

'Hello, Mrs Campion, how are you today?'

Eimear smiled at the clenched little woman in her black coat and knotted headscarf, pleased to note that the butcher seemed to be wrapping quite a quantity of meat for her. Whether Aran knew it or not, her funds were making a difference to the family: Achill and Dursey had come to school warmly dressed and fully equipped all this last term, no longer running back and forth between classrooms to share their books.

'I'm very busy Mrs Rafter, if you must know, that daughter of mine has me worn out.'

'Aran? With the knitting, you mean? But don't you think it's a wonderful idea?'

'Ah, the first few sweaters were grand. The ones for Mrs Mitchell and her friends. But we can't keep up any more.'

'Oh, but Mrs Campion, you must! I was talking to Aran only yesterday, and she told me she's got a stall booked, everything is ready . . . after all, there are fifteen of you, surely you can meet the order between you?'

'Thirty sweaters by the end of the month? It's obvious to me, Mrs Rafter, that you've never knitted a stitch in your life.'

Eimear's eye fell on the butcher's long carving knife, and she wondered whether he would turn her in if she plunged it into Molly's chest. Probably not.

'But Aran says she's sure she can sell them all, at a good price, think what it will mean to your families. I know it's hard work, but it can't be any worse than going out to fish in the freezing ocean. And if it goes well, think how many children might be able to stay on at school next year, maybe even the year after – including Achill.'

'Ah, what good does it do them?'

'It enables them to do the kind of thing Aran is doing now! Seeing the chance of a new venture, and acting on it. I know it's only a market stall at weekends, but it's a start. I'm sure the other women are very happy about it.'

'Aye, well, we'll wait and see what comes of it. We're to send the work over on the fish lorry Aran says, did you ever hear such nonsense?'

'I think it's a great idea. Charlie Doran has plenty of room and probably won't even charge, except for the extra bit of petrol maybe, to deliver to Islington.'

'More fool Charlie. Anyway, I'll not keep you, Mrs Rafter. I'm sure you're just as busy as I am.'

The old bag knows the school holidays are starting, Eimear thought, she couldn't let that jibe go if her life depended on it. Well, she may as well know the rest of it too.

'Did I tell you that Dan and I are thinking of going over in August?'

'No! Isn't it well for some.'

'We'd be happy to bring over any little thing you might want to send Aran.'

'Oh, she wants nothing, only the work. All sizes, all colours, we've had to send away to Cork for the right shades. Anyone would think she was our boss, that we had nothing else to do, no homes to run.'

'Yes, well, I won't keep you any longer from yours.'

Both Eimear and the butcher laughed as Molly departed, a prim old stick who wouldn't give them the satisfaction of admitting she was pleased. Yet she must be, surely. It wasn't every day the opportunity to make money knocked on Dunrathway's door, much less on the Campions', and Molly couldn't be more than forty-five or -six, she was well able to take it.

'Lamb,' remarked the butcher as he wrapped Eimear's order, 'dressed as mutton.'

Camden. It was only down the road, and although Petticoat Lane got more Americans, Leadenhall was prettier, Aran judged it the best and biggest market at weekends. Renting a stall there was not as cheap as she had expected, but if the investment succeeded she wouldn't need to send home quite so much of her wages, wouldn't feel quite so awful about wanting the things every teenage girl wanted. It was the first step on the path to freedom, and it was the first step on a path that might, some day, lead to something bigger. Something that meant she wouldn't have to take care of Ollie and Morag until they were pensioners. Much as she loved the children, revelled in Ollie's antics and Morag's big toothless smiles, she didn't want to mind other people's children for ever, always be on the fringe of someone else's family.

Some day, it would be lovely to have a little girl like Morag, a sturdy toddler like Ollie. But she was only seventeen. She would not have them until everything else was in place, and she could afford to care for them. In the Mitchell home nobody ever seemed to have enough time, in her own home there was never enough money; what she wanted was a life like Eimear Rafter's, marriage to a man like Dan. Eimear had married young, but she had got her university degree first, found work that left her with some time of her own, yet guaranteed her independence. Dan was the kind of man who would give her anything she wanted, but she never had to ask – and, if this market stall went well, Molly would no longer have to ask her daughter, or depend so heavily on her husband.

These next few weeks were vital. Passing exams was all very well, and had been a great encouragement, but putting theory into practice was another matter. The thought of actually raising her voice, inveigling people into buying her wares filled her with dread, but with any luck the handiwork should speak for itself. It must, because there was no point in selling anything inferior, anything you had to apologise for. She would make it a rule that everything was of the best possible quality, not just reliable but good enough that people passed it on by word of mouth. The women of Dunrathway were very competent knitters, but they must accept that these new sweaters were different, and better.

That was why Holly had bought the first one, and her friends had commissioned others, got this ball rolling. We're all going to work hard this summer, she thought, and learn a lot. I'll be way ahead when I go back to college in the autumn. This project involves marketing, accounting, working out overheads, dividends, profit margins. I'll deduct the rent of the stall, but I won't charge Mother and her chums for my time, because it's of such benefit to me. I'll model the sweaters myself too, so people can see how they look on an actual person, won't have to pull them about or try them on out in the open. It'll be fun! And it will get me into the life of this city, I'll meet lots of people. I don't feel nearly so restless now that I have something to call my own. I only wish I could have started sooner, but I suppose they're knitting as fast as they can back in Dunrathway, and anyway the stall doesn't come free until the end of the month. Thank God Walter was able to help me get it.

Who'd have thought he'd know so much about market stalls? I've never even been to Bermondsey or Cutler Street, where he says he started out. But he's been a great help, and anyone who owns five antique shops must know what he's talking about. He was right about getting a covered stall. The knitwear would be ruined on an open one if it rained, although this is the hottest summer I've ever known. That's the one thing I really miss about Dunrathway . . . the beach, and the sea, and the dolphins.

I'm sure Walter's right about how to rig up the lighting too – I'd never even have thought of that, much less known an electrician to do it for me. And I will get a moneybelt, like he says, I don't want anyone dipping into my bag while I'm busy with customers. Customers! Well, Walter calls his clients, nowadays, but it doesn't matter what you call them so long as you understand the ratio between what they want and what you've got. It was amazing the way he got all sparkly when he was explaining that, and how it fitted right in with what we learned at college.

God, I can't believe I've been accepted for next year, and might even be able to reimburse Eimear when she comes over in August. Partly, at least. She's been so good to me, and so have the Mitchells.

I don't know why they gave me those music lessons, when they heard they'd missed my birthday, but it was terribly kind of them. Not that six lessons could get anyone very far, but they did help; I'm playing much better now. And that, as Mr Becher says, is just the problem.

I am good at the oboe, and understand what he means about having to give it your all. But I can't. I wish I could, but I can't. He says that really great players have great passion, that that's the thing I keep reaching out for and losing again. If I could afford to continue with him, I'd get there . . . but how can I, with the children to mind, the housework to do, my studies and now this stall to run?

I know I'm turning my back on a great passion, just when I can hear it calling me. But maybe I'll find other passions – fall passionately in love with a man, perhaps, as Eimear did? She says half the men in the world are fools, and yet Dan is her vocation, in the same way that teaching children is her vocation. She loves them both.

Love. I love her, I love my father, I love Ollie and Morag, I love my oboe. But if I ever fall in love with a man, and have children with him, I hope they'll be able to do what they really love. I have to start a business, need money for myself and for my family – but maybe some day it will enable my own children to do what they really need to do, *have* to do.

When the driver of the fish lorry arrived, Aran thought quickly, and invited him to meet her for a drink at a pub in Islington. If she was as good to him as he was being to her, he might be even better, and drop the stuff off at her front door.

It took three pints, but he did, and her smile of thanks was so sweet he even said yes, certainly, he'd bring the next lot two weeks later. As soon as he was gone, leaving the boxes safely stashed in the Mitchells' basement, she threw herself upon them.

Oh, God, the smell of fish that rose from them! But nobody had thought to wrap the knitwear in plastic, and every sweater reeked of fish as she lifted it out with Holly, examining each one in minute detail, checking with bated breath for flaws.

But they were perfect. Molly and the other women of Dunrathway had been knitting for long enough to be technically virtuoso, and did not have the imagination, Aran suspected, to deviate from the instructions they had been given. Probably it had killed them to tone down their traditionally loud colours, relax their grim grip in favour of the softer style and looser stitch. But the result was actually easier and quicker to produce, and very much more fashionable. Yet it was still chunky and somehow distinctive, the kind of thing that could not easily be found in shops or boutiques, certainly not for such a modest price. With a little more thought and research on her part, Aran felt, it might even be refined into something quite unique.

'What do you think, Holly?'

'I think you'll sell every one of these. If this is a nation of shopkeepers, you're in business!'

Unlike Walter, Aran did not want to become a shopkeeper, yet she was certainly heading in that direction, and could put no name on the alternative. Anyway, for now it was enough.

'I'd better put these out to air, and hope the awful smell is gone by Saturday.'

At dawn on Saturday, Walter drove her to Camden Market, where in the warm opalescent sunshine other stallholders were already setting up shop, sipping cups of tea as they compared notes and exchanged friendly rivalries. It was a warm beautiful morning, and Aran felt the sun on her back through her T-shirt, suddenly realising it was the worst possible weather for sweaters. Sixty-five degrees already, at seven o'clock! But she must put the prettiest one on, and try to look cool in it.

'My God, you're a masochist!'

The girl at the next stall was grinning at her, and Aran could only grin back.

'Hi. I'm Aran Campion.'

'Hi. I'm Bronwen Reeves.'

Bronwen was not much older than herself, twenty at most, a thin girl in a light, muddled mixture of clothes, chiefly green cotton dotted with cream, her abundant red hair tied up anyhow around her tanned face and neck. On her stall stood a glinting plethora of glass: tall triangular bottles, squat little decanters, thick tumblers and thinner wine glasses. People would think of drinks, Aran thought, and buy those today.

'Don't look so doubtful, Aran! It's amazing what people buy here, regardless of the weather. Your sweaters are lovely colours, like ice-cream, you'll sell – well, maybe not the whole lot, but enough.'

Jesus, Aran thought, I'd better. I've got to clear my overheads at least, and make enough that Mother won't give up on me.

On me! That's what she'd say. I must think positive, and never say that again.

She blinked as a polystyrene mug of tea suddenly landed at her elbow.

'Here. Hi.'

'Hi. Thanks. Who are you?'

'I'm Thanh. Dith Thanh.'

'Nice to meet you, Dith. My name is Aran Campion. Thanks for the tea.'

'No. My first name is Thanh. In Viet Nam we put the first name last.'

Viet Nam! Now this, Aran thought, is what I like about London. I'd be waiting a month of Sundays to meet someone from Viet Nam in Dunrathway. He looks so different – and so young, too, even younger than me.

But as Thanh nattered in a high, musical voice she discovered that he was twenty-four, one of a family of eight war refugees who, like herself, were trying to establish themselves in a new country.

'Do you like it here?'

'Yeah. I like. Where you from?'

'Ireland. Dunrathway, in Cork.'

'Ireland. Bang-bang, boom-boom.'

People always said that, not knowing or caring the difference between the part that was at war and the part that might as well be on another planet. But then she didn't know the difference between North and South Viet Nam, either, and if Thanh had left then he probably didn't want to talk about his politics any more than she felt like talking about hers. Not that she knew very much – and anyway it was a nice sunny day, she was only seventeen, she couldn't be bothered.

'What are those?'

'Bamboo. Boxes, blinds, everything. My father make, I sell.'

'Hah! That's funny, my mother made my stuff too. With her friends.'

It struck her that her mother wasn't actually friendly with the other women in the knitting group – only acquainted, for a purpose. But if Thanh and Bronwen were being friendly to her, then she was going to be friendly to them. As cluttered as Bronwen's stall was, Thanh's was neat and organised, and she tried to arrange her own with an eye to the best features of theirs. Later, she'd find a style of her own.

By eight the market was beginning to hum, some early browsers already picking over the best bargains, eating doughnuts and swigging Coke in a casual way she found attractive. People were so much looser here than at home, where you sat down at table to eat a proper breakfast. But her stall was way down at the far end of the market, and it was a while before anyone made their way there.

'No worry. They come.'

Thanh smiled at her, with lovely clear green eyes and a nonchalant shrug. But he was a good salesman, not afraid to call out to people, coax them to examine his products, charm them into buying. Tongue-tied, she watched Bronwen begin to do it too, until there were quite a few people on either side of her, but still none at her own stall.

It was over seventy degrees now, far too hot. She wasn't going to sell anything. She might as well have brought her oboe, and used the time to practise.

'You make these?'

An American. Two Americans actually, middle-aged women in sweatpants and shirts, looking at the sweaters with mild interest.

'My mother does.'

'Uh huh. Where?'

'In Ireland.'

'Nice.'

But they moved on. God, she was going to have to do better than this, forget her shyness, chat and charm people a bit! With an effort, she set her mind to it the next time. And the next . . . but it was nearly noon before, finally, she sold her first sweater.

'I did it! I did it!'

Bronwen and Thanh laughed as she put the money into her leather pouch, thankful that Walter had warned her to bring change, get nice wrapping paper, remember the sellotape. Oh, but it was hard work!

And it was infernally hot. How anyone could buy a sweater was beyond her imagination, but gradually they did, sometimes taking an eternity to make up their minds, digging down into the whole pile and dragging everything about, wanting to haggle over the £12 which Holly had advised her to fix. And the questions! If she had to explain once more where Dunrathway was, she thought, she would scream. What did it matter where the damn sweaters came from?

But apparently it did. Everything mattered: and so she began to take notes, list all the queries. It was too late for tomorrow, but by next week she would have a sign on the stall, with information that everyone could easily read. Meanwhile, she could return Thanh's friendly gesture.

'Tea, Thanh? Bronwen?'

'No – something cold.'

Bronwen kept an eye on her stall while she went to get it, and had sold another sweater by the time she returned, bringing the tally to eight. Not a lot, but better than nothing.

'Thanks, Bronwen.'

'Don't mention it. Hey, why don't you come with Thanh and me when we close up? We're going to get a beer and a burger, go hang out by the river.'

Oh, bliss! Would Walter mind, when he came to collect her? Would he take the remaining twenty-two sweaters home in the car, and leave her to just unwind, dangle her feet in the water? She'd been on them all day – tomorrow, she'd borrow one of Holly's folding garden chairs. And, she supposed, eventually she'd have to find some form of transport of her own, some way of getting each day's supply to the market without depending on the Mitchells. They couldn't fetch and carry every weekend.

There was so much to be done, so much to be thought of. She knew her exhaustion was obvious to Walter when he arrived, looking rather starched in his blazer and trim moustache, but anxious to know how the day had gone.

'I sold eight.'

'Well done! Come on then, let's get you home.'

'Oh, Walter, this is Bronwen, this is Thanh ... would it be OK if I just went for a quick bite with them?'

He smiled, glad to see her making friends, and they smiled too, amused that someone should come to collect her, as if she were a child.

'All right. But be home by ten.'

Ten? That gave her four hours. Suddenly she was almost dizzy with heat and fatigue, the elated prospect of having a beer and hanging out with people her own age, like a normal teenager. Pulling the last accursed sweater from over her head, she dumped it on top of the pile, left him to cart the whole lot home and followed her new colleagues away to the water.

Dan and Eimear could hardly believe the difference in Aran when, in mid August, they arrived at Heathrow. Eight months of London had taken the child out of her, and it was a vivacious young woman who met them, her tanned skin highlighting the tangled curls that shone like silver coins, her clothes thrown together in a chaos of confident colour. With Oliver by the hand and Morag in a buggy, she pounced on them and led them away to the Underground, walking and talking at such a pace they had to hasten to keep up.

'A hundred and fifty sweaters so far ... did you bring the scarves and jewellery?'

Eimear nodded, feeling as if roles had been invisibly reversed. Word of Aran's enterprise had spread round the village and out to others, with the result that she had been charged with bringing over samples of assorted craftwork. A woman from Ferleague wanted Aran to sell the jewellery she made from pressed wild flowers, someone from Schull had the same idea for her handpainted silk scarves, a man in Bantry had become convinced that London would love his stained glass planters. Eimear's luggage was bursting with samples of all these items, plus lace and crochet, even tiny sculptures made from shells. Aran said she would consider everything provided it was of high quality and original design, but that henceforth she would charge a percentage for her time and labour; only the Dunrathway knitting group would continue to get those for free.

The group already had plans, Eimear informed Aran, for expansion. Nine more women wanted to join it, and they were going to appoint Shelagh Carney financial director, see if the bank would lend them enough money to buy wool on a commercial basis. If so, they would set about making up their own patterns, innovating in the way Aran suggested, scanning magazines to see what colours and textures were popular for winter and introducing items aimed at younger buyers.

'Great. I must talk to them about the signatures, too.'

'Signatures?'

'Yes. The handwritten labels have gone down so well I want to take them a step further, and get each knitter to work her name into the garment she's made. On the cuff, where it will be seen every time the wearer lifts a pen or a cup, even hails a bus. It will make the women feel involved, proud of their work, and it will give the products a personal touch. In future, every sweater will be visibly "Handmade by Molly Campion, Cork, Ireland", or whatever the maker's name might be.'

'You think people will wear labels on the outside?'

'Sure. Not labels, but logos. Something that tells the buyer they're getting something that isn't mass produced, something that has a really distinctive look, as if it was made specially for them, by an individual whose name they know.'

'Well, I must say, the grass hasn't been growing under your feet!' Aran grinned.

'I love thinking up new ideas – and the customers are going for them, too. I got Clare Keating's notice framed, with the picture of Dunrathway she painted on it, and all the information about the village, the group, even the sheep the wool comes from. It makes people look, take an interest, and I've even heard one or two say the

74

place is so pretty, they must think of it for a holiday.'

'Well, Dunrathway's isn't quite as pretty as Clare's picture of it, not this summer. There's still a lot of unemployment, people drinking and hanging round the pub ... even one or two of your former classmates.'

'Layabouts! Why don't they get together and paint the place, do it up and make it attractive to tourists? They could plant flowers, hang them in baskets, even open a café. Then they'd have something to occupy them – a purpose, and summer jobs.'

'They seem to be waiting for the government to give them jobs, tell them what to do. And their parents are happy to take the money the government gives them.'

'I know what I'd give them.'

Eimear smiled. 'You've given them something already – the knitters, anyway. But the younger ones don't want to knit, they say it's old hat, and far too hard.'

Aran sighed.

'You tell them that there's plenty of demand over here for Irish craftwork, and there'd be plenty of demand for it over there too if they'd only get off their butts and turn the village into a nice showcase for it. The hotel is a lost cause, but they could do up the guesthouses and open new ones, get the place into the guidebooks, give people a reason to go there.'

'Very good, madam. I'll tell them.'

Aran giggled. 'Oh, Eimear, I'm sorry, I didn't mean to sound officious! Oh, it's great to see you and Dan – how have you been? How's Sammy?'

'He's fine and we're fine. We've been really looking forward to seeing you, and meeting the Mitchells. It's so kind of them to offer us their spare room.'

'They're great. They've been endlessly helpful to me. And as you can see, their children are absolute angels.'

Ollie and Morag were being very good on the long tube journey, so sweet that Eimear longed to take them from Aran, sit them on her lap and cuddle them. How Morag smiled, how funny Ollie looked with his little feet jutting out over the edge of his seat! When the train pulled into the station at which they had to change to another one, she took the little boy's hand and helped him out, touched by the trusting way he put his pudgy hand in hers.

'Isn't he adorable?'

'He is. But he keeps me busy! What with him and his sister, the stall to run, the paperwork to do, all the letters I've got to write to Ireland, I'm up to my ears.'

'But what about your oboe, and your poetry?'

'Oh, I play as much as I can. I haven't any time for poetry, though.'

'Oh, Aran. You mustn't let it go.'

'I won't. I'll get back to it some day. In about twenty years, when I'm a lady of leisure.'

'But don't you have any fun? Have you made any friends?'

'Lots, at the market. Especially a Welsh girl called Bronwen and a Vietnamese guy called Thanh, you'll meet them later, Thanh sometimes helps me take my stuff to the market. He's a pet.'

'Is he?' Interested, Eimear searched Aran's face for a blush or one of those shy smiles of hers, that might betray she had found a first boyfriend. But Aran was struggling to get Morag's buggy through a turnstile, looking more like an angry wasp than a lovesick maiden.

'Jesus, you'd know these bloody things were designed by a man! Come on Morag, out you get, you poor little thing, don't cry.'

Despite her flustered exertion, Eimear noted Aran's gentle tone. For a girl who said she didn't want children, she was very good with them, careful and patient. But not with things that obstructed her.

'God, this is ridiculous! I can't get through!'

'Here, let me help.'

Dan put down his luggage, lifted Morag over the turnstile and then the buggy, with such calm ease that she smiled at him, at the way he managed Morag so that the child's unhappy cries were soothed, and stopped.

'Thanks, Dan.'

'Not at all. What do women bring men to London for, only to fetch, carry and fix things? I'm fully resigned to a week of trailing round after Eimear, with six shopping bags in either hand.'

He smiled at his wife, and Aran saw the same complicit look between them that she had seen before, on Eimear's birthday. Eimear was almost thirty now, but as visibly in love as a young bride, as Dan was equally in love with her.

Did she get it, I wonder? That thing that she wanted so badly, made the wish for? Did she ever get it?

Aran thoroughly enjoyed the busy week of Dan and Eimear's visit. During the day she had to leave them to fend for themselves, but in the evenings they went out, with the Mitchells, to bistros, little fringe theatres and concerts, shops and galleries that were open late.

'Oh, this is great fun, Aran, I'd forgotten how much there is to do in London.'

'Isn't there? I still haven't seen half of it myself.'

'But you're happy? You've really settled in here?'

'Yes. I have to admit I don't miss Dunrathway very much at all. Only the sea, sometimes . . .'

'Will you come home for Christmas?'

'Oh, no! The market will be far too busy!'

Aran didn't see the way Eimear looked at her when she said it, but she felt a slight sadness in her next words.

'But then, when will you come home? Your father misses you, you know. Your whole family does.'

'Oh, I don't know . . . I'd love to see them, of course, but when? How? I'm more use to them here than I would be there.'

'Couldn't you get just one weekend away from the market?'

'Come to it with me tomorrow, and you'll see just how much time and work it takes.'

Eimear went, with Dan, and was forced to admit that Aran was right. The crowds were vast, the buzz almost frightening, there were moments when she was carried along on the surging throng against her will, almost swept away. But what a great job Aran had made of her stall!

Clare Keating's framed painting did look great, and saved Aran having to tell people fifty times a day where the knitwork came from, who made it or what wools were used. Each sweater was tied up in a ribbon, with just one hanging loose overhead so that people could examine it, although Aran said she would wear another one herself when the weather cooled down, if it ever did. By then, each product would incorporate its maker's signature, and the display be enlivened by those other artefacts she had chosen from the samples: after a summer devoted to augmenting her mother's income, she would start to make a profit herself. But in winter there would be even greater demand for the sweaters, and Eimear thought that Molly stood to make quite a bit of money. Aran thought so too.

'At least, I hope so! To be honest, Eimear, I'd like to get her off my back . . . oh, I know that sounds terrible, but you know what I mean – I'll be going back to college, need new books and stuff. I want to keep a bit more of what Mrs Mitchell pays me. How is Mother? Is the money helping, making a difference?'

'Yes, it certainly is. Hasn't she written to tell you?'

'Well, she has written . . . but she doesn't say much.'

'Take it from me. She's doing very well, and she's delighted. The whole group is. Look, why don't I turn Dan loose, and help you on the stall? You'd need eyes in the back of your head with all these people.'

'OK! You can do the wrapping, and I'll do the talking.'

Eimear was amazed by the way Aran did talk, with such verve and polish, to her customers, The girl who had once been so shy was all chat now, outgoing without being effusive. She enticed people to buy, but she didn't push them, and smiled even if they didn't. There were many tourists, but lots of locals too, who she said might come back again another day. When she sold a sweater, she handed it to Eimear to be done up in attractive packaging, and popped a small sachet of potpourri into each parcel.

'They think it's a little gift, but it's actually just in case there's still any smell of fish! I air the consignments in Holly's garden, and the plastic bags have helped, but that lorry still reeks to high heaven. Did I tell you that Charlie Doran is on commission now?'

Eimear didn't know the driver personally, but mentally added his name to the list of people back home who seemed to constitute Aran's growing workforce. But they were adults, she was seventeen, it was laughable!

Still, they were earning and Aran was happy. Popular, too: whether she knew it or not, Thanh definitely had his eye on her.

'He fancies you, Aran! It's written all over his face!'

'He does in his eye.'

'I'm telling you! He hasn't stopped smiling at you all day.'

'Thanh smiles all day every day, at everyone. That's why I like him. But he's never asked me out, and I wouldn't go if he did.'

'Why not?'

'Too busy.'

'Oh, come on . . . wouldn't it be nice to have a little romance, a boyfriend?'

'Yes, Eimear. It will be very nice, when I have time, about ten years from now.'

Aran's face was serious, her tone final. Eimear didn't insist, but she couldn't help hoping that Aran would change her mind, and not leave it too late . . . if she wanted to have a family, particularly. She must want that, surely?

'You're pushing yourself too hard.'

'Eimear, I'm learning, and as of next month I'll be earning. I've got what I want, and I'm enjoying it.'

'My mother will be sorry to hear you're not playing the oboe more often. And I'm sorry you haven't written more poetry.'

'I play every day, for two hours! As for the poetry, I told you, I'll get back to it.'

'I hope so . . . I want a poem for my birthday, and another one for Christmas.'

'Well, I'll do my best, but don't hold your breath.'

Eimear saw from her face that there wasn't any point in holding it, for poems or music or boyfriends, any of the things that gave

78

sweetness to youth. Having come from a poor family, Aran seemed utterly determined to enrich it, and get away from it.

It will be a long time, she thought, before Aran comes home. I'm going home tomorrow, myself, but I don't want to go. She's happy here, but I don't want to leave her. The Mitchells are good to her, but Holly Mitchell is doing all the things I want to do myself. She's the one who's looking after Aran, and she's the one having babies. Ollie and Morag are so gorgeous, it's been torture to spend a whole week with them, and then have to leave. I wish they were mine, and I wish Aran was mine.

But they're not mine, and it doesn't look as if any child ever will be.

Chapter Four

Aran felt the wrench of Dan and Eimear's departure very keenly, and
sought some way to express it without offending Holly, who might
regard overt regret as a slight on her. Sitting down one sweltering
evening in the garden, she tried to write a poem, but it wouldn't come,
and in frustration she tore the pages to pieces. But later that night she
went back outside with her oboe, and it came then, some mournful
music that made itself up as it went along, and left her feeling much
better as she played in the dark; not comforted, but calm and
composed.

College began a week later, and she resumed her studies with a
will, pleased to find just how much the market had taught her.

What exactly she was studying for, she still didn't know, but
supposed that she would know it when she saw it. Now that she had
her own business, she felt less inclined to run anybody else's, and
began to wonder whether she could turn the crafts into something
more substantial. A shop? An import venture? But she didn't want to
sell other people's handiwork nearly so much as she wanted to create
and produce something of her own.

What, though?

'Maybe you should think about Dunrathway, Aran. You have so
many ideas for the place, what it could be with effort and imagination
. . . tourism might be the answer.'

'It's the answer for Dunrathway, Holly. But not for me. I've chosen
London, I like it and I'm staying here. This is where my life will be.'

'Well, I hope so, because I'll need you for quite a while yet, until
Morag is old enough to start school at least.'

Holly was so pleased with Aran she was prepared to offer
incentives to keep her: the basement that was being used for storage,
the phone on which calls to Ireland were permitted and always fully
accounted for. Despite the weekend venture Aran gave her full

attention to her job on weekdays, never slacking or cheating, caring for the children and doing all her own work in her own time. She was honest, reliable and incredibly industrious. Really she should get out a little more, socialise, date some boys, go to the discos Thanh and Bronwen suggested. She had so little time for fun, so much on her mind; there was something driven about her, some need that seemed to consume her round the clock. But she had acquired poise, the casual sophistication of other city teenagers – and, even if she did dress in Oxfam and army surplus, she looked more like her peers now, wore a bit of make-up to college, was becoming more confident and in command of herself.

If she was homesick or lonely, she never let it show, and her conversation had become more articulate and adventurous; it was a pity, Holly thought, that her mother couldn't see her nowadays, enjoy the daughter who was old enough to become a friend. But Aran didn't talk much about her mother, and the mother only ever seemed to get in touch about things connected with the knitwear.

And the father – what a shame he didn't come more often to the telephone that Eimear made available, because Aran's face glowed when he did. But his calls were rare and short, the sisters hardly made any contact at all and the brothers never did. The family was making no effort to remain united, and from experience Holly knew it was one of the ones that would fragment. The poor kid was very cheerful, considering – and a grand little worker, who could be trusted with the children at all times, in any situation. She would make a wonderful mother, some day, cherish her own children far more than she was cherished herself. For some reason she said she didn't want to marry for years yet, or have a family for even longer . . . but Holly thought that was something she had decided with her head, not something she felt in her heart. You only had to look at her with Ollie and Morag to see how she loved them, the way they responded to her, the warmth in every little word and touch.

Still, she was the kind to stick to something once she had made up her mind about it. She knew she should really become an oboeist, she felt the music, yet she had chosen to study business and start up a small one of her own. She was a pragmatist – not by nature, but by design, of necessity.

I'm not sure what she really wants, Holly conceded. But whatever it is, I'm sure she'll get it. Which is more than can be said for her friend Eimear. I've never met a nicer woman, or a more frustrated one.

It was a cool clear October morning, and the market was quieter than

81

usual. Muffled in a bottle-green sweater and one of the scarves from Ferleague, Aran stood sipping a mug of tea, reflecting and planning. After ten months, she had constructed a rewarding life for herself in London, and she thought she could see where it was leading.

And then, in ten seconds, the horizon dipped and skewed, lurched and rocked out of sight.

It was the hands that hit her first, the two dark hands with the long fingers that immediately announced a musician. They must do; that was what hands like those were for, created specifically to stroke a string instrument or a piano, their fine fingers so deft as they lifted one of her cardigans aloft, high into the air so she could not see their owner's face.

'How about this one?'

The voice was musical too, clear and distinct, with some inflection she did not recognise, some precisely enunciated undertone.

'No. I like this one better.'

She could see the young woman who spoke, a slender Indian in a sari, powder-skinned and very pretty. But it was a moment before her companion put down the cardigan to reveal his face.

Aran had seen many fascinating faces at the market, but never one so distinctive or so commanding. Tawny, Indian like the woman's, it was a young, fine face built on clear, strong lines, held high with great confidence. But it softened when he spoke, filling with a kind of smoky beauty, radiating all the molten warmth of the scorching summer gone by, the eyes smudged and glowing as charcoals.

'May we see the other one – this one here?'

Without waiting for an answer he picked up the rose cardigan and passed it to the woman, appraising it from under rich heavy eyelids and long black eyebrows. As he turned Aran was able to see his profile, the curve of his wide lips and smooth cheeks, the nose that was surprisingly assertive in one so young. But when he smiled she noticed that one of his large white teeth was slightly out of line, combining with a dimple in his left cheek to give him some childlike appeal, a precocious air of enormous charm and presence.

He helped the woman try on the cardigan, assisting her into it with such casual affection that she could feel the bond between them, the fond ease of long acquaintance. The cardigan was incongruous with the sari, but the woman surveyed it in the mirror with satisfaction, and peered to read the inscription on the sleeve.

'Oh, look, Ben, It's handmade, by someone in Ireland – in Cork? Where is Cork? Who is Orla Keller?'

Ben. His name was Ben. Aran etched it into her mind.

'Are you Orla Keller? Did you make this?'

Normally she directed enquiries to the sign on the stall, where people could read all the information they wanted. But he was different, and she couldn't.

'No . . . my name is Aran Campion.'

He smiled again, so blindingly she wanted to shut her eyes against the flash.

'Well, Aran Campion, that's a very hoarse little whisper. Are you shy, or are you catching a cold?'

She cleared her throat.

'S – sorry, I am a bit husky this morning.'

He didn't answer, turning back to the woman instead, inspecting her with admiration.

'It suits you, Rani. Let's get it.'

He put his hand into his pocket while the woman removed the cardigan, drawing Aran's eye from his face, framed by very black shoulder-length hair, down to his clothes. They were almost certainly from the King's Road, she thought, proclaiming someone with a taste for drama, artistic and strongly visual. A claret velvet jacket with enamel buttons flowed down over tight black trousers, partly covering a white muslin shirt of the loose kind worn centuries ago, and an embroidered scarf dangled to his waist. She was reminded immediately of Mozart, Keats, Byron, all the creative romantics Dan and Eimear had ever mentioned, even Bizet whose image she had never seen. But he paid for the woollen quite briskly, and wretchedly she wrapped it: it was obviously a present for his girlfriend.

'That looks lovely. Thank you.'

The dimple reappeared when he smiled, disarming and endearing, but it was his eyes that hypnotised her, pulled her into their velvety warmth. When he turned away, she had to grip the table to steady herself.

Thanh was watching from his stall as she drew a deep breath, and she knew he was laughing at her.

'Smitten? That is the word, I think? Smitten?'

Leaving her post, she went over to him.

'Oh, Thanh – did you ever – have you ever—'

'Seen such a man? Yes, actually. I have seen him before.'

'What? Where? *Where*?'

'At an Indian restaurant I sometimes go to, in the North End Road. He works there.'

'He works – in a restaurant – Thanh, can I take you out to dinner tonight? Is Indian food your favourite?'

She'd never tasted it. It was time she did.

'Yes. I like. But not tonight. I have date.'

'Oh, damn! You haven't really, have you? You're just trying to put me off.'

'No. I do have date. Very nice English girl.'

'Tomorrow, then?'

'Tomorrow Sunday. Restaurant not open.'

'Oh, God!'

She didn't care that he could see her agitation, and was finding it amusing.

'You never look at men before, Aran. You very cool. But no more.'

No. No more. She felt almost feverish, all her rules and plans forgotten, her mind frantically racing through ways to see the man – Ben – again.

She could ask Bronwen to come with her. But suppose Ben took a shine to Bronwen instead? Oh, she'd have to risk it, have to get to that restaurant! But Bronwen shook her head.

'I'm busy tonight too, Aran. Anyway, the guy already had a girl with him, he's probably a real heartbreaker – anyone who looks like that has to be. Forget him.'

'Oh, don't be so sensible!'

Bronwen and Thanh doubled with laughter, intriguingly: was that really her own reputation? Sensible? It appeared that it was.

'Look, I'm going to go to this restaurant, and I'm going to see this man again. Which of you is free, when?'

Finally Thanh volunteered for the following Friday. She had a class that night, but they would go afterwards, eat late and blow a whole week's worth of her mother's money if need be. This was an emergency, and she didn't care what it cost.

All she could think of was that skin like turf dust, those licquorice eyes, that smoky smile.

The week drifted by in an agonisingly long, slow haze, so maddening that she was tempted to pack the children up and take them to lunch at the Indian restaurant. But they might rebel at Indian food, and she wasn't sure how to manage it herself, what would be the right things to order. Besides, Ben might think they were her own children, that she was somebody's wife! Of course Thanh might equally look like her husband, or boyfriend, but she would make it clear that he wasn't.

What if Ben was not on duty on Friday? What if it was his night off? What if he only worked lunchtimes? What if he was a chef shut away in the kitchens, and she never saw him at all?

Oh, Jesus, Jesus Jesus Jesus. She was demented with anxiety, assailed by the new chords jangling in her head and heart as she replayed the scene in the market over and over again. He'd been very pleasant, but he had not really noticed her, she had not made any impact.

How did you make an impact?

By Friday morning, she had worked out exactly how. Taking the children with her she set off for the King's Road, where she went into a trendy swop shop and spent thirty pounds in twenty minutes, resolutely oblivious to the enormity of it. Transfixed, Ollie gazed open-mouthed as she emerged from the changing room in a tight beaded bustier, bright orange mini skirt and black leather jacket.

'Don't cry, Ollie! This is the new me! You'll get used to it.'

Ollie howled as she hauled him all the way back down the King's Road, heading for the bus home until she caught sight of herself in a hairdresser's window.

Demonstrably, Ben was a man who took notice of appearances. His clothes said so. His own appearance was highly dramatic.

'Cut it off, please.'

'*All* of it?'

'All.'

Half an hour later, her corkscrew curls lay at her feet, and she squinted at the shorn waif in the mirror.

'Wonderful.'

Even the nervous hairdresser had to admit that it was wonderful. The cluster of short curls that remained on top of her head thinned her whole face, gave definition to her neck, made her eyes bigger, her chin cheeky. And yet the whole aura was fragile. Fabulous.

'Now, what colours do you have?'

The hairdresser found, dubiously, that he was beginning to enjoy himself. Suggesting something that would wash out – just in case – he showed her a range of shades, and she selected a deep teal.

'Nobody ever asks for that.'

'Good.'

It was a bit unnerving, but when it was finished, it was thrilling. Nobody could ignore her now. The bill was pretty exciting, too, but recklessly she paid it, and left a large tip. Now she was a real London vamp.

Holly nearly fainted.

'Are you running away to join a circus?'

Aran did feel like running away, to anywhere Ben might suggest. But her tone was lofty; she didn't want to arouse Holly's suspicions in case it all went horribly wrong.

'I have a hot date tonight. Thanh is taking me out.'

Holly had met Thanh, and liked him. She knew Aran would come to no harm with him.

'Where are you going?'

'To an Indian restaurant.'

'All right. Just be home by midnight – and try not to let Walter see you, or he won't be able for his dinner.'

What did that mean? That she looked distracting, or dreadful? She decided it must be distracting, especially after she'd applied some of her new make-up. Her hand shook as she put it on; but this was very exciting, and important! Like the market stall, it had to be set up the right way, invested in, made to look enticing. When Thanh arrived to pick her up, she shot down to answer the door, and out of it before the Mitchells could see her.

'Bye!'

Thanh fell around laughing, all the way down the street.

'Stop it! I told you, I want to be noticed.'

'Don't worry, Aran. You will be.'

And she was. Ben appeared the moment they walked into the restaurant, and this time she knew she was making an impact. He didn't recognise her, but he did survey her, inscrutably.

'For two?'

'Yes please.'

Shamelessly she simpered at him, impressed that he seemed to be quite a senior waiter, loving every swish of his long white apron as he led the way to a table. His hair was tied back tonight, exposing his long dark neck, and she thought his walk was the most alluring thing she had ever seen. He held a chair out for her, and with difficulty she restrained herself from touching his hand as he gave her the menu, flicking it open with his unforgettable fingers.

'Now, Thanh, quick – tell me what to order.'

Familiar with Indian food, Thanh picked out something to suit her new style, a very spicy dish, with beer and raita to douse the flames. Aran looked as if she were about to ignite.

'Calm down, little one! Take it easy!'

'I can't! I was afraid he mightn't be here, or something would go wrong – but everything is perfect. Oh, Thanh, it's really sweet of you to do this for me.'

'No trouble. We good friends, yes?'

'Yes. We are. That's exactly what I want him to see, too. Or – well – you might flirt with me, just a little, for appearances' sake.'

'OK. But Aran, he has girlfriend, you know? Is maybe married. Mustn't get excited, hopes too high.'

But Ben was not married. She'd already glanced at his ring finger, but didn't really need to; there was just something about him that told her he was single. Besides, he was very young, not more than twenty. The girlfriend was only a passing fancy, might have been dropped already ... although he *had* looked very taken with her.

'Also, he Indian. Maybe he only like Indian girls.'

Now there was something she hadn't thought of. Well then, she'd get a sari, grow her hair back down to her waist, dye it black and dab a red spot on her forehead. She'd do *anything*.

'Aran, you crazy. Why you not relax, and we have a nice evening?'

Well, she would try. She'd never eaten in a proper restaurant before, unless you counted the ones the Mitchells and Rafters had taken her to, and she didn't count those. Tonight the venue was of her own choosing, and she was paying for it, so she would try to enjoy it. Make it nice for Thanh, too ... and truly memorable, for Ben.

But it was a different waiter who brought an array of little dishes into which she gazed bemused.

'Are these what we ordered? They don't look very filling – or very hot, either.'

Patiently Thanh explained that they were only appetisers, and showed her how to tackle them, with the dips and flat crispy bread. She thought they tasted fabulous, and was entranced by the romantic little candle that was lit for them, the sultry red decor of the place. But it was Ben who held her attention as he darted about, greeting other diners as they came in, showing them to their tables with graceful efficiency. Several seemed to know him, and she was fascinated by the way he talked and laughed with them, showing no sign of servility or reserve. But he did not return to her own table, and by the end of the meal she was starting to panic a little, trying to find ways of lingering.

'More coffee?'

She looked up rather desperately at the waiter who stood over her with a tall silver pot of it, and nodded.

'Please ... we're not in any hurry, are we, Thanh?'

'No ... we stay for the floor show, if you like.'

'Floor show?'

'Yes. That why so many people come here, Fridays and Saturdays. Your boyfriend play piano and sing, later, his girlfriend dance.'

The girl worked here? *With* him? Aran was as horrified by that news as she was elated to hear that she had been right, about those hands; they did play music. She could hardly contain herself until the main lights were finally dimmed, but when the spotlight came up it was on the girl, the one for whom Ben had bought the gift. If anything she looked even more lovely now, in a glittering silver jacket that was

87

open over her flat bare stomach, and very fine, full trousers cuffed at the ankles. Smiling exotically, she raised her hands and began to dance, not to live music but to a tape. Her long nails were painted red, her lips were the same colour, and Aran despaired – no matter how good she looked tonight, this girl looked better, not only because of her natural beauty but because of the sensual way in which she moved, her languid command of her luscious body.

Thanh was having a great time.

'She really lovely, Aran. You got big competition!'

The dance got faster, the girl began to spin and shimmer, and Aran saw Ben smiling from a distance, admiring and applauding as she whirled, finally, to an utterly entrancing end.

'Oh, God. He adores her. Look at him, you'd think he was seeing a vision.'

'Yes. He like her very much. But everyone like her.'

Aran could see that they did, but she couldn't bear much more of it, the girl's proximity and Ben's obvious infatuation with her. If it were not that she so badly wanted to hear him play the piano, she would have called for the bill and left. But then she saw him take off his apron, and go to where it stood.

She had known he was musical. She had known it, the very first moment. But only as he sat down and lifted the lid did she catch her first glimpse of the natural performer, the person who could hush an entire restaurant simply by brushing his fingers over the keys, playing a few notes that were barely audible.

But then they began to build up, into a classical piece unknown to her, filling the room with a foreign note so compelling that she forgot her disappointment, and simply listened. The mood of it was much bigger than the mood of any one person, and she felt swallowed up into it, invisible and insignificant. What matter, that he had not paid any attention to her? If he could play music like this, the only important thing was that she should pay attention to him.

God, what would Bizet's music be, in hands like his? Clearly he had classical training, but he had the other thing too – the passion, that had always eluded her. She had often heard it before, on radio or on records, but this was the first time she had ever heard it live, seen it in the flesh. No wonder the place was so crowded, so many people came here, specifically to hear him. But he should be up on a stage somewhere, out in a concert hall, not here in a little restaurant! His eyes were down on the keys, and she couldn't see what was in them, but she could feel it: the same intensity she felt when she played her oboe, the simultaneous sense of isolation and communication, the creation of something that was wondrous even when there was no audience, no one to listen. But everyone was listening, raptly attentive.

For ten or fifteen minutes he played on, other pieces that were equally new to her, some of them making her wish she had her oboe with her, and could join in them. But at last he looked up, with a slightly expectant, quizzical smile. Immediately, people in the room began to call out requests to him, and he chose a Patsy Kline song from amongst them.

'Crazy . . .'

The moment he opened his mouth Aran gasped, feeling his voice sink into her senses like the warm brandy Thanh was drinking, and had given her to taste. It was very rich and strong, but she wanted more of it, regardless of the effect it might have. Liquid and mellow, Ben's voice flowed on, twisting and turning into the song, drawing itself over her skin like silk. My God, she thought, crazy is the word for it; this guy is driving me crazy. I've never heard a voice like this, never seen anyone just throw back their head and let the sound pour out like that . . . he's a tenor, he's got perfect pitch, and this is the purest, clearest sound I've ever heard.

What on earth is he doing here, singing in this little restaurant almost as an afterthought, as if he were an amateur? But he has to sing somewhere. Look how he's enjoying it, doing what he was born to do! He knows exactly how to interpret these lyrics, how to reduce an audience to tears . . . but everyone is loving it, and he's loving it himself. He's *incredible*.

Slowly the song swirled and dipped to its sorry end, whereupon other people shouted out the names of the next ones they wanted him to play: the restaurant was officially closed now, and everyone who remained in it was obviously an aficionado, tuned into a repertoire of their own making. For a woman in a white dress Ben sang 'Love Me Tender' and Aran thought it was the most moving rendition she had ever heard, better even than the Presley original; if he should ever sing it for her personally, she would die.

But to her chagrin people in the audience wanted to sing themselves, and he encouraged them to come up to the piano and do so. She couldn't see the point of it, because nobody could hold a candle to him – oh, if only she had her oboe, though! But even without it, this was the best night of her life.

'Anybody know this one?'

He tinkled a few notes, and Aran drew in her breath: she did know it, very well. It was 'The First Time Ever I Saw His Face', one of her favourites, usually sung to perfection by Roberta Flack. She would love to get up and sing it with him; but she was rooted to her chair.

'Yes!'

Thanh had read her expression, and was pointing to her.

'Well, bring her up here then.'

Ben looked down, and everyone began to clamour, revealing to her why the restaurant put on this little cabaret; it encouraged people to linger over drinks, put them in a receptive mood, left them wanting more of everything. But she couldn't sing in front of them all, and resisted Thanh as he tried to push her to her feet.

'Go on, Aran! This is your chance! Go up there with him, where you want to be!'

For the first time in her life a spotlight swivelled onto her, and she was petrified as she stood up. She didn't sing as well as she played, and she certainly didn't sing half as well as Ben. But she could sing. And she would get closer to him, as Thanh said, right up there beside him. She had performed at Dan and Eimear's Christmas party – so, she could acquit herself here.

Ben smiled as she reached the piano, and quizzed her as to her preferred key and tempo. It was his way of weeding out people who didn't know what they were doing, she guessed; but she did know.

He played the first notes over again, from scratch, and adjusted the microphone so she could reach it comfortably, leaving a second one fixed lower on the stand to pick up the music. As she opened her mouth she felt so nervous she thought nothing was going to come out – but then, it did.

He listened for quite a while before he joined in himself, turning the song into a duet, knowing instinctively when and how to throw his own voice up against hers, under, over or right around it, bringing out the best in both. His was far stronger, but he allowed the sweetness of hers to shine, not dominating or dictating at all. It was a long song, and they were more than halfway through it before she dared look at him. Their eyes met, and she felt him telling her what she sensed herself: that they complemented each other ideally, were perfect together.

There was such applause when they finished that he didn't need to whisper, was able to ask her in quite normal tones what her name was.

'Aran Campion.'

He frowned. 'I've heard that before somewhere.'

'At the market. You bought a sweater from me last week, for your girlfriend.'

'My girlfriend?'

'Yes – the belly dancer, you bought her a cardigan.'

'Oh, so I did! It was her birthday. But Rani's not my girlfriend. She's my sister.'

His sister. Suddenly Aran wanted to sing the aria from *La Traviata*, hit a high C and smash every glass in the restaurant.

The house was in silent darkness when she got home at four o'clock in the morning, and she was both relieved and undermined. If Holly had waited up for her, she would have been in terrible trouble – but Holly hadn't, and so she had no one to talk to. That, she supposed, was the difference between London and Ireland; in Ireland someone would worry that you were out all night, wonder where you were. They would be angry, but they would care. Eimear would have waited up, and she would have cared.

She wanted to pick up the phone and call Eimear right this minute. There was no point in going to bed, because she had to be up again at six for the market, and anyway she was far too excited to sleep. Would Eimear go nuts if she was woken at this hour? Oh, God, she had to talk to her!

No. It wasn't fair. She would make some coffee, and try to simmer down. But by the time it perked and she had drunk a mug of it, she was wider awake than ever, unable to contain the urge to seize the phone.

It rang several times before a sleepy voice answered, almost comatose by the sound of it.

'Hello?'

Oh, Christ, it was Dan! Despite herself she choked down a giggle; he probably thought she was a farmer somewhere, summoning him out to deliver a parcel of piglets. He was going to kill her, but she was so euphoric she didn't care.

'Dan – it's Aran – I'm so sorry to wake you, but I have to talk to Eimear.'

'My God – Aran – what's wrong?'

'Nothing – oh Dan, just get her for me, please!'

There was a lot of mumbling before she heard Eimear's voice, sounding very alarmed.

'Aran, what's happened, what is it?'

'Oh, Eimear, it's wonderful, you won't believe it, I just had to call you, tell you, I've only just got home—'

'What? But it's nearly half four! Where were you? With whom? What were you doing?'

'I was out – at a restaurant, a cabaret—'

'You were out at a *cabaret*? Until *now*? Jesus Christ, Aran, are you mad? How did you get home? You're in *London*, for God's sake,

91

anything might have happened to you!'

She was right, Aran supposed; this wasn't Dunrathway, where people only ever shot each other by mistake. Anything could have happened. And it had!

'Eimear, I was safe, I was with Thanh, he walked me home, but the thing is, there was this guy, at the restaurant, he was at the market too, last week, he bought a cardigan, I thought it was for his girlfriend only she wasn't, she was his sister, anyway he was singing, and playing the piano—'

'Aran, have you been drinking?'

'No! Well, only one beer, and a tiny sip of brandy. Oh, Eimear, you should see him – and *hear* him, he's got the most amazing voice, I sang with him, five songs, it seemed to go on for ever, and then he and his sister sat down with me and Thanh, talking. I'd be there yet, if Thanh hadn't reminded me we have to get to the market this morning – Eimear, I'm in *love*!'

She was astounded to hear Eimear laugh.

'In love? There's been a change of plan, then?'

'What?'

'The last time we spoke about boys, Aran, I seem to remember you ticking me off severely, telling me you were a very busy young woman who didn't have time for them, and wouldn't have for at least a decade.'

'Oh. Well, yes – but Eimear, that's just the point. I said I wouldn't have time until I got my career sorted out, my life in hand. But now I have. I've found my vocation. I've found my *voice*.'

'What do you mean?'

'I mean – well, I don't know exactly what I mean, but I know that Ben Halley is my future. He's everything I want. I didn't know what I wanted until now, but suddenly I've got it.'

There was a pause.

'Aran, who is he, this person? Is he to be trusted? How do you know you'll even see him again?'

'I will see him, on Sunday, he's asked me out! He's picking me up after work and we're going to his sister's flat, I'm bringing my oboe, he wants to hear me play.'

'His sister? Well, thank God for that, I hope she'll keep an eye on you. How old is she? What does she do?'

'She's eighteen. A belly dancer.'

'*What*?'

'Yes, her name is Rani, she's beautiful – not as beautiful as Ben, though.'

'Oh, God. Look, Aran, I don't want to throw cold water on all this, but I'm going to have to call Holly Mitchell and speak to her about it. She can't let you go gadding about London with – with belly dancers.'

'Well, she doesn't know yet actually. But she can meet Ben and Rani if she likes, I'll give her their address.'

'Right. You do that, and then I'll give her a piece of my mind. I can't believe she's let you loose like this, a young girl, it's criminal negligence.'

'Oh, no, Eimear! It's wonderful! And Ben's got a motorbike, too! I've never been on one before, I can hardly wait.'

'Well, you just wait. Wait till I speak to Holly, and don't budge in the meantime.'

Grimly Eimear replaced the receiver, leaving Aran to wonder if she had done the right thing after all. Eimear was making such a fuss, but it was the kind her mother might make, not the kind she wanted.

And yet, she did want it. Delirious as she had been when Ben had invited her to Rani's flat, she had been slightly nervous too. After all, they could be mass murderers for all she knew. Well, hardly. Nobody who made such beautiful music could possibly be dangerous . . . still. Secretly she had to admit she was glad of Eimear's concern, and the safety precautions that would probably now be put in place. She wasn't a child any more, but she wasn't quite an adult either. Not one who could cope if things did go wrong, at any rate.

She certainly didn't want to end up in the kind of situation she had ended up in with Lorcan Miller. But that wasn't going to happen this time. She knew intuitively she could trust Ben Halley, was right in everything she thought and felt about him . . . and she was going to see him again, in less than forty-eight hours. Thirty-nine hours to be precise, thirty-eight and a half . . .

It dawned on her that it was nearly morning, and time to get her wares ready for market. She had spent an absolute fortune in the past twenty-four hours and, if she was going to continue to live this heady new high life, she had better start earning the means to pay for it.

It was desperately embarrassing, but after Holly and Walter had listened in silence to Eimear's monologue over the telephone they demanded to know the name of the Indian restaurant, and booked a table there for that same night. Aran was asleep by the time they came home, but on Sunday morning she was informed that Walter had met Ben, and had a long conversation with him. She could go to his sister's apartment that night, but he would drive her there, there would be no motorbike, and he would come back to collect her at eleven o'clock sharp.

93

She railed and protested, but was privately relieved, grateful to Eimear for having found a way to protect her, all the way from Dunrathway. Molly would have simply forbidden the excursion, but Eimear had managed it perfectly.

A pity about the motorbike, though . . . but by the time Sunday's market closed she had forgotten about that, and jumped into Walter's car with alacrity. Trembling with excited anticipation, she fluttered and stuttered all the way to Shepherd's Bush, where they located the basement flat with some difficulty. Walter firmly got out of the car with her, and invited himself in for a cup of tea.

Tea! The flat was so wildly bohemian she thought it could hardly contain anything less than opium, that nobody could possibly be harbouring anything so ordinary as a teapot among the clutter of cushions and junk. But Ben ushered them in with a regal flourish, and winked at her as he led Walter to a sag bag on the floor; the sofa was so strewn with books and records there was no room for anyone to sit on it. Tea was made and served by Rani, with such a geisha-girl smile that Walter looked rather unnerved as he accepted it. After one cup he coughed, stood up and left, with a final reminder about the strict curfew that was to be adhered to.

Ben politely saw him out, and it was not until he returned that she dared look at him properly, without fear of Walter seeing what was in her face and concluding that she had become an utter slut. But she had fallen passionately in lust with Ben Halley in that one minute at the market, and wholly in love with him that night at the restaurant. Had Rani not been in the room – well, it was a good thing that Rani was in it.

He was wearing a tie-dyed T-shirt, and jeans that made her want to do something dreadful.

'Thanks for coming, Aran. Your parents made such a song and dance, I was afraid you might not.'

'Oh, they aren't my parents. I work for them.'

'Oh? As what?'

'I look after their children.'

'What a chameleon! One minute you're a stallholder at the market, the next you're a child minder. One day you're a little blonde cherub, the next you're a siren with sky-blue hair.'

'It's not blue. It's teal.'

'Whatever. Anyway, I liked it better the way it was before. Well . . . the new style is very pretty, but the colour is weird.'

Weird? He didn't like it?

'You looked weird, the day you bought the cardigan.'

'Did I? Never mind. I'm glad I met you that day, and I'm glad you

94

came to the restaurant. Was it by chance, or how did you find out I worked there?'

Vanity warned her to say it was chance, but she was going to spend her whole life with this man, and didn't want to start it with a lie.

'Thanh recognised you and told me where he'd seen you.'

'And you came after me?'

'I – I guessed you were a musician, and wanted to find out if I was right.'

'How did you guess?'

'Your hands.'

He looked at her in surprise, and then down at them.

'A dead giveaway, huh?'

'Yes. And now that I've heard the music they make, I think you should insure them.'

He doubled with laughter, great peals of it like a church bell. 'For how much? Five million? Ten?'

She entered into the spirit of it as Rani began to laugh too, but something at the back of her mind was seriously trying to work it out.

'Say ten for the two pairs, yours and mine. Not that anything could compensate me if I weren't able to play the oboe, or you if you couldn't play the piano.'

'You'll play it for me?'

She patted the long box on the floor beside her.

'Yes. Later. I don't know you well enough just yet.'

'Then you must get to know me.'

Rani stood up. 'I'm going to my room to study, Ben. I know your life history, but I'm sure Aran will find it very novel. See you later.'

Aran noticed and liked the little bow with which she left them, the way she steepled her hands and pressed them to her forehead – and how good of her to be diplomatic, leave them to get acquainted. No wonder Ben seemed so fond of her.

He smiled as she left the room.

'Rani is studying medicine, which is what our parents want me to do.'

'But you don't want to?'

Oh, how cadenced his voice was, music to her ears! Expansive when he sang, but contained, almost clipped when he spoke, as if he were auditioning for a part in one of those romantic films about the Raj that Holly liked to watch on television. She wasn't sure what the Raj was, but it sounded fascinating, and so did he. But then, he actually was Indian.

'No. I don't. Our parents are both doctors, however, and had expected to produce a family of doctors. My father, who is British, is

95

a gynaecologist in Surrey, with a Harley Street practice to which he commutes twice a week. My mother, who is Indian, is a consultant at a hospital in Woking, and I have an elder sister who's just qualified as a cardiologist, and is working in Scotland.'

'But you're not interested in medicine?'

'No. Only in music. I had my first piano lesson when I was five, and knew even then, but my parents never believed me. They let me go on with the piano, but when I was fifteen I told them I wanted to be an opera singer, and they got rather impatient at that point.'

'You want to sing opera?'

'Yes. Badly.'

Aran didn't know anything about formal opera training, but she knew what he meant: she'd played the recorder since she was eight, and progressed to the oboe at thirteen. If she'd had formal training then, she might be as good now as she wanted to be – but she hadn't, and she wasn't.

'Why opera, Ben?'

'Because it's big! Big and dramatic! It has so much scope and challenge! It's beautiful, too . . . musically and visually. I don't know how anyone can bear to listen to these ratty little punk rocker songs, when they could be listening to opera.'

'But if you want to sing it, and you can't, you must be going out of your mind.'

'I am going out of it.'

He looked so fiercely angry that she might almost have been frightened, had she not understood.

'I nearly went out of mine, when I heard you sing on Friday night. Your voice is magnificent.'

'Yes, it is. But it isn't trained – and never will be now.'

'Your parents should be shot. If they're both doctors, they must have been able to pay for your training, or subsidise it.'

'Yes. It wasn't that. It was that my father thought opera was for wimps – even though he attends operas, he'd never let me sing in one. My mother thought it far too vulgar and uncertain a career for her only son. They kept trying to push me into medicine, in fact my motorbike was one of many bribes, before I left home and came to London with Rani. They're supporting her, but not me.'

'Do they know you work in the restaurant?'

'They know I do. She only does it for fun and extra pocket money. But I need the job. If I worked lunchtimes as well as nights I'd be able to afford a place of my own, but then I'd have no time to jam with other musicians or to write songs – not that I've written any worthy of a hearing, yet. Anyway, Rani is very young, like you, she wants me

96

to hang out with her this first year, until she makes her own friends and gets on her feet.'

She was touched by his protective tone, but baffled by his indolence.

'So you hang round with her and your musician pals all day? Listen to music, play it, but never write any of your own? Analyse arias?'

He laughed, and she loved the way his whole face changed, the unexpected mischief in it.

'I listen to opera, yes, but I listen to everything, study all kinds of music while I pray for the day when people will stop categorising it. Anything that has memorable melody in it is valid to me, it's just a question of scale. But I happen to prefer things on a grand scale.'

'Then you should pitch for that. But nobody starts off at the top, Ben. You have to be able to play Chopsticks before you can play a concerto, sing in the bath before you sing at La Scala.'

His brown eyes registered outrage.

'Aren't you a bloody sensible little thing. Tell me more about yourself.'

'Well, I'm from Cork, which is a coastal county in southern Ireland. My father is a fisherman, his name is Conor, I have four brothers and sisters, and grew up in a little cottage in our village. It could be quite a nice place if only people didn't – sort of mess it up. My best friends there are the Rafters, Dan is a vet and Eimear used to be my teacher. They're really interesting, know a lot about music, taught me about some of it and about other things, let me read all their books. I'd love to have stayed on at school, but I had to get a job – my family has very little money. That's why I have two jobs, one for me basically and one for them.'

'You must work very hard.'

'Yes, but I enjoy it. And my studies, at night.'

'What kind of studies?'

'Business. Not interesting in itself, but useful, unlike the oboe. I'd much rather have gone on with that, but I couldn't afford the luxury.'

'How can you bear not to go on with it?'

'Oh, I still play as an amateur, practise every day. I'll find some use for it eventually.'

'What's your favourite piece? What do you play best?'

'The fishermen's duet from *The Pearl Fishers*.'

' "*Au Fond du Temple Saint*"?'

'Yes – you pronounce it better than me or Luke Lavery! He was my music teacher, but not very good at French. Do you know what the name means?'

'It means At The End Of The Holy Temple.'

97

She considered that. 'It is a kind of holy temple, Ben. It makes me feel as if I'm in church.'

'That's how I feel when I sing or play the piano. Even at the restaurant among the crowd, I can feel Siva in the air, in me.'

'Siva is an Indian god?'

'Yes. Hindu. Not that we're very strict Hindus at home. I suppose you're Catholic, if you're Irish?'

Was she? Well, she was certainly a conscript, recruited into the Roman army at birth, confirmed eleven years later as a soldier of Christ. But she'd never been taught anything about other religions, had no more idea what was allegedly wrong with them any more than what might be right. Catholics were fighting Protestants in Northern Ireland, but God only knew what exact point of doctrine they disagreed on, what the Arabs and Jews disagreed on, or what they all felt was so exclusive to them. If she'd happened to be born in Saudi Arabia, she supposed she would be a Muslim today, not by conviction but simply by convention.

She thought for a moment.

'I'm a musician. I worship music, and if there's any other god, I think that's what he wants me to be. A musician.'

'Play your oboe for me now.'

He said it so quietly, she wasn't sure if he meant it.

'Will you sing with me?'

'Yes.'

She took the oboe out, and he looked at it, raising his dark eyebrows as he saw its quality.

'Do you know the tenor part?'

'Of the duet? Yes. I know it.'

He did know it. As she began to play and his voice joined with her, she heard just how well he knew it, not just the words but the character of the fishermen, their friendship, their rivalry. And she knew something else. Ben Halley was only nineteen, but ten years from now he was going to be a household name. He was going to be the most acclaimed singer in this country, in many countries, and he was going to be her lover. She had found her voice, and she had found the great love of her life. Greater even than the music, because he was its rhythm, its heartbeat, its soul.

Chapter Five

Aran felt that life with Ben Halley was, henceforth, inevitable. They would get to know each other, they would fall deeply in love and, the moment circumstances permitted, they would move in together. It was a simple matter of ironing out the details.

But it was not.

The details were difficult enough, because her working hours dictated that there were very few times she could be alone with Ben, although it was heartening to find that he did seek her company. But the more often she saw him, the less progress she seemed to make; every time she got to know one facet of him he revealed another, until she came to realise she had befriended an extremely complex person, elusive, contradictory and very wayward.

At his best, he was irresistible: clever, passionate, lavishly generous and wickedly funny. To those people and pursuits with which he was already involved he devoted his all, nailing them down with his loyalty and support, investing his whole heart and soul in them. But Aran saw that they had had to justify themselves first, earn his thought and his trust, because although he gave those things wholly he did not give them lightly. She found that she was being tested, put on some kind of probation she had not expected.

He made no demands on her, seemed to accept that he had to compete with her two jobs and her studies, that the children must be taken everywhere she went during the day, that the stall had to be run and night school attended. But she felt she would not fully capture his imagination until he fully captured hers, and was inexplicably frustrated that he should leave her completely free to choose her priorities.

When they did snatch some brief time together she was unable to anticipate what mood he might be in. His smile of pleasure when he saw her was always radiant, but one chance word could turn it sober;

the mobility of his face was very curious, as if two separate people were dwelling in it. At the restaurant he was extroverted, with his musician friends he could be very loud, both boisterous and bossy. But in her company he had a way of becoming still for brief interludes, so quiet that she could feel his concentration ebbing away from her, drifting somewhere from which she was excluded. He was not aware of doing it, so she could never accuse him of being rude or take issue with him, but she often felt some kind of invisible veil falling between them. Then, just as suddenly, he would ask her what the matter was, as if she were the one being difficult. She never knew what to say without sounding petty, but there were times when she wanted to throw the most childish tantrum, of which she sensed he would not approve.

Yet he could create spectacular scenes himself when he chose, and on the subject of music he often did choose. Aran was astonished one day when he took her to a friend's flat where three or four friends were playing guitars and other instruments, working hard on a piece that demanded greater skill and experience than they could yet bring to it. Violently he berated them all, cursed them for talentless blockheads, snatched one of the guitars and flung it across the room. For a moment she thought he was going to hit someone, or someone was going to hit him; but no, it all ended in laughter and the piece was attempted several times again until, to his equally vociferous satisfaction, it was conquered. Later everyone went to the pub and he bought them drinks; whether he had just been paid or was totally broke, he could spend money like a Rothschild. She began to wonder whether one of his ancestors actually had been a rajah – certainly, his imperious manner and his profligacy were befitting of one.

But his charm was warm and real. He introduced her to his friends and colleagues in a flamboyant way that made her feel very special, and although it meant they were hardly ever alone she found she was enjoying the lively new circle into which she was casually welcomed. None of his friends was quite so fanatical about music as he was, but they were rowdily enthusiastic, committed and dedicated. Nothing else was taken seriously, none of them read newspapers or cared less what was going on in the world, but they did know their stuff. Ben read biographies endlessly, of composers, conductors and singers who fascinated him, and even from the most offhand conversations she learned the most extraordinary things.

But he was not worldly, not remotely interested in her commercial studies, oblivious to daily realities and material pursuits. Given his extravagance she thought that strange, but he simply shrugged. When you had money you spent it, when you didn't there was always

100

some way to earn it. If necessary he would wash dishes or windows he said, but naturally it would not be necessary, because he was going to be a colossal musical success.

That arrogance alienated some people, but he said they were the kind of people whose caution or negativity was boring anyway, would only inhibit anyone who listened to it. But Aran did not find his confidence at all alienating. Even when Ben bragged or was outrageously domineering, his strength was attractive and inspiring to her.

Conversely, he was capable of being very gentle. Sometimes they went walking in the parks and squares with the two children in tow, where he would spend ages kicking a football to Ollie, help the little boy to sail his toy boat on a pond, throw Morag up in the air until she shrieked with delight. He could make both children chuckle and gurgle in seconds, tickling them or bouncing them on his knee, yet he never tried to ingratiate himself with them; sometimes his patience could turn to impatience, and she learned to anticipate his limits. He never got cross with them, but when he had had enough or they misbehaved he simply relegated them to invisibility, leaving her to deal with it.

Such expeditions were a joy to her, but they were also slightly trying, giving her the ridiculous impression of being out on a family jaunt. That was better than nothing, she conceded, but it was not what she wanted. If the infants were not there, would he take her hand, put his arm around her, devote his attention exclusively to her?

No. She thought he would not. She had become a friend, but not a girlfriend. It was going to take a long time to really get to know Ben, slip under his skin, compete with the music for his undivided attention. Sometimes Rani left them alone at her flat, but the only overtures he made were musical; just when she thought he must surely want to kiss her as much as she did him, he would ask her to play her oboe, fly into a rage because he had no piano. He was kind and affectionate, he made her laugh, but every once in a while she wanted to weep. Yet the music was always soothing when she made the effort, and even if she didn't understand him she remained hypnotised by him.

Crisp autumn weeks went by, the first cold snap of winter. Then, on Christmas Eve, he turned to her with his magical smile.

'I have tickets for a performance of Handel's *Messiah*. In a church. Will you come?'

She was thrilled. The invitation was belated and she had no idea what was the proper behaviour for a Protestant church, any more than he did, but none of that mattered once they got there; for the first time they were out on a date, the organ was playing and she was in heaven.

She could feel the reverence in him as he sat quietly beside her, his hand so near she ached to touch it, his face so close her own was almost brushing it. But when the *Hallelujah Chorus* began he did take her hand, his eyes burning like the candles, enquiring whether she was enjoying it as much as he was. Her smile told him she was, and she felt herself gripped in that one golden glance, confirmed in his affections. It was the first romantic thing he had ever done, the first ray of hope, and she thought he must feel the elation welling up in her like the voices of the choir.

Afterwards, they went to a little Italian bistro for a cappuccino, where she noted the delicate way he raised the cup to his lips in his long fingers, and was seized with desire. Intently, he looked at her across the table.

'Did you know Handel went blind, Aran, in his old age?'

Jesus, not another one! Bizet, Mozart, Schubert and George Gershwin all died in their thirties, Janis Joplin, Jimi Hendrix and Jim Morrison wiped themselves out with drugs, Beethoven went deaf and now Handel, he said, had gone blind. The entire orchestra pit seemed to be filled with tragedy, the stage strewn with corpses. Now, Ben Halley was about to meet a dramatically premature end too, because she was going to kill him. If he could hear what was in the damn music, and love it, why could he not hear and love what was in *her*? Would he never pick up the signals, attune to them? Oh, she had loved the *Messiah*, but it was him she worshipped!

Seething with frustration, she whipped her coffee into a whirlpool.

'Well, lots of people are blind to what they don't wish to see, Ben, deaf to what they don't wish to hear.'

'Yes, but Handel had to hire an amanuensis, Beethoven nearly went crazy.'

'Is that a fact?'

His eyes widened and darkened at her tone, strangely tart in this sweet-natured girl with the lovely Irish lilt.

'You seemed to enjoy the concert, Aran. Have I said something to upset you?'

'No. You haven't said anything.'

'You're sure?'

'Absolutely.'

'Well then . . . would you like to come home with me?'

More than anything, she would like to go home with him. But Rani would be there, and in Islington the Mitchells were waiting for her. Did she dare . . . would Rani perhaps . . . ?

'It's Christmas Eve, Aran. We could put on some carols.'

Carols. He only wanted her to listen to carols, help him decide whether every semi-quaver was in exactly the right place?

'No thanks, Ben. Holly won't let me stay out late until I turn eighteen. I'm afraid she's the boss.'

'That's a pity. You know I won't be seeing you again for a while? I'm going to Surrey tomorrow, to stay with my parents for a week.'

She was so disappointed already, it hardly seemed to matter.

'Well, have a nice time. We will – the Mitchells and I, Ollie and Morag are all excited. There's nothing nicer than a family Christmas with children.'

They finished their coffee and went their separate ways.

In desperation, Aran turned to Thanh and Bronwen.

'It's hopeless. It's been three months. We're getting on so well, but not getting anywhere. He must have a girlfriend, someone he sees all the time I'm at work.'

Bronwen conceded that it was more puzzling than promising. But Thanh was sanguine.

'In Asia things move slowly, Aran, and in India. Don't rush it.'

'But Thanh, I so wanted to be with him over Christmas and for New Year. He knows I'm alone except for the Mitchells, that my family is miles away.'

'So is his, and to a Hindu family is more important than this festive Christian season. Why don't you stop worrying for now, and come with us to Trafalgar Square tomorrow night? Big Ben will ring in the New Year, we'll get it off to a happy start.'

Bleakly she went with them, and felt like drowning herself in the fountains. She had worked so hard all this year, yet Molly did not praise her, Conor did not call her, Ben did not love her, nobody ever hugged her except Ollie and Morag, who belonged to somebody else. She was at home in London, yet it was not her home. Her studies were going well but they were no more than the means to an end, an end yet to be identified.

She must identify it, this new year of 1977, decide exactly what it was and how to get it. She was only seventeen, tonight, but unknown to Bizet and Mozart their lives had been half over at that age. Bizet had died from lack of appreciation, Mozart from exhaustion, alone and so impoverished he had been tossed into an unmarked pauper's grave.

It was a chilling thought, this lonely winter's night.

Ben Halley's Surrey home was large and comfortable, and his parents were pleased to see him. For all their differences they loved their only

103

son as he loved them and, at this particular moment, he was glad to sink into the bosom of his family.

God, it was turning into a nightmare, this business of Aran Campion! He had thought he had found his dream girl but, the moment he reached out to touch her, she turned into a virgin warrior from hell. Worse, it was his own fault. Some of it, anyway.

For several days he sat morosely by the fire, watching the rain run down the mullioned windows; when it stopped he mooched about the extensive gardens, glaring balefully at the birds who could sing so cheerfully, kicking at the occasional inoffensive shrub. Never before had he been in low spirits for more than five minutes.

But he had brought it on himself, made a hideous hash of something that had started out so promisingly. The first time he saw Aran Campion she had made only the most fleeting impression on him, the youngest stallholder at Camden Market but the prettiest and quaintest, shy but valiant in a kind of old-fashioned way. He had thought her small timid face very sweet, but forgotten it almost immediately. In a city of bedecked bouquets she was only a posy of daisies, amidst all the wild fauna she was no more than a doe.

Next thing, she had appeared at the restaurant. Or rather her alter ego had, sporting blue hair, black leather and an orange miniskirt. Had she not told him her name, given him reason to ask it, he never would have; visually she had turned into one of the rock 'n roll molls with which every London café was crowded. Only when she came up to sing had he taken an interest, thought that she was taking one in him too. Then, highly charged after that first duet, they had sat down to talk and he had found that there was more to her than met the eye; for some reason he had been reassured by her low-key tone. Even more reassured to discover her genuine interest in music, her amazing silver oboe and pure concentration when she played it. Everything he felt for music he felt for her, that night at Rani's flat as they embarked on their second duet, were absorbed into the experience they knew was uniting and consuming them both.

Then there had been a knock at the door and she had bounded away like a terrified kitten, home to the children she idolised. Since then the children had come between them time and time again, been taken everywhere, included in everything. They were only babies, but they stood in the way like giants, flanking and protecting her until he began to feel like Herod, ready to massacre the innocents.

But they could not be blamed at night, when it was her studies that claimed her, or at weekends when it was the market. In three months not one single day, not one whole night had been hers – his, theirs – without interruption. Invariably she quoted duties to be done, curfews to be watched, exasperating excuses that gave him to understand he was only a friend, a distant one at that.

Perhaps it had been a mistake to introduce her to so many of his own friends, so soon. But she seemed happy in a crowd, blending safely into its numbers, understanding that he had to sing with those people and play at the restaurant. He preferred to see her under such conditions than never see her at all – but why did she continue to see him, and in what light?

If she was afraid of him, or not interested, why had she dyed her hair and dressed up like a space cadet, sought him out that first night? Was it only friendship she wanted, because she was an immigrant, and lonely? But when he'd asked her home on Christmas Eve she had refused point blank, brought the Mitchells to her defence and said something about those perpetual, never-ending children. Handel's *Messiah* had been a stirring experience, but afterwards she had shown no emotion at all – and yet there was such feeling in her own music, a power that spurred him on in his, something that could be tremendously productive if ever she should choose to nurture it in him.

And that was the point at which Ben saw his real difficulties beginning. Aran Campion could be of use to him, and the selfishness of the thought disgusted him. To use a woman as a muse was bad enough, but it was worse than that: he wasn't sure he was worthy of her attention at all, because his own never lasted longer than the project it was invested in. He couldn't help it that his mind moved on so quickly, but it did, on to the next song, the next girl, the next exciting day. In two years he had got through six or seven girlfriends, which hadn't mattered because they were only experimenting too; but Aran was not a dabbler. She took things seriously, stuck to them, followed them through. If ever he did attract her, acquire her attention and affection, she would have him signing contracts before he knew it, signing his name in some register.

Despite her fragile looks and self-effacing manner he thought she had a very strong mind, one that might organise his life, give it the shape and direction he knew it needed. But if he let her do that, she would give even more . . . give all the love he felt in her, and did not want. Not for more than a week or a month, anyway; there were too many girls in the world to settle for only one. Aran was a lovely one, but there was a kind of dedication about her, something that would attach and devote itself to him, cling like a limpet. He was very attracted to her, but her single-mindedness was terrifying. When they broke up, she would be devastated, hurt in a way that hardly bore thinking about.

105

But then he had hurt his parents already, and would hurt them even more if he introduced an Irish immigrant into the family. A nursemaid who played the oboe. Guy would love that, for his opera-loving son. As for Deva . . . Deva had once been an immigrant herself, but that was just the point. Twenty-two years later she was a successful doctor and settled Surrey matron, married into a respected British family and ready to marry her children into others. The daughter of an Irish fisherman simply did not come into the picture; Deva was thoroughly anglicised, accepted and secure in her new culture. She retained her religion but never discussed it in public, never mentioned the long journey she had made home to Lucknow so that her only son could be born in India. This young girl would remind everyone of her origins, proclaim the struggle all over again . . . Deva definitely would not be pleased.

Yet he felt the need to consult his mother, ask her advice even though he wouldn't take it. It was curious, this history of inter-racial marriage in the family: Guy's great-great-grandmother had been Indian too, the sixteen-year-old bride of a soldier posted to Bengal to quell the Sepoy rebellion of 1857. She too had adapted to her new country, refused to hark back or pine for the land she had left. Establishing herself where she had chosen to be, she had declined to return to her homeland even as a widow to live out her long life in its easeful warmth. She was Mrs Halley, and she was British.

Aran, he suspected, wanted to be Mrs Halley too. Wanted to fit into her new country, rise above nostalgia, conquer it all in her quiet way. Unlike many of her compatriots, she didn't hang around Irish haunts, didn't cry into her beer or criticise everything that was not what it was at home. She was bright and brave, and he admired her, wanted her very much. Between them he sensed an affinity that might endure if he let it, a passion that could sing loud and long if it were unleashed. But would passion in his life beget passion in his music, or would it divert it, claim it and use it all up? Did it matter whether relationships endured, so long as music did? People only lived for a century at most, but great classical works lived for many centuries, for ever. He intended to compose some of those, would always choose his work over any woman, never allow himself to be distracted or restricted by domestic trivia. Aran took her work seriously too, managed it much better in fact than he did – but she was one of life's natural mothers, the kind of woman who had 'wife' written all over her.

She would surround herself with babies like Ollie and Morag, cease to give him priority once children came along. And, in turn, he could not give her priority. That was unreasonable and horribly selfish, but it was the case. He would make her very unhappy.

Perhaps she guessed that, and it was why she was holding off; to play second fiddle was not enough for her, would not be enough for her children?

Well, why would it be? It wouldn't be enough for him; in life as in music, he was a lead singer, would always take centre stage. The fact that she had yet to put him there was absolutely maddening. If he wanted her he would have to work harder, perform better.

Did he want her? Yes. He did, physically, emotionally, spiritually. He just wanted other things as well, for longer, and then there were certain things he did not want, things that would interfere as those children were already interfering.

Oh, damn! It was utterly confusing. Perhaps he had better return indoors, find his mother and listen to the speech about how music would never make him happy, an Irish nursemaid would never make him happy either. Listen to reason instead of discord.

He turned for the house, took ten steps and stopped dead. What had come over him? What did reason have to do with instinct, the instinct that told him he must risk Aran Campion? He wanted her and he was going to get her, be honest with her and then do his best to make her happy. If it didn't work, at least he would have tried. Life was short, and nothing was worse than not trying.

It was Twickenham weather, Walter said, dividing the seasons up as was his habit, according to Britain's great sporting events: Aintree weather, Ascot weather, Henley weather and Wimbledon weather. Twickenham weather meant short sharp days with a bite to them, and Aran pulled her collar up with one hand as she gripped her books in the other, making her way out of college into the dark. Tonight's class had been extremely instructive, taking her mind off Ben Halley for almost the entire two hours of its duration. But now she needed some exercise, and decided to walk home; London wasn't nearly as dangerous by night as it was invigorating.

She had gone no more than fifty yards before she changed her mind. The motorbike that came roaring up the quiet street behind her was, she knew instinctively, making straight for her. Stiffening, she gripped her bag and forced herself to turn around.

'Aran! Aran, wait!'

Ben. Relief flooded through her as he drew in beside her, his hair flying behind him, his hands encased in gauntlets, his body made bulky by a shell of black leather. If she didn't know him, she'd have run for her life.

'Get on and hold tight.'

He indicated the back of the bike and revved the engine

impatiently, ready to go the moment she was in place. To where? The speed with which he took off was so sudden it left her breathless, unable to ask.

London flew by so fast it was all she could do to hang on as they shot through it, heading south across the river, her attempts to speak swallowed up by the noise and wind. By the time they reached the open park overlooking Greenwich she felt as if she had been catapulted there out of a cannon, and slid off the bike on shaking legs, incoherent with cold and a kind of wonderful fright.

'Aran, we've got to sort this out.'

He took her books and her hand, his grip tight as he led her to a kind of little gazebo where they sat down on the grass and looked hard at each other. His directness was a massive relief to her, and she met it head on.

'Yes. If you mean us – our relationship – I would like to know where we stand, Ben.'

'Aran, why do you keep avoiding me?'

'Avoiding you? But you're the one who avoids me!'

'All right. Let's say it's mutual. Why are we doing it?'

'I don't avoid you, Ben. The things that get in the way are genuine things. I came to this country with nothing, Ben. I'm an immigrant and I have to work very hard. I have no choice. You're the one who fills up our every moment together with friends, pubs, parties, jam sessions, as if they might – might *save* you from me. Why?'

He looked down, with some shame in his eyes.

'Because I'm afraid of you. Scared stiff, if you want the truth.'

'Afraid of *me*? But you're not afraid of anyone! I've never met anyone with more confidence than you.'

Behind him she could see the city lights, and wondered that he should have taken her to a place he had liked so much on the one occasion she had been there before; by day the view was like a D.L. Lowry painting, filled with little matchstick men. Scurrying figures in the background, in the foreground a great open space, majestic command over the whole perspective.

'I am confident, Aran. Totally confident, in a big crowd. What I can't handle is being alone with just one other person. It scares me and I hate it.'

Suddenly her thoughts became very clear and ordered.

'You mean you need a big audience?'

'Yes. And I need to be in charge of it. You're the first person I've ever wanted to be alone with, and the first who ever looked like taking charge of *me*. That might be a good thing, but it might make me resent you too. Women are like toys to me, only to be played with.'

108

She sensed his distress, yet oddly felt none herself. Something began to relax inside her as she stretched out and took his hand, gently and comfortingly, in his.

'Go on. Tell me the rest of it.'

'I – I'd be afraid of using you, Aran. You have qualities that could . . . be helpful. I could take everything you have to offer, and then—'

'And then?'

'And then get bored.'

It was hurtful to hear. She looked down, trying to appreciate his honesty, disguise her wounded feelings.

'You know, Ben, it's funny . . . you always seemed the kind of person who would rush right into everything. But this sounds like something you've been thinking about.'

He smiled. 'Yes. For the first time and probably the last, I have. You're the one who usually does the thinking. You're grounded in a way I'll never be. You'd expect a commitment, wouldn't you?'

'Yes. Eventually, I would. But not now, I'm too young, there's so much to do first, I don't know myself well enough, never mind knowing you . . . I don't want to marry for a long time yet, and I don't want children for even longer.'

Amazed, he leaned back and looked at her.

'Really? But you seem so keen on the ones you look after.'

'That's different. I'm responsible for them.'

'But when you finish your studies, you'll do something else?'

'Yes. I'm not sure what yet, but my tutors say I'm ambitious.'

In fact she'd been surprised when they said it. She felt more as if she were moving away from something than towards it. She didn't see herself ever becoming wealthy, she just knew she didn't want to be poor. It would be wonderful to travel but it would be nice to fit in somewhere too, to belong to – to what? To whom? She wanted Ben so badly, but he didn't seem to want her. Not really want her, the way she wanted him.

'What will you do?'

She hesitated. Did she dare say it, tell him? He might run a mile. But if she didn't, she might never get the chance again.

She gathered all her courage.

'I'll do everything it takes, to make your voice heard all over the world. My future will be your future, if you'll let it.'

She was overwhelmed by the courage and confidence with which she spoke, and saw that he was too as his eyes slid off her like oil. She was pinning him down. But even if he didn't want to hear it, he needed to. He needed her.

She needed him, too. As he lay silent beside her and she felt his fingers in hers, his warm breath on her cheek, she knew they needed each other for different reasons, but that it was mutual.

It seemed like hours before he spoke.

'What exactly do you mean, Aran?'

'I mean I want to manage you, Ben. Manage you, look after you, make you.'

'Professionally?'

'Yes. And personally. It's all mixed up together . . . your voice moves me to tears, when you sing I feel . . . enthralled. United with you, part of you.'

He looked back at her, his eyes full of thought and concern, his hand massaging hers very gently.

'I think I can honestly say I'm a good risk professionally, Aran. I love to sing, love the way an audience responds, leap to life whenever or wherever there is music. I want to succeed and will work like a slave to do so. I won't be dictated to musically, but in every other respect I know I need someone who can give me direction, discipline, support – someone who understands what I'm trying to do, as I think you do understand.

'But as a man – a boyfriend, lover, whatever – I'm a very bad risk. I have no concentration, staying power . . . I'm drained after I sing, have very little left to give to anyone. I enjoy sex but have never yet been involved with anyone, in love. I'd never deliberately hurt you but I have to warn you, you'd never have an easy life with me.'

'No. I know that, Ben.'

'Do you? Do you really appreciate the demands such a life would make on you – the concerts, the tours, the late nights, separations, hanging round waiting for me? You'd always be in the shadows, never have stability or recognition . . . it would be very hard for you.'

'You're very honest.'

'I want you to know what you'd be getting into. I usually rush in where girls are concerned, but this is something we both need to consider carefully. Can we think about it for a while?'

'Yes. I know I'm a risk too, Ben. I'm only learning management skills and I've never had a boyfriend, I'm not glamorous or sophisticated . . .'

'No. But you are many other things. Wonderful, worthwhile things. You have values, integrity . . . things that are very rare in the music world, in any sphere. You make me feel that I can only succeed by rising to your expectations, your standards.'

'Oh, Ben. You make me sound so – earnest! But I do like to have fun too. Life is so exciting with you.'

He smiled.

'All right! I'll keep it exciting if you'll keep it serene. We'll complement each other.'

'Yes. I'll try if you will.'

His lips were very gentle when they finally touched hers. But only at first.

Nothing. Aran knew less than nothing about the music business. Walking down Kensington High Street with Ben and the children two days later, she told him so.

'Neither do I, Aran. I know lots about music, but nothing about getting started at it, making myself heard.'

'Right. So here's the plan. In five months' time I'll be taking my final exams, and I'm going to work like blazes to get my commercial diploma. During that time you're going to work like blazes too.'

'At what?'

'At writing five songs. One a month. You're going to forget all about opera and write five good, catchy, popular songs.'

'Forget about opera? Aran, I—'

'Five.'

'But you know I—'

'You're nineteen. You're going to start with the basics and learn those before you do anything else. You're going to listen to everything I tell you and not argue with one word of it.'

He stopped and laughed aloud in the street, so loudly that people stared at the strange youth with his bizarre clothes and his hand on a baby's buggy.

'All right. But what are they to be about? I'm hopeless at lyrics.'

She thought of her poetry.

'I'll do the lyrics. You'll sing them, compose the music and play it.'

'Then you'd better give me some idea what our first theme is to be.'

Our theme, she thought, is you and me. But who cares about you and me? These people don't; they care about what matters to them. All these people who don't belong to London at all, who have come here as I have and you have, looking for work and escape and excitement. People who succeed, and people who sleep on the streets.

'It's to be . . . something . . . about not fitting in.'

'Into what?'

'Well, look around you. You're half Indian and I'm Irish. Look at that guy with the Rasta plaits. Look at those Chinese women. How many blue-blooded British citizens do you see? How many languages do you hear?'

111

He caught on.

'Well then, if it's to be about not fitting in, then the song itself can't fit in.'

'What do you mean?'

'I mean . . . think what's in the charts at the moment. Abba, Gary Glitter, the Bay City Rollers. Punk and disco. I couldn't write anything like that. It would have to be something – big.'

'Right. Big, like London.'

'Yes. And different, like these people. Foreign, new to the scene as they are.'

He was on her wavelength. Suddenly she was so excited she could hardly contain herself.

'Exactly! New and different, because that's what immigrants are! Oh, let's get started right away, Ben.'

She could see he was as taken with the idea as she was herself, couldn't understand it when he hesitated.

'Let's? Will we?'

'We – oh, Aran, this is a great idea! I'd love to do it. I can do it. It's just that—'

'That *what*?'

'That my parents might not like it. My mother has been in this country for a long time, doesn't see herself as an immigrant any more. I wouldn't want her to think I was talking about her.'

'But Ben, I'll be writing the words. I'll take responsibility for those. Besides, a really good song makes everyone feel it's about them. Everybody takes it personally.'

'You're right. Let's do it.'

'By February 14? Valentine's day?'

He hugged her to him and kissed her cheek.

'Slavedriver. Yes. If I can find a piano.'

'Use the one at the restaurant. It's free during the day, I'm sure they'd let you.'

'They would. I'll tell them I'm working on a new repertoire.'

In two days, she couldn't believe how different they felt together now; how attuned and how comfortable. Walking on past Hyde Park they discussed the song some more, diverted occasionally by Ollie and Morag, until they reached Harrods and he seized her arm.

'Have you ever seen the food hall?'

She hadn't, but was bemused that he should have any interest in it. Food was simply fuel to him, eaten in haste whenever he thought of it.

'No. Why?'

'A feast for the eyes. Come on.'

They went in, down to the lower floor where the displays were indeed spectacular, everything so perfectly presented it might have been painted into place. Thrilled, the children ogled cakes and chocolate, but it was the cheese counter that suddenly caught Aran's eye. Filled with aromatic produce from all over the world, it had huge wheels of Dutch edam, massive blocks of Swiss emmenthal, slabs of Greek feta and crocks of local produce from individual English towns and villages . . . but nothing at all from Ireland. Aran scoured the labels, but could not see a single Irish item.

'Ben, would you mind the kiddies for a moment?'

'Sure. Are you going to buy something?'

'No. I'm going to sell something.'

Leaving him puzzled she leaned over the counter and asked the assistant to please tell the manager of the food hall that she wished to see him. Fearing she had a complaint in this emporium of high standards and impeccable service, the assistant hastened away to get him. Moments later, a suave man in a striped suit appeared.

'May I be of assistance, madam?'

It was the first time anyone had ever called her madam, and she loved the sound of it.

'Yes. I hope so. I want to buy a particular cheese, but you don't appear to have any in stock.'

'Which one is it?'

'It's an Irish one from Cork, called McGowan's.'

'McGowan's . . . ? Can you describe it to me? Is it hard or soft?'

To her horror Aran realised she didn't know what Annie McGowan might be making these days. But she could still taste that first one Eimear had given her, in a sandwich on Dunrathway beach.

'You mean you don't know it? It's very famous in Ireland.'

'Is it?'

'Yes – and London has a very large Irish population, including myself. We're all looking for it. I'm really surprised you don't have it, because there's considerable demand.'

She sounded most assured, and the man blinked.

'Well, if that's the case, we will certainly investigate. You don't happen to know whether it's distributed to other shops in Britain, through whom we might reach the manufacturers?'

Loftily, she shook her head.

'I'm afraid I would have no idea, because we only ever shop here, in your store.'

She knew she looked a most unlikely customer, but that was the great thing about this classy store; it took all its customers seriously, regarded them all as important.

113

'However, I happen to come from the village where it's made, and could put you in touch with someone there who might be able to help you.'

'That would be excellent, if you would be so good . . .'

Taking a pen and pad from her bag, she wrote down Eimear's number.

'Here you are. My friend Mrs Rafter can direct you to the – the company that makes it. I do hope you'll be able to get it.'

Slipping the piece of paper into his pocket, the manager assured her that he would do his best, thanked her for pointing out the omission and wished her a very good afternoon.

'Now, Ben, quick! Have you any change?'

'Yes – how much? For what?'

'For a call to Eimear, to warn her and Annie ' Gowan! We have to contact them before the manager does, this is such a top-notch shop I'm sure they do everything right away!'

Within minutes the call had been made and facts verified: Annie was indeed supplying her produce to the deli in Cork, and would be over the moon at the prospect of supplying it to London. Aran could not guarantee that an order would be placed, but she had created the potential for it. Ben couldn't believe his eyes or ears.

'Aran, you're amazing. You handled that entire negotiation like a real entrepreneur.'

'It's one of the things they're teaching us at night school, Ben. How to spot opportunities and act on them.'

'But there's nothing in this one for you.'

'Yes there is. Anything that benefits my village is an investment for me and for my family. You never know what might come out of something like this . . . if Annie did get an order, she'd get others, maybe her business would expand and she could take on extra people some day, offer my brothers a job if the fishing doesn't improve. You just never know.'

Ben had no idea who Annie McGowan was, what her cheeses were like or whether they would ever take off in London. But he could see that Aran was going to. This woman could sell ice cubes to Eskimos.

Writing that first song was such heaven and hell, such a powerfully bonding process that Aran thought she understood how parents must feel when they created their first child together, the bliss of conception, the suspense of pregnancy and the blue bloody murder of giving birth.

Somehow they made time for it, and consecrated themselves to it. But for the first week they did not write a note, did not put pen to paper because, she proclaimed, they must do their research first. Ben

114

looked at her as if she were speaking in tongues.

'What research? Is this a song or is it a science thesis?'

'Ben, if we're going to convey how displaced people feel, then first of all we have to ask them. We're only two people, our own opinions aren't enough. We have to go to the places where they live, talk to them and tune into the vibes. Come on. We'll start in Brixton.'

In Brixton they were swiftly invited to fuck off. Nobody saw any reason to tell two total strangers what they thought or how they felt. But then Aran hit on the idea of masquerading as a reporter from a newspaper, and was delighted to find that the charade appealed to Ben. He borrowed a friend's camera and assumed the role of photographer, she got a notebook and brandished it with the bravado she had learned at the market, and once people thought they were getting a public platform for their views they poured them out. Anger, frustration, disenchantment, disillusion, dispossession and disempowerment: the bloody government and the bloody housing, the bloody taxes and the bloody welfare, it all gushed from the mains in floods of rage.

Sobered to find how very lucky she was compared to many immigrants, Aran filled the entire notebook and read back through it several times before going, the second week, to Ben's flat. Even Rani was interested; during her first year of college, she admitted, she too often felt lonely and invisible, intimidated by the crowd into whose lifestyle she had somehow to fit.

Ben had spent the day at the piano in the restaurant, and the result this first night was two sheets of scored paper that Aran could barely read. So many notes were crossed out, changed and rearranged that it took her an hour to make sense of them on her oboe, and when she finally did she was dubious.

'It's very jangly, Ben. Discordant.'

'That's how those people sounded to me.'

'Yes, but—'

'Oh, for chrissake! It's not the Teddy Bears' Shagging Picnic I'm trying to write!'

It wasn't her first glimpse of his temper, but it was the first time he directed it at her, and she found herself thinking of something Eimear had told her. There was no point in arguing with a man unless you were truly angry yourself; you got better results by going at them sideways than head on. If you made them feel they were wonderful then there was some chance that they might be wonderful. This was only Ben's first shot at the music . . . in time it would come together. Besides, he had a point. Those people had not been interested in singing songs of praise.

115

'OK. Let me play it again and then tomorrow I'll start trying to find words that fit.'

'Right. Short sharp words. That's the tone.'

She laughed. 'This is going to be a punk rocker song after all!'

He glared furiously.

'The hell it is. The hell. It's going to be – well, if it were a painting, it would be a Picasso.'

Aran had seen Picassos in Eimear's books and London's galleries and suddenly she saw what Ben meant. To write words to fit, she would have to think more in terms of Emily Dickinson than Keats or Shelley. This was a spiky song, with no room for romance. God, he was right about needing a piano, too! If he had one here he could play these notes himself, if she were free during the day she could go to the restaurant – oh, well. They were just going to have to muddle along.

'Don't worry, Ben. When you've written more and you've got the lyrics to sing, it'll come together.'

'Yes, but the melody must dictate the lyrics, Aran, not the other way round.'

H'mm. That was putting her in her place. But she couldn't argue; people hardly ever remembered the words of a song, but they were always able to hum the tune. If she was going to collaborate on four more songs with Ben, she'd have to accept that his was the dominant role.

Well, she would dominate in other ways. When they got this small repertoire together he would try it out on the restaurant audience and, if it went down well, she'd start thinking how to bring it to somebody's attention, make a demo tape or inveigle someone from a recording studio into coming for an Indian meal . . . it hit her that she had an awful lot to learn. Who were these people and how did you get hold of them?

She listened to Radio Four but now she realised that was a mistake; she should listen to all the stations, because these first songs were going to be more suited to Radio One or the local stations. However, that oversight was easily remedied and, in any case, public performance was a very long way off. All she wanted now was to provide words for Ben to sing.

He was sitting on the edge of the cluttered sofa, leaning on his knees as he scribbled and muttered, sang little snatches and then swore to himself. She smiled at him.

'Will I play it once more for you?'

'Yeah.'

His tone was brusque but he listened attentively, stopping her

116

several times to go back over the previous phrase until, confused, she hit a wrong note.

'Oh, Jesus! A scalded cat would sound better!'

'Sorry.'

She cringed as he flung the sheet music on the floor and took a step towards her, his eyes black with fury. But as he reached her his face changed and he put his arms around her waist.

'No. I'm sorry. I get so angry. I don't know why.'

'Get as angry as you want, if it helps. After all these people the song is about are pretty angry.'

'So they are. Maybe that's why. Anyway, don't take it personally.'

'I won't.'

Drawing her to him, he kissed her, and she could feel his heart pounding in his chest, the physical manifestation of whatever he was feeling. He kissed her often these days, in a way that demanded to be taken further, but thus far it never had been. Maybe she wasn't responding properly, not giving him enough encouragement? Tightening her arms around him, she glued her body to his and felt him respond in turn. But then he let her go.

'Oh, dammit, Ben! What *is* it? What am I doing wrong?'

Pulling her down to the floor, he sat them both on cushions and took her hand.

'You're doing nothing wrong. And I don't want you to.'

'What?'

'You're only seventeen. Too young.'

'I am not too young! I'll be eighteen in April and anyway that's not the point, is it? God, I've heard of singers who sleep with girls as young as fifteen! You're a singer, you're supposed to be a sex maniac!'

He burst out laughing.

'Aran, I assure you I'm as keen on sex as the next guy. But I don't want to have it with you until – until the conditions are right and it can be something special. If it were just a question of sex we could do it here and now, this minute. But I want it to be more than that with you. I want love to come into the picture.'

'But I – don't you—?'

'No. Not yet. Not quite. Not until you – you've got more time for me. When you stop studying, in the summer . . . these songs will be finished by then, and we'll know whether we're going to work together.'

'In the summer? But Ben, I . . . oh, *Ben*! What am I supposed to do until then?'

'Do what I do. Sleep with somebody else.'

She was shattered. As was he: he had had no wish to be brutal, no idea he could say it so casually. Her face looked as if he had slapped it. Immediately he reached for her, but she recoiled.

'Oh, Aran. I'm sorry. I didn't mean it that way. I only meant that . . . that maybe you should get a little experience before you decide I'm the only person you want in the whole world.'

She could barely whisper.

'Who are you sleeping with?'

'Nobody in particular. Just a few of the girls who hang around the jam sessions, the pub . . . never the same one twice.'

She had seen some of those girls, met them: tall loud girls who shrieked with laughter and wore neon clothes, draped themselves over any man who came to hand. Long legs, tight skirts, red mouths. Groupies.

She stood up.

'I'd better go.'

But he pulled her back.

'No. Don't run away, Aran. That's not the answer.'

No. He was right. It was not. She had run away from Ireland, but she was going to face anything London could throw at her.

'Where do you sleep with them?'

'At their flats.'

'When was the last one?'

'About a month ago. Just before Christmas.'

'Well, I hope you enjoyed her, because she was the last one. If you want to see me again, then you're not seeing any other woman. *Is that clear?*'

Her face was like glass, and he took some time before replying.

'Yes. It's clear.'

'Good.'

Grabbing her things she stormed out and slammed the door. It was midnight when she got home, but instead of going to bed she flung herself down at the kitchen table and wrote a full set of lyrics in a hand trembling with anger.

The following night Ben's remorse was intense as he gathered her into his arms and kissed her deeply, contritely, his whole being begging for forgiveness.

'How are you? I've been so worried.'

'I'm fine. I've done the lyrics.'

She handed them to him and he put them down, carefully, without looking.

'I'm really sorry, Aran. I was a rat last night and you were right to get angry. Don't ever let me get away with it. But that episode

118

happened before – before we went to Greenwich. I'll never do it again.'

His tone was so childlike she had to smile.

'That's what Ollie says, every day of the week.'

'I mean it. I'm so fond of you . . . nobody else means anything. And I only meant that you were free to experiment, not that I wanted you to. Anyway, I worked really hard today, didn't see a living soul.'

'Did you get much done?'

'Yes. Quite a bit. I think you'll be pleased with it.'

She was very pleased, when he handed her a sheaf of paper and went away to make a pot of tea. Order had been imposed on yesterday's output and considerably more had been added; she could see the effort he had made at first glance. The music was still chaotic, but it was chaos that seemed to be going somewhere, had some purpose. Suddenly she couldn't wait to play it and hear him sing her pulsating words. When he returned with the tea she was already running through it on her oboe, and ignored his hospitality.

'Let's get started.'

Obediently he picked up her lyrics, read them twice and then fell in with what she was playing, putting his hand to his ear instinctively as if listening to the sound of his own voice.

'Stop – stop – this bar doesn't scan.'

'Yes it does.'

'No, it only has three beats – count them again.'

It took hours. Hours and hours, in which they argued interminably and she realised the extent of his perfectionism; he simply wouldn't compromise on anything. Many changes were made to her words, but very few to his music. And this was only a simple song, for piano! What he would be like if ever it were orchestrated, she hardly dared to think – one if not all of the musicians would surely jump up and beat him senseless. His adrenalin was vibrating, but she was exhausted, as physically drained as if she had run a marathon.

So this was why things were progressing so slowly between them. He would work at getting things right for as long as it took, recognising all his own shortcomings, attacking them from every angle until he mastered them. For the moment, all they had was the raw material of something she could only hope would be worth the wait.

'Are you happy with it, Ben?'

'Yes – in its context. But it's made me realise how inexperienced we are. We have so *much* to learn.'

'Yes. But we'd better try to pace ourselves or we'll kill ourselves.'

'I could go on all night.'

'You don't have to be up for work at seven! And I have a class tomorrow night. We'll get back to it the next night, OK?'

Belatedly he noticed how tired she looked, pale and almost faint with fatigue.

'You've done your bit. The lyrics are great. I can manage the rest by myself . . . thanks for putting up with me. Let me take you home.'

For once she was happy to go, realising as she got onto the motorbike how few people could put up with him. If ever they built a life together, it would require colossal stamina.

The finished song, entitled *Dislocation*, was first performed to an audience of romantic couples on St Valentine's night, and its reception was a shock that taught both Ben and Aran a lesson. Everyone made it quickly and callously clear that they didn't want an abrasive, confrontational song on a night dedicated to love and romance; they wanted something soft and sensual. Aran watched in horror as their attention wandered and they began to murmur amongst themselves: for the first time ever Ben had lost his audience.

It was a terrible blow and she was devastated, unable to look at him as he fought his way through the piece, insulted and ignored. Knowing his temperament, she waited for him to jump up, bang down the lid of the piano, stalk out in contempt – or worse, say something abusive and lose his job.

Abruptly, he did stop playing. The gathering went quiet as he surveyed it, became gradually uneasy. And then, to her vast surprise and relief, he smiled indulgently.

'So. You don't like it, huh?'

Some of the regulars muttered guiltily that they did, but he shook his head and laughed softly, with great good nature.

'Well then, let's go with the flow. How about this one?'

With a suggestive wink he switched to a slow, sexy rendition of *Strangers in the Night*. In moments the mood was rescued, romance was restored and everyone was back on his side, holding hands happily across their tables. Only Aran sat alone at hers, waiting for over an hour until he could join her.

'Oh, Ben. What a disaster.'

'Are you upset?'

'Of course! Aren't you?'

'Wait a minute.'

He got up, went to the bar and returned with a bottle of wine in one hand, a red rose in the other.

'Now. Give me a smile.'

She forced one.

120

'And a kiss.'

That wasn't so difficult. Despite herself she began to feel better.

'But I wanted to die! Didn't you?'

'At first. Until I realised what was wrong. It wasn't the song, Aran. It was just the timing. I'll play it again tomorrow . . . actually, it was a very interesting moment. It taught me something about judgement, how to manage these situations.'

'You did manage it very well, Ben.' Suddenly she laughed, and raised the glass he had poured for her. 'Well done!'

But she saw the release of tension as he raised his own glass and emptied it rapidly.

'Phew. Close call. Thought I was a goner.'

Only then did she realise that he was shaken, unnerved for the first time by the stress of a live performance.

'When everyone has left, will you play it again? Just for me?'

'Oh, you don't want to hear it.'

'Yes. I want to hear it and I want to hear you.'

When the room and the bottle were empty, he returned to the piano and played it with such force she was stunned. Rani and all the guests had long departed, but the staff who were clearing up stopped what they were doing, stood stock still and, when he finished, applauded so enthusiastically she knew he was right: the only thing wrong with *Dislocation*'s debut was its timing. It would be heard again, and attention paid to it.

For Aran's eighteenth birthday in April Ben made a wonderful fuss, arranging for a friend to run her stall so he could take her out to a village in the Cotswolds. Never having seen the English countryside before, she asked him to drive slowly so she could enjoy it, noting how different it was from Ireland, the immaculate way in which houses were maintained, roads signposted and buildings preserved. Several times they stopped to admire Tudor cottages, resplendent gardens and the small square churches she found oddly appealing, their interiors so burnished she could see her reflection in the brass memorial plaques, sense the long tradition of tended, tranquil dignity.

However, there was nothing dignified about her squeals as they drew up outside the inn where Ben was treating her to lunch: their table on a terrace overlooking the river was festooned in dozens of yellow balloons. So this was why he had been enquring about her favourite colour! Even the tulips on it were yellow, a lovely surprise that had been secretly arranged and put her in the sunniest of moods.

'Oh, Ben!'

'Happy birthday, my love.'

Love? Could he mean it, at last? She thought that perhaps he did as they sat there for hours, eating slowly as they discussed the two more songs they had written and the summer that would bring change.

'I can't keep on two jobs once I start trying to get your career under way, Ben, and you can't work as a waiter any more. We're going to have to go at it headlong. I want to tape these songs and get the tape into circulation, send it to radio stations and recording studios . . . you need to concentrate exclusively on writing and rehearsing. And we both need more equipment. Mikes, amps, proper acoustics . . .'

'Well, my friends have a lot of gear I can borrow. I could look for another job too, in a better venue – one of the supper clubs in the swish restaurants or hotels, maybe?'

'Good idea. You never know who might drop in there. But I can't decide what to do . . .'

'Why not give up the day job? If I got a better one I could support us both. You'd still make a bit of extra money at the market, but have lots more time. You'll have your diploma by then, too.'

'Yes . . . it's just that . . .'

'What?'

'I don't want to leave Holly in the lurch. And I'd really miss the children.'

He frowned. 'Would you?'

'I really would, you know. I've got so attached to them, to the whole family.'

'But you'd have me. We'd be living together.'

Living together! He was ready for it, wanted to make a home with her?

'You're sure, Ben? It's what you want?'

'Yes. I'm not talking about marriage or mortgages, Aran, children, security, any of that stuff. But I am talking about renting a place of our own, becoming a couple, giving it a shot. I've lost all desire for other women, in case you hadn't noticed.'

She had noticed, even if they hadn't lost theirs for him. Whenever he came to help her at the market, business boomed, his mere presence was enough to attract hordes of gorgeous girls all suddenly desperate to buy sweaters. He joked and flirted with them, as he did with every pretty girl who crossed his path, but she knew he had kept his promise, had been celibate since January. Been testing himself, she thought.

'I'd be enough for you?'

'Aran, I'm falling in love with you. We've been friends for months and now we're going to be lovers. I can sing anywhere in the world,

122

we'll travel, go to India, have a fantastic time. Let's stop talking about it and just do it!'

Love, travel, fun and romance. She was eighteen, and she was swept off her feet.

'Let's!'

He vaulted clear across the table, seized her and kissed her.

'Get your exams, quit your job and find us somewhere to live. Somewhere big enough to take a piano. I'll be twenty on July 15 and we'll move in together on that date, make love on our piano.'

She giggled.

'It had better be a grand piano, so!'

'Yes. As you Irish say, everything will be grand. We'll have a grand time, on a grand scale.'

She thought of Philip Miller's little office in Ferleague, and was dizzy with excitement. How life could change, from minor to major!

'I love you, Ben.'

'I love you too, Aran. I'm a bad person and I don't deserve you, but I will try to deserve you.'

On a glorious day in June Aran sat on a bench in Regent's Park, gazing enthralled at the diploma that was finally hers. The logo of the small college from which she had just collected it was not at all impressive, nobody would ever mistake her for an Oxbridge graduate, but it clearly proclaimed that she had learned enough about business to be taken seriously. She might not look as if she knew anything about venture capital, marketing strategy, resource deployment or commercial law, but this document proved that she did.

Ollie pulled at it, seeing great potential for one of the paper planes he loved her to make, but it was whisked from his grasp and rolled tantalisingly away into a little cardboard tube. He opened his mouth and made his protest loud and clear.

'Sorry, Ollie! I'll make you a plane when we get home.'

But Morag began to bawl as well, and she gathered both children up onto her lap, jigging them on her knee until their tears turned to smiles, their pink faces rounding out into small sunny orbs that she kissed and consoled as she brushed the tiny tears away.

'There now . . . who's got a big hug for Aran, h'mm?'

They cuddled into her as she rocked them back and forth, enraptured as always by the scent of their soft skin, the feel of their fat sturdy bodies, the trusting innocence of their big welkin eyes.

Tonight, she would have to tell Holly she was leaving, and try to explain it to Ollie who, at nearly four, was old enough to be distressed. They were great pals, and his baby sister was a delight, a happy placid little thing whose face always creased with pleasure when Aran touched or spoke to her. Leaving them, she thought, was going to be a terrible wrench – a prospect so awful that something contracted in her, shrank from it.

Well, she would have children of her own some day. Now that she had experienced the joy of them, she was sure of that. If she admitted the truth, she would have them sooner than she had thought. But she was barely more than a child herself, whereas Ben – Ben needed a lot of looking after, if his life were not to collapse into chaos. For the moment he was her child, her protégé, the one who needed nurturing. Thinking of the dimple that appeared whenever he smiled, she felt him tugging at her just as Ollie tugged at her, pulling her away with him.

Ben was good with children, but his life was not suited to them and would not be for a long time yet. Music was a nocturnal career and she could think of very few singers who fitted wives or children into it; even the ones who tried usually ended up on the front pages of the tabloid newspapers, waging horrible wars in the divorce courts, wrangling over custody and alimony as their shattered families were strewn around the world. Better to have no child at all than to do that to it.

When she had children, ten or fifteen years from now, it would be in the context of marriage, a solid home with a garden and a big kitchen, a life that would not be uprooted by the demands of work or the whims of those people who surrounded singers . . . Lord, what a lot of them there were! When Neil Diamond had visited London recently he had come with a whole entourage, dozens of minders, managers, producers, technicians; and then there were the fans, screaming, jostling, plucking and pushing their way to him in a frenzy of adulation that must have actually been very frightening.

Was that going to happen to Ben? In one way she hoped that it was, in another she did not want it to. Such hysteria was the mark of public success, but must be the way to private failure, because no one person could cope with it all, ever get any time or space with a wife or child. Eimear saw that already, had warned her in a long letter that she would have to fight to keep her own place at Ben's side, be prepared for constant onslaughts on his attention, many intrusions into their domestic affairs. Only if he succeeded, of course, became really well known – yet it was her role, and her intention, to see that he did.

With mixed emotions she smiled at Ollie and Morag.

'Isn't life a big risk, my little cherubs! But do you know that my dad risks his every day, every time he goes fishing? He goes out in his boat and does what he has to do, and that's what I'm going to do too.'

As always Ollie latched onto the word 'fishing', wanting to hear for the thousandth time about the boat, the nets and the mackerel that he could hardly pronounce. It all sounded very heroic and exciting to him. Getting up, Aran strapped Morag into her buggy and took him by the hand.

'Did I ever tell you about the day he got blown overboard in a big storm?'

'No,' said Ollie, his eyes rounding. 'Did he drown? Did he, Aran?'

'No! But the boat had to turn round and the other men had to throw a rope to him, haul him up over the side, he was so cold and wet you can't imagine . . .'

Fascinated, Ollie nodded at intervals as she recounted the story, heading for the bus which would take them into the city centre where, at this moment, Ben was auditioning for a new job. She had wanted to go with him, but knew that a girl with two children in tow would not enhance his chances.

It was in a very large, trendy restaurant, one that rather intimidated her when she reached it. As arranged, she did not go in, but waited for him on the street outside. As soon as he emerged, she saw that he had got the job. Wearing a black polo neck tucked into belted black trousers, his hair recently trimmed into a very attractive style, his new look was that of a French actor. Visually he was very versatile, conscious of meeting people's expectations.

'Fifty pounds a week, Aran, for four nights! We can get a flat, and our piano!'

We can get *our* piano. She loved the way he said it, the way he swept her into his arms and looked into her eyes, searching for approval, puckering his lips in the most comical way.

'Give us a kiss!'

She gave him a huge one.

'I'm so proud of you – what did you play – are the acoustics good?'

'I played one or two of the things we decided on, but not all. They said they wanted new stuff, so I gave them *Odyssey* and *Flight Paths* . . . they were really keen when they heard I'd composed them myself, want me to do more, said I had *class*! I couldn't really judge the acoustics because the place was empty – obviously, it'll sound different with a hundred and fifty people in it. But the sound system is excellent and I can come in during the day, use any of the equipment any time I want. Hey – did you collect your diploma?'

'Oh, yes. I wasn't trusting that to the post! Look.'

She showed it to him and he paused after he inspected it, fishing in his pocket for a minuscule package wrapped in tissue paper.

'I found you this, on the way to the audition.'

She opened it, and a fine silver chain unrolled into her palm, with a pendant in the shape of a clef.

'Oh . . . a clef, a necklet, my first piece of jewellery! I'll wear it for ever!'

With a smile he fastened it around her neck and touched his lips to the nape, brushing his hand through the hair that was still short, but back to its original colour.

'You'll wear it for a week and then tire of it, or lose it.'

She looked at him.

'Oh, no, Ben. Today is the first day of our future. I will wear it every day, to remind me how we began, how kind you are and how happy you make me.'

'I hope I always will, Aran. But let's not look too far into the future. Let's just play it by ear.'

Fingering the necklet, she nodded as she slipped her arm around his waist and fell into step with him.

'Aran! Your mother is on the phone!'

Holly called up the stairs rather impatiently and Aran came down rather guiltily; the news that she was leaving after only eighteen months had not been received with any great pleasure by the Mitchells.

'Hello, Mother. How are you?' From the clunking noises she could tell that Molly was calling not from Eimear's house but from the coinbox in the village.

'I'm disgusted, is how I am.'

'What's the matter?'

'What do you think? Your letter is the matter. Your behaviour, your – your Indian *singer*, that you're going to live with in a state of *sin*! The whole village will be talking! You can't do it on me, Aran! I forbid it!'

'But, Mother—'

'A wog, a coon, not even Catholic! He drinks, I suppose, and takes drugs? Lives on the welfare like the rest of them?'

'No, as a matter of fact—'

'Drugs, and discotheques! It's disgusting! He'll never marry you, you'll see, he'll leave you for the next little idiot who happens along, you'll come home here with a clutch of black babies and not a penny to your name. Well you needn't expect *me*—'

There was more bleeping and clunking as Molly inserted more coins into the phone, her fury flying down the line like a guided missile.

'Mother, he has a steady job, he doesn't do drugs, he isn't black, but anyway, if he were, then you should be pleased to think he won't marry me, since being black is such a crime. But I don't care what colour he is, I love him and I'm going to live with him.'

'You little fool.'

Fool? She thought how hard she had worked for Molly, and that maybe she was a fool.

'Mother, I'm sorry you feel this way. I hoped you might be phoning to ask if he was good to me, if we were happy, tell me you might like to meet him. We could come over for a day or two, you know, when we get settled. He earns fifty pounds a week.'

There was a strangled silence.

'Fifty?'

'Yes. He's a very good singer. This time next year, you might hear him on the radio.'

A longer silence, and then a scornful laugh.

'I'll not hear him on any radio, nor meet him either, because you'll not bring him next or near Dunrathway. No darkie is ever going to stay under my roof.'

Unexpectedly Aran felt hot pain at the back of her throat, tears trembling inside her.

'You're ashamed of him? Of me?'

'Isn't that what I said? Ashamed and disgusted. Now you just get rid of him, and let me know when you have. Then we'll see about you coming home for a visit.'

'I'm sorry, Mother. But if I can't bring Ben then I—'

'No. You can't bring him. Don't you ever do that on me. *Ever.*'

The line went dead.

The ground floor flat in Holland Park was bright, spacious and totally bare. It had a bedroom, bathroom, kitchen and sitting room, high corniced ceilings and a large black cat, complacently sitting on the back garden steps. Nobody knew who owned it.

They gazed at the bay window in front, and whooped with one voice.

'The piano! The piano goes there!'

Once that was settled, Ben didn't care about the rest of it. Aran could decorate any way she liked. Shyly she looked at the spot in the back room where the bed was clearly destined to go, and colour flew to her face. Life as a scarlet woman was going to be extremely exciting.

Mystified, Ben riffled through the paperwork the estate agent had given them.

127

'Can you make sense of all this?'

With some deliberation she took it and read every word, taking note of all the clauses, sub-sections, language designed to defeat.

'We've to put down a deposit, pay on the last Friday of every month, put all bills into our own names, repair any damages, refrain from sub-letting, commercial trading . . . the lease is for two years.'

Two years. She held her breath. But he didn't flinch.

'OK. Let's sign the damn thing and go look at some pianos.'

They signed, went and looked. Overnight London seemed loaded with pianos, big black glossy ones with spectacular price tags. They tried every single one they saw.

Finally he found a Steinway that spoke to him, sang his name aloud.

'This one.'

'Yes. But we can't afford it yet.'

'What? But Aran, we must! They have an instalment thing, we can pay for it a month at a time the guy says . . .'

'That's the wrong way to buy something, Ben. It costs much more in the long run.'

'Who cares? Aran, I've got to have this piano!'

She thought.

'All right. But we'll pay for it outright.'

'How?'

'Just give me a week, OK?'

'Well, I suppose, we can't move in until July anyway. But where are we going to get six hundred pounds in one go?'

'Trust me.'

Back in Islington she sat down and wrote to Dan and Eimear. It was an awful lot of money, she would understand if they felt it was too much, but she had paid back every penny of the funds they had given her to study and oh! They should see this piano, Ben's eyes when he played it! If they would do it, she would give them the very first copy of his very first record, prize seats at his every performance. Would they? Oh, please, would they?

Back came a cheque for eight hundred pounds, with a letter from Eimear.

'Dearest Aran,

Thank you for giving us this chance to start Ben off on what we're sure will be a wonderful career. When you get the piano and set up home together, we look forward very much to coming to London and hearing him play. You've told us so much about him we feel as if we know him already, and are delighted you have found someone in

128

whom you can put so much trust and confidence. Will you send us a tape, so we can hear his voice?

You must be so happy and apprehensive, all at once, starting out together! We wish you lots and lots of luck, everything that will make your lives fruitful and fulfilled. As I've said before yours will be a demanding part in the relationship, but I know you'll be able for it, and can't wait to see you, hear every little detail. It's such a shame you have to leave Morag and Ollie, but of course you must put everything into Ben for these next few years. If there's any other way in which we can help, you have only to let us know. Take good care of each other – and use the extra money for pots and pans! We're sure there are lots of things you need and hope it will be enough.

Much love,

Eimear and Dan.'

Aran clutched the letter, thought of her mother and wept.

Chapter Six

Oliver Mitchell lay face down on the floor, drumming his feet and screaming hysterically, his arms locked around Aran's ankles like manacles.

'No! Don't go! D-d-don't go!'

It was an appalling scene, and Aran's heart pounded as she struggled to disengage Morag from her shoulder, where the baby had battened on with the strength of a small gorilla, her hot tears pouring down the back of Aran's neck.

'Oh, please don't cry, I'll come and see you, I promise . . . please . . .'

Firmly, Holly removed both children, carried them away to the lounge and locked the door on their heartbroken howls. It was the only way.

'You'd better go quickly, Aran, before they break down the door.'

Wiping her eyes Aran hugged her speechlessly, picked up the last of her luggage and ran out to the car in which Walter sat with the engine running. As she got in she saw two stricken faces squeezed up against the window, clenched fists beating on it in paroxysms of bewilderment, and felt all the anguish of a convicted child abuser. Leaving these children was much worse than leaving her parents, the most painful thing she had ever done. How *had* she done it?

Stoically Walter reversed the car, turned and drove away.

'They'll get over it, Aran. Kiddies forget in no time.'

She knew they did, which made it even worse. As did the final kindness of the Mitchells, the supply of linen and household goods they had insisted she take, the box of groceries to start her off, the name of the doctor who had put her on the pill.

'You will be needing contraception I presume, at eighteen years of age?'

'Yes, Holly. Oh yes.'

She didn't need persuading. No way was she going to end up like Deirdre Devlin, whose second pregnancy was the talk of Dunrathway. But then contraception was a straightforward business in London, where you simply went to an anonymous doctor and then to a big anonymous pharmacy. In Dunrathway, Deirdre would have had to justify herself to Dr Conway, endure a long lecture and then – if he gave her a prescription – slink into the pharmacy to mumble at Mr Bennis as if she were trafficking in cocaine. In a neighbouring village, a pharmacist who stocked condoms openly on the counter had been visited by two women from a right-to-life group; while one of them distracted him, the other had used a hatpin to pierce every packet. Everyone found the tale hilarious except, presumably, the people who might have become pregnant had the deed not been discovered. Aran wondered whether the right-to-lifers would then have taken responsibility for the children, adopted them and coughed up the cash to send them to college.

In due course Walter turned the car into Holland Park, where he helped her carry in her things, pecked her on the cheek and left her. Ben's things were already there, but Ben was working with his friend Clem on the last of his five songs. Clem played a guitar, but his free time was limited, so it had to be today.

She smiled to herself. When she first met Clem, she thought from his effete manner and evident dislike of women that he might be gay. Ben mulled over this theory for a moment before grinning at her.

'No. Not really. I think he only helps out when things get busy.'

It was remarks like that that were going to make him such fun to live with. His irreverent attitude was so different to Molly's prim literal-mindedness, to Val's provincial snobbery, Achill's macho posturings. When Molly wrote one of her mournful letters, he would take it from her hand and make a paper dart of it.

'Dotty old crone. Mothers like her are the reason why man invented the aeroplane.'

Another day, when they were discussing contraception, Aran idly wondered how Molly had managed to limit her family. Again Ben grinned.

'God knows. But if I were her husband, I wouldn't be shooting blanks.'

He always made her laugh, and she wished he was here. Moving into this flat was no big deal to him, but it was to her. Sitting down on the crates in the middle of the sanded floor, she contemplated the black cat curled on the windowsill and waved rather forlornly at it, feeling suddenly and distinctly alone. But that was something she would experience often in the course of life with Ben – and meanwhile, here she was in her very first home of her own, the boss, accountable to nobody! Shaking herself, she stood up, did a tour of the flat and then unpacked everything, experiencing little tingles of pleasure as she eyed Ben's possessions, so intimate alongside her own. But there was nowhere to put anything, and impatiently she waited for the delivery men who were due with the piano, the bed and the wardrobe that had been purchased with Dan and Eimear's money. Ben had insisted on knowing where it had come from, and laughed when he heard.

'God, they must be as mad about you as I am!' And then he had written to the Rafters, thanking them and assuring them that they would be reimbursed. Aran was struck by his good manners and consideration; she had yet to meet his parents, but clearly they had raised him for some gracious role in society. Well, if they thought they had wasted their time, they were wrong.

The men arrived, first one set with the furniture and then the other with the piano. There were all kinds of shunting and grunting as it was manoeuvred in, whereupon a fussy little chap in a waistcoat set about tuning it; he had taken no part in the haulage but was always sent, he said, to tune instruments exposed to the rigours of transport and installation. While he worked, his panting colleagues suggested a cup of tea would be welcome.

She made some and handed it to them, wondering why they were looking around with such a curious air.

'Would there be anywhere we can sit down, love?'

As puzzled as they, she glanced about her. No table, no chairs! Her apologies were very giggly.

'Oh, well, that's nice, isn't it. A grand piano but no kitchen table. You'll make a great housewife, love.'

She laughed with them, realising they thought her one of the many Londoners who were just slightly off their rockers. But she tipped them as Holly always tipped people who delivered things, and beamed when they departed. Oh, how splendid that piano looked! Ben would be ecstatic when he came home. Home!

Strung up with anticipation, she waited until there was the sound of his key in the door – and then, voices. Dear God, on their very first day, he had brought friends with him? But she had to smile as he came in with Rani and Clem; really it was like Custer's last stand. Rani and Clem were not going to defend him permanently from being alone with her. Besides, he had brought freesias, and was hugging her enthusiastically.

'It came! Oh, look at it!'

Oblivious of the other things that had also arrived, he went straight to the piano and fingered its surface, its shape, its contours. It was only a baby grand, but his smile was enormous.

'What shall I play?'

Rani and Clem replied that he would play nothing until they got something to eat; they were starving and he had promised that Aran would feed them. He smiled winningly at her.

'Would there be any chance of a few sandwiches, sweetie?'

She had seen him do it before, knew his knack of persuading people to do things he was perfectly well able to do himself. But agreeably she made ham sandwiches and heated up two cans of soup. Sitting down on the floor in a circle, they ploughed into their impromptu lunch, rough and ready as it was.

'We're going to have to get a table and some chairs, Ben, a chest of drawers . . .'

'Yeah – Chopin, I think. The piano should be christened with Chopin.'

Clem thought it should be christened with one of Ben's own compositions, but no, he wouldn't dream of such cheek, Chopin would be inspirational, establish a level to be lived up to. Swallowing the last of his sandwich he returned to the bay window and sat down on the stool the shop had thrown in for free.

Aran drew in her breath as she always did when he began to play, with combined anticipation and apprehension even today, at home among friends. Whether he played alone or in public Ben had a way of bracing himself, closing his eyes as he tensed in readiness like an athlete on the starting blocks, drawing people into the sound as the athlete drew them into the spectacle.

Aran had never heard him play Chopin, but she had heard him say that the Polish composer was much more than the romantic virtuoso people thought; his chromatic melodies for the right hand were very taxing, making the left work equally hard to provide the harmony. Softly he played a few experimental notes and then set off into a nocturne, yielding his whole body to its gentle flow, flexing and bending over the keys without looking up, bringing to it, Aran thought, every single attribute the composer could have wished. Looking at Clem and Rani's faces she saw confirmation of what she had known from the first: Ben was really a classicist and would, in time, be recognised as such. It was a terrible pity to have to draw attention to himself with small, catchy songs designed for popular appeal – but it was an exercise in patience and humility too, one that would do him no harm. By the time he got to write musicals, film themes or even an opera, he would have a very thorough grounding, understand the basics to which people responded no matter what the

133

genre. In public, she did not want him to over-reach himself, but here in private she was amazed by the ease with which he did reach for, and attain, a much more complex standard. But then playing Chopin's music was one thing, writing its equal was quite another.

The nocturne fluttered to its conclusion and their applause was rapturous. As he lifted his eyes to them she saw how much he needed it, how important it was for him to engage every audience, even this teenaged group of three.

Clem was open-mouthed. An hour ago he'd been working with Ben on a pop song, thinking it the height of achievement; but he had been deceived. Ben was merely using pop as a platform.

'Halley, you've been taking the mickey.'

'Not at all, Clem. Didn't you hear the little blast of Rachmaninov in *Flight Paths*? Well, not Rachmaninov as he is known and loved, but the little twirl based on the Paganini Rhapsody? I can't see why the old shouldn't inspire the new – especially when I'm only nineteen, still learning from the greats.'

'Hendrix is my idea of great.'

'Hendrix, Chopin, Rachmaninov – what's the difference? Either your music endures or it doesn't.'

Clem, whose idols went back no further than one decade, found himself unequipped to argue. Seeing his resentful look, Aran chimed in.

'Ben only wants to mix it, Clem. Open up the straitjackets a bit. Why not? Maybe a time will come when everyone will be open to everything. You could have people going to a rock concert one night and an opera the next . . . why put lids and limits on things? Looking to the past is one way of looking to the future.'

He peered at her.

'What are you, some kind of Irish soothsayer?'

'Oh, Clem! Look, you see people wearing Levis one day and evening gowns the next, don't you?'

'What's that got to do with it?'

'Well, if people can wear what they like, why can't they listen to what they like? I mean, you'd be bored if you had to wear the same colour every day or eat nothing but hamburgers, wouldn't you? Who's to say that chips and champagne don't go well together, huh?'

'You're odd, Aran.'

'D'you think? Didn't you like the Chopin?'

'Well – yeah, I did. But I like *Dislocation* a lot more. And the other new stuff Ben's done.'

Had Ben told him that she'd written the lyrics? Just in case he hadn't she decided to say nothing. But wouldn't he be surprised if he knew that one set was based on Coleridge's poem 'The Legend Of Xanadu'! 'In Xanadu did Kubla Khan a stately pleasure dome decree – da da – down to a sunless sea – da *dah*!' She and Ben had had a brilliant time putting it together, mucking it shamelessly about and laughing their heads off. She was going to take liberties with Yeats, too, drag the whole lot of them out of their dusty graves until, like Ben, she found her own rhythm. For now they were only kids, having fun; they could do what they liked until commercial realities started calling the tune. But even then Ben wouldn't listen, and she would only pay lip service.

Rani wanted to know about Chopin.

'Is he another of your tragic geniuses, Ben?'

'Naturally. Stone dead at thirty-nine, Rani.'

Everyone grinned except Aran, who was beginning to be haunted by this litany of catastrophe. Looking up Coleridge in her old school poetry book, she'd found him extinguished at thirty-seven. It couldn't be constant coincidence.

'What happened to Chopin, Ben?'

'Consumption.'

Well, nobody died of that any more. Still, she must see about the heating, make sure this flat was kept warm . . . as yet, it didn't even have curtains. But it was summer, a hot bright day. Suddenly she wanted Clem and Rani to go away, leave her alone with Ben.

He played for another hour before they did, everything from Liszt to Leonard Cohen, but finally the pair stood up to leave and Rani kissed her brother affectionately.

'Happy birthday, tomorrow.'

Tomorrow, he would be twenty. And today, tonight . . . they would be lovers. Her stomach clenched at the imminence of actually getting what she wanted, her gestures were jerky as she closed the door on his friend and sister. When they had gone she looked at him, and rather desperately round the flat.

'So here we are – all on our own at last.'

He looked slightly desperate in turn. But then his face softened, his eyes grew thoughtful.

'Yes. At last.'

He drew her to him and she relaxed as she felt the warmth in him, the body language that told her he really did want to be here, was not going to bolt. His kiss was long and deep, and she looked into his eyes with sudden shyness.

'Nervous?'

'Terrified. But you mustn't be, Aran. I love you and I'm going to stay with you, do everything I can to make you happy.'

135

She smiled, groping for something normal and calming to say.

'Then wash the dishes.'

'Oh, bugger the dishes! Come on, find your oboe and let's get in tune.'

Funny. That was exactly what Eimear had said. That it took a little while for two people to get in tune, and she shouldn't take the first days – or nights – too seriously. But she was very keyed up. Maybe the oboe would be a good idea, first.

It was. As he sat down at his instrument and she stood up with hers, playing *The Pearl Fishers* by unspoken agreement, her whole body yielded and flowed, her spirit soaring as it joined his, their eyes and their hearts meeting, melding, blending. When they had finished, they smiled and sank down on the floor together.

'It is meant to be, Ben, isn't it?'

He stretched alongside her, and took her face in his hands.

'Yes . . . I've wanted you for so long, Aran. But I had to be sure you could trust me, and that I could trust myself.'

'Are you sure, now?'

He lifted his lips from hers and looked into her eyes.

'Yes.'

His voice caressed her heart, and she was profoundly reassured as he drew her close, stroking her back with his eloquent hands, kissing her over and over until she was loose and pliant, sliding her hands inside his sweater, feeling the taut smoothness of his skin, the growing ardour of his embrace.

'Aran?'

'Mmm?'

'Did – uh – did the bed come?'

She laughed aloud. 'Yes! It's in the other room.'

'Then let's go there . . . start slowly, pianissimo, until we're comfortable together?'

Her heart was thumping fortissimo as he picked her up and carried her to it, putting her down gently but then undressing her less gently, removing his own clothes with graceful haste. When he was naked, she marvelled at the beauty of his body.

'You're beautiful too . . . how did I ever hold back? But I can't do it another minute, I want to sleep with you and wake up with you . . .'

His voice was low and tender, his mouth curving with pleasure as she ran her hands down his chest and stomach and thighs, feeling the strength of his muscles, the length of his legs, the dips and curves and hollows. Adjusting her position until she fitted into him, she rolled with him between the covers, responding as he pulled her tighter, absorbed her into his arms, drew her into his heart and soul.

136

'Oh Ben . . . this is wonderful. You feel wonderful.'

He had never felt more wonderful than when he saw the flash of joy in her eyes, felt her tongue deep in his mouth as she kissed him with love and courage, every emotion he had known he would find in her. Entwining his legs around hers, moulding her to him, he was conscious of going further than he had ever been before, going somewhere he had never thought to reach.

But it was not beyond his reach, and it was not the dark prison he had feared. It was intense and exalting, open and infinite, light and weightless as the lips that touched every part of him, and told him he was free.

But now that he knew it, he did not want it. He wanted only to possess, and be possessed.

Aran woke next morning to see sunlight streaming through the uncurtained window, and Ben looking at her with his dark almond eyes.

'Mmm . . .' She snuggled against his chest and put the palm of her hand to his cheek. 'If that was a rehearsal, Ben, I can't wait for the concert at the Albert Hall.'

'Nor can I. You play the oboe beautifully, Miss Campion.'

She gurgled.

'Well, you give master classes! Oh, Ben. Are we really here, in our own flat, all by ourselves? I feel so – so strange, so different!'

'You are different. And you're going to make all the difference, to my life, to everything I do.'

Yes. She knew that she was. But not today. Today she wanted only to be young, to be alive, to be with him. Running her fingers through his black hair, she touched her mouth to his forehead and sat up, kicking the knotted sheets away with her feet.

'Let's do something ridiculous. Swim in the Serpentine, get tigers tattooed on our ankles, have breakfast at Claridge's?'

His eyes opened wide.

'And you used to be so sensible. I've corrupted you.'

'Corrupt me again.'

He seized her and complied with great pleasure, conscious of the huge relief he felt. So, she wasn't going to get up, make breakfast, organise the flat, play the housewife. Wasn't running off to see the Mitchell children either, phone her mother or attend to any of those duties he had feared might deaden the spontaneity of their days together. He had overestimated the bourgeois streak in her.

And he had underestimated the sensual streak. Wildly underestimated it, he thought as her silken skin glowed to the touch, her mouth and fingers melting his own, setting off like eager little explorers all over his body. In just one night she seemed to have learned an awful lot, and was laughing as she put it into practice now, checking to see whether it still worked.

It works, he wanted to yell as she carried curiously on, it works! If you don't stop this you're going to put me in *hospital*! But like a child let loose in a space centre she went on, pushing all the buttons until there was complete chaos, and she was amazed by the havoc she had wreaked. So was he; having prided himself on being a marathon man, he now seemed to be entered in some kind of artery-exploding sprint. Later, he supposed she'd learn about timing and pacing, but meanwhile this was unbelievable, and he told her so the moment he could speak.

And yet, hours afterwards when they still lay savouring the taste and feel of one another, he felt the need to test something.

'Let's take the bike and go off somewhere? Margate, Maldon, Marlow?'

'Mexico, Manchester, Missouri! Anywhere!'

They leapt out of bed, dressed and raced out to the bike. Jumping on behind, she held him tight as it zoomed away, but he did not feel her grip on him, did not hear her gasp as they sped out onto the open road, hurtling into the fast lane where they overtook everything in sight. Exhilarated, he felt only the freedom, heard only the powerful roaring engine.

Conor's letter went to Islington, but Aran asked Holly to forward it to Holland Park. Having left the children she could not bear to see them again until they got used to their new nanny, would no longer cling or cry in the way that rent her heart. But she felt no less a pang when she saw the handwriting on the envelope, the round awkward script of a man for whom communication was an ordeal. Inside was one page, with three lines on it.

'Dear Aran,
Your mother told me what she said but you mustn't mind. We hope you're very happy with your boyfriend and he looks after you. Come home to see us soon and bring him with you.'
Love,
Dad.'

Home. Aran thought of the cottage, the room in which Conor had probably laboured for hours over this letter. She thought of the hills and the harbour, the salt air and the long white beach, of Eimear and

Dan and the dolphins, the boats gliding home in the sinking sun. On her skin she could feel the breeze that was always south westerly, in her ears she could hear the gulls and the waves, in her mind she could see her father, pleading with her mother.

Pleading, to no avail. Molly had had no hand in this letter. Quietly, she tucked it away under the cooking utensils in the kitchen, where Ben would never find it.

Such a simple thing, a tape recorder! But it took Aran weeks to save up the price of one, weeks in which she was overwhelmed by the expense of running a home. Whoever said that two could live as cheaply as one had never met Ben Halley, never envisaged the way he left lights on, took two hot showers a day, chatted for hours on the phone, mislaid possessions that had to be constantly replaced. But when the first bill arrived, they fell around laughing over it.

'Look, Ben! The electricity people! They think we're real!'

It was all quite unreal, in the beginning, ridiculous to think they were grown adults who could run their own lives, vote, marry, pay bills and be responsible. They felt like impostors, playing house, having a great time. Meals were irregular, sex was wild, laughs were perpetual. Friends were invited, wine was drunk, music was loud and eternal. One day, there was a tremendous thumping on the door, and Aran opened it to find the man who lived in the flat overhead, a biologist whose existence was normally invisible.

'Who's playing that piano?' he demanded to know, in a state of great excitement. Hastily, Aran apologised.

'My boyfriend – I'm sorry, it is very loud. I'll ask him to cool it.'

'No! It's wonderful! I just came down to tell him he's superb!'

Without another word he stamped away, leaving Aran wishing she had the tape recorder and could get him to repeat his opinion into it. But it wouldn't cut any ice, she supposed; recording company executives would think she'd bribed a friend. However, recording company executives were going to get tapes in the post any day now and would discover for themselves just how superb Ben was. Despite the chaos she felt her life coming together like the skeins of a sweater, knitting into a pattern and a purpose; this was her man, her job, her future and his. Even when they fought, which they did frequently at first, she was invigorated.

There was no point in agreeing with Ben for the sake of peace, because peace was the last thing he wanted.

'Don't humour me!' he would yell, 'I don't want a perfect partner! I want your real opinions – come on, fight! Feel free!'

So they shouted and argued, over every little thing, and she discovered just how assertive he was. But if he was wrong he always admitted it, never sulked, forgot his defeats within minutes. Sometimes the air hummed with electrical storms, but invariably it cleared, leaving them refreshed and crackling with energy. Aran loved the panoramic way in which Ben talked about the future, his big breathtaking vision of huge concerts and international tours; but he never spoke about its material rewards, the things he would buy or give her – only the places they would go, the things they would do and see.

'India, of course, and Japan – don't you think Japan must be amazing, Aran? So many people, such buzz and colour, yet such delicacy, such constant striving for perfection. Think of their food, their art, their industry . . . we'll have a fabulous time there. Italy, too, France, Brazil – we'll do it all!'

His face glowed, his eyes sparkled when he talked like this. Yet there were quiet interludes too, private times when he would become subdued and withdrawn, times that were provocative to her until she recognised how precious they were to him, and learned not to intrude on them.

But he was considerate too, always appreciative if she cooked a meal or did the laundry, adamant that he did not expect it of her. Not that he would do it himself – things would simply be left undone and they would starve. But Aran liked running a home, enjoyed the domesticity so long as it was voluntary and studded with moments of abandon, sudden bursts of excitement. Ben was great for thinking up sprees and jaunts, adventures for which she was happy to drop everything else. One night they went to the Marquee Club to hear a very heavy metal band with Thanh, Bronwen, Clem and Rani, ate in some Chinese dive in Soho afterwards and drank themselves silly. Next morning, her stomach felt like a ploughed field, her head churned like a failed laboratory experiment and her legs folded under her as if filled with helium.

God, she thought, we danced and drank our brains out last night. We spent a fortune. We were noisy, wicked and disgraceful. But what a great time we had! I'm getting an awful taste for the good times. But we won't go mad like that again for a month. It's only fun when it's a contrast and can be kept under control. Ben would do it every night if he didn't have to work – but he does have to work, and it's up to me to see that he does.

But one day in August, Ben came back from the newsagent's, where he had been sent to buy milk, looking so distraught she couldn't imagine how he could entertain anyone at the restaurant that night.

'What's wrong? What is it?'

'Elvis is dead. Here.'

He handed her a newspaper and she took it with relief: that was all? She loved Elvis's voice and was very sorry to hear he had died, but after all . . .

'He was my earliest inspiration, Aran. My first idol. How can he be gone already?'

She looked at the page and knew immediately what she was going to find. Thirty-five, thirty-six? How old was Elvis?

Forty-two. Roughly twice Ben's age. Closely, carefully, she read the story. Drugs, again. Only legal ones, uppers and downers, but combined with all the other, inevitable things – stress, divorce, constant travel, junk food, minders and bodyguards bickering over every last piece of him until neither his mind nor his body belonged to him any more. A death that any fool could have seen coming. But nobody had seen it, intervened or tried to save him – or if they had, they hadn't tried effectively.

Ben was very upset, but even as she consoled him she felt something harden in her, something snap into place in her mind. This was not going to happen to him. Not ever.

That night she went with him to the restaurant, where he played what the audience wanted to hear – Elvis, exclusively. It was a mournful, lugubrious evening, but one that forced her to think very clearly. Next day, she insisted that Ben accompany her on a long walk, as far as Green Park and back.

He needed exercise, not just today but every day, after the nights spent among the food and wine and cigarette smoke. As yet he didn't smoke himself, and she was going to make sure he never took it up. Regular meals, in future, salads and healthy things. Fresh air, sleep, a decent diet and strict limits on booze. No drugs, not even grass, none of the stuff that circulated in their circle and might lead to stronger addictions.

But she let him talk on and on about Elvis, said none of this aloud.

'Of course he was brash and vulgar, Aran, but he was such a showman! He started out with nothing, hardly any education or experience of real music, but he taught himself . . . never composed any songs to speak of, but what a voice! What a voice, what a performer!'

'You'll have a great career like his, Ben. Only it will last longer.'

'I hope so, because I'm not getting very far as yet.'

'You will. We just need to plan it. Look, I think you should divide it into two halves. In your twenties, concentrate on the rock side of it – new songs with a classical twist to them, and your performance technique. That's the most demanding part physically. Also the part that will make you popular, well known. Study all the other male soloists: Elvis, Cliff, Neil Diamond, Rod Stewart, Bob Dylan, Leonard Cohen, David Bowie, Elton John . . . all of them.'

'But I don't want to be them. I want to be me.'

'Yes, but just to see how they do it! The women too, Carly Simon, Aretha Franklin, Maria Muldaur, Liza Minelli, Barbra Streisand . . .'

'What they have in common, you mean? Exceptional delivery?'

'Yeah. Yours is terrific already. You're a natural. All we need is to let people know you exist. Lots of people.'

'Well, I'm not touring the clubs and colleges for the next ten years. Haven't the patience.'

'No. But one slot on local radio would bring you to all of London. One play on national radio could make you a star overnight. One live performance on television, one video even, would—'

'Aran, how in Christ's name do I *get* on radio or television?'

'I told you before, you make a tape which I will circulate. Market. The video might take a while, but we'll do that too. Anyway, let's start with the tape.'

'Right. And then?'

'And then you perform live, tour, make albums, write all your own material so you can really put your heart into what you sing. I know lyrics aren't your forte, so I'll help with those. That's the ten-year plan.'

'Ten years?'

'Yes. Then you quit the stage while you're ahead. You diversify into musicals, film themes, anything you want. And then you write an opera.'

'I'll be thirty! Forty!'

'Exactly. Mature and experienced. You'll become a composer then, a serious one, full time. You won't have to worry about whether the disco ravers think you're still sexy. There's nothing more pathetic than a forty- or fifty-year-old man puffing round a stage trying to gyrate like the kid he used to be. Look at Bing Crosby, croaking away long after his voice is gone! You're not going to end up like that. You're going to sing for ten or twelve years and then compose for ten or twelve. Good stuff. Maybe opera will even be trendy by the nineties. Mainstream. Anyway, whether it is or not, you'll be able to afford to do what you like. Make your money early and make it big.'

'I'm not in it for the money.'

'No. But you don't want to die a pauper like Mozart, do you, with the bailiffs hammering on the door? You want to travel, don't you, buy a smashing piano, give parties, have a whole collection of Harley

Davidsons? Nice clothes, paintings, a big comfortable house for your – for your friends to visit?'

'Well . . . yeah. I know I do have expensive tastes. I do want to do it all, on a grand scale.'

'You will. You'll see. Only you have to be disciplined, Ben, and you have to get your first break. Let's get that demo tape made.'

'Walk into a studio you mean, tell them to hand over their gear and get me their session musicians?'

'No . . . we can't afford to do it professionally, obviously. I'll just have to get a good machine and do it myself, at the restaurant.'

'Who's going to listen to an amateur tape?'

'Everybody I'm going to barricade into their office and make listen!' He laughed. 'You're a nutter.'

'No, Ben. I've studied marketing. I can do it.'

Touched by her faith in herself and in him, he hugged her.

'You know, Aran, I was afraid I might tire of you in six months. Thought you'd have me making shelves and mowing the lawn. Now I can't imagine how I ever survived without you, or how I ever could again.'

'You couldn't, Halley. You'd fall to pieces in a flash.'

They both laughed, but suddenly they knew it was true.

Dan and Eimear strolled slowly on the beach, watching Sammy run into the dunes after rabbits, talking intermittently, hesitantly.

'I'm so sorry, Dan. I just don't see what more I can do.'

'Eimear, would you stop blaming yourself? It's no more your fault than it is mine. The doctors have said so. It's just nature. Fate. Anyway, there's still hope.'

'After ten years? Dan, we may as well stop kidding ourselves. There isn't.'

'It's not quite ten years. And you're only thirty-two. We must stop worrying about it, or it will become an obsession and never happen.'

'I don't think it ever will.'

'So let's say it won't. Haven't you got the children at school? Haven't you got me, Eimear, and I you?'

The wind blew her hair across her face, stung colour into her cheeks.

'Yes. We have each other. Have so much. I don't mean to sound ungrateful. I won't go on about it any more.'

'Please don't. Give me your hand, and all the news from school.'

'Oh, school is fine. Achill Campion is staying on till he's eighteen, he says – so are several of the others. They seem less keen on the fishing now, there's more talk of tourism, restaurants, guest houses

143

and what have you. Anything that keeps them at home is fine by me.'

'You're still sorry Aran went to England, aren't you?'

'Yes. But she is happy there, doing very well. Somehow she still finds time for the knitwear, and her turnover at the market is nearly three hundred pounds every weekend. Of course she only gets to keep about thirty of that, but it's not bad for two days' work, and the women in the knitting group are so glad she's managing to keep at it. Ben seems to be reliable, too. Much steadier than I'd have thought.'

'I hope so! Eight hundred pounds! How did you talk me into it?'

She smiled. Dan had taken no persuasion at all.

'I sat on your chest and mugged you, remember?'

'Oh, yes, so you did. I must say, I'm not looking forward to this tape they promised us. London's full of young rockers and Ben is probably just another guy who can pick out a tune to make a girl's eyes go starry. I bet it's his cute butt that really turns her on.'

'Dan! Aran's a musician herself! She can judge.'

'Yeah – well, we'd better not hold our breath for our eight hundred quid.'

'I don't care if we never see it again. I want to see her, though.'

'Eimear, Aran is a grown young woman now, living her own life in a different country. It's time to let her go.'

Looking at it logically, Eimear knew that Dan was right. She must move on, let go. But she couldn't.

'Remember we used to work over there when we were students, every summer, canning peas?'

'Uh huh. Peas, strawberries, corn, plums. I'd rather break bricks with a teaspoon than ever do it again.'

'Still, we had fun. But we always wanted to come home. Always did come home, even though you could have made so much more money once you qualified if you'd become a vet in Sussex or Hereford . . . d'you think Aran will ever come home, Dan?'

'No, Eimear. I don't. She has friends, a boyfriend, an income, a flat of her own. Why would she come home? To what, for what?'

'To – to her roots. For her family.'

'Eimear, get real. Molly Campion would blow Ben Halley out of the water if she ever set eyes on him. He's Indian, isn't he? A rocker on a motorbike, screwing her Catholic daughter silly?'

'Dan!'

'Sorry, but there you have it. Besides, there's no music industry in Ireland, no outlet for Ben or work for Aran.'

'You know, I heard of a new Irish rock group just the other day. On the radio. I believe they're called Yoo Hoo – You Two? – only kids playing school dances, but some woman rang the Gay Byrne show to say they're going to be huge.'

'One of their mothers! London's where it's at, Eimear. Always has been and always will be. Ireland is showband territory. The ballrooms of romance.'

'I suppose you're right. Still, that's an idea I must put to the youngsters who'll be leaving school next summer. A nightclub would be a great draw for tourists, especially one with live music.'

'They can get nightclubs in Birmingham or Barcelona. They come here for ballads and folk songs.'

'You're not being very positive, Dan.'

'I'm being realistic.'

'But then things will never change.'

'Oh, I suppose they will eventually. It's just a question of working the new into the old and vice versa. But it's not going to happen in time for Ben or Aran.'

Reluctantly, Eimear had to admit that her husband was probably right. Her golden girl was gone for good.

'Eimear, look! Look, way out there – they're coming in – sshh, don't frighten them!'

Scanning the horizon of the choppy autumnal ocean, Eimear could not make out what Dan was pointing to, until suddenly there was a splash and a spray of white water.

'Oh, the dolphins!'

'Yes. But look, Eimear, only one of them is jumping.'

'What's wrong with the other, do you think? Is it just lazy, or might it be injured?'

'It might. Or it might be caught in a net, something some fool fisherman threw overboard. Let's wait and see whether they come in any closer.'

Silently they waited as the black specks became definite shapes, streaking under the water until they were no more than fifteen or twenty yards away. Climbing up on a promontory rock, Dan edged along its length until they were immediately below his line of vision.

'They're OK. They're not hurt, or in difficulty.'

'So what's wrong with the quiet one? Is it Fred or Barney? Can you see?'

'I can see Fred, I think . . . only he's not Fred any more, Eimear. He's a she, and she is pregnant.'

Sammy came racing down from the dunes, barking as he flew over the sand to where something interesting seemed to be happening. Eimear flew after him lest he should frighten the creatures, and her thoughts flew after her.

The dolphins could do it. Deirdre Devlin could do it. Everyone and everything could do it, except her.

Yet dolphins were a symbol of luck and joy, who brought hope and joy to everyone who loved and lived with them, believed in their mystic powers. Quietly she stood waiting for Dan to climb back down from the rock, thinking how lucky she was in this loyal husband who loved her so much, who made her feel strong when she felt so vulnerable. When he rejoined her she took his hand and walked on with him, watching their shadow as the sun cast it down the beach, watching the dark form of the dolphins as they returned to the deep.

Finally Aran got the tape recorder, a complicated double-deck one that made her frown like a science boffin as she twiddled and fiddled at it, experimenting with all its functions until she was confident of getting exactly the results she wanted from it. Then, recklessly, she went out and bought a short black cocktail dress in a chain store.

Ben jerked his head up from the piano where he was rehearsing the night's repertoire, his face that of a man witnessing a spaceship coming in to land amongst his petunias.

'What – where – why – Aran, what *is* that?!'

'It's my little black dress, my little black shoes, my little black magic tricks with the warpaint.'

Aran's usual uniform was a muddle of clothes he had never quite been able to sort out, a kind of jumble rummage emptied at random over her head every morning. Tonight, with her blonde curls swept up in two silvery combs, she looked like someone who might be found attached to an arms dealer in the small hours of a Monaco morning.

'You look like a kind of harlot starlet.'

'Yeah. Well, it's a ritzy restaurant, Ben. I don't want to let you down.'

'But you're going to be sitting at a side table, making a tape.'

'I still want to look glamorous. Pack a bit of pzazz.'

She certainly did pack it, and they were dreadfully late getting to the restaurant, but he was in the height of good humour when they arrived. As always it was crowded, and she touched him on the shoulder as he made his way to the piano.

'Play perfectly tonight, Ben. Better than you've ever played before.'

Charged with energy, he kissed her for a split second longer than was decent and made his way to the raised dais amidst shouts and whistles of applause; in other such venues food was served with music thrown in, but since he had been playing here those priorities had been inverted. People came here for him.

146

The moment he took his place Aran felt the adrenalin run round the room, the rapport he established instantly with everyone in it, the contact of skin-to-skin, ship-to-shore. Setting up her equipment, she nodded, and he began to play.

Dislocation had been worked on many times since its first airing, honed and polished until tonight it shone sharp as a switchblade. Cutting through all preliminaries Ben plunged it straight into his audience, drawing gasps as it hit them at full force. Watching the reaction Aran realised it didn't matter any more what mood the audience might be in; this rock-hard, diamond-bright song now had the power to change any mood and dictate its own. As the microphone picked up the applause, she saw the needle rocket up to its maximum register. Catching his eye she signalled it to him and his eyes flashed back at her, his whole body seeming to gather momentum, draw in the power of the moment and radiate it back like a dynamo.

He was in top form. As his voice swooped like a swallow into the next song her stomach plummeted; it was like flying in a plane struck by a storm, spinning, falling, grabbing at gravity until suddenly it smoothed and levelled out, took up and off again ... Raising spirits high as flags on the fourth of July he took everyone with him, into a crescendo that erupted like a geyser and on into the night that left her reeling: his vocal range, she thought, could shoot down the stars one by one from the sky. Technically masterful, physically compelling, emotionally devastating, it all went into the slowly turning tape and left her feeling she had been struck by a thunderbolt.

Oh, if only there were someone influential there, someone from some part of the music industry, some cog in the wheel! But the people who surrounded him afterwards were shrieking young women in lurex dresses, brandishing their table napkins for him to autograph, clutching and crushing until Aran could no longer see Ben at all. It took every ounce of her nerve not to dash in among them, defend him from them, proclaim herself his rightful owner. But this was going to happen time and again, and she had to see how he would deal with it.

He loved it. His face was glazed with sweat when next she saw it, his smile wide and exultant, his eyes ablaze with gratitude as he acknowledged the adulation, every nerve leaping in his cinnamon skin. Standing up she raised her arms over her head and joined in the standing ovation, her heart palpitating as she saw a beautiful girl with waist-length hair kiss him seductively on the cheek. He did not reciprocate, but Aran saw the moment register in his consciousness, and made up her mind; she was going to speak to the management about the need for security. Ben's voice was common property, but his body was not.

Over the weekend she went to the market as usual, breathlessly recounting the event to Thanh, who could not get enough of it, and to Bronwen whose lack of interest was strangely hurtful.

'Sorry, Bron. I'm rabbiting on. You must be bored stiff.'

'Oh, no. Not really.'

For the first time Aran got a whiff of something she would encounter many times in the years ahead: envy, tinged with small resentment. Bronwen had seemed supportive at first, but today her face proclaimed that their friendship was finished. In the beginning, Aran's stall had made hers look good by comparison; now it drew many more customers and had netted Aran a handsome, talented boyfriend into the bargain. Aran couldn't see what difference Ben made to Bronwen, or that extra customers would hurt anybody's business, but she could see that Bronwen was inexplicably bitter. She was sorry to make such a discovery, in this big city where friends were so hard to find and keep, but there was no denying the truth. Only Thanh's friendship remained solid, selfless and supportive.

But Thanh was a man, and he had a girlfriend of his own. The 'very nice English girl' was called Beth and came often to help him with his bamboo wares, but she was quiet and Aran did not know her very well. Getting to know the English, she thought, was hard work, especially here in London where the tone was so coolly cosmopolitan. That Ben could generate such exuberance was really a tribute to his enormous charisma, because the English did not seem exuberant people, there was no trace of Celtic or Latin temperament about them. But once you did get to know them, perhaps their friendship would endure as their traditions and beautiful architecture endured?

However, the social conquest of England was another day's work. First, there were the tapes to distribute. Deciding to send them out in two batches, she posted the first six and sentried herself by the letterbox every day for a week thereafter, on tenterhooks.

Another week. Nothing. In the third week, she received one reply. 'Dear Madam, We regret we cannot accept unsolicited . . .' etc, etc. They didn't even have the courtesy to send their tape back, although something told her they had not even listened to it. But she said nothing to Ben, who had agreed not to ask.

Eventually two more replies arrived. Dear Madam ripped them open to be informed that one company's books were full and the other recommended the services of a professional agent. Aran didn't want to hire an agent to do what she thought she could do herself, but she tucked the idea away with one of the six remaining tapes. Let's see how they go first, she said to herself, when I deliver them in person.

It was late November. She had three weeks before businesses started breaking up for the Christmas holiday – and a lot of extra work at the market also, as that season approached. Stuffing the five tapes in her satchel she set off to beard the corporate lions in their dens, and it was then that she discovered the awesome power of the rottweiler secretary, a creature who made Moira look like a pet poodle by comparison.

No, said the first, Mr Spicer was not in the office today. Aran could see Mr Spicer sitting at his desk behind the glass panel of the door with his name on it, and glared pointedly at the silhouette. If Miss Campion would care to make an appointment, sighed the secretary, she would see . . . March, perhaps? March 29, 1978? Defiantly Aran made the appointment anyway, and knew it would be regretfully cancelled on March 28.

The next stop was a local radio station. A friendly young girl put down her mug of coffee, invited her to have a seat and left her there. After two hours she conceded defeat and headed for the BBC. Terry Wogan was very popular on Radio Two, and he was Irish. He would see her, take the tape and play it to Britain over breakfast next morning.

She got as far as a security man on the door. No, there was no question of seeing Mr Wogan in person, but if the young lady would care to leave her package for him, he would convey it to its destination. Of course it would have to be X-rayed first, what with the Irish situation, you never knew what might be in an innocent little parcel these days, did you? Cursing the 'Irish situation' under her breath, Aran left the tape and hoped against hope for the best.

Next day, at another recording company, she scored a direct hit.

Evan Hardy was her goal, and Evan Hardy was crossing the lobby as she walked in. She had no idea what he looked like, but the receptionist called out to him: there was an urgent call for him, would he take it before he went to his meeting? Evan took it, and Aran stood her ground until he had finished, whereupon she rushed up to him.

'Oh, Mr Hardy, you're the very man I wanted to see – my name is Aran Campion and I have a tape you should hear – a singer and pianist, his name is Ben Halley, it's a live performance at the Shot Snake and you can hear the applause on it—'

Evan took the packet as if it contained a live cobra, thanked her and handed it to the receptionist. When he returned, he would collect it and listen to it.

Really? Yes, really. Promise? Promise, absolutely, cross my heart.

It was the best she could do. Despondently she headed for home, kicked off her shoes and made a pot of tea. Ben was out rehearsing and a huge carton of sweaters sat accusingly in the hall, where the biologist from upstairs had very kindly taken delivery for her. Between now and Christmas, every sweater had to be sold, as well as the scarves, planters, shell sculptures and numerous other items that had yet to arrive. A stack of dirty dishes sulked in the sink, a pillowcase full of laundry shouted to be taken to the laundrette and out in the back garden the black cat was busy killing a robin. She ran out to save the bird, but it was already dead.

London was fabulous at Christmas. Hand in hand with Ben, Aran dodged and ducked through the crowds on Bond and Regent Streets, her neck craned up at the thousands of glittering white lights, swivelling back to the sparkling shop windows and up again until they reached Trafalgar Square, where a gigantic Norwegian pine swayed under the weight of thousands more lights. Ben was very taken with the spectacle of it, but she wondered whether the star at its pinnacle could really mean anything to a Hindu, especially a non-practising one.

'It's an omen, Aran. Your Trojan efforts will make me a star.'

Squeezing her hand, he kissed the face that was carmine with cold and looked into the large grey eyes he had come to love so far beyond his wildest expectations. Such big eyes, in that small face! But she spoke quietly, was a little subdued.

'I have tried, Ben. We both have. It's not our fault we haven't got anywhere yet.'

'Oh, Aran! Just think how far we've got, since last Christmas. Do you remember, we went to hear Handel, and then you gave me the brush-off?'

'I did not! You were the one who went to Surrey and left me all alone.'

He was silent for a moment.

'I have to go there again this year. My father is Christian, and my mother observes all the cultural traditions of this country. We have a big meal with a goose like everyone else, exchange gifts, watch the Queen's speech – my parents watch it, anyway. It's an institution.'

She fell silent in turn as she looked back up at the star, slowly comprehending that she was going to be left alone again. Completely alone, this time, without even the Mitchells to give her sanctuary. If she were married to Ben he would have to take her with him, but she was not. He had never even suggested that she meet his parents.

In the dusk her voice fell like a needle from the pine, softly to the ground, to be crushed underfoot.

'It's all right, Ben. I understand. Everywhere in the world, families want to be together on December 25.'

'Yes. It might be a bit of an ordeal for you, Aran. But you will come, won't you? They'll probably be a bit iffy at first, but they won't eat you, I promise.'

'What?'

'My parents. When you meet them. They'll make you sleep in the guest room, interrogate you like the Gestapo, but it's only for a few days . . . I'll get you through it. Rani will be there too, to help.'

'You – you want to take me with you? To Surrey?'

'Yes, of course! What did you think, that I was going to leave you by yourself at Holland Park, lock you under the stairs until I came back?'

'Oh, Ben! I – I don't know what I thought . . .'

'Oh, you goose, it's you we should be having for dinner!'

He held her to him, gazing at her with wonder. She had so much faith in him, professionally – so why so little, personally? Did she really need marriage, after all, to feel secure? Well, he was by no means ready for it, but perhaps he had better start thinking about it . . . just thinking, once in a while.

Gripping her about the shoulders he walked on with her, uncertain whether she was trembling with fright at the prospect of meeting his family, or the prospect of not meeting it.

The Halley house was huge, and Deva Halley's bearing was regal as she welcomed Aran into it.

'How lovely to meet you, my dear. Do come in and sit down.'

Gingerly, Aran sat.

'You know Rani, I believe? And this is our elder daughter Chanda.'

Chanda, the cardiologist Ben had mentioned, had brought her fiancé with her. A wine merchant in a navy suit that blared money, he glanced at Chanda and Chanda glanced, in turn, at Aran.

'You came down with Ben, on his motorbike?'

Reading her tone, Aran knew that she looked it. But she could hardly have walked from London, or worn a suit on the bike, if she had a suit!

But Deva and Rani were wearing saris, which somehow put her more at ease, and Ben was standing protectively behind her.

'Of course we came on the bike, Chanda! Would you like a ride on it, after lunch?'

His tone was arch, but Chanda neither smiled nor accepted. Like her fiancé she was conservatively dressed, slightly stocky, with a detached air about her. Anyone could tell that Rani was Ben's sister and that both had inherited their beauty from their mother, but Chanda seemed different. A chip, Aran wondered, off the old block? But as yet there was no sign of Guy Halley. With a gracious smile, Deva turned to her.

'I've put you in the little pink bedroom, my dear. Ben will take your things up for you. I do hope you'll be comfortable.'

She smiled, much more warmly than Aran had expected. On the way down, Ben had warned her that his mother might be difficult, a bit distant, but he had been wrong. If anything, Deva seemed to be paying more attention to her than to Chanda's fiancé, was making her feel very welcome.

'Ben tells me you come from Ireland?'

'Yes. From Cork.'

'Cork? Now, where is that? Do tell us all about it.'

Hesitantly Aran described it, relaxing as Deva nodded and smiled at intervals.

'Oh, but it sounds lovely! Don't you miss it?'

At that moment Aran found that she did miss it. Why today, she could not say, but Deva seemed to understand, and patted her hand comfortingly.

'I still miss India at times . . . I believe your Mr de Valera was very friendly with our Mr Gandhi?'

Aran had heard that too, but before Mrs Halley could tell her anything about it, Ben's father came into the room. Instantly, the atmosphere changed.

'Chanda! Charles! How are you!'

He went straight to them, a dark substantial man in a striped suit, polished and well-preserved. Noticing the air of authority about him, the firm way in which he shook Charles's hand while ignoring her, Aran suddenly felt on a par with the corgi which lay on the floor. But Deva intervened.

'Darling, Ben has arrived too, with this lovely young lady – Aran, this is my husband, Guy Halley.'

Guy Halley looked at her, and looked again.

'How do you do?'

By the time Aran managed to reply that she did very well – the wrong reply, apparently – Guy had gone on to greet Ben indifferently and start pouring drinks from an array of decanters on the sideboard.

'What will you have, Miss Campion?'

Frantically she racked her brains. What was the right thing? What was Ben having? 'A beer, please.'

'A beer. Ah yes, of course. You're Irish, I believe?'

She heard it all in those few words: the Irish, the beer, the drunken

Paddies. But his wife was Indian, he had Indian blood himself and his own son was drinking beer! When he handed hers to her, she took one very small, deliberate sip, and put it down. An hour later, when a maid summoned them all into the dining room, she had got no more than halfway through it.

With a smile, Rani showed her a bathroom where she might freshen up before lunch, leading the way through the imposing, formally furnished house.

'He's an old hatchet. Don't pay any attention.'

Gratefully, Aran smiled back. Rani had been so friendly, on her side from the first, and now she sensed that Deva was too. But the father and the other sister – it dawned on her that they were treating her exactly as Molly and Val would treat Ben. Oh, who needed all this nonsense!

Ben sat beside her at table, stroking her hand under it supportively when, finally, Guy looked at her again.

'So, Miss Campion, what brings you to Britain? What is it you do?'

'I run a stall at Camden Market. My mother and her neighbours knit sweaters, which I sell.'

Guy froze, Chanda froze, Charles froze. Even Deva registered wonder.

'But Ben mentioned – business studies—?'

'Yes. I got my diploma last summer.'

Everyone's relief was visible except for Guy, whose disapproval rolled down the table at her like a boulder.

'Last summer? You mean to say you haven't found a proper job yet?'

'Well – I'm going to manage Ben. His musical career, I mean.'

'His musical *career*? I *see*.'

Guy's smile was so deeply sarcastic that she was not surprised to feel Ben stiffen beside her, draw breath to defend himself.

But he did not defend himself.

'Father, Aran did very well in her exams. She's extremely bright, able and diligent. I'm going to be a singer, as I've told you before, and she is going to be my manager. If that doesn't suit you, then may I suggest you drop the subject.'

For a moment Aran thought his father was going to get up, come down to him and hit him. But then Guy sat back in his chair.

'Certainly, Ben. The subject is of absolutely no consequence.'

It felt like hours before the meal came to its merciful conclusion and they adjourned to watch the Queen's speech on television. Back in Ireland, everyone would be watching the Pope's Christmas blessing, the Urbi et Orbi ceremony from Rome; but here this event

153

had pride of place and, despite Ben's reluctance, she was interested to see it.

It was a mistake.

The Queen looked most dignified, but the moment she began to speak Aran was seized with a fit of the giggles. Such a squeaky little voice, like Minnie Mouse! Desperately she struggled to contain her laughter, but it was useless. With her hand over her mouth, she had to make a dash for the bathroom. Oh, someone should oil that voice, with honey or something, before the woman spoke!

When she came back, Ben was grinning from ear to ear, but his father's face was frigid. For the remaining twenty hours of her visit, he did not address another word to her. She had sat the family test, and she had failed.

But late next morning, Deva embraced her as she was leaving, and suddenly she understood why. Deva had been an immigrant, and knew what it was to be alone. Alone, assessed, and unacceptable.

But Deva had succeeded in her career, married Guy and become acceptable. Deva had got through, to the other side of the glass wall. Impulsively Aran hugged her, knowing she had found a friend.

There was no word from any of the people with whom Aran had left tapes. Not one word, from one of them. During the cold stark days of January she phoned or wrote to all of them, but the rottweiler secretaries snarled and barked at her, the ditsy assistants left her on hold and forgot all about her. Evan Hardy, she was curtly informed, had gone on holiday to Barbados. Day after day she listened to Terry Wogan, day after day hope faded.

With Ben she channelled her feelings into her music, and together they wrote an angry song about the music industry, brusquely entitled *Deaf.* Night after night the restaurant was full, yet the letterbox remained empty. For Ben's sake she tried not to get despondent; for her wasted efforts he got furious.

'Fuck 'em! Fuck every last one of them! Some day they'll be sorry!'

One tape remained. She was going to have to give it to an agent, after all – if she could find one of those who would listen to it. According to Clem, agents received up to a hundred tapes a month, and threw ninety-nine of them in the bin after listening to the first five minutes and charging a fortune for the privilege.

Yet people listened to her one last tape when she took it to the market, as she did every weekend, determined that someone should hear it. Often they asked the name of the singer and whether they could get it in the shops – how infuriating, to have to say no! If she had to say it once more she would scream.

154

'No.'

The man who was buying a sweater stared at her in disbelief.

'No? Really?'

'Really and truly. It should be, but it isn't. Sorry.'

The man dropped the sweater and simply stood there, watching the cassette go round as if it were slowly hypnotising him. Only when it finished did he snap out of his trance.

'Who's the artiste?'

Artist*e*? Was he French? But he sounded English.

'My boyfriend. His name is Ben Halley.'

'Ben Halley. Ben Halley.' He repeated it like a mantra.

'Yes. If you'd like to hear him live, he plays Wednesdays to Saturdays at the Shot Snake.'

'Does he? Excuse me, miss, but what's your name?'

'Mine? Aran Campion.'

He extended his hand.

'Hi. I'm Gavin Seymour.'

Gavin – God had sent *Gavin Seymour* in search of a sweater, to Camden Market?! Gavin Seymour whose late-night radio programme was a forum for new talent, with a vast cult following? She ripped the cassette out of the player.

'Mr Gavin, I mean Mr Seymour, Seymour, Gavin – would you take this? Would you?'

He took it with alacrity, smiling at the babbling little blonde.

'I was going to ask you if I could. I'll play it on Monday night, if I may?'

She knew the format. He played ten brand new tracks by totally unknown people every night, and listeners rang in to vote for their favourite. And here he was putting Ben into his pocket! Beside herself, she thrust the sweater at him.

'Oh, thank you! Thank you so much! Please take this too, or any other one you'd like! Take them all!'

He laughed as he put his hand in his other pocket and took out a wallet, a piece of paper and a pen.

'Thanks very much, but I belong to a rare species that doesn't accept – uh – gifts. Let me pay you for the sweater and then you'd better give me your name and address, phone number.'

For a moment she couldn't remember them, such was her shock, but finally they were safely stowed away with the tape. She didn't take her eyes off his dark, rotund figure until it vanished back into the crowd, or realise until much later that she had given him the very last tape. If he lost it or forgot about it, she was sunk.

But Thanh was adamant that he would do neither.

'He like very much, Aran. He play. And then I ring programme to vote.'

'You're such a good sport, Thanh! Will you really?'

'Oh yes. You must get everyone to vote, Aran. Sometimes people win by only one or two votes you know, can be very close.'

Later, when Ben arrived to help her sell her wares, she stuttered the news so incoherently it took him ages to make sense of it.

'You're sure? Gavin Seymour? Absolutely sure, Aran?'

'Yes! Yes!'

Between them they rounded up everyone – Rani, Clem, Deva, Holly and Walter Mitchell, Ben's musician friends, even people she hadn't seen since they had been in class with her. All of them promised to stay up all night, no matter if Ben's tape wasn't played until four in the morning, and vote for it.

It was wonderful of them, but it was unnecessary. Ben topped the poll by nearly two hundred votes.

Chapter Seven

Beautiful, Aran thought, was the only word for Ben today. It was a hot August day, the studio was like an oven, but hot weather suited Ben, brought out something spicy and smoky about him, something that charged her with electricity. With his eyes closed, one hand to his ear, he held the microphone lightly, gracefully in the other. His voice rolled like lava into it, but for some reason it was his wrist that held her eye; coppery and sinuous, it was incredibly sexy.

His wrist! Really she must need therapy, if even a flick of it could have such a lustful effect on her. But his whole body was moving, swaying up into the air like a charmed snake, his ebony eyes looking up at intervals to seek her out. He was quite a distance away, down on the floor while she sat up in the sound box, but she smiled and nodded, conveying her approval. He was recording his first single, and everything was going swimmingly. Everything, until he suddenly ripped off the headphones, threw the microphone away from him and screeched in livid fury.

'Bastards! Bastards, bastards, *bas*tards!'

What was wrong? His face was so tragic, his volume and vehemence so violent that despite her concern she had to laugh: it was almost operatic. But she had better go to him.

By the time she reached him he was waving the score in one hand, thumping it with the back of the other, yelling at the producer who was yelling right back. Around them the musicians sat stoically, waiting for the victory that, in their experience, usually went to the illustrious Myles Irving. But Myles turned to Aran in exasperation.

'You sort him. Give him a valium or something.'

He strode away, and she put her hand on Ben's arm.

'What is it? What's wrong?'

He was quivering with rage, exploding with emotion.

'It's impossible! You write a song – a simple little ditty – la la la –

157

and they screw it up! Speed it up, stamp all over it, chuck massive orchestration into all the wrong places! I can't sing this!'

'Ben, calm down.'

'I will not calm down! It's my song and I'll sing it my fucking way!'

'Ben, they're experts. They know what they're doing.'

But she knew what he meant. Two contracts had been offered to Ben after Gavin Seymour catapulted him to national attention, and he had chosen the one that offered less money but more artistic freedom. But even so, the recording of this first disc was a revelation.

She had almost fainted at the complexity of it, the monster that had been created overnight. Recording a song was just a tiny part of a vast process involving producers, technicians, art directors, lawyers, distributors, promoters, everything from copyright to sleeve design to accident insurance. Reading the contract was like reading *Ulysses*, as if it were deliberately designed to defeat all but the most determined. Panic-stricken, she had thought briefly of calling in an agent after all, but Ben had gazed at her in disappointment.

'Don't you want to do it? You've got your diploma, Aran, I'm sure you can. And I trust you! I'd much rather put it all in the hands of someone I know and trust.'

So she had floundered on, slowly deciphering the contract as if it were a wall of Egyptian hieroglyphics, discovering more than she'd ever thought could exist. But Ben's confidence buoyed her up until eventually she cracked the document, pronounced it sound and advised him to sign it with her heart in her mouth. If she'd missed or misinterpreted a single clause, the repercussions could be horrendous.

But Cedar Records seemed as keen to see Ben succeed as she was herself. Already the promotions team was at work, telling all the radio stations that 'white labels' were underway and that a sensational new disc would follow. They couldn't guarantee good publicity, they admitted, but they could guarantee some curiosity at least. Busily, a biography and some very creative photographs were being put together, and until this moment Ben had been exuberantly happy.

Aran thought the promotions people knew what they were doing and so, definitely, did Myles Irving. A slightly overweight man with thick white hair, perpetually clad in faded denims, Myles's professionalism had been obvious from the first moment he entered the studio, even if he was not already well known as a producer who had a remarkable way with new young talent. Since 1964, he had built up an enviable track record, had a whole stable of successes who had started off as Ben was starting now – cramped in a small hot studio, lost without his live audience, confused by technology and very reluctant to take orders, even when Myles was tactful enough to disguise them as requests. Ben was a perfectionist with strong opinions of his own, but so was Myles, and Myles was the expert. Furthermore, Cedar's rock label was only one of several: the company had a classical music division as well. If the partnership prospered, Ben might stay with this highly-respected outfit for a long time.

She smiled at him sympathetically, but went to what she thought was the crux of the problem.

'It's the speed, is it? That's your basic difficulty?'

His eyes were still glittering.

'Yes. It's like the charge of the bloody Light Brigade! There's no time to draw breath! This isn't the tempo I wrote it in, Aran, you know it isn't!'

She saw that exhaustion was taking its toll. Since February he had written ten songs, slaving day and night over them, feverishly putting together a repertoire for the winter tour that would follow the release of this single. Most performers worked their way up to that point over a period of a year or more, but he had been propelled to it at the speed of light, with no time to think or take charge of the suddenly hurtling juggernaut.

Amongst other sacrifices he had had to give up his job at the Shot Snake, and she knew he was missing the rapport with the loyal supporters who went there to hear him, the buzz they generated and the sympathetic atmosphere. Myles was patient – considering – but studio time cost money, he clearly wasn't going to humour Ben all day.

She tried to sound soothing.

'Look. Why don't you just try it the way Myles suggests? Sing the whole thing once, right through, and then if you're not happy with the playback we'll talk to him. There's no point in abandoning it halfway through, Ben.'

He considered for a moment, knowing she understood music, would fight for anything she knew was right. Anyway, he had agreed to this tempo in principle; it was only a fraction too fast, in some places.

'OK. If he'll just get them to slow down here' – he jabbed at the score – 'and here, the rest of it will be all right.'

Relieved, she beckoned to Myles, who was glowering over his glasses as he muttered with his colleagues, his shirt drenched in perspiration. A forceful man in his forties, he was making it abundantly clear that he did not need temper tantrums from young men half his age. After some further consultation with the session musicians, he came over and signalled for recording to begin again.

She knew it would be disastrous if Ben didn't fully accept her advice. But he did, with no hint of resentment, attacking the song with the verve it needed while clamping down this time on his instinct to linger over the disputed notes. From her vantage point, she didn't know which was the sweeter sight; Ben's tall brown body undulating into the rhythm, or Myles's ruddy face as a smile of satisfaction finally spread across it.

'Better. Much better.'

Yet recording went on for hours more, over and over until even Aran thought she never wanted to hear the wretched song again. By the time a halt was called everyone had only one ambition left: to get out to the pub and sink several pints of ice cold beer. Rounding up his troops, Myles led them across the road to it, cursing the choice of career that confined him to sizzling studios on hot summer days that were meant to be spent at the beach. Yet when he sat down he was pleasant and sociable, a mine of information about the whole exhausting business.

But what an exciting business, in spite of everything! In January Aran had been close to despair; now, only eight months later, she was thrilled with the turn things had taken, the wave of enthusiasm on which Ben had been swept up, the speed at which things were moving. The release of this single, entitled *White Web* with lyrics on which they had collaborated together, was generating momentum far beyond their expectations, interest and speculation within an industry that always kept tabs on anything Myles Irving was doing.

'But you stay out of it,' he advised her now as Gavin Seymour had already advised her. 'People won't want to see a wife or girlfriend, they'll want to think Ben belongs to them. Lyrics or no lyrics, manager or no manager, keep a low profile if you want to help his image.'

She knew Myles didn't take her seriously, even when Ben made a point of consulting with and referring to her; at nineteen she was a most unlikely looking manager. But she was learning fast, watching every aspect of the whole process with fascination, steeling herself for what everyone warned her would be a hard road ahead. Ben was having to adapt a bit too, frequent places and events the promotions people said he should be seen at, meet certain key people, wear and eat and drink things chosen to convey a specific impression. He thought this aspect of it all nonsensical, but since the competition was doing it she persuaded him that he must too. For the moment, anyway.

He had signed a contract for five years and Gavin Seymour had been very helpful about the things to watch out for – second rate session musicians, inferior sound equipment, inadequate rehearsal time, all the frustrations that drove some disillusioned young musicians and singers to drink and drugs. Once that happened, in his experience, a career could rarely be salvaged. Not that Cedar was a dodgy label – on the contrary – but you couldn't be too careful. Aran was very grateful to him, aware that she didn't know half enough about this minefield of a business. And if it weren't for Gavin, Ben wouldn't be here now, laughing over his outburst.

'You have the patience of a saint, Myles.'

'Yeah, and fortunately you have the voice of an angel, because otherwise I'd have put your teeth down your throat.'

Ben laughed, slightly giddy after the stress of the recording session and the elation of having completed it. The cheque he had received on signing with Cedar had made Aran's head whirl, but it was the actual act of singing that gave him real delight. With some of the money they were going to repay the Rafters, join a sports club where they could swim and play tennis, get some new clothes and things for the flat. But the only material thing that really interested him was the acquisition of a new motorbike. That, and the new possibilities for partying.

Her idea of partying was an interesting meal at a Chinese, Italian or Indian restaurant, his was a night on the tiles at a crowded club from which he would usually bring back a dozen people for more fun at the flat. Tonight, with the single under his belt, he would be raring to go. The money from Cedar was beginning to open up other possibilities, too: concert and opera tickets previously beyond their budget.

'Opera?' Cedar's promotions manager Jessica Hunter had shrieked.

'You're a rock singer! You can't be seen at the opera!'

Ben retorted that he could and would. Was there anything in his contract about it? No, but—

'Then I'm going! The *Magic Flute* is on at Covent Garden.' Off he had swept, leaving Jessica to have a seizure, but the *Magic Flute* had been fabulous, whirling them both up on a carousel of colour and drama. When this record was released, Aran suspected their entire lives might be about to take on those very qualities.

Myles was discussing the release here and now.

'September 20. We don't expect it to chart, naturally, but anywhere in the top fifty would be satisfactory. It'll need maximum exposure so your name will be well aired before the tour. Now, Aran, about lyrics – one person can't do them all. We were thinking of getting in a fulltime professional to work with you and Ben. That OK with everyone?'

Ben looked at her, and she thought before replying.

161

'We'll give it a try, Myles. But we'll want to retain final say and power of veto. Who did you have in mind?'

'Kelwin Hughes. Welsh chap, lovely turn of phrase, very experienced. I'm sure you'll get on well with him.'

'We'll do our best. But we'll still be writing most of our own material.'

'Sure. Just so long as we have fifteen songs by October. I know you've got ten already, but a concert tour is a very hungry animal, it consumes material at a tremendous rate. Ben can include cover versions of other people's songs to start with, but not more than ten per cent of the total repertoire. As of next year I want everything he sings written specifically for him.'

Aran had to concede that Kelwin Hughes might be necessary. If she spread herself too thin, attempted to run their home and business affairs and write all their lyrics as well, she would end up doing none of those things properly. Much as she loved matching her words to Ben's voice, she wanted time to play the oboe as well, visit the Mitchell children, do all the simple little things that were part of everyday life. Otherwise it wouldn't be a life any more, it would be a treadmill.

Reaching for her hand, Ben stood up and took his leave of his new colleagues, thanking them for helping him through the memorable day. Outside in the street, he turned to her and kissed her.

'Thank you too, Aran. It made such a difference that you were there with me, are able to handle all the conflicts and the practical stuff as well . . . God, I love you to bits!'

They glowed with happiness all the way home where, unexpectedly, Ben did not instantly start thinking about which nightclub to visit.

'Let's just go to bed for a while?'

They went, and stayed there all night, amazing themselves with the growing strength of their love, the deepening intimacy in which they lay twined together, tender and still long after their bodies were exhausted, smiling and cuddling together in the darkness. Shutting out the whole world, whispering and murmuring endearments, they discovered a new dimension that night, a depth of loving and bonding that took them to a new level, and left them happier than ever before.

'Are you looking forward to the tour, Aran?'

'Oh, yes, Rani! It's such a big break for Ben . . . only I wonder a little bit what it will be like living in hotels all winter, moving on every few days? We've been so comfortable at home lately, so close, and now there will be all these other people rushing us about, organising everything. It's all a bit overpowering.'

162

Rani and Aran sat together in a small busy bistro off Oxford Street, where they had spent a fun morning raiding the boutiques and chain stores for cosmetics and accessories, giggling like the carefree girls they were. It was a welcome break from music and medicine, and Aran got a great kick from being able to treat Ben's sister to lunch. She was so supportive, and becoming a great friend.

'Look on the bright side, Aran. You haven't seen much of Britain, have you? This tour will take you from Cornwall to Scotland, you'll get to see the whole country now.'

True. Very true. By spring she would have seen more of Britain than she ever had of Ireland.

'But it means giving up the market, Rani.'

'Well – you weren't planning to stay there for ever, were you?'

'No . . . but I enjoy it so much. It's the one little piece of my life that's still mine. Besides, my mother needs the income as much now as she ever did. The whole village does.'

'Then sell the products on to shops, or farm the whole project out to someone.'

That was an idea. If she could find a good reliable person to take on the stall, someone able for the importing and paperwork as well as the actual selling . . . someone from Ireland, maybe, who could use a start? That had always been Holly Mitchell's method and, according to what she heard from home, thousands of highly-qualified graduates were coming to Britain in search of work these days. A stall wasn't much, but it had certainly got her started.

'Thanks, Rani. I'm so close to it I wasn't able to see the solutions clearly, but that's exactly what I'll do. Farm it out to someone who doesn't mind selling sweaters knitted by a fascist!'

'What?'

'Oh, nothing . . . everything's been happening so fast, I don't know what I'm saying. Let's take a breather and enjoy our lunch.'

They ordered stuffed garlic mushrooms to start, followed by fluffy omelettes with French bread and white wine. Thoughtfully, Rani watched Aran despatch her mushrooms.

'You're looking really well, Aran.'

She flushed, pleased.

'Am I?'

'Yes. I'm so glad to see Ben making you happy, as well as making a success of himself. I was a little concerned for you, in the beginning.'

Aran paused to look back at her, candidly.

'Because – because Ben had had so many other girlfriends?'

'Yes. I never told you then, but they came and went like buses. He didn't seem to have any staying power at all.'

'Well, he was younger then, Rani. He's twenty-one now.'

'That's still young.'

'Yes, I suppose it is. But he seems to have developed great powers of concentration. For instance he knows that rock is only the first step to something much more substantial, but he's putting everything into it. I wondered at first whether he'd have the patience to pace himself, but he seems to understand that composing really great music takes far more experience than he's got yet. What he's got now is a foot in the door, and a goal for later on. By the time the next batch of young pretenders start yapping at his heels, he'll be moving on, not getting stuck in a cul-de-sac.'

'You have it all mapped out, haven't you?'

Rani smiled, but Aran hesitated a fraction.

'Well, yes . . . as much as I can. As far as work is concerned it's all panning out perfectly. Talk about a lucky break, with Gavin Seymour! We're starting to get better at what we do, we're having great fun and we feel fulfilled. It's fantastic.'

'But?'

'Oh, but nothing! I'm just an ungrateful wench who wants the sun, moon and stars all in one fell swoop.'

Rani reflected, sitting back between courses to toy with her long black plait.

'Marriage? Is that what you want, Aran?'

'Oh . . . you know, Rani, I used to say I didn't want it at all. Not until everything else was up and running. But now it is, much sooner than I'd expected, and suddenly the next piece of music I want to hear is the Wedding March! I love Ben so much. I'm beginning to have the most ridiculous dreams about white dresses and orange blossom.'

Rani dropped her plait and gaped at her.

'Aran, are you out of your mind? You want to get married at nineteen? My God, why don't you just have done with it and go to India, offer yourself up as a child bride! You should be down on your knees thanking fate you live here, in 1978, when women's lib has done away with the need to marry, we can have careers, earn good money and do what we want.'

'But that's what I want, Rani. A husband and a home. There has to be someone who still does!'

'You're off your trolley. Aran, you seemed so ambitious before – what's happened to you? Isn't it enough that you're living with Ben, writing songs, managing him? What about that diploma you worked so hard for, were desperate to get?'

'Oh, I am thrilled I got it, Rani, and I do still want to manage Ben. But I want to marry him too.'

164

'*Why?*'

Why? Because – because – now that she had to rationalise it, she found it very difficult. It wasn't anything she could put into words or make sound logical . . . it was just some need that had started to grow, some instinct setting her heart against her head, getting a sudden grip on her. She had no roots in this country, no family, and she was beginning to feel the need of both. The need of a home of her own, of status, of security. Commitment, domesticity, all the things that would counterbalance a musician's erratic life on the road, establish something fixed and permanent.

'A home, Rani. That's all. Is it so awful, so much to ask?'

'With an apron and a budgie and an aspidistra? Aran, it's too *little* to ask! After you've studied and worked your butt off, after ten years of Germaine Greer – do you realise that until very recently I could have been forced into an arranged marriage, made to become a housewife and produce six sons? But fortunately my mother wouldn't have let that happen anyway, because she's educated and liberated, a professional who knows the value of her work and her brain—'

'But she's married, Rani. A wife and mother as well as a doctor.'

'Oh, give it a rest! Can't you see how difficult it is to combine all those things? When I was a small girl, I can remember crying all night because my mother had gone out to work and wasn't there to tuck me in, read me a story . . . couldn't grasp why she had to do it, how there could possibly be anything more important than me. Ben missed her too. Then she felt guilty, was torn – just as you told me Holly Mitchell was torn. Aran, you've got the best of both worlds! Why can't you leave it at that, and be happy?'

Aran was forced to come clean, confess to the paranoia that sometimes shadowed her life with Ben.

'Because . . . I'm afraid Ben might tire of me, Rani. Leave me for somebody else. There are so many girls out there, so many traps and seductions he could fall into – oh, don't get me wrong, Rani. He's the most loving, affectionate guy in the world, kind and romantic and everything I could wish. But – it's just that—'

'That you're insecure? But he's been faithful, hasn't he, never given you any reason to doubt him?'

'No. None.'

'Then this is all in your overworked imagination. Anyway, if he ever did take a shine to someone else, I frankly doubt if a wedding ring would hold him back. Would you want it to, for that matter, if he didn't love you any more?'

'Oh, Rani! Don't say that!'

'Aran, you really are paranoid. You amaze me. I know Ben used to be an awful Lothario, but he's been with you for two years now. Why can't you give him the benefit of the doubt, and trust him?'

'I don't know, Rani. Maybe it's just a silly phase I'm going through.'

'Yeah . . . well, cut out the women's magazines and soppy movies. You've got a great relationship and a shower of confetti isn't going to make any difference to it. If you still want to marry Ben ten years from now, we'll review the situation then. But you won't catch *me* falling into the old tender trap. Marriage is fifties stuff, Aran, for the birds.'

She had to laugh.

'I'm a birdbrain, is that it?'

'Yeah. I'd have given you more credit.'

She smiled, thinking how right Rani was if you looked at it logically. Until recently she'd have made the same points herself, had the same attitude . . . why in God's name was her head filling with these notions of husbands, houses, sunny gardens and big warm kitchens, log fires and aromatic things simmering in saucepans? Why couldn't she stop studying fabric swatches and paint charts, gazing into estate agents' windows, furniture shops and bakeries with wedding cakes in them?

Ben would die laughing. Even if he wanted such fantasies, which he most certainly didn't, he was embarking on a lifestyle which was exactly the opposite. Tours, concerts, fans, hotels, planes, trains, roadies – nothing more permanent than a rainbow, more lasting than a joss stick. A new song and a new city every day, a whirling kaleidoscope of colour, a whole ice-cream parlour full of flavours.

Why settle for just one, of anything? Why stop at one concert, one record, one woman?

She couldn't think of one good reason why. Couldn't think of anything, lately, except wedding bells, wedding marches, wedding vows.

Rani snapped her fingers.

'Aran! Wake up! You're dreaming!'

Her head jerked up, her eyes flew open.

'Sorry, Rani. You're right. I am dreaming.'

It was a lovely autumn day, glowing with soft sun as the tour bus pulled out and headed in the direction of Oxford, a city that Aran had heard was one of the most beautiful in England. For the first few miles Ben sat beside her, eager and happy as he absorbed the reality of it, the fact that tomorrow night he was going to sing to a thousand people, the biggest audience he had ever faced. If he was nervous, he showed no sign of it, grinning at all the other people who were travelling with them.

'They're paid to do the worrying, Aran. Let's you and I just enjoy it.'

There were backing musicians, sound technicians, lighting technicians, costume and make-up people, a publicist, a whole team fielded by the record company. Aran knew that Cedar still didn't take her seriously, but she had to admit they were taking Ben very seriously, putting vast resources and experience into building up his name, planning this tour with great thought and detail. Oxford had been chosen for the first concert because its student population was open to new music, and was likely to appreciate the unusually classical twist to Ben's. Furthermore, it wasn't very far from London, he would not arrive exhausted, and a whole day had been allowed to set everything up. The road manager's name was Kevin Ross, and they had both taken an immediate liking to his relaxed manner, the reassuring way in which his friendly blue eyes twinkled from behind little round glasses. He was about thirty-five, an old hand at getting new talent on the road.

Kevin left them alone at first while the bus wended its way out of the London traffic, but then he made his way to where they sat and suggested that Ben might like to come and get acquainted with the rest of the crew, use the travelling time to discuss various aspects of the arrangements that had been made for him. Sociably Ben got up, leaving Aran to admire the passing scenery; her presence didn't seem to be required, and she decided against forcing it upon them.

The scenery was lovely as it turned gradually rural, spreading out into great golden fields hung with russet trees, the harvest colours of corn and chestnut under a mauve sky, punctuated by pretty villages in which swans floated on serene rivers and great redbrick houses stood in the secure dignity of many centuries. But gradually Aran's mind drifted away from it, back to the conversation she had had with Rani.

Rani was a modern woman and she thought Aran's wish to marry Ben alarmingly old-fashioned. Everyone seemed to think marriage old-fashioned these days; the magazines and newspapers warned constantly against it, expounding instead on the 'new woman' who found fulfilment in the office that was infinitely preferable to a home, a husband or a family. Anyone who 'settled' for the latter was as good as pronouncing herself brain dead and consigning herself to social extinction, a life of unspeakable drudgery. The 'new woman' was a corporate creature who rightly mistrusted all men, trading them in as frequently as she traded in her car, moving right along with never a backward glance. Her heart never got broken, because she never let anyone hold it.

In theory, Aran supposed, she might be right. In today's Britain marriage certificates seemed to be as disposable as Bic razors or paper hankies. No woman in her right mind took men seriously. If you carelessly let yourself fall in love with one, as she had fallen in love with Ben, you spent all your time justifying your heinous crime, asserting that you had no intention of becoming – shudder – a housewife. That wasn't the only thing Aran wanted to become, but it was one of them. Ben's professional success mattered greatly to her, but it was much more than a matter of making money or getting his talent recognised; it was all bound up with feelings and emotions, the faith she invested in him as a person, the vision she cherished of their life together. When she let her faith in him waver, even for a moment, it reflected badly on her judgement, on her consistency far more than his. As Rani had said, he had given her no grounds for the uneasiness she sometimes felt, no evidence that his love would not endure. Some day, they would marry, set up a home and a family no matter what the feminists said – was that really so terrible, so dated, so laughable?

She hadn't known at first it was what she wanted, but she did now. Somehow the certainty had crept up on her after she left the Mitchells, had something to do with the late nights Ben worked, the attention he attracted, the nightlife that had begun to make her head spin. It was all fun for the moment, but where would it end?

No. Molly was wrong when she said Ben would never marry her, Rani was wrong in ridiculing the whole idea.

Perhaps if Rani and Molly had not said those things, she wouldn't be thinking so much about them now. But their pessimism had taken root in her mind, and she was resolved to prove it mistaken. Maybe even by the time this tour was over, Ben would be longing for a quiet life in one place, cured of his restlessness and ready to make at least one thing permanent in his fast-moving life.

She looked up at him as he laughed and chatted at the front of the bus, perched on the arm of someone's seat, his face so animated and his dimple so endearing. There wasn't a bad bone in his body, she thought as he caught her eye and beckoned to her to join him; he was incapable of hurting her, of ever changing his mind about her.

She had better go and mix with these new colleagues of his, before they began to think her aloof, or pathetically shy. Standing up, she smiled at them all as she made her way through the swaying bus, linking her fingers into his when she reached him. Oxford was coming into sight in the distance, and as she saw the rising spires her spirits began to rise with them: this was the world she had long wanted to see, and nobody could deny that it looked wonderful.

Aran had never stayed in a hotel in her life, and couldn't understand why Kevin Ross was apologising for it, explaining that the best hotels were reluctant to accept bookings for singers who would scandalise the other guests and reduce the furniture to matchwood.

'But Kevin, Ben would never do that! I know he can be a bit boisterous at times, but he's not the least bit aggressive, never mind violent.'

'Oh, I know, he's your pet lamb. But lots of rockers are snarling thugs – or want everyone to think they are, anyway. Look at the Sex Pistols, who say they're yobs and proud of it.'

Their lead singer Johnny Rotten had actually said that, looking for notice on television. But Aran laughed as she thought of his contrived contempt, his churning hatred for everything and everyone; Ben was a baby by comparison. The only passions he ever expressed were making music and making love.

They were taken to their room, which turned out to be perfectly comfortable, though hardly big enough to contain Ben's excitement. The live performance wasn't until tomorrow night, but a rehearsal was scheduled for this afternoon and he was peppering to get to it. Hugging her to him, he beamed.

'Kevin says nearly all the tickets are sold – mostly because the single got into the top thirty and Cedar managed to generate so much publicity. But this is the part I'm really looking forward to, Aran. Singing live for real people, getting them to sing with me, making sure they have a great time – a fantastic time!'

He kissed her so enthusiastically she was swept up into his excitement, dying to see all these people coming to enjoy him and enjoy themselves. Night after night he would have to sing the same songs, keep them fresh for each fresh audience, but she knew he could do it. He was born to do it.

Over lunch everyone got together, like a temporary family with a common purpose, working out how best to approach Oxford. Should they start with one of the five familiar old favourites that Ben was going to sing, or *White Web*, or something else? It amazed Aran that such decisions could be so last-minute, but everyone seemed to be used to it, to have nerves of steel. Then, should he talk between songs, or simply switch straight from one to the next? Ben said he wanted to talk a bit, allow just six or seven of his hundred and twenty minutes on stage for spontaneous remarks, comment on whatever might catch his fancy. So the timing was arranged around that. Then there were the costumes, of which he would sweat his way through several apparently, the props, the lights, the amps . . . by the time they left the hotel and headed for the rehearsal, Aran was speechless with apprehension. But she kept it to herself, and smiled until her lips were numb.

Sitting up in bed two days later, Aran opened the first of the newspapers that had been slipped under their hotel door in the early hours of the morning and flew through it until she found the review. Beside her Ben lay with his face buried in the pillow, the duvet comically pulled up over his ears as he waited for the worst. The concert had gone wonderfully, except that he had got an electric shock from one of the cables, forgotten the words of the song he was singing and had to start it again. Aran thought most of the audience realised what had happened and was sympathetic, but he wasn't convinced.

She began to read aloud.

' "Ben Halley is the most recently discovered star in the Cedar firmament and last night Oxford was the first city to see whether he shines as brightly on stage as he does on vinyl.

' "Halley doesn't shine. He coruscates. From the moment he appeared his command of his audience was as obvious as it was instinctive, his relationship established by something you don't often see live these days – a smile that seemed to welcome everyone right to the very back row. Daringly dressed in a black leotard that made other performers' jeans look very unimaginative by comparison, he gripped the microphone by the throat and belted straight into the first of fifteen numbers apparently written for the express purpose of showcasing the finest new voice of the decade. Saying that Halley can sing is like saying that Bjorn Borg can play tennis – but while Borg's personality leaves spectators lukewarm, Halley's leaves them red hot.

' "For the first time in years rock has found an exponent who actually seems to love what he does, does it with style, flair and a vivid grasp of what music is all about. Balleting up the stage and racketing down it, Halley generates both electricity and empathy; even when a technical disaster caused him to forget the words of his penultimate song he bounced right back and took every member of the audience with him. A completely natural and charismatic performer, gifted with a great voice, an athlete's body and looks that don't hurt, he is also an exceptionally fine pianist. Cedar claims that he composes all his own music but this critic suspects that he must be in mystic communion with all the greats from Wolfgang Amadeus Mozart to Jimi Hendrix. There's hardly a conventional chord in his entire

170

repertoire and if Oxford was looking for originality it certainly got it last night. Whether you're seventeen or seventy, you will be dazzled by Halley's comet as it shoots across Britain over the coming months." '

The paper was snatched out of her hand, and Ben turned to her in disbelief.

'You're making this up.'

Smiling hugely, she shook her head.

'I am not. Read it for yourself. You're an overnight sensation and I am so proud of you I can hardly . . . oh, Ben! Wait till your parents see this, they're bound to change their minds now. Wait till Dan and Eimear see it, Rani and Thanh and everyone – let's see what the others say.'

There were two other reviews, in two other national newspapers that had considered it worth their while to send critics to Oxford. Both were glowing, and so was Aran's face as she read them out. One even mentioned the lyrics of *Dislocation*: 'penned by a person caught between cultures, going forward but looking back . . . could become an anthem for Britain's immigrant population.'

Slowly they repeated the word 'anthem', looked at each other and burst out laughing.

'An anthem? An anthem?! Like they sing at soccer matches? This critic must be crazy! Who is Jeff Barber, anyway?'

Neither of them had ever heard of him before. But they would hear of him again, and discover that he wasn't crazy at all.

The tour was gruelling and not every city was as receptive as Oxford. In Birmingham the audience appeared happy and enthusiastic, but next day a local newspaper denounced Ben's 'vocal sorcery' as being somehow fraudulent, his appearance as a decoy and his innovative compositions as 'schizoid'. In Liverpool he was firmly dismissed as 'no threat to the Beatles', and in Manchester a group of drunken punk rockers caused havoc, heckling and throwing beer cans up on the stage. Horrified, Aran wondered what injuries might have been sustained if the cans were bottles, and although Ben laughed it off it made her realise how vulnerable he was.

By the time they reached Scotland, where a five-day break was scheduled, she was ready to fly him back to London for a complete rest. But he wouldn't go.

'Let's hire a motorbike and check out Glasgow!'

Kevin Ross promptly vetoed that idea: he wasn't having his star turn end up in hospital or on crutches. To her surprise, and Kevin's, Ben nodded obediently and said OK, then he and Aran would stay

171

quietly at their hotel while the rest of the crew dispersed about their various pursuits.

'Good. There's plenty to see and do in Edinburgh. Aran, make sure he behaves himself.'

Aran promised she would, whereupon Kevin returned to London and Ben went out an hour later to hire a massive motorbike. The more she berated him for it, the more he laughed.

'Come on, let's get this show on the road! Are you coming with me or not?'

Reluctantly she got on to it, but as they roared away to Glasgow she found his defiance infectious. Cedar didn't own them body and soul, couldn't dictate every single thing they did!

Glasgow turned out to be a tough gritty town with a mind of its own. Aran thought she might have been a bit anxious in it by herself, but with Ben beside her she enjoyed it immensely, going roller skating, to the cinema and to a swimming pool where a group of squealing teenagers recognised Ben.

'Aw, but he's got a girl with him,' said one, disappointed.

Ben grabbed Aran by the waist and grinned mischievously.

'This isn't a girl, this is my wife.'

It was only a joke, but she was ecstatic. Even when Kevin Ross returned in a rage, issued a denial of Ben's rumoured marriage to the press and lectured them for hours thereafter.

'You're supposed to be his bloody manager, Aran! My God, this is what comes of letting a woman loose on a man's errand!'

'I can't gag him, Kevin. He was only teasing.'

'Yeah, and look at the damage it's done his image!'

She had to concede that it was bad for Ben's image. But it was a great boost for her morale.

When they got back to London at the end of January a mountain of mail was waiting for them, including a cheque from Cedar addressed to Aran, as Ben's manager. It was for an incredible amount of money. Thoughtfully, she looked at it.

'You know, Ben, the lease on this flat expires in April. We could buy a house.'

'A house? Oh, come on, love. You know I'm not into mortgages and all that stuff.'

'We wouldn't need much of a mortgage, with this.'

He went to the piano and began to play it softly.

'You can do what you like with any money we make, Aran. I really don't mind what you want to buy. But I told you in the beginning I didn't want to get involved in anything that would – sort of tie us down. Why

172

can't we just renew the lease here, or rent somewhere else?'

He looked at her mildly, enquiringly, but she felt the resistance in him.

'Because . . . well, we don't want to be gypsies all our lives, do we, moving from place to place?'

'Why not? What's wrong with a change of scenery now and then? Look, if this flat isn't big or comfortable enough for you, we'll rent a bigger one. On a longer lease, maybe. You can go shopping for nice furniture and have a great old time. How's that?'

She saw that it would have to do. Next week the second single was due for recording, after which he was to start making a video to accompany the third, then work with Kelwin Hughes on more songs before embarking, on her twentieth birthday in April, on a European tour. It was the wrong time to put him under stress or cause friction. Swallowing her disappointment, she went through the rest of the mail while he played quietly on, caressing the piano as if delighted to see an old friend. Spotting an envelope from Ireland, she brightened.

'Dan and Eimear are complaining that they still haven't met you – they want to know will we go over and see them at Easter?'

He looked at her eager face and smiled.

'Sure, if you can get me a few days off. I'd love to meet them . . . I suppose I'll be meeting your parents as well?'

She thought about it.

'Yes. It's time, Ben. Besides, I want to give my father a present. But there – there isn't room for us at my parents' house. We'll stay with Dan and Eimear.'

'Good. Let's give them a present too – a big one, to thank them for my beautiful piano.'

'You could get an even better one now, if you want.'

'No. I'm attached to it. I'm going to keep it until I wear it out.'

He stroked it in a way that made her breath falter. So some things were permanent, after all. Things he loved and wanted to be part of him. Putting down the letters, she went to him and wrapped her arms around him, leaning her cheek against his as he played on.

'I love you, Ben.'

He smiled and turned to kiss her. But his fingers did not leave the keyboard until the piece was finished. Then he took her hand.

'You were fabulous on that tour, Aran. So steady, so supportive . . . always there when I needed you, never complaining about anything. You must be worn out.'

She was. She thought a long warm bath would be the most wonderful thing right now, followed by an early night in their own bed.

But he stood up, also thinking.

'Since there isn't a bite of food here, let me take you out tonight? Somewhere wonderful. I know – we'll call Thanh, Rani, Gavin – let's all get dressed up and celebrate that cheque! We'll go to the Elephant On The River.'

He was trying so hard to please her, she hadn't the heart to resist.

' "Flaky . . . flashy . . . overproduced and overrated." '

Myles Irving was reading aloud from a music magazine's opinion of the new single. Ben, Aran, Kevin Ross and Kelwin Hughes were listening in silence .

Myles glanced up over his glasses. 'Shall I go on?'

Dumbly, they nodded.

' "A great voice – for weddings, funerals and bar mitzvahs. Won't fill any football stadiums though." '

Everyone glanced at Ben, but he sat immobile, his face and hands unusually still. Myles picked up yet another magazine.

' "Pushy, prancing and extremely painful." '

Aran thought there couldn't be much more, but there was.

' "A ghastly blend of Stravinski and supermarket rock, perpetrated by someone who can't decide whether he's a ballerina or a bricklayer." '

She touched Ben's hand, feeling tears stinging her eyes. Myles opened a newspaper.

'And finally – "inflated, bombastic, unbearable. Cedar should know better. This guy sounds like he's having dental work without anaesthesia." '

Feebly, Kelwin attempted a smile.

'Ben Halley, nul points. Maybe my lyrics were wrong for you, Ben . . . guess it's back to the drawing board.'

Ben leaned his elbows on Myles's desk, put his head in his hands and closed his eyes. For an agonising moment Aran thought he was weeping. For someone who wore black leather, rode a motorbike and had a great sense of humour, he could be very sensitive, withered by such scorn if she let him. She reached over and touched his shoulder.

'It's only your second single, Ben. And the live reviews – of the tour I mean – were terrific.'

He straightened up, composing himself with an effort.

'I'm sorry, Myles. Guess I've still got a lot to learn.'

Myles pulled himself together in turn.

'Sure. You're still very young – if anyone's to blame it's me. Overproduced, huh? At my age, I should be shot for that.'

Ben pushed his hair back off his face and sighed.

'I'll understand if you want to tear up our contract.'

Aran gasped. Fortunately it wasn't up to Myles to do such a thing, but Ben should never make such a suggestion, in the heat of the moment! She had better get him out of here.

'Come on, let's go get a sandwich and figure out why they didn't like it. We've got to take the bad reviews as seriously as the good.'

She hoped Myles or Kevin wouldn't come with them, but they both stood up wearily.

'Yeah. Let's go to the pub and get blitzed.'

So this was how it started. This was why musicians, actors, writers and painters drank themselves senseless. Unlike people who worked in banks or schools or offices, they were subjected to constant criticism, expected to be on top form every day of the year and to satisfy tastes that changed without rhyme or reason, please people they didn't even know. If the rewards were exceptional, so were the risks. Taking Ben's arm she began to lead him to the door. But suddenly he turned back, seized the pile of publications on the desk and held them at arm's length.

'Anyone got a match?'

Before she could intervene Kelwin produced a match and touched it to them. Solemnly, they stood in a circle and watched the pages burn until Ben dropped them into Myles's bin, clutched at Aran and began to laugh hysterically. Within seconds the tension dissipated and they were all laughing speechlessly, senselessly.

Much later that night, after at least six or eight whiskies, Ben thumped out a very drunken version of *Jailhouse Rock* on the piano while Aran sat on the floor sobbing. Kelwin lay snoring beside her, Myles was crashed in the kitchen and Kevin was being violently sick, for the second time, in the bathroom.

It was a complete mystery to them all when, a fortnight later, the reviled and detested single entered the charts at number nineteen; an even greater mystery when it rose the following week to number twelve. Myles was as much at a loss as anyone else to explain it, but he decided to gamble on it, spurred on by the sackful of fan mail that a secretary had had to be exclusively assigned to answer. It was time Ben made an album.

Deva was delighted.

'We should have had your voice trained after all. I admit it and I'm very sorry about it, Ben.'

He grinned at his mother.

'Well, if you had, maybe I'd still be struggling to become an opera singer.'

'Yes. I know that's what you really wanted. But I can detect little bits of opera in this music – it all sounded very noisy at first I must admit, but now my ear is attuned to it I can make out the idea. At least I think I can – was I dreaming, or was that a snatch from *Madame Butterfly* in that last song? Did I really hear it?'

'Yes. You did.'

Deva sat back in her armchair, looking very comfortable and matronly in the pink blouse and tweed skirt she had worn to work that day. Pink, she told Aran, was a colour that small children found comforting. But of course male paediatricians could hardly wear it.

'I remember the story of Madame Butterfly . . . didn't she marry an American sailor who left her when she bore his child?'

'That's right. She considered the marriage binding but he didn't.'

Deva sighed. 'Such a beautiful aria. *One Fine Day*. It always makes me cry.'

Aran glanced at Ben and saw him fight back the temptation to ask Deva why, if she found such music moving, she hadn't permitted him to make a career of it. But Ben was very fond of his mother and never recriminated. God, if his fans knew of this secret passion for opera! Yet, although the allusions were subtle, they were always there. Either the fans didn't get them, or they liked them. Liked them a lot.

Getting up, Deva wheeled the tea trolley over to Aran, invited her to another cup of tea and a cheese biscuit. But then she turned to Ben.

'So, darling, when are you going to marry Aran?'

Aran almost choked. Ben threw back his head and laughed.

'Oh, whenever the promotions people decide I should!'

Deva frowned at him.

'Ben, be serious. Aran has been a wonderful help to you and you've been living with her for quite a while now. I'd like to see things put on a – a more – on a proper footing.'

'Why? What's wrong with them the way they are?'

'Oh, Ben! All this bohemian behaviour is very frivolous, and becoming rather irritating. You're a grown man now, and Aran is a respectable young woman. I'm sure her parents don't think much of your attitude – do they, dear?'

Aran felt herself blushing as she lowered her eyes.

'I – well – I suppose my father would agree with you, Mrs Halley.'

Deva looked at her keenly.

'And your mother?'

'My mother . . . isn't . . . doesn't . . .'

She couldn't think what to say. My mother has a problem with black, brown and yellow people, Mrs Halley? She's dreading meeting

176

your son the darkie, who is going to shame her in front of all Dunrathway next month? If it weren't for the vast sums of money he's making he wouldn't be let inside her door at all?

A Rover car drew up in the driveway and she was saved from having to reply as Guy Halley got out of it, came into the hall and then into the lounge where they were sitting.

'Ah. Ben. How are you. Good evening, Miss – ah – Miss – um?'

He put down his Gladstone bag and headed for the drinks cupboard, but Deva's arm restrained him.

'Guy, dear, I think it's time you grasped your future daughter-in-law's name once and for all. It's Aran Campion and you may call her Aran.'

Guy went brick red. 'Daughter-in-law? What? When did all this happen?'

'Well, it hasn't yet. But I hope it will soon.'

Deva's smile swivelled sweetly from Guy to Ben and then to her.

'It must be wonderful to be earning so much money so young, Aran. When I was your age I was just a penniless student. I'm sure Ben knows it's all thanks to you. He's so disorganised he'd never survive without you – and all the money would be gone in a flash, on parties or heaven knows what else.'

Her gaze swept like an X-ray through her husband and son. Looking mutinous, neither of them answered her, but Aran caught her eye and was amazed when Deva winked at her, explicitly and complicitly.

Easter fell in the second week of April, just before the European tour which, Myles said, was in the nature of a reconnaissance trip. Even though the British tour had gone well, this one would stick with the same relatively small type of venue, none able to take more than two thousand people. Aran thought that was a vast number, but Myles assured her it wasn't. Kevin Ross had suggested letting Ben travel as a support to other, bigger acts, to get him used to bigger audiences, but after debate they'd decided against it, Ben wasn't the kind of performer who'd ever make a support to anyone.

'He hasn't got the right temperament, Aran. He's much better off having small audiences to himself than sharing huge ones. But what I want this time is a really top group of backing musicians – I'll talk to Kevin about it.'

Kevin agreed and was very vocal about the visual aspect of this tour as well. Ben was naturally dramatic on stage so – expense or no expense – he wanted a dramatic wardrobe designed for him. It was extravagant and it would have to be done in a hurry, but finally it was agreed. And something else was agreed too, after Ben and Aran got a nasty fright one day as they walked down the street after a visit to the Mitchells. Out of nowhere, five or six youths came up to Ben and surrounded him in a very menacing way, demanding to know why he was mucking rock music about, pushing and prodding at him until he became incensed and a fight threatened to develop. A passing policeman put an end to it, but Aran was unnerved to find that people were now starting to recognise Ben and feel free, apparently, to accost him. When Kevin heard, he made his mind up without debate.

'We're going to have to get you a minder.'

He was very surprised when Aran said she knew just the person.

'You know a heavy? A gorilla? Well, forgive me for laughing, but I wouldn't have thought you mixed much in the underworld!'

Ben was laughing too, but she persisted.

'His name is Thanh Dith – or Dith Thanh as he puts it. He doesn't look heavy at all, but he has a black belt in karate.'

Kevin agreed to meet Thanh and, after witnessing a demonstration of his expertise in the martial arts, made him an immediate offer. Without consulting Beth, Thanh accepted it.

'This great, Aran! Now I sub-let my stall like you sub-let yours and we all go to Europe together! I not let anyone near Ben, he safe with me!'

Ben thought the whole thing hilarious, but Aran was delighted. Delighted with Sinéad Kenny too, who now ran her stall at Camden Market for her. There had been some grumblings in Dunrathway about having to deal with a new person, but Sinéad had got the hang of it quickly and was, Aran thought, very tolerant of Molly's suspicious attitude. Anyway, when she went home at Easter she would smooth down what ruffled feathers still fluttered.

Before then, there was the question of finding a new abode. The lease in Holland Park was not available for renewal and so, while Ben was making his video, she set off househunting alone. Rents, she discovered, were rising rapidly in London.

'Economy's turning,' predicted the estate agent. 'Election coming soon I shouldn't wonder. High time too. Tories had better get their game together.'

Aran didn't know very much about the Tories, but if they were all like Guy Halley then she was most definitely going to vote Labour. Guy, a staunch Tory, predicted that Britain's recent 'winter of discontent' was about to put an end to the career of 'that nitwit' prime minister, James Callaghan.

It struck Aran that political careers were not unlike musical careers. One slip and you were gone. Anyone in either field with half a brain in their heads would be well advised not to get too fond of the

178

fame, money or influence that went with the territory. Myles Irving and several other people had advised her to see an investments expert about the money she and Ben were earning, but after a meeting with the one at their own bank she came away suspicious. He had advised her to invest in certain publicly-quoted companies whose stock did seem to be doing well; but when she checked them out she found that two of the three he recommended were owned by the same bank. Since Ben didn't want her to buy a house, which she thought the best way of all of investing the money, she did something so horribly sensible she had to smile at it herself: she put it in a post office savings scheme. The post office! That would certainly stun the fans, who probably thought he was living a wild life of fast cars and fast women. But at the moment he was too busy for any kind of spending spree, locked into studios from one end of every day to the other. If he wanted to have some fun when they got to Europe, she had budgeted so that he could.

After viewing several houses she saw one she liked, in an area she liked. Hampstead was hilly and airy, with a convivial atmosphere she thought Ben would take to, yet it had a villagey feel to it, was small enough that you might stand some chance of getting to know your neighbours. It was expensive, too; the thought that they could afford it made her slightly dizzy.

But the house was irresistible – and Ben had agreed that they could rent a whole house, by way of making up for not buying one. Built in 1830, it was a two-storey terraced house, painted creamy yellow with a blue front door, one of a row of similar houses all washed in lovely pale pastels. Inside were two deceptively large reception rooms, two big bedrooms and a smaller one and – the deciding factor – a big bright kitchen overlooking a square garden filled with pink tulips, two blossoming apple trees and a flagged patio. For a city dwelling it was very quiet, yet the estate agent assured her that nobody was likely to object to a piano being played; Hampstead was the kind of area where people did play them.

But it was an important decision and so, saying she must sleep on it, she left the man and went for a walk round the neighbourhood. Within minutes she found a bookshop she liked, a café where she lingered over a cappuccino, soaking in the friendly atmosphere, and then a house where the poet Keats had lived – not only lived, but allegedly written his 'Ode To A Nightingale' under the mulberry tree in the garden. Further on were houses once occupied by the writer John Galsworthy and the painter Constable, and then there was Hampstead Heath, with wonderful views and many Londoners out walking their dogs. Thinking of the money she had wasted last year on a sports club neither she nor Ben had ever had time to use, she surveyed the Heath optimistically; they could get air and exercise here whenever they had even half an hour to spare. After the European tour, they might even get a dog.

That night, she told Ben all about it.

'Hampstead? Bit out of the way, isn't it?'

'But Ben, it's beautiful! Just like Chelsea or Kensington, only the traffic isn't rushing everywhere . . . oh, Ben, do come and see it, please!'

'Is it big enough for the piano?'

'Yes! That was the first thing I thought of.'

He smiled. The day's work on the video had gone very well, he had discovered that he liked film studios much better than recording studios, had a bit of an actor in him. Quite a bit the director had said, actually.

'OK. Then let's take it.'

That was typical Ben. Once he was convinced of something in principle, he didn't want to be bothered with the minor details. Aran thought he would quite happily live in a shed or a tree house, on a river barge or in a high-rise apartment, so long as it had space for the piano and to entertain friends.

'Still . . . we've been so happy here, Ben. I'll be sorry to leave Holland Park.'

'Oh, for heaven's sake . . . didn't you say you wanted a house instead of a flat? I don't understand why women always get so attached to where they live.'

She didn't labour the point, letting her mind fill instead with visions of the new house as it would look when she filled it with flowers and soft furnishings, photographs and bric-à-brac . . . maybe even a few oil paintings? Surely his visual sense would make him take an interest in those. But first she had better organise a removals van, get the bare essentials over to Hampstead before they left for their short visit to Ireland and the European tour to follow. The real fun of settling in would have to wait until after they came back, at the end of the summer.

Settling in, on a five-year lease this time! Much as she was looking forward to going to Europe, she was looking forward to coming back even a tiny bit more.

Chapter Eight

She might have known it. Ireland was swathed in a thick fog as the plane began its descent into Cork, great wet heavy chunks of it streaming past the windows so that she was unable to show Ben anything of the beautiful coastline. But still she felt a thrill, the excitement of returning home for the first time in three years. Returning home with Ben, too, whose exotic clothes and looks caused quite a stir as they emerged into the arrivals hall, scanning it for Dan and Eimear.

But Eimear came running up to them alone.

'There you are! Oh, Aran . . .!' Without another word Eimear pulled Aran into her and stood hugging her, almost rocking her like a child, Ben thought, as he surveyed them bemused.

Eventually Aran disengaged herself and beamed at the dark, pretty woman whose white blouse and long pleated skirt made her look like a street urchin by comparison. A very fetching urchin, but a very muddled one.

'Eimear, this is Ben . . . Ben, Eimear Rafter.'

To their joint surprise Ben threw his arms around Eimear and kissed her dramatically.

'The lady of the piano! The wonderful woman I can never thank enough!'

Flushing, Eimear let herself be kissed profusely, struggling to apologise for Dan's absence.

'He was called out to an emergency in Baltimore – you'll meet him later – oh, I can't believe you're home at last, Aran. I've invited your whole family for dinner tonight. Since you're staying with us, I thought that was the best thing?'

Aran thought so too. Amongst eight of them Conor's shyness might not stand out so painfully, and Molly might find it difficult to be snippy. Whatever her reservations about Ben, she could hardly air them in front of him. But who, she wondered, could really resist Ben for long? With pride she noticed the way he took charge of the luggage and loaded it into Eimear's car, not letting either woman lift a finger, the way he offered to drive if Eimear was tired from the outward journey? Eimear said she was fine, but it was a thoughtful gesture.

The hour's journey to Dunrathway flew by as they caught up on all the gossip, and although he hadn't a clue what they were talking about Ben didn't interrupt or attempt to upstage Aran. Her face was glowing with happy vitality.

'What about the cheeses, Eimear? How's Annie McGowan?'

'Annie is supplying four shops in England now, thanks to you. She wants you to come and see her.'

'I will. I want to see everyone, show Ben everything. Starting with the baby dolphins!'

Eimear's mouth tightened a fraction.

'Those poor dolphins . . . d'you know people are talking about them as if they were circus animals, saying what a great tourist attraction they're going to be this summer?'

'Well – they might be, if people just want to go out and see them in a boat maybe. I mean, nobody would want to hurt them, would they?'

'No, I suppose not. But I'd hate to see them turned into some kind of star turn, harrassed in any way. Now that the new crafts shop is open and people have cottoned onto the idea of tourism it's like a kind of gold rush – your own brother Achill reckons he's going to make his fortune, amongst others.'

'Achill?'

'Yes. The bank turned him down for a loan for a guest house, so now he's come up with a new plan. He's going to open a funfair instead.'

'A *what*?'

'A funfair. Dodgem cars, shooting galleries, roller coaster . . . he went to a second bank and they approved a loan for that. He's also got involved with some electronics company, assured them that he can persuade every publican in Dunrathway to install a juke box and a big video screen.'

'Oh, Eimear! Oh, no.'

Ben was laughing. 'Great. Make sure he gets a copy of my new video, Aran. My records too.'

He was sitting in the back, and she whirled round to him.

'I will not! I don't want pubs in Dunrathway to be like the ones in London! The whole point of this village is its peace and quiet, Ben. It's the wrong *place* for rockers and bikers and noise!'

182

'I'd better go home, then, had I?'

'Oh – sorry I didn't mean it that way. *You* know what I mean, Eimear, don't you?'

'Yes. I'm intrigued by your music, Ben, and like some of it very much. But I don't want it imposed on me in public places, every hour of every day – not just yours, but anyone's. My idea of a pub is a comfortable place with a coal fire where people go to talk and socialise, not to have their ears blasted off by rock around the clock. If there's a demand for that, let Achill open a nightclub or discotheque. A mile outside the village, for preference.'

'Exactly. Pubs are for occasional live music at most – people playing tin whistles, banjos, traditional instruments. Ben, you tell Achill that when you meet him.'

'But he'll surely expect me to be in favour.'

'Well, make it clear you're not. Will you?'

He sighed.

'All right. I'll try, if that's what you want. But I don't want to get into an argument with your brother the moment I meet him. He sounds quite enterprising.'

Aran had to concede that he did. But juke boxes, dodgems, in Dunrathway?

'Look at it, Ben!'

He looked, and saw a small village nestling between a long white beach and soft, rolling green hills. Small white houses clustered together around a church spire and a harbour filled with fishing boats, bobbing serenely on calm grey water, the whole vista faintly draped with wisps of mist.

He had to admit that it was not exactly Las Vegas. If the residents wanted to turn it into Las Vegas, or Blackpool or some such tinseltown . . . well, Aran had often said herself that they couldn't live on fishing alone. But he was an outsider, it wasn't for him to judge or even comment. But the place was very pretty, and it might be a pity.

Aran and Eimear were still prattling on as they turned into the driveway of a bungalow on a hill, heatedly expounding their own concept of tourism which seemed to involve art galleries, good restaurants, fishing, diving, sailing and horse riding, painting classes maybe and tennis courts. If Achill went for a quick buck, they agreed, he would destroy the place.

So this was Ireland. One hour in it and you were caught up in a family feud already? Ben decided he would neither encourage nor discourage Achill Campion. Achill. What a weird name.

Aran glanced at Eimear as he unloaded the luggage and took it into the house which, she noted with pleasure, had hardly changed at all.

'Where – er – where should he put it, Eimear?'

Eimear grinned mischievously, but decided not to tease.

'In your room – it's the one at the end of the corridor on the right, Ben.'

Phew. Ben departed with a private smile of relief. He'd heard that the Irish could be odd about things like this. Single rooms for single people. It was a practice his own mother had given up . . . but something told him Eimear was not the prudish sort to begin with.

Aran hugged Sammy as he rushed up to greet her, barking and licking, wagging his tail as if it were a welcome-home banner.

'Hey, there's my boy! Do you remember me, Sammy?'

Eimear smiled at him.

'He seems to, but I can't imagine how. You've changed, Aran.'

'Have I?'

Her fair hair was short and curly, two long earrings accentuating her fine face as they brushed the shoulders of a rose-coloured velvet dress over which she wore an embroidered waistcoat. Because of the oboe her wrists and fingers were devoid of jewellery, but around her neck hung a musical motif, a little silver clef, and on her eyelids was a soft sweep of amethyst eyeshadow.

'Well, put it this way – I don't know that Philip Miller would hire you now! You look kind of – ethnic. Arty.'

Her mother, Aran thought, would make that sound like a crime. Arty-farty was Molly's favourite term for François Maurier, the Frenchman who farmed the oysters and was responsible for introducing such dubious items as aubergines and green peppers into Dunrathway, as if potatoes and cabbage were not good enough for it. Nowadays, Eimear said, you could get such items without having to make the two-hour round trip into Cork city.

'What do you think of Ben, Eimear?'

'I think he looks extremely handsome, has very nice manners and has a lovely speaking voice. But I'll have to wait until I get to know him before I can say any more than that. Does he always dress like a cross between Lord Byron and the Incredible Hulk?'

'Oh – yes, I suppose he does! I hardly even notice any more.'

Aran's smile was more than merely smitten, Eimear saw; it was the smile of a young woman in love. Very much in love. And Ben's smile, as he reappeared and put his arm around her, said the same thing. Together, they looked made for each other, radiating tender affection as they exchanged a little kiss.

'Can I tempt anyone to a glass of wine before Dan comes home?'

They both nodded, and Ben hastened to take the corkscrew from her.

'Please. Let me.'

'Well, such old-fashioned courtesy! I thought rock singers were supposed to swig wine by the neck!'

Ben grinned as he pulled the cork. 'At night, Mrs Rafter, I grow fangs and turn into a vampire. That right, Aran?'

Aran giggled, and it struck Eimear suddenly what was so different about her – not just her appearance, or the slightly shortened vowels which now modified her accent – but her mood. Aran Campion was happy. Positively, vividly happy.

'Please, Ben, call me Eimear. And tell me all about this video you're making. I did tell you how much Dan and I loved the tape you sent us, didn't I? You deserve to do well, with a voice like yours.'

'Well, thanks. But I wouldn't have got very far, or nearly so fast, without Aran. She got me heard on the radio, she went into all the nitty gritty of my contract with Cedar, she found us a new house when the lease on our flat ran out. She's even found me a bodyguard!'

Eimear nearly dropped her glass. 'A what?'

Aran's grey eyes were large and rather concerned as she explained. 'I know it sounds ridiculous, Eimear, but Ben needs a minder. People sometimes come up to him on the street and a few have been a bit aggressive. Not everyone likes his music or – or maybe the fact that he's Indian. Anyway I had this friend at the market – Thanh, you remember? He's a black belt and he's coming to Europe with us on tour.'

'Dear God. A black belt. I hope he won't be called upon to demonstrate how he got that.'

'So do we. But it's a precaution we need to take. Anyway Thanh is great fun, he'll keep me amused while Ben is rehearsing. Some of the tour is going to be recorded for an album – his producer thinks live performance is his greatest strength.'

Suddenly she remembered that the Rafters didn't have a piano. Lord. Ben would go mad without one, for five whole days. Unless . . . the rackety old one down in O'Brien's pub, maybe? If it was still there, it would be better than nothing.

Dan came in at last, and lit up at the sight of her.

'Aran! Don't you look marvellous! It's great to have you home, my pet.'

He scooped her into a tight hug, all smiles as he stood back to admire her and turn, with a blink, to Ben.

'Ben Halley, I presume?'

'Yes, sir. How do you do.'

They shook hands cordially as Aran and Eimear exchanged glances, stifling their laughter. Ben's thick glossy hair, navy velvet

185

jacket and maroon trousers made quite a contrast with Dan's old flecked sweater, grey corduroys and sadly thinning hair. But then Dan had been out on some farm all day, not had a chance to change or freshen up. Besides he was thirty-eight, while Ben was only twenty-two.

Aran saw from his expression that he was taken slightly aback by Ben's polite greeting, and dignified tone, the ease with which he was slipping into a new social situation. Probably Dan expected to be slapped on the back and addressed as 'mate' by a semi-thug who would shovel peas off his knife and get through a crate of beer before the evening was over. People were always slightly wary of Ben before they met him, and perplexed when they did.

Eimear began taking pots and pans off the racks on which they hung.

'I'm going to start dinner. A nice traditional roast, Aran, for your parents and brothers.'

Molly, Conor, Achill and Dursey. Would they be the same people she had left, or what would she find? The boys would certainly have changed, after all this time; Achill was eighteen now and Dursey fifteen. Nothing, she thought, would change Conor very much, he would merge with the furniture and leave the others to do the talking. In a sudden flash of insight she understood why he had insisted on calling his children such strange names – it was the only chance he had ever had to express his love of his family and of the sea, two things that blended and knitted together in his mind. The only chance he had ever had to take a stand on anything, say anything of which people might take note.

And Molly? Aran hoped her mother would be in better form nowadays, with the little cottage industry going so well, providing an income and a purpose. In her bag she had a cheque for her mother, enough for a small car or a holiday. Enough, perhaps, to make her smile?

After an hour in which Dan played several cherished items from his record collection for Ben while she chatted with Eimear in the kitchen, she saw the four members of her family walking up the hill in the falling twilight. How tall the boys had grown! But Conor looked more shrunken than ever, while Molly was tightly wrapped in the same black coat she always wore – but she couldn't be wearing it still, surely?

Yes. It was the very same one. For a moment Aran felt a little shiver, wondering whether everyone would fall into each other's arms talking all at once, or there might be an awkward silence. But nobody could be awkward in the Rafters' house. Dan leapt up to usher

186

them in while Eimear threw an extra log on the fire and left Aran to go out to them, putting her hand on Ben's arm in case he should feel obliged to dash precipitately into the breach.

It was Conor who fell first on Aran, embracing her with tears in his eyes.

'Child. Child.'

She fought back her own tears as she clasped him to her, smelling the strong soap with which he had diligently scrubbed away all trace of fish. For several moments nobody said anything, transfixed as if in a half-finished painting. But then Achill and Dursey pushed their way in behind him, ostentatiously wiping their shoes on the mat as Molly nudged them to do. Their good shoes, Eimear noticed, shined up like mirrors; everyone seemed to be dressed as if for church. But the boys' booming voices filled the hall and broke the silence.

'Hey, Aran! Jaze, you've changed!'

She smiled and kissed their round open faces, weathered by the elements to the colour and texture of terracotta. And then Molly; her dry wrinkled cheek felt like a crumpled ball of tissue paper. Holding her handbag in front of her, Molly surveyed her daughter from head to toe.

'Well, and isn't our little girl the young London lady!'

With resolve, Aran decided to take it as a compliment.

'Come on in, Mother – everyone, give me your coats and Dan will bring you in to the fire, it's lovely and warm.'

Conor wasn't wearing an overcoat, had never possessed one that she could remember, maybe because he was so inured to the weather. But the boys flung their anoraks off while Molly, with great deliberation, removed her headscarf. Like the Queen at Sandringham, she wore it everywhere she went. But when she removed her coat surely, she would be wearing something new and pretty?

No. A black twill skirt was unveiled, with a black cardigan buttoned up to the neck. If she had thought to compliment her hostess by wearing the silk blouse Eimear had once given her, there was no evidence of it.

Hospitably, Dan ushered them into the sitting room where Ben was waiting with the same expression he wore when confronting a new audience, a mixture of apprehension and determination that broke, instantly, into an endearing smile.

'Mother, Dad, boys – this is Ben. Ben, this is my mother and father, my brothers Achill and Dursey.'

Like a rocket at Hallowe'en he rushed forward, seizing their hands, encompassing them all in his vigorous charm.

187

'Hello – hello – how do you do, sir – Mrs Campion! May I call you Molly?'

Before Molly could bestow permission he had clasped her in both hands by the shoulders and was kissing her on either cheek. Open-mouthed, Aran watched her mother quiver like a small bird in a storm, touch her hand to her face as if to make sure it was still there.

'So this is Ben.'

At speed, Eimear thrust a glass of sherry into Molly's hand.

'Yes – isn't it marvellous he's found time to visit us at last? Aran tells me he has a very demanding schedule, even his own poor mother practically has to make an appointment these days!'

Conor gazed at Ben in wonder while the boys struggled to suppress obvious amusement. To their eyes, Ben looked as if he had stepped down off a cinema screen.

It wasn't until dinner was served, and some very tortuous preliminaries had been got through, that the atmosphere began to thaw. Realising the lucky chance that had fallen into his path, Achill grinned at Ben across the table.

'Dunrathway's a dull old place, Ben, but I'm going to liven it up. Juke boxes and video screens in all the pubs. Like they have in England. What d'you think?'

He crammed a forkful of potatoes into his mouth and chewed on them while Ben considered his options, aware of Aran's gaze as he did so.

'Well, it sounds like a good idea. How many pubs are there?'

'Five.'

'Then maybe you could do it in one. The one your own friends drink in.'

'Huh? But sure why stop at one? They're all dead as doornails. Five of them would be five times the craic. Five times the money, too. I've got an agency from a company in Dublin that makes the hardware.'

'But Aran tells me that people aren't so keen on piped music in Irish pubs as they are in Britain? She says there are some terrific live sessions, though.'

'Oh, yeah, well – that's mostly oul fellas playing spoons and tin whistles. Ancient history – eh, Mrs Rafter?'

Achill grinned cheekily at his former history teacher. But Eimear had long since got the measure of Achill Campion.

'We can learn a lot from history, Achill, as you'll appreciate when you're older. My husband and I don't hang round the pubs as much as your age group, but I'm afraid there'd be even less chance of us going into any that had juke boxes or videos in them. Sorry. Two customers lost already.'

Achill reddened, more in anger than embarrassment Aran thought.

'But what about the young people? What is there for them? Sure half of them are gone to London already – my own sister included.'

Aran considered while Conor kept his eyes fixed on his plate, Dursey gulped milk and Molly turned her knife over to check, surreptitiously, whether it might be silver.

'Well, London has a lot to recommend it, Achill. Only it's a big city, while this is a small village. People go there for one thing, they come here – or stay here – for another. A lot of the people who've gone to London will come home, if only for holidays, and they'll be delighted to find that it still *is* home. Still the place, the people, the customs they know and love.'

'And what about the rest of us, the ones who don't flit off but stay all year round? Are we to be pickled in aspic, framed in our flannel shirts as if Dunrathway were a time capsule? It's 1979 here like it is in the rest of the world, Aran. We want to move on the same as everybody else.'

'Well . . . yes, of course. But why don't you listen to some of Ben's music, Achill? He's trying to combine the best of the old with the best of the new. I'm sure the same thing could be done in Dunrathway.'

'Ah, we're sick of the old.'

'But anything that's endured for years must have strength and character! Old houses, old songs, old stories – people would throw them out if they weren't worth anything. Whereas everything that's new isn't automatically wonderful – new cars, for instance, lots of them are designed to fall to pieces after five or six years.'

Aggrieved, Achill sighed.

'I must say you're a great help. Here I am trying to get a bit of business going so I can earn a living, and you're all against me. Maybe I'll just go to London myself and take my chances there.'

Eimear looked alarmed, so did Conor and Molly. But Aran wasn't perturbed.

'If you want to come over you can stay with us, we'll help you all we can. But London's very competitive, Achill, full of immigrants. The streets aren't paved with gold like in the song – in fact they're paved with people sleeping rough on them. I think you'd get much further here if you'd just think your plans out a little more. Tourists come in all age groups. You've got to offer something to everyone.'

Surprisingly he was silent for a few moments.

'Well, maybe you've got a point there. I'll start with the juke boxes and the funfair – did I tell you about that? Then later I'll think about stuff for older people.'

'But Achill, older people won't come here if the place is noisy and tacky. Why not try something else for your own age group – tennis courts, canoeing, hill climbing, scuba diving? There are lots of natural amenities.'

'Well . . . you amaze me, Aran. I'd have thought you'd love to see juke boxes playing your boyfriend's own music. Think of the royalties.'

But Ben looked at Aran, and thought of something else.

'Tell you what, Achill. Why don't you and I go out for a few beers tomorrow night? If there's a pub that has a piano I'll play and sing a few songs, see what people think of live music. If they hate it, Aran won't say any more against the juke boxes. But if they like it, maybe you'll reconsider selling them. In this village, at least.'

'Is that a bet? That you could pack a pub for a whole night, without any amps or anything?'

'Yes. It is. I'll bet you a hundred pounds.'

'You're on.'

Eimear smiled as she served dessert. Clearly Achill had never heard Ben sing. But he was right about Ben standing to make royalties from juke boxes . . . yet Ben was prepared to lose them here, if he could please Aran in the process? Thoughtfully, she studied him closely, and was impressed with what she saw.

Only Molly Campion was not impressed, eating her meal in studious silence, addressing not one syllable to the young man with the big mouth and the ridiculous clothes.

Next morning Aran took Ben for a long walk round the whole village, stopping every few yards to exclaim over something she remembered, something new or some small detail that had changed. Every shop and every street corner seemed to yield one or other of the women from the knitting group, all of them dying to chat about Camden Market and Sinéad Kenny – a grand girl, they said, a grand girl. Wondering what 'grand' meant exactly, struggling to understand their richly unintelligible accents, Ben began to think the tour would never end. Even though he was wearing an ordinary sweater and denim jeans today, he was aware of being sized up, stored up as fodder for conversation once he was out of sight. But finally they reached the harbour, where Aran became very animated.

'There's a man called Jim Flaherty I want to find. It won't take a moment, Ben, honestly.'

It took ages, but at last Jim Flaherty was located under the hull of a boat he was painting on the quayside and engaged in lengthy discussion. It seemed that Aran wanted to buy her father a boat. Jim took off his woollen cap and scratched his head.

'For shark fishing? Ten or twelve passengers? With equipment? Well now . . . I don't know about that . . .'

But it turned out that he did know. Knew a man called Sullivan who knew a man called Corcoran, who maybe knew a boat that might be . . . there were an awful lot of mights and maybes, but he said he would see what he could do. No promises, mind.

Ben thought this very odd. In London, people would sell you something quick as they'd look at you. Here, you had to spend an hour persuading one person to talk to another, leave everything dangling until you heard – maybe – from them again. But Aran was grinning as if she'd already got the boat.

'Now, let's go and have lunch with Mother. I never got to give her her present last night.'

Last night Molly had been so frosty that Ben thought, today, he'd sooner have lunch with the Ayatollah Khomeini who, according to the Rafters' radio, was throwing his weight round Iran. A grim piece of work.

Molly opened her front door three inches.

'Oh. It's you. You'd better come in.'

In they went, into a tiny house reeking of fish. But Aran exclaimed over it.

'You've painted, and got new curtains! Oh, it looks much brighter!'

If this was brighter, Ben shuddered to think what it must have been before. But it was Aran's home, not his to criticise. Rummaging in her bag, she took out an envelope.

'Mother – Ben and I just wanted you to have this.'

Molly took the envelope and opened it gingerly, drawing out the cheque it contained as if it were a live grenade.

'Well. Isn't that nice.'

Aran's face was very eager.

'We thought you might like to get a little car, or have a holiday. You and Dad.'

'A car? But sure where would we be going?'

'Oh, I don't know! Into Cork maybe, to see Val? Or you could take a few weeks in the sun, go to Spain or Portugal in the summer.'

After a pause, Molly allowed that she might visit her sister, who lived in Mayo, for a few days. But of course Achill and Dursey would turn the place into a pigsty if she went away. A pigsty, that she'd have to clean up when she came back.

Ben neither wanted nor expected thanks for himself, but Aran's crestfallen expression was painful to behold. Pointedly he took her hand and held it.

'You have a wonderful daughter, Molly.'

He was determined to call her Molly, even though he expected her to say 'call me Mrs Campion' at any minute. Thank heaven they weren't staying here, with her!

Molly gazed at Aran.

'Ah, yes – I have three daughters, you know. But the other two are married, of course.'

Was that what this was all about? That he and Aran were not married? But they were happy, any fool could see that!

Suddenly Ben didn't want lunch. He wanted a double Scotch in the nearest pub.

He didn't drink Scotch. But now he knew why people did.

O'Brien's pub was full and the atmosphere, while lively, was indifferent to Ben Halley. Nobody had heard of him on any of the Irish radio stations and virtually nobody listened to the English ones. Everybody knew, of course, that Aran Campion was home from London with an odd-looking boyfriend, staying with the Rafters instead of her own family, but then Aran had always been a bit funny, never really one of the crowd. When Ben sat down at the piano, conversation carried right on.

The piano was upright, ancient and decrepit, its keys yellow with age and the cigarette smoke of thirty years. Aran thought that expecting Ben to play it was like expecting Martina Navratilova to play table tennis, asking Mark Spitz if he'd mind swimming a few lengths of the bath. But when Ben touched it, the effect was like the tip of a feather sweeping over her skin, sensitising every nerve in her body. Very quietly, he began to play Leonard Cohen's song, *Suzanne*.

A few people near him glanced round, lowering their voices a fraction. Most went on talking, some even more loudly, in competition, right through the first verse. But gradually the din quietened, gradually his clear voice became audible as conversations died away, until the whole room was hushed, people craning their heads to see where the song was coming from. Without looking at them, keeping his eyes down and making no attempt to command attention, he played on as if for himself alone. Without lighting nobody could really see him clearly in the thronged, dimmed room; without a microphone he was entirely dependent on the carrying quality of his voice.

At a corner table Aran sat with Conor and Dursey, watching Achill up at the bar with his friends. For as long as they could they went on talking and laughing, resolutely indifferent; but it was a long song and by the end of it they were getting hostile looks, being asked to shush so people could hear. When *Suzanne* finished there was no applause, but there was a very puzzled silence.

192

Where had it come from, who had played it so hauntingly? Not everyone liked or even knew of Leonard Cohen, but trying to ignore the atmosphere was like trying to ignore a ghost that had materialised in the midst of the throng, so unexpected a phenomenon that nobody knew what to say or do. Casually, Ben looked at the people nearest to him and apologised.

'Sorry. Didn't mean to interrupt.'

'Oh, but you didn't! That was lovely! Do you know another one?'

He waited until at least six people had asked for another before starting the one Aran had advised, the one everybody would know, *Hey Jude*. How he managed to coax its tricky notes out of the old piano she didn't know, but he did, nodding when people began to join in, humming diffidently at first and then confidently, smiling when he began to smile at them, encouraging their participation. By the time he was halfway through the song everyone was singing, pints forgotten on the tables as his voice soared up to the higher notes effortlessly, gliding as if on thermals of air.

This time there was thunderous applause. Someone sent Ben a pint, someone asked if he knew *Strawberry Fields Forever*, several people asked him who he was. Even Conor looked animated, while Dursey was laughing outright.

'Achill's going to lose his hundred quid!'

Achill knew that too, judging by the look on his face, but it was more thoughtful than resentful as he raised his glass and gazed at Ben speculatively.

People were clamouring for another song, in a way they would never clamour for more piped music, but Ben was demurring, insisting that he'd only wanted to try out the old piano, had no desire to disrupt their evening.

'Oh, give us a blast of Elvis!'

One of Achill's friends was calling out to him, a young fisherman of nineteen or twenty, slightly drunk and slightly belligerent. Sizing him up at a glance, Ben hurled himself into *Jailhouse Rock*, standing up at the piano the better to assail it, electrifying the entire room with the sudden change of key. Such was the force of his performance glasses began to shake on the tables, the decibel level deafening, the spectacle incredible as his lithe body ignited with energy.

The entire pub was rocking, riveted, awestruck.

'Jaysus, where did they get this guy? Is he going to be here every night? Why doesn't Liam O'Brien get him a decent piano? He should turn professional.'

Aran smiled as Ben suddenly slammed the lid down on the piano, his point made, and gulped his pint amidst protests. He wasn't going

193

to hog the whole night, he asserted, surely there must be others who
wanted to play or sing? Making his way over to Aran's table he sat
beside her and waited for Achill to join them.

Achill took his time, but finally came over.

'Well, bang goes my hundred pounds. Haven't got it on me right
now, Ben, but I'll get it before you leave.'

Ben threw his hair out of his face and turned to him.

'If you'll forget the hardware, I'll forget the money.'

To his credit, Achill needed no time to think about it.

'You were right. Live music does have more potential. If we could
find a few more singers like you, people would come for miles to hear
them.'

Aran didn't think there could be anyone like Ben. But it would be
interesting to find out.

'Why don't you see if you can come up with some, Achill? If you
could get people who'd bring business to the pub, Liam O'Brien
might put you on some kind of commission. Who knows? If any of the
pubs in the village ever comes up for sale, you could try the bank for
a loan again, open your own pub with live music, run talent
contests . . . it's an idea, anyway.'

Achill looked into his pint, and looked at the energised crowd
around them.

'Yeah. It is an idea.'

Ben had no idea why Aran suddenly seemed to want to get rid of him,
but she wasn't giving him much choice: he was to go off with Dan for
the day, see a bit of scenery and leave her alone with Eimear.
Reluctantly, Ben went.

As soon as he was gone, Aran made a pot of coffee and sat down at
the kitchen table.

'Eimear, what am I going to do about my mother? Why is she
acting this way?'

'You mean, why isn't she more pleased to see you, or meet Ben?'

'Yes. I know why she's not keen on him, I suppose, but she could
make a bit of an effort to get to know him. You like him, don't you?'

Eimear smiled.

'Yes. Dan and I think he's very charming and very gifted. You're
mad about him, aren't you?'

Aran's grey eyes were wide and frank.

'Yes. You might think it's just puppy love, Eimear, but it isn't. I
know we're young, but I feel that we're growing together, balance
each other. I'd do anything for him and I – I think he'd do anything
for me.'

'You think?'

'Yes – Eimear, is it really ridiculous to want to get married, in this day and age? Ben's work involves so much travel, meeting so many people . . . for some reason I feel we need something fixed in our life, something stable. A proper home of our own, a – a commitment, even a family some day. But his sister says he's not the marrying type, that I should be more interested in managing him than marrying him. I am enjoying learning about music management, delighted I got my business diploma – but I just don't feel it's the be-all and end-all of everything.'

'Well . . . I love teaching, as you know, but I love Dan even more. My marriage is very important to me. But it's a question of temperament, Aran. Some people are more suited to it than others. If you feel you are, but Ben isn't, you could have a problem on your hands. Why don't you just leave well enough alone for the moment? After all you've got lots of time, and people change a lot in their twenties.'

'I know. That's what everyone says. Put your career first and have a family later. But I – I'd love to have a family soon, Eimear.'

'Would you? Why, Aran?'

'I – oh, it's so hard to explain why! I know it's not logical. It's just some kind of instinct, some biological need . . . I never felt it at all until I started looking after Oliver Mitchell. He was just so adorable, and then when his sister was born she was even more beautiful. Even now, I'm always sneaking back to see them.'

'But people don't simply have babies, Aran. They have children who grow up very fast, turn into teenagers and then into adults. Babies are very sweet, but you can't flash-freeze them. They're cuddly bundles one day, confused adolescents the next. A major responsibility. Do you really think you're mature enough to take that on?'

'Well, I feel – I feel I have the energy now. Holly Mitchell was always so tired, but I never was. Ben was great with her children too, I'm sure he'd be even better with his own.'

Eimear swirled her coffee in her cup, thinking about Ben.

'Aran, Ben's very young too. His music is what matters to him at the moment. I don't think you should put pressure on him.'

'No. I haven't said anything to him. But he – Eimear, do you think musicians are unstable by nature? There are so many girls out there, so many distractions . . .'

'Aran, you're insecure and if you don't get a grip on it you always will be, because those girls, those distractions will always exist. You're going to have to learn to trust Ben – which, since you ask my opinion, means *not* getting married and not having children for several years yet. You're little more than a child yourself – a rather mixed-up one at the moment. I think London and Ben have all been a bit too much for you, too soon.'

'But I love London and I *love* Ben.'

'Then just relax and enjoy them both.'

Aran was silent, tugging at her earring, thinking that nobody really seemed to understand.

'What about Mother, then? Is it me or is it her?'

'No. You're right about that! Molly has worked so hard all her life, for so little reward, it's affected the way she sees things. Her three daughters have so much more than she ever had, she might be a tiny bit jealous. Or threatened.'

'But she's always been so – so grim. So negative.'

'She grew up in a grim, negative era. She didn't have the education or the freedom that might have broadened her mind a bit. She knows you and Val and Sher are all going much further than she ever did and that she can't control you any more. Her main role was always as a mother, and now it's nearly over.'

'But we all try to help her, give her things—'

'Yes. The kind of things she could never give you. That might make her feel dependent, as if things are the wrong way round.'

Aran considered that.

'I gave her some money yesterday, and she's been making enough from the sweaters to buy a few nice things if she wanted to. But she doesn't seem to want to.'

'Aran, her income was always uncertain before. It still is, really, because she doesn't know how long the sweaters will be popular or what might happen with Conor and the fishing. She's probably saving instead of spending.'

'Mm. Maybe. She has done the house up a bit, at least.'

'Well, if that's all she wants, just let her be. She could be menopausal too, at her age. A bit depressed.'

It hadn't occurred to Aran that her mother was in her mid-forties now . . . but she was. Facing the – what did the magazines call it? The empty nest syndrome? Yet when she, Aran, had visited the 'nest' yesterday, she had felt distinctly unwelcome. It had never been a warm, happy house, never sunny or smiling like Eimear's. This was exactly the kind of house she wanted herself – not just a house, but a proper home. The only thing missing in it was children . . . see, children did matter, whatever the career feminists said. Eimear really should have some, she would make a much more cheerful mother than Molly.

196

'How's your mother, Eimear?'

'Fine, thanks. She often asks how you're getting on.'

'Does she? Did you tell her about Ben?'

'Oh, yes. She wanted to meet him, but she's gone to Majorca with her bridge club for Easter.'

Now, why couldn't Molly do that? Play bridge and go to Majorca? Because then she'd have nothing to complain about any more, no right to sympathy? Suddenly Aran had a vision of her mother in Spain, dancing to flamenco music with a gigolo, and giggled. No. Molly would never dream of letting any sun or fun into her life.

But Conor might. His burden could be eased, if the new craft shop and Annie McGowan's cheeses and music in the pubs started drawing tourists, if Achill thought more about sports facilities, if a demand grew for shark fishing and pleasure cruises.

Had Jim Flaherty got the boat yet? She decided to go and find out.

'Eimear, will you come down to the harbour with me? Jim Flaherty said he might have some word today about the boat for Dad.'

The air was fresh and tangy as they set off together, much fresher than the air to which Aran had become accustomed in London. If only this village shook itself a bit, she thought, it could be such a nice place to live. At the moment it was a little like Molly, hostile to change, entrenched in its ways, dependent on hand-outs and faintly sorry for itself. Small and hunched around the harbour, it did not exude confidence or bonhomie . . . yet the eighties were coming, with a feeling of economic optimism. That was the mood in London anyway, if only it could somehow filter through to Dunrathway. Wouldn't a wine bar make a difference here, and a good restaurant! Five pubs in one village hardly showed evidence of much imagination. Five identical pubs whose common idea of lunch was a sliced-pan sandwich and soup straight from the packet.

As they walked they met several acquaintances, and as they talked Aran suddenly noticed how much more vivacious the women were than the men. Not invariably, but in general – Shelagh Carney who ran the knitting group's financial affairs, Bláithin ni Murchú who was Annie McGowan's enthusiastic new assistant, Aoife Bailey who couldn't stop talking about Ben's beautiful voice. When they ran into Paddy Clafferty, on the other hand, he simply wished them a good day and passed on, as did the lordly Joey Devlin. Even though the Camden Market enterprise had brought some prosperity to the place, Aran felt from their glance that they still regarded her as a little chit of a thing, if they thought of her at all.

However, Jim Flaherty had thought of her, and found out more about the boat.

'Forty-foot, clinker-built, over in Schull . . . a bit on the big side maybe, but sound as a bell. She'd need fitting out of course. Owner is looking for twelve hundred for her, probably get him down to eleven.'

'Could we go over to Schull this evening, when Dad comes back from work?'

'Well . . . aye . . . maybe we could. Got a car?'

Eagerly Aran turned to Eimear. 'You wouldn't lend us yours, Eimear, would you? Ben has a driving licence.'

'And it's time you had one, because I'll bet Ben isn't insured to drive my car. But I'll drive you over myself.'

Aran felt there was no end to the favours she owed Eimear, her blushes salvaged only by the thought of the present she and Ben had chosen for the Rafters and would give them before leaving: a piece of antique Chinese porcelain found by Walter Mitchell. Signed by the artist, it was exquisitely delicate.

She could hardly contain herself until evening arrived and Conor's trawler came into the harbour, heaving on a heavy swell. Conor was up on deck, braced against the wind as he winched ropes and unloaded crates, doing the strenuous work which, she knew, became much more difficult for men in their fifties, potentially crippling for men in their sixties. She had found this alternative at just the right moment, and his face was a study of joy when she told him about it. Leaving Ben to take a hot bath after his mystifying day on a farm, and Dan to cook dinner for him, she bundled Conor into Eimear's car with Jim Flaherty and they set off for Schull, a picturesque half-hour's drive away. Conor hardly uttered a word all the way there, but she sensed his rare excitement as Jim described the boat. Not that many people would want to go shark fishing, in his opinion, but if by any miracle they did then this was just the vessel in which to do it.

The boat was bobbing in the small harbour, painted white with its name, the Lady Gráinne, painted in blue on the prow. Moving with more speed than Aran had ever seen in him, Conor was out of the car and standing awed on the quayside by the time the owner emerged from the galley where he had been waiting for them. A laconic man in a dark green sweater and oil-stained trousers, he didn't seem in any great hurry to sell his boat.

'The wife says she wants a new car, but haven't we a perfectly good one already,' he indicated a 1971 station wagon with its fender hanging off. 'Can't get her out on the water at all. Nothing like it though. Nothing like it in the world.'

His name was Cathal Erskine and he was an amateur sailor, who owned the Lady Gráinne purely for amusement. Now that his sons were grown up, he wasn't getting much use out of the boat, which was too large for solo outings. He was fond of it, though, maybe when his grandchildren were a bit bigger—

'Brass fittings,' said Conor in wonder, eyeing them lustfully. But with Jim he took a long time to inspect the hull, the deck, the engine and the helm, the practical things that mattered much more. Casually Cathal produced the log book which testified to the boat's sound history, and said he knew a man who might be able to install shark fishing equipment. Only then did it dawn on Aran that equipping the Lady Gráinne was going to involve major work and expense – but, looking at her father's face, she made up her mind to do it for him.

After lengthy debate and negotiation, which seemed to involve everything from the long-range weather forecast to the price of eggs, Cathal agreed to take eleven hundred pounds for the boat as they saw it, all fixtures and tackle included. Rigging it out properly, Jim estimated, would require another six hundred.

Conor sank down despondently on the bollard to which it was moored.

'It's too much, child. I can't let you do it.'

Feeling like Santa Claus on Christmas Day, Aran took out her chequebook.

'Will you accept a sterling cheque, Mr Erskine?'

Mr Erskine supposed that he would. Ten minutes later they were all sitting round drinks in the pub, sealing the deal with a toast as was customary, and Conor was clutching his owner's papers to his chest with tears in his eyes.

'I'm going to rename her the Lady Aran,' he ventured, whereupon everyone gasped. It was bad luck to rename a boat.

But with rare obstinacy Conor stood his ground.

'Aran has brought me great good luck. I want everyone to know what a fine daughter I have. Here's health to the Lady Aran.'

He raised his glass and drank to her with such love and pride that she was unable to speak, her throat constricted by the simple happiness she had brought to his lined, weatherbeaten face. All the way back to Dunrathway, he held the papers tightly in both hands on his lap, the owner of a boat at last.

The last day of Aran's visit home was very busy. Val came to see her, sailing into the Rafters' house like an ocean-going liner; six months into her first pregnancy, she was enormous. For a full hour she poured out every detail of the pregnancy from blood pressure to Mr Patterson, her gynaecologist, the best man in Cork and such a charmer – no, not a doctor, but a mister! That was what you called them when they were very senior. Would Aran be a dear and get her some things from Mothercare in London? Would Aran do the decent thing and get married herself, give them all a day out? Val spoke as if Ben were invisible, had nothing to do with any mooted wedding at all, not even noticing when he left the women to gossip and went outside to kick a ball to Sammy. After five days, Aran knew he had had enough, was itching to get back to London, his friends and his piano.

Then Annie McGowan arrived with a huge basket of cheeses, so beautifully wrapped and presented that Aran saw the small, rotund woman had a natural eye for business. Annie now supplied ten shops in all, four of them in Britain, and couldn't thank Aran enough for her help.

'Oh, it was fun. Let me know if there's anything else I can do for you.'

'Indeed I will not. You got me started and the rest of it is up to me. Too many people in this village are willing to take too much help for too long. Of course the government encourages . . .'

The government encouraged everything but entrepreneurial spirit, Annie asserted at length – Lord, the paperwork a body had to fill in to keep them happy up in Dublin! The rules and regulations, the taxes, the busybody inspectors, the hours you'd be on the phone trying to get hold of anybody who knew anything about anything, you spent your whole day filling in forms and then had to stay up all night doing what you should have been doing in the first place. The minister should be shot, the bureaucrats should be hanged, the entire Cabinet should be horsewhipped within an inch of its life – Aran had never met anyone in her life who talked at such a rate as Annie or held such hilariously trenchant views. Of course people criticised the government in Britain too, but they didn't propose, as Annie was proposing, that all politicians should be sterilised immediately upon election so that the species couldn't propagate.

'Little men,' Annie snorted, 'tiny little men with tiny little minds. It's far from big jobs and big cars they were reared.'

With her puffy ankles propped up on a footstool Val agreed that her husband, the newsagent, had just such tiresome problems himself, whereupon Eimear concurred that Dan had too. But at least the self-employed didn't have huge chunks of tax stopped from their salaries at source, without even being able to argue their case! Laughing, Aran drank it all in, aware that she would have a lot of paperwork to do herself when Ben's European tour was over. Many British singers had left the country altogether, defeated by the government's avaricious pursuit of almost every penny they earned. Ben was a long way from being a tax exile, but it was a shame to see so much talent leaving its native country.

This was *her* native country. Right now she was enjoying it, talking and laughing with Annie and her sister here in Eimear's cosy kitchen, watching the wind whip the waves far down in the harbour below, the haze of fine sand blowing up into the bright green hills around it. After her long absence she was more conscious of things she had taken for granted before, the physical beauty of the Irish coastline, the lovely lilting accents, the humour and spontaneity of a closely-knitted community. Sometimes she felt such a stranger in Britain, so shut out . . . yet here, she had felt shut in. Yeats was wrong when he said Ireland was 'no country for old men' – it was no country for young women.

At least it hadn't been when she left it three years ago. Now she sensed it might be changing . . . or was she? Was this just a brief bout of the nostalgia all emigrants experienced when they returned home?

Home. Perhaps some day in the distant future Ireland would be home again, some day young people would choose to stay here because it was a confident, dynamic place to live. Taxes would be low, unemployment would be low, people would want to stay and be able to. If ever a music industry got under way Ben might even be persuaded to spend summers here, long golden summers out on Conor's boat with the children they would have by then.

But for now, home was in Hampstead and, although leaving her family and friends would not be easy tonight, she was looking forward to returning. Returning with Ben, who made all the difference.

'Yellow and blue, or blue and yellow?'

Ben surveyed the paint chart Aran held out to him and exploded with impatience.

'Who cares! We're going on tour next week, we'll be away three months so who the hell *cares*!'

They were completely at loggerheads. In one week Aran was trying to get the decor of the entire house under way so it would be comfortable and pleasant to come home to, studying colour schemes, draping fabric samples, arranging furniture and consulting with everyone from painters to carpet suppliers. In the middle of the chaos Ben sat at his piano, trying to compose a new song and psych himself up for the tour. He couldn't just *go*, he said; he had to get into the right frame of mind.

The right frame of mind seemed to be a very nervy one, a mixture of elation and tension that was making him unusually difficult to live with. At any other time he would have laughed off the domestic muddle, hardly even noticed the clutter of tea chests and things waiting to be unpacked, but now he went crazy when he couldn't find his manuscript paper, swore when the phone failed to arrive on the day it was promised, devoured the unlucky electrician who had to drill a wall in the room where he was trying to work. Aran knew he was wound up – knew that he had to wind himself up – but still she thought he might take some interest in her efforts. Was it really too much to say which colours he preferred?

'Ben, I know we're going on tour, but that's exactly why I'm trying to do all this before we leave!'

'Why can't it wait till we come back?'

She couldn't logically say why. All she knew was that she wanted everything decided and in place, a nice environment in which to eat and work and sleep, pictures on the walls, sets of glass and china in the cupboards, fresh linen on the bed, curtains on the windows, cutlery in the drawers, food in the freezer. She didn't want to return to an empty shell of a house in July, she wanted to come *home*. That was all she was trying to do, make a nice home for them both. Why was he being so unhelpful, so disagreeable? Unexpectedly, tears trembled in her eyes.

'All right. I'll decide the colours, I'll do everything myself. Just don't blame me if you hate it later on.'

He saw the quivering lip, and sighed as he stretched his arms out to her. He hadn't meant to upset her.

'Sorry. I'm a horrible brute and you can send me to bed without any supper if you like . . . come on, don't cry! It's only a tin of paint.'

'It's not only a tin of paint. It's our home and you're not a bit interested in it.'

She was right. He really wasn't. But he couldn't stand to see her face crumple, the desolate way she stood looking at him, the hurt in her voice.

'Yellow. Yellow with blue stripes, blue geraniums and matching blue spaniels. How's that?'

Her chin wavered tragically.

'You're making fun of me.'

'Oh, God – what do you want me to do, Aran? Lie down on the floor and weep? Kelwin Hughes will be here in an hour, I've got to have this piece finished by then!'

Bristling, she withdrew from his arms.

'Oh, finish it then! Make love to your bloody piano all night for all I care! Make love to bloody Kelwin!'

Rushing out of the room she raced up the stairs, into their bedroom and slammed the door. Oh, he was hateful!

Lying on the bed, sobbing loudly, she waited for him to repent and come up to her. He always did, on the rare occasions they had any little tiffs, apologising so•theatrically that she had to laugh and apologise in turn. He was irresistible when he clowned around, thrust a flower under her nose or clasped his hands piteously to his heart, grinning at his own performance.

But this time she waited in vain. Only the sound of the piano came up to her, and then Kelwin's voice from the hall. Ripping her oboe out of its case she began to play it at full volume, loud violent bits of everything she could think of. She was a musician too, she counted as much as he did!

But the piano was louder, and it drowned her out.

Chapter Nine

Little Belgium. That was what people had called it apparently, during the war. Poor besieged little Belgium. Leaning over the rail of the ship Aran looked at it, but all she could see yet was a grey blob on the horizon. Grey like the whole world, on this her miserable twentieth birthday. Ben couldn't have forgotten it, because he never forgot birthdays, so he must be ignoring it.

A hand touched her shoulder, and she turned round to find Kevin Ross. Once again Kevin was their tour manager, apologising for the ferry this time; when Ben was a bigger name they would travel everywhere by plane, separately from the crew and the equipment. But at least she would see a lot of Europe from the coach as they drove through it, and it was a very comfortable coach. Some day this tour would be a wonderful memory he said, so she should try to enjoy it.

She wanted to enjoy it. But how could she, when Ben still wasn't speaking to her? Glumly she nodded at Kevin, and he smiled in return.

'Still feeling sorry for ourselves, are we?'

'Kevin, it's my birthday and he's a bastard.'

He leaned on the rail beside her, looking concerned and rather queasy; he wasn't a very good sailor.

'Look, Aran. This is going to be a long tour. The last thing I need is friction on the very first day. People have no option but to pull together, get along as best they can. You're Ben's manager and you should know he needs your support. Whether you like it or not, I want you to patch things up with him.'

'How can I, when he won't speak to me?'

'Aran, he has a lot on his mind. Tomorrow night he has to sing in front of two thousand complete strangers, get them on his side and keep them on it. He doesn't even speak their language, can't talk to

204

them the way he talks to audiences in England, doesn't know what to expect. You mightn't think he's scared, but he is. Performing live is like lion-taming – you can be savaged if you're not in control, if you show any fear at all. His mood *has* to be positive tomorrow, or a negative vibe will spread right across Europe when the reviews appear. The tour will be ruined and, frankly, I'll hold you responsible.'

'But Kevin, he's down there in the lounge with the whole crew. You surely can't expect me to kiss and make up in front of thirty people!'

'If I send him up here to you, will you give it your best shot?'

She ran her hand through her hair, watching Ostend take shape like a developing photograph.

'I will if he will.'

Satisfied, Kevin patted her hand.

'Thanks. I know it's a personal matter, but this is a professional venture, very important for us all.'

He staggered away, groping cautiously for the hand rail even though the sea was calm; years of touring had exacerbated his hypochondria instead of curing it, and everyone had teased him when, ten minutes out of Dover, he had started swallowing Kwells. But he was a decent chap, very patient and very popular.

A few minutes later, Ben appeared, his hands plunged into the pockets of a silk windcheater, his skin saffron in the harsh noon light.

'Aran? Kevin says you're feeling seasick – are you all right?'

She wasn't seasick in the least, but suddenly she grasped Kevin's strategy. It was a way to reconcile without anyone losing face.

'Yes, I'm all right, but I need to stay up here in the fresh air. We're nearly there – look, you can see Ostend.'

He looked at it, soberly.

'Ostend. Then Ghent, Brussels, Lille, Douai . . . forty towns and cities in sixty days.'

She put her hand into his pocket and edged closer to him.

'Don't worry, Ben. You'll wow them all.'

He smiled at last.

'I will you know . . . if you help me. I'm sorry I've been so cranky.'

She laid her face against his shoulder and leaned into him.

'So am I. I want this to be a great summer, Ben, and for us to have a great time. Let's not fight any more.'

Hampstead seemed very far away now, and the house; Ostend was much nearer. Then Ghent, as he said, Lille and Douai and all the other towns she'd never even heard of before . . . really it was so romantic and exciting, like going on honeymoon! With thirty other people, admittedly, but in early July they would be leaving them, staying on somewhere sunny by themselves after the tour finished.

Anyone who wanted to return to England with the coach could do so, but several of the musicians and roadies were talking about holidays in Spain, Italy or Greece. Thanh had already decided on Rome and Beth was flying out to join him there. But she wanted to go somewhere remote, somewhere they could be totally alone.

'Aran?'

'Yes?'

'Happy birthday.'

He took her into his arms and kissed her, letting the last of his hostility fall away, relaxing his body into hers. In silence they clung together, savouring several minutes of perfect peace, watching their dreams materialise on the approaching skyline.

In Brussels, the music press spoke excellent English.

'What is your music saying to us, Mr Halley?'

'You draw heavily on the past, Mr Halley – does this mean you reject the present?'

'What do your contemporaries think of you?'

'Are these costumes really necessary? Why did you wear a mask in Bruges?'

'Are you a trained gymnast or dancer?'

'Are you married, have you a family?'

Jessica Hunter had done up a press release in several languages, but they weren't interested in it; they wanted to meet Ben for themselves, gauge how much of his exuberant stage personality was real. Belgium wasn't used to people who pirouetted on top of pianos, painted their faces like Egyptian kings, threw rose petals into the audience and combined the raunchiness of Mick Jagger with the innocence of Judy Garland, all in one astoundingly articulate body. Everybody had a theory about Ben – he was Brel, he was Piaf, he was Johann Sebastian Bach – but nobody really knew what to make of him.

In a black T-shirt, black trousers and red braces, Ben was giving his first press conference and finding it hard going.

'I'm not a trained anything. I'm just not able to stand still.'

'Have you a choreographer?'

'No.'

'Do you think Mozart would approve of being worked into your music?'

'Unfortunately, I'm not in a position to ask him.'

'Clearly you are also a fan of the late Maria Callas?'

'Yes. I wish I'd met her.'

'Who does your make-up?'

206

'My manager.'

He said it without thinking, and all eyes turned on Aran. Painting Ben's face like an Egyptian boy-king's had been her idea last night, just a fun notion inspired by the vivid colours she had seen in a cosmetics boutique. The mask in Bruges was something Thanh had picked up when they were browsing, more mundanely, for postcards. But Ben had loved both ideas and so had the audiences.

'You are a very young manager, Miss – ah? – Campion.'

'Yes, but I have a business diploma and am a musician myself.'

She wished Ben hadn't dragged her into it.

'Where did you meet Mr Halley?'

'In a flea market in London.'

'Is the relationship purely professional?'

It was an older journalist who asked the question she realised they were all dying to ask.

'Very professional, I hope – the entire crew is very professional.'

The moment passed, but she saw she was going to have to be on guard against that in future. Her private affairs were no more anyone's business than Ben's were.

'You also write some of Mr Halley's lyrics?'

'Yes. So does Kelwin Hughes.'

Jessica Hunter stood up. 'Ladies and gentlemen, thank you for your interest. It's been a pleasure. Now, we have to get to Lille I'm afraid, so if you don't mind . . .'

When they had dispersed, she summoned a waiter and Aran was dismayed to hear Ben order a vodka. It was only eleven in the morning . . . but the experience had been an ordeal she supposed, putting him under unexpected pressure. Jessica hadn't anticipated such extensive interest, scheduling individual interviews but not this fullblown conference.

Still, what fun, what a positive response! And Ben looked happier now that they were gone, laughing and joking, calling her over to his side so he could kiss her, tease her about her 'professional' interest in him. He was full of affection, full of excitement too, as Kevin imparted the encouraging news that the concert in Lille was booked out. *White Web* had sold extremely well in France, and she sensed his enthusiasm infecting everyone as he began to sing snatches of the *Marseillaise*, mimicking a French accent until they were all pleated with laughter.

'And zis is my manager, *mesdames et messieurs*, 'er name is Aran, she is purely professional, I do not love her, not one leetle bit, ah non . . .'

Jessica turned to her as he squeezed her to him, covering her in exaggerated kisses. Jessica wasn't noted for her sense of humour, and was wary of Aran.

'What you said was perfect – about your relationship being professional I mean. We don't want anyone thinking Ben is unavailable, that he has a common-law wife.'

Both Ben and Aran looked at her, horrified for entirely different reasons.

In Paris Ben bounded on stage as an Apache, wearing warpaint, feathers and not a lot else. Down in front of the stage, Thanh and a security man had to restrain several teenaged girls who tried to climb up to him, screeching deliriously. Watching from the wings, Kevin Ross found their cries music to his ears.

Not only were these extraordinary disguises giving the fans great visual mileage, they were enabling Ben to reinforce his point about mixing different eras and cultures, adding a different dimension to the show every night. Assembling the props and accessories had become a fun challenge for the entire crew, who had taken to bringing back a hat, a piece of lace or leather or fake jewellery every time they went shopping. Over the years Kevin had seen many singers, musicians and crews grow gradually more weary as a tour progressed, finding the repetition increasingly monotonous until their boredom was palpable and very counterproductive. But he couldn't imagine Ben ever shambling on in the same clothes the fans were wearing, ever looking as if he were there to mow the lawn or fix the plumbing. His voice was good enough that he could afford to do that, but it wasn't good enough for *him*.

He wanted his audience fully engaged on every level, wanted them to go away not only entertained but intrigued, speculative or even shocked. The range of leotards designed in London was only a base; with imagination they could be transformed into almost anything – and Ben's imagination was prolific. Now, each show had its own colour, its own theme and style. Each city felt it could expect something unique. After only seven shows Ben had already got through twenty-four leotards and twenty pairs of the soft ballet shoes he favoured and, although he was barefoot tonight, Kevin made a note about replenishing supplies. The cost of this tour was going to be higher than anticipated, but extremely well invested.

Last, but not least, the costumes both protected and revealed Ben. In them he was able to keep his own self as private as he wanted, while putting forward whatever aspect of it he chose to highlight, get into whatever mood took his fancy. Aran was enjoying doing the make-up too, and Kevin smiled as he watched her, watching Ben.

The two didn't know it, but this was a phase of their lives they would remember forever. As Ben rose higher in the spectrum of stars many things would distract and entangle them, knotting their lives into a web of administration, technology, accounts, investments, all that went with big business. Ben would become a business in himself, Aran would have to run it, and it would be a heavy burden to them both. But that had yet to happen. Tonight, they were young lovers in Paris, everything was fresh to them, free of complication.

Would their relationship endure, when that changed? Would they make the transition from minor to major, cope with the stress, the travel, the money that destroyed as many people as it enhanced? Kevin's own marriage had long since foundered on the rocks of constant travel, late nights and the eternal demands of the business. Half the crew were separated or divorced, two of the three musicians were embroiled in lawsuits filed by disconsolate ladies in London.

Aran was a strong person, professionally. She had a good brain and was learning rapidly. But Kevin didn't think she was nearly so strong on a personal level. While many women today clamoured for independence, professed it the most important thing in their lives, she was the kind who needed a great deal of love and security. Ben the singer was vitally important to her, but Ben the man was crucial. Sooner or later she was going to want a home, a baby, a wedding ring at the very same point, probably, at which Ben was going to be surrounded by hordes of gorgeous groupies who would be ecstatically grateful to spend just one glorious night with him.

Ben was very keen on Aran. Very. All the little gestures were there, the looks and touches, hugs and smiles, unspoken things that said everything. Her presence was the force that enabled him to express such a range of emotion in his music, everything from tenderness to passion, curiosity to omniscience, innocence to innuendo. Technically, he was a perfectionist, but he never chased melodies to the bitter end, never hammered anything into submission. He knew the importance of space and spontaneity – only those were the very things, ironically, that might one day rebound on Aran. Did she realise how much she had taken on? At twenty, it was unlikely. Tonight, her kite was flying high, and she probably thought it would fly high forever. But kites didn't do that; they swooped and swirled, soared skywards and then crashed to earth. Manipulating them took skill, patience and expertise.

Should he tell her that? Should he warn her? Kevin supposed that he should. But not now. Not when her face was alight with joy and youth and love. Everybody needed this moment in life, this period of

209

perfect happiness. Even if it was very brief, it was the stuff of memories, the memories that got you through later, when the flame flickered and the lights were dimmed.

Ben lay on his back, wearing nothing but the remote look that said the curtain had come down, the show was over. Beside him Aran sat propped up on her pillows, writing in the diary she had started to keep. She thought she would remember everything of this time, this magical tour, but everyone said she wouldn't. In a year or two, when she read her notes, looked at the old photos and cuttings, she would be amazed. So she was keeping them all, delighted that Ben had given her a camera for her birthday. But photographs captured only fleeting looks, scenes and moments; in these pages she could capture thoughts, ideas, feelings. Busily she scribbled away, until Ben stirred and put his hand on her leg.

Something about his wrist, as it pushed away the crinkled cotton sheet, caught her eye. His skin was so brown, the sheet so white, but it was the angle of the wrist, the construction of it, that caught her attention as it always did. Something graceful, something vulnerable.

'Wasn't last night incredible?'

She didn't know whether he meant the show, the celebration that had followed it or the memorable sex that had followed that. But they had all been incredible.

'Unreal. I've been trying to find words to describe it, but I can't.'

'I feel – I feel I've got my act really together now. Totally tight.'

'So do I. I was just thinking how much more scope the costumes and make-up have given you. You've got all the elements of opera.'

'That's exactly it. I'm beginning to realise that rock music can be anything you make of it. You don't have to be hostile or dirty or hate the whole world to make an impact. There's room for a lot more than that. I was afraid it mightn't be enough for me, but it is – for now, anyway.'

'Yes . . . well, some other performers used clothes the way you're using them – Elvis did, for one – but I can't think of any who jumped right out of their skins the way you did last night! Not many with voices like yours either, who could be a pianist and an athlete and a comedian all at once.'

'Was I over the top?'

'Totally. So was the audience. So was Kevin. But the notes and phrasing were very natural . . . every song had substance.'

'D'you mind not writing all the lyrics, Aran? Do you feel you should be getting more say and more credit?'

'No. Not now. I have too many other things to do. Writing some songs, and this diary, is enough for the moment. But God, I love it when you sing my words! It makes me feel . . . I don't know, the same way I feel when we make love. Part of something bigger than myself.'

'It's not too much for you? Too tiring?'

'No! I don't know how I could have been in such a rotten mood when we left Hampstead. How many other girls get to see the world this way?'

His lips parted in a smile, exposing the uneven side tooth that made her feel so weirdly protective. Jessica Hunter was always going on about how he should get it fixed, but she thought Jessica had a nerve.

'Well, we have the whole morning to call our own – or what's left of it. What time do we leave for – where is it? – Orleans?'

'At three. We've got five hours.'

He sat up and pulled her to him.

'Well, it's not much, but let's see what we can of Paris! Do you want a long luxurious lunch, or a sandwich and sightseeing?'

'Sandwich and sightseeing.'

'Right. Let's get moving.'

That, she thought ruefully, was the only problem. They had to get moving nearly every day, on to the next town, before seeing the one they were in. But after all this was work, not a holiday, and as work went it was wonderful.

France was fantastic. Spain was sensational. Germany was strange. Berlin took Ben straight to its bosom, but in Munich there was some shifting, some suspicion in the audience. Next day, half the reviews said that Ben Halley was bastardising rock, while the other half said he was bastardising the classics.

Too elated by twenty triumphs to care about one disaster, Ben burst into song.

'Fuck 'em! Fuck 'em all, the long and the short and the tall . . . !'

Everyone laughed and joined in except Kevin, one of life's great natural worriers. He didn't want Ben getting too big for his boots. In Switzerland he worried even more, when a woman critic denounced him to his face.

'You are breaking all ze rules, Mr Halley! All ze rules!'

'Madam, they were made to be broken,' retorted Ben with some asperity, while Thanh hovered anxiously, wondering whether the woman was actually going to turn violent. She was extremely agitated. But then she stormed away.

Maybe it was just the weather. It was late May, and getting very hot. Of all the cities they had visited so far, Aran thought Barcelona

211

was her favourite, while Ben was still puzzling over Salzburg. Many houses had their windows thrown wide open, revealing the same sight over and over: large women industriously ironing great mountains of sheets.

'What is Austria – the world's official laundry?'

But Salzburg was Mozart's home town and he wouldn't leave it without attending a Mozart performance of some description. The only thing, on the one evening at their disposal, was an open-air concert in a park. A medley dominated by Austria's other two giants, Johann Strauss the Elder and Younger, it concluded with a frenetic rendition of *The Blue Danube*.

'Huh. Tourist stuff.'

'You are a tourist!'

Muttering, Ben decided that Covent Garden was much better at Mozart. Until he got to the Opera House in Vienna and was forced to change his mind.

'Now there's a theatre! There's an orchestra, there's a conductor!'

Kevin wondered what he would do with Ben when they reached Italy, the home of opera. He'd insist on going to La Scala in Milan – want to sing in it probably, given half a chance. He would look at his own small venues and become disenchanted.

But when they got there, to Kevin's surprise and Aran's as well, Ben quailed.

'Oh, no. Too much, too soon. I won't be ready for this for ten years.'

Aran knew he meant as a composer, that he would never get to sing in such a place. Kevin didn't know what he meant, but thought somebody should explain that modesty was a virtue. In private Ben was still a very nice guy, but in public he was starting to get out of control. As the tour gathered momentum it had become champagne all the way, parties, invitations and adulation. On Jessica's advice he accepted everything and went everywhere, his profile rising like a balloon, until soon, Kevin thought, Aran would be very hard pressed to keep him anchored to reality.

Sitting at a café in Venice, savouring the sun on her back, Aran appraised Ben as he sat talking to Thanh and Kevin. The others were lazy and languid in the heat, but Ben was upright at the table, with a taut look about him as if he were poised to pounce on somebody or something. With only Florence, Rome and Naples to go, the tour was nearing its end – and Ben, she thought, was nearing the end of his physical resources. Young and fit as he was, nobody could sustain the pace or the stress for very much longer, especially not in this arid heat. After seven weeks under the microscope of critical assessment, he was virtually unable to relax; both mind and body were sucked almost dry.

He gives so much, she thought, and they take so much! Not just the fans, but the crew, the critics, the press, the local promoters, the hundreds of people who have been involved along the way. He's like some kind of specimen dissected in a laboratory. He badly needs a break, away from them all. Needs to replenish himself physically, needs spiritual nutrition.

For herself, the tour had been a lavish banquet. For as long as she lived she would never forget the sights she had seen: the full moon rising last night on the canals and lagoon, the moon that had only been a thumbnail when it rose over the silver waters of lake Geneva. A silversmith's shop in Amsterdam, a sherry bodega in Granada, a lemon grove near Eze, the taste of cherry beer in Bruges and the perfume of lavender at Grasse . . . memories flitted into her mind like butterflies, multicoloured, ephemeral, exquisite. In every town she had stashed away some tiny souvenir, a glass bracelet Ben had bought her in Milan, a rose that had been on their restaurant table in Nice, a pencil box from Innsbruck, a menu that everyone had doodled with cartoons one giddy night in Seville. Here in Italy she was looking for a little treasure chest in which to store every reminder of this shining summer, perhaps one of the tooled wood or leather boxes Jessica said she would find at the Straw Market in Florence. Ben laughed at the way she squirreled small objects away, everything from an onyx egg to a gauze scarf, but nothing would ever part her, she thought, from her tokens and talismen. Long after the press cuttings had yellowed and the photographs had faded to sepia, she would have her miniature memorabilia to touch and hold, to evoke the tingling taste of these days.

But Ben . . . either Ben would have a holiday, now, or he would have health problems. Since April he had lost half a stone, sweating it off on one stage after another, all but collapsing after last night's performance for which he had worn a Venetian carnival costume. It looked magnificent, but the voluminous folds of violet fabric were incredibly heavy, swathing his entire body, exacerbated by a densely draped turban, tightly cinched silver belt and a black papier-mâché mask. Under the hot lights he had been virtually mummified, gasping for breath during the interval, soaked to the skin by the end.

Thanh was talking about his forthcoming holiday in Rome. Now was her chance.

'We've been thinking of going to Greece.'

Greece, like Ireland, Scandinavia and the Slav countries, had been excluded from the official itinerary for one reason or another. There

213

was no point, Kevin said, in trying to cram an entire continent into one tour, to grapple with small or dispersed populations or with political obstacles. Greece's problem was that such a large proportion of its potential audiences lived on islands – small islands with sea breezes, exactly what the proverbial doctor would order. Ben wasn't particularly enthusiastic about it, but she thought it sounded ideal. Idyllic.

Thanh registered the look on her face, saw that she was trying to recruit his support, get Ben interested.

'Greece – sunshine, beaches, tavernas! Acropolis and bouzouki music! Oh, you have wonderful holiday there.'

Aran smiled at him, and at Ben.

'Should I go ahead and book it? We could fly from Rome to Athens . . . oh, come on, Ben! Say yes.'

She was hard to resist when she looked the way she looked this morning, her eyes shining like opals, her hair gleaming in the white light.

'Well, I suppose . . . but it will be so odd, just the two of us, after so many! Couldn't we stay in Italy with Thanh and Beth?'

He had got used to being part of a group, dependent on the adrenalin. But Thanh saw that Aran very much wanted Ben to herself.

'No – I on holiday in Rome, with lovely English girl! You go away now, after tour finish. You go to Greece with Aran.'

Suddenly Ben slumped backwards in his chair, too tired to argue.

'Oh, all right. We'll go to Greece. But not to any of those tiny remote islands where nothing ever happens.'

Aran thought one of those islands would be perfect – somewhere like Kéa, Sífnos or Euboea, all of which she had been surreptitiously studying in a guide book. They certainly couldn't go to the mainland, in July, everyone said it was an inferno.

A compromise, then. A big island. With quiet unsuspected little nooks in it.

'How about Crete? Everyone says it's lovely and there's lots to do – swimming, sailing, lots of things.'

Ben's body seemed to go slack suddenly as he drained his beer.

'Oh, all right. If we can fly straight there – I don't think I can face much more travel. Will you organise it then, muffin?'

She liked this nickname by which he sometimes called her. She liked organising these things for him, too; it made her feel needed, useful, grown up. When they got to Crete, he'd be grateful she'd chosen somewhere for him to unwind properly, somewhere undemanding.

'I will. Did you know the Pan pipes were invented in Greece, Ben? They were the earliest kind of oboe. It's a very musical country.'

'Is that so?'

She'd discovered this information only yesterday, but thought it might lure him in there – not that he was going to sing another note this summer, if she could help it. Singers who overworked their voices tended to suffer from throat nodules, which were not only painful but recurrent. Putting pressure on his voice would be like putting pressure on a Ming vase.

Leaning forward, Kevin expressed much the same thought.

'You need a complete rest, Ben. I want you to have a quiet break and do whatever Aran tells you.'

To everyone's surprise, Ben glared at him.

'Kevin, Aran's not my mother and I am not a child.'

Quickly, casually, Aran turned her attention to the view, to the dome of St Mark's, the gondolas drifting by.

'No, of course not. I'm going to swim and sunbathe and Ben can do whatever he wants.'

That was how you managed men, Eimear had said. You gave them the illusion of freedom and of being in charge, even when they were neither. Most of them couldn't actually manage for five minutes on their own, but they needed to feel they were running the whole show. It was just a little game people played – a silly game that feminists abhorred, but then they didn't have boyfriends like Ben.

And sure enough, Ben was all smiles again.

'Yeah. I want to hire a motorbike and maybe learn to water-ski. They'd have all that in Crete, wouldn't they?'

Not having a clue, Aran nodded nonchalantly.

'Yes – bikes, shops, nightclubs, everything you could wish for. Only three more concerts to go, and then you're free as a bird! Have you decided the themes for Florence and Rome?'

'Yes. A Renaissance theme for Florence and a gladiatorial theme for Rome. We'd better start sourcing the props.'

She knew that when he said 'we' he meant 'you', and grinned wryly at Thanh and Kevin. But he would be busy with rehearsals, he couldn't do everything himself; much as he liked to maintain an air of independence, he was in fact dependent on the whole team. Like a pyramid of circus acrobats, they all had to work together to keep him at the pinnacle. He had come a million miles from the North End Road, from the days when it was just him and his piano.

It was uncanny, Aran thought four nights later in Naples. As if he had been reading her thoughts, Ben concluded the tour by doing away with everything that had become part of his elaborate act. Wearing the plainest of black trousers and a white collarless shirt buttoned up to the throat, he simply went on stage, sat down at the piano under a single spotlight and began to play. Puzzled, the audience stirred uneasily. Many of them had bought tickets when word spread that they could expect a vivid spectacle, a feast of light and colour – yet the stage was dark, the backing musicians invisible, the tone decidedly stark. It took a long time for them to accept that the focus tonight was solely on music, and not all of them did accept it. Even when Ben closed his eyes, clasped the microphone with both hands and delivered the most intensely intimate performance of the entire tour, Aran sensed confusion. Why was Naples being denied what every other city had got? Was some kind of trick being perpetrated at its expense? Ben didn't explain, didn't speak at all, with the result that purists went away rapturous while those who had come to party went away angry and perplexed. Next day, the reviews were suspicious, concluding that 'Ben Halley is a classicist masquerading as a rocker, teasing and toying with those who came to see as well as hear him – toying, in fact, with the whole genre on which his career depends. If he harbours secret ambitions to sing in private salons or at the Albert Hall, then let him go back to England and do so.'

Kevin, who had begged Ben not to do it, was furious. Jessica Hunter flew straight back to London in a huff, and Thanh advised Ben to leave Italy immediately before he should have to protect him from the irate fans congregating in the lobby of their hotel next morning. Aran knew why he had done it, but didn't know whether to be angry, impressed or amused. It was very provocative of him, but he was entirely unrepentant. Grinning, he said goodbye to the crew, got into a taxi and headed for the airport. Four hours later his plane landed in Crete, where nobody had ever heard of him.

From the first moment she set eyes on it, Aran felt an affinity with Crete, something drawing her into its somnolent power. In the centre of the island great mountains rose out of the gleaming heat, mauve and blue and ochre, ribbed with the horizontal terraces of ancient irrigation, clustered with cubed white villages. From the foot of the mountains pale green plains fanned out into viridescent banana plantations and argentine olive groves, shining and shimmering all the way down to the topaz beaches, washed by the most brilliant blue ocean she had ever seen.

The hot dry air was very still inland, scented with honey and oleander, dipped in dormant silence. Every blue shutter was closed against the heat, every windowsill sentried with scarlet geraniums

216

and cats laid low by the heat. Between late morning and early evening nothing stirred, not a leaf flickered; only out on the coast was it possible to move in the rustling salt air. For the first full day Aran sat stunned in the sun, seeking the elusive shade that moved in tantalising tranches: the thermometer registered forty degrees celsius.

It was a form of paralysis, and she found herself sliding into it unresisting, acquiescent. Whatever Crete's charms, nobody could chase after them in such conditions, the idea of walking as far as the nearest shop or taverna made her head spin. Three days elapsed before she emerged from this coma, to find Ben lowering and lugubrious.

He was unperturbed by the heat, but his list of other problems was long. He was devoured by mosquitoes. He was depressed by the women in their black shawls. He was scalded every time he took a shower, poisoned by the saline water, drowned in the unfathomable plumbing. He couldn't find a piano. He couldn't understand a word of Greek and he couldn't begin to comprehend why Aran had taken him here.

'Darling, it's a rest cure. Why are you fighting it?'

'I'm bored.'

Aran frowned anxiously, too young to know that men all over Europe were saying the same thing at the same moment. While millions of women like herself lay blissfully sunning on every beach from Brighton to Biarritz, content with their novels and their ices, millions of men mooched and whined, scowling at the partners who had lured them to such deathly destinations. In every case without exception, it was all the woman's fault.

'Then get a motorbike and go for a run.'

He got one, upended it into a pothole and came back covered in scorching road rash. Sympathetically, she surveyed the damage.

'You poor thing. Maybe a swim would cool it off.'

She meant in the pool, but he plunged into the sea and emerged howling: the salt stung the cuts excruciatingly.

'I hate this place! I hate it!'

But she resolved to persist. In another day or two the warm torpor would soothe him as it was soothing her, slow and seduce him into the same state she was entering herself. Languid, drowsy, drifting into deep relaxation, she found Crete incredibly tranquil. Why must Ben fidget and fret?

Against her inclination she strolled with him one evening as far as the village square, a full kilometre away from their hotel. As they approached it they heard bells pealing, and found a wedding in progress.

'Oh, look. I wonder, is it different here?'

It was actually very similar to a Catholic ceremony, except that the priest wore a tall hat and a very long beard, while the guests pinned money on the bride's dress in the grounds of the chapel as she emerged like brides the world over, wreathed in smiles.

'Oh, her mother is crying – and look at the little flower girls, aren't they sweet?'

She could have watched for ages, but he led her away.

'Crete is part of Europe, Aran, I'm sure they do things much the same as anywhere else, we're not in Swaziland.'

'Oh, Ben! Crete feels totally different to me! It's strange and foreign and I love it.'

It was such a lazily beautiful island, the people were so pleasant, the scent of thyme and hibiscus hung on the air like opium, lulling her almost into a trance. In many ways the little coves and fishing boats reminded her of Ireland, but in Ireland the sun never seeped into your bones, nobody ever ate outdoors at night in a flimsy summer dress, or swam in a sea that was tepid even by moonlight. By the end of a week she felt dazed, almost drugged by the heat, the rich floral perfumes, the local wines that made her so sleepy she could hardly speak.

Admittedly, Ben was right when he said there wasn't much to do; the highlight of their day became the buying of melons from the old man who sold them from panniers on his donkey's back. In the evenings, they ate often at a beach taverna where the sea water swirled round their ankles as they picked their way through freshly-caught octopus and squid, sometimes accompanied by a local musician desultorily playing his bouzouki.

'Isn't it romantic, Ben?'

He glowered at her.

'Oh, come on . . . you just won't admit it.'

Reaching across the table where they sat nursing Metaxa brandies, she took his hand.

'Give me a smile?'

Reluctantly, crookedly, he did. At least she was enjoying herself, even if he wasn't.

'A bigger one! That's better . . . tell you what, why don't we go out on a boat tomorrow? There are cruises to the baby islands. I hear Dia is lovely, really tropical, it even has palm trees.'

Next morning they set off in the turquoise haze of dawn, in a wooden schooner out over the glassy sapphire water. Wearing only shorts and sandals, his eyes licquorice in his dark face, she thought Ben looked altogether beautiful. Despite his protests to the contrary the holiday was doing him good, the indolence replenishing his strength, the sultry heat caressing and balming his body. It was having the oddest effect on her, too; as the boat bobbed gently away to Dia she felt as if her mind was melting, her spirit floating off to some separate destination of its own.

Dia was like a furnace, the sand burning to the touch as they spread their towels and lay down on it. Other than swimming, there was absolutely nothing else to do.

'Isn't this paradise?'

Glumly he supposed that it must be, since everybody seemed to think so. Not that there were many people here to confirm it; they had the island virtually to themselves. Rolling onto her side, she kissed him, sighed contentedly and drifted off to sleep. Never in her life had she slept as much as she was sleeping in recent days. Not just sleeping, but losing things, forgetting things, wandering vaguely around like a zombie. The tour, she thought, had been more tiring than she had realised. Now that it was over she barely seemed able to remember her own name, string two coherent sentences together. Oh, well. This was what holidays were for.

When she awoke two hours later, Ben was sitting upright beside her, staring out to sea.

'Ben? Surely you haven't been there the whole time? I thought you'd go swimming, or exploring.'

'No.'

'Then what have you been doing? Reading?'

But the novel he'd brought lay in the beach bag, untouched.

'Nothing. Just thinking.'

'For two hours? About what?'

'About you.'

He looked intently at her, and she was flattered. Sometimes it was hard to keep his attention for two minutes, yet he had spent two whole hours at her side, uninterested in anything else? Definitely, this island had been a good idea. On the beaches of Crete, she sometimes suspected he was a little interested in the other women on them. Glamorous French and Scandinavian women, who wore lipstick and jewellery even when they were swimming, playing volleyball, disporting their lissom bodies.

Her own swimsuits were pretty, and she did dress up in the evenings – brush her hair and put on some eyeshadow, at least – but Crete was so casual, not the kind of place where you swanned around in all your finery. She thought the foreign girls looked overblown and out of place, tripping along the sandy lanes and rocky roads in high-heels, reeking of perfume when the air was already full of natural fragrance.

She snuggled into him.

'Let's have lunch.'

The boatman had given them a picnic to take with them: tomatoes, olives, slabs of white feta cheese and a little bottle of ouzo mixed with water. Huge fresh oranges, too, and a loaf of soft yeasty bread. Eating these things in the sand was a messy business, but she didn't mind, in the ocean air she seemed to be permanently hungry. Peeling an orange, she dangled a slice over his lips.

'Here – mind the juice!'

It ran down his chin and she leaned over, playfully, to lick it off. But he pushed her away and wiped his mouth with his hand.

'Oh, this is too sloppy. You eat it, Aran. I'm going to swim.'

He padded down to the water and dived in, striking out slowly at first but then cutting faster through the water, until he was so far out she could no longer see him at all.

It was their last night in Crete, and it was Ben's twenty-second birthday. To celebrate, Aran suggested they go into Heraklion for the day, to shop and see the ancient remains of Knossos. Local people said Chania and Rethymnon were much prettier towns, but both were over two hours away.

When they reached Heraklion, Ben wrinkled his nose and screwed his eyes shut.

'Ugh!'

Dismally, she was forced to agree. The city was polluted, teeming with traffic and horribly industrial. But couldn't they just make the best of it? Did Ben have to find fault with every single thing they did, every place they went? Until now he'd been complaining that their base in Stalis was too quiet, now he was disgusted that Heraklion was too noisy. She couldn't seem to get anything right.

'Well, there must be some little back streets, some parks and cafés somewhere. Oh, Ben, do take that look off your face, please!'

'Sorry.'

But the look returned as they trudged through the mess and muddle, sweating so that the dust stuck to them, ringing their eyes with soot until they looked like pandas. Eventually they reached a shopping area where Aran, in desperation, plunged into a cool, clean jewellery shop.

'Will we get something for Rani?'

He nodded listlessly as she selected a lovely, square gold bangle for Rani. Then another for Eimear. Then a brooch for Molly, earrings for Val, a scarf pin for Deva. Anything, to stay in the air-conditioned shop, out of the path of the lorries careening by outside. Anything to catch his interest – but, although he usually enjoyed choosing presents for people, nothing did.

'What am I going to get you, love? What would you like?'

Birthdays were important to him, he attached great significance to marking them. But not this one.

'Oh, please don't, Aran. I don't want anything, really.'

Against his will she picked out a pair of cufflinks, very contemporary in design, and asked the jeweller to engrave his initials on their backs. In silence they waited for the work to be done.

'They'll look great in a plain black shirt, or a white one – you'll get more wear out of them than you think.'

The jeweller took forever to do up each little gift separately in a package of blue and white paper, smiling as he attempted to chat in English. Then there was payment to be figured out, exchange rates to translate.

'Oh, just pay the man, Aran!'

His tone was so curt she didn't even wait for the change. It was like shopping with a total stranger, and she was wounded by his impatience when she was only trying to give him a gift. What had come over him, these past few weeks?

Stoically they slogged on to Knossos, where the museum and ruins were overrun by German, American and Japanese tourists exclaiming as they photographed everything in sight.

'Do we have to do this?'

'Not if you don't want to – I only thought—'

'Let's go back to Stalis.'

Miserably she sat beside him in the taxi all the way back, wondering how one of them could have enjoyed the holiday so much while the other enjoyed it so little. Not that they had quarrelled, as such, but neither had they been in harmony. Even in bed at night, he was somehow absent in her arms, having sex rather than making love. Everything she found so appealing – the tiny white chapels and villages, the slow pace, the quiet life – he loathed. Although he did not say it, she knew he was dying to get back to London.

Why? What was so terrible about a Mediterranean holiday? What was wrong with the hot sun, that suited his Indian complexion? What was wrong with her company? After all, she hadn't mapped out a fixed itinerary, insisted on relentless sightseeing or made him do anything he didn't want to. On the contrary, she'd never felt so lazy, so peacefully agreeable to his proposals; even when he'd gone off water-skiing by himself, she hadn't minded. Although he eyed the English and Danish girls in their plunging swimsuits, she said nothing, made no jealous scenes.

The whole summer had gone so well. He'd become a minor celebrity, made lots of money and met many new people, seen and done so much – what more did he want? She wasn't angry with him, but she was worried and upset.

It dawned on her that he had not given her a present, either, since the glass bracelet in Milan. Until then he'd found her some small thing everywhere they went, a love token, a memento, a gesture of gratitude for organising everything, oiling every wheel. At the end of this wild, wonderful summer they were, inexplicably, going to return to London in exactly the same grey mood as they left it.

Well, his new single and video would be coming out, and then there was the album to work on. Maybe that would brighten him up. Clearly he was happiest when he was working.

At the hotel in Stalis she busied herself packing, while he sat by the pool with his book in his hand. She didn't need any help, didn't mind doing the job he would only make a mess of, but she did mind that he didn't offer, didn't interrupt. In other cities there had been flowers, smiles, kisses.

Could she possibly coax a smile out of him, before they left? The flight was not until three in the morning; before that they were going to a village called Elounda for dinner. Elounda was reputed to be gorgeous, tucked away at the foot of a cliff, with a fish restaurant that jutted right out into the water. Under the stars, it would be heavenly.

She loved Ben. Loved his talent, his warmth, his wit and his generosity. She had never known him so out of sorts and she wasn't going to let him stay that way. Could he be ill perhaps, suffering from some bug he'd picked up? Back home, she'd make him see a doctor. Here, she was going to give it one last shot. Slowly and carefully, she took a shower, styled her hair, painted her nails and picked out a favourite dress. Made of coffee-coloured silk, trimmed with tiny spangles round the hem, he had often said how sexy and feminine he found it. And, since they would be travelling by taxi, she slipped on a pair of fragile, elegant sandals.

When he finally came up from the pool, he did smile, slowly and wistfully.

'You look beautiful, Aran. That dress is stunning with your tan. Men will be falling over you tonight.'

'Let them fall. You're the only man I want.'

Lightly he embraced her, brushing his lips over her cheek, smiling again as he espied the miniature bouzouki she had got for Val's impending baby.

'You always think of everything and everyone, don't you?'

'Well, the baby won't be able to play it for a while yet! But it's a way of keeping in touch . . . families crumble if you don't work at them, Holly Mitchell says. I've got little things for her children as well.'

Why that simple remark should silence him she couldn't imagine, but without further comment he changed into the clothes she had selected for him and they set out in the lucid evening for Elounda.

'My God, Ben, have you ever seen anything so beautiful in all your born days?'

He had not. Like Aran he could not take his eyes off the view from the cliff top over which they had to pass to reach Elounda. Snaking round terrifying bends, the road wound down into a glittering crescent of harbour lights far below; as the amber sun sank into the lilac sea the little village began to twinkle like Brigadoon, a vision so mystical it seemed conjured up by fairy forces. Strewn on the water like a handful of glow-worms, the last of the fishing smacks crept home in the twilight that was turning to rapid darkness, falling on Elounda like a sable cloak. Overhead, a single star studded the sky, a silver nugget of the night.

For several minutes after they took their seats in the restaurant Aran said nothing, gazing up into a canopy of dark green vine leaves, gazing down into the water where fish flitted so close she might have touched them.

'So this is what Dunrathway is up against.'

He looked at her over the menu a friendly waiter was giving him.

'Dunrathway is what?'

'Up against. You get dazzling views and sunsets there too, beautiful beaches, coves, mountains. But you don't get the weather. It's so much warmer here, prices are lower, waiters and shop assistants speak several languages, nobody steals your stuff on the beach . . . Greece has a lot of advantages. Selling points.'

He smiled despite his sober mood.

'Your mind never rests, does it?'

'Oh, it has been resting, really . . . look at all the stars coming out, Ben. There's an Irish legend that says each one is a soul. The soul of someone who's died and gone to heaven.'

'Like Margaret Thatcher?'

She laughed. Word from Britain was that the new prime minister was indeed very pleased with herself, making quite an impact already. To Aran's chagrin she had missed the election which had finally come in May, while they were in Spain. Irish residents were entitled to vote in it, but she had lost her chance to thwart Guy Halley.

Absurdly, she felt that her vote alone would have halted the Tories in their tracks.

Now that they were restored to power she could just imagine Guy smirking and swaggering, blustering about sweeping the homeless off the streets, packing the Paddies back to Ireland where they belonged. For a doctor, he had a remarkably unsympathetic nature. If ever she should have a child, she thought, he was the very last gynaecologist she would choose. Of course his own wife had not come to England destitute or desperate for work; she had come to study medicine, graduated from university the same year they were married. It never seemed to occur to Guy that most immigrants from what he called 'the colonies' came because they had been taught, even forced, to believe that England was the mother ship. For centuries, Britannia had ruled Ireland, India, the West Indies, Canada, Australia, South Africa, even outlandish places like Ceylon and Guyana. You couldn't simply lay claim to own them one day and deny all responsibility for them the next, not when you'd imposed your language, religion and social code on them. People had not only got into the habit of looking to London, but been coerced into it. If you could speak English, and your own country had been stripped bare, then it stood to reason that you might seek work in the country that had brought all this about. Aran knew very little about Margaret Thatcher, but while she admired any grocer's daughter who could rise to such a position of power she wondered equally how it would be deployed.

'I think the eighties are going to be different, Ben.'

'In what way?'

'Well . . . it's just a feeling. But every other decade seems to be active, while the ones in between are passive. I mean – the twenties, forties and sixties were all strong, memorable, energetic, while the thirties, fifties and seventies were sort of . . . soft. Wishy-washy.'

He wasn't sure what she meant.

'You think the eighties are going to be what – tough?'

'Yes – like this Thatcher woman! Pushy, confident, perhaps quite self-centred. And materialistic, like the Tories.'

'And how do you think that might translate musically?'

'I think people could have more money than before, to spend on records. Also that they'll want disposable songs, so they can keep buying new ones, show how prosperous they are.'

He looked down contemplatively, unhappily.

'I'll have a choice to make, then. Whether to write a lot of commercial stuff or whether to do what comes naturally, even if I end up in the wrong place at the wrong time.'

'I think you should be as commercial as you can while you can. Then, when you decide you've had enough, you'll be able to do what lies nearer your heart. I've told you this before, Ben.'

'I know. I wouldn't even have tried, if it wasn't for you. You can see things so clearly. I could never be so cool about it.'

'That's why I'm your manager. I tell you, Ben, I grew up in pretty dire circumstances and I never want to be in them again. My father says that money gives you power and freedom and he's absolutely right. Once you've got that, you've got any number of options.'

'I can see that. But I won't prostitute myself for any amount of money.'

'Oh, don't take yourself so seriously! Writing rock is fun, isn't it? You're twenty-two and you're having a great time. We both are. When you're thirty you can reinvent yourself.'

He swept his eyes slowly over her face.

'You're really indispensable to me, Aran. You keep my feet on the ground and my face to the future. I just wish . . .'

What? What did he wish? That he had got more into the mood of this island, more in tune with her? Eagerly she took his hand. It was not too late; this last night could still be marvellous.

'What's on your mind, Ben? What's bothering you? If it's the past few weeks, please don't worry. Forget about them and let's have a wonderful night tonight. We'll remember that and you can wipe out all the rest. You were simply tired.'

He didn't reply, pausing as the waiter brought their kalamari, with bread, lemons and a carafe of honey-gold wine. As soon as she took a first bite, Aran knew that the squid was straight out of the ocean; the lemons were so fresh their leaves were still glossy. For all its simplicity she thought Cretan food superb, and wished Ben would look a little more enthusiastic about it. But he seemed to have no appetite.

'Ben, it's delicious! Do try it, please . . . I can't enjoy it if you don't.'

He gripped her hand as she put down her fork, twisting it in his so tightly it hurt. In such a setting, how could he look as he did, so uncomfortable, so wretched?

'Oh, Aran. You can't imagine how awful I feel. I hate myself, I never knew such guilt . . .'

Briefly, he lifted his eyes to meet hers, and she was bewildered by the pain in them.

'Ben, it's only a holiday! I'm sorry you haven't enjoyed it, but that's because you didn't try.'

'I did try, Aran. I know it doesn't look as if I did, but that's the truth.'

'Well, if you say so . . . it's a shame, but I suppose it's not the end of the world.'

He drew a deep breath, hesitated and then spoke in a low, raw voice, as if he were arriving at the funeral of someone very dear.

'Aran, it is. It is the end.'

'It is – it is – what?'

'It's the end, Aran. Not of everything, perhaps – I hope. But it is the end of the road, for us.'

She sat dumbly, immobile. Had a hand reached down from the sky and struck her, she could not have been more confused, more confounded.

'Us?'

'You and me. Our time together, our . . . oh, God, how can I say it?'

'It?'

She knew she was making no sense, but neither was he.

'Aran, we've had two very precious years together. As my girlfriend you have given me great joy, as my manager you have been a marvel. But I – as your lover, your companion, I – I am – Aran, I can't go on. We can not go on.'

She could hear herself making some sound, but it didn't seem to be any recognisable word. Her hand lay in his like a small dead animal.

For a long time he looked out over the ocean, but then he wrenched his eyes back to her, wretched as a murderer's.

'It – it's the signs, Aran! All the signs are there!'

Signs? This was some game, like a map or a hunt, if you followed the signs you would end up safe, out of danger? You would no longer feel sick, faint with fear?

'W-what signs? What are you talking about?'

He still held her hand, was massaging it as if she were ill.

'Can't you see them, yourself? Can't you see what's happening to you?'

'No, Ben. I can't. Please tell me what's happening to me.'

Her voice was frail as a moth, weightless.

'Aran, you're – you're nesting!'

'Nesting.' The word fell to the table like a feather.

'Yes – brooding, nesting, whatever you call it when a woman wants to settle down with a man, marry him and have children with him. I can understand it, but I – I can't do it!'

A slight breeze cooled her cheeks, enough to clear her mind very fractionally.

'Explain to me, Ben. Tell me what signs you've seen. One by one.'

'The house. The furniture, the shopping, the decorating. The Mitchell children, the presents for them, for my family, for your sister's child that isn't even born yet. The wedding you wanted to watch. My mother and all the hints she drops. The way you've stopped organising me, become so serene . . . that dreamy look you have. The anxiety when I drink alcohol, when I look at any other woman. The way Kevin and Jessica refer to you. Those are all signs, Aran.'

Her face contorted. 'Ben, you're insane. Completely insane.'

'I wish I were. But it's been ebbing and flowing for weeks. It started with the new house, then the tour distracted you, then when we got here it all surged back again. I've seen it and sensed it every day, I never felt so claustrophobic as I have on this island. Aran, I adore you, but I'm suffocating.'

She could find no words. In the sultry night, the silence rose between them like a stalacmite.

'Oh, Aran . . . please don't . . . I love you so much, I can't bear to hurt you.'

He wasn't hurting her. He was killing her.

'Was it Ireland, Ben? Was it meeting my parents?'

'Yes. That, and the rest. Ties, roots, families. If you can tell me I'm wrong, I will believe you. But I don't think you can.'

She opened her mouth to tell him. No word came out.

'You see? You don't even realise you're doing it. But you are. At twenty years of age, for some reason I don't understand, you want a commitment from me. I truly do love you, Aran, but I can't give you that. If I did, I would break it.'

'If you loved me, you would not.'

'Then I can only admit that I mustn't love you enough. If this had happened in ten years time, it would be different. We'd marry, have children – but not now! Not now, I *can't*!'

She heard the pain and honesty in the words, saw the anguish in his eyes. But her mind had switched to automatic pilot, was moving without guidance.

'Then you'll need a new manager.'

He bit his lip, struggling, pleading.

'You don't think – there isn't any way – you could—'

'No. I couldn't.'

Their meal untouched, they sat like statues. After a long time he spoke again.

'We – I – Aran, if there's anything I can do—'

She stood up.

'No, Ben. As you say, there is nothing you can do.'

From Elounda to Heraklion airport, from Heraklion to Heathrow, from Heathrow to Hampstead, Aran did not utter a single word. As if

227

he were travelling with a corpse, Ben tried desperately to will life into her.

'You can have anything you want. Anything. I'll keep up the house, share all our money, phone you and come to see you. If there's anything you ever need you have only – Aran, say *some*thing!'

She said nothing, only clutched her leather case to her. The leather case she had found in Florence and filled with her little things: the gauze scarf, the onyx egg, the dead rose.

In the London light of early morning the house was pale and quiet when they reached it. At the foot of the steps she put down her case, took her key from her bag and turned to him.

'Go, Ben. Go to Rani. Don't come in. Don't come back. Don't ever call.'

He reached out to her, his eyes dilated with torment. But hers were blank, blank and empty as the marble eyes of a Greek icon.

Chapter Ten

It was what you would call a grand soft day, Eimear thought as she sat in her garden contentedly hulling strawberries. It hadn't rained since early morning, and now the cloud was breaking up for long enough to reveal patches of baby-blue sky. As was so often the case in Ireland, the sun would be shining by evening, for just long enough to show everyone what they had been missing before. This drove some people mad, but it only made her smile as she dropped the hulls into one glass bowl and the berries into another. Once you kept your cardigan around your shoulders, it was really quite pleasant.

How pretty the garden was, this year! In its centre the sloping lawn was striped and even, around the edges the phlox, heliotrope, zinnias and nasturtiums flamed with colour under the yew trees Dan had planted as a windbreaker, years before. Nearer the house the white and yellow roses were in full bloom, while Aran's little Cupid looked very demure in his bower of blue lobelia. Every once in a while Eimear gave him a bubble bath, scrubbing the lichen off until she imagined he was laughing, tickled by the soft brush as it whizzed across his chubby tummy.

Dear Aran. She would be home from Crete by now, tanned and happy after her days in the sun, inspecting all the work the decorators had done in her absence. Talk about the lady of the manor! When Eimear was twenty she had been in London too, but she had stayed in a hostel where you had to queue up to take a bath, label the food you put in the cupboard and sleep in a dormitory full of rigid, squeaking iron beds. But when you were in love it didn't matter where you lived, and she had been so deliriously in love with Dan, as Aran was now with Ben. Of course the insane passion calmed down a bit over the years, but even today Dan's footsteps gave her a little frisson of pleasure every evening; unlike most men in Dunrathway he preferred to come straight home from work without pausing at the pub.

Would Ben be like that? Would he mature into the kind of husband Aran deserved, devoted and dependable? Eimear couldn't quite shake off her anxiety about the circumstances of the relationship, couldn't envisage any musician settling into a steady routine. Yet Ben was a decent chap, solicitous of Aran, apparently aware of how lucky he was. If only they were both slightly older! Dan had sown a bumper crop of wild oats before buckling down, very belatedly, to his veterinary studies. By the time he married at twenty-six, he knew what he was doing, was ready to commit. And of course he had just been a nice, ordinary man – whereas Ben, God help him, was the answer to every maiden's prayer. With one flash of his beautiful brown eyes, he could probably have any woman in London.

Even if he didn't want them, he'd still have to fight them off. If Aran was older she'd be better equipped to deal with that, have more experience of the subtle ways in which women coped with men, and indeed with other women. But then she wouldn't be the innocent creature Ben found so appealing. Funny, how she had retained that innocence. Even last April, when she'd come visiting from London, she had shown no trace of the hardness that city life often engendered. Oh, she had a coat of varnish now, perhaps, but you only had to scratch it to see the cailin underneath.

Too young, definitely. Too young to be in such a serious relationship, and far too young for the family she strangely spoke of starting. What could have put such an idea into her head? Before she went to London she'd been quite adamant about *not* having one until she was good and ready for it. As powerful a force as nature was, equipping young girls to become mothers many years before they were emotionally able for such a responsibility, Aran had never seemed the kind to let nature dictate to her. Could her change of direction have something to do with Ben? Did she think a child would cement the relationship, establish some tangible bond between them, some common duty or purpose? If so, she was sadly mistaken. For every young man who shouldered the decades of duty born of a brief encounter, ten more denied it, fled from it. Somewhere in this village, for instance, was a youth who was the father of Deirdre Devlin's two children – maybe even two youths, because Deirdre refused to disclose any details of paternity. But she was the one left holding the baby, quite literally, her youth gone in every sense of the word.

Eimear didn't think Ben would abandon Aran in the same callous fashion, should she have a child, but she didn't think he'd appreciate having a gun put to his head either. It would weaken, not strengthen, his love for her. If he wanted a family, then he would have asked Aran to marry him, they'd be engaged by now.

230

A biological need, Aran had said. Well, that was understandable. The drive to procreate was incredibly strong. She felt it herself, all the time, tugging at her as if she were a small shrub in a storm, sweeping her away on its force. Sometimes it swept all reason with it, leaving her a shuddering wreck, weeping because she could not do it. But Aran was a much younger woman, not even married, living in a city that laughed at young mothers! Over there, women took control of their lives – and was control not the very thing she had claimed to want?

Well, girls went through these phases. No matter what they said, virtually all got broody at times. For no good reason they dreamt little dreams of babies, they imagined cuddly pink bundles of joy, sweet and fragrant in their arms. It was nature, instinct, some elemental thing. But then they got their wits together! And by now Aran must surely have got hers together. She had a fine new home in London, a challenging new career, a happy relationship and more money than was good for her, probably, at her age. It had all happened so fast, so fortuitously.

Was that it? Had she got too much, too soon? Did she think a child might anchor her, stabilise her in the maelstrom of her heady new life? If she had one, there wouldn't be so much dancing, drinking, pubbing and clubbing . . . maybe this was her way of trying to get a grip on it all.

Poor child. She was confused, deluged, deluded, trying to create order out of chaos. Life in Dunrathway had not prepared her for life in London; life with Conor and Molly had no resemblance to life with Ben. Probably Ben was confused himself. How many young men of his age were offered a large lucrative contract, promoted as stars, sent off to tour Europe? It was like winning a lottery. Hardly anyone could cope without a period of adjustment, a lot of sensible advice. The best thing Ben and Aran could do now was take everything slowly, do nothing rash.

Was that someone waving, down there in the harbour? Squinting into the westerly sun, Eimear stood up on tiptoe and peered out between the yews. Yes, it was Conor, chugging away in his new boat with four other figures. The slightest of them would be Dursey, who had taken a great shine to shark fishing. The others must be the three American men who had pitched up in Dunrathway this morning, enquiring about the boat they had heard they could rent.

Since it was Friday, the fleet had already despatched last night's catch to market, and was mostly idle. Conor must have a few hours to himself, and was making the most of them. Cheerfully Eimear waved back before he turned the Lady Aran round the headland and headed off down the coast, standing proudly erect on the deck, rejuvenated by a good ten years. Never before had Eimear seen him stand up straight, but since he got that boat he was a new man. Even his darned old sweater had been replaced by a new cable-stitched polo neck, smart navy to match the peaked cap he had bought. The Americans liked such little touches, he'd informed Dan, they expected you to look the part. And didn't he look it! Next thing, Eimear thought with a grin, he'd be wearing blazers and cravats, joining the yacht club over in Schull. Nearly every evening since the end of May he had had customers, some of whom had caught fine big specimen shark, and now his look could nearly be described as jaunty. Aran had worked wonders for him.

Well, the strawberries were done. Would they be nicer in a flan, or soaked in a little kirsch for serving in chilled glasses? Yes, that was the very thing, with a few mint leaves . . . lazily Eimear pulled some fresh from the herb patch and went into the kitchen to chop them into the fruit. Oh, damn, of course the phone would ring, just when her hands were covered in juice! Licking her fingers, she picked it up.

'Hello?'

At the other end, there was a kind of suction noise, a deep intake of breath. Billy Darn Devlin, she thought impatiently; the great goon is still trying to make obscene calls, as if the whole village didn't know it was him.

'Billy, it's teatime, has your mother not got a nice rusk for you? Run along now, and don't forget to put on your dribbler.'

Hanging up, she made a mental note to buy a whistle. Next time, he'd get nothing but a perforated eardrum. Oh, for the love of God, surely he wasn't at it *again*? Well, let him ring, she wasn't going to answer a second time. But the phone was right beside her, and its persistence was extremely irritating. Exasperated, she snatched it up.

'*Look*, Billy—'

'E – E – Eimear, no! It's me, it's A-A-Aran!'

'Aran?' But the voice sounded hysterical, like a lunatic's.

'Oh, Eimear! Don't hang up, it's me – ohhh!'

Suddenly Eimear was alarmed. If it really was Aran, she was in a terrible state.

'Aran, is that you? Where are you? What's wrong?'

Another muffled howl, some incoherent gulps, sobs, splutters. Instantly Eimear reverted into a teacher, firm, calm, in charge.

'Now, Aran, whatever it is, it can't be as bad as all that. Pull yourself together and tell me what has happened.'

'B-B-Ben!'

'What has Ben done? Have you had a little tiff?'

An explosion of grief.

'No, it's – I can't – oh, just come! Please *come!*'

Floods of tears, such torrents that Eimear was terrified. Whatever had Ben done, that was actually unspeakable? Surely Aran wasn't injured, he hadn't hit her or been violent? But she'd never have thought he was like that.

Yet Aran sounded almost demented, as if she were in agony. Abruptly Eimear glanced at her watch. Four fifteen. There was a daily flight from Cork to London at six.

'Is it really serious, Aran? You want me to come over there?'

'Yes, it is, I do, you must – I can't move, I need you, oh – !'

She couldn't *move*? Frantically Eimear shut the panic out of her mind.

'Right, Aran. Sit tight. I'm on my way. Are you in Hampstead, or what?'

'Yes, Hampstead—'

'Good. If I can catch the plane, I'll be there by eight, nine at worst.'

Hanging up, she tore away to pack a bag and raced back again to scribble Dan a note. Aran was ill, but he mustn't worry, she would call him as soon as she got there.

Oh, thank God it was summer, school was shut and she could just go! Jumping into her car she sped away, in such haste that it never even crossed her mind to tell Molly.

On first sight, Eimear thought that Ben had physically attacked Aran. Her eyes were swollen shut, her face inflamed, her chin askew almost as if it had been dislocated. Speechless, she pulled the girl into her arms.

'My precious! Oh, my poor baby, what's happened to you? There, there, don't cry, I'm here. Ssh, it's all right, I'm here . . .'

A pool of hot tears soaked through her blouse as Aran buried her face in it, clinging, crying, gasping for breath, soldering herself on so tightly Eimear could hardly breathe in turn. Where, she wondered desperately, was the nearest doctor? Aran needed medical attention.

'Come on, come with me, that's it, sit down here . . .'

As if she were an invalid, she steered her into the front room and sat her down on the sofa, kneeling in front of her and prising her hands gently away from her face. Under the tumbling fair curls it was arctic white, with two blazing red spots that looked feverishly afire.

'Now, I want you to take a slow, deep breath. Deep and slow, that's it . . . and another . . .'

Very gradually, the choking eased, the stuttering quietened, the heaving chest subsided. But still the head hung down, suddenly limp like a rag doll's, as if she had not the strength to lift it.

'Aran, look up. Look at me.'

She looked the way accident victims looked in hospital, when their

233

reflexes were tested. Obedient, but completely inert.

Standing up, Eimear took off her jacket, took the face in her two hands and kissed the curls on top.

'All right. Now, I'm just going to make a cup of tea. Where's the kitchen?'

No answer, only a stream of silent tears. Swiftly, Eimear found the kitchen, boiled a kettle and made a scalding pot of tea. Handing her a cup, she stirred two heaped spoonfuls of sugar into it, remembering that sugar was good for shock. Like a puppet on a string Aran lifted it to her mouth, sipped it and put it down.

'No. More. Drink it all.'

If it didn't work, Eimear decided, she was simply going to go into the house next door and ask for the name of a nearby doctor. But slowly Aran sank back into the sofa, her eyes losing their catatonic glaze, her hectic colour toning down.

'That's better. Now, sweetheart, you must try to speak. Tell me what happened – every little detail. You know you can trust me.'

Trembling, her eyelashes matted with tears, Aran stared at the opposite wall and spoke so quietly she had to strain to hear.

'Ben has left me. And I'm pregnant.'

Fully twenty-four hours elapsed before Eimear could say she had regained her composure, pieced Aran's tale of woe together and made some sense of it.

First and foremost, it wasn't definite that she was pregnant. She kept insisting she was, kept repeating that she 'knew it in her bones', but she hadn't had a test. She had merely been careless in Crete, forgetting her pills a couple of times because the heat made her lightheaded and lax. There was no point in even having a test for another few weeks; it was far too soon to tell.

'Aran, you're simply shocked and upset about Ben. Your mind is working overtime.'

'No, Eimear, it isn't! I can *feel* it! I know I am!'

'How can you know?'

'Because my body has gone haywire . . . I'm so sleepy all the time, so hungry, kind of tense and lethargic all at once. I feel so strange, dreamy, as if I were some other person. I can't describe it, but I'm telling you there *is* another person.'

'We'll see. I really doubt it, dearest. But if you're right, then you must find Ben and tell him immediately.'

'I – Eimear, I can't.'

'Of course you can. The record company will know where he is, won't it? And Thanh?'

234

'I don't mean that. I know where he is – at Rani's apartment. I mean I can't tell him.'

'Why?'

'Because I gave him to understand – ages ago, at the beginning, that I wasn't going to do this. He made it absolutely clear he didn't want children and, at the time, neither did I. Eimear, this is exactly why he decided to break up with me. He said I was nesting. Said he'd never felt so claustrophobic in his life.'

'Yes, but he can't have known—'

'No, he didn't know, but he sensed it coming.'

'But didn't you sense anything coming? Hadn't you any idea how he felt?'

'No! I knew he wasn't happy in Crete, but I thought he was only restless to get back to London. We didn't have any rows or quarrels, he was just moody. We did have a huge row ages ago, over doing up the house, but I thought that was all forgotten.'

Eimear sighed. Either Aran was too young to see the signs of disenchantment in a man, or she had refused to see them.

'So this was all a complete bolt from the blue?'

'Yes. He said he wasn't ready to settle down, that he loved me and was very sorry, but he simply couldn't do it. Eimear, I love him, I can't live without him! He's my whole life, I gave up the Mitchells and the market to be with him, his life had become my life – oh, what am I going to *do*?'

'Well, for a start, you're going to have to figure out where he's left you financially. Have you any means of support?'

Sadly, Eimear looked around the lovely new house that Aran had obviously worked very hard to turn into a home. So much thought had gone into it, it was so neat and pretty and happy. And now, it would have to go?

'He says he'll keep the house up and give me whatever I want.'

'Well, that's a mercy! But don't forget you helped him earn everything he has. You have a right to half of it.'

'Yes, well, I do want to stay here, and I don't want to fight over money. I think it would be fair to let him pay the rent and divide the rest up. But it's not that much, Eimear. We were spending an awful lot.'

'But there is something?'

'Oh, yes. Enough to live on until – until the end of next year, I'd imagine.'

'Good. If you are pregnant, the baby would be due – when? March, April?'

Aran tried to think it out, counting on her fingers.

'At the end of March I think.'

'So that would leave you plenty of time to find a new job afterwards.'

'I don't want a new job! I want *Ben!*'

Eimear poured another of the endless cups of tea that were keeping her sane.

'Well, maybe he'll change his mind and come back.'

Aran gazed at the carpet.

'I told him he was never to come back.'

'What? Why did you say that?'

'Because – because I didn't know what I was saying! I thought that if he didn't want me, then I wasn't going to let him know how much I – oh, why does anyone say anything? Why do people do stupid things in the heat of the moment?'

'I don't know. But I do know this much: if he is the father of a child then he has to be told.'

'But I told you, he doesn't want one and I promised I wouldn't have one! I didn't do it deliberately, my – my body did it, all by itself! Something took hold of it, it was as if something crept up behind me and pushed me over a cliff.'

Eimear considered.

'You did say you wanted to start a family, Aran.'

'Yes. I did say it and I did want it. But it was all sort of – subconscious. I didn't mean it, not with my head! Only with my heart – oh, God, I'm all mixed up.'

Clutching a cushion in front of her, pulling at a strand of its fabric, she gazed at Eimear with tragic eyes full of anguished confusion. In a simple summer dress, her face still swollen and sleepless, she looked no more than fifteen. The loss of love had come very early to her, and she had no strategy for coping – not, Eimear reflected, that anyone ever really had. Her own mother Hannah, the most dignified and composed of women, admitted to having grieved for two full years after she was widowed, said she would have lost her mind if she hadn't been obliged to resume teaching and care for her infant daughter.

Daughter. Could it really be that Aran was going to have one? Or a son? For one brief terrible moment, Eimear felt a pang of envy. Whatever the circumstances, a child was a child. The doctor would probably tell Aran she wasn't going to have one at all but how she longed to hear exactly the opposite, herself! Last night, talking to Dan on the phone, she'd almost been tempted to tell him what Aran suspected. Of course Dan would be pragmatic as usual, tell them both to calm down, but if it was true he would be thrilled. Aran would bring the child to visit, maybe even come back to Dunrathway for good . . .

236

'Aran?'

'Yes, Eimear?'

'What are we going to tell your mother?'

'Oh, Jesus!'

'Well, we have to let her—'

'No! Oh, Eimear, no! Not now, not until I have some idea what's going to happen! If she hears that Ben has left me she'll say it serves me right, she told me so, good riddance to him. And if I'm pregnant, which I am, she – she'll disown me! She'll say I'm a slut and a disgrace, like Deirdre Devlin. Dad will be so upset, too, he'll want me to come home . . . but this is my home!'

'Is it?'

'Yes! This is our house, mine and Ben's, all his things are here, look, even the piano. I couldn't bear to leave. Besides, Dunrathway is too small for me now, I'd never fit back in.'

No. If she were to be honest, Eimear had to agree that she wouldn't. Her brief bright life with Ben had ruined her for a small rural village. She would be constricted, dissatisfied and ultimately unhappy.

But what would she be here? A single mother with no job, or a job that meant putting her child in a crèche, having it minded by somebody else? Reared by a stranger? For some reason Eimear found herself strongly opposed to that prospect.

Oh, she must stop thinking along these lines. There was no baby. How often had she said those very words to Dan?

Sinking back into her armchair she was silent for several minutes, sorting out her feelings, camouflaging the guilt that was taking hold of her. On the sofa, Aran was still pulling at the cushion. On the table between them, a framed photograph of Ben smiled without a care in the world.

'What about Ben's parents?'

'Deva will be very disappointed. Guy will be very relieved.'

'And if they're to be grandparents?'

'They won't know. Nobody is going to know, because they'd tell Ben and he'd feel more trapped than ever . . . I can't see Rani any more, or even Thanh.'

'But then you'll be all alone, just when you most need your friends.'

'I don't care. Well – I do care, but I'm not going to blackmail him into coming back. Besides, I have you. You – you're not going home right away, are you, Eimear?'

No. She certainly wasn't going home until a pregnancy test was done, which meant staying two or three weeks at least. Stricken by Aran's fearful face, she smiled reassuringly.

'No, of course I'm not. I'll stay right here with you until you've seen a doctor, put your mind at rest and got over the shock – oh, my poor little pixie! I know how much Ben meant to you, but he was only your first boyfriend . . . there'll be others some day, you'll see.'

Unexpectedly, Aran's voice rose, shrill but resolute.

'Never! There will never be anyone but Ben Halley.'

'Yes there will. You're only twenty, you'll meet lots of good, kind chaps. I know it will take a while to get over Ben, but someday you'll wake up to find you have.'

'Never. I never want anyone else. I only want Ben.'

Like a lost child, she crumpled into the cushion, rocking and sobbing, repeating his name over and over.

Two days later, Thanh and Rani came to call, distressed and very sympathetic.

'Ben's just as upset as you are, Aran. He says it was all just too much for him, too soon. Why don't you let him come round to see you?'

'Try to stay friends with him, you mean? Make polite conversation and pretend I'm all right? Rani, I'm not all right! I'm distraught, I can't sleep or eat, if I saw his face for one second I – I'd – oh, don't you understand? It's all or nothing! I could never go back to being just his friend, or his manager, I—'

Her throat felt as if a hot coal was stuck in it, and she was unable to finish her sentence. Unable to explain how she felt, the rejection, the humiliation, the scalding sorrow.

Apart from being Ben's sister, Rani was such a practical feminist. She would worry about the career implications, but the pain and grief of losing Ben would be a mystery to her. Was he the only man on the planet, that Aran should think him indispensable? Had they not agreed that he was young and volatile? She would say it was bound to happen. And Thanh – he worked with Ben now, his loyalties would be torn. There was no point in prolonging this kind but pointless visit.

Wearily, she stood up.

'Will you tell Ben I'll write to him about our – our joint affairs? As soon as I'm able – I'm feeling – when I'm more together. It was very good of you to come. But Eimear is here, I'm really quite all right.'

They lingered a little, trying to get past the defensive barrier they saw being raised. But eventually they were left with no choice but to leave, and out in the hall she heard them conferring with Eimear, snatches of comment about her not 'being herself', not being amenable to logic.

Logic! What had logic to do with anything, when you stood knee-deep in the debris of your life, when the man you loved and trusted had taken a hatchet to your heart? Would Ben be logical, if she took a hatchet to his precious piano and chopped it to pieces? For a crazed moment she looked at it, and thought of doing just that.

But she hadn't the strength. She was too drained to do anything. As their voices drifted away everything seemed to drift with them, until she found herself lying on the sofa, clasping the cushion, her eyelids closing on blessed oblivion.

Dr Crofton was pleased, and the two ladies seemed pleased also. The older one, he assumed, must be the mother, her face illuminating with pleasure as the consultation progressed. She was very youthful, but very concerned and protective of the daughter who looked so pale and wan, her smile seraphically detached. Like most young mothers in the early stages of pregnancy, she was a little overwhelmed.

'Has there been any morning sickness? Would you like me to write a note for your employers?'

'Oh, no, thank you. I – I've given up work, for the moment.'

Dr Crofton thought that was unusual, and rather nice. Not many pregnant women these days could afford to rest and take care of themselves; on the contrary, they worked all the harder to prove their careers came first.

'Then I'd recommend an hour's walk every morning, and a nap in the afternoons.'

Aran thought she could sleep for centuries.

'No stress if you can avoid it, no smoking or alcohol, and if you have any queries just telephone any time you like. Now, let's make an appointment for your next checkup.'

He ushered them out to his receptionist, noting the way the mother took charge of everything, happily and efficiently. Unlike some single mums this girl obviously wasn't embroiled in any tussle with her family. She would be well cared for. Briskly, he bade them goodbye.

Out in the street, Eimear hugged Aran to her, her eyes filling with joyful tears.

'Oh, Aran, this is wonderful. You are pleased, aren't you? In spite of everything?'

'Yes. I am.'

'Let's find a nice café where we can sit down and talk about it.'

She steered her to a nearby one with pink curtains and white wicker furniture, ordering tea and cakes with a beatific smile.

'How do you feel, sweetheart?'

How did she feel? Very pleased. Very proud. Very tired.

'I'm so glad you're here with me, Eimear. I'm all excited and confused, don't know whether to laugh or cry – I'm a mother! I'm going to be somebody's mother . . . doesn't that sound strange?'

A mother. Overwhelmed in turn, Eimear sat thinking about it, turning the word round in her mind.

Next spring, on March 29 the doctor estimated, Aran was going to have a son or a daughter

'Wait till Dan hears! And Ben – Aran, you must tell him now. You must.'

'No.'

'But Aran, he—'

'No. I told you before, I won't blackmail him.'

'Oh, I do wish you'd stop saying that! Anyway, he's sure to find out. Suppose he comes to see you, maybe at Christmas, when it will be obvious?'

'If he comes of his own free will, then he can decide of his own free will.'

Eimear sighed. It was like trying to converse with a mule. But if she pressed the point now, there might be tears. She would return to it later.

'What about your parents then, and Ben's?'

'I won't be seeing his again, and mine are in Ireland.'

'But you'll have to tell them! Your own, at least. You can't hide a baby.'

'No . . . but there's no need to tell them right now. Dad would worry himself sick, Mother would go mad. She loathes Ben, Eimear. You know she does. When she hears he's left me and I'm expecting his child, it'll be the last straw. I just can't face her yet.'

'But what are you going to do? Who will look after you? I wish I could, but I have to go home, school will be starting soon – you can't be left here on your own!'

'Eimear, I'm not ill. I can look after myself.'

'You certainly can't. What if there were any kind of – emergency?'

'Then I'd call Dr Crofton the same way anyone else would call him. Besides, Holly Mitchell is in Islington. We're great friends, and she's a trained nurse.'

Eimear made a mental note to contact Holly as soon as possible. Aran was not Holly's responsibility, but she would surely help out if Aran was determined to stay in London.

'But don't you think it would be better if you came home with me? Dan and I would be delighted to have you, if it would be easier than staying with your parents.'

'Oh, Eimear. You're so kind. But I've made my life here. I'm not

240

going back to Dunrathway to be a burden on anyone, to be gossiped about or have Father Carroll coming to lecture me on the error of my ways.'

'Oh, you make it sound like an awful place.'

'Do I? I didn't mean to. But I'm trying to be logical, as you wanted me to be! I suppose part of my heart will always be in Ireland, but let's face it, Eimear, that's the kind of emotion that holds emigrants back. I chose London, my home is here and I'm staying here. As Holly once said, you can't run crying to Mummy every time there's a problem.'

'Then what are you going to do?'

She smiled vaguely.

'I'm going to enjoy being pregnant. Be a lady of leisure for a while.'

'And what do ladies of leisure do all day?'

'They read, they walk, they play their oboes and they figure out their futures.'

'Is there nothing I can say to convince you?'

'I'm sorry, Eimear. I know you're only concerned for me – oh, why are you? You're so supportive even when I must sound stubborn and stupid.'

She looked so puzzled that Eimear had to smile.

'Because you're you, Aran. Just because you're you.'

Dan was bewildered. 'The girl is off her rocker.'

'No, Dan – she still worships him, actually! Maybe that's why she wants to stay in London. Because Ben is there. I did argue as much as I could, but at the end of the day it's her own decision. She's in an emotional condition and I didn't want to upset her.'

'You should have insisted. Made her come back with you.'

'Dan, I'm telling you, I did my best. But I could hardly abduct her.'

'Hmph. Did you get Ben's address then? I'm going to write to him and sort this out.'

Gratefully, Eimear smiled at him. He was always so dependable.

'No. I didn't ask her, because I knew she wouldn't give it. However, I am going to phone Holly Mitchell, right away.'

Holly was shocked, mystified and instantly helpful. Of course she would visit Aran, once a week at least, Walter would drop in too and invitations would be issued to Islington, the whole situation closely monitored.

'Thanks, Holly. I'll be back myself at Hallowe'en and at Christmas. During the spring break as well, and for the birth of course. The baby is due at the start of the Easter holidays.'

'But Eimear, how did it happen? Why did she do it?'

'She says it was an accident. Personally I suspect she was insecure,

241

wanted a family life with Ben – either that, or nature is simply a very powerful force. Of course she wasn't to know that Ben would choose that very moment to break away. She's devastated about that, but happy about the baby. I'm sure he'd support it if he knew, but she won't tell him. Pride, and all the rest of it.'

'Oh, God. What about her parents?'

'Won't tell them either, until she has to. Very obstinate, but in a way I can understand it – you know what Molly Campion is like. I suppose she doesn't want to be nagged nonstop for nine months.'

Suddenly Eimear laughed.

'What's so funny?'

'Oh, I'm just thinking of Molly, knitting little bootees with a face on her like a thunderclap! She'll hit the roof when she hears.'

'Don't you think she should hear?'

'Yes, she'll have to, naturally. But I can't see her dashing off to London with an armful of roses.'

'Still, a girl needs her mother at a time like this.'

Disconcerted, Eimear paused. She had become so involved in the situation, was so concerned for Aran and so fond of her, she almost felt as if *she* were her mother.

It dawned on her that she had been feeling that way for a very long time.

It was arranged that Eimear and Aran should take turns to call each other every other day, and after Eimear's departure Aran found the system very comforting. Holly Mitchell began to call regularly too, so often that she realised Eimear must have spoken to her old friend. Weren't women wonderful, the way they rallied round! But to be fair Dan was equally supportive, and Thanh was trying to be. But Thanh didn't know about the baby, and wasn't going to know.

'Thanks, Thanh, but I'm fine. Really. There's no need for all this.'

After a few weeks his calls tailed off, and she knew she had hurt him. Hurt Rani and Deva, also; it killed her to think of losing every friend she had made, when friendship had been so rare in her life and was now so cherished. But she had to break free of every tie with Ben, and so she discouraged them until, wounded, they gave up trying.

It was sad, when they did, and she felt terrible for them, but it was a kind of relief. Every mention of Ben was torture, every reminder so painful that she set about exorcising his entire existence. In a burst of angry energy she packed all his clothes away, burnt the photographs she had taken in Europe and ripped the little clef from around her neck. But she could not bring herself to throw it away, fling it from her as she knew she should. After some thought she put it in her leather case with her other mementoes, climbed up on a chair and shoved the case on top of a wardrobe in the spare bedroom. When the removals men came for the piano and Ben's other possessions, she would give them the case to take away.

But they did not come. Night after night she gazed at the piano, waiting for this last link to go, but every morning it remained in place, and she was mystified. When Myles Irving called round to see her, she mentioned it to him.

'Doesn't he want it, and need it?'

'He's bought a new one.'

Oh. A bigger, better one, she supposed. Yet he had been so strangely attached to this one ... but then, he had once been attached to her, too.

'How is – how is the video going, Myles?'

'Very well. Haven't you seen it, on television?'

She hadn't. For some reason she had not turned on the television at all since Eimear left, nor the radio. She was nauseated by what was happening in the world, couldn't bear to watch the horrible news of murder and mayhem, listen to the gruesome details of starving children in Cambodia or the Yorkshire Ripper who had now butchered twelve women. Was this what she was bringing a child into?

'No ... I've been a bit out of it lately.'

'I'm sorry to hear it. In fact that's why I've come, Aran. Is there really no hope of a reconciliation?'

'Not to my knowledge.'

Myles sighed, and looked at her rather paternally.

'You were so good for Ben. He needs you, you know.'

'Perhaps. But he doesn't want me, Myles.'

'I don't think he really knows what he wants. What do *you* want?'

'I want to be left alone.'

'Oh, come now! You're too young to play Greta Garbo.'

I'm not all that young, she thought wryly; I'm going to have a baby. After that, I'll have to make some kind of decision, decide what I want to do. But for now, all I want is peace and quiet.

'I'm taking a little time to myself, Myles. I gave up two jobs to manage Ben and now that one is gone too. Fortunately I'd saved a little money, so I don't have to rush into the next thing – whatever it might be.'

'I can get you a job tomorrow, if you want it. With a management company that handles most of our big names.'

'Oh, Myles. Thank you. But I don't think I'm cut out to work for anyone else. I'm too – too bossy!'

'H'mm. Well, I don't think you are. You get things done very quietly and tactfully. You're a good organiser, that's all.'

Well, yes. She certainly wasn't the type to scream and shout at people. But she did like to be in charge, couldn't imagine taking orders from anyone. Anyway, she wasn't going to work in the music industry, where news of her pregnancy would get around.

'Do you know what I'm doing at the moment?'

'No. What?'

'Playing my oboe and writing poetry.'

'Any that could be put to music?'

'No. Just silly stuff I throw away.'

'You wouldn't consider doing some more lyrics?'

For Ben, did he mean?

'No . . . I can't concentrate these days, Myles. I haven't any drive.'

He scrutinised her thoughtfully.

'You really loved him, didn't you?'

'Yes. I did.'

'Well, he's a fool. Most young men are. I hope he'll grow out of it.'

It was very sweet of Myles to come to see her, but if he didn't stop talking about Ben and go soon, she was going to sink down and sob with the effort of speech, the sheer exhaustion of it. Did all pregnant women feel this leaden fatigue? Did their heads swim when they smelled the aroma of coffee, did all their guests stay for hours, drinking gallons of it?

'I hope he'll find a new manager. He needs order and discipline in his – well, in his work if not his life.'

'He was hoping you might change your mind. Hoping I might persuade you. But I'd be wasting my time, wouldn't I?'

'Yes.'

'I thought so. I suppose I can see your point of view. But it's a pity, Aran. A great pity.'

'I couldn't do it, Myles. Could never manage Ben as if he were a – a stranger, or a commodity. Maybe that's not very professional, but that's how I feel.'

At last he stood up.

'Very well. I'll say no more for now. But if you change your mind about it, or about writing lyrics, you know where to find me.'

'Yes. Thank you.'

Affectionately, he embraced her.

'Take care of yourself.'

Suddenly she wanted to lay her head on his chest and weep, explain why she must take care of herself and why she could not see him again. Couldn't see any of these people who were being so good to her.

'Myles?'

'Yes?'

'Say hello to Thanh for me, will you? And Kevin?'

'Why don't you say it yourself? You're not going to drop us all, are you?'

'I – I'd rather make a clean break. In case Ben might think I was – you know, hanging on.'

He grimaced as he put on his overcoat.

'I only wish Ben had hung on. You're a sorry loss to him, and he's going to realise it one fine day.'

On a soft sunny day in September, when she was ten weeks pregnant, a letter arrived from Ben. She recognised his handwriting and trembled as she sat down to read it.

He was missing her. He was anxious about her. He could understand why she did not want to see him, but could not understand why she had hardened her heart against Rani and Thanh. They were her friends, had committed no crime. Could they not all get together perhaps, some time in the future when she was feeling better? He hoped for her compassion, her eventual forgiveness.

Meanwhile, was she well, was she busy? Why would she not accept Myles's offer of a job? Not that it was to be construed as putting any kind of pressure on her; he would pay the rent until the lease expired five years hence, split their assets and provide any extras she might require. She mustn't worry about money, she must think of getting out and about, keep up her music, try to accept that it was all for the best. He was going to get a flat of his own, but could always be contacted through Rani, or his mother in Surrey.

It was a kind, generous letter, and she could hear his voice in every word of it. Oh, if only she could feel rancour or bitter acrimony, tear it up and thrust him from her memory! But for every brief burst of anger she felt hours of sadness, heartache, aching loss, and his concern only made things worse. On every page she could scent his skin, see his fine elegant hand, his face as he paused for thought . . . how long had it taken him to compose this? Had it been as hard to write as it was to read?

She must try, Eimear had said, not to think of him. Not in this agonising way. But how could she not, when she was carrying his child? For almost an hour she read and reread the letter over again, searching for clues to his mood, some indication that he regretted his decision, would come back to her . . . but there was none.

245

His child. For the first time undiluted pleasure stole over her as she thought of it, the tiny face that was forming, the limbs beginning to curl and flex, the eyes that would open and see her in the spring. Her baby, Ben's baby! Why had she wanted to throw away those mementoes, when she would have this? Slowly, in a kind of trance, she went upstairs and tucked the letter into the leather case, removed the silver clef and hung it back around her neck. Then, for the first time, she spoke aloud to the child.

'Do you like music, little one? Will I play for you?'

Her oboe lay downstairs, on the piano, and she picked it up gently, caressing it with her lips. *The Pearl Fishers*? Yes. Their baby would like Bizet.

Baby girl, or baby boy? Her mind drifted away on the music, visualising the child, slipping into deep dreamy harmony with its small spirit. Some day it would play this oboe, sing this song, lift the lid of Ben's piano and bring it back to life. It would be a beautiful baby, a happy baby . . . were its lungs filling with air already, as hers were filling, was the music making it smile?

For more than an hour she played to it, thinking, wondering. What did it look like, at ten weeks? Minuscule, of course, fragile as a flower; but did it have lips, ears, fingers and toes? A mind, a soul, senses that could distinguish one sound from another? Why did she know so little about it? Maybe because it hadn't seemed quite real, until now? But it was real today. This bright sunny day, that was theirs to share. Putting down her oboe at last, she patted her tummy.

'Come on, muffin. Let's go out for a walk.'

Where was the bookshop, that she had found the same day she found the house? Not very far. It was so warm she didn't even need a coat as she set off in search of it, enjoying her pregnancy just as she had told Eimear she would.

Would people think her careless and indolent, if she didn't worry about finding work until after the birth? She should worry, of course, should be planning and organising; but that kind of reality seemed somehow remote for the moment. Crete must have done something strange to her, because she still felt in thrall to its slow pace, its benign aura. Walking down the street in the sunshine was all she wanted to do, and she was free to do it. For some unknown reason she was starting to feel wonderful.

There was the bookshop. She went in and smiled hugely at the man at the desk, a thin elderly man with glasses on the end of his nose, wearing a green waistcoat over a very white collarless shirt.

'Do you have any books about babies?'

He smiled back. It was nice to see a new face in the

246

neighbourhood, especially such a happy one.

'Yes, many – on the middle shelf on the left, at the end.'

As she browsed through them she realised that this was a Jewish shop; some of the titles were actually in Hebrew. Wasn't London marvellous, the strange things you could find in it! However, all she needed just now was a simple guide in plain English, with lots of illustrations.

Illustrations! Was this really the same person who had worked out Ben Halley's complex contract, got a diploma in business studies and could calculate the rental of premises by the square yard? She must be going soft in the head. But here was her book: an A – Z handbook of motherhood, with dozens of coloured pictures. Giggling, she almost felt like a child herself as she took it to the old man, exchanging pleasantries while she paid him for it. So this was what life was like, when you weren't working? You could stop to chat with people, look at things in windows, take note of houses and gardens and the first autumn leaf as it twirled slowly to the ground? But it was luxury, it was bliss! And she was going to make the most of it, take the baby to see Keats's house and Galsworthy's, to Kenwood House which was also within walking distance, filled with paintings, fronted by a little lake . . . Kevin Ross had told her there were even concerts in it sometimes, and a coach house where you could have coffee.

Uh. The very word made her queasy. But she could have milk, or something, if she went there right now. Yes, why not? It would be a nice serene place to look through the book, find out what was happening to her body and her baby. What a pity she didn't look pregnant, yet! But she would soon, she would be able to show off and go shopping in Mothercare as she had done for Val, last April. Val's baby was the same age now as his unborn cousin, but she'd been away when he was born, heard none of the details except that his name was Paudge. Short for Padraig, but what an abbreviation, it sounded like porridge!

She'd sent Val the little gift she'd bought in Crete, but had received only a perfunctory note of thanks, no phone call or invitation to be godmother. Counting Sher's children she now had one niece and three nephews, but never saw any of the children, didn't feel like a proper aunt at all. Never mind. She was going to be a mother.

Walking on, she reached Kenwood House where the coach house did indeed contain a charming little restaurant. Settling down with her book, a glass of milk and some biscuits, she began to read. Yes! She had been right, some women did know they were pregnant well before they had a test. Some did develop aversions to certain foods and longings for others. Most felt tired in the beginning, but that wore

247

off after the third month – oh, she was nearly there, she wasn't going to sleep for ever after all. And look, here was the baby at ten weeks: it did have budding fingers and toes, a brain, eyes and ears. It was amazing. Why would people say her own brain was turning to slush, because she was interested in it? Well, she was interested, whatever they might say, she was intrigued and fascinated and – and *thrilled*. Of all the work she had ever done with Ben, this was by far the greatest.

Wouldn't he think so? Wouldn't this baby mean more than any song he had written, any audience he had ever conquered? If he knew, if he could see it flickering into life, would he still say his music mattered more, or his freedom? Would he want other girls more than his own little girl? Prefer to party with the boys than play with his own little boy?

Oh, God. Maybe Eimear was right. Maybe she should tell him, give him the choice.

But if he turned it down, if he walked away from her and from their child, she could not bear it. She was not bitter now, but she would be bitter then. Crippled with bitterness, she thought, consumed with it, her whole life seared with blazing anger. Whereas if she gave him the benefit of the doubt, she could still respect him, believe that he might have behaved with honour, accepted the child and learned to love it.

He had always behaved honourably. He had been honest and fair. That was why she still loved him, could welcome his child and love it in turn. But if he rejected it, she could no longer love him. Every sweet memory would be soured, every moment of the life they had shared would turn to ashes in her mouth.

No. It was too great a risk. It was better that he did not know. As long as she had her illusions, she could have the baby, be happy. Never totally happy, without him, but happy in the way older people sometimes were when they learned to live without something they had once wanted.

Eimear had done that. She had wanted something, wished for it with tears in her eyes, but she had not got it. To this day you could see it in her face at times, some kind of yearning she camouflaged the moment she was conscious of letting it show. What could it be? Was it something she had lost, or something she had never found? Not a lover, because she adored Dan; not an abandoned career, because she adored the . . .

The children. Suddenly Aran sat very still, staring at the book, realising she had found what she was looking for.

Chapter Eleven

Mothers, Ben thought in exasperation. They counted so much in Indian culture. But they didn't have to be Indian to make life a misery.

'And how is Aran? Have you been in touch with her? What is she doing? What about the lyrics she used to write? She was so talented. I liked her so much. Oh, Ben, I do wish . . .'

On and on it went, Deva's gently relentless onslaught on his every sensibility, until he cursed the day he had ever let Aran meet his mother. With Rani it was different; she was young, modern, she knew that people didn't make lifetime commitments these days on the strength of youthful flings. Whereas Deva couldn't let go of the idea that a man who kissed a girl had to marry her – and Ben had done a lot more than kiss Aran Campion.

'Two years, Ben, more than two. I can't understand it.'

'Well, everybody else can. My own father can give you a dozen good reasons why it wouldn't have worked.'

Deva responded as if Guy's opinion counted for as much as the corgi's. Men were always evading things, sliding out of the muddles they created, never knew what they wanted until they got it, whereupon they decided they didn't want it after all. Guy was an idiot, and now Ben was taking after him.

'Mother, Aran is an intelligent capable girl, she knew from the start how I felt – as a matter of fact she felt the same way.'

'Ben, she loved you. And I thought you loved her.'

'I did! But she was changing. If we'd gone on we'd have ended up hating each other. I mean, can you really see me going to the supermarket on Saturdays, digging the garden, coming home at five o'clock every evening? Can you see Aran putting up with me when I didn't?'

'She put up with quite a lot as it was. She was too good for you, if you ask me.'

He hadn't asked her, but that didn't deter her. From her point of view, he had succeeded professionally, but he had failed in what really mattered. And now Aran was all alone in London, shying away from contact with the Halleys, struggling on by herself .

'Fortunately she won't be alone for long. She'll soon find someone who appreciates her.'

Deva glanced at Ben as she said it, and was gratified to see him frown; like most men he had a possessive streak in him, didn't want anyone else to have what he had thrown away. Was it any wonder the world was in the mess it was! What Aran should do now was flaunt a new boyfriend, make him jealous; but she wasn't the hardened kind of girl who could do that. She was the kind who would take a long time to get over her first love.

But perhaps she'd better say no more about it, for now, or Ben would stop coming to Surrey. Lightly, she changed the subject.

'Have you written any new songs?'

He frowned again. He hadn't. But he had a song in the charts, with a video that was making his face as recognisable as his voice; he could go nowhere any more without Thanh to protect him from the fans who accosted him in every public place. Was that not enough? Was his own mother going to start nagging him as Cedar was also nagging, querying his lack of output the moment he paused for breath? With an American tour planned for next year, Kelwin was already churning out lyrics with professional facility, but where, Cedar kept demanding, was the music to go with them? Could they have some ideas please, some samples, and could they have them soon?

He smiled rather irritably, provocatively.

'I'll have a couple of new ones by Christmas. A couple of new girls, too. Stop fussing, Mother.'

Deva decided to do just that. The new songs, she thought, would be just like the new girls. Ephemeral, transitory, disposable. Ben had no idea how much he needed Aran.

Eimear was able to return to London for only two days at Hallowe'en, but was reassured to find Aran looking well, with the serene aura of pregnancy about her. So serene, in fact, that she seemed to be living in a world of her own.

'So have you thought any more about the future? About what you're going to do after the baby is born?'

'Not yet. I'm just taking each day as it comes. Walking a lot, going to concerts, art galleries, visiting Holly and the children.'

She smiled angelically, leaving Eimear at a total loss. What could you say to someone who simply wasn't listening?

'What about Ben? Have you heard from him?'

'Not since his letter – oh!'

Suddenly she winced and put her hand to the front of her smocked dress. Instantly Eimear was at her side.

'What? What is it?'

'Nothing . . . only I think the baby is kicking. Sort of – fluttering. Here, feel it.'

She guided Eimear's hand to the spot and they stood in silence, waiting for the next faint flutter.

'Oh, yes! It is! Oh, Aran. I feel as excited as if I were having it myself.'

Quietly Aran leaned against her and put her head on her shoulder.

'In a way we're kind of having it together, Eimear. You're the only one who knows about it, apart from Dan and the Mitchells. I'd never manage without you. You will be with me when it's born, won't you? At the hospital?'

'At your side. I wouldn't miss it for the world. Unless – unless your mother comes over, and takes over. After all it is her right, her duty really—'

'No. It's Ben's baby, and she detests Ben. I don't want her to be there, saying hateful things about him. You and I are going to have this baby between us, Eimear, and not tell her until then. Promise me?'

'Aran, I can't promise such a thing! She and Conor are your parents, you must—'

'Please, Eimear. I want you with me, you and Dan.'

Aran's tone was pleading, almost desperate, and Eimear wished with equal desperation that she could agree.

'But I can't, Aran. You've got to tell them.'

Reluctantly Aran wrote, and braced herself before opening the reply that arrived a week later, feeling almost the way she had felt the night Lorcan Miller attacked her. Instinctively she was sure it was better to say nothing – unless Molly was going to rally round, for the sake of the child? Her grandchild, that might soften her attitude, dilute her moral outrage?

It was a slim chance, but it was not impossible. After all, the letter had been addressed to both parents; Conor would have some say in their response, surely. In fact it would not have killed Conor to go up to the phone kiosk in the village and call her immediately, say something affectionate and encouraging. But perhaps he had needed a little time to think things over. Apprehensively she opened the envelope.

'Dear Aran,
Your father and I cannot tell you how shocked we are by your terrible news. Of course it was bound to happen, but that makes it all the worse. Why wouldn't you listen, when I said he'd never marry you?
Well, now he's gone and here you are left to see the joke. I hope it will teach you not to mix with that type of person again. Meanwhile, we must decide what is to be done. As you are in London there is a good chance it can be handled quietly and nobody need know about it.
Your father thinks you should come home and have the child here, but as I have explained to him that is out of the question. One Deirdre Devlin in this village is quite enough. If you could hear the way the boys talk about her! Your father agrees that that would not be very nice for you.
So I have spoken to Father Carroll, who tells me there is an excellent home for young women in your position, near London, run by Irish nuns. I am enclosing their address so you can contact them and they will make arrangements, both for the birth and for the adoption. I'm sure you realise that this is the only course open to you and will be sensible about it. A good home will be found with two Catholic parents who can raise the child properly, and you will be free to start over.
I hope you will start over, as you have been a good daughter in some ways, we never thought you would bring any shame on us. But nobody knows about it except Father Carroll, who says he will pray for you as we will ourselves. We haven't told the boys, and of course you mustn't tell the Rafters. As a teacher who holds a responsible job alongside Father Carroll, I'm sure Mrs Rafter would be very shocked.
We are glad to hear you're not in need of anything, and will try to get over to see you if we can. Let us know when would be the best time. Father Carroll says you will feel much better when you go to confession and receive absolution, and that the nuns will help you to find work after the event.
Mam and Dad.'

It was the longest letter Molly had ever written. Stunned, Aran read it several times, digesting everything in it, searching for what was not in it.

Love. It was not even signed with love, only with Molly's spiky signature. Conor had not signed it at all. Not added a single word of his own, not even asked how she was, mentioned the boat she had given him or scrawled the X that symbolised a kiss.

Nothing.

And suddenly she knew why. Molly had lied. Molly had not told Conor. Not told him, because he would fret and worry, want her to come home immediately, have the baby in Ireland, return to live with them. He would want everything she did not want. Three of her five children were off her hands now, there was no place in her house for an errant daughter or for a baby. A baby that she might have to look after, if its mother were lucky enough to find a job.

Well, she needn't worry. Her daughter was not going to be a burden to her, and neither was her grandchild. Without reading the letter again, Aran tore it up and dropped it in the bin.

Hannah Lowry was adamant. They would all go to London for Christmas: Eimear, Dan and herself. Eimear needn't even think of trying to work out any other arrangement, because it was as simple as that. Christmas only got complicated when people wouldn't co-operate and made others feel guilty for their own selfishness.

'I'll enjoy London thoroughly, Eimear. When people say they have to spend Christmas in their own homes it generally just means they won't make the effort to enjoy it anywhere else. Now you tell Aran you'll be there and that I'm coming with you.'

Eimear was very grateful to Hannah for simplifying what might have been a problem, and to Dan who took exactly the same view. They were all going to London and wasn't it a good thing too; for once nobody would be able to disrupt his Christmas dinner. Any emergency calls would be handled by Fiach O'Sullivan over in Leemanway and that was the end of it. Besides, Aran was six months pregnant now, it was high time he saw her and talked some sense into her, said the things that were too tricky to say over the phone.

'Such as?'

'Such as telling Ben Halley that he's going to have a child to support.'

'I'm sure he would support it, if he knew. But you won't convince her, Dan.'

Dan was sure that he would – until he arrived in Hampstead, and saw the way Aran's face closed over when he broached the subject. Ben was gone, she said, and that was that. But she listened with interest as Hannah began to talk, over Christmas lunch, of her life as a single mother.

'Of course, Eimear was two when her father died. I didn't have to go through the most demanding stage on my own, the midnight feeds or the teething – heavens, she cried like the rain! I used to worry myself sick, thinking it couldn't be only the teeth, that there must be something seriously wrong with her.'

'But there wasn't?'

Aware that she had Aran's full attention, Hannah kept talking.

'No. Not then. But she got measles when she was four, and was

253

very ill then. I slept in her room with her, on a mattress on the floor, every night for a week, listening to make sure she was still breathing. I don't know how I kept my job, because I couldn't give it my full attention, used to be half asleep in the mornings. But of course I couldn't afford to lose it, or to be ill myself – who would have looked after her then?'

Who, indeed? Aran pushed her food back and forth on her plate, forced to address the questions she had not addressed. Enquiringly, Hannah fixed her gaze on her.

'Do you drive, Aran? Have you a car?'

'No, Mrs Lowry. Not yet. I thought I might learn last summer, only I was away, and then when I came back I was a bit upset, didn't feel able to concentrate.'

'Well, you'd better learn as soon as possible, because you'll be spending the next fifteen years or more driving your child everywhere, to school, to other children's houses, to parties, music lessons, picnics, whatever – there'll be no time for a social life of your own.'

Eimear smiled.

'Aran has gone into purdah already, Mother. Hasn't seen any of her friends for months.'

'Is that so? Well, that's a pity, because single mothers have to rely on their friends a lot – for babysitting, for sudden emergencies, for all sorts of things. Of course, if they have children themselves, then you can return the favour. I can remember six or seven children running round my house sometimes, whooping like red Indians, tearing it apart! Do you know many mothers, Aran?'

Horrified, Aran realised that she didn't know even one, apart from Holly Mitchell whose life was already full to overflowing.

'H'mm. I'd recommend that you get to know some, then. You can't raise a child without a great deal of help. But at least you're secure financially, I gather?'

'I – yes, I am – for now.'

'For now?' Hannah raised her eyebrows. 'Might I ask what you mean, Aran? For how long?'

'F – for about a year.'

'A year! Good heavens, child! What are you going to do then?'

'I – I haven't quite decided yet—'

'But you must decide! What about medical expenses, school fees, food, clothes, life insurance? The older the child gets, the more it will cost. Would you consider selling this house and buying a smaller one?'

'I don't own this house, actually, it's only rented . . .'

Dismally Aran's voice trailed away. Hannah was putting things in a very cold light. But undeniably she knew what she was talking about.

'Rented? So you don't even have any equity? Well, I must say – oh, dear, it's none of my business. No more wine, Dan, I'm talking too much!'

Aran's face was creased with concern.

'Please go on, Mrs Lowry. I want to know what to expect.'

'Perhaps it would be kinder not to tell you.'

'Please. I need to know.'

Hannah glanced at Dan and Eimear.

'Well, I don't want Eimear to think she was ever anything but a great joy to me. But she was a great worry too, and a great responsibility. Ideally a child should have two parents, to share the job, because it's twenty-four hours a day, seven days a week. But much as I worried about my ability to do it, I worried about her a lot more, growing up without a father. At Christmas, on her birthdays, at school plays and sports events, her first dance, her first date . . . it was so sad sometimes, to look at her all by herself. It nearly broke my heart, the day she graduated from college, the day she got married, with no proud father there beside her.'

Silently Aran gazed at Eimear, not seeing the look Hannah exchanged with Dan.

'I hadn't thought of all that.'

'Hadn't you? Tell me, Aran, how old are you now?'

'Twenty.'

'Twenty. So I was nearly twice your age when I had Eimear. Yet even then I found it very difficult to cope, without her father. I don't mean to sound discouraging, Aran, but I must warn you that bringing up a child alone is very demanding, and can be as hard on the child as on the mother. Will you take my advice and remember one thing?'

'Yes, Mrs Lowry – what is it?'

'The child's interests. You must always put the child's interests before your own. Always.'

Biting her lip, looking very lost, Aran nodded.

'Yes. I will remember that.'

'Thanh, do me a favour, will you?'

'Sure, Ben. What you want?'

'I want you to call Aran. Invite her to this party – housewarming, New Year, whatever you like to call it.'

'OK. But why you not ask her yourself?'

'Because I think you might stand a better chance of persuading her.'

Thanh smiled and sighed simultaneously. Ben's efforts to establish a friendship with Aran were frequent and sincere, but they were not getting very far. It wasn't that Aran was angry, or bitter; it was simply that she was incapable of settling for anything less than what she had had before. Mere friendship was worse than nothing, to a woman still as much in love as he suspected she was. That was why she preferred a clean, complete break.

Without much hope, he telephoned her, and was taken aback to be answered by a man. A friendly man, who sounded Irish.

'Just a moment, I'll get her for you.'

As soon as Aran came to the phone, he could hear the reluctance in her voice. But her New Year wishes were cordial, even if she did not extend them to Ben.

'Ben having New Year party, Aran, in his new flat. He want you to come – big social event you know, lots of interesting people to meet.'

'Thanks, Thanh. But I have some friends staying with me. We've already made arrangements for that night.'

'You bring friends with you.'

'No. We've booked a restaurant table. Thanks anyway.'

Her tone was so firm that Thanh didn't even attempt to argue. But he thought Ben would want him to come back with as much information as possible.

'Who your friends?'

'Oh, they're from Ireland. Nobody you'd know.'

'Well, we sorry not to meet them, or see you.'

'I'm sorry, Thanh. But it's for the best. Wish Rani a happy New Year for me, will you?'

'Yes. But what I tell Ben?'

'Tell him – tell him his piano is going to waste.'

Despondently, Thanh hung up and went to tell Ben.

'No good. She not come. She have friends staying.'

'What friends? Who are they?'

'She not say. But very nice Irish man answer telephone.'

'Irish man? Who is he?'

'I tell you, she not say!'

The look on Ben's face prompted Thanh to make himself scarce. Now that he was general minder and factotum, he had plenty of work to do, and plenty of places in which to hide out in this enormous new flat. But, large as it was, he could still hear *Dislocation* as Ben began to play it a few minutes later, so loudly that the walls vibrated.

It was a huge party and, as Aran expected, it was reported in several of the gossip columns. But she waited until Eimear, Dan and Hannah

256

had returned to Ireland before sitting down to read them.

'Over two hundred people crowded into the new Kensington home of rock star Ben Halley . . . amongst them producer Myles Irving, tour manager Kevin Ross, lyricist Kelwin Hughes, publicist Jessica Hunter, radio personality Gavin Seymour . . .'

There were photos of all of them, skewed lurching photos obviously taken at the height of the revelry, when people were brandishing bottles and kissing everyone in sight. To look at Kevin and Jessica, anyone would think they were having a passionate affair, Kevin lewdly embedded in Jessica's cleavage, Jessica unprecedentedly glam-rock in a skirt that would barely suffice as a Band-Aid. But of course they were just good friends – which was the caption under the photo of Ben.

'Just good friends: Ben Halley and actress Sasha Harwood sizzle at his housewarming party.'

Aran had never heard of an actress named Sasha Harwood, but knew that was what they all called themselves, the London girls who made careers of attending parties. Undoubtedly Sasha had worked her way in through a friend of a friend, her path smoothed by her bright wide smile, her tiny lurex dress, her racehorse legs and gleaming black hair – exceptionally long black hair, that Aran had seen somewhere before.

At the Shot Snake. Suddenly Aran remembered her vividly. The girl who had pushed her way through the crowd to kiss Ben, the night they'd recorded the demo tape that had found its way to Gavin Seymour.

Ben had not responded then. But he was responding now, his eyes locked with Sasha's, his arms wrapped around her in a way that said it all. If Sasha was just a good friend, then she, Aran, was Ludwig van Beethoven.

So this was why he had invited her – not even in person, but via Thanh. To show off Sasha and make it clear he was enjoying his freedom, was not regretting his decision or going to change his mind? Tears blurred her eyes as she stared at the photograph, but the message was crystal clear.

How long, she wondered, had it taken them to warm the house?

For twenty minutes or more she sat with the paper on her lap, tears spilling down her cheeks onto the bulge in the front of her dress, wondering how many more of these photographs she would see in the years to come. Would it always be Sasha, or was she just the new model for 1980?

Probably. Sasha, Annabel, Fiona, Felicity – even their names were predictable, these 'actresses' who prowled London by night, stalking their easy prey, paralysing and devouring it. And God, Ben was so easy! Photogenic, sexy, what the papers called 'great copy'. Probably Jessica would tip them off about each new girl, get every story into every publication. And, some day, their child would be old enough to read. What would she do, then? How would she protect it? Even if she never named the father, never told the child or anyone else, somebody would find out, work it out. Aran Campion had a child and, if you did your mathematics, that child had been conceived in Crete in July 1979 when she was with Ben Halley.

Aran did not panic easily, but she began to panic now, facing for the first time the implications of what she had done. Some urge, some need had made her conceive a baby. Pride would not let her tell Ben what he did not want to know, but he was going to find out – maybe from a newspaper reporter. Then what? Regular cheques from his solicitor, and a child growing up in the knowledge of his indifference? Or a shotgun wedding, prompted by Deva, regretted by everyone? A tug-of-love, ten years from now? Or a runaway teenager, off to claim its father?

At the very best, a child born and raised in secret, in fear of discovery, without the father that Hannah said was so important. But what right had she, to do that? And *how* was she going to do it?

For six months she had managed to conceal her pregnancy, by avoiding every single person she knew, by opting out of the music world and the life that went with it. With luck she could survive for the remaining three months, give birth in a quiet discreet hospital and be home before anyone heard about it. But one day she would be pushing the pram and she would run into Rani; or she would be at the school gates just as Kevin drove by, or Myles, or Ben himself.

Oh, dear God, what had she done? And what was to be done next? She must wake up, she must plan, organise, think this out. And above all, as Hannah had said, she must put the child's interests first.

Early in February, one cold day when the rain was coursing down the windows, Aran answered the telephone warily, fearful as she always was now of what she might be going to hear.

It was Molly.

'Aran? Did you get my letter?'

'Yes, Mother. I got it.'

'Then why haven't you answered me?'

'Because I – I needed time to think. About what you said.'

'And have you thought?'

'Yes. I have. You needn't worry, Mother. There won't be any scandal, nobody is going to know.'

258

'Indeed they are not! You're a sensible girl, Aran, you can imagine what it would be like for me if anyone here knew. Bad enough to have my daughter living in sin, bringing her coloured boyfriend here to Dunrathway under my nose – but then he runs off and leaves her pregnant! Of course your father is – is too upset to even talk about it.'

'Yes. I thought that must be why he hadn't been in touch.'

'I haven't told anyone else – Val or Sher or your brothers. I thought that was the best thing.'

'Yes, Mother. That's the best thing.'

There was a pause.

'So you've made arrangements? For the – the birth?'

'Yes. Everything is arranged.'

'And do you want – should I – come over? I'm quite prepared to, you know, I wouldn't have it said that I ever left you to—'

'No, Mother. Holly Mitchell is a nurse, she knows people, has taken care of all the details. Other friends will be there too, I'll be quite all right.'

'I see. Well, if you're sure—'

'I'm sure.'

'Good. That's settled, then, and we'll say no more about it. It's all for the best, you know, you'll see that when you're older.'

'I can see it already.'

'And afterwards, you'll get a new job, won't you?'

'Yes. There's always something in London.'

She could hear Molly's exhaled sigh of relief quite distinctly. Along with her sweaters, she had successfully exported her problem.

'You're a hard worker, Aran, and apart from this one thing you've been a good daughter. I'm praying for you, that everything will be all right, and that God will forgive you. You won't ever do anything like this again, will you?'

'No, Mother. Never.'

'There you are. You've learned your lesson already. I only wish you had listened to me in the first place.'

Aran thought she would scream.

'Well, I'll say goodbye then. Let me know when – when it's all over, won't you?'

'I will. Thank you for calling me, and give my love to Dad.'

'Yes – well, he's away at sea a lot at the moment. But I'll tell him when I see him.'

Abruptly, she hung up .

For the first six months of her pregnancy, Aran had avoided reading the newspapers, listening to the radio or watching television, doing anything that might confront her with Ben's face or the unbearable sound of his voice. But in the last three she found herself scanning them all in the desperate hope that she would see or hear him, find some evidence that he had tired of Sasha Harwood and was ready to reassess his decision. Even now, it was not too late. If only he would come back to her, discover her pregnancy, stand by her . . . oh, she would give anything, if only he would. Night after night she lay alone in her bed, thinking of him, missing him even more than she had in the first shell-shocked months.

Every day she looked at the piano, ran her hand over its contours as once she had run it over his, wondering why he did not want it. How he had loved it, at first! Could he really love the new one as much? And what of his new management, at the same company where Myles had offered to get her a job? In retrospect she knew that Myles had been devious, but well-meaning, trying to bring them back together. But now Ben was just one more name on that company's list. They couldn't possibly give him the personal care or attention she had given him – could give him still, if only he would give her reason to.

In ten years' time, he had said. In ten years, it would have been different. They would have married then, and had children. They would have been a family. It was not that he did not love her, it was only that he was not ready – oh, why could he not be ready? What did he need Sasha for, or anyone? Vaguely she remembered something that Eimear had said to her, that day in Dunrathway when they had sat talking and laughing together; men, she had said, matured at a different rate to women. Emotionally they were light years behind. It had seemed so funny, that distant day. But now she knew it was true, and it was a source of infinite grief to her.

Oh, Ben! Come back, come home. Please come home.

With every ounce of her strength she wished for him, fingering the silver clef at her neck, touching the photograph that stood on the table in the front room, wandering desolate about the empty house. The beautiful house that would never be a home, without him.

But a week after Molly's call the first daffodil bloomed in the garden, followed a few days later by tulips, pale pink among the yellow bells; her heart lifted as she looked out at all the colour, feeling the first warmth of spring on her skin. And there was pleasure in the oboe as she played it each morning to the baby, standing at the window where the gentle sun could touch her. The baby had no room to kick freely any more, but she was sure it was listening, absorbing the music as it gathered its strength to enter the world. The baby who, like Eimear, would never know its father.

Its father. As she lay in bed early one morning thinking of Ben, something came to her, and she padded downstairs in her bare feet to search for something she had put away. Where was it, what had she done with it? Had she thrown it away, in those first distracted days?

No. She had not, and eventually she found it: the tape she had made last year, travelling through Europe with Ben, recording his live performances along the way on the tape recorder that had been such an invaluable investment. All his best songs were on it, all the applause and the atmosphere of those memorable nights, and she smiled as she put it on, adjusting the bass and treble until the sound was just right.

'Are you listening, muffin? Do you want to hear your dad? He has a beautiful voice . . . and that's him playing the piano, too. You're going to play like him when you grow up, you're going to sing like an angel, so you just listen to this, now.'

She supposed she must be mad, talking to an unborn infant who could not possibly understand, but as Ben's voice rose pure and clear she felt oddly peaceful, sensing his presence and the child's, the harmony of the family unit. For the first and last time they were all together, as close as destiny might ever permit them to be, sharing the music that was their unbreakable bond.

Every day for the rest of her pregnancy Aran played the tape to her baby, finding comfort and inspiration in every note, smiling to herself as she paced back and forth reciting names aloud, wondering which one would best suit her son or daughter. Conor had named her after an island, perhaps prophetically since she was so alone now, but *amhrán* was also the Irish word for a song. What songs would her child sing, what joy would it bring?

On the morning of the spring equinox, March 21, she felt a twinge. Just a small twinge in her back, but Dr Crofton had told her to take no chances. Immediately, she phoned him, and then Holly Mitchell. Holly said she would be there in twenty minutes to take her to the hospital where Dr Crofton would meet them, and Aran beamed as she picked up the phone again to call Eimear.

'Eimear, I think the baby is coming – yes, now, today! I know it's early, but you—'

Cutting her short, Eimear said that she and Dan were on their way. There was a flight at ten, they would be there by lunchtime, and under no circumstances was Aran to have the baby before they arrived.

She laughed.

'I'll do my best! Hurry!'

They arrived four hours later to find Aran sitting up in her hospital bed, talking to Holly, looking apprehensive but elated.

'Oh, I'm so glad you're here! But you needn't have rushed after all, Dr Crofton says it won't be for ages yet. This evening, or early tonight.'

Flustered and wildly excited, Dan raced away in search of Dr Crofton, and was appalled to be told that he had gone to lunch.

'Lunch! How can he be, his duty is here with this young girl, how can anyone eat at a time like this!'

Nothing would convince Dan that everything was under control; for the first time his habitual calm deserted him completely as he paced up and down, ran out to buy flowers, came back to accost Dr Crofton, went out again for champagne and came back with a huge teddybear instead. Eimear and Holly laughed as he staggered in with it, but Aran was deeply touched by his anxiety. Finally Walter Mitchell arrived, and was instructed to take him away to the nearest pub for a stiff brandy. Looking equally anxious, Walter did as he was told.

But they were back long before Aran was taken at last to the delivery room, clutching Eimear's hand, frightened when she saw the medical staff in their gowns and masks. Eimear was nervous too, but kept her voice low and steady; as Aran said, they were going to have this baby together.

If it ever came! For Aran's sake she prayed that Dr Crofton was right about everything going smoothly, no complications being expected. But Aran was breathing rapidly, wincing, her hair damp with sweat, looking very small and scared as she tried to do what the nurses were telling her and remember her breathing technique. Firmly, Eimear held her hand as she began to breathe in the same rhythm.

'That's it . . . just hang on to me, try to relax . . .'

But her own tension mounted as the first hour went by, the second and then the third – God, would it never end! Although she was in pain, Aran refused to have an epidural, but Eimear herself was beginning to wish someone would stun her into merciful oblivion. If this baby didn't come soon she would insist on the epidural, because even a fit, healthy young mother could not go on like this for much longer.

But Aran struggled on, determined to miss nothing, do everything she thought best for the baby. After four hours she was exhausted, after five the entire medical team was exhausted. And then, just as they all began to reconsider their options, everything happened at once.

Eimear knew she would never forget the look on Aran's face as her baby came into the world, drew its first breath and yelled at the top of its lungs. It was a small dark baby with perfect features, and it yelled again as it was put into her arms. Dazed, blissful, she held it to her, her eyes vast with wonder and delight.

'It's an opera singer!'

Faint with relief and emotion, Eimear laughed giddily.

'It's a girl, Aran. We have a little girl.'

If she had loved Ben Halley, Aran could find no words to describe what she felt for his daughter. For hours on end she cradled the baby, touching each tiny finger in turn, nuzzling the soft fragrant skin, euphoric with love and pride.

'Isn't she beautiful? Isn't she just beautiful?'

Dan and Eimear thought they were both beautiful, mother and child, as they rested together after the ordeal of birth. As pale as she had been the night before, Aran was rosy now, the pain forgotten in the warm light of morning. Wrapped in a white shawl, her little girl lay sleeping peacefully, her pink mouth slightly open, curved as if in a smile. A cot stood at the end of the bed, but Aran was cherishing every moment, could not bear to put her down.

'Look, Eimear, such long eyelashes! And she has a dimple – oh, she's opening her eyes!'

Briefly, the baby stirred, regarded them all thoughtfully for a moment, and went back to sleep. But there was no mistaking the brown eyes, the black eyelashes, the dimple in the dusky cheek; she was heartbreakingly pretty, and she was Ben's. Everyone saw it clearly, but nobody could bear to say it. Gently, Dan reached down to touch her face with his finger.

'My God, she's so perfect, so gorgeous. What are you going to call her, sweetheart?'

Aran beamed.

'Rhianna.'

'Rhianna. Is it Irish, or Welsh? Or Scots?'

'It's a Celtic name. It means little maiden.'

Dan gazed longingly at the infant.

'Well, baby Rhianna, are you going to come up and say hello to me?'

Aran handed the child to him, and smiled as he took the bundle gingerly into his arms, peering at it very tenderly.

'She's so light! She weighs nothing.'

'She weighs six pounds and five ounces, as I can testify to my cost. But it was worth every moment . . . oh, Dan, men don't know what they're missing! Having a baby is the most fabulous experience, I just can't tell you how happy I am.'

But Aran didn't need to tell him, or Eimear; she was radiant, her face changed overnight from a girl's to a woman's, with a fulfilment in it that told them this achievement was the highlight of her life. For a few moments Dan said nothing, until he sensed Eimear's almost palpable ache and handed the baby to her. Without protest Rhianna snuggled into Eimear's shoulder, and Eimear's eyes were very bright, her hands trembling as they enfolded her.

'Oh, Rhianna. We've waited so long for you. So long.'

Her voice was barely a whisper as she murmured into the fine dark hair, stroking and clasping the baby while Aran watched protectively. But her daughter was in safe hands, the safest, most loving hands a child could ever need.

It had all been discussed so often, down to the smallest detail; but Dan and Eimear wanted to discuss it yet again, to satisfy themselves that Aran was absolutely sure. But, sitting in an armchair with Rhianna on her lap, Aran insisted that she was.

'I've thought about nothing else since Christmas. I'm alone, I'm unemployed, I'm going to have to find work and start over from scratch. You're happily married, there are two of you, you're mature and you can look after her much better than I can. You can give her a proper family home, in a small safe village by the sea, in a country where there are no mass murders, no rampaging thugs.

'Hannah will be like a grandmother to her, she'll have a dog, a pony, lots of little friends her own age. And, now that you're giving up work, Eimear, she'll have what she needs most of all – a mother who doesn't have to fit her in with anything else, who isn't too tired to play with her, read to her, teach her everything she needs to learn. I know you're going to be wonderful at it, and love her every bit as much as I do.'

Aran spoke calmly, quietly, but Eimear knew the battle she was fighting, and could not believe it had really been won.

'What if you change your mind, Aran? What if you find the sacrifice is too much, and want her back?'

'Eimear, I will want Rhianna every day for the rest of my life. But I will never take her. All I ask is that you and Dan devote yourselves to her, give her a secure happy childhood and let me see her as often as I can.'

'Without telling her who you are?'

'Without telling her anything until she asks. Maybe by then she'll be old enough to understand . . . but she will grow up as Rhianna Rafter, and you will be her parents.'

264

Parents. Dan and Eimear sat together, holding hands, unable to believe that it was happening. But if it was, then they were going to do everything in their power to prove themselves worthy of it. Giving up work would be a terrible wrench, Eimear knew, for many women; but teaching other people's children was nothing compared to raising one of her own. She wanted to do it, wanted to spend every waking hour with Rhianna, wanted to give her job to some young graduate who needed work much more badly than she did. Dan's income was perfectly adequate, and he was utterly dependable; if people thought she was crazy to put this child before her career, well, let them. This child was her only hope of having a family, becoming the mother she so desperately wanted to be.

But still Dan was worried.

'What if Ben—?'

Aran's expression became guarded and masked, as it always did when Ben was mentioned.

'Ben is on tour in America with his new girlfriend. He has no idea he has a daughter. If he had, he'd be horrified.'

'Oh, Aran, how can you know that?'

'I know. Only one thing truly matters to Ben, and that's his music. He'd take financial responsibility, but he would never come back here to settle down with us, to be a father in any real sense. He – he isn't mature, Dan. He's a wonderful man in many ways, but he's a musician first and foremost. Restless, unstable – I'm sure Rhianna wouldn't hold his attention for any longer than I did.'

They heard the hurt in her voice, and had to concede the point.

'But where does this leave us all legally?'

She had thought of that.

'Well, we can make it all formal if you like. I suppose it would be called long term fostering. But I'd rather think of it as a private adoption – without any lawyers or paperwork, because our trust and friendship is central to it. You'll be Rhianna's permanent guardians, with my full consent, and I'd like it if you'd let her be called Rafter. I don't want the press to ever start digging or leave any way for anyone to connect her with Ben.'

Dan drew breath to discuss the details further, but at that moment Rhianna drew breath too, and began to cry. That cry did something to him, something fundamental. He felt it in Eimear too as she tensed beside him.

'All right, Aran. Let's simply say it's a private adoption, mutually agreed by everyone.'

Nodding, Aran didn't reply as she got up to walk the child up and down, soothing her in a singsong voice. At just ten days old, she was a sunny baby, but occasionally she screamed loud and long for no apparent reason. Anxiously, Eimear peered at her.

'Is she hungry, Aran?'

'No! She's just exercising her lungs. Aren't you, cherub? You only want us to stop talking and pay attention to you.'

. That was exactly what Rhianna wanted, Dan saw, his heart tightening as he looked at her. And it was what he wanted; like her mother, the little girl had taken a strange and immediate hold of him . . . yet she was so unlike Aran!

Something in the way she cried, with her head thrown back for maximum volume, told him that Rhianna Rafter was going to be a handful. And he couldn't wait to hold the handful, to call it his own.

'But we'll have to put something in writing before she can be baptised, Aran.'

'I suppose we will . . . why don't you go to see Thomas Allen, then, over in Leemanway? I'm sure he can draw up whatever document is necessary, and I'll sign it. But Dan – it's not documents I'm interested in. It's that you and Eimear really want to do this, feel able for it. I don't want you to take Rhianna just out of – of pity or sympathy. I want to know that you really want her. *Need* her. That you'll love her even when she's crying or bold or cheeky, even when she's driving you crazy.'

Hugging Rhianna to her, she smiled.

'Because you will drive them crazy sometimes, won't you, muffin? You're an angel, but sometimes you'll be a little devil!'

Dan knew she would. Even now, watching the small fists flail, he was almost tempted to laugh.

'She certainly knows how to command an audience!'

As if realising that all eyes were now upon her, Rhianna sighed in satisfaction and cuddled complacently into Aran's arms.

'Yes, Dan. I think she's going to need a lot of attention. You will give it to her, won't you?'

'Yes, Aran. If you're sure about this, we will.'

'I am sure, Dan. If I were in Dunrathway, if my sisters were nearby, if my mother could be – but I'm here in London, Ben is gone, I have – I have no choice! If she's to have a real home and family, then she will have them with you.'

Yes. He would see that she did. For their sake, and for his wife's, he was going to take this child, this chance that Aran was offering to them.

'But how will you cope, when – when we go? What will you do?'

She looked at him soberly, her eyes dark as graphite, more adult than he had ever seen them.

'I'll grow up, Dan. I'll find work, forget Ben Halley and get my life back under control.'

She sounded firm, and very controlled; but at that moment something vanished from his vision: the shy girl he had come to love so much. Now, the only child in the room was Rhianna. Rhianna, whose father had taken the last of Aran's girlhood with him, all her illusions, and all her love. The kind of love that nobody ever found twice.

But Ben was so young. Too young, to know the value of it. And nobody could blame Ben for simply being young. Thoughtfully, Dan looked at Rhianna again.

'Is there anything you'd like to give her, Aran? Any small memento, to take to Ireland?'

She shook her head. The only thing she wanted to give her child was what she couldn't give her – security. A home, a proper family.

But then she went to Eimear, placed the baby in her arms and reached up with her own, fumbling at the clasp of the silver clef at the nape of her neck. Taking it off, she held it out to Dan.

'Will you give her this? When she – when she's older?'

'Of course.'

For her sake he kept his voice steady. If the tears started now, they would never stop.

'And – and maybe music lessons, if she ever wants them?'

'Everything. We'll give her everything it's ever in our power to give her.'

There was a laden silence, a struggle in all their hearts.

Cradling the baby, Eimear did not speak, her thick brown hair hiding her face so that neither Dan nor Aran could see it. But Aran knew without being told; her daughter would have everything, everything. But what would she have? Without Rhianna, without Ben, what would be left to her?

Nothing. Nothing only grief, grief and the fading memory of lost love. With all her heart she wanted this child, wanted to give it the life that Aran could not. But it was too much. She could not take Rhianna. Slowly, she stood up.

'No, Aran. She's yours. She belongs to you.'

But Aran looked at Rhianna, and at Eimear.

'She has always belonged to you, Eimear. Long before she was born, she belonged to you and Dan. I had her for you.'

I had her for you. For years the memory had lain suppressed in Dan and Eimear's common memory, but now it came back to them both, the candles on Eimear's birthday cake, Aran's young voice in the falling dusk, promising them that it would happen.

'Of course it will! I promise!'

But she had not even known what she was promising. How could she know, any more than she could know, now, what she was doing?

How could she know?

Over the remaining few days before Dan and Eimear took Rhianna to Dunrathway Aran spent every moment with her, assembling toys and clothes, every small item she thought might be a comfort. Out in the garden she took photographs, and then Eimear took several of her, standing under the blossoming apple trees with Rhianna in her arms, sitting on the grass holding her hand as she lay on a rug, pointing to a swallow as it flew overhead. Then she made a tape, one that would surely mystify any other listener, of her daughter's small cries and murmurs, all the sounds that were already distinctive to her ear. Finally, as she bedded the baby down for the night, she snipped off a lock of her dark hair, wrapped it in tissue paper and laid it in the leather case that contained all her memorabilia of Ben. Amongst them was the wooden pencil box from Salzburg, and she smiled; the day Rhianna started school, she would give her that.

But inexorably the day of their departure arrived, a day that Eimear found the happiest and most agonising of her life. She could not contain her tears as she kissed Aran goodbye, took Rhianna from her and got into the taxi. But Aran's eyes were dry as she released the child with a last kiss, inhaling the scent of her silken skin. Burying her face in the baby's, she lifted it after five or six seconds, and let her go.

Wordlessly Eimear slid into the car as she turned to hug Dan, tightly and trustingly.

'Take her, Dan. Take her home, where she belongs.'

It was the third day of April, a cloudless blue morning perfumed with new grass and apple blossom, and Dan thought he would carry those fragrances with him for the rest of his life, as he would carry the responsibility of those words, and the memory of Aran's face as she said them.

Rhianna slept all the way to the airport, and by the time they boarded the plane Eimear's tears had given way to the joy that was stealing into her soul, the process of bonding and loving that had already begun. But Dan's fingers tightened on the silver necklet in his pocket, his heart clenching with pain as he thought of the girl they had gained, and of the girl they had lost. As often as humanly possible, he and Eimear would see Aran again, but he did not think they would ever see the same person again.

Chapter Twelve

America was mystified by Ben Halley, and Ben Halley was mystified by America. At first sight, it did not look radically different: the language was the same, the food was recognisable, the buildings were not exotic or soaked in the impenetrable legend of centuries. But as the tour progressed he began to find that its attitude, its mindset, was the antithesis of anything he had experienced in Europe.

Even in the bigger cities, in Boston, New York, Atlanta and New Orleans, he sensed the wariness in the audiences. They were not hostile – on the contrary, they were extremely polite – but from the moment he stepped on stage he felt the chasm between him and them, the gulf between his culture and theirs. His music was very popular, especially *Dislocation* which the blacks and Hispanics had adopted as their own, but his video had not been released on this side of the Atlantic, and his appearance was a shock. Even New York didn't know what to make of it, while in Houston the critics were openly derisory. Frequently he was invited to appear on television chat shows, but many were confrontational and two ended in chaos.

'Christ, Kevin, this is a disaster. What the hell are we going to do?'

But as ticket sales were solid, Kevin was sanguine.

'Stick with it, Ben, only tone it down a bit. Well, you'll probably be OK in San Francisco and Los Angeles, but I think you should drop the costumes everywhere else. The make-up, too. They'll feel more comfortable if you just wear jeans and a shirt. Americans like to know where they stand.'

Reluctantly Ben dropped his colourful disguises for denim, and the make-up which his professional assistant could not do half as well, in any event, as Aran had done it in Europe. But then, although the audiences were clearly more at ease, he began to feel even less so. In ordinary clothes, with his hair cut short, all the magic seemed to evaporate until he felt like a lumberjack, a truck driver moonlighting as a performance artist.

'I hate this, Kevin! It just isn't me! And I'm still not making any contact with them, not really connecting.'

If only he could talk to his audiences, he felt he might yet establish communication with them; but they didn't understand his accent, didn't get his wry wit or humorous innuendo at all. They simply wanted him to shut up and sing, get on with the show, or what was left of it after all the props and visual witticisms had been exorcised. That simplified things no end for the crew, but left him restless and dissatisfied.

'I don't know why they bother coming to see me at all, Kevin.'

'That's the point, Ben. They don't really come to see you. Only to hear you. They love the clarity of your voice, and I think Kelwin's lyrics suit them too.'

Kelwin's lyrics did suit them, but Ben wasn't at all sure whether they suited him. Undeniably, Kelwin was slick, upbeat and highly polished, yet his words did not sink deep into Ben's consciousness, he did not sing them with the same conviction he had sung when – when Aran was involved. In Europe he had often come off stage faint with fatigue, dizzy with elation, feeling that both he and his audience had been wrung emotionally dry. In America, he was aware only of high technical standards, glossy professionalism and an acute lack of – of what?

'I don't know what, Ben. The reviews are positive, improving all the time. What more do you want?'

'I can't articulate it, Kevin. Something is simply missing.'

Kevin thought it more likely that someone was missing. Sasha Harwood was great for publicity, the American photographers couldn't get enough of her, but she didn't affect Ben the same way Aran affected him. Everyone could feel the sexual chemistry between the two, yet nobody felt the affair would last. Where Aran had been warm, Sasha was too hot to handle, and Kevin thought she would soon burn herself out. Yet he couldn't take his eyes off her, and neither could Ben.

When a five-day rest period was reached at the end of April, Sasha prevailed on Ben to take her somewhere she had always wanted to go, to the gambling tables of Las Vegas. Kevin had no objection to that, but Thanh was dubious.

'You not get much rest there, Ben.'

'Oh, who cares? I'm so bored on stage, I can sleep there! Come on, let's go.'

He flew off as if a fuse had been lit under him, checked into an ostentatious hotel of Sasha's choice and, not knowing the first thing about roulette or blackjack, lost two thousand pounds on the very first night. But Sasha's charms compensated for that, and the next day he lounged complacently by the pool, eating one of the enormous American meals that Thanh thought sufficient for an entire family.

'Why you eat so much? You got nothing else to do?'

Stung, Ben replied that he had, rented a Harley-Davidson and zoomed off into the desert on it. But Sasha remained in Las Vegas, polishing her nails on her sun lounger before embarking on the first of several spectacular shopping expeditions. Thinking of the gauze scarf and glass bangle with which Aran had been content, Thanh gazed awestruck at the mountain of clothes, shoes, handbags and jewellery that accumulated at breakneck speed; apparently Ben had made the mistake of giving Sasha her own credit card.

'She only want you for your money, Ben.'

'Yeah, well, I only want her for her body, Thanh.'

Horrified to hear it in one way, Thanh was pleased in another. Ben was a fool, but at least he was an honest fool. There wasn't going to be any snap marriage in Reno, or any costly divorce back in London. Personally he couldn't wait to return there, see Beth and start planning their October wedding. Furthermore, he wanted to check out the rumours that were beginning to reach their ears from that city, some talk of a German company making a bid for Cedar, wanting to buy the company lock, stock and barrel – not because it was good, but because it was too good. He knew nothing of big business, but he knew that buying the competition was a common and effective way of dismantling it. Kevin was worrying already, in his neurotic way, but as yet Ben hadn't given it a thought. That, he said, was what he was paying his management company to do.

The American tour concluded in Seattle, where a belated thought occurred to Thanh.

'Was Aran's birthday last week, Ben. She twenty-one.'

'Yeah. I know.'

'Oh. I thought you forget.'

Ben frowned, and then smiled crookedly, ruefully.

'No. I didn't forget. I sent her some flowers.'

Flowers? Well, at least he hadn't forgotten, had made a gesture and an effort. But Thanh thought of the far more extravagant things he had bought Sasha, and reflected that really Ben Halley was for the birds.

Amery Cheam III did not think Ben Halley was for the birds. Amery Cheam, alone among Americans, thought he was intriguing and extremely original. Which was exactly what he was looking for. If the decision had been solely up to him, he'd have contacted young Halley immediately after seeing him in concert in New York, but first there had been the damn blasted board of directors to persuade, a process that would have scalded the heart of a stone. But finally, inevitably, Amery got his way. Picking up the phone, he instructed his secretary to track the singer down – now, immediately, before he left for London. He was somewhere in Seattle, it shouldn't take more than five minutes to get hold of him.

Four minutes and fifteen seconds later, he heard the clipped voice, English and yet not quite English, responding to his call from somewhere that sounded very noisy. Of course, these singers were always surrounded by their people, never alone for two minutes at a time.

'Mr Halley? My name is Amery Cheam III. Of Cheam Marine.'

'Cheam Marine?'

He didn't sound as if he'd ever heard of Cheam Marine. But then that was precisely why Amery wanted him.

'Yes. Yachts. Boatbuilders. Rhode Island, originally. But I'm calling from New York. Wondered if you might have time to stop off here on your way back to Britain. Bit of business I'd like to discuss with you.'

'Business? With me? Well, Mr Cheam, I think I'd better give you the name of my management company in London—'

'No. Never mind your management, for now. I want to talk to you, first. In person.'

'But—'

'About music, Mr Halley, About my boats and your music.'

Ben was bewildered. But he wasn't averse to the idea of talking about music. And Sasha wouldn't be averse to stopping off in New York.

'If you could just give me a little more information?'

Briskly, Amery gave it to him. Five minutes later both parties hung up, each equally interested in meeting the other.

Even by his own rapidly rising standards of luxury, Ben had to concede that Amery Cheam's New York mansion on the Upper East side of Manhattan made his new flat in Kensington look, by comparison, like a Salvation Army hostel. Panelled in oak, carpeted in V'Soske Joyce, hung with silks, tapestries and what he strongly suspected were real Rembrandts, it purred with money. Not just money, he noted, but style, confidence and character. Amongst the Rembrandts were several paintings by contemporary American artists, between the leatherbound classics were numerous novels by young Europeans, and the records stacked by the music system included the most eclectic assortment he had ever seen. If Amery Cheam was in his late fifties, as he appeared to be, he was not letting the grass grow under his patrician feet.

'Champagne? Scotch? Bourbon? What can I offer you, young man?'

Ben opted for vodka, and was brought a large Stolichnaya in a cut-crystal tumbler stacked with ice. Of course he should have brought Kevin Ross with him, Jessica Hunter or any one of the various people who might have the faintest notion how to conduct this meeting, but he was glad he had come alone. He was getting a little weary of being 'handled' like a child, told what to say and do, having all his decisions made for him. Without even Sasha squeaking breathlessly beside him, he felt like a stowaway on a ship departing for some unknown but exciting destination.

Amery Cheam was a tall, cordial man with blue eyes and white hair, classically dressed except for an eccentric waistcoat patterned with nautical knots. Amused by the mixture of the conventional and the egregious, Ben smiled as he sipped his Stolichnaya, reclining in a leather sofa so large he thought it would swallow him whole.

'Well, Mr Cheam, here I am. I think I know why, but I'm not altogether sure.'

Amery removed a clear plastic folder from his desk and handed it to him.

'What do you think of these?'

Opening it, Ben took out a dozen photographs, eight by ten, in full colour. Each depicted a yacht; some racing through flying spray, some drifting on azure tropical waters, others moored at anchor in nameless harbours.

'I can't comment technically, because I know nothing about yachts. But they're certainly works of art.'

'That's it. Works of art. Every boat we build is a work of art, Ben – I may call you Ben?'

'Certainly.'

'Every boat. Always has been and always will be. Custom made, designer fitted, hand finished. Cheam boats are the best boats in the world, my boy.'

For no reason that he could think of, Ben recalled Conor Campion's face – was it really only a year ago? – as he stood in the cabin of the Lady Aran, touching the brass fittings with wonder. Compared to these vessels, the Lady Aran was a floundering tub, but there was no doubt that owning her had done something to Conor. Boats, he supposed, must do the same thing for some men that

273

Harley-Davidsons did for him. Something liberating, challenging . . . something that Amery Cheam could detect in his music.

'The best, you say? Does everybody say that?'

'Everybody. Even our competitors. If you have time, I hope you might come back here in the summer, so I can take you out in one.'

'I'll make time.'

'Good. Now, as I told you over the phone, we don't advertise very much. In fact we've never advertised at all before, on television. But 1981 is our centenary year, so we're going to do three things: sponsor a race, make a documentary for visitors to our marine centre in Rhode Island, and mount a very high-quality advertising campaign. Of course it'll be handled by one of the agencies on Madison Avenue, but I wanted to get in ahead of all the gung-ho young fellers in their braces – what d'ye call 'em? What's the new word?'

'Yuppies.'

'That's it. Anyway, they'll have their own ideas for the visuals, but I have mine for the music. The theme. I'm a great lover of music, and I don't draw distinctions between the new and the old. Either it's good or it isn't. And I think yours is very good.'

'Thank you.'

'So, what we need is a theme. The same one for the television commercials, the race and the documentary. Have you ever seen *The Onedin Line*, Ben?'

'Yes. My mother is addicted to it.'

'Well, that's what I have in mind. A piece of music that everyone will recognise the moment they hear it. Something powerful, beautiful, unique – like our boats. Only the thing is, these are racing boats. That's where you come into the picture.'

'Is it?'

'Yes. The moment I heard you, saw you, I knew you were capable of much more than you're actually doing. Am I right?'

'Yes, sir. You are.'

'H'mm. Well, here's your chance to do it. You're young, but you respect the old, you understand how to be popular and contemporary without jettisoning tradition . . . I've acquainted myself with all your music, you know, studied it very carefully. Had the critiques flown out from London and read 'em all. Very interesting.'

Suddenly he laughed, and Ben knew he had indeed read them all, including the ones he had set fire to in Myles Irving's office. Grinning into his vodka, he laughed in turn.

'So you know I'm a risk?'

'Yes. Always did enjoy taking a risk. I'll give you two months, Ben. Two months to come up with something I can play to my board of directors and to the puppies – yuppies, these fellers on Madison. No lyrics. Just music.'

No lyrics. Ben felt the most profound sense of relief. Just pure, plain music.

'What d'ye think?'

'I think it's the answer to a prayer, Mr Cheam. I've wanted to do something like this for a long time. But it will take resources other than my own – an orchestra, and a studio for recording your demo tape.'

'Of course. You write the piece, choose your musicians, and leave the rest to me.'

'But I can't. My management company will want to know what I'm doing.'

'You tell 'em you're writing a theme for me, and that they're to call me. As we say here in America, my people will talk terms with your people.'

Ben wasn't remotely interested in 'terms', thinking that this was such an incredible opportunity that he should be paying Amery for it, not the other way round. He didn't want to talk commerce at all.

'I can't believe you're willing to take this kind of chance on a rock singer, Mr Cheam.'

'Like your style, my boy. Like your style, like your voice, like your face.'

He summoned his manservant to replenish their glasses, toasted the success of the venture and then, motioning to Ben to follow, led the way into another room, a salon elegantly but sparsely furnished, dominated by a grand piano. A concert grand, shining in the spring sunshine pouring in between the damask curtains on the four high windows.

'Care to try it?'

The lid was already raised, revealing that this was a test, just to make sure. Without hesitation Ben sat down at it, closed his eyes and played two pieces: first an experimental, untitled one of his own, and then an excerpt from the controversial work of the Argentinian composer Mauricio Kagel. Closing his eyes in turn, Amery listened reverently.

'Ah, yes. What's that called?'

Ben smiled and took a deep breath.

'I'm afraid it's called Variations Without A Fugue On Brahms' Variations On A Theme Of Handel.'

'Yes. I've heard it before. That young South American, isn't it? Kagel?'

'That's right. But he's not so young, he's nearly fifty – I mean—'

Too late, Ben wondered if he had put his foot in it. But Amery laughed.

'Younger than me, but more than twice as old as you. How old are you, Ben?'

'I'll be twenty-three in July.'

'Too young.'

Too young? To write like Kagel, did he mean? To be entrusted with his theme, after all? But Amery Cheam must have a fairly accurate idea how old he was. Candidly, he looked at him.

'I'm sure I can do it, sir.'

'I'm sure you can. That wasn't what I meant. I meant that you're too young to feel the way you feel.'

'The – the way I feel?'

'Yes. The way your music tells me you feel. Not angry with the world, like most men of your age, but angry with yourself.'

Angry with himself. What on earth made this man, this virtual stranger, say a thing like that?

Or, more to the point, how did he *know*?

Ben was very boisterous on the flight home, singing aloud on the plane, flirting with the stewardesses, laughing uproariously at the inflight movie which was a touching tragedy about a nun in love with a priest. But he wouldn't tell anyone what Amery Cheam had wanted to see him about, deflecting enquiries into a review of the American tour, which in commercial terms was pronounced a success. But he thought it would be quite some time before he toured America again; demonstrably it was a country that preferred to hear him than see him. However, as Kevin pointed out, the large audiences had been excellent experience, ideal preparation for his next major appearance in Britain, at an open-air summer concert in London where he would share the bill with several other acts. Proceeds would go to charity and up to twenty thousand people were expected to attend; with any luck it would be a sunny day and everyone would have a great time.

Back in London, Sasha suggested she return with him to his flat rather than to her own. After all, they had been together for six months now, it was time they thought about living together on a more solid basis.

He took her home, explained that he didn't want to live with anyone on a solid basis, and ended the relationship.

Three days later, Myles Irving called a meeting in his office at Cedar's headquarters. It was crowded with his numerous protégés, but the convivial mood sobered as Myles officially broke the news they suspected was coming: Cedar had been bought, in its entirety, by Schwabbe Music Inc. Formal notice would follow, informing them that they were all now the property of the German audiovisual giant.

As yet nobody was sure what the implications might be, but Ben was not alone in his dislike of the word 'property'. Songs could be bought, copyright and contracts could be bought, but how could people be bought? Was there no opt-out clause for those who might wish to avail of it?

'Not until your current contracts expire. I'm sorry, but that's the way the cookie crumbles. Your managers will go into all the fine print with you.'

Running his hand through his permanently dishevelled hair, hitching up the jeans that sagged perpetually under the weight of his paunch, Myles opened his drinks cabinet and produced anaesthesia for the shock. Schwabbe was a very healthy, vibrant company, but the atmosphere was funereal. Having been big fish in a relatively small pond, the assembled singers and musicians now felt the reverse might apply; Schwabbe already had a large body of talent to which they were being appended, with no guarantee that their individual careers would continue to be nurtured.

It was some consolation to hear that Myles himself had also been 'bought' and would continue to produce them, but Kevin Ross was ashen. Catching his eye, Ben wondered why.

'Bad news, huh?'

Kevin took off his glasses and polished them distractedly.

'Yeah. Schwabbe is very hot on hardware – tapes, records, videos – but not at all keen on live performances. They think touring is too expensive, that television will wipe out the need for it eventually.'

'But live performance is the whole point! Audiences, atmosphere, everyone singing along having fun – you can never generate the same mood in a studio.'

'They're not interested in mood. They're interested in the economics of technology.'

The economics of technology. Suddenly Ben wished he was a lyricist and could write a scathing satire on that. Thank God some instinct had warned him not to tell anyone about Amery Cheam's proposal. Tomorrow, he would visit his management company and see that it was set up as a private venture, never became anyone's property but his own. Consolingly, he put his hand on Kevin's shoulder.

'Don't worry, Kev. I'm sure you'll be managing my tours for a long time yet, and everyone else's.'

Kevin grimaced.

'Maybe. But if you want some advice, Ben, make the most of this outdoor charity concert next month. I don't think there'll be many more like it.'

The huge bouquet of yellow roses had long since died, but Aran kept the card that had come with them, puzzling it over and over. 'With lots of love from Ben on your big birthday.' What did that mean? Love in the sense that people signed it on any communication, without particular significance? Love, as in affection? Or love, that still lingered in the way they had once known it?

But Ben couldn't mean that. If he did, he would be here, he would be living with her. He wouldn't need the freedom he claimed he needed. He wouldn't need Sasha Harwood. Probably the roses had been suggested by Thanh, sent to ease Ben's conscience, But, a year after their separation, she was glad they had been sent. Nowadays, she was glad of every reminder, every tiny ray of hope. What had possessed her to slam the door on him, shut out all his pleas for friendship? Pain, she supposed; pain and pride. Last summer she thought she couldn't have borne to set eyes on him again, now she would give anything to see him. Yet if she ever did, she knew she would be unable to sustain a normal conversation, unable to restrain herself from throwing herself at him, doing everything in her power to rekindle the passion she could never forget, never replace.

Holly and Walter Mitchell were becoming impatient with her, telling her frequently that it was time to get on with her life, make new friends and get out of the damn house to which she was so unreasonably attached. But how she loved this house, even if Ben was not in it! Holly and Walter hadn't grown up in a cold, cramped fisherman's cottage, they took warmth and light and space for granted, knew nothing of what a garden meant to someone who, as a child, had been forbidden to play in the tiny back yard for fear of damaging the few precious vegetables. Even now, she couldn't get over the big pine wardrobe which contained only her own clothes, the kitchen in which she could cook whatever she liked without her brothers knocking pots over, her mother telling her to hurry up and that she was doing it all wrong anyway. This house didn't smell of fish, its windows didn't rattle, its bathroom was not a soggy battleground invaded by seven squabbling people every morning.

But she was trying to get out of it. She was taking driving lessons, attending concerts at Kenwood House and the Wigmore Hall, visiting Camden Lock to make sure Sinéad Kenny was running the stall properly. But she was no longer involved in it actively, no longer wanted anything to do with the sweaters her mother continued to knit so industriously. Soon, she knew, she would have to make up her mind what she did want.

Ben! Ben was all she wanted, Ben and their baby. Without them, there was no point to anything else.

From Ireland, Molly wrote that Conor was off shark fishing again for the summer, that Dursey was helping him, that Achill had abandoned his plans for funfairs and video screens to go into partnership, instead, with an older friend who had bought a pub. It was to be a musicians' pub, was being stripped down to its original stone, its fireplace opened up, wooden furniture installed for convivial evenings under its thatched roof. Of course Achill's idea of music was now something called Celtic rock, so it would surely fail, because nobody wanted that kind of noise. But at least the project was keeping him off the streets. Aran was glad to hear it, and thought it had great potential, but it all seemed very distant to her.

It was very distant. It was six hundred miles away. Six hundred miles, between her and her baby . . . every week Eimear wrote faithfully, enclosing news and photographs of Rhianna, reporting every tiny development, every cherished smile. Aran wept over the letters, treasured them, ached to touch and hold her daughter. Yet she knew that was what she must not attempt to do, not until she could do it without wanting to snatch her back to London, where she could offer her nothing of the life that Dan and Eimear were able to. Eimear had given up work, but she must find it, and Rhianna was far better off with Eimear in Dunrathway than with a paid minder here in London. Even at the worst moments Aran knew she had done what was best for her baby, and was soothed by that knowledge. Rhianna would never give her first smile to a stranger, her needs would never be fitted in around the demands of an office or a desk or a shrilling telephone.

But what a thing it was, to have a child! Even though the child was not here with her, Aran felt strangely fulfilled since giving birth, felt the accomplishment of it; the achievement of a driving need. A primal need, that had nothing to do with current concepts of femininity or feminism, something that no amount of equality legislation could budget for. Even if she had been able to keep Rhianna, had worked perhaps for one of those companies that had a crèche on the premises, she would never have been able to concentrate, give her employer's needs priority over her daughter's. Holly Mitchell managed it, millions of women managed it, but she simply wasn't such a woman; she was the kind who believed in a secure, traditional, two-parent childhood, at home in the child's own house. Who ever would have thought it? She certainly hadn't thought it at first, in her

279

teens. But she thought it now, had been convinced of it from the first moment she knew she was carrying Ben's beautiful baby.

Christmas. Dan and Eimear thought she might come to visit at Christmas, that the new Rafter family would be well established by then. Of course it would be painful, but it would be reassuring too, a vindication of her belief in them. Thomas Allen would have finalised the formalities by then, it might even be the moment to tell Molly . . . but Aran didn't want to tell Molly. Molly had advised her to have the child adopted, and simply been told that she had done so.

Molly wasn't interested in her grandchild, and was not going to be given the opportunity to recriminate, to criticise, to lament Rhianna's likeness to her father. If she guessed, when she saw the Rafters' 'adopted' new infant, that would be her just reward, and she would have to live with it. But Molly rarely saw the Rafters these days, and even if she did guess Aran did not think she would make many eager visits to see Rhianna. On the contrary. It had been plain for a very long time that Molly had had her fill of children.

It was that rarest of Irish treats: a sunny day with real heat in it, the kind that entered your bones and repaired the ravages of rain, of damp, of the long dark winter. Holding Rhianna aloft so that she could see the sea and the boats between the yew trees, Eimear revelled in the increasing weight of the baby, the warm soft body that felt so elementally part of her own. At thirty-four she felt ten years younger, bathed in the joy that the baby had brought.

'What do you think, cherub? Will we go pay a social call on Grandma this morning?'

Hannah loved being called Grandma, loved Rhianna, thought the whole situation absolutely marvellous. What a sensible girl Aran Campion was, and how selfless! Her door was permanently open, she said, and Eimear must bring the child as often as possible.

Despite the hot sun Eimear wrapped Rhianna up warmly in her buggy and threw a blanket in the basket underneath; sunshine on the way up to Fenner Hill did not necessarily mean sunshine on the way back. The child would probably sleep all the way, but even when she slept she delighted in showing her off, hearing people exclaim over her long eyelashes and adorable little mouth. Hannah's house was little more than a mile away, but the route traversed the village and, on the way, they would encounter lots of friends and neighbours.

Eimear had hardly got beyond her own front gate when she heard a voice calling her. Looking round, she saw Annie McGowan, red in the face, waving as she hastened across the large unkempt lawn which, because of her cheese-making, she never had time to tend.

'Eimear, wait! I want a word with you!'

Puffing, Annie caught up, bent down into the buggy and beamed at Rhianna.

'Oh, will you look at the little thing, isn't she sweet . . . are you in a hurry, Eimear, or can you spare me a minute?'

'Yes, Annie, of course. We were only going for a walk.'

'Well, I was just wondering – do you still have Aran Campion's phone number in London? I know I had it somewhere myself, but I can't find it for the life of me, and I need her advice about something.'

'Aran's advice? About what, Annie?'

'Oh, well, I'm sure she's far too busy to be interested herself, what with her rock star – did you see him on the television, last week? Would you credit it! – anyway, the thing is, I've had a call from this man in Manchester—'

Eimear laughed. Annie's tongue was always miles ahead of her.

'Slow down, Annie!'

As much as she could, she did.

'A man in Manchester, you see, who owns a whole string of food shops, in Leeds, York, Bradford, Hull, Liverpool, all these places, I don't remember the names of half of them, but he saw my cheeses in London and he wants to take them, there are so many Irish people in the north of England he says—'

'But Aran's in London, Annie. I don't quite follow.'

'Eimear, I need an agent! Someone over there to see the supplies arrive in good order and reach their destinations, visit the shops and get to know the managers, maybe even do a bit of marketing in other areas. Aran would be perfect, but since she's all tied up with her young man I thought perhaps she could recommend someone, you know, the way she got Sinéad Kenny for the sweaters—'

Eimear considered.

'Actually, Annie, Aran isn't with Ben any more. It wasn't my business to tell anyone, but they broke up some time ago.'

Annie looked at her quizzically.

'Is that so? Well, I must say, I think that's a shame. He was a nice lad, and she was mad about him – he seemed mad about her, too. What happened then?'

'Oh, it's a long story.'

'Is it? Well, I hope she'll get over it. But meanwhile, I must ask her—'

Belatedly Annie paused to absorb what Eimear was saying.

'But if she's not looking after the young lad's career, Eimear, then what's she doing?'

'As it happens, Annie, she's looking for work.'

Complicitly, they smiled simultaneously.

'Well now, isn't that a lucky thing! Would she be interested, d'you think?'

'I'd say she might well be, Annie. Ben was very generous with her, but his largesse is coming to an end.'

'H'mm. But does she drive, Eimear? There'd be a lot of travel.'

'She's learning. No licence yet, but I believe she has applied for her test.'

'Well, I'd better wish her good luck, so! She did me a great favour once . . . come on, Eimear, be a dear and get me her number now.'

Aran was interested. Interested and grateful and enthusiastic. Working for Annie wouldn't be like working for a boss. It would be like working for a friend, one who said she wouldn't interfere or even see her very often. Aran could make whatever hours she chose, wear whatever clothes she chose, pursue whatever ideas or opportunities she might spot. So long as the cheeses were properly monitored on their travels around Britain and the customers were happy, Annie would be happy. If Aran should find any extra outlets for them, that would be a bonus, and be treated as such. Knowing the quality of the product, Aran thought she would find extra outlets, and was glad of the chance to use her initiative, get her brain back into gear. Glad of the work she could help to create in Dunrathway, too; already Annie had five people working with her in a newly-converted barn at the back of her house, and more sales would mean more jobs. Some day, she thought with a smile, she might even take a few samples of Annie's produce over on the ferry to France – imagine if she could get it into even one shop or supermarket over there, where they boasted of having a different variety for every day of the year! It would be like selling the proverbial sand to Arabs, the ultimate proof of her skill and Annie's.

Of course she was going to need a car. But that was easy. Taking a chunk of her dwindling savings out of the post office, she consulted Walter Mitchell's advice and then bought a year-old station wagon with lots of space in the back, plus a set of insulated picnic boxes that would keep the cheeses cool.

The supplies came from Ireland by refrigerated lorry, but inevitably there would be odd batches to move from one place to another, shopkeepers looking for another dozen or two to keep them topped up over busy weekends. Annie would pay for petrol, for overnight accommodation and any other expenses incurred . . . what a lot of Britain she was going to see, in the course of her new work! Not with Ben, this time, not with a fun crew of roadies, but all by herself. If it was lonely work – well, it was work, it would enable her to visit Rhianna at Christmas. Thinking of Rhianna, Aran wondered what on earth she would have done with the child in this situation. How did mothers manage jobs that took them away from home three or four nights a week, as hers would, every week?

Let someone come up with a satisfactory answer to that one.

For the summer concert Ben decided to dress up as a satyr, in a costume composed of leaves and foliage, ideally suited to the hot day and woodland setting. As he pranced on stage the audience – much larger than anticipated – laughed with him, and his spirits soared. Unlike the Americans, they knew he was joking, thought him amusing rather than decadent, were flattered that he had gone to so much trouble for them.

The performance was a huge success, and he was bemused to receive a letter from Schwabbe Inc. a week later, outraged at the suggestive tone he had set. Was he trying to corrupt the young? Had he no idea of his responsibility as a public figure, a teen idol? In future he would consult them, at their London office, before doing anything so lewd or in such blatantly bad taste. Lest he forget it, his image reflected on their image, and his contract still had two years to run. By way of countering the damage, the cover of his next album would depict him fully clothed, in a suit selected by their public relations people, in some quietly respectable environment. There was no mention of how well he had sung, how enjoyable the day had been or how much money had been raised for the charity – even though all those things also reflected on their image.

Once, he would have been furious, rung them up in Cologne and gone through them for a short cut. But now, after just one vehement oath to clear his head, he went to his piano, played the first bars of the provisionally-entitled Cheam's Theme, and played them again.

Oh, yes! *Yes*. It was by no means finished, but what there was of it sounded, in his far from humble opinion, positively celestial. Unlike the *Onedin Line* theme with its evocation of trading vessels, billowing schooners and mountainous seas, this was contemporary music for fast, featherlight yachts; but the surge of the water was in it, the flying spray, the rushing adrenalin and the soaring thrill. Working only from Amery's photographs, he had got the basic structure down, all he needed now was the promised day's sailing in the speediest craft, so he could experience every sensation at first hand and work it into the music. Only three weeks remained of the eight Amery had given him, but now he understood the deadline: like the yachts he was racing to an exciting finish, one that made his heart race with them.

It was a difficult challenge, stretching him to full capacity, and he felt both proud and fiercely protective of what he was achieving. No matter what his management company might fear to the contrary, no corporate honcho in Cologne was going to touch it, dictate it or profit from it. This project was *his* baby, satisfying every driving urge in him, fulfilling the deep need he had known all his life.

It was August before Aran passed her driving test, got into her new car and headed north, quaking with terror as she negotiated the terrifying motorways full of speeding traffic. But after the first hour or two she began to relax, thinking what a luxury England's roads were compared to Ireland's potholes, which no amount of road tax ever seemed able to repair. Here, you got twice the quality for half the price, petrol and insurance were much cheaper too, and when you bought a second-hand car it wasn't riddled with pothole damage. When emigrants shed nostalgic tears for Ireland, it surely wasn't for the driving conditions there.

She had shed many tears herself, since giving birth to Rhianna, but after five months her system was getting back to normal, telling her it was ready to settle down and be sensible. Even if her new life was going to be nothing like the life she had known with Ben, it would be independent and honourable; she could look Margaret Thatcher in the eye and say she was no burden to the State, no Irish layabout or immigrant relying on welfare. Her child was safe and well, and its mother had rejoined the workforce. Even Guy Halley could have no cause for complaint. She was very lucky to have got this job and, for Annie's sake, she was going to make the most of it.

Annie worked so hard herself, supporting her unemployed husband and the four sons who were all at college in Cork, getting the degrees which, effectively, were tickets to America or Australia. Yet she never complained – so, at twenty-one, how could Aran Campion complain? Even if she didn't have Ben or Rhianna, she had her health, her house, her new horizons. She had ambition, someone had once said; all she had to do was dig down into herself, find it and wind it up again.

You could do that, couldn't you? Even if you didn't feel as passionate about cheese as you did about music, even if you didn't love Annie McGowan the same way you loved Ben Halley, you could pretend you did, you could almost convince yourself. Could *definitely* convince yourself, because your customers wouldn't believe anything you didn't believe yourself. It was all a question of attitude.

Besides, even if the midlands and the north were not as exciting as London, they were still a sight better than Ferleague on a wet

Monday. Had the Beatles not emerged from Liverpool, had Emily Bronte not written *Wuthering Heights* in Yorkshire? Manchester had a magnificent cathedral, Harrogate was famous for its flowers, there was the Lake District to explore and the stunning Castle Howard to see. People were said to be friendly up there too, and Annie was going to pay for petrol and accommodation – all things considered, this was a damn good job, with lots of potential. In the hotel rooms at night, she would still be able to write poetry and read the books she couldn't get enough of – if only she'd known, the awful day her parents took her out of school, how easy it was to educate yourself! Once you could read and write, you could do anything.

Of course, Rhianna would learn to do a lot more than read and write. Dan and Eimear would give her as much education as she wanted . . . and maybe, by the time she got it, Ireland would have some use for it. She wouldn't have to leave the country if she didn't want to. What would she want? What talents would she have, what tastes? What—

Firmly, Aran checked herself. Even if she couldn't help thinking about Rhianna at night, she must help it during the day, especially on busy motorways where you needed all your wits about you. Until she reached Manchester at least, she had to put the little face out of her mind, the face that was Ben's face.

But then she found she was thinking about Ben instead, about Sasha Harwood who had been replaced by a Chinese fabric designer called Kim Chang, about Kim Chang who had given way to a trainee architect called Charlotte Lucas . . . three girlfriends in one year was a good sign, Eimear said, it showed he was working the restlessness out of his system and wasn't greatly enamoured of any of them.

But how could he be? They surely didn't play the oboe, didn't write lyrics, didn't know Bizet from a bull's foot. He might be infatuated with them, but he couldn't be enamoured. Could he?

Oh, God. She had to stop thinking about Ben and Rhianna. She *had* to, or her mind would buckle like a cardboard box.

At first, Molly thought her imagination must be running away with her, until she remembered that she didn't have any imagination. Even as a child she could remember being told that, and it was true. She didn't distort things, didn't see them in any way other than the way they actually were.

Yet it was hardly credible. Aran couldn't have done this to her. Couldn't possibly . . . it had only been a very brief glimpse, and the infant had been wearing a hat, was buried up to its chin in a rug. Babies all looked alike, if they were put on identity parade nobody

285

would ever assign them to their correct parents.

There was no need to be sneaking round the town like this, going into every shop for superfluous bottles of milk and wasteful packets of butter, in the hope of seeing Eimear Rafter again. When they did eventually meet, by chance, she would see that the baby's nose was totally different, its skin was lighter, its eyes were actually blue or green.

They had to be. Because, if they were not, how could she ask the question that begged an even worse one?

If Aran had given her child to Eimear Rafter for adoption, the whole town would want to know the answer to that: why had she given it to her former teacher instead of her own mother?

Even when Conor was out at sea overnight, in the most dangerous weather, Molly always slept soundly. But now she was awake all night every night, gripped in a nightmare of her own creation. She had told Aran to have the baby adopted. She had made it perfectly clear she wanted no hand or part in it. Unlike Deirdre Devlin's mother, she was not prepared to help, turn the clock back twenty years, endure the privations and aggravations of motherhood all over again. Aran hadn't asked her to, but if she had asked, the answer would have been no. Aran knew that, and that was why she hadn't asked.

But the Rafters! Was there not a single family in Britain that would have taken the child, in Dublin, in Galway, Donegal, Wexford, anywhere?

Was this Aran's idea of punishment, of retribution? Or had the Rafters, in their desperation for children, talked her into it? And what if Conor found out? Oh, Jesus, Mary and Joseph, what if Conor found out?

She must find out, before he did.

Steeling herself, Molly forced herself to walk up Fenner's Hill one Friday morning, timing her departure by the Angelus bell. Eimear Rafter usually visited her mother for lunch on Fridays, and she would intercept her at the little grotto that was screened by trees, where nobody would see them. On wet days Eimear drove up in her car, but today was fine, perfect weather for walking.

By twelve fifteen Molly's nerves were mangled. By twelve thirty she was ready to rush down to the Rafter bungalow and demand the truth. But finally she heard footsteps, Eimear's voice talking to the child, the child gurgling and jabbering in return. Suppressing the urge to leap out at them, she emerged from her apparent devotions at the statue as nonchalantly as she could. But her eyes flew to the baby. Again it was wearing a hat, but it was sitting up, smiling a smile

286

that brought Molly's heart to a standstill. Ben Halley's smile, greeting her the first time they met, in Eimear's house. There was absolutely no question about it, no room for any doubt whatsoever. This was Ben Halley's child, her grandchild.

With supernatural strength she wrenched her mouth into a smile, greeted Eimear and bent over the buggy.

'So this is the baby . . . I'd heard you'd adopted . . . is it a boy or a girl, Mrs Rafter?'

Her hands locked to the buggy, Eimear steeled herself in turn for the moment she had known would come one day. The moment she and Dan had discussed and rehearsed for months, knowing there was nothing Molly could do about it. Rhianna was perfectly safe.

'A girl.'

'A girl. And how old is she?'

'Nearly six months, now.'

'Six months. And – and what's her name?'

'Rhianna. Rhianna Rafter.'

Icily calm, she forced herself to smile, and Molly smiled in turn, feeling as if her lips were being wrenched apart by forceps.

'Rhianna. That's a – a very nice name. An Irish name. But you – you wouldn't really think she was Irish, to look at her.'

Firmly, Eimear faced her.

'Wouldn't you, Mrs Campion?'

Hastily, Molly drew back.

'Oh – I only mean – what I mean is – you must have had her out in the garden all summer, she has such a lovely colour.'

'Yes. She's been out in the sun a lot.'

'Aye. And did you – did you – have much trouble adopting her?'

'No. None at all. Dan and I were considered very suitable.'

'Oh, naturally. A teacher and a vet, with plenty of money. She couldn't have gone to a better home.'

They eyed each other.

'I'm glad you think so, Mrs Campion. Actually, I've given up teaching. I wanted to spend all my time with Rhianna – especially since she's the only child we're likely to have.'

She was amazed that Molly had the nerve to say what she said next.

'Ah, dear, isn't that sad! No little brothers or sisters.'

Pulling the buggy out of her reach, Eimear glanced pointedly in the direction of her mother's house.

'No, Mrs Campion, I'm afraid not. Not all of us are as lucky as you, with five children.'

Eimear knew. Molly saw that she did, had heard all about the letter advising Aran what to do, and how to do it discreetly. The advice that Aran had followed, almost literally, to the letter.

With a last narrow look at Rhianna, Molly backed off and wished Eimear a good afternoon. With all the cordiality she could muster, she returned the compliment, and they went their separate ways. But, when they reached their destinations, both women were trembling violently.

God's punishment, Molly muttered. That's what it was. God was punishing her as she deserved to be punished, for letting her granddaughter be adopted by what she had expected to be a total stranger. God had put the idea into Aran's head, Aran had sent the child back to Dunrathway, and now Rhianna Rafter was going to appear in front of her every day for the next eighteen or twenty years, a testimony to one and all that Molly Campion had failed in her Christian duty to her daughter.

Oh, God, who was going to notice, who was going to realise that the Rafter baby was Aran's baby, by the boyfriend everyone had seen, the one with the unforgettable face? Slow as he was, Conor would not be the first to realise, but surely he would some day, maybe not now, but in a year or two, or three. What would he say, what would he do? How would he ever understand why she had done it – and would do it again, if only the child could go to some distant destination?

Even after having seen the baby, seen it clearly, Molly still didn't want it. She had raised five of them already, she had slaved to feed and clothe them, been tied to nappies and bottles and duties she had thought would never end. She had worked and worried all her life, and only in very recent years had she come to know any rest or respite. She was entitled to speak her mind, to reject what she couldn't undertake, turn away from what had never come naturally. Even if Aran had helped with the sweaters – helped a lot – she didn't want her back in the house, and she didn't want her child by a half-Indian rock singer.

It was better to be honest about it than to lie about it. Even if it looked like a harsh decision to an outsider, she didn't regret it. Not in any moral sense. After all, baby Rhianna would be much better off with the Rafters, would grow up in a much nicer house and have far more advantages than she ever would have here with her tired, ageing grandparents. She would be kindly treated and properly raised.

No. Molly's conscience was clear on that score. Adoptive parents were well checked by the social workers, and usually extra attentive to their charges. But on the question of Conor, it was vibrating with shock and worry. Oh, why hadn't she told him Aran was pregnant, at the outset?

Because he might have rushed off to London, that was why. Rushed off in a foolish panic, dragged the infant home with him and maybe Aran as well, insisting that they could all muddle along together somehow. But he was the one away at sea from one end of the week to the other. It wouldn't have fallen to him to look after the child while Aran went out to work – if any could be got – or to babysit at night as well, while Aran gadded about to pubs and parties like all the other young folk. His life wouldn't have gone right back to where it started, shut up in a small house with a screaming baby.

So, she hadn't told him. And now here was his grandchild under his nose, in his own village, with its big brown eyes and smoky skin. Even if by any miracle he didn't put two and two together, one of the neighbours would, let the information slip maybe even by accident, in the belief that he knew of the adoption and condoned it.

Oh, this was a nightmare. A nightmare that was going to go on and on for years. For ever. To her dying day, Molly Campion would be known as the woman who let Dan and Eimear Rafter take her granddaughter, refused to help her daughter, didn't want a coloured child under her roof. And Conor, who was blameless, would be included in the blame, the shame.

Desperately, she filled the kettle and put it on for a cup of tea, pacing the kitchen as she tried to think clearly. It wasn't very dark. Only a little bit Indian. And Eimear was dark herself, she had brown hair and brown eyes. Maybe all would be well, maybe nobody would notice.

But if they did, what would they say? What would they say in the shops, the pubs, the church? Would she be shunned by the knitting circle, or gossiped about behind her back?

With hideous irony, it dawned on her that people might talk about her exactly as she had so often talked about them. That they were going to talk about her for sure, in scandalised tones completely devoid of all Christian compassion.

'Oh, Mother, you should have seen it. It was unspeakable.'

'In what way, Eimear?'

Hannah Lowry was composed as she brought their crab mousse to the table with some hot toast, poured two glasses of Muscadet and passed one to her quivering daughter.

'In the – the way she looked at Rhianna. With such distaste, almost with – with revulsion.'

'Oh, come now, Eimear. You're exaggerating.'

'No, Mother, I'm not! First she squinted at her, then she stared outright, but she didn't touch her even once. She must be the only woman on earth who can look at a baby without putting her finger to its cheek, taking its hand or asking to pick it up. But there was no contact, no baby talk, not a single question about Rhianna's weight or health or anything. She didn't even know her name! She never asked Aran what her own grandchild was called.'

'But that would be unnatural. Maybe the only way she could deal with the trauma was by pretending it hadn't happened. She might be in some kind of shock.'

Eimear smiled wanly.

'Well, she certainly is now. She scuttled away like a bat out of hell – oh, Mother, what am I going to do?'

Hannah sipped her wine reflectively.

'Darling, you're going to calm down, that's all. You knew this was bound to happen, but there's nothing to worry about. Molly didn't want Rhianna to begin with and it certainly doesn't sound as if she wants her now. Besides, Mr Allen has dealt with all the documents, you and Dan are her legal guardians, everything is perfectly in order.'

Eimear sighed, but she did feel calmer.

'Yes. You're right. It just feels so odd, having Rhianna's grandparents so near yet not treating them as such. I'd have thought Conor would take some interest, if not Molly.'

'Well . . . he's had a long hard battle to bring up his own children. Maybe Aran thought it was better not to upset him, put him under any obligation he might not be able to meet.'

'Yes – but I'd like him to know he can come and visit Rhianna any time he wants. Just see her, without having to bring presents or get involved or anything.'

Hannah considered.

'Look, Eimear, Aran didn't want to drag him into it and I think you should respect his wishes. But if you're worried about it, why not ask Molly over for tea and talk to her about it? Then everyone's mind will be at rest.'

'Yes. I think that's a good idea, Mother. I will ask her over.'

Ben spent only one weekend sailing with Amery Cheam in America, but came back highly invigorated, returned to his piano and began putting the final varnish on his theme music. A week before the deadline, it was finished, ready to be brought into a studio, rehearsed and recorded. But he could not use Schwabbe's facilities and so, at considerable personal expense, he booked private time in an independent recording studio. And, the moment he heard it spring to life, saw the energy sweeping through the orchestra, he knew he had written a wonderful piece of music. Tucking the demo tape lovingly into layers of protective packaging, he despatched it to America with inexpressible pride.

A week later, the phone rang. Amery Cheam was thrilled. Thrilled to bits, as the campaign team had been when they heard it that morning; it was the perfect soundtrack for the documentary, television ads, race award ceremony, everything. Mingling the new and the old, it conveyed all of the company's tradition and history, yet it was dramatic and exciting, it would take Cheam Marine right through into the twenty-first century.

The twenty-first century! Ben felt like climbing the Post Office tower and shouting those words all over London. If all his other music to date had been for fun, this piece was for real, for posterity. A work of genius Amery said, that would be treasured for ever. Picking the phone up again the moment he put it down, Ben dialled Charlotte Lucas's number, bursting to tell her the great news.

But there was no answer. Strange, because Charlotte had said she was taking work home with her tonight, would be at her flat all evening . . . puzzled, Ben glanced down at the desk diary to make sure he'd got the number right.

But it wasn't open at L for Lucas at all. It was open at C for Campion. In his breathless excitement, he had somehow dialled Aran at their old house in Hampstead.

Molly arrived for tea with her face set as if in aerosol fixative, but as she divested herself of the black coat and headscarf that Eimear privately called her widow's weeds, she revealed the silk blouse that Eimear had given her nearly six years earlier. Like a white flag raised from a wartime trench, it seemed to denote that she was prepared to negotiate.

Yes, she said, she was prepared to negotiate. Negotiate and surrender. Since Aran had done this dreadful thing to her, she was going to accept it and say no more about it. Which was the point, actually: it would be best if Eimear said nothing about it either.

Eimear pointed out that she had no intention of discussing Rhianna with anyone. Her parentage was none of the village's business, but in any event she couldn't imagine anyone being tactless enough to ask. Molly was creating problems where none existed.

Molly cleared her throat. Of course Mrs Rafter was right, it was only that – well, the thing was—

Was what?

Was that she had judged it best not to upset her husband by telling him about this whole sorry affair. Of course she would have, if she had known the child was going to end up in Dunrathway, but since

Aran hadn't seen fit to tell her – well, Mrs Rafter must understand, surely? For everyone's sake, it was best that Conor remain unenlightened. He would only fret and worry and feel so bad about it, start beating a path to the Rafters' door and demanding to see Rhianna at every opportunity. People might notice if he did that, and – and – well, it would all be so upsetting.

Reeling, Eimear realised that Molly had only one thing on her mind. Gossip, scandal and public opprobrium.

'Please don't worry, Mrs Campion. Your secret is safe with me. As is your granddaughter. Wouldn't you like to see her – now, since you're here, in private? She's taking her nap, but I could—'

Molly recoiled as if Eimear had poured the scalding tea over her lap.

'Oh, no! I mean, no thank you. I'm sure she's a nice little thing, but – well, to be perfectly frank Mrs Rafter, I think it's best if we don't establish any contact that can't be continued. I won't be coming here again, and if we meet on the street we'll just be neighbourly and leave it at that. If that's all right with you?'

'Yes. Of course it is. I'm sorry, but I only thought . . . wondered whether you might . . .'

'No, Mrs Rafter. I don't. I've had five children of my own, the first of them when I was only nineteen years of age, and I was the eldest of eleven myself. Until these last few years, there's never been a day in my life when I didn't have a child clinging to my skirts, crying, demanding . . . I'm sorry, but the truth is that I've had enough of it. More than enough.'

'I see.'

Dimly, Eimear began to think that maybe she did see. The old girl had had a lot on her plate, as she said, for a very long time. And it would be a relief to Hannah, to know she could enjoy playing grandmother to Rhianna without fear of being challenged. If it was sad in one way, it was all for the best in another. Except for poor Conor, who would never know what he was missing.

But then, Ben didn't know what he was missing either.

Counting the days, Aran was looking forward to Christmas more than ever before. Only four months to go – three months, two months, one month! – and she would see her darling daughter. Of course Dan joked that she wasn't a darling at all, she was a little demon who delighted in flinging her toys on the floor for Sammy to chase, pulling the contents out of every cupboard she could crawl into and yanking out what hair remained to him by the roots. And could she yell! It was a wonder the police hadn't been up to enquire why the Rafters were driving their child into such frenzies of rage.

But the poor baby was teething, Aran thought indulgently, you only had to look at a photograph of those red cheeks to see that she had every grounds for complaint. And one little tooth up already, right in the middle of her lower gums! Oh, it was adorable. As she drove from Leeds to Bradford, from Bradford to Hull, she compiled lists in her mind of the presents she would bring her, envisaging with huge anticipation the child's wonder on Christmas morning.

However, the shopkeepers in these towns were more interested in the cheeses they were getting, and she was coming to know and like them all very much. Whereas London's shopkeepers and counter assistants were remote and anonymous, these people seemed to enjoy their work, get some fun out of it, always have time for a chat and a laugh. They were happy with the produce too, open to a new variety that Annie was trying out, pleased with any suggestions for displays or sampling sessions. Would it be an idea to link up with a wine merchant in each area, perhaps, organise some cheese and wine evenings where they could jointly promote their products in a congenial atmosphere? She must see about that, in the new year.

Must get in touch, also, with Sinéad Kenny. Sinéad would be thrilled to hear what had happened in Manchester the other day, when a customer in one of the delicatessens had come up to her as she was talking to the proprietor. Excusing herself politely but enthusiastically, she wondered if she might ask where Aran had got that lovely sweater?

Next thing, her eye had fallen on the sleeve and she had been able to read the information for herself: 'Handknitted by Orla Keller in Dunrathway, Co. Cork'. Oh, she said crestfallen, what a pity. If those sweaters were available in Britain she would buy several for the boutique she owned.

Oh, but they were available, Aran assured her, and if she was genuinely interested she could arrange a supply for her – or just a few samples if she liked, to see how they went? The woman looked at the sweater again, examining the handiwork closely, and said she would take fifteen to start with. Any chance of getting them in time for Christmas, no?

Oh yes. Certainly. Aran would drive them up herself next week. Names and phone numbers had been exchanged, and now all she needed to do was get them from Sinéad. Fifteen for the woman, plus five for herself, to wear in every new town and city from now on. Even if relations with her mother were very strained, that was no reason to penalise the entire co-op. Rhianna lived in Dunrathway too, and she wanted the village to thrive more than ever.

But despite the new contacts and friendly faces, it was lonely work driving around in the murky dark days of winter, staying in hotels and inns where, before leaving, she always asked to see the catering manager and presented him with a sample selection of McGowan's cheeses. None had yet expressed interest, but there was no harm in trying, and she lived in hope. Imagine if Trusthouse Forte should place an order, or Park Hotels or Ramada Inns! Heavens, Annie would expire of joy.

Of course the handful of Irish-owned hotels in London had taken some for their restaurants, been very supportive in fact, and that was a milestone already. But they were not big national groups, only small steps on a long road that stretched into eternity. However, eternity only stretched as far as Preston this morning, and as she drove up to it she switched on the car radio. Even though Ben's voice was often on it, she could listen to him with pleasure, and loved to hear any mention of what he was doing.

The news was on. Urgent news, to judge by the horrified tones in which it was being read, Liverpudlian tones on a local station:

'– after being shot several times at point-blank range, the singer was taken to Roosevelt hospital but did not recover from surgery. This morning a spokesman for the British music industry said that it has lost one of the finest, most prolific and best-loved talents—'

Swerving the car violently, she barely made the emergency lane before losing control of it. What singer had been shot? Who was prolific and loved? Oh, no, don't let it be. Don't let it be.

'The assassin, who will be charged with first-degree murder later today, is believed to have acquired the .38 calibre gun in Honolulu before returning to stalk the star for several days in New York—'

New York. She had read in a music magazine that Ben was in New York. Sitting in the immobile car, she felt icy fingers of fear all over her body.

'– his widow Yoko Ono, his sons Sean and Julian—'

John Lennon. It was John Lennon. John Lennon had been murdered. She heard herself repeat the name aloud, faint with a mixture of horror and compassion for his family. His little boy, Sean, was only five.

The report continued and gradually she pieced it together, understood that a fan for whom John had signed an autograph earlier in the day had come back that night and shot him dead, right in front of Yoko on the doorstep of their own home. God, what must that do to a woman, to witness her husband's murder!? And how could she shield her small child from the brutal details?

She had been only four when John F. Kennedy was shot, but she could remember that day in Dunrathway, with everyone running about in tears, the funeral on television with the pictures of his veiled widow, holding the little girl's hand while the even smaller boy saluted his father's passing cortège. Everyone had thought it was terrible, talked about nothing else for days. Yet there would be far less sympathy for John Lennon, who was also a husband and father; many of the women who had mourned Kennedy would say Lennon was only a rock singer, decadent and depraved by definition. Certainly Molly Campion, who had been distraught about Kennedy and still refused to believe the stories about Marilyn Monroe, wouldn't care less about John Lennon, unless maybe to remark that it was good enough for him, it was one less drugged-out junkie in the world. Never would a rock star be considered for what he was: a human being, a parent, a pacifist, and a great talent whose music had brought nothing but happiness to humanity. Kennedy had invaded the Bay of Pigs and taken the world to the verge of war, but John Lennon would never be forgiven for a few indiscreet remarks and ultimately harmless photographs.

And now John was dead, at forty. In recent times Aran had tried not to think so much of music's endless tragedies, of the starving Mozart or the grotesquely bloated Elvis, of Schubert struggling to afford a piano and then dying when he got it. But she thought of them now, and thought of Ben. Of course Thanh was devoted to him and would never let any crazed fan get near him with a gun – yet somebody had got to Kennedy with a gun, despite a fleet of bodyguards and the protection of an entire intelligence network. Maniacs had got to Abraham Lincoln, Martin Luther King, Princess Anne whose bodyguard had been seriously injured while protecting her. To all kinds of people.

That was the risk such people took, by virtue of their position. The risk Ben took every time he went on stage before a live audience. Her skin crawled as she thought of it, and thought of Molly's righteous disdain for him, for their child.

Chapter Thirteen

Eimear was waiting at Cork airport on Christmas Eve with Rhianna in her arms, and Aran struggled frantically through the throngs of returning emigrants to get to them. Oh, Rhianna! Scooping the baby into her arms she hugged her wordlessly, fighting the tears that threatened to spill over the soft pink cheek, realising immediately how much heavier and sturdier she had grown in nine months. Fearfully Eimear stood watching, wondering whether the baby might make strange, but Rhianna latched onto her mother like a limpet and bestowed her with a big, gummy smile.

'Oh, she's gorgeous! I could *eat* her!'

With immense gratitude Aran looked at Eimear, deeply touched by all the signs of her love and care for Rhianna: the child's health and happy smile, her clean face and brushed hair, the padded pink suit into which she snuggled warmly. Even tiny mittens and a minuscule scarf, and a bunny rabbit that she clutched triumphantly.

'She looks wonderful, Eimear. Wonderful. And so do you.'

In fact Eimear had never looked better, radiating an aura of deep content, wearing a red coat that brought out the dark lustre of her eyes and clear complexion. But where was Dan?

'Circling outside in the car, waiting for us. It's so busy today he couldn't find parking.'

Aran refused to part with Rhianna, leaving Eimear to push the luggage trolley while she carried her outside, stroking her back with her hand, pushing her nose into her cheek, peering into the bright inquisitive eyes that seemed to be assessing her. Gently, she lifted up the hand that held the bunny.

'Is this your little friend? What's his name?'

'Um,' said Rhianna, and thrust the soft toy into her shoulder.

'For me? Are you lending him to me?'

'Um.'

Oh, she was beautiful! Strangled with emotion, Aran said nothing as she held her tightly; she had known the first few minutes would be torture, but was determined not to cry. Dan and Eimear deserved better than that.

Dan's black Renault appeared and she saw his face light up the moment he beheld her. And didn't he look terrific, too! Despite Rhianna's teething and all the sleepless nights it entailed, he seemed rejuvenated, fresh and full of energy. Embracing him in her free arm, she felt the strength in him, the warmth of his affection. And as always she felt the bond between him and Eimear, the love that grew with every passing year.

Settling into the back of the car with Rhianna on her lap, she nuzzled and murmured into her ear, whispering baby talk that made everyone laugh.

'Oh, come on! Surely I'm allowed to be silly for a few minutes?'

Grinning, they said she was allowed to be silly for as long as she liked. And then came all the news, of Rhianna and Hannah, Rhianna and Sammy, Rhianna and all her little friends, her funny gestures, her daily development. Rhianna, who had transformed their lives. Drinking it all in, she felt more than ever the sense of family, the sense of unity she had always known with the Rafters. And, although she had informed her own family that she would be staying with them, knowing that Conor would be upset if she didn't, fate had ordered things otherwise. Sher was home from America, with her husband and three children, and the cottage was full. Even Dursey had had to be farmed out to a neighbour to make room, and Molly was distracted with the chaos that had descended on her. Three enormous American children, roaring their heads off, eating her out of house and home! There was nothing for it but to accommodate Aran with the Rafters.

As they drove into Dunrathway she was curious to see a new stone building, roofless and only half complete, evidently abandoned by workmen for the festive season.

'What's that?'

Dan and Eimear beamed.

'It's a bistro. At least it will be by next summer. Not a restaurant, but a bistro – can you imagine? Dunrathway is rocketing up in the world!'

Aran smiled, pleased. If anyone had used the word 'bistro' five or even three years ago, they'd have been thought pretentious snobs, reminded that it was far from bistros they were reared. But now, this little waterfront building looked as if it was going to be charming.

Eimear turned round to her.

'Things are moving at last, Aran. The old schoolhouse is being turned into a small hotel – a nice one, this time – there's this bistro, the new craft shop, the shark fishing, the knitwear and cheese, the new vegetable shop that even sells samphire and stem ginger, all sorts of stuff. There's the pub where Achill is going to organise the music and the bakery does baguettes now, pitta bread . . . the fishing is still dicey, but we're going to get a lot more tourists.'

She was delighted to hear it, even though some of the streets still looked a little seedy, there was still litter and houses badly in need of painting.

'Yes. There was a proposal a while ago that some of the unemployed youngsters might clean things up, help the old people who can't manage their gardens, but finally it was decided that that would be going too far.'

'Why?'

'Oh, the kids thought they'd lose their dole, and the council said jobs would be threatened.'

'But the council hasn't the money to do the maintenance itself.'

'Yes, but they said if the kids did it their own employees would be out of a job.'

Aran didn't see how you could be out of a job you weren't doing anyway. Dunrathway's local council had been notorious for years as one that never tended open spaces, mended roads, cleared up rubbish or planted trees. What it did do, exactly, was a mystery. And yet, all day every day, the pubs were full of able-bodied young men playing darts and snooker, huddling in the dark over their sixth pint or their tenth. A quarter of Ireland's total workforce was unemployed, but there was always money for drink. Lots of it.

Well, maybe by the time Rhianna turned into her teens in 1993, that would be different. And the village had so many other things going for it – the fresh sea air, the excellent school, the low crime rate. Oh, there was petty crime, you wouldn't leave your car unlocked, but you wouldn't get shot or stabbed either. Rhianna could walk safely to school, unlike so many British schoolgirls whose violated bodies were regularly found on moors or wasteland. Naturally people expected returned emigrants like herself to sing Ireland's praises and Dunrathway's in particular, but all she could say was that every country had its good points and its bad ones.

She had chosen Britain, but would be happy if Rhianna chose to stay here. Even if prices and taxes were high, spirits usually were too. Turning the baby round on her lap to face her, she smiled at her.

'And what are you going to be when you grow up, little girl? H'mm? Are you going to amaze us all?'

Rhianna gurgled happily, reminding her of Morag Mitchell who, she thought in retrospect, had been the cause of all this. She had never wanted a baby until she discovered how sweet it was to hold one, felt nature tugging at her with its fat tiny fist. Oh, if only she could keep her daughter here on her lap with her, keep her forever . . . but the logistics were impossible, and Eimear would have a routine set up when they got home. She must remember that, and try not to interfere. In all real respects, Eimear was her mother now, and Dan was her father. The father she wouldn't have if she were in London.

Finally they reached the bungalow, where the Christmas tree shone in the window as it had shone that day years ago, the day she had got the oboe and Molly had given her the mohair sweater . . . the day she had gone to see the dolphins, also. Emerging from the car, she stood looking for a moment down over the harbour and the white-flecked ocean beyond.

'How are the dolphins doing, Eimear?'

'I'm afraid they've turned into the one tourist attraction I'm not quite happy about. Of course I suppose they'd leave if they felt stressed – but so many people went out to see them last summer, they must have been exhausted. The boatmen made a lot of money out of them, but they let people chuck coke cans and plastic bags into the water, too.'

Aran winced, thinking of the baby dolphin or one of its parents choking in agony on a coke can. Why did the boatmen let people do that? If the dolphins died, or went away, they would be greatly impoverished by the loss. Did it actually have to happen before they would see it?

But it hadn't happened, they would say. Ah sure, it hadn't happened at all, and wasn't she the right little fusspot, home from England with her pernickety ideas.

Molly's cautious greetings were lost in the general confusion as Aran walked in the door of the cottage that evening, to be grasped by Conor and swallowed altogether by Sher, who had not seen her sister for eight years. At twenty-eight Sher was a handsome honey-blonde, making Val look dowdy and Aran feel shy as the three sisters talked all at once.

'And little Aran, still not married! What are we going to do with you at all?'

Proudly Sher produced her husband, daughter and two sons for inspection. The family had gone through a rocky financial patch, Aran knew, but things were better now, and to Molly's visible horror, Sher was hinting that she might come home more often in future. Looking huge in the tiny front room, her children were whooping at the top of their lungs, playing with Val's baby son as if he were a football. Val's husband was there as well, and Achill. Twelve of them . . . but only Molly knew there was a thirteenth, up in the Rafters' bungalow. She caught Molly's eye, but Molly dropped it like a guillotine on her grandchildren. The ones whose existence she couldn't deny.

'Darren, take your finger out of Paudge's ear! Shelley, you'll break that vase – Lance, take it away from her. Achill, get me those good glasses down out of that cupboard – yes, yes, of course I mean those ones!'

Darren, Shelley and Lance. Sher's husband was called Norbert, too, which was definitely going to raise a few giggles in the pub. But they looked like a happy, healthy family, with thick hair and neon teeth, boundless energy and assertive voices. Lance, the eldest, sounded like a foghorn as he addressed his grandmother.

'Hey Moll, when's dinner? We're starving!'

Moll. Aran shook with laughter, and Molly glared at the child. The evening meal was called tea, here; as far as she was concerned they had had their dinner hours ago. Surely she wasn't expected to cook twice? And the biscuits they were consuming, the fruit, the juice! It was like Fota Wildlife Park.

Edging his way through the stampeding horde, Conor came over to her and laid his hand on her knee.

'Are you all right, child? Are you well?'

She looked up at him and smiled.

'Yes, Dad. I'm very well, and very glad to see you.'

He cleared his throat.

'I – I'm sorry there isn't room for you to stay here with us. I wish you could. But – well, you can see the problem. Not that I'm not pleased to see Sher too, of course I am—'

His blue eyes were anxious, and she patted his hand.

'It's all right, Dad. I understand. And I'll be back again tomorrow, to have Christmas dinner with you.'

Fortunately Christmas dinner was served at lunchtime in the Campion household, which meant she would be in time to have it again with Rhianna, Dan, Eimear and Hannah at four o'clock. An orgy! But she wouldn't miss Rhianna's first taste of plum pudding for the world. What a shame Conor wouldn't be there too. How he would spoil his little granddaughter . . . and then, want to take her home with him. Whereupon Molly would pack her bags and leave for Brazil.

'Will you come to Mass with us, in the morning?' His face was pleading.

'Yes, Dad. I'll meet you at the church door at five to eleven.'

Pleased and reassured, he nodded. But she knew he would not ask whether she ever went to Mass in England; unlike Molly, he considered religion a private matter. All he wanted was his favourite daughter at his side this one day of the year. How glad he was she had bought his boat for him while she had been able to afford it. Now he only worked for Paddy Clafferty on the trawler eight months of the year, and was his own boss for the other four. When he built up the shark fishing a bit more, he might not have to work for Paddy at all, brave the winter weather or haul those heavy crates of fish.

After a lot more noise and sporadic chat with her sisters she stood up to leave, smiling as she looked at him, festooned in grandchildren.

"Bye, everyone. I'll see you all tomorrow.'

Over the din, they hardly heard or noticed as she slipped away, burrowing into her duffel coat against the sudden cold outside. The night was sharp and starry, but as she walked round the harbour the chill she felt was more in her heart than in her bones. Unlike Sher, she would never slip easily back into the family again, a secure matron with a family of her own; yet despite the Rafters' great kindness she was not blood-bonded to them, was not really their daughter or really Rhianna's mother. Halfway between the two houses, she hardly knew which was home, where she belonged.

If home was where the heart was, then she belonged with Ben, and Rhianna belonged with them both. If things had worked with Ben . . . but they had not.

Why not? Why, why? Where was he this Christmas, who was he with? With his parents, and Charlotte Lucas? Was Deva putting Charlotte in the pink bedroom, this year? Or in Ben's?

What a sad time Christmas could be, for all its cheer. Somehow the celebration seemed to sharpen the sorrow, for anyone who had any. Here in this village families were reuniting, some with children who had been away even longer than Sher, but next week they would all be sundered again, lonely lives would resume in faraway countries, grandparents would look round for the toddlers who were gone, houses would ring hollow in the dark January nights.

With her hands in her pockets she stood looking out over the black Atlantic, at the white moon hanging low over the horizon. But then she remembered that Eimear had said she could bath Rhianna and put her to bed, have her all to herself this first Christmas Eve. Eimear, who knew how she felt, and understood.

Oh, but thank God for Rhianna. Thank God for her.

* * *

301

Lying on their stomachs on the floor, Dan and Aran were laughing as they helped Rhianna unwrap her Christmas presents under the tree, and Eimear smiled to herself as she watched from the kitchen where things had to be got under control. The whole morning smelled of Christmas, of roasting ham with cloves and honey, of pine needles and nutty sherry, herbs and onions and almonds. It was the happiest Christmas she had ever known.

Shrieking gleefully, Rhianna was rosy with delight in her cherry-coloured smock bordered with green holly leaves, making a dustbin of Dan as she flung the ribbons and wrappers into his outstretched hands. As ever on Christmas morning, Dan was dapper in a check suit and waistcoat, but his hair was tousled, his whole face flushed with fun, like Aran's beside him. Aran, who had given them this priceless gift . . . with the sun flashing in her springy curls, gleaming on her glossy lips, she had no idea how lovely she looked today. Sitting up, she brushed the pine needles off her white sweater and looked across the room at the blazing log fire.

'Look, Rhianna – there are fairies in the fire!'

Wide-eyed, Rhianna turned to look.

'See them? Little ballerina fairies, with golden wings and scarlet slippers . . .'

Eimear remembered that childhood game so well, sitting on her mother's knee as Hannah pointed out the shapes in the flames. It had kept them amused for hours.

Rhianna was too young to remember it today, but she would remember in future years, long after the toys had been forgotten. But today's toys were only simple ones; at nine months they didn't want to confuse or overwhelm her. And anyway, it was bunny she loved, bunny who went everywhere, his ears soggy from constant chewing.

But eventually Aran stood up, looking regretfully at her daughter.

'I'm sorry, muffin, I have to go to Mass. I'll be back soon, I promise. But Grandma is coming to see you, and Luke Lavery and Annie McGowan. Will you be good while I'm away?'

'Um,' agreed Rhianna.

Aran winked at Dan as she left the room. Eimear had made him promise not to argue with Luke, with whom he was at loggerheads over all the new development in the village. Dan thought it was great, but Luke said that bistros and baguettes, amidst all the litter and lounging youths, looked absurd. It was like a woman putting cosmetics on her face before she had washed it.

Anyway, she would miss the row if they did have one, miss playing her oboe for Luke too, because he would be gone by the time she returned from Mass and the first of her two lunches. Annie would be gone too, but she'd go round to talk business with her tomorrow. Blowing a kiss, she left him with Rhianna, noticing that Eimear did not immediately dive on the child. Eimear was afraid, she admitted, of turning into one of those possessive mothers who appropriated her baby's every smile, monopolised its affections and excluded the father. It would be so unfair to Dan, and maybe even cause friction in their happy marriage.

So Dan continued to play blissfully with the baby while Aran let herself out, feeling as well as hearing the stillness outside. It felt as if the whole world was sleeping, with all the shops shut and normal life suspended; but then the church bell rang and she hurried down to the village, her heart warming to see Conor's happy smile as he waited for her by the door.

The ceremony was uplifting and cheerful, the dark church illuminated with the light of candles and newly polished brass, and afterwards the entire Campion family walked home together, all except Val with her husband and son, who were driving over from Cork to join them for lunch.

Lunch was madness, with thirteen of them crowded round the kitchen table, the youngest on their parents' laps, the rest wedged elbow to elbow, barely able to raise their hands high enough to reach their plates. Molly said thirteen at table was bad luck, but there was nothing could be done about it; even if he was sleeping with neighbours, Dursey couldn't be expected to eat with them today. And, in a hectic way, it was fun.

Until Val finished her food and looked at her sister.

'I hear the Rafters have adopted, Aran?'

Molly was standing at the oven, with her back to them, but Aran saw it stiffen, felt her own face freeze.

'Yes. A little girl. Her name is Rhianna and she's nine months.'

Idly, Val picked a piece of turkey from between her teeth.

'And Eimear has given up teaching?'

'Yes.'

'Silly fool.'

Aran coloured.

'Why do you say that?'

'Well, can you imagine, being stuck at home all day with a baby! She'll die of boredom.'

'But Val, she's not bored at all. She's loving it. After all, she'd been teaching for twelve years, the same curriculum every year. Don't you ever feel like giving up work?'

Everyone knew she felt like it, because she often said so herself. Serving behind the counter in Finbarr's newsagency, counting out

303

penny sweets to dithering children, did not fill her life with radiant joy. It was murder on the feet, too.

'Well, the odd day maybe – but then how would I run my car, where would we get the money to go to Bundoran every summer? We'd have to pay an assistant. I bet the Rafters are having to tighten their belts.'

Aran nodded.

'Yes, a bit. But Eimear says it's worth it not to have to go out in the dark on freezing mornings, to be able to play with Rhianna and not be exhausted by other people's children – anyway, with taxes as high as they are, insurance, union dues and all the other deductions, she wasn't exactly making a fortune.'

Val looked resentful.

'Hadn't she ten weeks off every summer, not to mention another four between Christmas, Easter and mid-term breaks? I call that money for old rope.'

Aran grinned.

'Then maybe you should have made more of your Leaving Cert, should have become a teacher yourself.'

Val frowned at her, but Sher intervened peacably.

'I tell you frankly, I'd quit work tomorrow if I could. The way things are, I get up at six, fix breakfast for the five of us, drop Lance and Darren off to school after I've organised everyone's clothes and lunches, got myself ready and taken Shelley to the playschool. Then I spend the day checking in hotel guests who are tired and cranky after long flights, wrestling with the computer system they're going to change soon anyway, and then I rush off to pick the kids up again. Then I do the shopping, the laundry, the cooking, the cleaning, supervise homework, take Lance to his football and Darren to his baseball, bath Shelley and get everyone's stuff ready for the next day. Then my boss, who is a bad-tempered stressed-out monument to ambition, switches me to the night roster and I have to change the whole system to Plan B. I already have an ulcer and I expect to have a nervous breakdown the minute I get time for it.'

Pointedly, Val looked at Sher's tan trouser suit, and then at the cramped room in which they sat.

'Think of the money you're earning.'

'Yeah. It covers the health insurance for the medical expenses it's going to cause. I tell you, as soon as Norbert gets a promotion, I'm giving it up. Norbert loves his computers and his office politics, but I can think of a dozen other things I'd rather be doing. You can only be bored if you have no imagination.'

Aran nodded. That was what she thought too. Lucky as she was to have her job with Annie, she couldn't imagine consecrating her whole life to cheese. And then she had a lot of freedom, she didn't have to clock in, wear shoulder-padded suits or kow-tow to any power-crazed boss. She could have picnic lunches and fit in an occasional visit to local places of interest.

But she'd still rather be with Rhianna.

Rhianna! Suddenly she couldn't wait to get back to her. What on earth would her sisters say, if they knew they had a niece only a mile away? Would Val say she shouldn't have dreamed of having her adopted, should have given the child to her if she couldn't cope herself? Somehow, she couldn't see Val offering to take Rhianna in a million years. Sher might have. But Sher lived in America.

With a pang, she looked at her father. He certainly would have helped. Only his help would have been worse than useless. Poor Dad, who always meant so well.

After helping with the mountain of washing-up, she kissed him goodbye, thanked everyone for their presents and returned quietly but speedily to the Rafters' bungalow.

Luke and Annie were gone, but Hannah was there, jigging Rhianna on her knee with no concern at all for her navy velvet suit, which had traces of something sticky on the shoulder. Somehow, Aran was touched as she looked at her.

'Hello, Mrs Lowry. Happy Christmas.'

Hannah beamed.

'The happiest in years, Aran.'

Something in her tone sounded conspiratorial, and as she looked at Dan and Eimear she saw that they too were looking positively beatific.

'What? What is it?'

Dan glanced at his wife.

'Go on, Eimear. You tell her.'

Blissfully, Eimear sat down and indicated that Aran should too.

'I thought Christmas Day was the best day to tell everyone. Aran, I'm pregnant. After twelve years of marriage, I'm going to have a baby.'

'Pregnant? – oh, Eimear! Oh, that's wonderful!'

'Yes. And it's all thanks to you. I don't know what happened exactly, but as soon as I had Rhianna I – I felt different. Happier, and much more relaxed. I wasn't worrying any more about conceiving. And now I have.'

She was thrilled. Rhianna was going to have a brother or sister, after all! And, as Eimear said, she had contributed in some strange way to making that happen. She had kept the promise she never

305

knew she was making, nearly six years before.

'Oh, I don't know what to say! When is it due?'

'In June.'

A summer baby, in the summer of her life. Her face was radiant, and Aran could feel the happiness in everyone, in the room, in the whole house.

No. Not a house, but a home. A proper home. That was where Rhianna lived, with a proper family. Going to Hannah, she lifted the infant off her lap and held her up in her arms.

'Aren't you lucky! Do you realise what a lucky little girl you are?'

'Um,' said Rhianna, gazing into Aran's grey eyes with her big brown ones, showing off her two teeth in a triumphant smile.

The new year of 1981 began well for Ben, but by March he was having his doubts about it. First came an unexpected phone call from his sister Chanda, to tell him that Charles's wine import business had run into a spot of bother, and to ask whether he could lend them – well, rather a lot of money actually, until this frightful recession bottomed out. Ben agreed to the loan, but he was provoked. Chanda's husband loathed him, he knew, and deplored his chosen career as much as Chanda herself, who had taken to using her married name since he had brought Halley into such disrepute. Pointedly, he made the cheque out to Chanda Halley, and smiled grimly as he enclosed it in a get-well-soon card.

Then came five even more provocative weeks in the recording studios, struggling with Myles Irving to make his new album under Schwabbe's stringent conditions. Schwabbe wanted it to be strong and punchy, they said, but they also wanted it to be inoffensive. Some of Kelwin's lyrics had been sterilised until they were virtually meaningless, and the new words tasted like sawdust as he sang them. Technically, Schwabbe expected high quality, but they expected it on a chokingly tight budget. In promoting the album, Ben was to follow an exact list of instructions – wear this, say that, go here, don't do this, that or the other – but of course he must be seen to have integrity. Worst of all, Schwabbe didn't refer to it as an album, they called it 'the product'. But when 'the product' was finally released in May, there were serious problems with distribution. Some shops got huge supplies, others got none at all.

Dreading the promotional tour that was reluctantly scheduled for the end of May, with endless restrictions on personnel and equipment, Ben flew clandestinely off to New York to see Amery Cheam. Cheam's Theme had been recorded over December and January, and was to be launched at a gala weekend in Rhode Island, in June. But his management company was not optimistic about Schwabbe's reaction to it, and only Amery's excellent spirits kept his own up.

'You didn't write it in Schwabbe's time, my boy, you didn't use their studios or their musicians. You own the copyright and there's nothing they can do about it.'

Generously and good-naturedly, he took Ben to Lutèce to celebrate. But despite the excellent steamed lobster, the amazing Chablis and the ancient brandy with which they regaled themselves, Ben could not fully relax. When Schwabbe heard about this venture there were going to be what Aran used to call 'ructions'.

'Well,' mused Amery, pulling on a long cigar and surveying him with his candid blue eyes, 'if there are, you won't have to fight them on your own. Cheam Marine has a fine team of lawyers.'

Ben was very grateful to him, but also very apprehensive: the last thing he wanted was a legal battle on his hands. Why hadn't Aran thought of this, written some protective clause into his contract?

Because she had only been nineteen then. Because she hadn't known he was going to write anything this good this young. Because nobody could have foreseen that Cedar would be bought by Schwabbe. She had done her best and it was not fair to blame her. After all, if she was still his manager she might have figured out a solution even now, whereas the damn management company had too many clients to give enough time to any one of their individual problems. To put a team of lawyers on this one might cost more than it was worth, they said; since it was a classical piece of music it was hardly likely to make Ben Halley a whole heap of money. Ben was uninterested in whatever money it might make, but that wasn't the point. The point was that this music was his brainchild, his baby. He did not want to see it taken into German custody.

After watching the documentary film to which it was being married, and going into detailed discussion with the videotape editor, he thanked Amery and flew back to London. On the hall table in the Kensington flat, Thanh had left the accumulated post in a neat stack. Schwabbe's logo was on the second envelope in the pile.

Who, he wondered, was the mole? A musician, a technician, a studio secretary? No matter. They would have found out soon enough anyway.

But he had not told them himself, the letter accused, and that was the worst of it. He had been secretive – was that a euphemism for dishonest? – and duplicity was not in the tradition of the German workforce. Mr Halley would meet with their chief executive next week, armed with his explanations and his lawyer.

Ben immediately phoned his lawyer, and his management, with a sinking heart. They'd do their best, they promised, but the situation didn't look too good. Not good at all.

On his newly slashed budget, Kevin Ross was doing his best, but the false economy was obvious to everyone. On the first night of the promotional tour, the lighting wasn't right, the amps were inadequate and the musicians' morale was low. Kevin, terrified that he might soon lose his job altogether, was twittering with nerves. For the first time ever, Ben felt that he didn't want to go on stage, couldn't deliver the high-octane performance the audience expected and deserved.

But when he did go on, in khaki overalls and a tight belt he thought many of the fans might interpret correctly, the applause was deafening, so loud and continuous that he was unable to sing or even speak for fully four minutes. What had brought this on?

But then he remembered: just a couple of small pieces had appeared in the music press about his fight with Schwabbe to be let perform as he wanted to perform, and about the piece of music he had written privately, to which Schwabbe now wanted the rights. This was the audience's way of telling him they were on his side. London's entire Hammersmith Odeon was vibrating with sympathy and support, the atmosphere full of affection for him.

Silenced and very moved, he simply stood still until they subsided, bent to pick up the bouquet someone had thrown on the stage, and thanked them in the Indian manner, with his palms pressed together in front of his face. And then he found his voice.

They sang with him all night, showing him that they had learned the words of the new songs as a gesture of solidarity, cheering and waving the lighters that Schwabbe wanted banned as a high insurance risk. Ever since he had first sung to fifty or sixty people at the North End Road, he had always felt a great sense of friendship with his audience, but tonight he felt something even deeper and stronger: a sense of family. It was not a huge venue, but it was filled to capacity, and so was his heart. Afterwards, he was besieged by fans of all ages, wanting autographs, wanting to speak to him, and instead of letting Thanh hustle him protectively away he stayed with them, talking to them for hours at the stage door, letting them come as close as they wanted. With John Lennon's murder still fresh in their minds, Thanh and Kevin fretted themselves into a frenzy, but he wouldn't be moved. No matter what his problems with Schwabbe, these were the people who really mattered.

England was magnificent in early summer, Aran thought as she drove along with the window open, listening to Schumann's piano concerto in A minor on the radio. Robert Alexander Schumann, who couldn't play the piece himself, because a finger injury had ended his career as a pianist. He'd become a great composer instead, but he'd also become a manic depressive, tried to drown himself and finally died in an asylum – for a change – at the age of forty-six .

But his music was beautiful, as was this cloudless blue sky, with the sunlight rippling through miles of sizzling yellow rapeseed, pale green corn and undulating buff-coloured wheat. Over the redbrick orchard walls great boughs of apples and plums hung ripening amidst their white blossoms, here and there a flock of geese strutted across a village green, in the distance creamy cows lay supine in the noonday heat. Keeping an eye out for a river where she might have her picnic lunch, she eventually came to a clear stream bubbling under a bridge, and stopped the car.

Poor Schumann! He surely couldn't have wanted to drown himself in a stream such as this, on such a heartwarming day, unless some very great chill had touched his mind. Spreading her skirt on the grass, she arranged herself comfortably, bit into a pear and wiped the juice from her chin as she considered the view.

She sensed she wasn't far from a village, and smiled as she thought of the quaint names the English gave them: Stow-On-The-Wold, Middle Wallop, Upper Slaughter, Small Dole, Bishop's Itchington. Some were barely a blink, others were postcards from paradise, but all were lovingly preserved, their honeystone and hollyhocks glowing as if in amber. Time and time again, when she stopped to picnic, she heard Grey's *Elegy* in her head, felt the drifting daylight, smelled the still earth and the drowsing animals . . . for all the humming motorways, many parts of England were still an enchanting timewarp, and every month it seemed to change colour: April was yellow with primroses and daffodils, May was pink with blossom, June was lilac and July was red with poppies. Then the exhausted white heat of August, the dun fields of September, the ochre of October . . . she had seen the full cycle now, and felt wholly in tune with it.

Rhianna was nearly fifteen months now, walking and talking, leading Sammy a dog's life as she tried to ride him round the garden. And Eimear's son Emmett was celebrating his birthday, a week old today. Poor Emmett, Dan said laughing; Rhianna thought he was a toy they had got for her personal amusement, and wanted him lined up on a shelf with her other dolls at night. Emmett was going to have to stand up to his lusty sister, Dan suspected, as he grew older – and that brought him to rather a delicate question. At what stage did Aran want Rhianna to be told about her natural parents? Or did she want her to be told at all? The matter had often been discussed, but never fully decided.

Aran mulled over it thoughtfully as she finished her pear and nibbled absently on a miniature pork pie, one of those English delicacies that looked as if they were imported from the middle ages. If she were thinking only of her own wishes, she would have told Dan that Rhianna should know as soon as she was old enough to understand. But then she would need to be old enough to understand, also, why her mother had done it. That really meant waiting until her teens – but then, dear God, what to say? Simply that she was adopted, or that she was, specifically, the daughter of Aran who came to see her all the time, and Ben Halley the singer, who was unaware of her existence?

Well, she had been christened Rhianna Rafter. And on her birth certificate Aran had reluctantly put 'father unknown' in case the nurse or registrar leaked Ben's name to the press. It was unlikely, but not impossible . . . it might slip out even to a friend some night, after a few glasses of wine. But now, Dan, Eimear and Molly were the only ones who knew.

How would Rhianna feel, if she discovered Molly, living only a mile away? How hurt might she be to find that her grandmother had no interest in her, taken no part in her childhood? What would Hannah feel then, after contributing so much to it? And what in heaven would Ben say, if a daughter materialised out of nowhere? Gazing into the water, throwing crumbs to the ducks bobbing on it, she reflected with great care.

There was no easy solution, but she must find the one that would hurt least, cause least distress to everyone. How long would it be before Rhianna needed to see her birth certificate, read the name Campion on it? Another fifteen years probably; at sixteen there would be things like exam entry forms, a driving licence, a passport.

Sixteen, then. Dan and Eimear could tell her the general situation when she was maybe fifteen, and the specifics when she was sixteen. There was plenty of time to prepare what she would say to her then, explain why the twenty-year-old Aran Campion had not been able to keep her, furnish the father and stable home she needed.

But Ben? Was there anything to be gained by naming Ben?

No. Only mutual shock, perhaps, and a scandal in the press if Ben were still as well known as he was now. If Rhianna turned out badly, she might even want to go racing after his money. If he had other children by then, she might feel excluded or jealous . . . oh, if only people could see into the future, know who and where they were going to be in it! She couldn't imagine ever loving anyone else in the way she had loved Ben, or having children with anyone else – yet she would love to have other children, and Eimear said she would learn to love someone else.

But whether she did or not, Rhianna wasn't going to turn out badly. She was going to grow up loved and secure, with Dan and Eimear, emotionally equipped to clear this hurdle when she came to it. That was why she was with them, because they were mature, able to deal with things, wise and experienced.

They would help her to understand why her mother had acted as she did, to accept that it had been for the best. Perhaps she would be puzzled or even angry for a little while, but gradually they would work out their feelings and their relationship – Rhianna, Eimear and herself, as three grown women. It would all settle down and be happy again.

But I must work at it in the meantime, she thought. Must work really hard, so that when she finds out she'll already like and trust me – maybe even love me, a little. I must say and do all the right things, build up sixteen years of friendship between us. I haven't much to give her, materially, but I could give her the things I wanted from my own mother – ideas, interests, a spirit of independence and adventure. I could make her laugh, and help her to learn. I could be her friend.

I will be her friend, if she'll let me. But what's going to happen when she discovers Conor is her grandfather? She'll think he didn't want her . . . and he'll be so hurt, so bewildered, if she confronts him. He'll feel cheated, so disappointed in me. Oh, I wish I could tell him! I'd do it tomorrow, if it weren't for Molly.

Racking her brains, she sat on the riverbank, feeling the sun on the nape of her neck, consoling, comforting. On a day like this, it was possible to believe that everything would work out. The future, as Dan was fond of saying, would take care of itself. And for the moment, her daughter was happy and healthy.

Much as she missed Rhianna, it felt natural that she should be in Ireland with Dan and Eimear, in the home that had always felt as if it was her own. She was so lucky, compared to other young mothers who were forced by circumstance to give their babies to strangers and never see them again. She would see Rhianna twice every year, at Christmas and in the summer – maybe even a little bit more, if Eimear could bring her to London occasionally.

Of course she'd probably have to give up the Hampstead house in 1984, when the lease and Ben's financial help expired. Find somewhere smaller, cheaper . . . it was as if her life was moving

311

backwards instead of forward. But the more of Annie's cheeses she sold, the more chance there would be of affording a flat with an extra bedroom. Maybe even one in the same area, because she didn't want to leave the friends she had made, move on yet again. During the week she drove all over England, but on Fridays she returned to London, took a shower and went out to the music group she had joined. Just an amateur group, without illusions or ambitions, but it was enjoyable and sociable. After they played for two hours, she often invited two or three of them home for supper; she loved cooking and they loved her chicken with walnuts and apricots, her crispy cabbage tossed in hot oil with garlic. It was a new life, only a green shoot as yet, but precious to her. On Saturdays she was free to browse in Mr Rudelstein's bookshop, on Sundays she went for long walks or, in winter, to concerts in the churches, to galleries or to the markets.

Sinéad was still selling the sweaters in Camden, but that wasn't going to last beyond the end of the summer. Now that eight boutiques in regional towns were taking them, she thought she would be better employed as the co-op's fulltime marketing manager. One night they had gone out for a pizza and had a long chat about what strategy to adopt. Was it worth aiming for big shops like John Lewis, Marks & Spencer, Top Shop or Miss Selfridge? In the end they thought no; the knitwear was too individual, much better suited to small boutiques. So Sinéad was going to get a car, and some young lad from Kilkenny was enquiring about taking over the stall, which seemed destined to remain in Irish hands. He made woodware, bowls and pitchers and things from bog oak, but he was willing to continue the silk, glass and shell artefacts as a sideline.

So young Turlough from Kilkenny was happy, the crafts people in Cork were happy, Sinéad was happy. The Rafters were happy, Hannah was happy and, out on the Lady Aran, Conor was happy. Even Molly, with her problem under wraps, was perilously close to it.

Gathering her things, Aran stood looking down into the stream for a few moments before getting back into the car. Smetana's *Libuse* was on the radio, and the presenter chattily informed her that Smetana—

'Went mad!' she chorused. 'Went mad, and died in an asylum!'

Never had Ben known such pleasure or such pride – or such relief – as he knew that weekend in Rhode Island. Up to the very last moment, he was petrified that Schwabbe would seek an injunction, preventing Cheam's Theme from being played at all. But they held their fire, and in the hot June sunshine five hundred guests congregated for a champagne brunch, to be followed by the launch of the documentary film and the music, and then an afternoon's triumphant sailing. The Americans knew how to do these things very well, with great fanfare, and he made up his mind to enjoy it. Later, if Schwabbe took the music away from him, they would never be able to take the memory.

But he felt unusually shy, even with Thanh beside him, Amery steering him round to meet his friends and clients. This project was so different to anything he had done before; it was serious music, real music that couldn't be leavened with a laugh or a witticism, a deprecating aside to the audience. He never took his rock music seriously, but today he found that people were taking him seriously. They were looking at him rather oddly, too, wondering why Amery had chosen him, wondering why he wasn't living up to his exuberant stage image. He didn't know any of them, but he was desperately anxious that they should like the music, vindicate Amery's faith in him.

At noon they gathered in the marquee on Cheam Marine's waterside grounds, a marquee made of specially filtered fabric to keep the sun out, cooled by dozens of whirring fans. After a brief speech, Amery gave a signal and a giant screen opened up behind him, with Cheam's logo on it. It was the same nautical knot that enlivened his waistcoats.

And then the music. Ben could hardly hear the first notes himself, they were so soft, just a little splash in the silence. But then the sound began to rise and grow, filling up with the wind instruments, setting out on the seven-minute voyage which, at this moment, loomed like eternity. As he heard the oboe, he thought of Aran. Aran could have been part of this – should have been, he knew. But she didn't play professionally, would have refused . . . oh, he was just making excuses.

The music embarked with the yacht on the screen, pushing it, lifting it, twisting and teasing as it gathered force. The photography was astonishing, so realistic that he felt as if he were on the yacht, leaning far out over the side with every muscle braced, speeding over and under the spray, concentrating all his senses with split-second timing. He knew nothing about sailing, but that was one reason why Amery had picked him; if a complete novice could convey the thrill of it, how many more novices might become hooked? Not that these people were novices. They were key clients, seasoned sailors who would detect any flaw, any anomaly in the mood of the music.

But there weren't any flaws, Amery had assured him there weren't. Holding his breath, he watched until his eyes hurt, waiting for the yacht to cross the finishing line. Just another few minutes to the

313

crescendo, the first sight of land, the waiting flotilla emblazoned with flags in the harbour.

And there it was. The peaking tension, the vision of victory, the jubilant camaraderie uniting the crew as the yacht flew far past its competitors. The music had captured every nuance, every emotion, every angle of the precision engineering. Like the hull of the yacht it sliced through the water, like the wind it grew fierce and threatening, like the sun it emerged blazing and brilliant.

Like the sailors he had given his all, more than he knew he possessed.

Amery was first on his feet, beating Thanh and the rest of the audience by a fraction, leading the standing ovation that Ben knew was for the music, but felt was for the whole crew: the photographer, the editor, the musicians and the conductor, everyone who had combined their talents to produce such a memorable experience. But everyone was looking at him, the applause drumming like a hailstorm, the smiles the kind Americans lavished on their favourite idol, success.

This could go to my head, he thought wildly. This is tremendous, and if I'm not careful I—

Was this why Aran took me to Crete, after that European tour?

Was this why we stayed at that simple hotel, doing simple things? To keep me in touch with reality, keep my feet on the ground? I hated it, but suddenly I think I understand it.

Jesus Christ, why didn't I understand it then?

Two weeks later, Schwabbe declared war. They owned Cheam's Theme, and they were going to fight in court for it.

'Fine,' Amery replied over the phone, adopting Winston Churchill's stentorian tone. 'We'll fight back. Whatever the cost may be, we shall fight on the beaches, we shall fight on the landing grounds, we shall fight in the fields and in the streets, we shall fight in the hills; we shall never surrender.'

'No,' agreed Ben, laughing in spite of himself, 'we shall not be moved.'

But the situation was hideous. Nobody really knew who owned Cheam's Theme, and efforts to negotiate had run into a brick wall. Did Schwabbe really own it, as they owned copyright to Ben's other work, for ten years from the date of completion? Did Cheam Marine own it, because they had commissioned it? Or did Ben own it, because he had written it in his own time with his own resources?

The project had started out so innocently, the carefree result of Amery's imagination and Ben's desire to rise to it. The music was not

314

for any commercial purpose other than an advertising campaign, it was not intended to release a record for general sale. If Cheam did own it, then Amery was happy to let Ben do what he liked with it from 1982 onwards; by then it would have achieved its purpose and any further performances would be a bonus, keep Cheam Marine in the public mind. If Ben owned it, then all Amery would ask was that he never sell it to any other company or allow it to be used for any other advertising. But if Schwabbe owned it, Ben felt, then they really did own him, body and soul.

Of course they should have clarified all this at the outset, drawn up documents and pinned everything down. But it had been a labour of love, a gesture of faith and friendship! And even now, Amery's friendship was rock solid.

'I'll take all the blame, my boy. I'll say I put you up to it and that the only money that changed hands was for expenses.'

That was true. Ben had turned down his offer of a flat fee, preferring to keep the whole thing out of the financial arena. There was something about this one piece of music that no money could buy. It was an experiment, a mere toe in the water of classical composition, he had never expected it to be so hugely successful. If it hadn't been, would Schwabbe still want it? Would they be prepared to pick up the pieces, stand over a failure? Oh, no. They would say they knew nothing about it, wanted no part of it. They would say, he was sure, that what he did in his own time was his own business. They – they were bastards!

'Bastards!' he shrieked aloud, 'bastards, bastards, *bas*tards!'

Picking up a Japanese vase, he flung it at the wall, and watched with fury as it smashed to atoms.

Chapter Fourteen

'Of course,' Dan observed, dropping the newspaper on the lawn after reading the piece aloud, 'it's not just the money. It's the insubordination. That's what's really bugging them. Ben broke rank, stepped way out of line.'

Eimear nodded, thinking he was probably right. Big companies were so tyrannical these days, exploiting all the clout they carried against their employees. In a recession, employees feared for their jobs, had to keep their heads down and their mouths shut. Trust Ben Halley to challenge the record company that liked to exercise complete control of its workforce.

Shielding her eyes against the April sunshine, she turned to Aran. 'How old is Ben now, Aran?'

'Twenty-five in July.'

Old enough to know better, really. But he'd only been twenty-two when he got into this mess. It had taken a year to bring the work to fruition, and nearly another year for Schwabbe to get a court hearing.

How quickly Aran could answer her question, though! She was twenty-three now herself, but physically she still looked like a fragile little wisp, especially at this minute as she lay on the grass, her eyes dreamy and distant. Her small wistful face was devoid of make-up, her lips slightly parted, her curls blowing in the breeze as she plucked at a fold of her pale pink dress with an absent air. Until a few minutes ago she'd been quite animated, rolling and tussling with the children, but her energy had suddenly abated like the wind, was coming now from some other direction.

Eimear raised a quizzical eyebrow, and sighed to herself. It couldn't still be Ben. Surely not, after three years, with a new boyfriend and a successful career, everything going for her? She had even spoken of bringing Thierry to Ireland with her for Easter: he was French, and very charming by all accounts. But alas Thierry managed a supermarket in Boulogne, which would be thronged with English daytrippers over the holiday weekend, so he couldn't get away. But she and Dan hoped to meet him in the summer, if they could afford to go camping in France with the children. The theft of Dan's car while he was visiting his parents in Dublin had put a question mark over the possibility of a holiday, and left their liberal views rather dented: the police had shrugged and said there was no point in pursuing the thieves. Dublin's jails were overflowing and stolen cars, these days, were very small beer. Eventually the abandoned wreck had been found, burnt to a cinder, and the insurance did not fully cover the cost of replacement.

But brooding over it was not going to change it. Feeling thankful that she didn't live in Dublin, Eimear surveyed the tranquil garden scene, thinking that it looked like a painting, that only their clothes distinguished them from characters on an Edwardian lawn. In his deckchair, Dan lay in a pose of rare relaxation, Sammy at his feet, Aran stretched a little further away, watching Luke Lavery push Rhianna on a makeshift swing he had constructed between the yew trees. Chirping to himself, baby Emmett was crawling over the grass, making for some booty he had espied amidst the lunch leftovers on the patio.

Like Dan, Emmett was fair-haired, with green eyes and a complexion that would soon be freckled. Nobody could possibly take him for Rhianna's natural brother, and Eimear thought that Luke Lavery had probably guessed, by now, where they had got Rhianna. Annie McGowan had a knowing air, too; but neither she nor Luke ever said anything, asked any tactless questions. In this little community, they were almost unique in their ability to mind their own business, and Eimear knew they would never drop any hints anywhere, ever make any idle gossip.

Rhianna was whooping loudly on her swing, demanding that Luke push her higher. At two, Rhianna was no shrinking violet, but for once Aran's attention was not pinned on her daughter. Sitting up, she asked Dan if she might have a look at his newspaper, and Dan passed it to her with an indolent grin.

'Here you are. And yes, there is a photograph. He looks very sexy.'

Blushing, Aran smiled as she took it from him. Dan was a terrible tease – but a great friend, and a great father.

Yes. There was a photograph, and Ben did look sexy. Sexy and defiant and – and very like Rhianna, a naughty child who could never be made to repent. Entering the courtroom with his chin high, he was smiling slightly, revealing his uneven tooth and his dimple, wearing a jacket and shirt by way of concession, but no tie. Thanh was beside him, his expression bland, his eyes guarded, and she sighed as she recalled the bright, open personality behind the watchful exterior. Dear old Thanh, whose friendship had had to be sacrificed; to this day she regretted it, and missed him very much.

But Ben could not feel as confident as he looked. After twelve days the hearing was completely bogged down, tied in legal knots, costing a fortune and going nowhere. If he won, he would only get back what he felt he owned anyway. If he lost, he was facing a very fraught year with Schwabbe before his contract mercifully expired. What fools they were! How could he compose hit songs for them, how could he perform at his best, under such circumstances? He would loathe and resent them – yet, she knew, he would put the fans first. For their sake he would continue to put everything into his music, strive for the number one hit that still, strangely, eluded him. Schwabbe probably guessed he would, were gambling that the fans wouldn't keep their promise to boycott their 'product', because they couldn't resist Ben's voice. To punish Schwabbe would be to punish themselves, and Ben would only lose out financially.

Further down the page there was another photograph, of his mother Deva, his sister Rani, producer Myles Irving and tour manager Kevin Ross, all looking as if they were on their way to a funeral. For the hundredth time she wondered whether they blamed her, thought it was all her fault for advising Ben to sign with Cedar and accept those copyright conditions. But they had been reasonable conditions at the time, and Cedar had been an eminently reasonable company. There would have been no fuss over this classical piece if Schwabbe hadn't come on the scene.

What was it like, the music? Obviously it was very precious to Ben, but was it really as good as rumour reported? It had been heard all over America, on Cheam television commercials, but no record had been cut, it was not available for sale. She knew, because she had tried everywhere to get it. In fact Ben's lawyers had pulled a clever but risky stroke, informing the hearing that Ben intended to endow the copyright on a philanthropical music organisation in London, which would use the proceeds of any public sales to award a scholarship to an inner-city child. That sounded well, and knowing Ben she didn't doubt his generosity, but might it be construed as a kind of bribe? An attempt to get the court on his side, to secure some of the respect which, as a rock star, he would otherwise be denied almost automatically?

Oh, what a mess! And yet he had made no move to drag her into it, had never mentioned her name in connection with his contract. On the contrary – he had remembered her birthday in the middle of it

318

all. Once again a big bunch of yellow roses had arrived, and she had called his management company to convey her thanks.

She'd left a message of support as well; even though it might get lost among the hundreds pouring in, it was safer than phoning him in person, risking a conversation that would fizzle into casual chitchat. The roses were so fragrant, she wanted her memories to remain fragrant too.

But it was time to stop dreaming. Time to give Thierry a chance and, as Eimear said, give herself a chance. It surprised her that she had met a new man, taken a liking to him, but she had. Thierry Marand, who managed a supermarket in Boulogne and had taken a trial range of Annie's cheeses, her one and only success in France so far. The other managers had been curt, some even derisive, but Thierry had come out from his office as soon as she asked to see him in her phrasebook French. Come out with a friendly smile, looked at the produce and then looked at her. A man of medium height, with thick reddish hair and twinkly eyes, he'd taken off his white coat to reveal an attractive physique, and asked her if she'd like to have some lunch. She could still remember the oysters, the bustle at the outdoor café, the whiff of salt on the breeze, Thierry's eyes clear and green as the water . . . in spite of herself she had enjoyed that first date. Enjoyed it enough to agree to another, and think of him in the meantime. He was a charming man, courteous and kind in a way that dispelled her shyness. His attention was flattering in the beginning, but now it was more than that; it was comforting, and rather touching. And it was fun, now, to have a cross-Channel romance. Boat trips, embraces on the quayside, weekends that were piquant with the impending sense of separation. She didn't let herself think too much about him for the first few weeks, but now she looked forward to every reunion, loved it when he phoned or sent flowers. Ben's birthday roses were not the only ones perfuming this lush summer.

Where would it end? She had no idea. All she knew was that she felt happier, more alive, more like a young woman again. She was making Thierry happy too, getting closer to him, savouring his smile every time he met her at Boulogne, or she met him at Folkestone. Eimear was pleased, Holly was pleased, and she was pleased herself. It wasn't a blazing romance – yet – but it was warming her soul.

Daydreaming, she was startled by something cold and moist on her ankle, and looked down. Baby Emmett beamed toothlessly up at her, busily smearing the remains of his chocolate yogurt, already covered in it himself. As Dan said, it was a mystery how there was always more yogurt on the child than could possibly have been in the pot. Leaning forward, she scooped Emmett up and mopped him with a tissue, murmuring to him, sucking his fingers until he gurgled with delight.

But instantly there was a shriek, and Rhianna came bowling across the grass, her ribbons flying in her hair, Luke Lavery forgotten. Ripping the yogurt pot from Emmett's small surprised fist, she plunged her hand into it, streaked some across her face and thrust the face at Aran.

'Me too! Me too, Aran! Me first!'

Pushing the baby out of the way, she clambered up on Aran's lap and installed herself in pride of place.

Schwabbe owned the copyright to Cheam's Theme. That was the court's decision, and Ben felt his soul disintegrate as it was announced. Saying nothing, feeling violated, he listened to the fine being imposed on him for breach of contract, to the fine imposed on Amery Cheam for collusion, to the ban imposed on Cheam Marine from ever using the music again unless they were prepared to buy the rights at full value. Of course the value had soared since the case started, with so much publicity, and dully he realised that that was why Schwabbe had not taken action earlier. The music had become a cause célèbre, discussed over desks and dinner tables around the world. If only for its notoriety, it was now worth a fortune.

Was this how women felt when they were raped? Was this how the American Indians had felt, when they were photographed? That some priceless thing, some part of their soul, was being stolen? Something intangible, that could never be replaced.

Lawyers jostled around him, talking about the appeal they would never lodge, because he could not bear to go through this again. Outside, fans and reporters surged up to him, microphones were thrust into his face, Deva and Rani were swallowed up in the crowd. Silently Thanh hustled him away to his car, and drove him home to Kensington.

Shortly afterwards, Amery Cheam arrived, as had been pre-arranged regardless of the outcome. His face was pale under its permanent tan, but his demeanour was fierce.

'Thieves, pirates, gangsters!' he raged, accepting a Scotch as he subsided into an armchair, bristling with anger. 'They robbed you, Ben, robbed you blind!'

Ben took a long pull on his vodka, and searched for a small smile.

'Yes. But look on the bright side, sir. Everyone has heard of Cheam Marine now. You got a lot more advertising than you expected.'

Amery swallowed his Scotch and accepted a refill.

'Oh, yes. We came out of it fine. The penalty was nothing to a company like ours, and we'll pay yours for you. But this isn't about money, Ben.'

'No. It isn't.'

'What are you going to do about it?'

'What can I do? If I contest it, I'll look petulant, maybe lose you more money, go through months more of litigation. Public sympathy might even wear off. So maybe the best thing is to accept it with good grace.'

Amery raised an eyebrow and studied him thoughtfully.

'I'd have put you down for a fighter, Ben.'

'I would fight, if I . . . if I didn't feel the music has been tainted. Been reduced to a commodity, stripped of its real value. Its value to me, as the first decent thing I've ever done.'

'It's a lot more than decent. It's superb, and it's a crime to steal it from you.'

'It didn't belong to me. That's what the man said.' Wryly Ben pulled on his vodka again, and grimaced as if it had been spiked with acid.

'Well, it will belong to you some day. In 1990, to be exact. And you'll write other pieces, now that you know you can do it.'

'Yes. I can do it, and I will do it, as soon as this godawful contract expires.'

Amery frowned.

'How did you get into it, in the first place?'

Ben looked at him for a moment, considering. But Amery had become a very good friend. He had a right to know.

'I got into it when I was very young, and Cedar was very reputable. I couldn't afford a lawyer, and we'd never even heard of Schwabbe.'

'We?'

'Myself and – and the girl who was my manager at the time.'

'Girl? I hope you mean a grown woman, with some business sense?'

'No . . . well, I mean yes, she did have business sense. But she didn't have experience. She was only nineteen.'

'Nineteen? Good God!'

Astounded, Amery groped for words adequate to his horror. But then he saw the expression on Ben's face.

'Ah. I see. You should never mix business and pleasure, my boy.'

'Perhaps not. But we all make mistakes.'

Amery smiled, feeling the Scotch slowly dispersing his anger, the court verdict recede a little in his mind.

'Well. It takes maturity to admit to a mistake. Do I gather that this one was worth it?'

For a little while Ben was silent, twisting a lock of black hair around one of his long fingers, lowering his lashes over his clove-dark eyes.

'She didn't make the mistake. I did.'

'Oh?'

Amery was a widower, with no children of his own. But something in Ben's tone made him feel fatherly concern.

'She did her best for me, and I let her go. That was the mistake. Not the contract. The – the letting go.'

'Why?'

'Why did I do it? Because she was ready to marry, and I wasn't.'

'Then you were right. To marry in such circumstances would have been a much worse mistake.'

'Yes. That's what I thought. I felt I might be unfaithful, and cause her a lot of pain. In fact I knew I would. So I – I ended it.'

'And now?'

'And now I can't blame her, for Schwabbe or anything else. I took the risk, and I have only myself to blame.'

Gazing into his glass, Amery mused on this for a moment before looking back at Ben, appraisingly.

'You know what I think, young feller?'

Ben smiled a little. 'No, sir. What do you think?'

'I think you're going to write damn good music some day. Damn good.'

Surprised, Ben tried to figure out what made him say that. Amery could be rather enigmatic at times, saying things that seemed beside the point. But the man had been his guest for nearly three weeks now, since flying over from America for the court hearing, and he was beginning to glimpse the depths in him. The depths that could be quite profound, on occasion. Amery was much more than merely astute. He raised his glass to him.

'Thank you for your faith in me.'

To his further surprise Amery stood up, crossed the room and joined him where he stood, by the fireplace. Then, hesitating for just a moment, he put his hand on his shoulder, diffidently but affectionately.

'I have great faith in you, my boy. Great faith. And I have a small confession to make.'

'A confession? About what?'

'About this music that's been taken from you. You feel very badly about it, don't you?'

322

That was putting it mildly. Ben felt as Charles Lindbergh must have felt when his child was kidnapped, as any parent must feel when their child was wrested away from them. Looking down, he said nothing.

'I knew it might happen, Ben.'

'You *knew*—?'

'Yes. But I also knew what would happen if we tied the whole project down legally, commercially. You wouldn't have felt free. You wouldn't have written as well as you did. You needed to feel it was your baby, not mine, not Schwabbe's. You needed to know the same freedom a man knows when he sets sail in one of my yachts, out on the infinite ocean.'

Biting his lip, Ben nodded.

'So I let you do it. It was a calculated risk on my part, and it was worth it. Now I know what you're capable of, and you know too.'

'But—'

'Never mind the buts. The thing is, you've done it. And you'll do it again. When your contract expires next year, I want you to let me help you negotiate a new one. Not with Schwabbe, obviously, but with a company that's right for you. One that still has heart and soul, in these greedy, soulless times. If we can't find one, I'll set one up for you.'

'You – you'll what?'

'Set one up. I'll put my best lawyers on it – not Cheam Marine lawyers, but my personal team, who know a thing or two about contract law. We'll hire anyone you want, this Irving fellow you say is so good, this guy Ross . . . buy them out of their contracts with Schwabbe and any other personnel you want to take with you.' Amery paused to smile. 'Getting even is much more satisfying than getting mad, Ben.'

He felt the blood drain from his face, as it would surely drain from Myles's and Kevin's if Amery could get them out. Being released from Schwabbe would be like being released from Alcatraz.

'But – but why? Why me? Amery, why are you taking such an interest in me? You're nearly sixty, I'm a rock singer!'

Amery stood up and began to pace the room, holding his glass aloft.

'Have you read any history, Ben?'

'Yes – musical history, that is.'

'Then you'll know that lots of them had them.'

'Who had what?'

'Musicians. They had patrons. People who believed in them and helped them. That's what I'd like to do for you, if you'll let me. You have great potential and I'd like to see it fulfilled. I want you to be able to continue with what you're doing now, because you love live

323

audiences and they love you, but I also want you free to experiment with other stuff. By the time you're ready to quit rock, you'll be on your way to the next phase. The serious phase, when you'll come into your own. Your next recording deal must allow you to develop . . . and it will, if you'll trust me, take my help?'

Bewildered, but very moved, he didn't know what to say.

'I don't have a son, Ben. Or a daughter. It's one of the great regrets of my life. Tell me, what do your parents make of your music?'

He smiled slightly.

'Not a lot. At least, my father doesn't. He hates it.'

'Uh huh. I thought that might be the case. He never showed once at the hearing, did he, to support you?'

No. Guy Halley had had much more pressing things to do. Deva and Rani had taken time off to be there, but Guy had not even telephoned. That was hardly surprising, but it was hurtful. As he stood reflecting on it, Thanh's wife Beth entered the room to tell them dinner was ready. Being American, Amery liked to eat early.

'Amery, I have to say I'm a little taken aback by all this. Could we discuss it over dinner?'

Beth, who ran the apartment, led the way to the long mahogany table that was often surrounded by friends. Ben loved to entertain, but didn't feel equal to hosting a large gathering tonight. Except for Myles, Kevin and Gavin Seymour, his friends seemed a little superficial in comparison to Amery.

Over his carrot and orange soup, Amery talked quietly and knowledgeably about music and musicians. Not just the classical ones Ben knew he admired, but Art Garfunkel, Bessie Smith, Bob Marley. He did not, he said, believe in putting people in labelled boxes. But that was what happened to them, if they did not foresee such a fate themselves, and circumvent it. Unless Ben paved the way now, took evasive action, he would be pigeonholed for life. Cheam's Theme had been a step in the right direction, but now that Schwabbe owned it they would either sit on it, or tart it up to the point of embarrassment. Ben listened in silence, recognising that his weakness was Amery's strength: he had vision, but Amery had perspective.

But over the Dover sole with mangetout and gratin potatoes, Amery let him do the talking. The talking that was freer and more wide-ranging than it had been with anyone, Ben thought, since Aran Campion. Was that why Sasha hadn't lasted, or Charlotte, or Kim? Because they had nothing in common? Whatever the reason, he hadn't been seeing much of anyone lately. Amery seemed to have noticed that, too.

'Tell me about this girl who negotiated your contract, Ben. If it's not too painful?'

He smiled at the ambiguity.

'Well, the contract was more painful than its author! Aran was a lovely girl . . . innocent, honest, very hardworking. Perhaps she aimed a little higher than she was able for. But at nineteen you don't know your limits, do you?'

Amery sipped his Montrachet slowly.

'She was ambitious for you?'

'Yes – like you, she had great faith, and was very supportive. I think she was trying to prove herself, too. She didn't have much education, so she set out to get more. And she did get it. Then she – she felt under a little pressure I think, to help her parents in Ireland, to become a career woman like all the women these days. She was good at selling things, getting ideas off the ground. But I always felt music was her real love. Music and poetry and – and me. Her instinct was to marry, to be a wife and a mother.'

'But you weren't ready?'

'No. I never lied to her about it. But she was still devastated when we broke up. I did everything I could to cushion her, help her, but she never spoke to me again.'

'Not a word?'

'Not a syllable. She even dropped our mutual friends, my mother and sister – everyone. Myles Irving offered her a job, at my request, but she turned it down.'

'I see.' Amery looked as if he was about to pursue the subject, but after a long, keen look he sat back and said nothing.

'It was just bad timing. I'd have married her eventually, but there were so many other things I needed to do first.'

'Needed, or wanted?'

'Needed.'

Accepting coffee from Beth, Amery lit a cigar.

'Yes. There were so many things I needed to do too, when I was your age. Unfortunately, by the time I got round to the things my wife needed, she was no longer with me.'

'I'm sorry. May I ask what happened?'

'Hodgkin's.'

After a moment he got to his feet, took his coffee and walked slowly through to the other room. Uncertain what to say, Ben followed him.

In the middle of the floor the Bechstein stood gleaming. Unlike those pianos which were more decorative than functional, it was closed to keep the dust out, no ornaments or photographs stood on its lid. For want of words, Ben went to it.

'Shall I play something?'

Amery sank into an armchair.

'Please. Anything you like.'

Seating himself, he decided at random on George Gershwin. *Rhapsody In Blue*: Amery knew the piece backwards. It had been first performed in 1924, the year of his birth. And from the way Ben began to play it, he could tell that he also knew its history, knew it was intended to be a piano solo. The clarinet, the orchestration, had been added later by some meddler called Grofé. Ben was playing the original version.

And he was answering the question that Amery had not needed to ask. Playing with everything their conversation had brought to the surface, the love, the loss, the memory of sweetness.

How far he had gone, beyond the anger of two years ago! Today he had lost something priceless, but today his anger was tempered with whatever came after anger; the assimilation, the reconciliation with oneself. He was maturing, learning the hard way as Amery had done. The pain was in the music, but so was the strengthening character.

Dan and Eimear decided they couldn't really afford France. But they could afford England, if they stayed with Aran. Would that be all right with her?

Delighted, Aran arranged her work around their visit, so that they could be together as much as possible. It wasn't until a full week after their arrival that she realised what she had let herself in for. Rhianna Rafter was an absolute demon.

'Sweetheart, please don't do that,' Aran pleaded with her one warm evening, as the two-year-old pulled nasturtiums out of their beds by the roots. Rhianna yanked out another handful.

'Rhianna, I said not to do that.' Uselessly, Aran attempted to put some authority into her tone. But she was incapable of disciplining the little girl she saw so rarely, and wished Dan had not taken Eimear out for a walk. Emmett was no trouble, but his sister's face was mutinous. Thrusting out her lower lip, she put her hands comically but defiantly on her hips.

'I want them.'

'Yes, but they're flowers, they're for everyone.'

Furiously Rhianna flung down the ones she had already pulled and stamped her foot, her black curls bobbing with rage.

'They are not! They're only for me!'

'No, darling—'

Rhianna threw herself down on the patio and began to scream at full throttle.

'They're for me! Me-e-e! They're mine!'

'Oh, muffin – look, why don't we go inside and draw some flowers?'

She reached for the child's hand, but Rhianna snatched it away and ran into a corner.

'Go 'way! Leave me alone! I want my bunny!'

But bunny was nowhere in sight, and tears began to pour down her face. That, of course, was the moment at which Dan and Eimear returned, and although she had done nothing Aran felt as if they had caught her beating the child. Anxiously Eimear's eyes flew to her, but Dan sized up the situation and sternly suppressed a smile.

'Are you being naughty, Rhianna?'

As if by magic the tears vanished, to be replaced by a cherubic smile. Although the little girl fought against the frills and flounces in which Eimear loved to dress her, she seemed to know their worth.

'No, Daddy. Me good.'

Dan gazed at the mangled nasturtiums.

'Bedtime, young lady. Go get your pyjamas.'

Sweetly, obediently, she ran off. But at the kitchen door she stopped, dodging Dan's eye, and stuck her tongue out at Aran. It was by no means the first such episode and, although her daughter was very dear to her, she had to admit she was exhausting. Dan called her a 'punk prima donna' and now, she thought ruefully, she knew why.

Over the following week Rhianna was found scribbling on the wallpaper with her crayons, painting Emmett's face with glue, stuffing marbles into Aran's oboe and chopping up Eimear's silk scarf to make a bandage for bunny, whose arm she said had been broken by baddies. Her imagination was terrifying, her energy appalling.

Yet her smile was adorable, her charm unlimited. Despite her many tantrums Aran loved having her, and in her more mellow moments it seemed that Rhianna loved being there. When the time came for her to leave, she wound her arms tightly around Aran's neck.

'No. Me not go. Me stay here with you.'

Oh, if only she could! But even as she nestled her into her shoulder, Aran saw her wicked smirk, and realised the child was playing her off against Eimear. At two and a half, she could summon quite a range of emotions in grown adults. And sure enough, Eimear succumbed, bribing her with a chocolate bar to let go of Aran. Pocketing the chocolate, she kissed Aran demurely, and went.

But how quiet it was, then! For several nights Aran lay in bed, longing for her, brushing away the tears, aching for the little dimpled face. When Thierry phoned late one night, he found her sobbing.

'What's wrong?'

She sniffled. 'Oh, nothing. I'm just feeling sorry for myself.'

Pleased, Thierry assumed his absence was the problem. Should he come to visit, then, next weekend? Would she like that?

Yes. She thought she would like it, and she did. Even if he was not Ben Halley, he was good and kind . . . not unlike Dan, now that she thought about it. He had a sense of humour, and he took her to concerts even though he knew nothing about music. Looking into his warm hazel eyes one evening, she found a lot of comfort in them.

He came often to London again during the autumn, and she went twice to Boulogne. Just to please her, his supermarket stocked a range of Annie's cheeses, and although she knew they hadn't really earned their place she was pleased. He was going out of his way to be good to her.

Holly Mitchell met him at Hallowe'en, and was impressed.

'Of course, I have a thing for men with moustaches! But he really is nice, Aran. Attractive, considerate, gainfully employed . . . and single and straight! I wouldn't leave him on ice too long if I were you. How old is he?'

'Twenty-eight.'

'Ripe for the plucking. And he speaks English . . . he could get a job here.'

'So he says.'

Unlike most Frenchmen, Thierry Marand did not consider France the only civilised country on the face of the earth. He would be happy to move to England, he said, if – if things were getting serious? He hoped they were, because he was ready to settle down and have children.

Children. Aran dreamt alternately of children, and of Thierry, until the two were hopelessly mixed in her mind. Rhianna's eyes, Thierry's eyes; Thierry's deep voice, Rhianna's piping lisp. In November, Conor phoned unexpectedly, to thank her for the holiday he and Molly had finally taken with her help. They had gone to the Isle of Man, it had been wonderful . . . but she thought of the granddaughter she had denied him, and felt only guilt. Then Dursey came on the line, her baby brother who was now nineteen, the nicest of all her siblings. He had fished with Conor for the summer and was working with Annie for the winter . . . as he spoke she thought of her fragile family ties, and how time was slipping away.

Early in December Thierry called again, his voice resonant with meaning, asking whether he might come over for Christmas?

Yes, she said. She would very much like him to come for Christmas – not the actual day, because she always spent that in Ireland, but for New Year?

It was arranged, and three weeks later she departed for Ireland in a suddenly tranquil frame of mind. As ever, Eimear welcomed her with open arms.

'Oh, Aran, all these presents for the children! You're going to have to cut back . . . we're expecting another one.'

Her face was full of happiness, and at that moment Aran made her final decision. She wanted some of that happiness. She wanted to be loved as Eimear was loved, and she wanted another baby of her own. As Dan could give Eimear all those things, Thierry could give them to her.

When she returned to Hampstead, after a painful parting from Rhianna, she sat down with him and discussed it seriously. First, she told him honestly, there was something he must know. She had a daughter in Ireland.

Yes. Taking her hand, he nodded. He had thought there must be something like that, some previous relationship. Not many young women of her age lived alone in lovely Hampstead houses like this one, or spent so much money on plane fares and long-distance phone calls. But he would be glad to include the child in their life together, and hoped they would have many more. Aran could work or not work as she chose – only she had sold tons of cheese already, how much more did she have in mind? If she preferred, she could devote herself to their family when it came, enjoy being a mother, playing her oboe, writing her poetry. He, Thierry, would command a good salary and take great care of her. He loved her, he said, and his kiss told her that he really did.

On the first day of 1983, they became engaged. For the first time in longer than she could remember, Aran was truly happy.

'Rani!'

Shopping for fruit and vegetables in Berwick Street market, Aran literally stumbled on Ben's sister, and flushed in confusion. They had been such friends, until she had shut the door between them. Of course she'd had to do it, but Rani didn't know that, and her smile was cautious.

'Aran – how are you?'

She smiled over her armful of fruit and spring flowers.

'I'm very well. I've just got engaged – look!'

Rani looked at the diamond on her finger, and laughed in spite of herself.

'That was always what you wanted, wasn't it? The aspidistra and the budgie. Oh, well – I'm happy to hear it. I know you had a bad time with Ben.'

'Yes . . . Rani, I'm sorry I wasn't able to see you after that. I really wanted to, but there were things, problems – look, would you like to come and have a coffee? I'd love to talk to you.'

Rani put down her heavy shopping with the grace she had never lost, looking beautiful in a saffron sari, and considered.

'Yes. Why not? Ben will want to know who the lucky man is.'

Ben. Aran could see his face in hers. But then she saw it in Rhianna too, all the time. Nudging their way through the crowd, they found a small café and got some tea. Stirring a slice of lemon into it, Rani looked at her critically.

'Better. Much better than the weeping waif I last saw. I'm sorry my brother made you unhappy, Aran, and glad to see you've got over him. Tell me about your fiancé.'

'He's French. His name is Thierry Marand, he's twenty-eight and he's applying for jobs in London at the moment, because we're going to live here. We're getting married in August.'

'Good. I'm not into marriage myself, as you know, but you deserve some happiness after what you went through. But why did you drop us, Aran? My mother and me, I mean? We were on your side.'

'Yes. I know that, Rani. I can't tell you why, but please believe that I had a good reason. Will you accept my apologies, and tell your mother how sorry I am? Thanh, too. How are they?'

'They're fine. Mother is still working, Thanh is married to Beth and they both work with Ben. Can you stand the mention of his name, or should I not mention him?'

'Oh, no. I've got over that stage. In fact I felt awful for him when he lost the copyright to that music he wrote – did he take it very badly?'

'Yes, but not in the way you'd expect of him. He didn't throw a tantrum. He was more upset on the inside than the outside . . . it seemed to change him. He's still wild on stage, but he's quieter now in private.'

'Where is he? What's he doing?'

'He's in Scandinavia at the moment. His records sell very well there. In fact he's had number one hits everywhere but here.'

Aran knew that, and thought it very odd. Lots of number twos and number threes, but no number one.

'He still sends me flowers you know – every year, on my birthday. Will you tell him I appreciate it, but that he must stop now? Thierry wouldn't like it! Besides, we're house-hunting. The lease in Hampstead runs out next spring, so I'll be moving.'

'I'll tell him. I'm sure he'll be pleased for you. He felt very guilty, you know . . . I've never fully understood why he did it.'

Aran sighed.

'Temperament, Rani. You warned me yourself that he wasn't stable, or ready to make a commitment. But – but what about you? Any nice doctors lurking in the wings?'

'No way! Oh, I date men now and then, but I – I'm not sure that I really like them very much.'

Good heavens. 'What do you mean?'

'I mean – well, I don't know if you've ever watched *Crimeline*? No? Well, you should, Aran. Then you'd see exactly what I mean. Ninety per cent of the crimes committed are by men, and ninety per cent are against women. It takes this huge police force to control just one half of the population. The male half. When women are involved it's only ever petty crime, or if it's serious it's some man has put the woman up to it. Women let themselves be brainwashed by men.'

Aran found she couldn't argue with that. She was fed up herself of seeing women beaten, burgled, raped and assaulted by men, seeing children abused by them, people assaulted, money stolen, property vandalised – all, as Rani said, by the male half of the population. Whenever you read about a crime you simply assumed a man had done it, and he nearly always had.

'But there must be the occasional decent one, Rani. Ben is, and so is Thierry.'

'Yes, I suppose. But I've yet to find one I can respect. It would take twenty strong horses to drag me to the altar! I stick to my studies and treat them with the contempt they deserve.'

Aran smiled.

'You must be nearly finished your studies by now?'

'Yes. Next year. Then I'm going to work in India for a few years. My mother has fixed me up in a hospital in Uttar Pradesh where she has contacts. She was born in Lucknow, you know. So was Ben.'

'Yes. He often mentioned wanting to go and see India . . . Japan, too. Did he ever get to either one?'

Rani laughed, her white teeth quite dazzling. 'Not yet! But I'm sure he will, he travels so much. And what about you? You were keen to see the world once as well.'

'I was. But life changed after he left. I've been to France, though, and we're going to St. Tropez for our honeymoon.'

'Lovely. And after that?'

'I – I'm hoping to have a family. At the moment I work for a cheese manufacturer in Ireland, I'm their agent over here, but if children come along I'll give it up.'

'Oh, you'll regret that! Never give up the day job.'

'But children are – oh, never mind! We'll never agree on this subject. Look, Rani, I have to go now, but would you like to come

331

round to dinner sometime? I feel terrible about not having seen you for so long. I'd like to make it up to you. If you're free – say next Saturday? – we could have a good gossip then.'

She hardly dared hope that Rani would accept, would overlook the insult and the years of silence. But after a moment Rani nodded.

'Yes. I am free. That would be very nice.'

Amicably they parted company, and Aran headed for home with a feeling of mingled pleasure and relief. It was sweet of Rani not to hold her bad behaviour against her, and for all the difference in their attitude to things it would be wonderful to resume their old friendship. So long as she remembered never to mention Rhianna. Not only would it be unfair to ask her to keep such a secret, it would horrify her to learn that any child existed. Rani liked children the way W.C. Fields said he liked them – lightly boiled.

Only four venues: the Falkner stadium in Copenhagen, the Ice Stadium in Stockholm, the Scandinavium in Copenhagen and the Drammenshallen in Oslo. Two gigs in each, eight nights in total. On a tour as short as that, there was no room for error. You had to get right into the groove and make your impact instantly. Ben did make it, and the voltage was fantastic. The interview schedule was pretty fantastic too; nineteen of them in eight days, for radio, television and print media. Schwabbe believed in getting their money's worth out of a tour. Although every concert was sold out, the revenue barely covered the cost of staging them, and in Schwabbe's view the human dimension, the personal contact, didn't matter. Tours were simply a vehicle for making money by selling records 'off the back' of the publicity they attracted. So Ben Halley, who was so keen on live tours, had better earn his keep.

With the end of his contract in sight, Ben could afford not to give a flying fiddler's what Schwabbe thought or said, but as always the blood pounded in his veins the moment he heard the fans chanting, stamping, calling his name. They were what he thought of even when he was writing the music, alone late at night in his Kensington flat, they were what kept him going through the long sessions with Kelwin, the interminable rehearsals, sound checks, interviews, flights from one city to another. The fans who saved up to come and see him, travelled miles, queued for tickets, went hungry, got soaked in the rain, wrote letters, threw flowers, treasured autographs. The vast majority, he knew, had ordinary jobs in humdrum offices, factories, hospitals, and he felt it was *his* job to brighten their lives in the way they said he did, with all the colour and brilliance he could muster. Together, they always had a great time.

But it was gruelling. Who could blame him if he fell into the arms of a pretty girl afterwards, made love to a bottle of vodka? There was more vodka than sex, now that AIDS was known to be a killer disease, and safe sex didn't light up his world in the way the other kind did. However, some of the girls were good company, just to talk to; they made him feel less lonely in the foreign cities he never got time to know. They took his mind off his problems with Schwabbe, and the vodka ensured he got some sleep. As usual Kevin Ross was nagging him about it, rabbiting on about his heart and his liver, but then Kevin was famous as the world's worst hypochondriac.

Kevin lived like a monk these days – no booze, no sex, no sun, no smoking. What exactly he did do for relaxation was a mystery, but whatever it was it wasn't working. For all his health cares and scares, he was a bundle of nervous tension. At least Ben still had some fun, whereas Kevin had none, and would probably worry his way into an early grave for his pains. If the vodka carried Ben off equally early, well, at least he could say he'd lived a little. Lived a lot, actually.

Aran used to nag about the vodka, too. Well . . . not nag exactly, as Kevin did, but worry, fuss a bit. What would she say if she could see him here tonight, in his hotel room in Gothenburg, drinking all by himself at three in the morning? Nothing, he supposed, because Rani said she was engaged to some Frenchman. Some Frenchman who'd given her a diamond ring and was going to marry her in August, father the family she wanted. Lying on his bed, gazing into his glass, he found it a sobering thought.

He could see now why people wanted families. Not that he wanted one of his own – yet – but he understood the attraction. A family put a shape on your life, gave it a point, a pivot. You could get very self-centred when you didn't have anyone to consider except yourself, and you could get very blue when you came home, yet again, to an empty apartment. A big luxurious apartment, but an empty one. Even if you brought a girl back with you, she didn't want to hear your woes, didn't really care if you were tired or worried or depressed.

Was he depressed? Studying his vodka, he thought that maybe he was. It wasn't like him, after a successful gig; usually he would be on a high, out celebrating and unwinding with the gang. Perhaps he was working too hard, in need of a break.

A break. It wouldn't be possible to take one for many months yet, with so much work stacked up before breaking free of Schwabbe. But Amery Cheam had said something about taking one this summer, and he smiled to himself as he thought of the man who had become such a close friend. Was going to become his manager, by the look of it, after he retired from Cheam Marine on his sixtieth birthday next

333

year. It was a curious relationship, but he liked and trusted Amery very much, respected his business expertise and deep love of music. Like Aran Campion, he lit up whenever he discussed the future, had so many eager ideas, clever plans . . . and he understood Ben Halley, in a way his own father never had. Somehow Ben had become his protégé, a very warm affinity had developed between them.

Amery wanted to do some sailing this summer. Not on his own yacht, because he was getting on a bit for racing, and certainly not on a cruise ship – God forbid, with all those blue-rinsed widows aboard! – but something relaxing, refreshing. But for all his money, he had confided to Ben, taking vacations was not easy. His wife was dead, his friends were very busy, he hated tagging along with married couples. Sometimes he travelled alone, but it could be lonely. Thinking of him, feeling rather lonely himself, Ben suddenly had an idea, and wanted to talk to him.

What time was it in New York? He glanced at the blue digits on the video. Only nine or ten. Stretching over, he picked up the phone.

'Amery? Hi. It's Ben. I hope I'm not dishturb – disturbing you?'

'Not at all, my boy. I was just thinking about you.'

'Were you? It's nice to know somebody is.'

'H'mm. Are you calling from Sweden, Ben? It must be late over there.'

'It's three. Three thirty.'

'How many drinks have you had?'

'God, Amery, I dunno . . . a few, I guess.'

'Well, I don't think you should have any more. Why don't you take a hot shower and go to bed?'

'Hah. You sound like Aran. Aran Campion. Did I tell you she's getting married? My sister rang with the good news.'

There was a pause.

'Well, you let her go, Ben, so I hope you can be happy for her.'

'I can. She deserved better than me.'

'If I detect a little self pity in your tone, I hope it's just the vodka talking.'

'Huh. Is that my thanks, for doing you a favour?'

'What favour? Calling me when I'm about to turn in with my novel and hot chocolate?'

'No, no. I mean your holiday. I've found the perfect thing for you.'

'Oh?'

'Yeah. Shark fishing. Aran's father in Ireland. He has a boat, takes people out in the summer . . . groups of them, to fish for blue shark.'

'Is that so? Well, my boy, perhaps you haven't drunk as much as I thought. That sounds like an interesting idea.'

'Don't you think? You'd make friends with the other guys, have ready-made boozing buddies in the evenings, with a common interest – get out on a nice stretch of the Atlantic, too, off the beaten track. I think you might enjoy it.'

'I might indeed. I'll certainly think about it, if you'll think about getting some sleep.'

'All right. It's good to talk to you, Amery.'

It was good, and Ben felt better as he hung up. Amery sounded so protective, as if he were somehow taking care of him across all the thousands of miles. Which was a comfort, because he really wasn't much use at taking care of himself. Downing the dregs of his vodka, he rolled over and fell asleep where he lay, his arm curled around the unfamiliar pillow.

It was very exciting, and Aran enjoyed planning her wedding tremendously. As often as he could, Thierry came over to help her with it, laughing at the way she fussed over the little details, pleased by the pleasure it was giving her. Every time he saw her she looked happier and lovelier than the last, and he felt their relationship deepening, her affection growing stronger every time she came to claim him, joyfully, at the airport.

Holly Mitchell's help was enlisted, the restaurant was booked, the cake was ordered, the dress decided upon and, finally, the invitations were sent out. The ceremony was to be at Hampstead town hall and, between his family coming from France and hers from Ireland, they estimated they would have forty guests. Rani was amongst them, but regretfully she decided against inviting Deva. Deva would hardly come without Guy, who would refuse to come, and besides Deva had wanted Aran to marry her son. God, guest lists were so complicated, it would take Solomon to figure them out! And of course there was no point in asking Molly's advice about anything. Molly simply wasn't the kind of mother who would take an interest, get enthusiastic – in fact it would be a miracle if she didn't turn up in black, criticising London and the heathens who got married in registry offices. As for Conor . . . trying to visualise him giving her away, making a speech, entertaining the guests, she smiled wryly. Conor would simply stand there, benign but quite useless. No matter. He would be there, happy for her in his quiet way, and Dan would assume most of his social duties.

Thierry would look after everyone, too. Dear Thierry, so solid and reliable, so loving and lovable. He didn't have Ben's charisma or startling looks, but he had other qualities – was, as Holly put it, 'excellent husband material'. Already he'd found a job in London, and brought his parents over to meet her. They spoke little English, but were very friendly, very impressed by London, very happy with his choice of wife. Sitting in Holly's kitchen one evening in May, she confided that she was very much looking forward to joining the Marand family.

'Mrs Marand. Mme Marand. Which d'you like better, Holly?'

'What's wrong with Ms Campion?'

'Oh, you sound like Rani! You know I'm old fashioned about this kind of thing, Holly. Thierry is a fine man and I want everyone to know I'm his wife. You took Walter's name, didn't you?'

'Yes, I did. If you want to be Mrs Marand, then go right ahead. But tell me, Aran, what are you going to do about Rhianna? Do you want her at your wedding, or would it cause complications?'

'I want her very much, Holly. She's going to be my flower girl. There won't be any difficulty . . . would you let Morag be a flower girl too?'

Morag was seven now, one of Aran's favourite people. Quiet and self-contained, she would be quite a contrast to Rhianna.

'I'd love to! She'd enjoy it so much. Thank you for thinking of her, Aran.'

'Well, it was she who got me into all this, really . . . the moment I saw her I knew I wanted to have children myself. And then Rhianna brought so much happiness to Dan and Eimear. You know their new baby is due next week?'

'Yes. For a woman who thought she'd never have any children, she's certainly making up for lost time!'

'Yes. She loves it. She won't be bringing the new baby to the wedding, but she's bringing Emmett – and you'll bring Ollie for him to play with, won't you?'

'Well, Ollie's a bit old for him. But he'll look after him.'

Ollie, at ten, had calmed down into a charming child, but still looked like the Milky Bar kid, and asked endless, astonishing questions.

'Val and Sher are bringing their children too. God knows what kind of bunfight this wedding is going to turn into. If I had any sense I'd get married in plastic overalls, because my dress is going to be ruined!'

They had shopped for it together, eventually finding exactly what Aran wanted in a small boutique in Islington. Ballet length, made of cream silk, its ruffled sleeves were caught up with rosebuds and Holly had laughed when she saw it.

'Get a crook and a collie, and you'll be a Dresden shepherdess!'

But Aran thought it highly romantic, and knew Thierry would love it. Rani, of course, would tease and scoff. But Rani wasn't the one getting married.

Married. It was a serious undertaking. Suddenly her face sobered, and Holly looked at her closely.

'Aran, you are sure, aren't you? About Thierry, about this marriage? You mustn't do it, you know, if you're still harbouring any thoughts of Ben Halley. It wouldn't be fair to him, and could make you both very unhappy.'

'Yes. I know that, Holly. I've thought about it a lot. An awful lot. But I'm twenty-four now, I can see that Ben was the kind of man you fall in love with, not the kind you marry. He was a shooting star . . . exquisite, exciting, but not enduring. I'll never regret having known him, or having had Rhianna, but Thierry – Thierry is *real*. He loves me, he makes me feel secure, protected . . . I can see now that there's a big difference between being a girlfriend and being a wife. I'm going to be a good wife, and a good mother.'

'Will you miss your work, when you have children?'

'Yes. I'll miss Annie and all the customers. But it – it wasn't really a career that consumed my imagination. It had nothing to do with music or poetry.'

'Still. It gave you a lot of independence. If it didn't take you so far away from home, for such long stretches, I'd advise you to keep it on.'

'No. It wouldn't work. Anyway, Thierry will be working hard, I want to be there for him when he comes home in the evenings – I know all about coming home to an empty house. Every worker should have a wife, whether they're male or female!'

True, Holly thought, very true. The current au pair was pretty good, but still, it was always nice when Walter got home. Especially if he got home first, had a hot meal ready or a drink waiting. He was a hopeless cook, but it was the thought that counted. The feeling that someone was thinking about you, waiting for you.

'So you're going to be a fulltime housewife?'

'Yes. I'll continue to do a bit of work for Annie, just around London, until the first baby comes. But I hope it will come soon.'

'I'm sure it will. But don't give up your music, Aran, or your poetry. You'll need something of your own when your children start school, make their own friends and start leading their own lives – which they will, sooner than you think.'

'I suppose so. But I haven't written any poetry for ages, Holly. Anyway, I'll have my children to myself for ten or twelve years, and I want to enjoy them. Do everything that Eimear does with Rhianna.'

Fair enough, Holly supposed. Maybe it wasn't quite the life she'd be content with herself, or have expected for Aran, but then an outside career had its drawbacks too. Even if Aran and Ben had stayed together, if she'd continued in the music business . . . anyway, she hadn't. She'd chosen Thierry, who was a good man, honest and devoted to her. His hazel eyes were humorous, his French accent romantic, his ruffled auburn hair rather boyish, yet there was something steady and upstanding about him. He would make a fine honourable husband. Most women would kill for such a man.

Most women.

'Aran?'

'Mm?'

'You do love Thierry, don't you? He – he isn't just a substitute?'

'For Ben? Heavens, no! Holly, it's been four years. I've grown up. I genuinely love Thierry, in a completely different way. He would have been all wrong for me a few years ago, but he's right now.'

God, Holly thought, he is. It's all such a matter of timing and luck. It's a miracle how two compatible people ever happen to come together in the right place at the right time. Staying together is another matter, and they need all the help they can get. Love is so hard to find, and Aran is right to recognise it when she sees it, act on it when she finds it.

She smiled. 'I think I'm going to get very dressed up for your wedding, Aran, and wear a huge hat.'

'Absolutely! You've always been the most elegant woman I know. I'm counting on you and Eimear to be graceful and colourful – an antidote to my mother, who will be grim as death, and spend the next six months telling Dunrathway what a frightful place London is.'

'But she must be pleased for you?'

'She's pleased I've met someone respectable, to make an honest woman of me. A shame, of course, that he has to be French. That's better than Indian, apparently, but—' she mimicked Molly's accent – 'is he Catholic? It's not *mixed*, Aran, is it?'

'What did you tell her?'

'Well, Thierry is nominally Catholic as it happens, but I told her the truth. That it is mixed. A man and a woman. You can't get two more completely different species than that.'

At the end of her pregnancy, Eimear was also at the end of her patience.

'Dan, will you take that thing away from Rhianna before I lose my reason!'

Luke Lavery, a sadist with a warped sense of humour, had given Rhianna a toy drum for her fourth birthday. She had been marching round and round the kitchen, beating it, since five o'clock. It was now twenty to seven.

Rhianna shrieked as Dan took it away from her and shut it into a cupboard. Shrieked her head off, until Emmett began to wail in sympathy and Oscar, their new puppy, barked in chorus. The noise was earsplitting.

'Oh my God – come on, the lot of you! Get straight to bed before I – Rhianna, stop that *racket!*'

Dan sat down at the table and shook with laughter.

'Well, we wanted it and we've got it. Kids, a family. What fun. Just think what it'll be like when the next one arrives.'

Eimear thought briefly, and shut her eyes.

'An asylum. That's what it'll be like. A lunatic asylum.'

Yes. It was always Rhianna, of course, who started the noise. She was the loudest little girl they had ever seen, or heard, in their lives. Sometimes she banged the drum with one hand and thumped the table with a fork in the other, sometimes she sang as well, a penetrating version of *Frère Jacques* that made their eyes water. They were saying novenas that Luke wouldn't give Emmett a drum for his birthday too. Or a rattle to the new baby, to complete the orchestra.

A scan had ascertained that the baby was a girl, and they were going to call her Sorcha. As he helped Eimear bath the toddlers and put them to bed, Dan surveyed his wife affectionately.

'Think of London, love. A whole weekend without the drum.'

'Yes – oh, thank God! But Dan . . . Aran has invited Ben's sister to the wedding.'

'Has she?'

'Yes – she couldn't not, I suppose, now that they're friends again. But – I just hope—'

'Oh, Eimear. Ben's sister doesn't know us from a hole in the wall. Rhianna will mean nothing to her.'

'No. It's just that she – she looks so very like him.'

'Eimear, get a grip. Nobody even knew Aran was pregnant.'

'No. Oh, why wouldn't Aran tell him, when we wanted her to? Everything would be so much clearer now.'

'Maybe it would. Or maybe we wouldn't have Rhianna.'

'Should we – are we – doing the right thing, do you think? I could always ask Mother—'

'Eimear, your mother is going to mind the new baby while we're away, which is very kind of her. But she is seventy-six. We can't ask her to take Rhianna and Emmett as well.'

'I could ask Annie.'

Tucking Emmett into his bed, Dan straightened up.

'Eimear, Rhianna is our daughter and that's all about it. We can't spend the rest of our lives being paranoid. What's done is done.'

'Yes, but I – oh!'

'Oh what?'

Putting her hand on her back, Eimear eyed him with some asperity.

'Oh, Dan, dearest, would you ever get Annie in here right now to babysit, and then get me to the hospital?'

Wide eyed, Emmett sat up.

'Hopsital! Get Mummy to the hopsital!'

'Me too!' whooped Rhianna's voice from the next room. 'Me coming too! Me take bunny! And drum!'

The month of June was blue and balmy, and at the end of it Amery came to stay with Ben in London. After many weeks of negotiation by telephone, he had put together the bones of a recording deal with a small new British label based in Chalk Farm, and wanted to see what Ben thought of it. For several days they talked it over, weighing up the advantages and disadvantages of signing with a new company which had energy and imagination, but not a lot of money.

'It's exactly the reverse of your current situation with Schwabbe, but I think it has potential, Ben. They're willing to take on Myles and Kevin, if we can get them, and they're very into live performances. They don't have any other big names yet, but that means they'll concentrate on you. If you're interested, I thought we might go see their studios and talk to them in person.'

The company was called Flinders, after the Australian mountain range from which its founder came. An intense but likeable man of forty, his name was Jake Rowan and he was extremely keen to get Ben Halley. Flinders was only five years old, but it was growing, with an office in Sydney and another proposed for Seattle. Jake knew Ben's work virtually off by heart, and brought his two partners into the talks which followed. They were very long talks, over many days, covering every aspect of Ben's past, present and future work. Eventually lawyers would have to come into them, but first of all everyone simply wanted to sound each other out, take personality readings.

Much of the conversation took place in Jake's office, but a lot also took place in nearby pubs, over restaurant tables and in their respective flats. Ben was adamant about certain things he wanted, or didn't want, while Amery raised some issues that seemed rather obscure. But Jake's response demonstrated an encouraging degree of sensitivity: he was a tough negotiator, but he understood music, was horrified by all the restrictions Schwabbe had imposed on Ben.

340

After a week, they decided they liked him and his partners. But Ben was very nervous.

'I can't afford another mistake, Amery.'

'No, my boy. You can't. Take your time.'

Myles and Kevin were summoned to join the talks, and impressed everyone with their immediate willingness to take a drop in salary. Not that Jake was tightfisted, but he simply didn't have the large sums of money they had always commanded as top professionals. Signing on his computer, he printed out a balance sheet to show them the exact situation. If Ben joined Flinders, and did well, they would prosper accordingly, but meanwhile he could only offer them artistic freedom by way of recompense.

A second week of talks ensued. In the heat of early July, everyone was exhausted, but they felt they were making progress. Even Jake allowed himself to think so, although he had never met anyone as obdurate as Amery Cheam in his life. When it came to protecting Ben's interests the man was like granite, his blue eyes impenetrable as the Great Barrier Reef. Yet Amery was not formally Ben's manager, there was no documentation between the two. One day, Jake took Myles aside to question him about it. Myles shrugged laconically.

'I don't know much about Amery either, Jake. All I can tell you is that Ben has formed some bond with him, has come to rely on him, and trusts him absolutely.'

They were all on the brink of agreement when a problem arose. Jake said that Flinders could not afford Dith Thanh. It wasn't that Thanh's salary was out of range, but it would cost too much to keep him on the road with Ben, travelling everywhere, costing a lot in overheads.

Amery's face froze. 'Ben must have a bodyguard. Dith Thanh is indispensable. A fundamental part of the deal.'

Jake fiddled with the reddish hair he wore in a ponytail, closing his eyes in thought for a few moments.

'We could provide the services of a security guard, as and when the need might arise.'

'No. Ben is guarded round the clock, at all times, by his live-in minder. Not just on tour or in concert, but in the studios, in public places, at home, everywhere. Thanh stays.'

'But we can't afford him. I'm sorry, Mr Cheam, but we really can't.'

Amery considered.

'OK. You pay his salary, I'll pay his running costs.'

Astounded, Ben turned to Amery. He had been about to propose paying Thanh out of his own pocket. His security was not Amery's concern, and he was stricken by such generosity.

341

'No, Amery. This has nothing to do with the music. Let me worry about my own security.'

Looking at him from under his snow-white eyebrows, Amery held up his hand.

'Leave this to me, Ben.'

As if he weren't there, Amery continued to negotiate with Jake until agreement was reached: Flinders would pay Thanh and he, Amery, would take care of transport, accommodation, whatever extra expenses Thanh might incur in the course of his duties.

Afterwards, when they got back to Kensington, Ben had it out with him.

'Amery, you're my friend, not my financier! No way am I letting you pay Thanh's bills!'

Idly, Amery glanced at his watch.

'What date is it? The fifth? Well, that's close enough.'

'Close enough to what? What are you talking about?'

'To your birthday. July 15, isn't it? Consider this my birthday present to you.'

'Amery—'

'Please, Ben. I want to do this. Your safety is very important to me.'

He said it softly, lightly. But Ben saw that he meant it, and was more moved than he could express. Handing him a glass of the Glenlivet he kept specially for him, he sat down and looked at him.

'Why, Amery? Why are you doing all this for me?'

Appreciatively, Amery waved the Glenlivet under his nose before taking a sip.

'I've told you why before, Ben. You've struck a chord in me. A very deep chord. You have no idea how much pleasure your music gives me, and your company.'

'Oh, Amery . . . I only hope I can live up to your faith in me, and be just as good a friend to you. I feel as if – as if you were adopting me!'

'Well, you have your own parents, of course. But you could look on it that way, if you like.'

Warmly, Ben smiled at him.

'I do like. As soon as we work out this deal with Flinders, I'm going to write a song for you.'

'Well, then, let's get a move on. Are you happy with Flinders, with Jake Rowan? Can you have confidence in them?'

'Yes. I think we've found the right people. What do you think?'

'I think this could be Jake Rowan's lucky day.'

They discussed it for the rest of the evening, held further meetings with Myles and Kevin next day, and called the lawyers in. Getting Myles and Kevin out of their contracts with Schwabbe was not going to be easy, but Amery was adamant that he would manage it. And amazingly he did manage it, within twenty-four hours.

Dazed with relief, nobody could thank him enough, and his eyes sparkled. He wouldn't say how the battle had been won, but clearly he had relished it. That night, Ben took him out to dinner at the Savoy.

'And now, my boy, it's time for my vacation. I've booked a week in that place you suggested – what's it called again?'

'Dunrathway.'

'That's it. I'll be flying to Ireland day after tomorrow. Any chance you could come with me, no?'

'I wish I could. But I've got a concert at the Rainbow this weekend. Anyway, Aran's father probably wouldn't be too keen to see me! I'll come over to the States later on, though – in August – we could go to hear Pavarotti at the Met?'

Amery beamed.

'Excellent. We'll finalise everything with Jake tomorrow, arrange for you to have a month's break between leaving Schwabbe and starting with Flinders. I know it's not a big company, my boy, but I think you're going to be much happier there.'

'Yes. I can't thank you enough for your help, Amery, but I want you to know how much it means to me. How much your friendship means to me.'

A gentleman of the old school, Amery merely nodded. But they both felt the link tighten between them.

Lying on the floor of her sitting room in Hampstead, playing Scrabble with Thierry, Aran smiled as she waited for him to make his move. Because English wasn't his first language, he was allowed extra time.

'Only three weeks to go, Thierry . . . are you nervous?'

He looked up at her.

'Not at all. You're the bride. You're the one who's supposed to be nervous.'

'Well, I'm not a bit. We're going to have a lovely wedding. Are you sure you like the music we chose?'

'You mean the music you chose? Yes! I like the music, the restaurant, the food, the flowers . . . everything. I like London and I like my new job. But I love you.'

He reached out to touch her hand, and she held on to his.

'I'm sorry about last weekend, Thierry. I know my mother wasn't much of an advertisement for marrying her daughter.'

'Oh, never mind your mother. Everyone else was friendly. Especially your younger brother. I liked him a lot.'

'Yes. Dursey's turned out well. And I've never seen Dad in better form. He loves the summers, out on that boat of his. But I think he'll have competition from the other boatmen, now that they've driven the dolphins away. They'll all turn to the shark fishing instead . . . isn't it a shame, about those beautiful dolphins?'

'Yes. A great shame. But I saw many other things that made you happy. Your older brother's musicians in the pub, your friends' new baby, your little daughter.'

'Isn't she gorgeous? I knew you'd like her, and she'd like you.'

'I look forward to seeing a lot more of her, and to having such a daughter ourselves. Well, maybe not quite so noisy! But one as pretty and as sweet.'

'We will. The moment I saw baby Sorcha I said to myself, I'd like to order one of those, please!'

'Then you shall have one. And Rhianna will come often, to play with her. Have you made up your mind yet, about the house we saw in Chiswick?'

'Not really . . . not yet. I do like it, only I wish – I wish it had room for the piano.'

'But why? You don't play it, and it only reminds me of my predecessor. He isn't going to come for it now, is he?'

'No, but I hoped – I hoped maybe Rhianna would learn to play it one day.'

'But Aran, she lives in Ireland. It would be much more practical to get her one over there, if she wants one.'

'I suppose you're right. It is a reminder, and it's not fair to you. I'll find a new home for it.'

'I think it would be better. Only I don't want to insist. I know Rhianna's father was important to you.'

'He was. Thierry, you do understand that everything I told you was in confidence, don't you? Everything about Rhianna, and Ben?'

'Of course I do. Your secret love child with the famous singer, that I must never mention to anyone! I never will, Aran, you can trust me. But I am glad you told me, and I think you did the right thing for her.'

Gratefully, she looked at him.

'Do you, Thierry?'

Getting up, he came over to where she lay and lowered himself to her side, putting his arm around her.

'Yes. She is secure, happy and much loved. If only we had met in time, perhaps you would have been able to keep her . . . but you were alone, you were not to know.'

'It was fate, Thierry. Rhianna was always destined to be with Dan and Eimear.'

He kissed her cheek. 'Well, you are destined to be with me. Am I enough for you, Aran, after such an exotic romance?'

Leaning into him, she let her fair hair brush his freckled face. Although he was French, he had the lighter complexion of the north: even Molly had admitted that he could 'almost pass for Irish'.

'Yes. You are enough, Thierry. I will be a good wife to you, and a good mother to your children.'

'I know you will, Aran, as I will be a good husband and father in turn. Perhaps you do not feel quite the passion for me that you felt for Ben Halley, but you – you do love me, don't you? You understand that love takes many forms, and grows with time?'

'Yes, Thierry. I do know that, and I do love you.'

Their game forgotten, they lay on the floor, thinking of the future to be forged, the life to be shaped and shared.

Chapter Fifteen

I might as well give up, Eimear thought, annoyed. It was a perfect day for painting when I started, but now look at it. The front door will end up like a haystack, with the wind blowing leaves and dust into the wet paint. Why can't the weather people ever warn you about things like this, instead of going on about their isobars and isotherms? I suppose I could do the inside of the door, though. Then Oscar will have nice new paint to scratch off . . . Lord, those zinnias will be blown to bits. Just when the garden is looking so nice, you get a wind like this. I hope Dan had the wits to bring the children's jackets with him.

On the patio, Sorcha's pram was beginning to rock violently, as if some malevolent force was trying to throw her out of it. Packing up her paintbrushes, Eimear hurried to take it indoors, and peered down at the rather puzzled-looking baby.

'Well, at least you're not down on the beach, getting sand in your eyes! Come on, let's make a cup of tea.'

Transferring Sorcha to her bouncer in the kitchen, she put on the kettle and looked out the window a little anxiously. On the sections of the beach that were visible between the yew trees, there was no sign of Dan or the two older children.

Well, if he had any sense – which he had – Dan would be already hustling the kiddies back up through the dunes, abandoning their search for shells and stones. The sky had turned from innocent blue to a dark hostile grey, the wind was churning up whitecaps on the ocean, and he had lived long enough on this coast to recognise the signs of a storm. Sometimes they wondered why they lived there; on other European beaches people would be toasting in the sun at this moment, sipping cocktails, revelling in the July weather that never really warmed the heart of Dunrathway. Being a Saturday, the trawlers were fortunately not out, but she could see the few pleasure boats turning around, making hastily for the safety of the harbour.

The tourists would be disappointed, but probably console themselves over hot whiskies in the pub that Achill Campion had made so attractive. Even during the daytime, there was always a bit of music and craic to be found in it.

By the time she finished her tea Eimear heard the front door opening, Dan coming in with Rhianna and Emmett, the door slamming on a gust of wind behind them. Emmett was thrilled with the sudden meteorological drama.

'Big wind, Mum!'

'Yes, sweetie. I think it's going to be an afternoon for the cartoon videos. Or we could get your paints out and make a birthday card for Grandma.'

Diving into a cupboard, Emmett rummaged happily for his paintbox, and Eimear cringed as Rhianna espied her drum in it.

'Oh, no, sweetie, Sorcha is sleeping. Why don't you get your paints out too?'

'OK. Drum later.'

Yes, Eimear thought, I'll give you your drum later, when you're about twenty-six. Settling down at the table with them, she resigned herself to a messy afternoon, smiling as Rhianna began to hum to herself. She always sang while she did other things, but at least she had added a few new songs to her repertoire, they only got *Frère Jacques* five or six times a day now. Quietly, blissfully, Dan sloped away to watch the racing on television.

It was about four o'clock when Eimear saw some huge white thing flying past the window, swooping eerily before it vanished. It gave her a fright, but then she laughed: it was only one of Pat McGowan's shirts. Often she and Annie ran across to each other's gardens to rescue laundry on stormy days, but she had forgotten to do it today. Pat's shirts were going to end up flying from the church spire, because Annie had gone shopping in Cork . . . what a day to pick! Biting her lip, she stared out the window with a mixture of fascination and apprehension, watching clouds the colour and shape of aubergines flowing across the sky as if hurled by some furious celestial force. Gathering speed, the wind was tearing at the trees, overturning garden furniture, banging and thumping on the walls like a belligerent drunkard.

As the clouds massed and lowered they seemed to suck all the light out of the day, became one vast purple bruise, streaked with a dull greenish hue at the edges. More than angry now, they were vicious, venomous, promising retribution for whatever sins the wretched mortals of Dunrathway had committed. But this couldn't be just a local storm, Eimear thought, and soon Dan came back into the room to confirm her suspicions; the racing in Dublin had been interrupted by a wind so powerful that the horses were unable to run into it. It was unusual, in July, but by no means unheard of. As a child she had witnessed a famous storm that had flattened all the crops to a pulp, ripped half the roof off the church and overturned all the caravans in a field full of holidaymakers. Many had been badly injured. She supposed she should pull the curtains so as not to have to watch this one, but it was only mid-afternoon, and against her will her eyes kept returning to it.

At five, there was a terrifying thud in the garden, so loud that the children jumped and Sorcha woke up crying. The rain was thundering down now, so heavily that at first they couldn't see through it, couldn't determine what had fallen or broken. But then, sadly, she saw what it was.

'Oh, Dan, look. Aran's little cherub, that she gave us one Christmas . . . oh, what a shame.'

The stone cherub and the plinth on which he had stood lay strewn in smithereens on the grass, the scattered fragments far beyond repair. Further back, the yew trees were bent almost horizontal in the gale, exposing massive white waves mounting on the horizon beyond. Shivering, she thought of the boats that had been out earlier; it was a good thing they had not chanced their luck. Even with the double glazing, the lights on and the central heating, the house felt gripped in some savage fury as the wind roared around it, the distant sea rose and crashed in huge plumes that shot up like snarling fangs. Used as she was to rough weather, Eimear felt a kind of evil in the air.

'You were wise to come home when you did, Dan. So were the boatmen.'

'Yes. We saw them all heading for the harbour, didn't we, kiddies?'

Solemnly Rhianna and Emmett averred that they had. Like all the local children, they were growing up keenly aware of such things. At four, Rhianna was already able to distinguish one boat from another, knew most of their names. But then she looked at Dan, suddenly uncertain.

'Not see Lady Aran.'

'What?'

'Lady Aran not come back.'

Eimear froze. Standing on the lawn with Rhianna and Emmett earlier that morning, they had waved to Conor Campion as he set out in the clear sunshine, taking a party of Americans to fish for shark. As usual he had waved back, with the gesture that had become a regular feature of the summer seascape.

'Dan, call the coastguard.'

Without question or hesitation, Dan went straight to the phone. He had not seen the Lady Aran returning either. Of course she might easily have slipped in unnoticed, but – within moments, he was conferring with someone at the harbourmaster's office in Castletown Bere. When he put down the phone his face was bone white, silhouetted against the black sky outside.

'They know. The lifeboat has gone out, and a helicopter is standing by at the marine rescue station in Shannon. It'll take off as soon as the weather permits.'

Sensing the tension between their parents, overawed by the pounding tempest, the children fell silent. Looking at Rhianna's suddenly frightened face, thinking of her grandfather, Eimear reached out to comfort her.

'Come on, sweetie, sing us a song.'

'No, Mummy. Me not sing. Not sing now.'

The storm raged long into the night, and by ten Eimear could stand it no longer.

'You stay here, Dan. I'm going down to the harbour.'

He implored her not to go. If there was any news, they would have heard. Half the village was already gathered down at the harbour, they could see the lights and torches from where they were, and Eimear Rafter's presence was not going to change anything. In such a gale, there was a real danger of people being blown off the pier. It had happened before.

'I'll be careful. But I've got to go. Molly Campion will . . . it's not just her husband, Dan. Dursey was on the boat as well.'

'I know. So was that man – the American who was mixed up in Ben Halley's court case.'

Amery Cheam. Eimear would have remembered his name even if she hadn't heard it mentioned in the village; there had been mild interest when he booked into the new hotel. Putting on layers of weatherproof clothing, she got into her car and forced it out into the black shuddering night.

Molly was standing by the harbour wall, impassive, Achill at her side amid a cluster of neighbours. Taking a hip flask she had brought with her, Eimear offered it to her.

'Brandy, Mrs Campion. It'll warm you up.'

But Molly shook her head and so, surprisingly, did Achill. A tall young man of twenty-two, he looked at Eimear from under his thick curly hair.

'Thanks, Mrs Rafter, but we're all right. There is one thing you could do, though.'

'Yes, of course, Achill. What is it?'

'Would you ring Aran in London, get her home here to us? And Sher in Florida, if I give you the number? Val knows already, but the weather's so bad she can't make it yet from Cork.'

'Yes, I will ring them . . . but Achill, let's not alarm them yet. The lifeboat might – the helicopter is coming—'

He nodded, but then led her away, out of Molly's earshot.

'No, Mrs Rafter. It's too late. Even in summer, nobody lasts in the Atlantic for six or seven hours.'

'But Achill, they might just be stranded on board, you don't know—'

'There's been no radio contact. Not since five o'clock. My mother knows they're gone, we all know it. My dad and my brother and the four Americans. They're all dead.'

She knew they were. Yet her mind clung to visions of lifejackets, people swimming, being miraculously winched from the heaving ocean. Over the years, people had been rescued once or twice before.

'They did have lifejackets, didn't they, Achill?'

'Yes. But my dad couldn't swim, nor Dursey either. Dad always said fishermen should never learn to swim, it only prolongs the agony. They won't have drowned, Mrs Rafter. They'll have frozen to death.'

Five o'clock, he said. Five hours, since then. Yes. They would have frozen to death. Unless you were spotted and saved very quickly, that was what happened in these waters. Endangering their own lives, the men on the lifeboat were out searching for dead bodies. If the helicopter had been able to take off immediately . . . but it hadn't.

Quietly Eimear nodded, and put her hand on his arm.

'All right, Achill. I'll go and phone your sisters.'

'Thank you.'

But still she hesitated, staggering into the teeth of the wind, pausing to question the men who were directing the onshore end of the search. Wasn't it possible – maybe the radio had only – ?

No. Their eyes told her that it wasn't possible. Eventually she returned to Molly, gave her an awkward hug and went back to her car. As she drove home, tears streamed down her face.

Dan knew. She saw that he had known for some time. A small boat, caught in a storm such as this, would never come chugging safely home next morning. The waves were of a height and strength that would have reduced the Lady Aran to matchwood. But why hadn't Conor turned her round, when he saw the storm gathering? Had he tried, but been too far out? Had the engine failed? Had one of their number been blown overboard? Why hadn't he come back with the others?

'We'll probably never know, Eimear. But we're going to have to ring Aran and Sher. Would you like me to do it?'

'You – you ring Sher, Dan. I'll ring Aran.'

In such circumstances it seemed unreal that the lines were not down, that she could get through to London so quickly. But she did.

'Hello?'

Eimear drew a deep breath.

'Aran, it's me, Eimear. I'm sorry to call you so late, but—'

'Rhianna! What is it, Eimear? What's happened to her?'

'No, sweetheart, it's not Rhianna. It's your – your father, and your brother.'

'Dad? Achill, Dursey?'

'Conor and Dursey. They – they're missing. At sea. There's a huge storm.'

'Missing?' Aran exhaled it in the same flat tone Achill had used. A fisherman's daughter, she knew immediately.

'Missing. You mean they're dead, Eimear. Dad and Dursey are dead.'

'I – I – yes, Aran. Achill thinks they are.'

There was a long silence. Then a strangled sob.

'No!'

With all her might Eimear wished there were not six hundred miles between them, wished she could take her in her arms.

'Aran, I – we – look, get Thierry. Tell him to bring you to Heathrow first thing in the morning, and we'll meet you off the first flight.'

The voice became high pitched.

'Was it the Lady Aran, Eimear? Was Dad out on the boat I gave him?'

'Yes. With Dursey and four Americans. One of them was the man who commissioned that music Ben wrote, the music there was the row over —'

'Amery Cheam?'

'Yes.'

Without another word, Aran hung up.

Ben was sitting at the head of his dining table, presiding over a late-night gathering that included Myles, Kevin, Jake, Kelwin Hughes and several other associates. Really it was a working dinner, which was why no wives or girlfriends had come along, but at this stage the wine was flowing and they were having fun. Harmless fun, there was no need for Thanh to frown as he came in looking perturbed.

'What's the matter, Thanh? Caught a fan climbing up the drainpipes, have you?'

Discreetly Thanh whispered in his ear, and he leapt to his feet very indiscreetly.

'Aran? On the phone? What?'

Bewildered and disturbed, he went out to the telephone, feeling something coil in his stomach. After four years of silence, it must be some very urgent thing that had impelled her to phone.

'Aran? My God, are you all right?'

It took him several minutes to absorb the reality of her voice, piece together what she was stuttering. When he did, he summoned Thanh, went out to his car and was driven away to Hampstead. In the dining-room, the conversation went on for nearly half an hour before his guests realised their host was not coming back.

After a surreal night, for most of which they sat stunned around the kitchen table, Ben, Aran and Thierry arrived at Heathrow at first light next morning. The bad weather had created a backlog of passengers waiting to get to Ireland, and by the time they got on a flight everyone was aware of Ben Halley in their midst, craning their necks to wonder at the expression on his normally friendly face. Aran was glad when the violent wind began to rock the plane; although it was terrifying it diverted attention away from him, and he sat slumped in the inside seat, hidden from view as much as possible, gazing out the window.

But although he did not look at her, the tension between them was electric. The tension of two people who had loved each other dearly, thrown together after four years: they could almost hear each other breathing. Tightly wedged in a row of three seats, they could not help touching, their arms and legs briefly brushing and then twitching away, acutely conscious of Thierry beside them. Highly conscious of it himself, Thierry was possessive, taking Aran's hand, assisting her with every small thing, letting his status fall on the air like a mantle. He had never expected to meet Ben Halley, and the atmosphere was razor sharp.

Sitting between them, glazed, she forced her mind away, ahead to what was waiting in Dunrathway. It wouldn't focus on the tragedy there, but kept rushing to Rhianna. If Ben should see her, he would think he was looking in a mirror.

But she had had to tell him about Amery, she'd had no choice . . . he would have heard from someone else, would have come to Ireland anyway. What were Dan and Eimear going to say, when they saw him? How were they going to cope? What were they all going to *do*?

The scenario was so terrible she could hardly bear to think of it, and then there was guilt as well, guilt that such thoughts should overtake her sorrow, take precedence over Conor and Dursey. Her father was dead, her brother was dead, and yet she kept seeing Rhianna, flying out of the house, coming face to face with the father who—

Oh, Jesus *Christ*! By the time they reached Cork airport she was speechless with terror, quivering as they emerged into the arrivals area. Eimear was there; when she saw Ben she closed her eyes and looked as if she might faint. Suddenly realising the situation, Thierry volunteered to drive, and silently she gave him the keys. Her face was almost transparent.

Nobody said anything as the car set off. All Aran could do was squeeze Eimear's hand, as if to say that everything would be all right. But Eimear did not respond, and the tension heightened with every interminable mile. Aran felt as if they were all trapped in a glacier.

In Dunrathway they went straight to the harbour. Jumping out of the car before it had quite stopped, Aran plunged through the gathered throng, searching frantically for her mother and brother.

For the first time ever, Molly embraced her daughter, folded her possessively into her arms. Enveloped in a black scarf against the strong wind that was still blowing, she looked hollow, drained of all hope. The lifeboat had returned, but only to change crew; there was no news. Taking Achill's hand, Aran huddled between them, and stayed there even when Thierry came to join her. Confused by Ben's arrival, Achill gazed at him, and after some seconds Ben found his voice.

'Amery. Amery Cheam. He was my friend.'

Achill nodded, wondering at the ebullient rock singer who had once played the piano in the pub. His clothes were still strange, his hair shoulder-length and rather wild, but today his eyes were dead. When he spoke again, so was his tone.

'Your father. Your brother. I'm very sorry. And for you, Mrs Campion.'

He reached out to touch her shoulder, and Molly surveyed him without interest. She had been down at the harbour all night, all morning, standing on the same spot for twenty hours. Val had arrived, pleaded with her to wait in the fishing sheds or the lifeboat station at least, but still Molly stood like a statue. It was obvious that she was on the verge of collapse, and Val had gone to get her some tea.

After some conference with the men on the pier, Thierry took charge of the situation.

'They say there is no point in waiting here, and they are right. It is very cold. We will all go to the hotel – Mrs Campion, you must have something hot to eat.'

Molly protested, but she was overruled; the hotel had a large front window from which they could see everything. Eventually they all made their way to it, with several supportive neighbours, but nobody could eat. Seated by the window, they watched the distant dot on the horizon, rising and falling, coming and going: after a long delay the helicopter had finally come. But, in radio contact, its pilot reported nothing.

In the middle of the afternoon Sher arrived from America with her husband, as white and silent as her sisters. Like them, she knew it was only a question of time, of whether the bodies would be found before the search had to be called off. Sometimes bodies were washed up days or weeks later. Sometimes they were never recovered. Taking one look at her mother, Sher spoke firmly, decisively.

'Mother, you must go home. It could be hours, all night . . . Val, take her home.'

Surprisingly, Molly staggered to her feet and let herself be led away at last. But Aran refused to budge. Seated between Ben and Thierry, she held both their hands, accepting comfort from the one while attempting to give it to the other. Ben's devastation, she sensed, was equal to her own. In turn, she felt the strength in his grip, the sympathy he did not need to voice.

How strange it seemed that he should be here alone. She had so rarely ever seen him alone. But he had refused Thanh's offer to accompany him, not yet phoned Rani or any of his friends. As she had guessed, he was thinking only of Amery, and was very quiet.

Four years. Was it really that long since they had been together? Yet there was no distance between them today, and despite their extreme physical awareness of each other she did not sense awkwardness. United by their common grief, they were simply there, waiting. Waiting and waiting and waiting. Vaguely she was conscious of Dan and Eimear conferring in a corner, Thierry bringing coffee, being practical and helpful. But she felt suspended, apart from it all.

At six, the hotel's proprietor came running up to their group. There had been a call. The lifeboat had found the wreckage.

An hour later they saw the boat coming in, and hastened out to the pier to meet it. Shuddering, Aran watched an ambulance drive down the pier, a police car, a surge of activity. A policeman came up to Achill, and then Achill took her aside.

'One of the Americans. They've got one of the Americans.'

Instantly, Ben rushed forward, his face phosphorescent. But it was not Amery. It was a man called Perry Fleming. Perhaps a hundred people were gathered round, hushed as the covered body was lifted onto a stretcher and then into the ambulance. Aran watched as a tearful blonde woman got in with it; his wife, his widow. The men's families had arrived from America during the course of the day.

She touched Ben's arm.

'Did Amery have a family, Ben?'

'No. He had nobody.'

Nobody. She realised then that he was going to stay here for as long as it took, was going to wait until he could claim Amery's body. Somewhere among the large crowd there must be someone from Cheam Marine, one or maybe more of Amery's friends and business associates, but he had made no move to find them. Clearly he felt the weight of some almost filial responsibility. The grief of it, too; his brown eyes were liquid with tears.

'Were you very close to him, Ben?'

'I loved him.'

In silence they stood together, staring down into the salt water.

By nightfall another of the American men had been found, and as the light faded the search was called off. They were told it would resume in the morning, and advised to go home. Thinking of her mother, Aran knew she must go to her – but then, where was Ben going to go? In the circumstances he might reasonably expect the Rafters to ask him to their house, tell him that he was welcome to stay with them. But Dan and Eimear were hanging back, their expression tortured.

Anguished, she turned to Thierry.

'Thierry, I'm going to stay with my mother tonight, but there's no room there for anyone else. Do you think you could – would you mind – booking in here, to the hotel? Ben will need a room too.'

To his eternal credit, he understood immediately.

'Of course. I'll get rooms for us both.'

Her heart heaved with relief as he went out to the reception desk. But within minutes he was back, wearing a look that made her catch her breath.

'The hotel is full. The American families . . . the people from the media . . . they haven't got a single bed left.'

Wildly she tried to think of other alternatives. But the previous hotel had long since closed down, and there wasn't another for fifteen miles. Uninterested in the subject, but sensing that for some reason she was concerned, Ben looked at her and then glanced across at the Rafters.

'Perhaps Dan and Eimear—?'

'No! I mean, no, Ben, they can't – they – they've got no space—'

355

A little perplexed, he raised his eyebrows.

'But they had lots of space the last time I was here.'

'Yes, but they haven't now, they – they've got three children.'

Her words were almost inaudible, her whole body shaking. At all costs she must keep him away from the Rafters, but the strain of it, the strain of everything, was close to overwhelming.

Never, she thought, would she be able to repay Thierry for his next suggestion.

'What about your friend – the woman you work for, who makes the cheese?'

Annie! Annie's sons were away at college, she had room – desperately Aran scanned the crowd for her. But Ben was frowning, baffled.

'When did the Rafters have three children? They didn't have any before, you told me they—'

Standing up, she located Annie and ran over to her, almost pushed the woman into a corner.

'Annie – please – I – we have a problem. Could you possibly give Ben and Thierry beds for the night?'

Annie knew. Annie knew about Rhianna's father. She sensed it as Annie looked at Ben, and nodded.

'Of course I can. I have lots of space, Aran, don't fret yourself.'

She all but wept with gratitude.

'Oh, thank you!'

But they exchanged a long look. Annie's house was only two hundred yards away from Dan and Eimear's. Often, Rhianna ran across the field that separated them to visit with Annie.

But Rhianna would be asleep now for the night, tomorrow Dan and Eimear would see that she was not let out.

Or the next day. Or the next? How long was it going to be, before Amery's body was found? How long was Ben going to stay here? How long could she possibly endure this?

Firmly Annie went over to Ben and Thierry, introduced herself and informed them that they were to be her guests. After a brief conversation Ben found himself led away, sandwiched between Annie and Thierry. When they were gone, Eimear almost tottered up to her.

'Aran, this – this is a nightmare. I know you had to tell him about Amery, I know you're upset, but – but what are we going to do, if Ben sees Rhianna? What are we going to do?'

'Oh, God, Eimear. I don't know. I just don't know.'

All night Aran hovered around Molly, clenched with anxiety, hating herself for not devoting her attention exclusively to her family. Would

356

it have been safer to send Ben to Hannah Lowry's house, up on Fenner's Hill? Yes – but in her panic she had not thought of it in time. Besides, Annie had a husband, whereas Hannah was a widow living alone, he might have refused to embarrass or encumber her. Now, her heart was pounding, her mind running wild around the unthinkable possibilities.

But her mother needed her, everyone did, she must concentrate . . . somehow she got through the endless evening until Sher led Molly away, and she became conscious of her own enormous fatigue. But then she had to share her old room with her sisters, fighting down the fear she couldn't voice, shivering with horror as they all thought of the same unspeakable thing. Somewhere out in the black ocean, Conor's and Dursey's bodies were . . . none of them said it, but none of them could sleep.

At five she abandoned all effort, and sat up with a jolt. If she didn't get out of this room she would scream, suffocate. Dressing in the dark, she crept out of the house and went down to the beach. In winter the sky would be pitch black, but on this July night it was charcoal, already streaking with a paler grey, and she walked with her head down, weeping quietly. What a death they had had. What a death; she thought her mind would disintegrate at the vision of it.

And then for a crazed moment she imagined she saw them, Conor and Dursey, two male figures materialising at the water's edge. She could even hear their voices – as she opened her mouth to cry out they began to run towards her, ghostly, terrifying.

It was Ben and Thierry. She sobbed as she saw their faces, and they hastened to her side.

'Aran – it's us – we couldn't sleep—'

Taking her into his arms, Thierry held her tight, protectively, letting her cry freely against his chest. He was being wonderfully supportive, and she clung to him, feeling Ben's eyes on their joint shape. But he said nothing.

Silently they walked on until they reached the hotel, which was beginning to stir. Thierry insisted she must eat some breakfast, and although she knew she would be unable to she let him lead her inside. Sitting down in the lounge which had become the centre of the vigil, all three of them huddled round cups of hot coffee, feeling that their ordeal had gone on for a month, a year. Again Thierry took her hand, Ben took the other, and they sat together watching the dawn come up. A pure white dawn, tinged with silver and azure, calm and windless. After forty hours the storm had blown itself out, the sky was innocent, serene.

Some time later Achill arrived, with news of Molly she supposed.

Overpowered by exhaustion, their mother had accepted a sleeping pill from Sher, but was in a state of great agitation.

'How is she, Achill?'

'Aran, it isn't Mother, it – it's – one of the fishermen has—'

Everyone looked up, and Achill bit his lip fiercely.

'On the beach . . . down at the cove . . . it's Dursey.'

Dursey. Without asking, Aran understood, and could not speak. Down on the sand, her brother's body had been washed up by the tide.

It was a blur after that, a muffled cocoon in which protective hands and voices wrapped her, not wanting her to know, not wanting her to see. But she went to the beach, and did see, swaying slightly when the blanketed form was strapped onto the stretcher. Dursey had been in the water for a day and a half.

Someone's arms were around her, someone led her away. She had no idea who it was.

And then the boats were out again, many of them, combing the coast for the remaining three. The other American, Amery Cheam, and Conor. A lifejacket was discovered, a floating plastic box from the galley, an airtight tin of tobacco. And then, at noon, Conor. From the way the paramedics spoke, she knew Thierry was not going to let her see her father. When the boat came in with his body he held her back, as Achill held their mother, crumpled against him like a handful of seaweed.

But Ben saw Amery. Saw the white hair floating on the water, the battered body that had been his friend's, as it came washing grotesquely in on a wave. By the time it reached the beach he was already there, wading in up to his waist, stretching to take possession of the man who had loved him like a father.

The rescue team tried to restrain him, but he helped them lift Amery up himself, carried him, put his hand to his ice-cold face. His touch was very gentle, but Aran saw the fierce pain in it, the pain that would haunt him as hers would haunt her, for ever.

That evening the five coffins were assembled in the church and a service was conducted. It was a terrible ordeal for the wife whose husband had not been found, but bravely she attended it, accepting the possibility that perhaps he never would be. Aran's family sat in the front pew as Father Carroll came out on the altar in the mauve robes of mourning, but she was up in the organ loft with Luke Lavery, and Ben. Thierry had not wanted her to do it, but she felt the same need Ben did, the need to say goodbye in the only way they could. Far below she could see Molly, Achill, Sher and Val and their husbands, Hannah Lowry and Annie McGowan. It had been decided that no children should be brought to such a traumatic spectacle, and like the other parents Dan and Eimear stood alone.

She had not thought to take her oboe from London, but Luke had loaned her one, and he eyed her anxiously as she stood waiting, listening to the prayers, watching Fr Carroll bless her brother's coffin and her father's, Amery's and the two others. The two American men had been Lutherans, and nobody was sure what Amery's religion might have been, but a joint ecumenical service was deemed appropriate.

It was not a long service. Tomorrow morning, there would be a full funeral mass for Conor and Dursey, they would be buried together in the graveyard behind the church, and then the Americans would be flown home to their native town of Chicago. Amery, too; Ben had located the representative from Cheam Marine and was making all the arrangements, would accompany Amery's body back to New York for cremation. This evening's service was more in the nature of a reconciliation to their fate, a kind of acceptance of the wishes of the gods. Sitting immobile at the organ he had played for many years, Luke waited for Fr Carroll to say his words of condolence, and then laid his hands on the keys.

Not knowing the words of the Catholic hymn, Ben stood with a sheet of paper before him, looking at Aran as she raised the oboe to her lips. In the short time available to them, they had discussed this moment with trepidation, but she was adamant that she could get through it without shedding a tear. It was impossible to play the oboe without complete breath control, and any moisture would make the internal reeds of the instrument swell, rendering it useless. Steadily, she raised it to her lips, and began to play. *Nearer My God to Thee.* That was the traditional hymn for obsequies, and for some unknown reason it had particular associations with death at sea. The passengers on the Titanic were reputed to have sung it as the boat went down, taking them with it. Anguished, Ben waited for the right moment, caught her eye and then joined his voice to her music.

All over the world, he had sung to thousands of people, but tonight, for the first time, his voice cracked. Aran swung round as she heard it, but kept playing.

No, Ben. Do it. If I can do it, you can do it.

After two or three tortured seconds he began again. Rigid with determination, closing his eyes, he lifted his head and sang the first eight words. Down in the pews, heads turned, there was an intake of breath. Pure and clear, golden as the burning flames of the candles, his voice floated down, transfixing everyone with the pain in it, the reverence, the soaring strength. Closing his eyes, Luke played on, unable to look at either of them, but the voice did not break a second time, the oboe did not waver. Slowly, stoically, the song went on, tearing them to pieces, taking their souls away together, binding the anguish to common purpose. Completely silent, the congregation listened, feeling every word and note in their hearts, overwhelmed. Never, for all the spiritual experiences in this church, had they encountered anything so harrowing. Poignant as a knife, Ben's voice sliced through the air; sweet as a baby's breath, Aran's oboe wafted under it, bore it down to the coffins, up to the heavens.

Trembling, Luke Lavery struggled to stay in tune with them, but Ben and Aran drew on the strength they had promised each other, exchanging the resolve they needed, getting each other through. When they finished, Aran knew her father would be proud of her, and saw in Ben's face what he was thinking about Amery. On the last few slow words, the whole congregation joined in, as if they could not bear the pain, had to help them, share the sorrow on all their shoulders.

Only then did Aran look at Ben, and ache for him. It was his twenty-sixth birthday. But then Luke stood up, his throat working, and came to stand beside him. Again she put the oboe to her lips, again they composed themselves. Huskily, Ben whispered something in her ear, and she nodded. The first notes flowed and swirled, and then Luke and Ben began to sing together, the baritone and the tenor. *The Pearl Fishers*, 'at the end of the holy temple'.

For the rest of their lives, none of them would ever know how they got through it, how they were the only people in the church who did not weep. Several times, Luke's voice broke, but Ben's rose over it, soothing the sob, stroking the sorrow away. Playing as she had never played before, Aran watched him sing with the most inexpressible beauty she had ever heard.

Cruelly, flashbulbs went off as they emerged from the church. Ben Halley was news, and so was Amery Cheam. Instinctively she tried to shield him, but then a flash went off in her own face: one of the photographers recognised her as Ben's former girlfriend.

Furious, Thierry tried to get her away. But it was Ben himself who blocked her path. Reaching for her hand, he held it with a pleading look.

'Aran – please – I'm leaving after your father's funeral tomorrow – I must speak to you.'

Desperate to get away from the chaos, she said the first thing that came into her head.

'In an hour – I'll meet you at Annie's house in an hour.'

Someone jostled him out of her view, and then Thierry steered her to someone's car, put her into it, took her home. Molly's house was crammed with people, and it was nearly two hours before she was able to persuade Thierry not to come with her.

'I don't want you to be alone with him, Aran.'

'Thierry, please, I won't be alone. Annie will be there, and her husband – if you'll just stay here with the family, I promise I'll be back as soon as I can.'

Very reluctantly, he let her go. As she ran her heart was thumping. Ben at one house, Rhianna at the next – and the three of them, a family! What would he say if he knew, if he found out?

He was waiting for her in Annie's garden. Before she could say anything, he took her arm.

'Let's get out of here.'

Seized with sudden urgency they sprinted away, down the back roads and past the school, into the sandy lane that led to the far end of the beach. Breathless, they reached the big rock that Aran remembered, and sat down on it. For a moment she was sure he was going to take her in his arms, but instead he gripped her by the shoulders and looked into her eyes.

'Do you love him?'

Steadying herself, she looked back at him.

'Yes.'

His grip became so tight she winced.

'You're sure?'

She wasn't sure of anything. Conor was dead, Dursey was dead, all she knew was that Thierry was helping her cope, making it bearable, Thierry was her rock.

'Ben, we're engaged. We're getting married.'

His grip loosened a fraction, but he still held her.

'Don't, Aran. Don't do it if you're not sure.'

Her lip trembled.

'Ben, he loves me. He's sure about me, in a way that you never were.'

Stiffening as she said it, she saw them all in her mind's eye, Sasha and Kim and Charlotte, every girl in every photograph. And how many more, that she had not even seen?

Thierry would never do that to her. Never, ever. Thierry wanted her to be his wife, wanted to have children with her. Thierry wouldn't leave, wouldn't drown, wouldn't die . . . dimly, she realised she was very confused. And so was Ben, his eyes strange, his face full of sorrow. They were both totally confused, torn by everything that had happened.

361

Wrenching his eyes off her, he gazed at the sinking sun.

'Are you still angry, Aran? Angry that I wasn't sure?'

Abruptly, her eyes filled with tears, her throat hurt.

'Ben, please. I'm too tired, there's too much pain . . . it's the wrong time for this.'

Half of her wanted to push him away, half of her wanted to pull him close, slide down into the sand with him. But then he leaned back, lowered his voice.

'And the Rafters? Are you the reason they won't speak to me?'

'What?'

'Dan and Eimear, who gave me my piano! I want to talk to them, but they've been avoiding me ever since I got here. Are they angry that I didn't marry you?'

Her head swam as she thought of them, thought of Rhianna.

'No. They're not angry with you.'

'Then what is it? Why are they acting as if I had something contagious? If you won't tell me, I'll go up there to their house, ask them myself. Ask them about this man too, and this marriage.'

'No! You're not to go near them!'

She saw in his face that she sounded hysterical. Suddenly he looked concerned.

'Aran, what is it? What's wrong with you?'

She pulled herself out of his grasp.

'Leave me alone, Ben! Leave us all alone!'

White and taut, she whirled away from him and ran up into the dunes. Ran until her legs ached, until the cottage came in sight and she could see Thierry, hastening out to catch her as she collapsed into him.

For a week afterwards, Aran stayed in Dunrathway, and was plagued by twisted, unnerving dreams.

They were not dreams of the sea, of storms or sharks. Those were things you accepted, when you grew up by the ocean, when your family lived from it. The Atlantic was dangerous and unpredictable, it could kill and it had killed many times; if you chose it as your way of life then you must accept its moods, its power. Urban people were shocked by such tragedy as had happened, but she knew it was inevitable, lamented only that her own family should have been chosen.

Her dreams were of innocent things. Innocent daisies in a field, whose petals suddenly turned into teeth and snapped at her ankles, biting and chasing her as she ran away from them. The Rafters' puppy Oscar, becoming a tiger as she tussled with him, devouring

362

her. Songbirds changing into vultures, trees towering over her, swallowing her in their foliage, strangling her with their branches. Thierry, some kind of rope or chain in his hand, rushing at her as she backed into a corner, crying and screaming.

In reality, Thierry could not have been nicer, more comforting or caring. He took time off work, stayed with her, held her when she wept, held the whole shattered family together as if it was his own. Shepherding everyone through the funeral and its aftermath, he ran errands, made phone calls, cooked meals, held the fort in a way that endeared him even to Molly.

But of course their wedding would have to be cancelled.

'Cancelled?' He looked at her in the way people did look at you when you were bereaved, in mourning, and lowered his tone gently. 'You mean postponed, Aran. It will have to be postponed. We will fix a new date later, when you are feeling stronger.'

Yes. That was what she meant. Postponed. Nodding automatically, she set about doing everything that was expected of her. Spending time with her mother, Achill and her sisters, thanking everyone who had taken part in the search, come to the funeral, sent flowers. There was a lot of talk, a lot of activity, she had little time alone. But in the evenings she walked barefoot on the beach, thinking of Dursey whose young life had been extinguished, of Conor whose half century had amounted to so little. Thinking of the things they might have done, and hadn't.

Then, in Dan and Eimear's garden, she sat with Rhianna on her lap, feeling the life in the child's wriggling body, the energy that soon propelled her away to run across the grass, jump on the swing, yell lustily in the settling twilight. The adults were dignified, solicitous, around her, there was a feeling of walking on eggshells; but Rhianna darted about shouting and laughing, oblivious. She knew the men were dead, but didn't understand, was not affected. Her grandfather and her uncle. But that meant nothing either. Like all small children Rhianna was a savage, free of care, free of convention. Her laughter rang in the shadows.

And Ben. Aran thought of him as she watched their daughter, wondering. She had thought – she didn't know what she had thought. But she had not thought he would leave as he did, immediately, to accompany Amery Cheam's body to New York.

Yet he had. Putting his hand to her face, in full view of Thierry, he had simply expressed his condolences, and gone.

It was five days before Thanh became sufficiently worried to phone Rani and ask whether she had heard from Ben. She said she had

363

heard. He had phoned from Ireland, explained what had happened and where he was going.

Yes, Thanh said, Ben had phoned him with the same message. But had she heard since?

No. She hadn't. With mounting anxiety Thanh rang Myles, Kevin, Jake, even Deva although he didn't want to worry her. They all knew Ben was in New York, but no, none of them had had any contact with him since he arrived there.

Leaving Beth stationed by the phone in the apartment in Kensington, Thanh went to the airport and took the next flight to JFK.

Plentiful as it was, the alcohol in Amery's apartment was having no effect on Ben. Certainly not the effect he wanted. And, although the couple who ran the apartment knew him well enough to admit him and let him stay there, as he had often done before, he felt they were watching him. Watching, and disapproving. Taking only his credit cards, he went out, found a bank and withdrew a large sum of cash.

With cash it was easy. Walking all the way from the Upper East Side down to Greenwich Village, he went into Washington Square and soon located what he was looking for.

In denims, a baseball cap and dark glasses, nobody recognised him, nobody even glanced as he slid the folded money into the guy's hand and took the small package in exchange. Half an hour later, he had checked into a small anonymous hotel and was sitting on the floor, gazing at the first line of cocaine, wondering how and why he had resisted for so long before.

Chapter Sixteen

'French or Italian?'

'What?'

Thierry made eating and drinking gestures with his hands.

'Dinner, Aran. I'm taking you out, remember? I know French and Italian are your favourites, but which would you prefer tonight?'

'Italian.'

He picked up the phone and booked a table at the Pontevecchio in Earl's Court. It was expensive, but nothing was too much trouble these days, nothing was too good for Aran. In the month since they returned from Ireland, he had done everything to console her, cheer her up.

'Why don't you put on something nice?'

She looked down at what she was wearing, a striped T-shirt and short cotton skirt. Not good enough for the Pontevecchio, she supposed, or for Thierry who liked her in long loose dresses, pretty pastels.

'All right.'

Upstairs, rifling her wardrobe, she came across the beaded orange bustier she had never got round to throwing out. Lifting it off its hanger, she held it up to her in front of the mirror.

My God, she thought, did I really wear this once? With my hair dyed teal? What a little tart I must have looked. Thierry would have run a mile. I'd be lost without him, if he ever did run off . . . but he never would. Not from who I am now.

Selecting an ivory dress that buttoned up to its sweetheart neckline, she brushed her hair, put on some make-up and, when she came downstairs, was rewarded with his gratified smile. Wearing a beige jacket with a check tie and cream Chinos, he looked very well himself, and she knew they made an attractive couple.

The restaurant was elegant, full of mirrors and paintings, other couples getting the weekend off to an enjoyable start. Having spent the day working in Cambridge, eating nothing, she found she was hungry.

'Have the *fettucine linguine*,' he counselled, 'and how about a bottle of Pinot Grigio? Or would you prefer a Trebbiano?'

They chose the Pinot Grigio, and the first glass went straight to her head. Woozily, she smiled at him.

'You spoil me.'

Pausing over his *antipasti*, he put down his fork and laid his hand on hers.

'Of course I do. I love you.'

'I know. I'm sorry I've been a bit moody lately.'

'You've had a dreadful experience. It's perfectly natural.'

'I'll try to start pulling myself together.'

'Yes. I think what you need is something to look forward to. Let's start thinking again about our wedding.'

The wine was coursing gently through her veins, making her mellow, more relaxed than she had felt in weeks. He felt so warm and strong beside her, so comforting.

'I was looking forward to it being in summertime . . . I can't wear that dress in winter. Maybe next spring? April? That's only eight months away.'

'Oh, Aran. Buy another dress, and we'll marry at Christmas.'

'But my mother wouldn't come then. It has to be at least six months before – between—'

'Oh. Yes, I see, I'm sorry. All right. Let's fix a date right now.'

To her surprise he took his diary from his pocket and consulted it.

'The fourth of April is a Saturday. How about that?'

She nodded, noting the way he patted his moustache with his napkin when he finished his *antipasti*, beamed at the waiter when his *osso buco* arrived. He liked his food.

'Yes. The fourth of April, then. I'm sorry about the delay, but—'

'I don't mind, Aran. Now that I know what the reason is, I can wait.'

'But of course that's the reason, Thierry. What other reason would there be?'

'Oh, none, I suppose. I just – look, why don't we get some red wine with the meat?'

She was surprised to find that they had already finished the white. One bottle was really enough. But if he wanted another, she didn't greatly care. It was a warm August evening, her resistance was low. They waited while the waiter brought some Velletri, and he tasted it in his very French way, then nodded with satisfaction.

'Ah. What was I saying? Oh, yes. The delay. Your mother being

366

widowed.' He leaned forward intently. 'It is your mother, isn't it? Only your mother, and not that bloody man?'

She laughed and spluttered all at once.

'Bloody man? What bloody man?'

'That damn Halley man. Rhianna's father, who upset you so much before mercifully leaving for America.'

Ben. Ben who had disappeared, never got in touch since, not even via Thanh or Rani, to ask how she was.

'No, Thierry. I give you my word, there has been absolutely no contact between us since then. I was a fool to even meet him that day.'

'H'm. That's what I told you at the time.'

She didn't want to talk about Ben. Didn't want to hear his voice, singing in the church, didn't want to think about death or funerals any more. Ben was gone, as Conor and Dursey were gone. Resolutely she turned her attention to the excellent *abbàcchio*, and finished it.

Afterwards, while they were lingering over the last of the Velletri, a flower seller came in. Thierry promptly bought a bunch of red roses.

'Oh! How kind of you!'

She leaned across to kiss him, and encourage him as he eyed the dessert menu enquiringly.

'Go on. Have whatever you like.'

He ordered *tiramisù*, coffee and two sambucas.

'Oh no, I can't drink any more.'

But the wine had long eroded the last of her willpower, and she sipped the sambuca when it came, feeling very warm, dreamy. Thierry's face was flushed, too, his voice a little veiled. When he pulled his chair closer she could smell his fresh cotton shirt, his soap and shampoo, all mixed with the alcohol. He was very masculine – very seductive, suddenly. She edged nearer to him.

'Are you going to stay over, tonight?'

Yes. He had a flat of his own, near her house, but as he looked at her hair curling around her face, her lips gleaming in the candlelight, he thought tonight was definitely a night for staying over. And it pleased him greatly that she had been the one to suggest it. Complicitly, they smiled at each other, and he took her hand again.

'Mm. I am. We'll take the phone off the hook.'

'Oh? OK. But no one will ring. It's late.'

'He might. He's so persistent, I'd have punched him if he'd been in the room.'

The glass tilted, she felt the sambuca trickling down the back of her hand, her breath like spun glass.

'He – he phoned? Ben phoned?'

His face crumpled, knotted with remorse and anger.

'Oh, damn, Aran, I'm sorry, it's the drink—'

She pulled herself upright, felt her body hot and damp, heard her voice cold and still.

'Tell me.'

He looked ready to cry.

'No, it doesn't matter, he said it didn't matter – Aran, I'm sick of this! Sick of his ghost, hovering between us! He left you, I'm the one who—'

'Thierry, tell me.'

He felt her gaze like a branding iron.

'It was weeks ago, you'd gone to Leicester, I was doing a bit of weeding for you, in the garden – he only asked if you were there, I said no, and that was that. He didn't even give his name, but I recognised his voice.'

'But you said he was persistent.'

'Not in person. But some other guy phoned – twice after that – sounded Chinese or something, said he was his bodyguard. The second time, I told him you were always away working during the week but that I'd give you the message.'

'You bastard.'

His face flickered with hurt.

'Aran, I'm not a bastard, I'm your fiancé, any guy would have done the same in my place.'

She overturned her chair as she got up, grabbed her bag and ran outside to hail a taxi.

The night security man knew the drill. Anyone who came asking for Ben Halley was to be told they were in the wrong building – particularly breathless young women. It was a lie, but it was the only way to deal with them all.

'I'm sorry, madam, but you're mistaken. Mr Halley doesn't live here.'

For a moment she thought maybe she was. But Rani had described it exactly, down to this marble lobby with this uniformed man. She plunged on.

'He does live here, and he does know me. If you won't let me up, then please call Dith Thanh and tell him I'm here. Mr Dith is his bodyguard, he lives here too.'

Oh. So she did have some inside information. Knew that the bodyguard's last name came first. Most of them fell at that hurdle. Relucantly, he picked up the internal phone.

'Mr Dith? I'm very sorry to disturb you at this hour, but there's a young lady, a Miss—'

'Campion.'

'A Miss Campion here, very insistent I'm afraid – oh. All right then.'

Still sceptical, he showed her to the lift and, when she fell out of it moments later, Thanh was waiting for her, his finger to his lips.

'Sshh – other residents, Aran. Not like noise.'

Obediently she tiptoed down the corridor, but as soon as they were inside the apartment she fell on him, hugging him, babbling.

'Thanh! Oh, Thanh, I didn't know – where is he, how is he?'

Thanh pursed his lips.

'He not here. Out on Harley Davidson, maybe pub, club, maybe drinking. Very dangerous.'

'But why aren't you with him?'

Thanh sighed as he led her into a large lounge, furnished expensively but haphazardly, dominated by a grand piano.

'Sit down, Aran. You like drink?'

'No – I think maybe I'd better have some water, though.'

He brought her a glass, and she saw accusation in his eyes.

'Oh, Thanh, I'm sorry. I know you probably don't believe me, but I have missed you, missed you very much – there was a reason, but I can't tell you what it was.'

His face softened, his green eyes lightened a little as he lowered his wiry body onto a chair at the other side of a glass coffee table.

'I sorry too, Aran, about your brother and father. Why you not call me back, when I call you?'

'I didn't know you had, not until tonight.'

'Well, you pick good night to come. Ben very difficult. Not well.'

'You mean, he's ill? But you said he's out—'

Again Thanh sighed, and surveyed her at some length before leaning forward.

'Aran, I trust you, OK? I tell you something, but you never tell anyone else?'

'No. Of course not.'

He studied a painting on the wall behind her head.

'Aran, Ben cracking up.'

'Cracking *up*? What do you mean?'

'Doing drugs. Cocaine.'

'Oh, my God.'

'Cocaine, vodka, all together . . . last month, he nearly die in New York. Missing for whole week. Police have to help me find him, in crummy hotel, very sick, lot of trouble. Big trouble.'

Cocaine. And the police. She could imagine what trouble, and what lengths Thanh must have gone to to get him out of it, get him home.

'But the police – didn't that give him a fright?'

'Yeah. For few days. He promise to never do it again. But now he doing it. Out at night, not let me go with him, come home stoned. Aran, he going to kill himself.'

'Oh, sweet Jesus. What can I do, Thanh? He called me, you know, it must have been from New York, but I wasn't – I didn't – have you spoken to him? Has Rani?'

'Sure. We all talk to him. No listen.'

Biting her lip, she thought for a while.

'Did he ever try drugs before?'

'No. Only since Amery die. He very upset about that. Amery get him new contract, now he blow it. I tell him Amery very angry.'

Suddenly she was angry herself. She'd lost her father too, but she wasn't taking cocaine.

'Thanh, can I stay here? Wait with you, until he comes home?'

'Yes. Please. I very glad if you wait. Then you see for yourself. But he not come until three, maybe four in morning.'

'No matter. I'll wait.'

Nodding, he went away to make some coffee, leaving her to look around the apartment. Such an apartment! Wandering around it, she saw just how much money Ben had made, the scale on which he lived. Her mother's cottage would fit into one of the bathrooms.

He was a fool. And some angry thing was clawing at her chest.

When Thanh came back he filled her in on a great deal of detail, everything Ben had been doing since they parted, his friends and his music, his bitter row with Schwabbe, his close association with Amery Cheam who would have become his manager. Amery, he told her, had left all his money to charities and music foundations, but Ben had inherited his apartment in Manhattan.

'Not good, Aran. New York wrong place for Ben.'

But any city was the wrong place, she supposed, for a drug addict. They could even get them in Cork – *addict*? The word swung in her mind like a hangman's noose.

By the time they heard the motorbike down in the street, over four hours later, she had worked herself up into a state somewhere between fire and ice. Apprehensively, Thanh glanced at her.

'He maybe have girl with him, Aran. But you no worry. I take care of girls.'

Brittle as she felt, she had to smile distractedly. How did Thanh take care of them? Push them down the incinerator chute? Any method of disposal was fine by her, but Thanh's face was drawn, nervous, and she wondered how long he could be expected to put up with it all.

Ben was singing as he got out of the lift, some loud snatch of opera, until Thanh rushed out to quieten him and lead him inside. There was no sound of a woman's voice or footsteps, but she could tell that Ben was high, argumentative, truculent. Whatever Thanh was trying to tell him about her being here wasn't registering.

Well, it was going to register. Standing up, her heart hammering, she turned to face the door. When Thanh got him inside, hauling him by the sleeve of his leather biker's jacket, he stopped dead, his eyes brown and shiny as chestnuts.

'Oh, wow! Muffin's here! Thanh, you shit, why didn't you—'

But Thanh had dodged through another door, and gone. Unsteadily he lurched at her, his face lighting up, his arms reaching out.

Picking up the pot of cold coffee, she threw it over him.

Gasping, he fell backwards, coughing and flailing. For a moment it occurred to her that he might throw something back, but then, maddeningly, he began to laugh. A rasping mindless laugh, that showed her what this beautiful talented man was doing to himself.

'Aran! Hey, Aran—'

Marching up to within striking distance, she raised her arm and slapped his face with all her force.

'Oh! Hey, stop—'

She hit him again. Raising his arms he began to defend himself, trying to catch her hand, but he was uncoordinated, unable to stop her as her palm landed on his face again and again, leaving stinging red marks. Then it became a fist, and thudded into his midriff.

'Uh! Ow! Jesus—'

She was astonished by her own strength as she swung her arm back once more and threw a punch that decked him on the floor. As he struggled to his feet, she grabbed him by the hair, held him with one hand and slammed her knuckles into his face. Panting, possessed by fury, she remembered Lorcan Miller. She had broken Lorcan's ribs.

She had broken something now, too. Blood was gushing from Ben's mouth and nose. But she felt no pity, wasn't sorry at all.

Making some muffled noise, he raised his hand, gaped at the blood on it and staggered away to the kitchen, hunching his shoulders sideways in case she should come at him again. A few seconds later, she heard water running.

Thanh must hear it too, she thought, must have heard all the noise. But he didn't interfere, he let me do it. He approved. Collapsing on the sofa, exhausted, she waited.

He was white as ice when he reappeared, clutching a wet towel to

371

his mouth, squinting at her narrowly. One eye, she thought with satisfaction, had the makings of a real shiner.

'You've split my lip. And broken my tooth.'

His voice sounded as if it had been soaked in tar, black and sticky.

'What did you say? Your diction isn't very clear.'

'I said you've smashed my fucking mouth.'

'That's a pity. The girls won't fancy you much with a great gummy mouth.'

The towel was turning crimson, and he hobbled back to the kitchen, reaching for a fresh one as she followed him in.

'Here. Do it properly.'

Turning on the cold tap full blast, she took him by the scruff of the neck and plunged his head under it, held him there until he began to gag and choke. He was soaked to the waist. When she let him up for air he shook himself like a sheepdog, spraying water, blood and coffee across all four walls.

'You bitch. You total, perfect bitch.'

'You fool. You total, perfect fool.'

He was tall and fit, she supposed he could hurt her now in return if he had a mind to. But Thanh was nearby, she only had to yell, and anyway she felt no fear. None. For all the bikes and leather, Ben Halley hadn't a violent bone in his body. In fact it seemed that she, in her nice dress with the sweetheart neckline, was the violent one. Unexpectedly she felt giggly, giddy. If his fans could see him now he would die, expire of shame and humiliation.

But he really was bleeding a lot, his eye was closing already. She sobered up.

'Do you want a doctor?'

'No, I don't want one, but I damn well need one, don't I?'

His voice was very thick, his lip in ribbons. Leaving him where he stood, she went out to the door through which Thanh had dodged and called him back. When he saw Ben his hand flew to his own mouth.

'Oh my God Aran, you kill him.'

Ben glared. 'Some bodyguard you are. Some great fucking bodyguard.'

Hastily Thanh telephoned an all-night medical service and then returned to his boss, dabbing ineffectually at him with cold compresses while Ben flinched and swore. Aran regarded him coldly.

'If you use any more of that language I'll take a hammer to your piano.'

He stopped swearing.

The doctor arrived, examined the damage and asked whether Ben had been drinking. Grudgingly, he nodded.

'H'mm. Then I can't give you a painkiller, which is unfortunate as your nose is fractured and you need three stitches in that lip. You'll have to see a dentist in the morning, and get your nose X-rayed.'

Ben howled with pain while his nose was patched up and his lip stitched, and then Thanh escorted the doctor out, whispering something as he put a large banknote into the man's hand.

'Now, I think maybe we all get some sleep. Aran, you stay in spare bedroom?'

She nodded, and he took her to it, thoughtfully furnishing pyjamas, towels, a toothbrush. She got into the bed, and slept like a baby.

Waking late next morning, with a hangover that did not diminish her grim sense of achievement, she went into the lounge to find that Thanh had taken Ben to get further medical attention. His wife Beth greeted her dubiously before starting to clean up the debris, which was considerable; had she really done all this? Then Beth indicated a note on the table, in Ben's handwriting.

'I suppose it's no use asking what I did?'

She picked up the pen beside it.

'You did drugs,' she wrote curtly underneath. And then, because she still didn't know why he had called her: 'Ring me when you're clean.'

After some juice and a shower she was ready to leave, but hesitated as she passed the open door of Ben's bedroom. She shouldn't – but she had to, just a quick peep.

The room was large and bright, cluttered, done in modern, masculine décor. Curiously she wandered around it, looking at books, tapes, objects brought from foreign travels – and then, a photograph. Just one, a small one in a polished marquetry frame.

It was of herself.

For ten or fifteen seconds she looked at it, her heart racing. And then she went home to face Thierry.

He was at his flat, broody and fretful.

'You went to him, didn't you? You stayed all night?'

'Yes. In the spare room. We had a fight, and I fractured his nose.'

'You what?!'

'Split his lip, too. A doctor had to come and stitch it.'

He couldn't believe his ears. But his relief was enormous.

'I'm sorry about what I did, Aran. But I—'

'It's all right, Thierry. I'd have done the same thing myself. Forget about it.'

They kissed and made up and then, as if still sensing some danger, he took her out for a long walk, talking all the while about the wedding, the honeymoon, the house yet to be bought and furnished. Was it not all very exciting, enticing?

She smiled at him, smiled at the other couples walking on the Heath. But all she thought of was the photograph, and Rhianna, and the cocaine that Ben Halley was never going to touch again. If and when their daughter ever came looking for her father, she wasn't going to find him in jail, in a clinic or in a cemetery.

It was nearly four weeks before he rang, on a russet Saturday in September. His voice was very soft.

'I must see you . . . can you come over?'

'When?'

'Now.'

She was there before noon, apprehensive, elated, her mind buzzing with things she must say, not say, maybe say. When he opened the door she stood on the threshold, looking at him.

'Are you waiting for me to carry you over it?'

They both laughed, and she came in, noting immediately that there was no sign of Beth or Thanh. Barefoot, he was wearing a navy sweater and jeans, smelling freshly laundered, his hair recently cut to chin length. His nose and tooth were fixed, but his lip was scarred. Leaning against the wall with his hands in his pockets, he surveyed her in silence.

'So you – you want to talk to me?' She heard her own voice, squeaky, splintered.

'No. I don't want to talk to you.'

His smile was slightly shy, enquiring, as he held one hand out to her. But he didn't move, and she realised what his gesture was saying to her: this was her decision.

She took one step towards him, a step she knew was going to change the direction of her life. Instantly, his face fragmenting with emotion, he took the other.

Engulfed in his embrace, her neck almost snapping from the force of his kiss, she fell to the floor under him, her mind and body rioting, completely out of control. As were his; he was tearing her dress off, hurting her, suffocating her. Her nails gouged his back as she pulled his sweater off, she was blinded by a flurry of clothes, tears of pain, his hands gripping her with the superhuman strength of death. And it was a kind of death, something transcended, something killed and reborn. His violence was annihilating, her cries unearthly as he entered her, extinguished her, extinguished

374

the person she had been, would have been,

Their bodies burned, their muscles throbbed, their lips bled, the agony was unbearable. It was a minute, a year, a century, it was exquisite, it was demonic. His fingers dug through to her bones, her teeth bit into his shoulder, their skin scorched until she sobbed, and could take no more.

They both wept, knowing that such moments were stolen from the gods.

Afterwards, they were paralysed, pinned to the floor, unable to speak. For a long time Ben lay with his face on her breast, shuddering, drenched in sweat, and she had not the strength to hold him, her arms limp, her eyes glazed. The rest of her life seemed superfluous.

But then she began to shiver, burrow into him for warmth, the salt stinging her eyes, her body bruised and battered. Slowly he raised his mouth to hers, kissed her, his lips velvet on her skin. Wordlessly she put her hand in his, and he got to his knees, his feet, helped her up.

She had no recollection of getting to the bedroom, but the bed was bliss when they reached it, warm and soft, balm to their naked skin. With one hand he held her tight, with the other his fingers caressed her spine. His breath touched her cheek like ash, glowing, dissolving.

'I love you.'

She pushed her hands into his hair, and the weight of his head forced one of them into the pillow; the left hand, the diamond ring digging into her finger. It was painful to them both.

Reaching for the hand, he lifted it out, and held her gaze questioningly, fleetingly, before slipping the ring off. Then, with a smile spreading into every corner of his face, he rolled over and dropped it on the floor.

Day faded into night. They made love again, and again, in the bed, in the shower, back in the bed. She felt as if she had been in a crash, a holocaust, could not imagine walking or talking ever again. But it was much gentler now, had to be; they were sore, tender, exhausted.

Around midnight he got up, and went to make something to eat. Her eyes followed him out of the room, watching his wonderful back, his wonderful legs, the beautiful body that had created Rhianna.

He came back with a tray of sandwiches and some milk. She peered intently into her glass.

'White vodka?'

Curling up beside her on the duvet, he looked down, shamefaced.

'No. No more drugs. You're the drug, now.'

'Why did you do it? Why, Ben?'

He hesitated.

'I was unhappy.'

'About Amery?'

'Yes. Amery and – oh, Aran. Do we have to talk about it?'

'I think we do. But maybe not now.'

'Please, not now. This day has been too perfect. Let's just—'

Suddenly, surprisingly, he started to laugh, look at her with wonder.

'I suppose it's Kermit's turn to beat me up tomorrow?'

'Huh?'

'Kermit. Your frog.'

She thumped him.

'Don't call him that! He's a dear, good man and he's going to be dreadfully upset – oh, Ben, how am I going to tell him?'

He snuggled closer to her.

'I don't know, but you're usually quite good at getting messages across. You could sock him in the jaw and send him spinning back to France.'

'Ben, stop it. I love him.'

He sat bolt upright. 'You what? Aran, you don't, you can't!'

But she nodded. 'I do. I love him. I'm just not *in* love with him.'

'Why did you agree to marry him?'

'Because I wanted . . . I thought I wanted . . .'

'Marriage? Security? Children?'

'Yes.'

'Do you still want them?'

'Yes. I suppose I do, some day. But I don't want them so urgently, so soon. I don't *need* them. You know, when my father died, I thought of all the things he never saw, never tasted, never experienced. He was married, but I don't think that ever made him really happy – and Dursey never even got a chance to find out what might make him happy, discover who he was or what he wanted. I realised I had let myself get bogged down somehow, that it was too soon, I was only twenty-four. Life clipped Dursey's wings, but I don't have to clip my own.'

Taking the tray away, he turned to her.

'I'm glad to hear you say that, Aran. But in fact Amery's death had the opposite effect on me. I saw how lonely he had been, saw what it was to be without a family. He was successful and he had a lot of money, but nobody loved him, there wasn't a single relative at his cremation. I don't want to end up like that.'

376

'You surely don't mean you're starting to want the things I'm starting not to want?'

'No. Not yet. I still have a lot of living to do first, as you do. But if you'd care to stick around for – oh, say five or ten years – I might go down on my knees some day and beg you to marry me.'

His tone was light, but she raised her eyebrows.

'That depends entirely on how many more Kims and Sashas and Charlottes you plan to bag for your trophy collection before then.'

'Oh, Aran! After today? What would be the point?'

'You tell me. What was the point before?'

'I don't know, but the point now is that I'm twenty-six. My needs are changing, my priorities are changing – please, Aran. Give me another chance?'

It was out of her hands, really. After today, her whole life was bound up with his, with him. She could exist without him, but she couldn't live.

Dursey hadn't lived. Conor hadn't lived. She was going to live. Not marry Ben, after all, but *live* with him.

Thierry was distraught. Thierry ranted, raved, stormed up and down, his face distorted by pain, his voice made harsh with hurt.

'I knew it! I knew you were going to do this to me!'

She sat on the sofa, her hands in her lap, her distress forcing her gaze to the floor.

'Thierry, I'm not doing it to you. It's not anything I can help. It – it's life, it's nature, it's chemistry.'

'Chemistry! And how long will that last? Will the chemistry still be there when you're ninety?'

She thought he was beginning to sound very faintly like Molly.

'I don't know. But there's only one way to find out. I have to find out, I have to risk it. I'm so sorry.'

The diamond ring lay on the table between them, winking as his eyes were winking, wet with tears. She knew the wound was very deep, knew how it felt when you loved someone, and they left you. Her words came like an echo.

'I still love you – I still care, want to see you – can't we be friends?'

'Friends? I don't want you to be my friend, I want you to be my wife! Aran, you agreed to marry me!'

'I know. I meant to marry you, I was going to – if my father and brother hadn't died, if Amery hadn't died and Ben hadn't come – oh, Thierry, you were wonderful then, I'll never forget how good. But I can't undo what has happened.'

'You let it happen!'

She knew she had. For the love of one man, she had destroyed another. People survived moments like this, but they did not survive intact. Some part of their soul was withered, and never grew back. Not pristine, not perfect. Not at all, sometimes.

'Thierry, what can I do, what can I say? If there's anything, tell me, and I'll do it.'

His face flushed, his hazel eyes darkened with bitterness, with the contempt she arguably deserved.

'You can do what you're planning to do. Leave me alone. Just leave me, here in this country that I came to for you – you didn't think of that, I suppose? Didn't think of the job I left, the friends and family, the life I'd built?'

Put like that, her selfishness appalled her. She would never do this to anyone again, was unspeakably grieved that she had done it even once. And to Thierry, who cared, who was genuine, who deserved so much better.

But this was what people did to each other, in the battle of the sexes that nature waged. This was how they hurt each other, damaged and maimed. Some day she would have to find a way of warning Rhianna against behaving as she had behaved. You didn't realise, when you were young, you didn't know how it felt until it happened to you.

But it had happened to her, before. She had known, and yet she had done it. She was ashamed. If anything ever went wrong between her and Ben, again, she would be better off alone. Thierry was showing her her own strength, her power to injure and kill. He'd trusted her, and she had crushed his trust, beaten it to dust. But she couldn't fight Ben. Fighting Ben was like fighting herself.

'I won't insult you by asking your forgiveness now, Thierry. But I'll try to earn it, and will ask you then.'

His face looked like a child's or small animal's, uncomprehending, not knowing why he was being hit, maltreated, abused. All he had done was love her, respect her, work hard, offer her the things Ben Halley never had, and maybe never would.

Aran did not see Ben again for several days, asked him not to get in touch until she sorted out her thoughts. She had acted on impulse, and now the implications were hitting her like a thunderbolt. They had to be figured out and faced.

She was so desperately in love with him it took her breath away, made her wonder if she might be going slightly mad. She only had to think of his eyes, his voice, his touch, to feel her mind and body seized with passion, fire flashing through her veins like a fever. The poets were right; it was a form of illness, incurable and maybe fatal. It took hold of sane, sensible people like herself and turned them into tottering wrecks, unable to put two coherent words together. In the car she thought she was dangerous, she heard people hooting at her and saw them mouthing oaths as she forgot to indicate, changed lanes, took wrong turns. Her mind was somewhere between London and lunacy.

It wasn't too late. Thierry would understand if she came back, forgive and forget, put the whole episode down to nerves. She could still salvage a normal, happy, uncomplicated life for them both. That was what everyone would advise her to do. That was what anyone with a lick of sense would do.

Finally she sat down at home one evening and made herself write a list, as all the pop psychologists in the magazines said you should when faced with a difficult decision. So. Ben's good and bad points, Thierry's good and bad ones.

Thierry came out winning by a mile.

Thierry was love, commitment, stability. Thierry would always be there when she needed him, he was strong and responsible, he didn't do flits and he didn't do drugs. He would never make her unhappy.

Ben was madness, a loose cannon that had already gone off once and might go off again. He drank, he womanised, he did cocaine. Even if he had done neither recently, even if he promised never to, he didn't have the iron discipline such abstinence took. He was gorgeous and funny and immensely talented, but he was insecure, contrary, mercurial. He gave a lot, but he took a lot. He was wealthy, but capable of losing everything overnight. Life with him would be as exhausting as it was exciting. She would never be free of anxiety.

And then there was Rhianna to think of. Thierry had already accepted the child, was prepared to include her in their life, love her even though she was Ben's. Whereas being with Ben would mean either continuing to hide Rhianna, in case he rejected her, or owning up to what she had done. Then what? Even if by any miracle he was delighted to discover he had a daughter, he might want to take her from the Rafters. Might spoil her with gifts and goodies, turn her into a confused little showbiz kid. But he was more likely to throw a fit.

That was the trouble with Ben. You just didn't know what he might do. He was wonderful, but he was bad news.

She read the list over and over. And then she threw it in the bin. She was muddled. She was mad. She was Ben's until the heavens cracked open and the sun crashed from the sky.

But she did negotiate. She went to Ben and laid down the law, hoping he wouldn't laugh. He could call her bluff, see she was possessed, would never leave him.

But he didn't. With great solemnity he agreed to all her terms. They would live in Hampstead, buy the house if it was for sale, put down the deepest roots they could.

'Right.'

There would be no more women, no more drugs, not even spirits of any description. When he wanted to party, he'd do it on wine or beer. But he wouldn't do it too often.

'OK.'

Thanh would accompany him everywhere, and he would do as Thanh told him.

'Yes.'

In due course – some time in their thirties – they would have children.

'We will.'

They would save as much money as they spent.

'Uh huh.'

And now he would devote all his attention to his new contract with Flinders, live up to everything Amery Cheam expected of him.

'Absolutely.'

Satisfied, she nodded, caught his eye and they both burst out laughing.

'I mean it, Ben! I mean every word of it and if you don't behave yourself, I'm telling you, you'll be one very sorry little boy.'

'I know I will. I'll need crutches, next time. The services of an undertaker.'

'You've got the picture, yes.'

God, it was like talking to a child! His meek expression was impish already, his charm irresistible as he thrust his cheek at her and pointed to a spot on it.

'Give us a kiss.'

They kissed and hugged, and her happiness would have been complete if only she could stop thinking of Thierry, and Rhianna.

Over the next few months Ben moved back into the Hampstead house in fits and starts, incredulous when he saw the Steinway.

'You kept it, all this time!'

'I thought you might come back for it, but you never did. Why not?'

'I don't know . . . well, to be honest, I felt it was a kind of link with you. But what'll we do now? There isn't room for the Bechstein as well.'

'We could give one to a music school, maybe? You choose which.'

He chose to part with the Bechstein, and they soon found a good home for it. But Aran felt a stab as she said the words. A good home. That's what I sent Rhianna to, she thought, and now she won't be able to come here any more. I'll only ever see her in Ireland, and I'll have to do that in secret. I can't risk letting Ben see her.

His heavy workload meant that it was November by the time Ben was fully installed, with Thanh and Beth in a rented house nearby. One evening she cooked a meal at home, secretly savouring the domesticity of it, and they discussed what they would do in the forthcoming year. In 1984, it looked as if Aran's predictions of social prosperity might finally be going to come true, the recession was ending. Ben eyed her speculatively.

'I need a new manager. It's becoming urgent.'

She thought about it, and shook her head.

'No. Business was never really my first love. You need someone much tougher and more ruthless than me.'

He grinned. 'You can be tough, in my experience.'

'Maybe. But I don't enjoy it. What I'd like to do is start writing lyrics for you again.'

'Would you? That would be great, if Kelwin could be persuaded . . . maybe Jake could assign him to someone else. He's very good, and I don't want to hurt his feelings.'

'He's never written you a number one.'

'No – but it's the music that gets hits, not the lyrics. Well, I suppose they're interdependent, but I've always felt – oh, anyway. Let me talk to Jake. Meanwhile, you could give a hand with the fan club. They're up to their eyes.'

'What, you want me to answer your love letters from besotted teenagers?'

'They're not all teenagers, by any means. You'd be amazed. There are sacks of mail every day, from all sorts of people – you could do it in the mornings and then write lyrics in the afternoons, or work out whatever schedule suits you.'

It occurred to her that she could do worse than intercept perfumed billets-doux written on pink paper, complete with photographs of the smitten senders. It would be one way of keeping control, and of monitoring the pulse of his popularity.

Agreeably, she smiled.

'OK. I'll volunteer, after the new girl takes over my work for Annie in January.'

For no reason she thought of Oliver Mitchell, running to greet her that first day, yelling about a 'new one, 'nuther one!' And now Ciara Keane was coming from Bantry to market Annie's cheeses: yet

381

another emigrant, but one with a job at least. Really she should be running an agency, like Holly. But writing lyrics was going to be so much more fulfilling. What should she write about first?

'Ben?'

'Mm?'

'Do you remember how you felt when Amery died?'

'Do I? How could I not? I'll never forget it, or him. He helped me and encouraged me so much more than my own father ever did. You can't imagine how I miss him – oh, I'm sorry, of course you can. But I feel as guilty about him as you do about Conor. I was the one who suggested that trip to Ireland. I know it wasn't your father's fault, it was just a terrible accident, but it haunts me.'

'It haunts me too, Ben. I gave Dad that boat, and – and I feel his death achieved so much more than his life. It brought us back together. If you could write some music that expresses what we both feel, I could write words to go with it.'

'I could. I'd love to. I'd promised Amery I'd write him a song, and I'd like him to have a memorial. But Jake would have a seizure if I said I was writing a requiem.'

'What's wrong with a requiem? Does everybody not experience death, lose someone they love? We could write a song expressing what they all feel. After all lots of love songs are sad – I don't mean we should write anything mawkish or mournful, but we could do something that reflected Amery's strength, Conor's simplicity.'

He sat back and thought about it.

'It's an idea, Aran. Let's try it. But let's assume that Jake will hate it, everyone will hate it, we'll end up with something that gets locked away in a drawer. It'll just be for us, not a commercial venture.'

'OK. We've got nothing to lose, and it might make us feel better at least.'

Maybe she'd write a song for Dursey too. Something about life being stolen, wasted, untasted. But one thing at a time. Let's do this first, for Amery and Conor, for peace of mind.

They accepted Jake Rowan's immediate veto of the idea, and worked on the song in their own time, content to think that it would be played here at home at any rate, their friends and families would hear it. Aran thought that she could even send a tape to Molly, who was slowly recovering from the shock of being widowed. Her relationship with Molly was still strained, always would be as long as Rhianna existed, but still she thought of her with sympathy. Molly who had never enjoyed her family, but was now alone except for Achill.

What was she feeling or thinking? Wishing she had made more of her children when they were young, while she had them with her? Wishing she had kissed Conor that day fifteen or twenty years ago, the day he did return safely from the storm? Aran wrote to her briefly but regularly, phoned her now that Molly had finally got a telephone. In return her mother told her that she was going to give up the knitting. She was weary of it, and Conor's insurance had left her better off than when he was alive, financially. The co-op could well manage without her.

'What will you do?'

'I thought I'd visit Val for a while, then maybe go to see Sher in America.'

Family ties, Aran thought. After all these years, Molly's family was starting to matter to her. But America – Florida? Somehow Aran couldn't see her basking in the sun, swimming, having fun with her loud noisy grandchildren. In fact it was easier to imagine a nun in a gambling casino, a priest in a brothel, a rabbi tucking into a plate of roast pork. Aran didn't envy Sher one bit.

Ben wanted to spend Christmas in Amery's apartment in New York.

'It'll be quiet there, we can work on the song in peace.'

Aran couldn't say no, couldn't tell him how she longed to go to Rhianna. But in January he would be incarcerated in the studio all day and all night, laying down tracks for a new album. She could slip away then for a day or two.

But Thanh and Beth were coming to New York with them. It was a city, as Thanh said, where Ben wanted watching. On December 23 she phoned Thierry before she left.

'I just wanted to wish you a happy Christmas.'

'I'd rather you hadn't, Aran. How could it be happy without you?'

Oh, guilt. If only there were something she could do, some way to make it up to him! Holly was accusatory about what she had done to him, Dan and Eimear were appalled that she was back with Ben – not only because he was unreliable, which he was, but because he was Rhianna's father. All she could do was promise never to bring him to Dunrathway, and hope for the best. She gave them all kinds of assurances on both counts, and took her oboe with her to New York. Ben had written a part for it into the piece they were composing for Conor and Amery.

The apartment was stunning, the city fascinating, and in spite of herself she found the trip invigorating.

'But what are you going to do with this place, Ben? You can't keep it like a shrine.'

'Our friends can use it. Amery was very hospitable, he'd like to see it alive and in use.'

Wow. Wouldn't Val be thrilled, when she found she could have a roof like this over her head, any time she cared to visit New York! It would be great for the Rafters too, and she thought with irony of Rhianna running around it. Rani and Deva could come too. Deva was thrilled to see her son back with Aran Campion, had made as little secret of her pleasure as Guy had made of his disgust.

'Pay absolutely no attention, my dear. My husband has no idea what a godsend you are to our son. I hope he will make you happy this time – he's a fool if he doesn't. But I think he knows now how much he needs you, and appreciates that you gave up a much more deserving man for him.'

She said all this in front of Ben, who wrinkled his face comically and made some wicked remark about Kermit. But Thierry was still in London, and Ben was conscious of the fact, unaware that Aran's memories of her time with Thierry were like blancmange, soft and sweet, insubstantial. Bland, to be truthful, only it was a truth she never confided to him.

On New Year's Eve Ben got drunk in New York, but only on champagne, so she let it go. Two days later he spent a fortune on hi-fi equipment, but she let that go too, glad that he at least had something to show for the money. Still . . . when they got back to London she consulted Rani and got the name of the hospital she was going to work at in Lucknow. Through that she got the names of some children who needed medical attention, and arranged for them to have it. Every time Ben blew money on a luxury in future, she'd find another child. Things were so cheap in India, the price of a motorbike over here could save a life over there. Some young life like Dursey's.

But wasn't she lucky, Val and Sher wrote, to have landed such a wealthy chap! Sher's tone was cheerful, Val's was envious. Yet Val had scoffed at the idea of a rock singer years ago, been condescending to Ben when she met him, and would dread to be seen in public with him. She saw the money, but she didn't see the risk her sister was taking, Ben's temper tantrums, the speeding motorbike, the vodka he longed to swig by the litre.

He wasn't finding it easy to kick his habits, but he was trying and she was proud of him. One night they lay tenderly entwined in bed, exploring each other's bodies in a way that torched her with lust. Suddenly he leapt up and threw off the covers.

'The piano! My piano!'

Stark naked, he ran downstairs to it, and when she caught up with

384

him she exploded in laughter. Feverishly he was playing little bits, writing them onto manuscript paper and playing them again, looking absolutely ludicrous in his birthday suit. Hastily she pulled the curtains before some passer-by should see him in all his glory, making love to his music instead of to her.

But he finished Amery's song that night, and it was sensational.

Jake wouldn't record it, Myles wouldn't hear of it. It was a very fine song, but it had all the commercial appeal of a funeral. It would *be* his funeral, if it reached the public.

'But it says in my contract I can experiment!'

'Not with suicide.'

'Bugger you both!'

He was as furious as Aran was philosophical. They'd expected this, hadn't they? Jake had said no from the outset.

'Yeah, but I was sure he'd come round. Your lyrics are so different from Kelwin's, they've got real meaning, sensitivity . . .'

'They've got the kiss of death, then! Let's leave it for now. You won't be a rock singer for ever.'

He stamped and muttered for days, but eventually the requiem did end up in a drawer. Resolutely forgetting about it, but feeling better for having written it, Aran stole away to visit Rhianna for a weekend, leaving Ben distracted with other work and Thanh guarding him like a clockwork soldier.

It was a very fraught visit, largely thanks to Luke Lavery who'd given Rhianna and Emmett tambourines for Christmas. Aran couldn't believe how the Rafters' once orderly home had turned into mayhem, how Eimear was screeching like a harridan above the racket, her hair askew and her brown eyes frazzled.

'Out, out to the garden – take the tambourines, take the drum, take the dog – does nobody ever listen to a *word* I *say*?!'

'Heavens, Eimear, calm down. I'll give you a hand.'

Eimear spun round to her.

'It's all Luke's fault, he knows she's musical and he encourages her, he's driving me crazy – a piano next he says – Aran, you can have Rhianna back. Take her to London, take the baby, take them all!'

Eimear's eyes were wild, Dan was laughing, it really was chaos. In black bootees and red tights, Rhianna looked like the little devil she was, a kind of punk cherub, giggling and squealing. But she was musical, in a horrible high-pitched way.

'I can see her winning one of Achill's talent contests in the pub.'

'Yeah. So can we. In the pub at five, in jail at six. Either she will or we will. God, Dan, open some wine before my mind snaps.'

Aran considered.

'You know, Eimear, if Rhianna does want musical training later on – serious training I mean – you must tell me. I'll give you the money for it.'

'But what would you tell Ben it was for?'

'I'll figure it out, if he even notices. He throws money around. But he'd consider Rhianna an important investment, if he knew.'

'Oh, Aran . . . I don't know how you can stand the stress of not telling him.'

'Telling him that I gave his daughter to you? Eimear, my mind freezes.'

'But he might accept it. Might even think you'd done the right thing.'

'Look, he wasn't there when I did it. It's my responsibility, and I know it's better for her to be here with you. You – you do love her, don't you? Even when she is a pest?'

'We adore her. She's so precious to us, you can't imagine.'

But Aran could imagine, and wasn't going to risk disrupting this family for anything. Even though she secretly winced to hear Rhianna call Eimear 'Mummy', wished she could mother her little girl herself, she couldn't unravel the ties that had been forged, would never make any of them feel insecure. It must be enough that she was able to see the child, cuddle and play with her, participate in any important decisions. Eimear was very generous about consulting her, and Rhianna was happy as the day was long.

Meanwhile, she had other duties in Dunrathway. First she went next door to see Annie, and then she went down to the cottage on the waterfront. After a long suspicious pause while Molly waited to recognise her knock, the door creaked open a fraction.

'Ah, Aran. I thought maybe you were too busy with the Rafters to bother coming here.'

On the defensive, already. Not five seconds in the house, and she was having to defend herself. She bit her tongue as Molly surveyed her.

'You look well. But red's not your colour, Aran, you really shouldn't wear it. I suppose you got that hairdo in London?'

No, she felt like shouting, I got it in bloody Botswana! Why must Molly always do this, use that tone that implied she could do nothing right? Was it going to be this way for ever, prickly, sparring over nothing? She was goaded to frankness.

'Well, Mother, black is certainly your colour. Wasn't it great not to have to get a new coat for Dad and Dursey's funerals.'

Molly looked at her sharply, and there was a truce after that. But the visit was a disaster. Aran noticed there was no sign of Achill.

'Where is he, at work?'

'Oh, aye, it's the pub morning, noon and night. The musicians and the barmaid – that little Keegan one, a right slattern she is.'

Lovely. Next thing Achill would move out to live with his 'slattern' and his negative, critical mother would wonder why he'd gone away on her. As in her teenaged years, Aran found herself groping for neutral, trivial subjects. Ben couldn't be mentioned, because Molly detested him, Rhianna couldn't be mentioned because she simply pretended the child didn't exist. Mention of Conor or Dursey would produce a flood of self-pity.

'How was your stay with Val?'

'Hmph. A babysitter, that's all I was. She asked me once too often so I packed my bags and came home.'

How often, Aran wondered, was too often? Twice?

'When are you going to Sher?'

'In April.'

'Well, I'll buy your ticket for you, and give you spending money.'

'Aye. That's nice. Imagine me going on a plane at my age. I hear they're very hot and stuffy, your feet swell up.'

Your lip will swell up, Aran thought, when I put the carving fork through it. She smiled amiably.

'I have to go now, Mother. I'll drop in again tomorrow. Maybe we could go to the pub for lunch.'

Gin would do it. She'd have six gins for lunch tomorrow and not feel a thing. Letting herself out, she skirted round the harbour in the direction of Fenner's Hill, noting how quiet the town was. The boating tragedy and the dolphins' departure had cast a pall, this would not be a good year for tourism.

When she reached Hannah Lowry's house the lawn was starred with crocuses and primroses, and Hannah came hurrying out to meet her in the driveway. More than twenty years older than Molly, she was wearing lipstick and perfume, hugging Aran as she ushered her in, plying her with questions.

Was she playing her oboe, writing poetry – oh, lyrics, really? How interesting, how challenging! She must tell her all about them, and the name of whatever genius had done that gorgeous hairstyle – no matter that she was nearly eighty, she still loved to see a good cut, a bit of style. And what did Aran think of this new Boy George, wasn't he a scream? Another wild minstrel boy, just like Ben. Was Ben well, were his records going to be put on these new CDs now? Hannah wanted all the news from London as she poured sherry, as elegant as ever in a tweed burgundy suit.

I'm glad I gave your daughter my daughter, Aran thought. Not glad that I had to, but very glad that I did.

Chapter Seventeen

For Aran's twenty-fifth birthday Ben surpassed himself. A massive basket of freesias, a lewd birthday card and then a casual glance around the house.

'Let's do it. Let's buy it.'

Oh, yes! She hadn't said any more about it, but the lease was about to expire. The only problem was, she didn't know whether the owner would sell, or what price he might want.

They rang to enquire, and an hour later the estate agent rang them back. The owner was willing to sell. For £300 000.

'T-t-three hundred thousand?'

Ben didn't even flinch. 'Just see if you can beat him down a bit. If not, I'll have to make sure I have a big hit this year.'

After some further negotiation she talked the tag down to £285 000.

'Oh God, Ben, it's still an awful lot – you said you never wanted a mortgage—'

'I don't. Tell him I'll give him £275 000 cash.'

By lunchtime it was agreed. The house was theirs as soon as they signed the paperwork. Her head was whirling like a carousel.

'Oh Ben, I love you to *bits*.'

But that was why he'd bought it for her, without the least interest in it himself. She'd love him even if he hadn't a penny. She had loved him then; otherwise he might still be a waiter moonlighting at the piano in the North End Road. He hugged her to him.

'It's for parties, you see. Wild drunken orgies. Starting in about eight hours' time.'

'What?'

'A surprise party, for your birthday. Everyone is coming, so I thought I'd better give you enough notice to get a bit of glitter.'

'Oh!'

She wanted him to come shopping with her, but he said no; he might be mobbed in Harvey Nicholls, kidnapped by some determined fan. What he actually meant was that the caterers were coming while she was out, and the balloon man and the florist. Twenty-five was a quarter of a century, a biggie.

'But I never shop in Harvey Nicks!'

He fished in his pocket and handed her a credit card, tied up in a tiny silver ribbon.

'Well, make your début.'

She flushed. Thanh had told her all about Sasha and her magic trick of making money vanish. Surely he didn't think she'd do that?

'Aran, sweetheart, if you shopped till you dropped you still wouldn't spend in a year what Sasha spent in an hour. Just go, and have fun!'

Off she went, only to end up in Miss Selfridge. It would take rather more than one day, she thought, to get the hang of Harvey Nicholls. But she bought a dress, shoes and a woven belt, feeling wickedly extravagant when the bill totalled £80. The instant she came home, Ben whooshed her up the stairs.

'Bath. Hair. Face. It'll take you all your time to get ready.'

Lying in the bath, she wondered what was being hidden downstairs. There was a lot of noise, muffled thumps and rustlings, she got the feeling there were other people lurking somewhere. Oh, Ben was brilliant at birthdays! She still couldn't believe they were back together.

But when she came downstairs, all dressed up, he had disappeared. The house had gone deathly silent. Where was he, where was Thanh? A little anxiously, she threw open the door of the sitting room. It was in darkness.

'Ben?'

The lights came on, and there he was, at the piano surrounded by Thanh, Beth, Rani, Deva, Myles and Kevin, Sinéad Kenny and Gavin Seymour, all their grinning friends.

'Happy birthday, dear Aran, happy birthday to you . . .'

Shrieking and laughing they all dived on her, kissing, hugging, dressed to kill. The double doors were open, and at the far end was a huge buffet festooned in flowers, with a white birthday cake in the shape of a clef. The entire room was full of white and yellow balloons, the sound of popping corks and singing voices. She felt like a child in Disneyland.

'Oh – I – I – think I'm going to cry!'

But no, there had been tears enough last year. She laughed instead as they sang the whole song, and then Ben stood up to toast her as Thanh put a glass of champagne in her hand. It was going to be a happy night, a great night.

It was wonderful. Holly and Walter were there, her friends from the music group, Mr Rudelstein from the bookshop, Jake Rowan and – and Dan and Eimear! She ran to them disbelieving.

'How did you get here?'

'We swam,' said Dan drily, and gave her a huge kiss. Then a present, lots of presents from everyone, songs and music and laughter. After a breathless while she got Eimear into a corner and discovered the awful fright Ben had given them.

'We nearly died when he rang us – we thought he'd found out about Rhianna. But he was inviting us here, he even gave us the tickets. He might be iffy, Aran, but he's marvellous.'

Iffy – God, there was a whole table full of spirits. Vodka, whisky, everything. She could smell cannabis too, from Clem's direction. But then Ben came up and put his arm around her.

'Only champagne. All night, I promise.'

'You're a pet and I'm crazy about you.'

He stuck to it too, didn't drink much at all but played the piano instead, *Jailhouse Rock* and *Demolition*, all the old favourites. Everyone was dancing, the roof was lifting, Rani was rocking with Mr Rudelstein who, at seventy, said he couldn't wait for her to do the belly dance she'd promised him. And far from missing Guy, who'd pleaded work, Deva was talking animatedly to Kevin Ross, waving a plate of prawns until one actually flew off. At about ten, Ben surrendered the piano to Myles and came to dance with her.

'Good party, huh?'

'Fabulous!'

She was spinning to *Good Golly Miss Molly*, cracking up at Ben's explanation that her mother couldn't come because her tiara was at the cleaner's, when she thought she heard the phone ring. A minute later Beth came up to her.

'It's for you.'

Molly. Molly had rung to wish her a happy birthday, and she felt guilt springing up, shut the door on the noise as she went out. But it was Thierry.

'I just wanted to wish you a happy birthday – I called earlier, but you were out.'

Thanh hadn't told her, or Beth. So Ben must have answered the phone, not given her the message, doing unto Thierry as Thierry had done unto him. He sounded sad, and she felt sad for him.

'Why don't you come over? We're having a party.'

'Oh, no. He'd go mad.'

'No, he wouldn't, I promise – there are so many people here he won't even notice. Please do, Thierry. I'd like to see you.'

His voice was wistful. 'I'd like to see you too, Aran.'

'Then come!'

'All right, I will. If you're sure.'

She wasn't a bit sure, but she'd talk to Ben, he wouldn't deny her anything tonight. And, after a mouthful of curses, he did give in. Provided she didn't dance or dally with Kermit, he could come.

He arrived with a bottle of wine and a little gift in a packet, looking mournful.

'I was going to post it. It's only a book.'

Shakespeare's sonnets. She was very touched. Brushing her lips to his cheek, she brought him in and introduced him to several people, put a glass in his hand. He began to brighten a bit.

Ben was back at the piano, watching like a hawk as he sang with two other well-known rock stars, so she left Thierry and went to dance with Thanh. Oh, it was great to be back with this whole crowd, wild as they were! Poor Thierry would have given her a party too, but she hoped he didn't feel she would ever compare his generosity with Ben's. He was a terrific guy in his own right, his own way.

But he'd melted into the crowd, she couldn't see him at all.

It was a very busy summer. When Ben finished recording his first album for Flinders he went on a tour of Spain and Italy, and Aran inhaled the Mediterranean air with delight, revelling in the sharp smell of pine and lavender, the bright colours. Scarlet, bitter lemon, ochre, turquoise and veridian, all set against blinding white . . . then the dusty browns and pinks of Tuscany, the mad medieval city of Florence. Everyone thought of it as a dreamy place, but in fact it was frantic, the fans were wilder than in any other venue. And such noise! After the silence of Venice the traffic seemed insane, but during the day they escaped into the Boboli Gardens, the Uffizi Gallery, the beautiful Baptistry with its golden panelled doors. She had never thought she'd be lucky enough to see this gorgeous, bewildering country again, and she made the most of it.

One day they went with Kevin Ross to Siena, where there was an awesome cathedral to be seen, of striped black and white marble. Ben wasn't big into cathedrals, but unlike many rock singers he was open to culture, to the classic pieces of art and sculpture, aware that the painters and architects were the equivalent of Mozart or Beethoven. When they finally sank into chairs on the square in Siena he looked a little tired, but she thought his exhaustion was more physical than spiritual. Touring was so draining, disorientating.

'Are you all right?'

'Sure, I'm fine.'

But at that moment two schoolgirls spotted him, came running over for autographs, and soon there was a crowd; even in this timeless old town he could get no peace. Thanh and Kevin tried to keep order, but he signed every scrap of paper with a ready smile, appreciating the adulation, feeding the monster. They went back to Florence without even having had their cup of coffee.

But he didn't resort to vodka, uppers or downers or anything else. Wine with food, beer with the crew, but that was all. He was working hard at it and knew she was watching him.

'How'm I doing?'

His grin was contagious. 'Great! We'll need a separate truck to bring home all your brownie points.'

Thanh can guard him against everything else, she thought, but I can protect him from himself. He'll be fine so long as I go everywhere with him, keep him under surveillance.

But when they got back to London in July Dan phoned to tell her Rhianna had the mumps, and she was stricken with guilt. Of course Dan and Eimear would take care of her, but she wished she could go to the child, confide her anxiety to Ben. He was her father, they were a family in blood if not circumstance . . . but apart from anything else, how would they cope with Rhianna even if they did have her? Did you take a four-year-old out of nursery school, disrupt her routine, expose her to the heat and noise and crude company of the roadies? Or did you stay home with her, leave Dad to run wild abroad, seeking solace in groupies?

For the thousandth time, she reminded herself that she had done the right thing, had had no way of foretelling the future. But she hardly slept for a fortnight, until Dan called to say the tot was demanding her drum, so they reckoned she was over the worst. Yet in her dreams Aran saw a flushed little face, heard a fevered little voice calling for Mummy.

'I'm here! I'm here!'

She was sitting bolt upright in bed, panting, running with sweat. Roused from a deep sleep, Ben was reaching for her.

'What is it? A nightmare?'

'Yes – no – just a dream, Ben. It was just a dream.'

He took her in his arms. 'It's all right. I'm here. I'm here.'

Rani was due to leave for Lucknow, a fully-fledged doctor at last. Ben wanted to invite her for dinner before she left.

'Just the three of us. There'll be a bigger dinner in Surrey to celebrate her graduation, but I'd like to have her to myself for an evening.'

Family ties, again. Ben had always been very fond of his sister. They chose a warm evening in late July and Aran cooked a special meal, but when Rani arrived she seemed subdued, almost downcast. Concerned, Ben hugged her.

'What's the matter, poppet?'

Rani smiled wanly, looking small in her sari, as if she were shrinking into it. At twenty-five she was a beautiful, confident woman, but tonight there was something vulnerable about her.

'I've just had my shots, that's all. I'm a little under the weather.'

'Oh, you poor thing.'

They tried everything to cheer her up. For a while it seemed to help. But as the evening went on her spirits flagged again. Aran thought maybe some music would soothe her, so Ben went to the piano and began to play a light, pretty piece of Strauss.

Rani burst into tears and began to sob piteously.

'Oh, Ben, stop, you're upsetting her.' Aran turned to Rani and took her hand comfortingly. 'Is it leaving home, Rani? Is that what's bothering you – your family and friends?'

Rani nodded, her kohl running down her face. She seemed unable to speak.

'But it's only for two years. We'll write to you all the time, you'll soon settle down. Think of the lovely hot sun, the new experiences, the new people you'll meet.'

Rani put her head in her hands, leaned her elbows on the table and sobbed her heart out.

'T-that's just it!'

Mystified, they gazed at her. Eventually she leaned on Ben's chest, clinging to him like a child, and looked up at him as if her big brother could make everything right again. But still there was something hesitant in her voice when she managed to find words.

'I – I have met someone new, already. Here in London.'

Aran was open-mouthed. A man, did she mean? Rani Halley was crying over a man?

'Oh, is that all? Rani, don't be silly! You've said a million times yourself, they're not worth weeping over! Come on now, have a cup of tea and calm down. You're a new woman, a feminist, you know your work is more important than anything else.'

'No, it isn't! Not now! I mean, yes it is, but he – he's important too, he's very important, I love him!'

Ben was inclined to laugh.

'My man-eating sister is in love? And who's the hero of this amazing hour?'

Aran frowned at him. 'Stop, Ben, leave her alone. She's just a bit

394

overwrought because India is so far away, so exciting – but you'll love it when you get there, Rani. You even speak Hindi, don't you?'

'Yes – but I don't want to go! I mean I do want to go, I am going, but I can't go without him.'

'Without who? Who is he?'

Rani gulped, looking soulful and nervous all at once.

'Thierry. Thierry Marand.'

Aran was aghast, Ben looked as if he would explode.

'Aran's ex? *Kermit*?'

'Y-yes! We met at your birthday party, but I didn't want to say anything, I was afraid you – oh, Aran, I feel awful, I'm so mixed up.'

For a minute they all sat in silence, digesting it. Then Aran giggled hysterically.

'Rani, I don't believe this. The last time I saw Thierry his life was in ruins, and the last time I spoke to you you were a diehard feminist.'

Rani roused herself a bit. 'I'm still a feminist. I still believe in careers and equal opportunities and civil rights and—'

'And budgies and aspidistras!' Aran was laughing outright.

'Oh, all right! I admit it, I do want to marry him. But I can't, I'm going to In – India—' She began to sob again, while Ben began to fall around laughing.

'Take him with you! Take the damn man with you, out of my life! Am I doomed to see him on every corner for the rest of my days? Well, Miss Campion, so much for your lovelorn swain whose life I was given to understand I'd destroyed. Nine months later he's seduced my sister!'

'He didn't seduce me, I – well, I felt so sorry for him, he was lost at the party, so I went up and started talking to him, oh, what am I going to do?'

'What does he want to do?'

'Well, he says he can't come to India because he's only been a year or so in his job here, he came here for Aran and now he can't dig up the new roots he'd only just put down, I think he suspects I might change my mind like you did. But I won't. He's wonderful, I don't know how you gave him up, he's so kind and thoughtful, he takes such care of me—'

'Takes care of you? Since when did you need taking care of?'

'Well, I don't really, but maybe everyone does, a bit – he needs me, you see, and I need him too. But India needs me, those poor children—'

Ben was fighting to contain the hilarity, Aran was still incredulous and beginning to feel a little bit miffed. Of course poor Thierry couldn't be expected to leave England after he'd already left France.

But poor Thierry hadn't languished quite as long as she'd feared he might.

'Rani, he's a supermarket manager. He'd be worse than useless if he went with you, he'd only distract you – pull yourself together! These are the first two years of your career! They're important!'

Another helpless little sob.

'It's easy for you to say that, Aran. You weren't in love with him the way I am.'

Aran glanced at Ben. 'Is that so? Did he say that?'

'Well, yes actually, we discussed it all one night. He says he only realises now how you felt about Ben, why you could never get over him. But if I go to India, I'll never get over Thierry. My life will be ruined.'

Ben was smirking from ear to ear.

'Rani, dearest, if it's such a great passion, I'm sure he'll wait for you. What's two years to a man who's found his beloved, his destiny?'

'Oh, you can laugh. You were just as bad yourself, when Aran wasn't around.'

'But she's around now, isn't she? After four years apart, here we are together, a shining example to you both.'

Rani looked a little more hopeful. 'Do you think Thierry would wait, like you did? I mean, it's too late for me to back out—'

Aran thought she was hearing things. 'Back out? Of your work? Rani Halley, it's your priority, you can't mean that.'

'Well, I've got two priorities now, we want to marry and have children – is that so awful?'

It certainly would have been awful, Aran thought, if I'd ever listened to *you*. If you ever marry Thierry – my fiancé, no less – I'm going to give you a damn budgie for your wedding present. The nerve of you, of him! And then a babygro I suppose, the year after that. Pink or blue, with teddies or bunnies? The Lindo wing for Mrs Marand, Daddy will deliver Precious?

Thinking of Guy, she was convulsed. His blue-blooded British son-in-law had gone bust, while his rock singer son was making a fortune. Chanda was divorced, Ben was happy. Guy had a half-Irish granddaughter and now he was going to have half-French grandchildren.

The gods weren't being very good to Guy.

Rani spent her remaining few weeks at home in a sorry state, unable to decide whether she was doing the right thing. Thierry had said he would wait for her, but two years was a long time. Up to the very day of her departure she was plagued by doubt, turning to everyone for reassurance. Her parents assured her she must go, that everything would be fine, but Aran wasn't so sure.

What if Thierry didn't wait?

For Rani to waste her training and talents would be a tragedy. But it had taken her as long to find a man she could love as it had taken her to become a doctor. What if her career cost her the only love of her life? Was there some helpful chapter in the feminists' rulebook about what to do then? Ben found the irony of her plight hilarious, but Aran knew he was as concerned as she was. After the first shock of discovering their relationship, they felt sorry for them both, and found themselves in the ridiculous position of promising to 'mind' Thierry while Rani was away. She departed for Lucknow in floods of tears.

But Aran had never been happier. Writing lyrics was a pleasure, and writing them for Ben gave everything extra flavour, extra purpose. Once or twice she tried collaborating with Kelwin Hughes, but the experiment was not a success. Kelwin had his system and regarded her as a threat to it; after a few attempts they abandoned the attempt. But other big names had signed with Flinders since Ben chose that company, so Kelwin was in increasing demand to write for them. Like Thierry, he did not languish jilted for long.

In the autumn, Ben decided to revamp his image. Jake worried about changing what was already successful, but he was adamant: if you didn't adapt you got left behind. Cutting his hair short, he decreed a more forceful, macho look on stage, leather instead of lycra, boots instead of ballet shoes or bare feet. Aran was bemused.

'Why?'

'Because if I look harder, I can get away with singing softer songs. Get your oboe, Aran. We're going to work on that requiem again.'

For weeks they played and sang together, on their own and with other musicians. She loved participating, loved the way he interpreted the words she'd written, but didn't see the point of it all.

'Here's the point. We're going to do this song live at the Ally Pally.'

'We? What?'

'My concert at Alexandra Palace in November. We're not going to tell Jake or anyone except Kevin, and the musicians who will be sworn to secrecy. You're going to play with them – on your own too, for the solo part.'

The very thought terrified her. But it thrilled her too, to think the requiem would be heard in public at last. As for playing on stage – well, Hannah Lowry would probably say it was high time she did. She set her mind to practising round the clock, driven by his faith in her.

But the Ally Pally! Jake Rowan would be apoplectic when he saw her coming on stage, Myles would go through her for a short cut. As for the audience – oh, sweet Jesus.

'Aran, this song is for Amery, Conor and Dursey. Just imagine they're in the audience. You're only playing for them. Forget everyone else.'

But for a week beforehand she could hardly eat or sleep, high with nerves, impervious to Ben's confident encouragement. Still, she asked Sinéad to come along and tape the event – if by any miracle it was good, she wanted Dan and Eimear to hear it.

On the night, the venue was full. For the first half of the concert she sat backstage, watching everything go according to plan, a little bit encouraged to hear enthusiasm and applause. The audience liked Ben's new look, was in a good mood. And then, halfway through the second half, it was time for her to slip into her seat amongst the backing musicians, feeling horribly conspicuous even in a sober grey dress. Raising his microphone, Ben turned to her.

'And now a new song, written by Aran Campion who plays the oboe in public for the first time tonight.'

With one ear she heard claps and whistles, with the other she heard Jake swearing, quite clearly from the wings. They'd had to get someone to divert him while she took her place. Ben continued to chat nonchalantly.

'This is a special song for three very special people. We'd like your opinion of it, so will you listen carefully?'

The audience shouted that they would, and he sat down at the piano. As Aran put her oboe to her lips she looked out at what seemed to be a million people. But only three mattered.

The first sweet notes made her smile as she looked at Ben in his chunky leather jacket and cheeky red trousers, but then there was a tricky fugue that took all her attention, and she was aware of silence falling. They were listening all right. Listening so you could hear a pin drop.

It was five minutes long – far too long to record, as Jake had mentioned amongst his other objections – and they were halfway through before she began to relax, discover that she was enjoying this. Enjoying it hugely. Even if the audience hated it and it was never heard again, she could say she had played it, done it. For Conor's sake, for Amery's and Dursey's, she gave it all her attention, all the emotion their memory brought to mind, everything she possibly could. Around her she could feel the other musicians' support, across the stage she could feel Ben's approval. He was looking at his keyboard, but she knew his mind was on her, and that they were perfectly in tune.

His voice got stronger as the music gathered force, staying on top of it so he was never swamped, every word was loud and clear. Every word she had written, about strength and simplicity, about three men who loved the sea. She was so proud of him, and although she'd never met Amery she thought he would be too.

It took courage to do this, to try a new song so different from the others, to risk Jake's fury and the audience's displeasure. He was going to get a right roasting later tonight. And, when the requiem was finally finished, there were a few seconds of bewildered silence before the audience reacted.

Lots of applause, lots and lots of it, but a few catcalls too, some angry boos and whistles, some people feeling confused or gypped or both. Ben stood up and faced them, went to the edge of the stage with his microphone.

'So what do you think? Should we record this song?'

Puzzled, the audience stared at him. It wasn't often that established stars asked their opinion about what they should do. Ben grinned at them.

'Come on, hands up! Who wants to hear this song again? How many of you?'

Wondering, Aran gazed at him herself. He hadn't told her he was going to do this. But then she saw hands going up, some dubious at first, then more resolute as the majority wish became apparent. They did want him to record it. Him, and therefore her?

He was thrilled.

'Are you sure?'

'Yeah!' they yelled.

'Absolutely sure?'

'Yeah!' Louder.

'Totally sure?'

'Yes! Yes!' They were laughing now, but decided, determined. About seventy per cent of them had their hands up, some were dragging their reluctant friends' hands into the air.

'OK then, let's do it! Let's make this requiem a number one hit! Because I'll be sacked if it's not, and it'll be all your fault! I'll say you people at the Ally Pally made me do it, and you were wrong!'

Laughing herself, Aran wondered at this rapport he had, this great genius for getting an audience on his side. But it was time she made herself scarce. Standing up, she began to edge off the stage, just as he turned to her and, to her horror, a spotlight shone in her face.

'Does this lady deserve special applause? This lady who wrote the words and played the oboe?'

They replied that she did, and she couldn't believe it – thousands

399

of people clapping her, at the Alexandra Palace! Shyly she looked at them as she took a bow, noticing that the other musicians were clapping too. What a night! But she ran off stage as fast as she could, and left Ben to get on with it.

Jake Rowan was in the wings, with steam all but coming out of his ears.

'You brats! You – you little brats! I'm going to have Ben Halley's head on a plate for this!'

'Oh, Jake! They liked it, it worked!'

'Yeah, but what if it hadn't?'

'Then you could have had his head on a plate.'

He eyed her as a fox might eye a rabbit. 'Did he put you up to this or did you put him?'

'We – we were partners in crime. But Jake, you will let him record it now, won't you? Please?'

'Do I have a choice? I must say, he's one clever cookie. I was sure they'd loathe it. Five minutes long for chrissake, and a requiem!'

'Yes, but Ben's fans know he's oddball, they've always let him experiment on them. They like to feel part of things, you know, included. That's why they're so loyal, always learn the words of his songs and sing along with him . . . I bet they'll all buy this record, just to show they were right about him tonight.'

'Hmph. Next thing I suppose it'll be Scottish dirges or mazurkas or something, we'll have Tibetan monks chanting their way into the charts.'

'Well, why not? Remember that Belgian nun in the sixties, *Soeur* Something? There's room for everything, Jake. The charts aren't the exclusive monopoly of loudmouths with attitude.'

'And what's Mr Halley?'

But he was starting to smile reluctantly, and she knew they'd won. As she headed for Ben's dressing room he called after her.

'Hey, Aran.'

'Yes, Jake?'

'You play a mean oboe. You will play it when we record this bloody thing, won't you?'

Oh, yes. Oh, wow. Oh, wait till Dan and Eimear heard! And Luke and Hannah and – and Mother!

But Mother was missing in action. To Aran's surprise she'd gone back to Florida and announced her intention of staying there for Christmas. Sher's letter a week later was shrill.

'Why me? Twice in one year, she picks me. She's driving the kids crazy, Norbert has taken up golf, I'm going round the twist – she hates the sun, hates the traffic, the food, everything on television, and yet she comes back for more. I don't know what I did to deserve this.'

Ben laughed as Aran read the letter aloud to him. They were both dizzy with delight after their success at the Ally Pally. She knew it was his attitude as much as anything that had won the day, but he insisted it was her oboe and her lyrics.

'You've no excuse now. You'll have to play more and write lots of songs for me.'

So she did, fuelled by the memory of their magical night and anticipation of the record they were to make together. It was scheduled for March, on the first album of 1985. Depending on reviews, Jake said it might then be released as a single. *Might*. But that was good enough for Ben, who had fought and won his argument about the length of it. Jake argued that nobody had an attention span of five minutes; he retorted that it was patronising the fans to say that about them, that they would sense if they were being treated like morons and reject a tight little soundbite that barely made sense. Wasn't Rossini's *William Tell* overture twelve minutes long, wasn't Ravel's *Bolero* fourteen minutes?

'Yes, but they're classics.'

'They are now. They weren't when they were written.'

So Jake gave in, and Ben was much impressed.

'That's the difference between Schwabbe and Flinders. That's why Amery chose Jake for me. Even when he's beaten he doesn't take it personally or hold a grudge. He still reckons the song isn't commercial, but he'll promote it wholeheartedly.'

This victory was a great start to the new year, and although Aran heard one or two negative comments most people were generous in their enthusiasm. Even Thierry said he would buy a copy, much as it grieved him to support the man who had stolen his first fiancée away from him ... knowing he was teasing, and thinking of Rani, Aran began to meet him occasionally for lunch or coffee. Ben wasn't nuts about that, but supposed he'd better learn to like his future brother-in-law.

'So long as he behaves himself. If he leches at you or lets Rani down, I'll kill him.'

Two years was a test, but so far Thierry seemed to be passing it, much to Guy Halley's chagrin. He wanted a professional man for his daughter, not someone 'in trade'. But Rani's letters remained full of Thierry, dreamy soppy missives that amused them no end. How the mighty were fallen!

In February Aran went to visit the Rafters once again. Ben looked at her quizzically.

'Again? What is the great attraction over there?'

'Mother, of course,' she replied archly, but she felt terrible. If only she could tell him, take him with her!

Rhianna was getting bigger and bolder, talking a mile a minute, beginning to latch onto Aran as someone who seemed to take special interest in her. Flying down the drive, she bounded into her arms with whoops and kisses.

'Aran, I've got a pony! Come see!'

Tugging her by the hand, she led her out to the field that separated the Rafter bungalow from the McGowan farmhouse, and sure enough there was a little Shetland contentedly cropping the grass. The pony had been promised for her fifth birthday, but she'd inveigled Dan into producing it sooner.

'Only six weeks sooner, but God almighty Aran, she had us driven demented.'

Dan lifted her up and held her while she trotted around bareback, clutching the pony's mane, never taking her eyes off her mother.

'Are you watching me, Aran?'

'Yes, muffin! I'm watching you.'

As usual Aran took photographs to add to the stack she kept in a shoebox in the attic. Ben had never been in it, but still she lived in terror that he would find them. With every passing week and month, her secret seemed to grow bigger, her guilt greater. But always Rhianna's smiles reassured her. Their little girl was having a wonderful childhood, much healthier and more secure than anything they could offer her in London. And there were Emmett and Sorcha too, little siblings to play with, keep her from getting spoiled. She liked lots of attention.

'Will I sing for you, Aran? Will I sing now?'

Aran said yes, whereupon she instructed Dan to lift her down off the pony and began to warble *The Teddy Bears' Picnic*, right there in the middle of the field.

' "If you go down to the woods today, you're sure of a big surprise" . . . come on, Aran! Sing it with me!'

And so the three of them stood there absurdly, herself and Dan and the child, singing the ditty like drunks at closing time. As she looked at the mite in her blue jeans and pink sweater, with her big brown eyes, bobbing curls and rosebud mouth, Aran hardly knew whether to laugh or cry. Dan saw her lips quiver.

'You OK, sweetheart?'

'Oh, yes Dan, I am . . . it's just . . . she's so cute, isn't she?'

'Yes. Particularly when she's asleep.'

'Oh, Dan!'

402

But after two days she could see his point. Rhianna was exhausting. The reality of such a lively child, she had to admit, really was a fulltime job.

'Happily, she'll be starting school in September.'

Aran looked at Eimear as she spoke, wondering how some women managed three children and jobs as well. They must be shattered – and maybe short with the children, sometimes? Not that anyone could equal Molly in that department. Molly sat her down when they met, and delivered some news.

'I'm thinking of selling this house.'

'Oh, are you? Well, a bigger one would be nice, and more comfortable for you and Achill.'

'Achill has nothing to do with it.'

'But he– ?'

'He can get a flat like all the other young folk. There's one vacant over Sweeney's shop. Let him entertain his young one there, and see how he likes having to pay all his own bills.'

'Mother! You don't want to live alone, surely? At your age?'

'My age? I'm only fifty-six.'

Aran blinked. Molly had always made such a thing about her age, dressing and thinking like an old woman, that everyone had come to believe she was one.

'So where are you thinking of moving to?'

'America.'

'*America*? I thought you meant down the road!'

'Well I don't mean down the road. I mean Florida. The – the weather's better.'

The weather? But Sher had said Mother complained on an hourly basis about the heat, the insects, the food and the 'coloureds', until finally she'd pointed out that if Molly continued to call black people that she'd end up in court charged with racism.

'Are – are you going to move in with Sher?'

'And those children of hers? I am not. No, I thought I'd get a little place of my own. Maybe you could give me a hand, since that singer of yours is doing so well.'

Well, yes, she would give her a hand. She wouldn't even tell that singer of hers, but use whatever royalties she might earn from the requiem. She'd told Molly about it, but been brushed aside. Rock music was no place for a requiem, it was sacrilege and Molly didn't hold with it at all. So Aran didn't explain that it was a memorial to Conor and Dursey.

But this was a more serious matter. She couldn't say she'd pine to death if Molly went to America, but she was worried for her. Despite

403

her cynicism Molly was frighteningly naïve, could be a danger to herself abroad, travelling with a closed mind, a total lack of sophistication or humour. And Sher couldn't babysit her round the clock.

'I will help, if you really want to go, but I think you should give it a bit more thought.'

'Why? Sure what's to hold me here? Nobody ever visits me at all, I'd be better off in the sun.'

There was a grain of truth in it. Apart from her children's duty visits, few people did come to see Molly. After all her years in the knitting group she had made no close friends, and although six of her ten brothers and sisters still lived in Ireland they didn't come either. Yet Aran was amazed that her mother would take such a radical step as to leave the home she knew, the village that was safe and familiar. The only thing she'd ever said she enjoyed in America was some prayer meetings she'd discovered in Sher's local church.

So why was her tone so firm, her arms akimbo across her chest in a way that defied debate? Thinking of Florida's high crime rate, Aran looked at her anxiously.

'Well, if you're sure about this, but I think you should consider—'

'I'm sure. I'll sell the house and you can give me the rest. I can live on the insurance money and maybe even find a little job.'

Aran knew there was other money too, a lump sum that Paddy Clafferty had decently given Conor's widow even though the accident had not happened on his boat. But—

'What kind of job?'

'How do I know? Won't I see when I get there?'

And that was that. Molly sold the house and emigrated three months later, in the same summer that Ben had his first number one record. *Atlantic Requiem* entered the charts at number five and reached the top spot the following week, where it remained until the end of July. Ben's twenty-eighth birthday was the excuse for major celebrations, and Aran couldn't believe how much she had enjoyed recording with him.

'I want to do it again! Will you write more parts for an oboe?'

He looked at her quite seriously.

'Yes, but only if you're prepared to play them with me, on stage.'

Oh. The more she thought about that, the more convinced she became that rock concerts were not for her. One was fun, but on a regular basis, no. She was happier at home with her lyrics, or helping Ben backstage with his costumes and make-up.

Furthermore, there was the fan club where she worked two

mornings a week, and the voluntary group she had joined to help find work for the homeless. Many of those who slept on the streets wanted to get off them, and many were Irish. Holly Mitchell was involved as well, very good at locating jobs, persuading employers and writing references. Thirteen-year-old Ollie often had to give up his bed to passing strangers, camp in his tent in the garden while Mum sorted out her 'lame ducks'. But Ollie was a great fan of Ben's now, easily bribed with autographs which he sold to his envious friends.

'They'll be collector's items soon,' Ben remarked one day as he signed another batch.

'What do you mean?'

'I'm going to be thirty in two years' time. Now that I've had my number one hit I can rest in peace, and start thinking about quitting rock.'

'But Jake thinks your new song might reach number one as well! And what about your audiences, that you love?'

He blew a kiss into the air.

'Farewell my lovelies! Unless you're prepared to come with me into the realm of classical music.'

So, he had remembered her advice of years ago. But not opera, surely? The loss of Amery had matured him emotionally, but she still wasn't sure he was ready for that.

'Not yet. But if I can do some film themes, and then write a musical or two, I'll be looking at opera in the nineties. Maybe a rock opera first, but then a real one, eventually.'

'Won't you miss the fans?'

'Yes. I'll miss them a lot. But they won't want to see me doddering out on stage when I'm eighty-six . . . now's the time to think about bowing out gracefully.'

Still, he looked a little wistful. She put her hand on his shoulder.

'Well then, let's make sure you enjoy the rest of these heady days. And get a few gold discs to put on the walls!'

Atlantic Requiem looked as if it might even go platinum. Its success amazed everyone, and Aran had heard whispers that it might win an Ivor Novello award for its originality.

'Right. If you can put up with everything for another few years, we will enjoy them.'

She knew what he meant by 'everything'. The people who crowded their home night and day, the nightclubs he still frequented, the tours when he was mobbed by girls, sometimes made irascible by exhaustion, the stress of always having to be on top form. Once or twice he'd reached for the bottle, but she'd snatched it away from him, and there had been some memorable rows. But they were very happy.

'Ben, I'm having a great time writing lyrics. I feel like I'm in full flow at last! And I want to write lots more. But when I turn thirty maybe we – maybe we could think about—'

He grinned. 'Getting married?'

'I was going to say having children.'

Even as she said it, she wondered if she deserved it. She had given away their first child. But the biological clock would start to tick . . .

He thought for a while.

'Yes. OK. When the touring is over and I can be at home more often. If I'm going to be a father I might as well be a good one.'

Immediately Rhianna flashed into her mind, Rhianna who was at school now, proudly flourishing the pencil box from Salzburg. Baby Rhianna who, incredibly, was already as tall as her Shetland.

Atlantic Requiem did go platinum, They were delirious. And by the following summer Ben Halley and Aran Campion had a gold as well, for a cheeky song inspired by a particularly dull dinner party they'd attended one night. Hosted by a friend of Chanda's, they knew Chanda had asked them to it on behalf of the friend's twenty-year-old son, who was mad to meet Ben. Chanda made no secret of the fact that she wished to socially ingratiate herself with this family.

'Do come. It'll be a super evening.'

Apart from the son, it was turgid, but for the sake of peace they endured it. Toying with her sugary dessert, Aran realised with something of a fright that this was what she'd once almost settled for, even wanted: staid evenings discussing Smallbone furniture, property prices and Jane Grigson recipes. By the time she got home she felt as if she'd escaped from prison, while Ben was wrathful that he'd wasted a whole night of his precious time. But they'd had enough wine to be a bit giggly.

'It was so politely, horribly competitive! Let's do a song on it – a spoof!'

They sat up all night writing words and melodies, and polished it off by the end of the week. It was called *Angel Whip*, and it started with Ben trilling brightly like Julie Andrews. Nobody was expected to take it seriously, and they were incredulous when Myles and Jake cracked up, recalling awful dinner parties they'd attended themselves. Even more incredulous when it was recorded, whereupon it turned out that half the country must have suffered equally horrendous events. Ben became the voice of bored Britain, corpsing audiences when he minced on stage in an apron, polishing a silver spoon assiduously as he sang. Even Kevin Ross stopped worrying for long enough to laugh, and the gold disc put an even bigger grin on everyone's face.

Later, there was a spin-off to it. An Italian film producer contacted Ben to say he was about to make a satirical comedy, and wondered if Ben would be interested in doing the music for it. He said he'd love to, if Aran could do the lyrics?

Yes, the producer replied that that was what he meant, both of them, the team who had done *Angel Whip*.

'Team! Do you hear that, muffin?'

Aran heard it, and loved it. She didn't want any limelight, could never face audiences the way Ben did, but felt they were really blossoming now, together. They applied themselves to the project, and in the interim a letter arrived from Sher. Molly had – was Aran ready for this? – Molly had joined a sect. Some kind of cult with a charismatic leader based in Miami, a man who made Mussolini look like Mother Teresa. The group's beliefs were blatantly fascist, and furthermore Sher was very concerned that Mother might be taking a ride on the financial dodgems, 'because of course the whole thing is a money racket. She's gullible and she's going to get ripped off.' Horrified, Aran wrote to Molly, but received no reply.

And then, suddenly, it was time for Rani to come home. Aran couldn't believe that two years had flown by so quickly. For Rani, she knew they had been long and difficult, but constructive. She'd gained a great deal of medical experience, contributed much to India and survived her painful parting from Thierry. Devoted as a dog, he had waited patiently, and on the day of her arrival he dashed off to Heathrow with flowers in one hand and an engagement ring in the other. Aran cocked a curious eyebrow at the box.

'My diamond, I suppose?'

'No! Well – I got the jeweller to swop it for a ruby.'

Ben put a Mercedes at his disposal, Aran put a bottle of champagne in it, and by the time they got back from the airport they were already engaged. But the champagne was untouched, because Rani's sojourn in India had turned her into a strict Hindu. Ben was agog when he finally stopped hugging his sister for long enough that she could tell him.

'The belly dancer doesn't drink any more?'

'No, and I'm very glad Aran made you cut down. It's so bad for you, Ben. Even worse for women.'

Worse for women? Aran thought Germaine Greer would strangle Rani if she heard that.

* * *

407

Rani's wedding was scheduled for the autumn of 1986, and Aran sat at her dressing table one morning, wondering what to wear. Knowing Guy Halley, his daughter's marriage would be a dressy affair. Maybe it was time to hit Harvey Nicholls with the credit card.

From the bed, Ben gazed at her speculatively as she sat pondering in her little floral camisole.

'You know, I think I'd like to give you something nice to celebrate all those great lyrics you've written. Would you like a serious piece of jewellery?'

Automatically her hand flew to her throat. 'Oh, no, I'm not old enough, I'd look silly—'

Their eyes met in the mirror, and they realised they were thinking the same thing at the same time. Ben frowned.

'Well, the only thing I've ever given you is that silver necklet, years ago. You know, the clef? Where is it, Aran? How come you don't wear it?'

'Oh, I – I lost it, Ben.'

He was silent for a moment.

'But you said you never would. You said you'd wear it every day.'

'Well, I took it off when we split up, and then I couldn't find it.'

Flustered, she held her breath. She was a hopeless liar. His eyes seemed to be chiselling into her.

'That's a shame. I thought it meant something to you.'

'Oh, it did! It meant a great deal. I – I was very upset.'

'Perhaps we could find another one, then.'

Oh, no, not another one, when Dan and Eimear had given Rhianna the original only this year! At six they thought she was old enough to wear it on special occasions. Quickly she turned round to him.

'I'd rather not, Ben. The first one was unique. I don't want a copy.'

'All right. I suppose there's no point, if you're only going to lose whatever I give you.'

She knew he was hurt, and floundered for some excuse to make him feel better.

'It's just that – well, I'm so careless to lose something so precious, maybe the money would be better spent on something I couldn't lose.'

'Such as?'

'How about – how about a trip to India? Rani says it's so fantastic, and you've always wanted to go.'

Just in time, he was diverted.

'Yes . . . if you'd prefer that, we could go.'

'It'd be lovely, and we'd both enjoy it. The serious jewellery can wait till I'm forty.'

He smiled then, and she smiled back. But she thought of the silver clef, touching Rhianna's fragile throat. Rhianna thought her Mum and Dad had given it to her, the Mum and Dad who treasured her.

Rani's wedding was indeed a stylish occasion, formalised at Woking town hall and celebrated by a hundred and fifty guests at her home. She looked dazzling in a scarlet sari shot with gold, wearing the little red caste mark that Aran didn't quite understand. But she understood well enough when Thierry's parents were cool to her, and was sorry when Guy Halley was cool too. Would he never thaw?

It distressed her that he could not accept her, could find no word of affection or congratulation for Ben, not even when he heard the music Ben had composed specially for his sister's wedding. But Deva was warmly welcoming as ever, and Chanda was cordial in a way that said she respected her brother's success – financially, at any rate. The party was less of an ordeal than it might have been, and afterwards the happy couple flew to Goa on their honeymoon. Waving them off, Aran was thoughtful.

'Nostalgic, huh? Thinking that this could have been you?'

'No, Ben. Not at all. I was just wondering what Rani's going to do when she gets back. Start work, or start a family?'

'Oh, she's only twenty-seven. She's hardly going to waste all those years of study.'

'No . . . but Thierry is keen on children.'

She smiled at his departing back, happy for him. The unhappiness she had caused him had weighed greatly on her conscience. But how curious, that Rani should be the one to console him! Rani had changed a lot, been tempered by her experiences in India as well as by the unexpected power of love. She seemed more rounded, less forceful than before but a good deal deeper.

Feeling Ben's arm around her, she squeezed it affectionately.

'So when are we going to India?'

'Not for a while. I've got that tour of Canada in the spring, and summer will be too hot. We'll have to wait nearly a year.'

But she knew the time would whizz by, with the Italian score to be finished, Rhianna to be visited, homeless people to be helped, the fan club to be run and Ben's new manager to be taken in hand. Aran didn't want to cramp his style, but there were things that Ben would never think of discussing with him – things that Ben hardly knew existed, like health insurance, pension plans, investments. If she didn't make sure Larry Becker went into all that with the accountants, nobody would. Ben was much more interested in Canada, where he would work his way from Vancouver east to Montreal, and in the huge party he wanted for his thirtieth birthday next July. She smiled to herself; even now when she was writing lyrics and had helped him to reach number one in the charts, she couldn't entirely shake off her sensible streak.

In December, when the film music was down on tape, she told him she was going to Dunrathway for a few days.

'But your mother's not there any more.'

'I want to see Achill, and the Rafters.'

'Oh, OK. I'll come with you.'

She nearly went through the roof.

'Oh no!'

'No?'

'I mean, you'd be bored, you've got that video to make, you can't possibly come.'

'I could make time – Aran, what is it? Don't you want me with you?'

'Yes, but there's nowhere for you to stay. Dan and Eimear only have one single bed to spare, it's a fold-up—'

'There's the new hotel.'

'Oh, Ben . . . look, why don't you just get on with your work? I'll only be gone three days.'

The expression on his face never left her mind all the way to Dunrathway. What was in it? Annoyance? Disappointment? Suspicion? Oh, God. This was becoming a nightmare. She was going to have to tell him. He'd be thrilled to hear he had a child.

He'd be furious.

He'd love her.

He'd leave her.

She was white with fear and strain by the time she got there, looking at the Rafters' happy faces, wondering how they'd look if Ben ever took Rhianna away from them. She must tell him. She couldn't tell him.

But then her little daughter was in her arms, cuddling up to her in a chubby embrace, so fragrant, so sweet.

'Aran, I'm going to be the Virgin Mary in the 'tivity play.'

She had to smile. Rhianna was a most unlikely Virgin Mary.

'Are you, my muffin?'

'Yes and Sorcha is going to be the Baby Jesus.'

Again it sounded funny. At three and a half Sorcha was a strapping Baby Jesus. But Aran's heart ached, wishing she could be there at the nativity play, at Christmas, at all the childhood events she was missing. These baby days, these innocent days that never came again.

'And – and what's Emmett going to be?'

'A shepherd. Mummy's getting him a new tea towel.'

'A tea towel?'

'Yes!' Rhianna cuffed her affectionately. 'For his head! He has to wear it on his head, silly!'

Emmett scowled. What a sight they would all be, if only she could see them. There would be photographs. There would be a tape, or a video, if she sent Dan and Eimear a camcorder early for Christmas. But there would be no memories. Sadly, she traced her finger around Rhianna's neck.

'Will you wear your little silver necklet at the play?'

'Aran! Virgin Marys don't wear necklets!'

She sighed, and supposed that they didn't. But these brief visits were too precious to waste, she had to be positive, make the most of every minute. But it hurt so much! Could Molly possibly have been right, that it would have been better to give Rhianna to strangers? No. Nothing could be worse than never seeing her again – and suddenly Aran thought of something. Molly hated seeing Rhianna, hated the evidence of Ben, evidence of sin, reminder of her own unoffered help. Was that why she had gone to America?

After several hours with all three children, plus Oscar, she told Eimear she was slipping down to the village to see Achill. He was renting a flat overlooking the harbour with his girlfriend – another reason for Molly to go? In her book couples didn't live together, not unless they had been very badly brought up and then failed in their Catholic duties.

'That's fine, sweetheart. Dinner will be ready when you get back. Why don't you bring him with you, and the little Keegan girl?'

'Thanks. I will if they're free. I'll phone to let you know.'

Achill's flat was in a side street near the pub, a couple of dark but comfortable rooms filled with the hardware he loved, a video, stereo, large television, stacks of computer games. Pleased to see her, he brought her in and introduced her to his girlfriend Aisling, whom he was supporting since she became unemployed.

Aisling was a curvy creature with masses of red hair and a strong handshake; Aran thought her very pretty and pleasant. But what had happened to her job in the pub?

'They've let four of the staff go since last summer. It was a bad season, and the winter's been even quieter.'

Even though Achill managed the pub for the friend who owned it, he hadn't been able to save his girlfriend's job. Sorry to hear it, Aran thought she'd send them a good big cheque for Christmas. Not that Achill would expect it of her; a big, blue-eyed man with ruddy cheeks, he was very independent.

'If I could get a bit more overtime we'd be able to make up the shortfall, or if Aisling could even work part-time. There's just not enough to do at the moment.'

'Why, Achill?'

'Because the dolphins left I suppose, and then there was the – the accident. Word got round. Just when we'd got the new craft shop and bistro and everything, the tourists stopped coming. Dwindled, anyway. After all the effort everyone was making, it's pretty demoralising.'

'Well, I hope the dolphins were a lesson to everyone about exploitation. They've gone to another village, I hear?'

'Yes, in Kerry. We think they're the same ones, anyway.'

'Then what you need here is a new attraction. What about the music nights at the pub?'

'Well, yeah, they're still going pretty well. But it's very hard to get good musicians all the time, and the best ones tend to go off, travel abroad.'

'Then you need something to attract new ones. What if you were to run a series of competitions next summer – best singer, best player, in lots of different categories? Rock, jazz, blues, folk, classical?'

'But where would we get the prizes? We used to offer cash prizes in a sort of general category, but there's none to spare at the moment.'

'You could get sponsors. Beer and wine companies. They have the facilities to promote competitions too, get entrants from further afield. In fact anyone who sells anything to pubs could help – crisp and peanut manufacturers, coffee suppliers, soft drinks, whatever. And maybe you could get some big musical names interested. If you invited them down from Dublin or wherever for a nice weekend here, the hotel could put them up and they could present the prizes. Think of all the tourists you'd get if Bono or Christy Moore ever stayed here!'

'If!'

'Oh, look, you'll get some if you try hard enough. All you need is one to get you started.'

Achill brightened eagerly.

'What about Ben? If we got a rock weekend organised, would he come and present the prizes? God, it'd be mobbed!'

Oh, no. What had she done? It was a perfectly natural suggestion, but it was impossible. How long was she going to have to live like this, keeping people apart, making excuses and apologies? How long before she forgot herself and let something slip? How much more secrecy, deceit, suspense?

'Oh, Achill . . . I wish he could, but his schedule's so full. I tell you what, though. He'd put up a prize – money for the winner, a trip to his recording studios in London, whatever you like. Autographed videos and albums for the runners-up. He'd sign T-shirts for every contestant and get his rock star friends to sign some too.'

'Jeez, would he? That'd be great!'

'Yes, and then you might get publicity, other names could be encouraged to come, or do the same at least.'

Achill's mind was beginning to work overtime judging by the look on his face. In moments his discouraged stoop had gone.

'You're great, Aran. I wish we all had brains like yours.'

'Hah! Look, we'll talk more about it over dinner, if you're free to come up to the Rafters?'

They were, and they went gladly. But when they reached the cottage that had been their home Aran and Achill stopped to look at it, unable to believe that another family lived there now. Of the seven Campions, only Achill remained in their village. The tiny house bore no trace of their existence, no testimony of Conor's struggle to keep its roof over their heads . . . how hard he had worked, and Molly too. Aran could almost smell her childhood, the fish and wool and oilskins, the dampness, the scrawny chickens in the back yard. It had not been idyllic, she did not want to live in those conditions again . . . and yet she felt guilt in her sense of freedom, and a sharp pang for her father, for the youngest brother she had hardly known. She glanced at Achill, but his face was impassive; Molly had been hard on him too, but when there was friction he had always gone off to the pub, never taken things to heart the way she had. He was hardly aware how much Molly loathed Ben, had no idea there was a granddaughter whose existence Molly denied . . . men, she thought, were slow to notice the subtleties of family relationships, to get caught up in emotional undercurrents. There had been nothing intense between the boys and their mother, and therefore Achill felt no ambivalence now, would not understand hers.

'Do you miss them, Achill?'

He looked surprised. He was not without feelings, but he never discussed them.

'Yeah – well, poor old Dad, what a way to go. I suppose Mother could be a bit cranky at times, but she never had it easy.'

'Do you write to her? Do you visit Dad and Dursey's grave?'

No. His silence said that he didn't. It would take at least ten pints, she supposed, to get any of her brother's thoughts or feelings out of him. Yet he was her brother, her one remaining root in the sandy, shallow earth of home; without him she would come here in future only as a visitor, a transient. For both of them, and especially for Rhianna, she didn't want that. And some day he might marry Aisling, there might be children. Nieces and nephews, Rhianna's cousins . . . only how would she manage things then, bring them together? Gazing at the cottage, she thought that things which had not mattered before were beginning to matter now. And Rani, also, might have children. Deva had been deprived of the granddaughter she would have loved, Ben's little girl. The solution to one problem was starting to look more like – oh, God! Were they all going to find out some day, were they all going to hate her for what she had done? Ben, Rhianna, Deva, Rani, Achill, all of them?

She realised Achill and Aisling were waiting for her. Walking on, she tried to lift her tone.

'How's the fishing these days, Achill?'

'Same as ever. Fucking great Spanish trawlers still cleaning us out.'

Even as they rounded the harbour, they spotted the huge hulk of one in the evening mist.

'Coastguard must have arrested her, if she's in this far. Some things never change.'

No, Aran thought, looking round the streets that were once again shoddy, the dispirited harbour. Things never change unless you make them, and go on fighting for them. Please go on fighting, Achill. I know I don't live here, but I want you and Aisling to be able to stay. You like it here, you belong, you mustn't get defeated or discouraged the way our parents were. I want my child and yours to grow up in a—

I *want* my *child*.

Chapter Eighteen

'You must do it, Ben! You must!'

'No! It will only cause trouble, there'll be a row over it!'

'So what? It's better than ignoring the whole situation isn't it, pretending it doesn't exist?'

'Since when is it my job to meddle in local politics?'

'It's not meddling, it's simply acknowledging the separatists, letting them know you're not indifferent to them.'

'But I am indifferent! Not to them as people, but as agitators – I don't understand Quebec's problem any more than I understand Syria's or Sri Lanka's or Argentina's, I'm only a singer, I can't get involved in every hassle in every country I tour.'

'It's not getting involved, it's only a gesture. One verse of one song, you'd learn it in half an hour.'

'I don't speak French.'

'Neither do I, but I've gone to the trouble of writing it in French so the least you could do is sing it. I'm the one who had to look up all the words and translate them, and anyway it's not provocative, it's open to several interpretations. Oh, please, Ben. It would mean a lot to them.'

He looked furious, striding up and down the hotel room waving his hands with black resistance in his eyes, but Aran stood her ground. Most people in Montreal spoke French, so all he had to do was learn six lines in that language and they would love him for it. She knew he wasn't political, but unless he took such small risks he would appear cold in countries that were hot with conflict . . . he took them in his music, so why not in the words? She'd gone to such trouble to write them, they wouldn't bloody choke him.

He looked at her as she sat on the bed, holding the page, her hair damp from the bath. With no make-up on, she looked very young and wishful.

'Oh, here, give me the blasted thing.'

She stretched out her arm in its dressing gown and he snatched the page, peered at it rebelliously.

'What's it mean? How do I pronounce it?'

'Il était une fois une voix . . .'

'Eel aytayt oon-eun – it's double Dutch! I'll never remember it!'

She giggled. He was like an angry little kid, stamping and pouting.

'Sure you will. Read it again.'

'Eel aytayt eehoon – oh, bugger this! Why don't I just strangle a live cat, it'd sound the same!'

'You're not getting out of here till you do it. If you can pronounce *Au Fond du Temple Saint*, you can do this.'

He glanced warily at her, and after twenty tortured minutes he did do it. Not great, but not bad.

'Right. Now, we'll go do the soundcheck, and then you can relax until tonight.'

Of course he wouldn't relax, not with his first night in Montreal coming at him like a Ferrari, a huge audience in the Forum, Kevin Ross fussing and fretting as if the city were on fire. He gives so much, she thought, looking at his taut muscles as he pulled his T-shirt over his head and went to take a quick shower. It's been a great tour, but still there'll be new critics in the Forum tonight, they'll ridicule him if he gets it wrong, query his meaning if he gets it right . . . they're cannibals, they feed off him, dissect every little part of him and then, if they don't like him, there's always somebody else. He's been singing almost non-stop for six weeks, running round stages like a lunatic, rushing from one side of Canada to the other, yet he's got to be fresh, sparkling, perfect. I don't know how he does it.

But he loves it, and I love him.

The Forum was packed with thousands of bodies sweating already in their own warmth, but the sudden silence was electric as the single spotlight fell on the gigantic stage. For a moment there was nothing and then, as if from nowhere, Ben was standing in the middle of it. He was great at dramatic appearances.

In the front row, Aran swallowed and clutched Larry Becker's hand. No matter how many first nights there were, she was always nervous. Even tonight, when they were not doing Amery's requiem and she did not have to be part of it herself. Looking up, she watched Ben rip the microphone off its stand, thrust it to his face and then survey the audience, in the way he had, for just two or three unnerving seconds.

'Bonsoir Montreal!'

416

'BonSOIR!'

They erupted immediately, and Aran was very glad he'd agreed to that first word of French. The disputed song didn't come until the end, it was a kind of parting gift, but his impact was made *now*. She could see the grin on his face, the energy coiling in him as he threw back his head and threw out his left arm in a way that seemed to invite every single person in the stadium to join him, to enjoy this night as he was going to enjoy it. And in moments she was enjoying it herself, dazzled by the lights that changed colour so that his latex costume looked yellow, orange, red, his leather jacket looked black, brown, navy . . . it was a very sophisticated set, making him seem distant, remote as a god and yet vulnerable, isolated. In the orchestra pit the musicians were invisible, yet she knew he was communicating with them on a different level, depending on their timing, on everything being in exactly the right place. It looked so easy, but it would take everything he had. Behind her she could hear shouts, cries, screams. It was a huge audience.

At any moment, anyone in it could do anything. They could throw a rose or they could throw a petrol bomb, a knife, turn hostile or use the occasion to make headlines of their own. Like a soccer crowd, their slightest displeasure could be lethal; yet their pleasure was so moving, it made her almost weep to feel them swaying in rhythm with him, like a giant field of wheat in the summer sun. They had never met him and never would, but they loved him. He was never afraid. The bigger the crowd the better he sang, and over the years she thought his voice had got even better, acquired a kind of yearning quality which, as the critic Jeff Barber put it, 'reaches the parts other voices can't'. Jeff had been a very good friend to them since that first concert in Oxford, and often travelled abroad with them, writing despatches that were occasionally tough but always fair. Aran knew he was somewhere in the audience tonight, scribbling busily, noticing everything.

But it was a fabulous night. Every little thing was in synch, the crew working superbly together, every change smooth and every note right. Savouring it, her body tingled at the clarity of Ben's voice, her mind registered this as something she would always remember, a night when their love and their joint talents were at the peak of perfection. After two hours Ben was still fresh, the audience was still stamping and screaming, everyone was totally caught in his power and charisma. He has the world at his feet, she thought; he has everything he has ever wanted.

Saving the song with the French lyrics for last, he sat down at his piano and introduced it with a smile.

'This one's for Quebec, this one's for you.'

They roared with delight as he began to play, but automatically she tensed, wondering what hash he might make of the words. Oh God, oh well, it was the thought that counted – and then she heard something that jarred on her ear, something that was neither music nor applause. Something that made her spin round into the blinding glare of the lights.

In the centre aisle, quite close to her, something was happening. There was a commotion, but she couldn't make out what it was – a shout, a blur, a – a man running very fast, towards her, amidst screams that were changing pitch. In a split second, there was mayhem. She grabbed at Larry.

'What is it – who is it—'

He pushed her down in her seat as he jumped up, Kevin rising beside him, climbing at speed over people's laps as they fought their way out to the aisle, but the man was moving faster, racing past them until he was right in front of the stage, only three or four feet away from her. He had a gun in his hand, and he was pointing it at Ben. Ben who couldn't see him, but was frowning, aware of some disturbance.

Her cry froze in her throat.

'No – *Ben* – no—'

The man raised his other arm and gripped the gun in his two hands, holding it straight out the way policemen did, taking steady aim. And still Ben couldn't see, didn't know.

Nobody knew what happened next, but as the shot rang out the man fell forward, tripping on something that flew at his legs and brought him down, some small dark shape moving at the speed of light. Aran stepped on it as she ran hysterically to the orchestra pit, tried to claw her way up to the stage that was much too high, crying as her fingers slipped down its sheer surface. Ben had been shot, Ben had been killed, and she couldn't get to him; in the midst of the pandemonium there was a kind of deathly silence, everything happening very fast and yet distant, unreal.

The musicians were scattering, the entire audience was standing and screaming, but all she could see was the cliff wall of the stage, so high nothing was visible above it, only the lighting rig in the roof. And then some man was pulling at her, lifting her off her feet as she struggled in his grip.

'No! Let me go – he's dead – they've killed him—'

But the man carried her back out to the aisle, oblivious to her sobs, and dumped her roughly on the ground where other security guards were converging round the two struggling figures on the floor. One

418

was the man who had shot Ben, the other was Thanh. They were both fighting to reach the gun that had fallen out of reach, but then a guard picked it up and Thanh was hauling the attacker upright, twisting his arm behind his back to breaking point.

After that it was all complete confusion, Kevin Ross's arm around her and someone else's voice in her ear, the security men lifting the struggling figures and leading them away, lights going on and noises on the stage. The stage where Ben—

'OK, let's all calm down. Please go back to your seats.'

His voice, speaking as calmly and nonchalantly as if to his mother. Aran's whole body buckled with relief, tears poured down her face as Kevin took her to the side near the wings, where she could see him at last. He was very drawn, but he was standing up, looking out at the surging sea of bodies. Frightened and uncertain, they looked back.

'Come on. Sit down. Calm down. Nobody's hurt.'

He couldn't know whether they were or not, but they took his word for it, gazing collectively at his right hand as it went to his left arm. The sleeve of his jacket was torn, but only Aran and those at the front were close enough to see that there was blood on it. Thoughtfully, he inspected it.

'Pity. I rather liked that jacket.'

She heard the feeble dizzy laughter, knew everyone felt as faint as she did. But if he was injured, he wasn't concerned. Or wasn't showing it, adding to the panic. Instead he took a step forward, nodded to the musicians and waited for them to regroup. Glad of some direction, shaken but visibly relieved for him, they picked up their instruments as bidden.

Awestruck, Aran realised what he was thinking. The show must go on. They've come all this way, they've bought their tickets, they're getting what they came here for. Leaving the mike in the stand where he didn't have to hold it, he abandoned his piano solo but signalled down to the orchestra pit: number twenty in the running order, a gentle ballad chosen for its soothing qualities. It was a reserve song, kept handy in case things got too hectic. And unbelievably, the musicians began to play it, he began to sing.

Every word was clear as glass. Not a note faltered, not a word did he forget, his colour even returned a little as his own voice reassured him that he really was all right. Mesmerised, the audience fell utterly silent. What she felt for him at that moment was indescribable, so much love and pride she was weak with it.

But blood was oozing from his arm, she could see people wincing in the front rows, agog. When he finished the song they rose as one

419

and gave him a standing ovation that lasted until he was forced to quell it.

'Will you forgive me if I don't do an encore tonight?'

He always did, because every audience demanded it, but this one was spellbound beyond caring. Nothing he did now could possibly top what he had just done. With a smile and a wave he left the stage amidst deafening applause as she fought free of Kevin and ran backstage to him.

He literally fell into her arms.

'Sorry, muffin. 'Fraid I didn't get to sing your French lyrics for them.'

And he passed out.

It was only a flesh wound, but it made headlines round the world. Sitting up in his hospital bed next morning, where he'd been kept for observation, he was virtually invisible among the people around him, the flowers and cards and gifts. Jauntily, Kevin and Larry were reading him faxes from Jake and Myles in London, reports from newspapers in every language. But Aran sat like a statue, her hand tightly in his, her eyes on Thanh.

'We'll never be able to thank you, Thanh. Never, ever.'

It was Thanh's lightning response that had deflected the bullet, caused it to go through Ben's upper arm instead of his heart. Aran was prostrate with gratitude, and she never wanted Ben to sing in concert again.

He was laughing at her.

'Is one nutter not enough?'

The man who had shot him was, as far as the police could ascertain, a nutter. Acting entirely alone, he'd offered no explanation, no motive. Later today he would be charged with attempted murder. Pale from loss of blood, Ben seemed otherwise unconcerned.

'That's the chance you take. The world's full of them. Hey Thanh, pass me the phone. I think I'd better tell Jake about the raise you're getting.'

Thanh smiled modestly.

'No need. This my job.'

'Bullshit. The guy could have shot you. I'm going to have you dipped in gold.'

Everyone laughed, but it was a jittery laugh; nerves were badly frayed. Aran wanted to do two things very much – cry all over Ben, and then get him out of this hospital, on a plane and home to London. All the papers said his behaviour under fire had been incredible, but she could think of no more horrendous end to his wonderful

Canadian tour. His public career, because nothing was worth this.

At noon his doctor said he could leave: the hospital was besieged by fans and the administration was anxious to be rid of him. It took an hour to smuggle him out through an emergency exit into a waiting car and back to the hotel, which was also awash with fans. The manager came flying up to him, ashen, directing staff to clear a path. When finally they got to their room, it was afloat on flowers and champagne. And only then, as he sank down on the bed, did Aran see the toll taken. Putting his head in his good hand, he leaned forward almost to the floor and began to shake violently.

'Jesus Christ. I thought I'd had it, Aran. I really did.'

Kneeling down, she took him in her arms, kissing his cheek, caressing him with all the reassurance she could muster.

'I know. But you're all right. Everybody is. We're just in shock, a bit. I think you should lie down and try to sleep.'

Without protest he nodded, let her help him undress and get into the bed. His arm was stiff and sore, it was all very awkward, and she realised he was collapsing with fatigue. Looking at her, his eyes were large and dark, searching for comfort.

'Get in with me. I need a cuddle.'

She got in and stretched out beside him, holding him close, hearing the delayed shock in his voice, the tears.

'Why do you think that guy would want to kill me?'

'I don't know, love. I don't know.'

She wrapped herself around him, snuggling him into her until he felt warm and safe. For a little while he murmured into her shoulder, but then his lashes fell dark on his face, his breathing slowed into sleep. Watching him tenderly, she gave thanks for his life.

His life that Thanh had saved, risking his own. For all the fans, for all the joy, for all the fame and fortune, was it worth it?

Back in London Ben did not refer to the incident again, but he was unusually quiet, and Aran knew he was thinking about it. An attempt on anyone's life, she supposed, could not but affect them, cause them to reflect a little on the nature and purpose of that life. So she gave him extra care and attention, was understanding when their sex life suffered a bit; all Ben seemed to want for the moment was to lie gently in her arms, looking at her, thinking.

When his arm was better he played the piano a lot, was at home more than usual, and she loved that. The house felt different when he was in it, happy and alive. He was a slob to live with, but he was so sunny and funny, and he seemed to miss her whenever she went out. When she did go, particularly to the fan club office, her attention kept drifting back to him and to that terrifying night.

I knew it would happen, she thought. I always felt that someone might try to harm him some day. Now that they have, I'm almost glad; at least it's over, and they didn't get him. But there are plenty of other maniacs out there, that no amount of bodyguards can protect him from. What a good thing he'll be thirty soon, now he can give Jake and the others an unarguable reason to stop touring. He can concentrate on film scores and start getting into the classical stuff he's always wanted to do. It'll be rough on Kevin, I guess, but I think Jake and Myles are secretly interested in experimenting with him. We'll find another niche for Kevin, maybe he's had enough of life on the road anyway.

Thank God Thanh was there that night, so quick, so brave. And thank God Amery Cheam insisted he always be there, everywhere; he said he was indispensable and he was right. It's almost as if Amery were still protecting Ben. He held on to Thanh for him and he brought me back with him . . . he must have been a wonderful man. I wish I'd met him. Maybe we should go to his apartment for a little break? Ben's not saying much at the moment, but I know he's strung up.

Tentatively she put the idea to him, but he turned it down. He didn't feel like New York at the moment, he said, and besides a composer from Durham was using the place, trying to write a Broadway musical. People were always using it. Ben was so generous that it had become a cross between a hotel and an artists' colony, filled with wandering minstrels, writers and singers of all descriptions. But that was exactly what Amery would have wanted, and even though the hospitality was sometimes abused Ben never ceased to offer it.

The house in Hampstead was always busy too: Aran never knew who she'd find making tea in the kitchen or whistling in the bathroom. When Larry Becker called a meeting to discuss the 'Canada episode' she wasn't surprised that it met there: Larry, Jake, Myles, Kevin and Ben, sitting round looking variously anxious and determined. Ben was far too valuable a property that he should be exposed to danger again. Fixing a tray of beer and sandwiches, she carried it into the front room and joined them.

They all had their own ideas, and their strong personalities resulted in a lot of shouting, particularly from Myles whose white hair seemed to fly into a rage all of its own, and from Larry who, as Ben's manager, bluntly said he wasn't taking any crap from anyone. There would be hi-tech, wall-to-wall security from now on, random searches at concerts, whatever it took. Larry was a short guy with tufty eyebrows and a cigar perpetually in his stubby fingers, which he jabbed at people to make his point. Jake and Kevin were inclined to digress, think of all the ifs and buts, and Ben let them all rant on, unusually silent as he sat with one leg crossed at right angles over the other, rubbing his eyebrow occasionally with his finger. Aran supposed he was wondering how to tell them he wouldn't be doing any more concerts, that he'd be thirty in July and that meant a whole new ball game. Eventually, realising they had lost his attention, they turned to consult him.

'How do you feel about it, Ben? What do you want to do?'

'Right now, I want to take a break. Four weeks, maybe six.'

'Sure, sure. Just finish the new single and you're free as a bird. But in the long term?'

He sighed, and Aran thought he was evading her eye a little.

'Well, we've been giving that some thought for quite a while – for years, actually. The plan was that I'd quit rock at thirty and move into other spheres. I've already done a film theme, as you know, and I want to do more. I also want to write an opera.'

They nodded dutifully, humouring him; this had long been one of his little hobbyhorses and, while they knew he was serious, it was on the back burner, safely distant.

'Yeah, right. But what about the concerts?'

He *was* avoiding her eye. Definitely.

'I'm cutting down. In future there'll only be one tour a year, in winter, lasting not longer than three months. You can make whatever security arrangements you like, but they'd better be good because they're going to be in very big arenas. The demand is there and it's time I played them. Wembley Stadium, Knebworth, Madison Square Gardens, the Rock in Rio festival . . . I want to do Australia too, the San Remo song festival, the Nep Stadium in Budapest. Ten biggies, over the next ten years. Then it's curtains for rock, I'm off to La Scala.'

Their eyes lit up like Christmas Eve on Fifth Avenue. All except Aran's. She was speechless.

Larry was scribbling in a pad on his knee. 'Great. Great. I'll talk to the promoters. This kind of thing takes years to fix up.'

Kevin was incredulous, his eyes whirling behind his glasses.

'Aren't you scared? After what happened?'

Ben sat back and regarded him evenly.

'No. But if I quit now, everyone would say I was. That's why I'm not quitting. One looper isn't going to dictate to me or to the millions of fans who've made my career what it is.'

'But there may be other loopers!'

He waved his hand dismissively.

'So deal with them. We all take the same risks – me, Jagger, Clapton, Cliff, Rod, the whole lot of us. The women take them for chrissakes, that little Kylie Minogue kid, people you'd knock over with a feather. I'm damned if Ben Halley is going running for cover.'

Aran sat gazing at the ground, dumbstruck. She knew, and he knew, that they were going to have a massive row over this. He hadn't even told her, hadn't breathed a word! She was going to break his bloody neck. She was just not having this.

She looked at them all. 'Well, gentlemen, I have to tell you that this comes as news to me. Ben and I have not discussed it. So you'd better put everything on hold until we do.'

Uh oh. They eyed each other, sensing trouble in the trenches, and she knew what they were thinking: damn interfering women, always throwing spanners in the works. Only Kevin looked sympathetic, even though he stood to lose most if she won. The others assumed Ben was going to get the sharp end of her tongue, but that he would take care of her. Silence her.

She stood up. 'So why don't we call it a day for now. We'll get back to you when our final decision is made.'

She emphasised the 'our'. Reluctantly, they stood up, muttering amongst themselves as she ushered them out into the hall, handed them their jackets and shut the door firmly behind them.

The instant they were gone, she rounded on him.

'You bastard. You utter bastard.'

He grinned sheepishly, but didn't look repentant.

'Sorry, muffin. But—'

'Sorry isn't good enough! You did this on purpose! You've been planning it for weeks without saying a word to me!'

'Yes, I have. I knew you'd throw cold water on it if I said anything. But Aran, I can't quit now. I can't!'

'Why? You want to make sure the next nutter with a gun scores a bullseye, is that it? You want to get killed?'

'I won't get killed. Every precaution will be—'

'No precautions are foolproof! None! And what about your opera, your film themes, musicals, that you've been talking about for years? Ben, what the hell *is* this?'

'It's one tour a year. That's all. Three months on the road, and three months writing for it. The other six, I'll be doing other stuff, new stuff.'

'You don't need to do one tour! You don't need to do this at all!'

He sat back down on the sofa and looked at her with a mixture of imprecation and defiance.

'I do need it. I love it, Aran. I can't sit home all year writing. I have to sing, have to have an audience. It's my – my nerve centre. It's what music is all about.'

'Wouldn't it be good enough for you to be in an audience, at the opening night of your film or opera?'

'No. That'll be great, but the real buzz is being on stage yourself. Singing, playing, doing it, being it. It's all up to you, you can make people laugh or cry at will, make them happy, give them a great night they'll never forget.'

She thumped a key on the piano and faced him furiously.

'I see. It's the adrenalin, is it? The applause and the adulation, the power—'

'Yes, if you will. Those people are my life blood, they want me and I want them.'

'So. You are a drug addict after all.'

He nodded.

'Yes. I admit you could put it that way. I'm hooked, I'm addicted, I can't live without it.'

'But you'll *have* to, some day! You've said yourself you can't crawl on stage when you're eighty, and they won't want you to.'

'I know. But thirty is too soon, Aran. You heard me tell Larry I'll stop at forty. It's over then, I promise you. *Finito*.'

She didn't know what to say, where to turn. He didn't often defy her outright, but something in his face told her he was going to fight her for this. Fight her all the way.

'And what about me? Am I to not only put up with this, but go on writing lyrics for it?'

'Yes, of course! You've only just started, you've got lots of talent, I want you to record with me even if you won't play live. I'm depending on you!'

'Flattery will get you absolutely nowhere.'

'Oh, Aran, come on. Please. We're a team, aren't we?'

'I thought we were, which is why I can't believe you informed your colleagues about this without consulting me.'

'All right. I'm sorry about that. But there was no point in going round in circles.'

She thought of something else.

'And when I'm thirty, what about the children we were going to have?'

'We will have them. I won't be away much, but when I am we'll all travel together, in comfort—'

'Children go to school, Ben.'

'Not till they're six. That gives us eight years already, before the

425

first is old enough. When we have a family it won't be disrupted, I promise you.'

Calculating, she found he was right. If she got pregnant at thirty she'd have her 'first' child at thirty-one, she'd be thirty-seven by the time it went to school and he'd be thirty-nine. *Damn*.

'Your mother will be horrified. And Rani. They're very worried about you.'

'Don't I know it. They've rung every day since Montreal. But that's just it, Aran. I can't sit home all day because the women in my life are worrying about me. I do appreciate it, but I'm not a little boy.'

No. And yet he looked like one so often, especially now when he wanted something, was trying to wheedle it out of her.

'Oh, bloody hell!'

Laughing, he looked at her hopefully. 'Does that mean yes?'

Try as she might, she couldn't resist. He wanted it so much, so desperately. She sighed despairingly.

'You're out of your mind, and I must be out of mine.'

He had her in his arms before she had time to say anything else, was hugging her so tight she couldn't breathe.

'Muffin, you're magic. Sheer magic. I love you to bits – let's go to bed. In fact let's not bother with the bed. Mr Steinway can join the party.'

She went on about it for ages, didn't let him forget that she was doing him a major favour, that he owed her one. She was seriously concerned for his safety . . . and yet, she kept remembering that night in Montreal, not the moment he'd been shot but the moment after it, when he'd sung clear as a bell, the blood dripping from his arm, the crowd rising and her immense pride in him. He belonged on stage, she acknowledged, the way a fish belonged in water. He was so happy there, she couldn't deny it to him . . . to him an auditorium was like a church, it was where you transcended yourself, fulfilled everything the gods expected of you. And they had given him such great gifts, who was she to stifle them?

Who was she? His lover, his friend, his partner. The most important person in his life, maybe even his muse at times. He loved her very deeply, and she saw now that no other woman would ever matter to him again. No one else, only his music, that was a living being to him, a rival far too strong to fight. But she loved it herself, and found she did not want to fight it. You couldn't fight something you understood. It would be like fighting a cloud in the sky; even when it was dark and full of rain, you needed it. It would always be so, and you accepted it.

For a while she was quiet and pensive, working on lyrics that fell into place that summer as never before, in rhythm and harmony. When Ben's birthday came round she almost didn't want to celebrate, to disrupt the peace, but with his family's help she finally roused herself, and gave him a night to remember.

Thirty! But they felt the same way together they had at nineteen or twenty, full of fun and energy, still playing at being married. Playing at life, in a way, making music that kept them young, and yet incredibly paid the bills. There were peaks and valleys, days when neither of them could write a note and the oboe sounded as bad as the piano, so awful that they shrieked; yet they could work till midnight, till they got it right. He loved her lyrics that let him say things he couldn't say in reality, she loved the way his music flirted with her words, sometimes squared up to them and then pirouetted away, his voice classic as a Rolex. He was the sound and she was the sense, they felt made for each other. There were times when they fought like tigers, times when they felt transported to a distant galaxy.

And there were times when Ben was scared. He never said it, but she saw it. Not only scared of being attacked again, but of hitting a wrong note, writing or singing something that people would hate. He thought that meant they would hate him, that the love affair was over, the chimera would collapse. His anxiety attacks were terrifying, she often watched helplessly while he tore up manuscripts, banged his head down on the piano, yelled that he was falling off the tightrope. Once he gripped a glass of water so tightly in his hand it shattered, slashed his palm to pieces. Once he lay on the floor as Oliver Mitchell had done, screaming. One memorable day he seized Gavin Seymour, whose casual visit had interrupted him, and shook him until she had to prise him loose.

He shouted, he kicked the piano, he banged his fists on the wall. But time after time she calmed him down, pointed to his gold discs, played something soothing or joked him out of it. And he did the same for her, on days when ideas were scarcer than diamonds in a drugstore. If their life floated light as a bubble on the surface, it was anchored to something very strong underneath; even if they lost everything overnight, never wrote another song, they knew they'd still be together. For better or worse, for ever.

Rani set up practice as a family GP that summer, Achill wrote that he'd got sponsorship and it had been a great success, thanks very much for the prizes and the winner will be over to tour Flinders in September, can he stay with you? Aran was pleased and touched, it was the first letter Achill had ever written to her. Then an odd letter from Molly, saying she'd become some kind of minister or official in

427

her weird church, that God had chosen her for sanctity.

'Chosen her for the loony bin,' Ben replied to that, so tartly that Aran cracked up; the mother who had weighed so heavily on her youth never seemed so much of a problem when Ben was around. And Molly did seem to be happy, in her way.

But Rhianna. Oh, Rhianna. Night after night Aran thought about her, saw her face in every passing cloud, heard her voice in every note Ben sang. Much as she had missed her as a baby, she missed her even worse now, ached when Eimear sent a photo or school report, any news at all.

She'd missed her seventh birthday, been in Canada at the time, and now she wondered how and when she would see her again. She couldn't let another Christmas go by, another birthday – another day, she felt sometimes, another hour. Tentatively, she said something to Ben about maybe going over to see Achill.

'Achill?'

'Yes, well, he is my only brother. I might drop in on Val as well.'

'And the Rafters?'

'Y-yes. Naturally.'

'Am I invited?'

Oh, Jesus. This was it, this was the terrible problem. Every time the phone rang, she flew to answer it in case it was Dan or Eimear, talking to Ben, letting something slip which, at a stroke, would ruin their lives. Hers and Ben's and Rhianna's, Dan's and Eimear's, everyone's. The anxiety sat like a cat on her shoulder, getting bigger and blacker, leaping up out of nowhere to claw at her.

Casually, she looked at him.

'Oh, Ben, you know you don't like it there, I always go alone.'

He regarded her thoughtfully, unnervingly.

'Yes, I know you do. I just thought you might like to bring me with you sometime. I'm sure I could help Achill with his project, and I'd love to see the Rafters.'

Yes, but they would die if they saw him. Sometimes, Aran suspected, they even died a little when they saw her, lived in fear that she would tell Ben even now, take the child away. Fleetingly, she had seen it in their faces, staring at her over Rhianna's shoulder as the child sat on her lap, wriggling and giggling, recounting all her little bits of news. Despite the infrequency of her visits Rhianna always loved to see her, regarded her as a firm friend. But how was she going to get away to her now, with Ben breathing down her neck, the excuses running out?

'Yes, well maybe we'll go later then, after we come back from India.'

428

Again he looked at her, with something that shrivelled her heart. Something she was imagining, creating from nothing but guilt. They would never return to Ireland together, and she wondered if he knew it. Wondered if he wondered why.

And so another visit was put off, another of Rhianna's childhood summers slipped through her fingers, the pony, the hay in the meadows, the splashes in the sea where Dan was teaching her to swim. Aran could see the slivers of southern Irish light in her mind, feel the cold waves washing her body, hear the happy shrieks that had once been her own. With a smile that betrayed nothing of the heaviness in her heart, she prepared to go to India.

It was a grainy day in September, and by the time they reached the airport Ben was in one of his mad-musician moods, ranting on about the crowds and chaos and confusion as if it had all been designed to thwart him personally. Several people recognised him and asked for autographs, delaying him so that it fell to Aran to organise the luggage and join the throng trying to check in, then find a lounge where they could wait without being hassled. Thanh and Beth were travelling with them, and did what they could to help, but Aran felt as if responsibility for everything rested entirely on her shoulders. Ben had a way of detaching himself from the practicalities, had got used to being escorted through airports and pampered on planes, when he travelled on tour every detail was taken care of by unseen hand, and all he had to do was simply arrive.

But this was a private holiday, and although she was fond of Thanh and Beth, glad of their help, she wished in a way they didn't have to come, felt she was never going to be alone with Ben. She never really would be, she supposed, until he stopped performing in public; at the very least Thanh would always be there, watchful as a yeoman of the guard. Beth wasn't strictly necessary, but Ben said it wasn't fair to leave her at home while her husband went off to India, and of course he was right. He was paying all their expenses, nothing was too much trouble after what Thanh had done for him. And Thanh was excited; as a Buddhist he couldn't wait to see India.

Eventually the long-delayed flight departed, and Aran began to relax when Ben did, warmed by his winsome smile.

'Sorry. I don't know why I got so flustered.'

'Neither do I. I'm the one who got the visas and the tickets, did the packing, booked the hotels, organised everything.'

'Yes. You're a marvel, muffin, and I promise I'll behave better when we get there. Nobody will recognise me over there, we won't have any bother.'

That wasn't why they were going to India, but it was a thought. Ben's records didn't sell there, he was virtually unknown, they'd have some peace. Just so long as he didn't react to it the way he'd reacted to Crete . . . but even if he did, she knew it wouldn't be fatal this time. Their relationship was much stronger now, underpinned in a way it hadn't been then. Even Guy had accepted them as a couple. She wished Val would stop writing those occasional miserable letters, echoes of Mother, saying she had all the responsibilities of a wife without any of the rights. Val said she should insist on marriage, and sometimes Sinéad Kenny said the same thing; even Myles had winked at her one day and said maybe she should take the bull by the horns.

But why? They were happy, they were going to have children, they were united in spirit. Ben made her soul sing, which was a lot more than Val's husband seemed to do for her, and besides she'd learned that pushing Ben to do anything was the surest way to make him not do it. He needed to feel free, needed the illusion of being in control even when he wasn't.

Deep down he knew how much he needed her, needed everyone who supported the act the public saw on stage, but if he admitted it then maybe he wouldn't be able to do it any more, would no longer be able to dictate the mood and responses of the people who idolised him as if he were a god. Gods weren't supposed to have minders and mothers and normal families, normal lives. They were young and strong, never captured or cornered.

It was a long way to Lucknow, with a change of plane at Delhi. For the latter half of the journey Aran was fascinated by the landscape they were flying over, but before that she left Ben to watch the film, thinking about him and about their daughter. There had been a row in Dunrathway a little while ago, over whether or not Rhianna should make her Communion with the rest of her class. Dan and Eimear were not religious, didn't want to impose Catholicism on her, and the child herself had no interest in the event apart from the money to be made out of it: the tradition was to visit people after the ceremony, amass a small fortune and then blow it on goodies. The Rafters didn't think that was very spiritually uplifting and neither did Aran – on the contrary, they thought the greasing of small palms encouraged greed and the little bridal dresses encouraged vanity. But then Hannah Lowry rowed in with her opinion, which was that Rhianna shouldn't be singled out, made to feel different from the other children. She must make her Communion with the rest of them. Then Rhianna herself stamped her foot and said she wasn't wearing any stupid frilly dress, she wasn't going; whereupon Fr Carroll stormed up to the

Rafters to tell them they were raising a young heathen.

The upshot was that Rhianna made her allegedly holy Communion in her everyday clothes, which scandalised the entire village, and Eimear sent the money saved on an expensive outfit to St Vincent de Paul. People were asked not to give her gifts of money, but some did anyway, so half of that also went to St Vincent de Paul and the rest was shared with Emmett and Sorcha, leaving Rhianna with six pounds and a scowl that prompted Dan to tell her she was a very selfish little girl. In return Rhianna gave him a mouthful of cheek that got her sent to bed early, crying; as a spiritual event the whole thing was a fiasco.

But what bothered Aran was that she hadn't been there for it, hadn't been able to talk to her daughter about what it was all really supposed to be about, that reaching the 'age of reason' meant thinking about other people besides yourself. Of course Dan and Eimear had, but *she* hadn't. She had not seen her daughter at all, for so long now it was like a physical pain. A pain that got worse every day, and seemed incurable. To add to it, she knew Rhianna didn't miss her, on her Communion day or any other; the child's short memory of her was fading, she was just a friend from dim and distant London, who might come again some day or might not.

But instead she was going to India, a destination which was a kind of spiritual pilgrimage for Ben. He was even less religious than the Rafters, in any formal sense, but he was very curious about the land of his birth, had a feeling of heritage about it. Unlike Rani he didn't speak Hindi, unlike Molly he wasn't superstitious, and yet this trip meant something to him, was much more than just a holiday.

Was that why he'd been tense at the airport? He could face huge crowds, but in India he would face part of himself, the land where his Bengali great-great-grandmother had met her British husband and first mingled two bloods, two cultures. India had no interest in him, but maybe that was why he was interested in it, to see the life men of his age lived there, the life he might have had if Deva had not gone to England, retraced the steps already taken by her husband's ancestor.

Whatever the reason, he was quiet on the plane, and took her hand when it landed.

'I'm glad you're here, muffin. I'd be lost without you.'

And then he meekly fetched a trolley, like any ordinary tourist, loaded the bags onto it and whistled for a taxi. For the first time in years, there wasn't a fan, a limo or a promoter in sight. Nobody at all, to whisk him away into the limelight. She wondered how long his humble mood would last.

It lasted. He didn't seem to mind at all that Aran had not booked them into a wildly expensive hotel in Lucknow, because everyone had warned her that the poverty in India made westerners feel decadent and guilty; the more you tried to escape physically, the worse you felt mentally. Many people tried to escape it, but she didn't want to feel cut off, have to walk round with her eyes glued to the ground. India was poor and they weren't going to pretend otherwise.

Her first impression was of people everywhere. Thousands of them, millions, milling around in all directions, overflowing off the pavements into the streets, which smelled of jasmine and cows and coriander, as well as a lot of things she decided not to think about. Lucknow was industrial, not India's most beautiful city by any means, but she was very struck by the expressions on people's faces, even in the commercial sector: they were so alive! Laughing, talking, arguing, all in sing-song tones that made her smile. Indian music drove her mad, she thought it monotonous and yet slightly hysterical when she heard it in London restaurants, but here the real music was in the voices on the streets, the women's lovely tinkly laughter, the way everything sounded so much more upbeat than it could possibly be. Sentences ended on a kind of lively question mark, everyone looked so animated, far more than they ever did in England. She had heard that Indians were masters at dissembling, yet there was nothing passive or inscrutable about these faces, the eyes shone and spoke in a way no commuter's ever would on the London underground. And the colours! No dark pinstriped uniforms here, it was all reds and yellows and luminous whites, people's clothes looked impossibly clean in the dusty air, yet it wasn't a bit like Austria where Ben had felt it all to be so ironed and starched. For the first few days they just wandered around, glad that Lucknow's climate was relatively cool, awed by the stunning mosque that stood on a hill making the citizens look like ants. What architecture, what riches amidst the poverty; everything was on a huge scale.

The Mughal buildings were magnificent, and she felt Ben slipping into the mood of the city, which was a renowned centre of classical Hindustani music and Kathak dance. He was by no means as dark as the local people, but he blended with them, taking the sun easily until his skin was a rich tobacco shade – its natural shade really, that only needed a few days to emerge. Nobody took him for a foreigner, whereas her very fair hair was the object of glances, and he laughed when she smothered herself in sunblock, not needing it himself at all. Again she thought it delicious to be able to wear light silk or cotton dresses, a real treat for anyone who'd grown up in a country where

432

you wore woollens even in summer. It made her mood light and airy, made her understand how the people could be so good-humoured even when they had little or nothing. There was prosperity in Lucknow, but there were sights that horrified her too, things that even silenced Ben in mid-sentence.

On the third day they went to visit his aunts and uncles, a whole clutch of them who lived near to one another, the brothers and sisters Deva had left behind. Middle-class merchants and matrons, they were every bit as welcoming as Rani had said, seizing him as if he were their prodigal son.

'And who is this?'

'This is my girlfriend Aran.'

He introduced her with pride and she was passed round for inspection, handed tea in a bowl while the women touched her hair, not believing it was natural.

'It is natural,' Ben insisted, 'everything about Aran is.'

It still surprised her at times that he liked her look, which wasn't all the leggy look of Sasha Harwood or the sophisticated gloss of Charlotte Lucas. She'd never been to a beauty salon in her life, never had facials or manicures or wore fitted clothes like theirs, but she supposed she must be doing something right if only by accident. A little overpowered by all the chattering relatives, she stayed close by his side, trying to make sense of the rushing conversation. They spoke very little English, but bits of Hindi were coming back to Ben, things his mother had taught him but he'd never practised. It was funny, to hear him struggling in Hindi!

'What are they saying?'

'They're saying you're a sweet little thing and we must stay for dinner. Either that, or they're telling us Margaret Thatcher has been kidnapped by a band of guerilla chimpanzees – I'm really not sure!'

It was a dinner invitation, extended to Beth and Thanh as well; even here they were shadowed, protected. Cousins joined the throng and the whole thing was chaotic, but great fun. Delicious, too, foods and spices Aran had never smelled or tasted before, cooked with great fuss and served with triumphant smiles. How weird for Ben to have a family branch like this . . . she saw he was thinking the same thing, looking at them as if into a mirror, at the kohl-rimmed eyes that were examining him in turn. He was a curiosity, and yet he did not look out of place, seemed to easily absorb the tones and gestures.

They'd brought gifts, and after the meal other gifts were produced in turn, a beautiful bolt of white silk for Beth and a deep blue bolt for her, hand-carved cigar boxes for Ben and Thanh, a marble chess set and then two dolls in national costume.

'Are these for us? What are they saying now?'

'I think they're saying the dolls are for our first-born daughters.'

He smiled at her, and her heart almost stopped.

From Lucknow they went on to Agra, where the Taj Mahal left them both speechless. Seeing it in reality had nothing to do with seeing pictures of it, they couldn't get over its beauty, its awesome grandeur or its almost serene sense of sadness. Demented with grief after the death of his wife Mumtaz Mahal, the Shah Jehan had built it in her memory three hundred years before, and to Aran it felt as if there was sorrow in every stone. It was the first time she had sensed sorrow in India, and she knew Ben felt it too as he led her round by the hand, lingering far longer than was his wont. Often he became impatient while she gazed at things, but not here.

'Jehan must have been literally stone mad about Mumtaz.'

'Yes . . . don't you ever dare die on me, Aran, or it'll cost me a fortune.'

What? What did he mean? Was this his way of telling her he felt the same about her, would go out of his mind if anything ever happened to her?

Dreamily, she laid her head on his shoulder.

'Don't worry, Ben. I'm not going to leave you.'

He kissed her suddenly, more passionately than was proper in a Muslim shrine, and they stood quietly together, looking down into the long rectangular lake reflecting the vast white dome and the smalt-blue sky. The water was clear and calm, but from nowhere she had a flash of her father and brother, flailing, their bodies filling with water and their minds with fear.

He felt her shiver and turned to her, but when he did she saw the same thought in his own face: Amery. Amery who had lost his wife, and been lost in turn.

It had done something to Ben. She could feel the difference in him. But his lifestyle remained the same, there was still no room for a child in it. The more she thought about their child, about the erratic contact that confused Rhianna, was so painful for everyone, the more she felt the pressure that had been mounting for a long time. Seeing Rhianna was her greatest joy, but she was doing it at everyone else's expense.

Chapter Nineteen

En route to the sacred city of Varanasi, Ben was subdued, and Aran sympathised. She'd got over a mild stomach upset herself, but he was suffering the effects of a fiery curry which had left him stretched listless on their bed all of the previous day, ghostly under the mosquito net. And now Thanh was driving their rented car at breakneck speed, bursting to see the Buddhist shrine of Sarnath. Everyone felt a little queasy.

But Varanasi would be worth it. As well as Sarnath there were many spectacular Hindu temples along the banks of the Ganges, a river imbued with such mystical legend Aran could hardly believe she was going to see it. Chafing Ben's hand, she willed him to perk up, miss nothing of the scenery which was so different to Kathmandu's dark green valleys; the plains were flat and tan now, planted with cotton, mustard and rice. After a while, he began to look out the window, take an interest in the creaking carts driven by thin ragged men in turbans.

'It's really pretty bad, isn't it? Rani and Deva said it was, but somehow it doesn't seem real until you see it for yourself. These people look as if they can barely keep themselves alive.'

It was terrible, and everyone felt terrible; still Aran was surprised to see him so thoughtful.

'Well, we are doing something. There's the hospital in Lucknow.'

'What? Rani's hospital, do you mean?'

'Yes. We've sent quite a bit of money there over the last few years.'

'Have we?'

She smiled. He left all the business finances to Larry, all the domestic finances to her, glazed over with boredom whenever anyone tried to go into the details with him. Money was great as a commodity in his pocket, but as a concept it was a complete mystery. Other people understood the system, and he left them to it.

435

'Yes. Whenever we get something, so does the hospital. But we could do more – will do it, even if it's only a drop in the ocean.'

'But why didn't you tell me about the hospital? We could have gone to see it when we were in Lucknow.'

'I did tell you, years ago. But I didn't suggest going to see it because – well, I thought maybe you'd find it a bit depressing.'

'Oh, Aran! What kind of heartless creature do you think I am?'

'I don't think you're heartless at all. I just know you're squeamish.'

He looked at her curiously, as if seeing for the first time what a lot went on behind the scenes, the way she ran his life so smoothly he didn't even know she was doing it. After a moment, he lapsed back into silence.

Eventually they reached Varanasi, checked into the Pallavi hotel and recovered from Thanh's assault on their equilibrium. Aran felt a little dizzy, and under surveillance.

'Why are you looking at me like that?'

'I don't know. I just am.'

It wasn't that he was moody; he just seemed slightly withdrawn, contemplative. Divested of the glitter of stardom, it was as if he was assessing himself, adjusting to the fact of being a mere man, absorbing realities that had never touched him before.

Thanh and Beth went off to see Sarnath, but they took things slowly that day, sitting in a little courtyard with cool glasses of lassi under a palm tree. The air was warm and moist, making it difficult for her to concentrate on the guidebook she was reading, but more than anything she was aware of his dark eyes searching her face at intervals. She couldn't remember when she'd last seen him sit so still, say so little. After a light meal they turned in early that evening, standing by the window for a few moments, looking up at the sky netted with stars. In bed, he was very tender.

Next day they set off with their batteries recharged, conscious that the monsoon season was coming and they had only ten days left in India. The temple they most wanted to see was a fairly long walk away, quite small, but patterned with the most beautiful faded mosaics. Covering her head and shoulders with a wide gauze scarf, she let him lead the way in and found to her delight that some sort of service was in progress.

Near the front, on what she supposed was an altar, several robed monks were lying face down on the floor, chanting in unison, looking at first sight like one large grey blanket with a row of sandals at the end. She didn't know whether to stand, sit or kneel, but he motioned to her, steepled his hands to his face and dropped to his knees beside her.

They were the only people there, and although she understood nothing of what was going on she felt a sense of privilege. Did it matter who or what people worshipped, anywhere, so long as they respected something, aspired to rise above themselves? The temple was full of peace, and for a moment she thought of Molly, worshipping a very different god in a very different country. Molly had not given up Catholicism – you couldn't, she maintained, once you were born into it – and she still adhered to the teachings of Rome. But in her increasingly rare letters was something neither peaceful nor respectful of others, a growing note of zealotry, talk of being singled out, chosen, special. Sensing the humility here, Aran was aware of a sharp contrast, and felt a little frightened. Sometimes Molly used words like 'cleansing' and 'purifying' in a way that reminded her of Eimear's history lessons in Dunrathway. The Nazis had used those words a lot too.

Ben was praying. She'd never seen him do that before, never really knew what it meant to him to be a Hindu except that he was a pacifist, loathed violence and conflict of all descriptions. Despite his hot temper he had never hit or hurt anyone, ever.

What was he praying for, to which god? Siva, she supposed, as Thanh had prayed to Buddha yesterday, Molly prayed to Jesus – not that Molly would believe it if she saw him kneeling now, or have any time for his 'false god'. For her the monks' ceremony was more cultural than religious, but she felt drawn into it just the same, and knelt in silence until it ended. Then the monks stood up, all in a row, and she was a bit nervous when they turned and saw her, a foreign woman in their temple without invitation. Should she leave?

But the monks smiled, their eyes surprisingly friendly behind their little round glasses, yet she nearly died when one of the older ones beckoned to them.

'What do they want? Should I go outside?'

'No, I think they just want to talk to us. Come on.'

She followed him up to the man who had beckoned while the others filed out through a side door, their arms folded into their wide sleeves, nodding polite adieux as they went. Then the one who had beckoned greeted them, in English, asked where they were from. Were they interested in the temple, would they like to see it properly?

Oh, yes please. So he took them on a guided tour, pointing out things they mightn't have noticed at all and explaining their significance, giving them a little potted history as they walked around. He was very sociable, said he had been a farmer once, and then told them all about the local agriculture.

It was so interesting she wished she had a tape recorder, but thought she would remember the event for ever if not the details, his young-old face that could have been anywhere between forty and sixty. Whatever his physical age he was young and agile in spirit, very fit mentally, making occasional philosophical remarks that were really food for thought. She felt nourished in his company, saw that Ben was thinking too, very pleased that they had stumbled on this.

And then the monk left them, after giving them a full hour of his time, brushing off thanks and wishing them an enjoyable stay in Varanasi. They sat down on the wide rim of a pillar, and looked at each other.

'Wasn't that amazing?'

'It was . . . especially that it should have happened today, at this minute.'

'Why? Is it a holy day, or something?'

'Yes . . . in a way it is, Aran.'

'What do you mean?'

'I mean . . . that . . . there's something I want to ask you. Something I need to ask, that I've been thinking about for some time.'

He took both her hands in his, so earnestly that she felt a sudden frisson: his demeanour had been not dissimilar that awful day in Crete, the day he said he couldn't go on with her.

But surely not – not now? Was she mistaken, in this deep bond she felt between them, stronger than ever? But she couldn't be, nobody could mistake such a thing, be so wildly off the mark. She felt a little faint.

'What do you need to ask, Ben?'

'Will you marry me?'

It was so unexpected, she was stunned.

'M-marry you?'

'Yes. Now, right away, while we're here.'

He knew he didn't need to say he loved her. His eyes said it.

'I – I – Ben, are you serious?'

'Yes.'

'Oh, Ben – I – yes! Yes! If you really want to, of course I will. But it's a huge commitment. Are you ready? Are you sure?'

'Very ready. Very sure. After a mere eleven years, I am.'

And suddenly she realised she was too. She didn't have an engagement ring, didn't have a wedding dress or any preparations of any kind, he hadn't gone down on one knee to make a pretty speech. And that was how she knew she was ready. She'd marry him wearing a sack, standing in the middle of an open field. She'd live with him in a mud hut and love him till the end of her days.

Radiant, she touched his face.

438

'What brought this on?'

'Amery brought it on. Then the guy who tried to kill me. Then India . . . the more I thought about it the more it all added up. This is the right place and the right time for us, Aran. If – if you don't mind not doing the bridal bit, not having a reception or guests or any fuss?'

'On the contrary – although I must say it's the first time I've ever known you to turn down a good party!'

'We'll have one later, at home.'

'M'm. But Ben, how do you do it here? I mean, how do people get married in India? What do you have to do?'

'Well – unless you're very keen to have a Catholic ceremony, I'd like us to have a Hindu wedding. Here in Varanasi, in this very temple if possible.'

'Oh . . . I'd love it. Will they accept me, or do I have to get baptised first or something, swear to be a good Hindu wife?'

'No! They'll accept us both just as we are. I'll find out where the monks live and talk to our friend. But Aran – if I go tonight, will you think it over while I'm gone? I know we're on holiday, but this isn't a romantic gesture. It's serious. It's for life.'

For life. Our life, our future, all our days together. She reached up and kissed him, the scarf sliding off her hair so that the sunlight touched her cheek.

Three days later, Aran and Ben were married by the *purohit* in the temple on the banks of the sacred river Ganges. Beth and Thanh stood on either side of them, legally witnessing the ceremony, placing garlands of flowers about their necks after their vows were exchanged. Then the holy man blessed them, embraced them and wished them many healthy children. As they turned from him, a monk at the back of the temple plucked at a sitar, and they were very touched that, upon hearing Ben was a singer, this simple music should have been offered. Aran thought she would not exchange it for the entire London Symphony Orchestra, and knew Ben could not have been happier if Maria Callas had materialised to sing an aria.

As they emerged from the obscurity into the bright light outside, Thanh told them to stop, and went down the steps with his camera; unless he furnished proof nobody at home would ever believe it had happened. Yet it had not been difficult to arrange, all they needed was their passports, and Ben had found a beautiful ring of chased rose gold to put on Aran's finger. Together they smiled for Thanh, and then Aran laughed, feeling both silly and happy in her sari.

She'd never worn one before, and nearly strangled herself trying to get into it, but Ben was thrilled when he saw the yards of pale yellow silk, edged with a few tiny stars, her head and arms draped with a fine veil for the temple.

'You look fabulous. I think I'll keep you this way at home.'

She laughed again, wondering what Rani would think of the sight she presented. Deva, too – she was Mrs Halley now, like her new mother-in-law, she had a whole new family. Guy would blow his brains out when he heard, and possibly Ben's as well.

Thanh took his photographs, the monks were thanked and went off full of good cheer. And it was as simple as that. A few minutes later, they strolled back to their hotel, Thanh procured some champagne and the four of them drank it out in the courtyard, standing up with the rose petals still around their necks. Then they changed and went for a long walk, just the two of them, by the banks of the wide swirling river, looking at the ghats and the dhows sail by.

His lips brushed her cheek. 'Happy?'

She was carrying her oboe, and by way of answer she sat down on the grass and began to play it. Gounod's *Ave Maria*, wafting across to the bank on the other side, carrying pure and clear across the water that did not mean death, but life.

'But you can't have! Not just like that!'

'We have. Just like that.'

Eimear sounded as she might on the first of April, certain she was the victim of a prank.

'But a wedding takes months to arrange! There's the church to book, the hotel, the food and flowers and clothes, the guest list, the presents, the music, the bridesmaids, the honeymoon, the cars, the cake—'

'We were already on honeymoon, we had no guests, and I wore a sari.'

'A sari?!'

'Yes. Yellow silk. I got it in a market the day before.'

'A market?!'

'Well, I did start out in one myself. There's nothing wrong with markets, is there?'

'No, but – oh, Aran! What have you done? What is your mother going to say?'

'Congratulations, I hope.'

They both burst out laughing, Eimear on the Irish end of the line and Aran in London.

'Well, I must say, you're two very dark horses. I wish you'd told us, we'd have sent a telegram – oh, I'd love to have been there, it must have been beautiful.'

'So beautiful, you can't imagine. I'm sorry I didn't tell you, but I didn't know myself, and you wouldn't have been able to come anyway, would you?'

'No, but we – Rhianna—'

She heard Eimear bite her tongue, but guessed what she was thinking. Rhianna had been mooted as a flower girl once before, for her wedding to Thierry Marand. The 'right' wedding, to the wrong man for the wrong reasons.

'Eimear, I want to talk to you about Rhianna.'

'Oh, God. Oh, Aran – you – you haven't – you're not – ?'

'Oh, I'm sorry, Eimear. I didn't mean to sound so blunt, or frighten you. Look, we can't discuss it over the phone, but I'm coming to Dunrathway next Saturday. Will you arrange to be at home, with Dan, and for Annie to mind the children? We have to sort it out, and it has to be done calmly, quietly. I'll rent a car, but I won't be staying overnight.'

There was a long silence.

'All right. I'll do as you say. But—'

'Please, Eimear. Don't panic. Everything will be all right, I promise you. Not easy, but all right, eventually.'

'You kept a promise to me once before, Aran. I hope you can keep this one.'

'Yes. I can and I will. I'll see you on Saturday.'

On Saturday morning Aran got up at six o'clock, and when she was dressed she woke Ben.

'Ben. Darling. Wake up.'

His eyes opened slowly and he motioned to her to stop shaking him.

'What is it? What time is it?'

'It's early. Listen, I have to go out. Are you recording today?'

'Yes, but where are you going?'

Hating to tell a lie, she hesitated.

'Shopping. To Camden Lock – the best time is when it opens at eight. Will you be home for dinner tonight?'

'Depends. Probably not. We might work late and eat out – at Langan's maybe. I'll phone to let you know and you can join us.'

'OK. We'll plan on a late supper and I'll see you then. Go back to sleep now for a little while.'

Instead he sat up a little and looked at her, pushing his hair out of his face, rumpled and slightly bewildered.

'It's lashing rain. You'll be soaked.'

'Never mind. I'll take an umbrella. 'Bye, love.'

Before he could reply she dropped a kiss on his cheek and was gone, walking quickly down to Hampstead Road until she saw a taxi and hailed it, asked the driver to take her to Heathrow.

The rain poured down the windows, and she was glad the driver was taciturn at this early hour, because she did not think she could speak to save her life. What was there to say, on this terrible day, this day already wet with her tears, grey with the sadness to come? Wretchedly she sat looking straight ahead of her, down the empty streets, wrapped in the pain already endured, the pain yet to be inflicted.

For once the plane to Cork was half empty, bumping a little as it lost altitude over the ocean that had taken Conor and Dursey, Amery and its other victims. Grim and dreary, as Cork was grim and dreary when she reached it, curtains pulled in houses still silent with sleep. Halfway to Dunrathway she stopped at a truckers' café, sat over hot tea for forty minutes, not wanting to arrive too early. Not wanting to arrive at all.

Shortly before ten she turned into the Rafters' driveway, knowing they would hear the car and come out as they always did, Dan and Eimear and the children . . . but when the door opened only Dan stood there, his face like death.

Yet he kissed her, tried to smile.

'Aran, sweetheart. Come in.'

It was better inside, and worse; she could hear the three young voices in the kitchen, the sounds of breakfast, glimpse Sorcha warm and snug in a fluffy romper suit. For one second she stood stock still. She couldn't do it. She couldn't.

Trembling, she glanced at Dan. He too was shaking.

'I – I – oh, Dan, I'm so sorry, I can't bear it—'

Even in his distress he was able to comfort her as he always had, let her lean on him a moment, patting her hair while she stemmed the tears, forced them down. Later, they would all cry. But not now.

Eimear appeared, composed and very pale, embracing her without meeting her eyes. And then the children, one after the other, running into the hall to climb up on her, thrust their milky lips at her, smelling of food and sleep. Sorcha, the baby who was nearly five now, Emmett wearing pyjamas and a cowboy hat, and Rhianna. Rhianna her daughter, their sister, grown too big to climb, her large brown eyes level with her waist. Beautiful brown eyes, sparkling at the sight of her.

'Aran! Aran! You're back!'

Her legs buckled as she drew the child fiercely to her, kissing her over and over, capturing every little detail in the beloved face she had not seen for so long. Soft dark skin, melting into her own, the new teeth that were all in place now, white and straight; the rosy lips, the long legs that had lost their baby fat.

'Muffin. Oh, my muffin. My muffin.'

The arms were clamped around her neck, no longer dimpled but pliant and strong, full of healthy energy, but she clung as if she were the child, her lips glued to the bright fresh face.

'Did you miss me, darling? Did you?'

'Yes, Aran, guess what? Emmett got the measles, he had all these big red spots, he had to have mittens so as not to scratch, he looked so funny! And Sorcha's got a new trike, but I can ride my bike without the stabil – stabil – you know, things, Grandma's taking us to a gym – Mummy, what's it called again?'

'Gymkhana.' It was Eimear who answered.

'A gymkhana, to see the ponies jumping, in Cork next week—'

Her heart was breaking. Tearing in two, splintering.

'Aran?'

She couldn't bear it, the way Rhianna looked at her suddenly, candidly, curiously.

'Yes?'

'Why haven't you been to see us for ages? Were we bad? Did you not love us any more?'

Oh God. Oh no, not this, not now. All three of them were looking up at her, wondering, a little accusing.

'Of – of course you weren't bad. You're as good as angels, and I love you all to bits.'

'Then why?'

'Because – because I live in London. It's a long way off.'

Rhianna brightened, drew herself up importantly.

'I know where it is. You have to go on the plane.'

'That's right. On the plane.'

Her heart was thumping so loudly she didn't hear the knock at the door, didn't notice Annie McGowan come in until the woman was standing before her, her face telling her immediately that she knew, and was heartbroken.

'Annie. Oh, Annie, it's so good to see you . . .'

Her breath trailed away on a sob. Once she had worked for Annie, now she wanted to lean on her motherly bosom, cry, implore her to find some way out of this dreadful day. But Annie only shook her head, hugged her briefly before turning to the children. Any lingering now, her look seemed to say, and we will all be undone.

'All right, kiddies, get dressed quickly now and off we go, you're going to help me make cheese today so wear your old clothes.'

Emmett and Sorcha ran off, but Rhianna didn't.

'Do we have to, Annie? I want to stay here with Aran.'

Wistfully, she put her hand in Aran's. Her warm hand, tight and innocent. And then a hopeful smile, up at her.

'Can I stay, Aran? Please?'

Eimear's voice sliced between them like a hatchet.

'No, Rhianna, go and get ready, quickly.'

Startled, she flew off, and Aran tottered into the kitchen. Eimear poured coffee, which nobody drank, waiting for the three of them to reappear, and then leave with Annie.

They came back washed and dressed, lined up like little soldiers, holding their hands out solemnly for inspection. Barely looking, Eimear nodded approval, and they trooped away. At the door, Rhianna stopped, turned round, and blew Aran a kiss.

'Bye, Aran. See you later.'

She shot to her feet and raced after her, caught her up in a hug like a vice.

'Bye bye, darling. Promise me you'll be good?'

The curls nodded dutifully.

'And – and—'

The little girl looked at her gravely.

'What?'

'I love you, Rhianna. You're my very special girl. Very special.'

'I love you too, Aran.'

With a last hug, she ran after her brother and sister.

The tears poured down all three of their faces, but somehow they got through it, spoke coherently, made arrangements. When Rhianna was sixteen she would be told everything, given the choice of where she wanted to live. Between now and then, Aran would never see her again, never visit Dunrathway, never telephone or make any contact at all.

Once a year, Eimear would write with an update, unless there were any emergency in which case every rule could be broken. Other than that, the long friendship between the two families was over.

'It's horrible, Eimear, and I hate every word of what I'm saying to you, but it's the only way. I miss her so much, want her more and more every time I see her, I'd end up kidnapping her if we went on any longer as we are. I've come so close to telling Ben, so often, within a whisper of it – but if he knew he had a daughter, had lost nearly eight years of her life, that she was here with you – I'm sure he'd take her, ruin her little life, destroy your family. I can't do it to her, or to you.'

She could hear Hannah Lowry's words as she spoke. 'The child's interests. You must always put the child's interests before your own. Always.'

Eimear swallowed.

'She's going to be very upset, Aran. She asks about you all the time. And she's old enough to miss you now, to realise you're not coming back.'

'I know. You'll just have to keep putting her off until she forgets. Children do forget. Walter Mitchell said so once, and it's true.'

It sounded very hard, but she had to be hard, be firm. It was that or collapse, run off with Rhianna today, terrify the child and leave the Rafter family smashed to pieces. In London, Rhianna would sob for weeks, for months, inconsolable for her Mum and Dad, her brother and sister, her pony, her dog, her home. She would come to hate her and Ben, never forgive them, never understand.

Dan looked at them both.

'Couldn't we just phone each other, once in a while—?'

'No, Dan. Every time you call I wait for you to let something slip to Ben, I wait for him to ask how your children are, piece it all together somehow. Every time I call you I want to talk to Rhianna, hear her voice, torture myself with it. I love you both very dearly, I always will love you and treasure every little thing you've done for me, for my daughter. But we can't communicate any more. Not until 1996.'

'Oh, Aran. Eight years. And then what?'

'Then Rhianna will be needing her birth certificate for one thing or another, she'll be old enough to – to maybe accept what I did, why I did it. You can either prepare her gradually, or tell her all in one go, whatever seems best as she goes along. But not a word till then.'

Looking at Dan's sad eyes, Eimear's wet and anguished, she felt like both a murderer and the victim of one. On the air, the child's fragrance still seemed to linger, she could hear the voice that was no longer lisping now, but clear. Clear as an oboe in a Himalayan village.

'If she ever needs anything, you must let me know immediately. That, or illness, are the only exceptions. Especially if she wants music lessons or voice training, special classes at school, anything of that nature.'

'We were thinking of getting her a piano, actually. Mother gave her a keyboard at Christmas and Luke's been teaching her to play it. She loves it.'

On the spot, Aran took out her chequebook and wrote a blank cheque.

'Then get her a good one, please.'

'All right. We will.'

'Yes. And – and when she is sixteen, you know – even if she does want to see me, to meet Ben, she'll still have two more years of school here. I hope we can all be reasonable then and share her, make her feel she has two homes and that she'll be welcome and loved in both.'

'Of course. She could spend holidays with you, maybe she'll even—'

'What?'

'I was going to say maybe she'll even have little siblings in London by then.'

'I hope so, Eimear. I truly hope so, because the only way I can get through this is by having another child. I was going to wait till I'm thirty, but I'll be twenty-nine next April anyway, I'm sure Ben wouldn't mind if it was a bit early now that we're married.'

'I think you should, Aran. Ben is obviously much more stable now, has made a commitment to you. If you had another child it might help – ease—'

Ease the pain of losing this one. Could it? At this moment she didn't think anything could help. When Rhianna was a baby, when Ben was not around, she'd at least been able to see her often and freely, which had been a huge comfort. But henceforth she wouldn't even have that any more. She just could not keep up a life of deception, snatch stolen visits and then tear herself away again, leave Rhianna wondering what it was all about. Couldn't prolong the agony she knew Dan and Eimear secretly suffered, or remain on the sidelines of a family to which she would never fully belong. If she had a baby now, her best friends wouldn't know, wouldn't see it, she wouldn't see them any more. Wouldn't even see Annie or Achill any more, unless they came to London, and she didn't think Annie would. Her cheeses travelled, but she did not. Even Val, Sher and Molly in America . . . Conor and Dursey were dead, it was all over. This part of her life was finished. Annie had guessed that this morning, known somehow it was the last day, the last time.

This village would become a memory, these dear friends, this first daughter. Apart from Rhianna, it was Eimear who hurt the most. Dan and Eimear who'd given her her oboe, brought her into their home, taught her things and given her the books that had opened up the world to her. That was why Rhianna must stay with them; they were wonderful, natural parents, their house was a home. Rhianna's home, where she belonged.

Aran Campion had another life to go to. In a way she had another child; she had Ben. Weeping, she stood up.

'I – I'm going to go now. Don't say anything. Please. Just don't say anything.'

446

They didn't, but they rose with her, put their arms around her and held her in silence. Dan trying to be brave, Eimear still so lovely, but looking forty today, for the first time. In Eimear she could see her own youth vanishing, feel something dissolving between them. Always they would love each other, but Eimear was no longer her mother. She was Rhianna's.

London seemed as unreal as a stage set when she got back to it, incredulous that she could have travelled such a huge distance in one day. The house was empty, only the answering machine flashing with Ben's message: dinner at ten, at Langan's. Grateful for the quietness, she went upstairs and lay on their bed for nearly an hour, crying it all out, emptying her heart so it would not overflow when she saw him. Then she took a bath, changed her clothes and tried to repair her face, erase the evidence.

It didn't work. He noticed the moment she walked in, smiling brightly at Myles and Jake and Thanh, at their wives, at the big loud group in which she hoped she could disappear. Making room on the banquette beside him, he looked at her sidelong.

'What's with all the make-up?'

'Well, we're out to dinner, aren't we?'

'Your face is puffy. You look very tired.'

'I'm fine. How did the recording go?'

Somehow she kept it up till they got home, thankful that for once he didn't bring everyone back with him. Instead they went straight to bed, where for the first time ever she was unable to make love with him, hardly able to respond at all.

'What is it, muffin?'

'Oh . . . we don't always have to have sex to have sex, do we?'

'Isn't that a very Irish thing to say! No, we don't, but you're not just tired, are you? Something is wrong . . . come on. Tell me what it is.'

She wanted to, so badly. She wanted to roll into his arms and tell him, every single thing, the terrible things she'd done today, the terrible woman she was. But she couldn't. Pushing it all down into her heart, into the past, she fell into a cold black sleep.

It was bound to happen, Aran supposed. The joy of being married to Ben got all mixed up with the pain of losing Rhianna, and she was very confused. One minute she was writing lyrics for some bright music he'd composed, the next she was putting her pen down sadly, seeing Rhianna's face as she came home that evening, expecting to see her. What had Dan and Eimear told her, how had they explained, how had she taken it?

447

She would lose her mind if she kept it up. Work was the answer. So she wrote feverishly, helped Holly with the homeless, ran the house like an army camp, went into all the business dealings with Larry Becker, answered thousands of letters at the fan club. Since the attempt on his life, Ben's popularity had soared, they poured in from Europe, America, everywhere from Chester to Chile. She planned the next tour with Kevin, entertained guests, painted the hall, dug the garden and planted hundreds of bulbs . . .

'You haven't played your oboe much lately.'

'Jesus Christ, Ben, haven't I enough to be doing!'

Then, sorry she'd snapped at him, she played it for hours at a stretch, sometimes forgetting he was there, until her mind drifted and the music took her back again . . . then she'd fling it down, furious with herself. Puzzled, he'd look at her as if they had swopped spirits; he was the calmer of the two now, she was the restless one, churning.

'You're doing too much. Why don't you let Beth run the house?'

She didn't want Beth. There were enough people around already. Beth helped once a week with laundry and so forth, but she didn't need a fulltime housekeeper, she needed peace and privacy.

He persisted. 'God knows we can afford home help.'

That did make her smile a little. The stock market had crashed spectacularly, the day after their return from India, and amidst all the consternation Ben had turned to her looking vaguely worried.

'Had we any money in it?'

'No. Larry's got us into all sorts of other investments, but I'm afraid I made sure they were all very dull and boring. And safe. Our personal savings are in the post office.'

'The post *office*?!'

She had to laugh. 'Yes. In a long-term account with a high yield. Safe as houses.'

Relieved, he said she was very odd, but a lifesaver. It made her feel better about the mess she'd made years before, getting him into the disastrous contract with Schwabbe. No matter how often he reminded her she hadn't known Cedar would be taken over by Schwabbe, she still felt responsible, and she was cured of her ambition to manage every facet of his career. She had her experience of Philip Miller's office, she had her little diploma; but Larry Becker had studied economics at Oxford, business management at Harvard. He was a heavyweight. Still, Larry hated to see her coming, and she hated it when he called her a 'bantam' – even though she didn't dictate what he should invest in, she vetoed what he shouldn't. She was proud of having vetoed the stock market.

* * *

Ben toured Australia that winter, playing to huge audiences in Sydney, Melbourne, Adelaide and Perth, and Aran's heart was in her mouth even when Thanh assured her security was tight as a drum.

'Aran, you no live this way for next ten years. You learn relaxing. You take up yoga.'

In desperation she did take it up, and was astonished. Not only did it help her accept the risk, it helped her cope with the rush and stress too, made her more philosophical about everything. Even Rhianna: she began to have glimmers of hope in the dark nights, calm moments when she felt she had been right, that in time she would learn to let go. Or learn to live again, at least.

She was glad when the party to celebrate their marriage was deferred until spring of the next year, merged with her twenty-ninth birthday. By then she was able to control her muddled emotions, enjoy it for Ben's sake and truthfully tell him she was feeling better. Not knowing what was wrong with her, he was concerned, probing, protective. He was, to everyone's amazement, a devoted husband.

It was a relief not to have to lie to him any more, not to have to watch her back. Or only at odd moments. One day in the early summer of 1988 she was sitting in the garden, playing her oboe, when he came up behind her and gently kissed her neck.

'You haven't been home for a while.'

'This is my home, Ben.'

'I mean Dunrathway, that you were always dashing off to.'

'I – I'm losing contact with it. I can't keep track of everyone any more.'

'The Rafters haven't rung for a while. A long while.'

'No . . . they're busy, they have three children. I suppose our lives are different now, we don't have the same things in common nowadays.'

'Maybe not. But you know you're free to go whenever you like, don't you? I'm sorry if I inhibited you before.'

She spun round and made herself smile.

'What's this? Are you trying to get rid of me? Is Sasha stashed away somewhere?'

'Please, Aran. That isn't funny. Or fair.'

It wasn't. Once Ben made up his mind to do something, he went at it headlong, and he had made up his mind about her. People said rock stars made a mockery of marriage, but it wasn't always true. Paul McCartney had been with Linda Eastman for twenty years now. And Ben always liked to beat his rivals' records.

Achill wrote. He was organising a rock festival for August, a whole

449

week this time, would there be any chance . . . ? Aran ticked off his requirements with pleasure, packed up a crate of rock memorabilia she'd got Ben to autograph, the leather jacket with the blood still on the sleeve, unreleased discs, other things she got his famous friends to sign. Some ghoul would treasure the jacket she supposed, and she was glad to get it out of the house. The man who had tried to kill Ben was jailed, but he didn't have to testify at the trial, because as Larry told the court he hadn't seen a thing from the stage. But there was such sympathy for him, total strangers had written . . . only Molly failed to refer to the event at all. Confounding Sher's suspicions and Aran's worries, Molly did not lose all her worldly goods to the cult. She was, she proudly wrote, one of the people who encouraged others to make donations, decided how funds should be deployed. Aran shuddered, but wrote back anyway, telling her all about her Hindu wedding.

There was a resounding silence.

Aran knew then that there would be no more letters, that she had lost her blood mother as well as her adopted one. The last parent, the last link . . . but soon, she would be a mother herself. The baby would come, the new baby and the new start, making it all better. Her own family, her own child in her arms.

Rani was pregnant. Crowing with delight, she arrived one autumn evening with Thierry for dinner, and they only had to look at her to guess.

'You're going to have a baby.'

'Wrong. Guess again.'

Ben grinned. 'You're having a miniature doctor, or supermarket manager, born in a white coat with a chart in his hand.'

'No.' Thierry was smiling so widely, looking so dazed Aran wondered if he'd been drinking.

'What, then?'

'Three babies. We're expecting triplets.'

Three! But it would be pandemonium, round the clock! How would Rani run her practice in the middle of all that? She'd get no sleep, she'd be a menace to her patients.

'Oh, I'll figure it out. Maybe get an au pair, maybe pack it in altogether . . .'

'Rani Marand, you'll do no such thing. This is what men are always accusing women of, losing career momentum when they get pregnant, going to pot when they have babies! And Thierry will be hard pressed to support five of you on one salary.'

'Well, I might work part time. But how many women have three children all at once?'

'Not many. But lots have toddlers close in age. They cope, they stay at work, either because they have to or because they need the stimulus.'

'What could be more stimulating than triplets?'

She looked so indignant that Aran laughed, but she wondered too. Which chapter of the feminist handbook covered triplets? Rani seemed fated to eat every word she'd ever uttered. But then, in front of them all, Thierry volunteered the answer.

'Darling, I wouldn't dream of putting you under such pressure. You trained for years, you earn more than I do. I'll give up my job and look after the babies.'

He beamed at his brilliance, and Rani looked ready to hack off his head with her fish knife.

Rhianna's three cousins were born the following summer, making Ben an uncle to baby Guy, baby Freddie and baby Amy. Guy senior was sufficiently flattered to thaw a bit towards his daughter's French 'tradesman' husband.

'Of course he's not a tradesman any more. Hmph. I don't know which is worse, a man in trade or a man in an apron.'

But he held baby Guy as he spoke, at the christening down in Surrey, which was performed with sacred water from the Ganges. It was a weird compromise; Rani was Hindu, Thierry was Christian, but they had agreed to bring the children up in both faiths and then let them decide for themselves. Aran was impressed by that.

Guy turned to her accusingly.

'And I suppose you'll have my own son at home next as well, making up feeds for my next grandchildren?'

It was a hurtful thing to say. She wasn't pregnant. But she was stung to retort.

'Well, better a house-husband than a rock singer, wouldn't you say?'

He gathered up his eyebrows as if to strike her with them, but Deva saw her lip quiver, and intervened.

'Aran will be a wonderful mother, when she chooses to be, and you'd better be kind to her or she'll never let you see your grandchildren at all.'

That shut him up, and then Deva took her arm, led her away to take a little walk around the grounds.

'I'm sorry, my dear. It's just his way. He's very sensitive about – certain things.'

Aran thought Guy was as sensitive as his beloved Iron Lady. But Deva genuinely was, always had been. She trusted Deva. What a pity

Guy wasn't a paediatrician, and Deva a gynaecologist . . . not that anyone in their right mind could entrust either their body or their baby to Guy, she didn't know how his practice was so successful. Technical expertise maybe, but certainly no sympathy.

Still, Deva was a doctor, and she was understanding. She decided to confide in her.

'I have chosen to be, Deva. A mother, I mean. But it doesn't seem to be happening.'

For a moment Deva said nothing, only looked at her, assessing her anxious expression, her wistful grey eyes. Then she patted her arm.

'Don't worry, Aran. These things can take time.'

Aran thought of Rhianna, conceived in no time.

'I've been trying since we were married, almost.'

'But that's scarcely two years. You're still young.'

'I'm thirty.'

'And isn't that nice, that you've had a few years to enjoy being Ben's wife! He's very happy, I'm happy for you both, and you should be happy for yourself. Don't spoil it . . . once the children do come along, you know, you won't have nearly so much time with him.'

Aran thought she understood. Some marriages suffered, some husbands felt neglected, when babies reigned supreme. That was when all the demands started, the friction . . . unless you were like Dan and Eimear, keeping romance alive, working at it. It was a question of many things, but attitude was one of the most important.

'I'll make time. If you think the fans adore him, you haven't seen me in action!'

'That's the spirit. You stop worrying now, and let the future look after itself.'

'You don't think there's any cause for alarm, then?'

'No. Maybe later, if nothing has happened, I can refer you to one of my colleagues – or refer Ben! Maybe his plumbing is wonky, it wouldn't surprise me after the – the life he's led. God knows where he'd be today, if it weren't for you.'

'In the Betty Ford clinic, or pushing up daisies.'

They both laughed at her frankness, and the laughter lightened her heart.

The spring equinox, March 21, Rhianna's tenth birthday. Aran sat at the kitchen table, holding the annual letter and photograph that Eimear sent to confirm that all was well. It was a brisk letter, carefully short and to the point, but the photograph said much more. All five Rafters were standing outside their bungalow, a happy healthy family, windblown, smiling at the camera held, probably, by Annie. Rhianna stood in front of Dan, his hands resting on her shoulders, her head level with his chest. She was tall for ten, with her father's slim leggy physique, his dimple in her left cheek. Her hair was longer now, curling down to her shoulders, and there was a certain independence in the way she stood with her hands in the pockets of her shorts, her sandalled feet firmly planted apart, her smile cheery and confident. She was a visibly happy child, and Aran was torn between pleasure and misery. She would allow herself only this one day, carry the photograph around with her and then stow it away in the attic, wait another year for the next one. Another year.

Ben had gone to the recording studios, in a very positive frame of mind. In just a few more weeks the copyright on Cheam's Theme would revert to him, and the thought was inspiring. He was going to work hard now on several new pieces, sonatas and rhapsodies, until he had enough material to release his first classical album. The piano solos and instrumental pieces would come as a shock to many of his fans, but Jake and Myles were full of enthusiasm, refreshed by the challenge it presented. Larry Becker was hysterical, convinced they were all on the road to ruin.

Aran didn't have any lyrics to write, but she was to play the oboe on two of the orchestral pieces, which was one of the things they'd been discussing this morning. That, and the 'kiddie problem' which he knew had become a source of acute concern to her. He kept his tone deliberately light, jocular.

'We could get a couple off the peg.'

'What?'

'In India. Rani says there's an organisation where you can sponsor children. You send money to a particular child in a particular village, and in return they send you letters, photographs, school reports and so on. There's a lot of personal contact, and we could even go to visit some day if you liked. Why don't you think about it, muffin? It might help, until we have our own – it would certainly help them, anyway.'

Until we have our own. He hadn't given up hope, didn't appear to be worried, and the tests they'd had showed no reason why either of them should be. Besides, he said airily, hadn't her friend Eimear waited years, hadn't it all worked out well for her?

Yes, Aran said. It had all worked out well for Eimear.

Maybe it would for her, too. Hannah Lowry had had her first child at thirty-seven, Eimear had been well into her thirties when Emmett was born. She wished she could stop worrying, casting a blight on their otherwise wonderful marriage. But she couldn't, and she knew why.

The gods were punishing her. Telling her body that it was not to produce a second child when the first had been given away, pulling her mind to Rhianna when it should be on Ben. Something was locked inside her, seized up. Her emotional currents were flowing backwards, not forwards. Sometimes she had very strange dreams, thought she could hear a piano playing, a small voice singing *Frère Jacques*, and she lived in terror that she might utter the child's name in the night.

Getting up to make some more tea, she read the letter again. Rhianna was indeed playing the piano, Eimear said; Luke was sure a musical career lay ahead of her. That wasn't surprising, with Ben's genes, she was in the school choir and had the makings of a soprano. A punk soprano, Eimear added, a soprano with attitude. If she got into classical music she would be like Nigel Kennedy, cavorting round the stage in Doc Martens, a little rip with a big mouth.

But she was only ten. Aran wished she could stop wishing the years away, and yet pushing them away.

Chapter Twenty

But the years did fall away and, as Aran had once predicted, the nineties were different to the eighties. People were much more cautious about how they spent their money, and it took Ben a long time to make an impact on the world of classical music. There was scepticism, the *Cheam Collection* got mixed reviews, Jeff Barber wrote that Ben Halley was no longer credible as a rock singer. That hurt, but he persisted, and the fans remained loyal. Some even went with him, crossed the bridge from rock to rhapsodies, wrote that they were learning to love this whole new dimension.

But while he recorded in both fields, he only performed rock live, touring South America and then behind the newly opened Iron Curtain. That was fabulous, the fans so fresh and keen that there was a kind of love in the air. Aran noticed the difference in the faces as they walked the streets of Prague and Budapest, vitality everywhere, gratitude for life and freedom, nothing like the jaded languor of the West. The concerts were loud and wild, the buzz driving Ben on, soaking up every smile as he pranced and danced, loving it, loving them all. Aran was afraid he'd feel flat when he came home, but no; he threw himself into writing a rock opera, and told Larry to put Moscow on the list for next winter.

Then Japan, for 1994. His plans were endless, for everywhere except Germany.

'Isn't that a bit childish? I mean, I know Schwabbe were sods, but why take it out on the entire German nation?'

'I'm not taking anything out, I just don't want to be reminded of all the aggro . . . God, I was miserable then, Aran. I never thought I'd enjoy singing again. But here I am, tra la la!'

She smiled, thinking how young he still looked, how full of vigour. He had to work a bit at staying fit now, watch his diet, and they bought a red setter to take for walks on the Heath. The nightclubbing was less frequent, less frenetic, neither of them was able to handle hangovers any more. Sometimes two beers lasted him a whole night, which was fine by her. And then there was another visit to India, to see the two children they'd sponsored in Bombay. They were gorgeous kiddies and her heart went out to them, filling with mixed emotions.

Ollie and Morag Mitchell were frequent visitors, Ollie a handsome university freshman now, Morag demure in her school uniform. Rani was knee-deep in work, but Thierry dropped in occasionally with Guy, Freddie and Amy – the only children, Aran thought now, who would ever play in her house or garden. She spoiled them appallingly, laughing when Ben sang scales with them, nearly weeping to see how good an uncle he was. The role seemed to come naturally to him -- but then it was a fun role, with no responsibility.

The rock opera was performed in the spring of 1993 at a theatre in Drury Lane, a mad affair with a libretto written by a taxi driver Ben had 'discovered'. He was in heaven, interfering with everything, screeching at everyone from the conductor to the costume designer. Naturally he had to sing the lead, leaving three of his rock star friends to fight over the other main roles, furious that Kate Bush was out of the country.

'She'd be perfect for the witch who does sorcery by computer!'

'I'm sure,' Aran said serenely, 'she has far more sense.'

On the opening night he was wired to the moon, and Aran cringed when she saw Jeff Barber sailing in. Ben hadn't let her attend any of the rehearsals, wanted it all to be a surprise, and it certainly was: the curtain went up to reveal him in a spacesuit, painted in Star Trek make-up, suspended from an invisible wire so that he seemed to be walking in space. Bursting into song, he announced that his name was Voyager, clasping his chest for all the world like Placido Domingo. There was laughter at the comic story, but the power of the music he'd written was undeniable. To her surprise and Larry Becker's, the venture was a hit, made no money but lost none either.

'I told you! I told you I could do it!'

The euphoria lasted for weeks, and he said everyone had better watch out now, the next one would be for real. Pavarotti would beg to be in it, José Carreras would go down on his bended knees for a part. Out of my way, Mozart!

And then the letter came. Aran was sitting at her desk in the fan club office, going through the post with the two other girls, when her hand froze to a pink envelope with an Irish postmark on it. Dunrathway. For a split second she thought there must be some emergency, that it was from Eimear, but then she absorbed the rounded handwriting, remembered that it was addressed to the office.

Inside were two pages of ruled paper from a school copybook.

'Dear Sir or Madam,

I am thirteen and I am a big fan of Ben Halley's. Well I am a big fan of opera really and am going to be a soprano when I grow up. But I love rock too and Ben Halley is my favourite. Can you please tell me how a person goes about getting his autograph? Some people in my village have it because they've won contests in our yearly festival, but I can't because my parents are very strict and won't let me enter the contest, it's in a pub. I'm only allowed go to the Opera House in Cork and not to pubs. They won't let me have Ben's records in the house either, they say he's not suitable. So I listen to them at my friends' houses and we all think he's great. We wish he'd come here to the festival some time, he sends prizes to it every year. An older boy from Galway won his jacket once.

By the time I'm old enough to enter the contest it'll be too late, I'll be an opera singer by then. There's a classical music section but that's no good because the prizes are different, there isn't anything from Ben for opera singers.

So I got the fan club address out of a magazine and think you must be really lucky to work there, do you actually see him sometimes? If you do will you please give him a big kiss from me and tell him I would love to have his autograph, please please. I will love you for ever if you can get it.

Yours faithfully, XXXX

Rhianna Rafter.'

She had read thousands of them, thousands of identical letters from identical girls all over the world, varying only in detail but united by their common tone, starstruck, pleading. But never before had she heard the voice of a young opera singer, or seen her daughter's handwriting.

Trembling, she got up and went out to the bathroom, locked herself into it and read the letter four times, five, six. Oh, Rhianna! Thank God you didn't think to ask Achill, he might have given you our home address! Ben might have opened this, read it, written to you!

But of course Rhianna couldn't know Achill. She was a schoolgirl and he was a pub manager. Dan and Eimear were obviously keeping her on a tight rein, well away from him. Keeping her away from Ben's music, in case it all got out of hand. Yet Rhianna clearly had a teenage crush on him. On her *father*.

Leaning against the cold wall, she held the letter to her, so weak she felt she would slide to the floor. But if ever she needed her wits, she needed them now. She must contact Eimear immediately.

Twenty-four hours crawled by before she was able to do it, the next day when she was at home alone and knew Rhianna would be at school. Eimear's voice was jagged with shock when she heard her.

'Aran! What's wrong?'

'I've had a letter from Rhianna.'

'*What?*'

'It wasn't written to me personally, it was to the fan club, looking for Ben's autograph.'

'Oh, my God.'

'Eimear, she has a crush on him. I'll send you a photocopy, you'd better read it for yourself.'

'But we've done everything . . . we don't even let her buy his records out of her pocket money.'

'She said that. But she listens anyway, at her friends' houses. Eimear, what are we going to do?'

'I – I don't know. I'll have to talk to Dan. Maybe forbidding it is only making it worse. They always want what their parents forbid.'

'Then try to distract her. Get her interested in Michael Jackson, Prince, someone else. Please!'

'Yes. They're all like that at the adolescent stage, they get notions, it's their hormones . . . oh, God.'

'And she's interested in opera too, just when Ben's written one and going to write another! If we don't put this fire out we'll all be burned to death!'

'Yes, but how are we going to put it out?'

'I don't know, but you were a teacher, you're her – her mother. Think of something! We can't have her fantasising about Ben!'

'No – don't panic – I'll sit on her round the clock, keep her so busy she won't have a moment to herself. Don't worry, Aran. Dan and I will manage this somehow.'

'All right. I'll leave you to it . . . Eimear?'

'Yes?'

'Does – does she ever ask about me?'

'I – she – she used to. But she's forgotten now . . . five years is a long time to a child.'

A long time to a child. And an eternity to a mother.

For months afterwards Aran relived the horrific scenario, waiting for the day Rhianna might write again. Someone else might open the envelope next time, send off the facsimiled autograph they sent to everyone who asked for it . . . but nothing came, and in time her panic subsided, under the surface. Whatever Eimear had done, it seemed to have worked. For now.

But it was only a matter of time. Only three years, until she would have to face the girl, face Ben, tell everyone the truth. Was she going to lose them both then, husband and daughter, the only family she had left? It might be even less than three years, if anyone put a foot wrong. The ice was so thin she hardly dared draw breath.

And still no baby, no other child to buffer Ben's shock when he found out, console her for the lost years. When Eimear's next letter arrived she could hardly endure it, the guarded news that everything was 'under control', the photograph of the tall teenager, fourteen now, willowy. But what a change! In ankle boots, black leggings and a denim jacket, Rhianna stood with one hand on her hip, her head tilted quizzically, her ears pierced with half a dozen earrings. Cropped to the scalp, her haircut exposed a long neck and the most exquisite wide eyes, strong lips and cheekbones. She wasn't smiling, but she was wearing the silver clef. In a postscript Dan said she was taking the bus into Cork twice a week for voice lessons, had reduced Hannah Lowry to tears last Christmas with her rendition of *Scarlet Ribbons*. That was quite a feat, because even in her eighties Hannah had all her faculties, was not a bit frail or sentimental.

He had been just as moved himself when the girl sang it, a cappella, captivating even her little sister Sorcha.

Scarlet Ribbons, Aran thought. Scarlet ribbons, for her hair. Only her hair is gone now. Her childhood is gone.

Writing a real opera was not at all the breeze Ben thought it would be. It was extremely difficult, not least because he wanted to do the libretto himself this time, but couldn't come up with the right storyline. The plot changed every week, but although he had never done words before he didn't want Aran's help, was determined to master the technique. Then there were so many interruptions: the tour of Japan, a charity gala with several other stars, private performances commissioned by wealthy socialites for their sons' or daughters' lavish birthday parties. Larry wanted him to think about investing in property, buying a new house for tax purposes; but Aran didn't want to move to any plush pad in Surrey. For what? The Hampstead house was more than large enough, for just the two of them, and she loved it, felt it kept Ben's feet on the ground. It was lovely, but not vulgar, not spectacular.

On a wet morning in the February of 1995 she stood in the lounge, looking at a painting Ben had given her. A circus scene, it depicted two trapeze artists with their arms outstretched, flying towards each other in mid-air, each dependent on catching the other. It was very beautiful, arresting, somehow touching. What if one fell, one failed, let the other crash to the sand far below?

She could hardly bear to look at it, and yet she looked at it all the time, willing them safely into each other's arms. But then she felt Ben's arms, encircling her gently from behind.

'In a brown study, are we?'

'I suppose . . . sorry. Did you want me for something?'

'I want . . . yes. I do want something.'

'Well, you've picked a good moment. I wasn't doing anything.'

'No. That's what I want, muffin. I want to know why you're not doing anything. Why you won't tell me what's wrong, what's holding you back. Is it the child?'

She flinched.

'Perhaps it is. It's so hard to write songs when – when there isn't a song in my heart. A baby's cry would be the sweetest sound in the world, but I'm never going to hear it, am I?'

'Oh, Aran. Maybe you're not. But you've got me, you've got so much. Isn't it enough?'

It should be. Did she need a baby, really, or did she only want one? Wasn't her music her baby, and Ben? It wasn't fair to him, when they had love and friends and success, every other thing in the world. And it wasn't right, to tinge these days with regret, when they might be their last days together. When he heard about Rhianna, she had no idea what he would do. Where he might turn.

'It should be, Ben. I wish I could help myself.'

'Can I help? Can't you talk to me?'

'Talking about it won't change it.'

He said no more, but looked at her quizzically the way Rhianna looked in her last photograph, his head tilted slightly to one side. And then, unexpectedly, he let her go.

She felt terrible after that, knowing he was worried about her and that she was making their home less than happy. Unable to make any progress with his opera, he began to stay out overnight on occasion, with Myles or Jake he said. She trusted him, but still she felt her mind drifting into pockets of doubt, hating herself for it. He wouldn't stray for no reason, she felt sure, but was she giving him reason? Driving him away, back to his old ways, his old flames? For a while he seemed distant, not himself at all, and she couldn't fathom what was going on in his mind. Sometimes he looked at her very strangely, as if he really was seeing someone else.

Then, out of the blue, there was a sudden burst of creativity. All in a rush the opera began to come together, as if his biorhythms were right or he had found inspiration. Had he? And if so, what or who was it? Afraid to ask, she felt a gulf opening between them, inhibiting communication until they could hardly discuss the opera at all. More and more, he buried himself in it.

Their once sparkling sex life was dimmed, and she became convinced that he had found someone else. I can't ask him, she thought, I can't talk to him, and now he can't talk to me. He has a new muse. I am destroying myself.

In the late slow summer he was away more than ever, working at the studios he said, and then Thanh began to act strangely as well, evasively. Thanh knew.

Thanh was her friend. He must tell her.

'Who is she, Thanh? I know you're always loyal to Ben, but please tell me! Please.'

She could see and hear herself, fretful, obsessive. But Ben was obsessive too, broody, giving birth to his new baby, his opera. Or – oh, God! Was his girlfriend pregnant? Was that what was wrong with him? If it was, she thought she would lose her mind. The thought of him fathering a child with someone else drove her almost to insanity. Grasping at Thanh, she pleaded with him to tell her, loathing the unfairness of her suspicions, the paranoia she couldn't hide.

'Aran, you crazy. You think this way, you ruin marriage.'

Thanh had two children himself now, was so calmly and simply happy with Beth that sometimes she almost felt envious of them. It was a feeling she hated, often sensed in other people when they looked at her, at her husband and home, her travels, her music, health and wealth. But envying other lives didn't change your own, only soured it. Forcing herself to stop, she thought that Conor would be ashamed of her.

In October, Ben suddenly cancelled his winter tour of South America. Larry was incandescent with anger, and she was fired with fear. It must be something – or someone – very powerful to make him do that, to keep him here in London.

'I want to concentrate on my opera. Get it finished, on stage by spring.'

Backers were found, a conductor was found and then a venue – St Clement Dane's church, where small operas were often staged. Much as Ben would have liked a bigger venue, Larry wasn't letting him take the risk even if a theatre would have. But with a cast of virtual unknowns, the theatres were not about to bank on the value of Ben's name alone. Working on a small scale came as a shock to him, but he consoled himself with the quality of the singers he had found.

'They may not be Pavarotti or Caballé – but they could be in the future. Imagine if they could say my opera was their first break!'

Despite her misgivings she began to share his excitement, and feel happy for him. After nearly twenty years, he was about to fulfil his ambition.

'Oh, Ben. I'm so proud of you. I really am.'

He smiled, just about.

'Perhaps you should wait till you've seen it.'

He wouldn't let her see the rehearsals, said it would be unlucky to even discuss it, but then he did something that touched her very much. He fixed the opening night for her birthday, April 19. She would be thirty-seven. Old enough, she thought, to trust him, to have sense and know that he still did love her, that they would work their way through this difficult time.

Reflecting on it, she decided to postpone the other drama, the real drama, until summer. He'd have settled down again by summer, Rhianna would have the long holidays, and it would be done. If it was going to break their hearts, at least they would have this joy first, this happy memory.

Eimear's annual letter came in March, around the time of Rhianna's birthday, more guarded than ever. Rhianna, she said simply, was 'being sweet sixteen': in other words she was staying out late, developing a taste for boys and parties. She wanted a motorbike, she had become vegetarian, she wore the weirdest clothes. But she was well. All was well, and the 'other thing' would sort itself out, Aran was not to worry.

Aran wished Eimear and Dan could come to the opera. Ben's big night, all thanks to their kindness of years ago, the piano, the support. But if she invited them everything would be impossibly awkward – Rhianna might even want to come too, and then what? Rhianna was seriously into opera now, studying rigorously, but there was no photo this time. Aran consoled herself that she would see her in person in the summer, and was tormented with pleasure, with heart-stopping fear.

For now there was still a glimmer of hope, but soon, almost certainly, there would be horror instead, pain and bitterness and maybe even hatred. Years of hatred, for the mother who had given her away. For the father too, the father who might try to upstage Dan, disrupt her warm close family.

Or might dismiss her, reject her? Ben was so good with his nephews and niece, so affectionate with everyone, yet Aran's throat went dry as a desert, her whole being clenched against the future.

* * *

462

Ben was impossible in the weeks before the opera opened, plagued by nerves, visions of failure and disaster. Thinking of the infinitely worse trauma to come, Aran set her mind to encouraging him, reminding him that it was only a start, the first of many operas. She wanted to help, to comfort, but even the title sounded tentative: it was called *First Night*.

'First and last, maybe.'

'Oh, don't be a pessimist! You said the rehearsals are going well.'

'Yes, they're wonderful – oh, muffin, I'm sorry, but you can't imagine the stress I'm under at the moment. I – I'm terrified.'

'Ben Halley is terrified?'

'Petrified. Will you promise me you – you'll try to like it, at least? Keep an open mind, even if you hate it at first?'

'I won't hate it. I'll love it madly.'

He came to her and took her hand, gravely.

'I love you. I love you madly.'

She dropped her eyes, ashamed.

'I know you do. And I know I've been – difficult, at times. But I am trying to come to terms with it, Ben. Even if we're not going to have a baby, we have each other, and I love you very much.'

Embracing, they stood together, saying nothing, letting the current flow from one to the other. She thought then that she was wrong, that there was no other woman, no new family. The very word was unbearable.

On April 19 Ben was quaking, but Aran felt a kind of calm. It was all in the lap of the gods now, final. Even if it all went wrong, Ben had tried, and in time he'd try again. Never in his life had he lain down or given up, been beaten by a problem. He'd lost Cheam's Theme and the man who inspired it, he'd lost her and even lost himself for a time, he hadn't fathered a baby, but he ... it struck her that he had experienced quite a lot, learned a lot. He was mature enough for opera now, could handle the complexity of it.

Good luck calls and cards arrived all day, and he looked at them woefully.

'Maybe we won't go. Maybe we – oh, dear God, what have I done?'

'You've done your best.'

But they dressed in a kind of stoic silence, his hands shaking as he fumbled with his black dress tie.

'Here, let me. Calm down. You look so gorgeous, I'd seduce you if I weren't a married woman.'

That made him smile, irresistible in his black suit with a striped gold waistcoat. There'd been a huge fuss about what to wear. She had

463

chosen a strapless black dress, daring, sexy. There would be photographers, and she wanted to look good for him – for whoever might think she was 'only the wife'. Then, thinking that black was her mother's colour, she brightened it with gold shoes and evening bag, scarlet lipstick, a satin jacket lined in red. But he looked dubious.

'I hope all this black isn't prophetic.'

Taking him by the shoulders, she looked him in the eyes.

'Ben, stop it! It's only an opera, your first attempt! You're going to enjoy it if it kills me!'

And then they set off in a long black car, Thanh at the wheel, impassive.

There were such crowds, such noise and chaos that it seemed hours before they got through the grounds and into the church. Myles, Jake, Larry and Kevin were in the seats reserved for them and their partners in the second row; the one in front was reserved for Ben and herself, Thanh, Beth, Rani and Thierry, Deva and Guy. Guy was resplendent, puffed up like a peacock.

'Always knew it, my boy. Always knew you'd make something of yourself.'

Aran thought Ben was going to punch him, but instead he kissed his mother and Rani, even Chanda who had come with a party of friends. There was a lot of chat, the whole building filled with excited rustlings, bright light, anticipation. When she saw a programme on Deva's lap she could hardly contain herself.

'Have you read it? Do you know what it's about?'

'Yes. We all do, but we're sworn to secrecy . . . you'll love it, Aran, I promise you will. Ben wrote it specially for you.'

For her? But he'd said nothing, given her no idea it had anything to do with her. Dearest Ben, so brilliant at birthdays! She turned to kiss him, and he took her hand.

'Happy birthday, my love.'

And then the lights were going down, a hush falling, the orchestra tuning up. The curtain rose, and a young girl was standing on the stage.

Not so young, a grown woman of nearly thirty in fact, but made up to look far younger. Standing alone, wearing a plain dress, she held her hands low in front of her as she began to sing. The opera was in English, would at least be intelligible.

'The boats are sailing, the gulls are flying, I will fly . . .'

Something about horizons and distances and departures, Aran thought the woman looked very small and alone, having to carry the first vital scene by herself, make an impact on the critics.

The set wasn't much help, either, an unremarkable cluster of cottages around a waterfront, the backdrop not unlike Dunrathway—

Dunrathway! Electrified, Aran leaned forward, almost falling over to see, her body turning to water.

And the mezzo soprano sang on, packing a suitcase as she looked out over the sea of faces, blowing kisses over her shoulder as she set off, carrying it into the wings. Then she was gone, already the first scene was over . . . Aran clutched at Ben, but couldn't speak.

Oh no. Oh, no.

A new backdrop, split in two. On one side, a bright house with two children in it, on the other side a market scene, the mezzo soprano crying her wares to a crowd of extras, laughing and flirting with them until one of them stopped to talk; a dark man, the young tenor Ben had mentioned. Together they began a duet, then suddenly the woman dropped his hand, flew across to the children, flew back to him, hesitating . . .

Finally a full duet, so soaring and yearning Aran could not believe how she felt, the way *The Pearl Fishers* still made her feel, her eyes filling with tears as she saw what Ben had done. Through a blur she watched the singers kiss, leave the stage and then run back together to kiss again, separate reluctantly with their hands touching till the final moment.

It must have been thirty minutes, but might have been thirty seconds before the first act was over, the curtain going down on applause Aran knew was for the quality of the music and the singing, regardless of the libretto. But it was her libretto, it was her they were singing about. All around her she felt the silence, everyone looking at her.

'Drinks,' barked Guy, whereupon they all leapt to their feet and followed him away, leaving her alone. With Ben. After a pause he took her hand, biting his lip, looking into her face.

'Are you – are you very shocked?'

She nodded dumbly. She couldn't understand why he had done this, what it was all about, what was going to happen next. Her life wasn't the stuff of opera, and surely he wasn't going to chronicle the tenor's rise to stardom? Her help behind the scenes, her slavish devotion? She would look a complete fool and he would look a vainglorious idiot, when the audience realised this was auto-biographical. They would be laughed out of London.

He squeezed her hand.

'Please don't panic yet, Aran. It's all under control.'

But his eyes were scanning the audience behind her even as he spoke, so anxiously she felt her whole life was whirling out of control,

465

in front of all these people. She had to drag words out of her mouth.

'The – the music is magical.'

Pleased but anxious, he put his arm round her shoulders and they sat there together, ignoring the people rubbernecking around them until Thanh and their family came back, tiptoeing into their seats like frightened rabbits. Only Guy looked smug, and she thought she could guess why: he was going to be glorified somehow now, portrayed as a stalwart supporter of the young singer. Faintly she remembered Ben in Kensington High Street, telling her he would never depict his own parents in music, hurt or embarrass them in any way.

The audience settled and the curtain rose again. But the tenor wasn't there, only the blonde mezzo, who looked different now, had changed in some way. Older, maybe? Embarking on a beautiful aria, she began to sing of the young man from the market, of her great love for him, of some fate that had driven them apart. There had been a quarrel, he had left her, she was alone again now. Flushing violently, Aran waited for the spotlight to swivel off her, move to the tenor waiting in the wings, as he surely must be waiting, ready to claim all the attention.

And then the mezzo spun round, flinging her hands up in supplication, and Aran saw what was different. She was heavily padded. Heavily pregnant.

The seat seemed to vanish from under her, she felt as if she was sitting on air.

What now, the singer asked the audience, what shall I do now? He no longer loves me, and I am alone. I am expecting his child. I want it, I will have it, but how will I care for it? I am poor, I have nobody in this country, I must work, and then who will look after it? Who will raise it, love it?

The first backdrop came down again, and there was the village on the water. In one of the cottages was a light, with a face in each window, a man and a woman. A man and a woman singing poignantly of their long childless marriage, their wish for children.

Aran felt disembodied.

Desperately the mezzo ran back on stage, slender again now, the baby in her arms. The couple came out, and she thrust it into the woman's arms: will you take my child? You were my friends, when I lived here: will you help me? Please take our baby, love it as you loved me, treasure it and keep it safe. Then all three sang together, exchanging promises, parting with pain in their faces.

A voice from the wings. The tenor's voice, distant, but rising on an anguished note of loss. I have made a mistake, a terrible mistake, I must find this girl I loved. Where is she, will she have me, what will I do if she will not? I will die.

Slowly he emerged, saw the girl and ran to her, joyful, reaching out. But as the older couple went back in behind the backdrop, carrying the baby he did not see, another man came out. A baritone, reaching for the girl from the other side of the stage.

There was a struggle. First the girl was pulled between the two men, then she went to the baritone, then the tenor came at them both, aggressive, almost desperate. While the two men fought she sang in an aside, telling the audience the child was a girl, a beautiful daughter, just like her father. As she sang the baritone was pushed out of the way, into the wings, and the tenor came to claim her, beg her forgiveness for having deserted her.

Aran watched the second act as if through frosted glass, only dimly aware of the tears in Rani's eyes and on Deva's face, of Guy and Thanh and everyone around her, immobile. When the lights came up the applause was tremendous, but Ben was wan and silent.

None of their group got up this time except Thanh, gliding out to the edge to keep people away. Myles and Jake were somewhere behind, their voices excited, saying that the libretto was catching attention now, everyone wanted to know how it would end. Would the lovers get back together, stay or part when the girl's secret was discovered? What of the child, hidden away, growing up with the couple only to discover she did not belong to them? Would she seek her natural parents, accept them or despise them?

Unable to look at Ben, Aran felt Deva's hand on her knee. Deva's brief touch, saying she understood, forgave her, loved her no matter what she had done. But she couldn't reply, couldn't move.

The last act. The lovers sat on either side of a wide table, singing the two harmonised parts of one song, sometimes synchronising and sometimes contrasting, both older now, wearing wedding rings. The duet reverberated like an echo, rising and falling, reaching out and dropping back. But never together, so that there was an aura of something wrong between them, off key. Their faces were full of love, and the set was the back wall of a lovely room, but the room was bare.

Aran didn't think she was actually breathing as it vanished, was replaced by the old waterfront house again, where unseen children were chorusing. Two adult voices rose over them, shouting, laughing, then hushing suddenly, conveying fear as they whispered together, telling of the eldest girl who had grown up. What should we do, will we tell her now, will we wait? She will ask, we must tell her; no, we must wait, she is ours to the last.

467

Our girl that we love, and cannot bear to lose. Oh God, Aran thought, oh God, oh God, oh God.

The stage went dark. Completely dark, the tenor's voice swirling out of the obscurity, singing to itself. I cannot bear it, it sang: my wife is unhappy, she wants a child and we have none. She is getting older, soon it will be too late, I must do something. I must go to our daughter, to the child I discovered many years ago, the child who may hate me. I am stupid, I am worthless, but I must find my daughter. Our daughter.

On the edge of their seats, the audience almost groaned aloud as his solo ended like a prayer, was lost in the dark. And then one soft light rose, pooled around the figure of a young maiden.

Rhianna. Aran shuddered violently as she craned to see, wiped the tears to find out who had been found, given the honour of the role. How had Ben found her, *how*? And who was she? Who was going to play their daughter on this stage, this first spine-chilling night?

The girl was tall and slight, so frighteningly like Rhianna that Aran thought for one sickening moment it actually was her. But this girl was older, her voice and gestures were trained. Dressed in jeans, Docs, a black T-shirt, she took her hands out of her pockets, pushed back her spiky hair and began to sing in a voice silvery as a waterfall, tremulous as a teardrop.

My father came. My real father, who never came before, because he loves me, let me be. For many years he resisted, left me where I was loved and happy, but now he wants me. He needs me, my parents need me. Nature's parents, my first parents.

But my other parents, my lifelong parents! I love them, will not hurt them. What will I do, what will they say?

The light grew stronger as she advanced to the front of the stage, looking out, fingering a necklet, wondering. Her father said her mother could no longer go on, keep the secret that was consuming her, but what was she to do? She was young, shattered by what he had told her, afraid to move.

First she looked out into the audience, searching with her eyes, looking for reassurance. Would her second parents understand, forgive her, if she went to the first?

And then she looked down, directly to where Ben and Aran sat. Throwing back her head, stretching out her two hands, she sang the aria straight at them, so vivid and close that Aran could see the tears glistening. Come to me, be mine, don't be afraid. I will not hate you. I will love you, as I love the others. We will talk, we will share, we will grow together. We will be one family. Only come to me, come. Come now.

* * *

What matter if she wept, Aran thought as she stumbled to her feet, annihilated. Everyone was weeping. Thanh would cope, Ben was beside her, Ben would explain why he had done it when they got backstage, *how* he had done it, how he had known.

She couldn't see, couldn't find her way, couldn't breathe. But he took her hand, and she clung to it as they fought through the crowd, gasping as she bumped into people and objects. Myles's stunned face flew past, Jake's voice and Larry's, a blur of confusion. And then they were backstage. Abruptly, Ben stopped.

'Look at me, Aran.'

She looked. Her throat was blocked, burning.

'Tell me you love me. Tell me you still love me, that I did the right thing?'

Unable to speak, she locked her fingers into his, and for a moment they paused together. Then he knocked on a door.

The soprano's dressing room, Aran assumed as the door was wrenched open. But a lovely dark girl stood in it, crying uncontrollably. Crying like a child, as she threw herself on her mother, reached blindly for her father.

Not the soprano, but Rhianna.

For an eternity they stood there, devastated. Then Rhianna pulled them in, and Ben shut the door, left Thanh to protect them from the hands and faces and voices. It was a very long time before anyone spoke.

With her face buried in Aran's hair Rhianna quivered and wept, their tears mingling, their words incomprehensible. And Ben wept, holding his wife, holding his daughter, choking. Holding everyone together, until Rhianna lifted her head, looked at her mother.

'Aran.'

Was she Aran? Was this Rhianna? Really Rhianna, in her arms? Not in Ireland, not in an opera? Not in Dan's care, Eimear's domain?

'My little girl.'

Clinging to her, Rhianna smiled through the wet veil.

'I'm sixteen.'

Of course she was, but it was her tone that Aran couldn't grasp; warm and open, with nothing accusing in it, nothing bleak or bitter. Dizzily, she sank to a chair, holding the girl's hand, turning her from side to side.

'Let me look at you.'

Rhianna stood back with a kind of candour, wiping her streaked make-up with the back of her hand while Aran inspected her fit firm figure, her flushed oval face, the short hair and long eyelashes . . . and the necklet.

'Ben gave me—' Uncertainly, she stopped. How much did Rhianna know? How had all this come about? As she looked from daughter to father she saw them glance at each other, and realised that she was the one in the dark. She had thought she was the only one who knew, but she was the only one who didn't.

'I – I think you'd better tell me. Both of you. All of it.'

The room seemed to revolve as she thought of the tenor's song, about how he had known for a long time . . . how long? How much?

Ben was leaning against a table, his back reflected in the mirror, grasping the edge of it. His face had everything in it, defiance, anxiety, pride and pleasure, all overlaid with a kind of frantic need.

'I found out on the day of the funerals.'

The funerals? The day they sang in the church, twelve years ago? Twelve years? Her eyes flew to Rhianna, but immediately he reassured her.

'It's all right. She knows. We've had many long talks about it since last summer.'

Aran was completely at sea.

'Do you remember that day, muffin? We went to the beach, and I wanted to know why you were so tense, why the Rafters wouldn't speak to me. You told me to leave you alone, and ran away.'

She remembered. Vividly.

'So after you left me, I decided to ask them. To go to their house and simply ask, because something was wrong, I was worried about you. When I got there their car was gone, I didn't see any sign of them, but there was an older woman in the garden, watching a little girl on a swing.'

On a swing. Luke's swing, between the yew trees. Annie.

'They didn't see me, so I just stood at the gate, watching the child until I noticed a little boy as well, blond, freckled, very different . . . the more I looked at the girl, the more I saw it, the more certain I became. Except for the curls she didn't look like you, but she – she was me. I knew she was mine. I can't describe how I felt, Aran. I just can't describe it.'

'And you – you never told me. You never told me.'

'No. My first impulse was to run after you, confront you, but then I began to think about it, to wonder why you'd done it. It took all night, but by morning I thought I understood. You'd had my child, after we parted, you were alone and frightened, you were no longer even working with me, had no money. So you – you did what you did. And then I kept thinking about the child's face, how happy she looked, and I realised I'd seen her where she belonged. She had a real home, she was secure. I had no right to interfere.'

'But – but you—'

'I was wretched. When I thought of all you must have gone through, of what I'd done and what I'd lost, how I was the only person taking Amery home for cremation – that's when I fell apart, when I got to New York. If Thanh hadn't come, I think I might have killed myself. Not consciously, but . . . I might have.'

Twice. Thanh had saved his life twice.

'Then there was Thierry, the thought of that as well as the rest – you know how I was then, Aran. The night you came and attacked me was the best night of my life. You dragged me up from the depths, you gave me a reason to recover, to live. You—'

'I kept running back to Ireland, and you knew why?'

'Yes. I never pushed you, never tried to make you explain if you didn't want to, or thought it wiser not to. But I did try to give you – little openings, little chances, if you needed them.'

She remembered. *'What's the great attraction over there? I'd like to see the Rafters. Why don't I come with you? They haven't written . . .'*

'I had to do it, Ben! I had to leave Rhianna with them, I couldn't do it to them, or to her!'

Tears sprang up again, but he didn't go to her, because Rhianna already had, was stroking her hand like a mother.

'I know. We both know, Aran. It's all right. Anyway, I let it lie for a long time after that, for much the same reasons as yours. But then it got worse for you, I could see you were miserable, more so as the years went by without any new child. It was eating into you. I had to do something. I had to act, before we – you – fell apart.'

'So you went to Dunrathway.'

'Yes. Last summer, several times. I told you I was staying with Myles or Jake and I told them to cover for me if you called.'

'And – and what happened?'

She couldn't visualise it, couldn't imagine the horror when he arrived.

'First of all, I wrote to Dan and Eimear. A long letter, explaining everything, asking them to call me at the studios. After we all got over the shock and they knew I wasn't going to cause trouble, we decided I should meet Rhianna, tell her everything. Eimear said you'd been close to doing that anyway, this year.'

'Yes. We were.'

'So she prepared the ground, sat Rhianna down and broke it to her.'

Faintly, Aran gazed at her daughter. 'Oh, my God.'

Rhianna nodded. 'Yes. That's what I thought. The world just caved in. I'd never even suspected . . . and then it was Ben as well, Ben Halley whose voice I adored, the singer I'd once had a crush on. It – it took me a week or two to sort things out, to remember how you used to come, visit me when I was little. Dan and Eimear were a huge help, they let me cry for days without taking offence, they were just there for me all the time . . . they're here tonight, you know. We're going to see them later.'

Later felt like next year, infinity. Aran couldn't get her mind beyond the here and now.

'Yes. Anyway, the next thing was to meet Rhianna myself. That was something else, wasn't it, Rhi?'

Rhi? He had a pet name for her, already? And she was nodding, smiling at him like an old friend?

'So we met. The first time was incoherent, just tears and more tears. That went on until there were none left, and then we began to get acquainted, to discover we liked each other. Liked each other more every time, began to discover all we had in common, how much music meant to us both. And then we started to wonder about you. What to do, how to tell you. We kept talking about it, but nobody could figure out how to go about it until Rhi took me to meet Luke Lavery, and he took us both to the Cork Opera House. One of Rhi's favourite singers was performing, and when she told me she wanted to be a soprano herself one day, sang for me that night, I knew.'

'The opera.'

'The opera, loud and clear, the secret announced to the whole world so there'd never be any press speculation, any sordid stories in the media. I wanted to tell everyone Rhi was my daughter, and I wanted to write a role for her. Some day she'll sing it herself.'

'But who – who sang it tonight?'

'Sive Sullivan, who I first heard in Cork that night. She's ten years older than Rhi, but still very young in operatic terms. We thought she'd be perfect, and then I thought of you and Holly, always trying to create openings in London for Irish talent . . . I hoped you might be as pleased as Sive was when I offered her the part.'

Rhianna nodded. 'Wasn't she amazing? We couldn't believe what she did with Ben's music, with our lyrics.'

Aran gazed. 'Your lyrics?'

'Yes. Well – Ben found the words difficult, so I helped him. I hardly knew how at first, but once I got into it I started to feel much better. The rhyme and rhythm just seemed to come naturally, and then I found I was beginning to see reason in the story as well. I could understand what you'd done and why, feel how hard it had been for you – and for Ben. Sometimes we got so upset we could hardly go on.

472

But it brought us together, and I – I hoped the libretto might be a kind of greeting gift for you. Then when rehearsals started, he brought me over here to be in on them.'

'He – when?'

'Six weeks ago. Mum and Dad took me out of school, they thought this was more important. I've been staying with Holly and Walter Mitchell.'

So this was why there'd been no photo, in March. Rhianna had not been there. Eimear had . . . well, she'd go into it all with Eimear whenever she could speak normally.

Together they looked at her, conspirators, Rhianna's eyes sparkling with tears and fears.

'So here we are. We left the scene so quickly, God knows what the audience thought . . . but what do you think, Aran? How do you feel? Did you – are we – are you angry with us?'

Angry? She felt as if she were witnessing a miracle, participating in one. As she reached for Ben she thought of Amery, and as she embraced Rhianna she thought of Conor and Dursey. Of the whole family, together.

Five hours later, at nearly four in the morning, the house was still alive and full of people. So many of them Aran was overwhelmed; not only had Dan and Eimear come over, been in the audience with Rhi, Annie had come too, with Achill and Aisling who were still getting over the news they had been told only a few days before. Ben's parents and sisters were there, well over it, since Ben had apparently told them at Christmas. Guy still seemed slightly dazed, but she couldn't tell whether it was because of his teenaged granddaughter or because his son 'amounted to something'. On the floor, the early newspaper editions were full of it – not only Ben's daughter, his beautiful music and Sive who had sung it, but the fact that Rhianna had collaborated on the lyrics and intended to sing the role herself some day.

'Real music,' Guy growled. 'Proper music.'

But Guy was inaudible for the music around him as Ben played his early song *Flight Paths*, singing with Rhianna. Aran ached to talk to her, to start work on the relationship that would probably take weeks or months to develop, but in her daughter's face she could already see one of her father's most beloved facets, his warm forgiving nature.

Everyone was joining in the song, humming if they didn't know the words, even Myles, Jake and Kevin who'd finally laughed and admitted that Ben had slipped one over on them. Until tonight they'd never suspected what the opera was about. But now all three were listening intently to Rhianna, looking at her speculatively, and Aran had to smile: they never missed a chance.

Thierry was nodding off, exhausted by his day of triplets, but Hannah Lowry was wide awake. Upright and dignified, she rested her hand on her cane, looking at Aran with immense satisfaction. Nearly ninety, she had insisted on flying to London, not only to see the opera but to see Aran, make sure there was going to be no discord in the Rafter family. But there wasn't. Aran set her mind at rest about that, promised that Rhianna could come and go as she pleased, that there would be no friction between Eimear and herself. Hopefully Rhi would come to London often now, but she had two years of schooling to complete, so her visits would be confined to holidays for the moment. Besides, as Rhi said herself, Ireland had a healthy music industry now, Dunrathway was famous for its festival which attracted talent from all over the world: she didn't need to go to London. Wanted to go, yes, wanted to visit her parents and maybe have a few chats with Myles Irving, but that was very different from having to go.

And something else had been settled, when Rhi got her mother to herself for a moment, took her hand in her own long fingers.

'Aran . . . would it be all right if I went on calling you that? It's just that I – I don't want to hurt Mum and Dad.'

It was fine, Aran said, looking at Dan and Eimear as they sat talking to Deva and Guy, flanked by Luke Lavery who had also done so much for her, encouraged Rhianna when she wasn't there to do it herself. Luke had such a fine voice, but his real talent was the way he coaxed music out of others, made their voices heard.

Sinéad Kenny was there, looking intently at Kevin Ross, Thanh and Beth were there, Sive Sullivan and Holly and Walter with their children. Morag was arguing with Rani and Chanda was arguing with them both, but it was to Ollie that Aran turned for a moment.

Little Ollie, shouting about 'a new one, 'nuther one'. And then she looked at Ben and Rhianna.

Dearest Ben, with whom she might be able to have another one, at last. Now all the weight and worry were gone, she felt nothing but peace and joy . . . only they had a new one, one they had yet to get to know.

I still want a baby, she thought. I'd still like that, so much. But Rhianna already has a brother and sister, and Ben and I have everything we need.

474